$2 75

THREE NOVELS

OF

F. SCOTT FITZGERALD

BY F. SCOTT FITZGERALD

THREE NOVELS OF F. SCOTT FITZGERALD

THE GREAT GATSBY

With an Introduction by MALCOLM COWLEY

TENDER IS THE NIGHT

(WITH THE AUTHOR'S FINAL REVISIONS)

Edited by MALCOLM COWLEY

THE LAST TYCOON

AN UNFINISHED NOVEL

Edited by EDMUND WILSON

CHARLES SCRIBNER'S SONS

New York

CONTENTS

THE
GREAT GATSBY

INTRODUCTION
THE ROMANCE OF MONEY

ALTHOUGH FITZGERALD regarded himself, and was regarded by others, as a representative figure of the age, there was one respect in which he did not represent most of its serious writers. In that respect he was much closer to the men of his college year who were trying to get ahead in the business world; like them he was fascinated by the process of earning and spending money. The young businessmen of his time were bitterly determined to be successful and, much more than their successors of a later generation, they had been taught to measure success, failure, and even virtue in monetary terms. They had learned in school and Sunday school that virtue was rewarded with money and that viciousness was punished by the loss of money; apparently their only problem was to earn lots of it fast. Yet money was merely a convenient and inadequate symbol for what they dreamed of earning. The best of them were like Jay Gatsby in having "some heightened sensitivity to the promise of life"; or they were like another Fitzgerald hero, Dexter Green—of "Winter Dreams"—who "wanted not association with glittering things and glittering people —he wanted the glittering things themselves." Their real dream was that of achieving a new status and a new essence, of rising to a loftier place in the mysterious hierarchy of human worth.

The serious writers also dreamed of rising to a loftier status, but— except for Fitzgerald—they felt that money-making was the wrong way to rise. They liked money if it reached them in the form of gifts or legacies or publishers' advances, but they were afraid of high earned incomes because of what the incomes stood for: obligations, respectability, time lost from their own work, expensive habits that would drive them to earn still higher incomes; in short, a series of involvements in the commercial culture that was hostile to art. "If you want to ruin a writer," I used to hear them saying, "just give him a big magazine contract or a job at ten thousand a year." Many of them tried to preserve their independence by earning only enough to keep them alive while writing; a few liked to regard themselves as heroes of poverty and failure.

Their attitude toward money went into the texture of their work, which was noncommercial in the sense of being written in various new styles that the public was slow to accept. The 1920s were the great age of literary experiment, when the new writers were moving in all directions simultaneously. Some of them tried to capture in words the effects of modern painting (like E. E. Cummings); some used the older literary language with Shakespearean orotundity (like Thomas Wolfe); some worked at developing a new language based on Midwestern speech (like Hemingway). Some tried to omit all but the simplest adjectives (again like Hemingway); some used five or six long adjectives in a row (like Faulkner); some ran adjectives and adverbs together in a hurryconfusing fashion (like Dos Passos). Some approached their characters only from the outside, some gave only their inmost thoughts, their streams of subconsciousness, some broke a story into fragments, some told it backwards, some tried to dispense with stories. They were all showing the same spirit of adventure and exploration in fiction that their contemporaries were showing in the business world. That spirit made them part of the age, but at the same time they were trying to criticize and escape from it, and many of them looked back longingly to other ages when, so they liked to think, artists had wealthy patrons and hence were able to live outside the economic system.

Fitzgerald, on the other hand, immersed himself in the age and always remained close to the business world which the others were trying to evade. That world was the background of his stories and they performed a business function in themselves, by supplying the narration that readers followed like a thread through the labyrinth of advertising in the slick-paper magazines. He did not divorce himself from readers by writing experimental prose or by inventing new methods of telling or refusing to tell a story. His very real originality was a matter of mood and subject rather than form and it was more evident in his novels than in his stories, good as the stories often were. Although he despised the trade of writing for magazines—or despised it with part of his mind—he worked at it honestly. It yielded him a large income that he couldn't have earned in any other fashion and the income was necessary to his self-respect.

Fitzgerald kept an accurate record of his earnings—in the big ledger where he also recorded his deeds and misdeeds, as if to strike a book-keeper's balance between them—but he was always vague about his expenditures and was usually vague about his possessions, including his balance in the bank. Once he asked the cashier, "How much money have I got?" The cashier looked in a big book and answered without even scowling, "None." Fitzgerald resolved to be more thrifty, knowing that he would break the resolution. He had little interest in money for itself and less in the physical objects it would buy. On the other hand, he had a great interest in earning money, lots of it fast, because that was a sort of gold medal awarded with the blue ribbon for competitive achievement. Once the money was earned he and Zelda liked to spend lots of it fast, usually for impermanent things: not for real estate, fine motorcars, or furniture, but for traveling expenses, the rent of furnished houses, the wages of nurses and servants; for entertainments, party dresses, and feather fans of five colors. Zelda was as proudly careless about money as an eighteenth-century nobleman's heir. Scott was more practical and had his penny-pinching moments, as if in memory of his childhood, but at other times he liked to spend without counting in order to enjoy a sense of careless potency.

In his attitude toward money he revealed the new spirit of an age when conspicuous accumulation was giving way to conspicuous earning and spending. It was an age when gold was melted down and became fluid; when wealth was no longer measured in possessions—land, houses, livestock, machinery—but rather in dollars per year, as a stream is measured by its flow; when for the first time the expenses of government were being met by income taxes more than by property and excise taxes. There were still old solid fortunes at the hardly accessible peak of the social system, which young men dreamed of reaching, but the romantic figures of the age were not capitalists properly speaking. They were hired executives, promoters, salesmen, stock gamblers, or racketeers, and they were millionaires in a new sense—not men each of whom owned a million dollars' worth of property, but men who lived in rented apartments and had nothing but stock certificates and life-insurance policies (or nothing but credit and the proper connections), while spending more than the income of the old millionaires.

All these changes and survivals, as refracted through different personalities, are mirrored in Fitzgerald's work. In dealing with the romance of money, he chose the central theme of his American age. "Americans," he liked to say, "should be born with fins, and perhaps they were—perhaps money was a form of fin."

2

One of his remarks about his work has always puzzled his critics. "D. H. Lawrence's great attempt to synthesize animal and emotional —things he left out," Fitzgerald wrote in his notebook, then added the comment, "Essential pre-Marxian. Just as I am essentially Marxian." He was never Marxian in any sense of the word that Marxians of whatever school would be willing to accept. It is true that he finally read *Das Kapital* and was impressed by "the terrible chapter," as he called it, "on 'The Working Day'"; but it left in him not so much as a trace of Marx's belief in the mission of the proletariat.

His picture of proletarian life was of something alien to his own background, mysterious and even criminal. It seems to have been symbolized in some of his stories by the riverfront strip in St. Paul that languished in the shadow of the big houses on the bluff; he described the strip as a gridiron of mean streets where consumptive or pugilistic youths lounged in front of poolrooms, their skins turned livid by the neon lights. In *The Great Gatsby* he must have been thinking about the lower levels of American society when he described the valley of ashes between West Egg and New York—"A fantastic farm," he called it, "where ashes grow like wheat into ridges and hills and grotesque gardens; where ashes take the forms of houses and chimneys and rising smoke and, finally, with a transcendent effort, of men who move dimly and always crumbling through the powdery air." One of his early titles for the novel was "Among Ash Heaps and Millionaires"—as if he were setting the two against each other while suggesting a vague affinity between them. Tom Buchanan, the brutalized millionaire, found a mistress in the valley of ashes.

In Fitzgerald's stories there could be no real struggle between this dimly pictured ash-gray proletariat and the bourgeosie. On the other hand, there could be a different struggle that the author must have regarded, for a time, as essentially Marxian. It was the struggle that I have already suggested, between wealth as fluid income and wealth as a solid possession—or rather, since Fitzgerald is not an essayist but a story-teller, it is between a man and a woman as representatives of the new and the old moneyed classes.

We are not allowed to forget that they are representatives. The man comes from a family with little or no money, but he manages to attend an Eastern university—often Harvard or Yale, to set a distance between the hero and the Princeton author. He then sets out to earn a fortune equal to those of his wealthy classmates. Usually what he earns is not a fortune but an impressively large income, after he has become a success in his chosen profession—which may be engineering or architecture or advertising or the laundry business or bootlegging or real estate or even, in one story, frozen fish; the heroes are never writers like himself, although one of them is described as a popular dramatist. When the heroes are halfway to success, they fall in love.

The woman—or rather the girl—in a Fitzgerald story is younger and richer than the man and the author makes it even clearer that she represents her social class. "She was a stalk of ripe corn," he says of one heroine, "but bound not as cereals are but as a rare first edition, with all the binder's art. She was lovely and expensive and about nineteen." Of another heroine he says when she first appears that "Her childish beauty was wistful and sad about being so rich and sixteen." Later, when her father loses his money, the hero pays her a visit in London. "All around her," Fitzgerald says, "he could feel the vast Mortmain fortune melting down, seeping back into the matrix whence it had come." The hero thinks that she might marry him, now that she has fallen almost to his financial level; but he finds that the Mortmain (or dead-hand) fortune, even though lost, is still a barrier between them. Note that the man is not attracted by the fortune in itself. He is not seeking money so much as position at the peak of the social hierarchy and the girl becomes the symbol of that position, the incarnation of its mysterious power. That is Daisy Buchanan's charm for the great Gatsby, and it is the reason why he directs his whole life toward winning back her love.

"She's got an indiscreet voice," Nick Carraway says of her. "It's full of—" and he hesitates.

"Her voice is full of money," Gatsby says suddenly.

And Nick, the narrator, thinks to himself, "That was it. I'd never understood before. It was full of money—that was the inexhaustible charm that rose and fell in it, the cymbals' song of it. . . . High in a white palace the king's daughter, the golden girl."

In Fitzgerald's stories a love affair is like secret negotiations between the diplomats of two countries which are not at peace and not quite at war. For a moment they forget their hostility, find it transformed into mutual curiosity, attraction, even passion (though the passion is not physical); but the hostility will survive even in marriage, if marriage is to be their future. I called the lovers diplomats, ambassadors, and that is another way of saying that they are representatives. When they meet it is as if they were leaning toward each other from separate high platforms—the man from a platform built up of his former poverty, his ambition, his competitive triumphs, his ability to earn and spend always more, more; the girl from another platform covered with cloth of gold and feather fans of many colors, but beneath them a sturdy pile of stock certificates representing the ownership of mines, forests, factories, villages—all of Candy Town.

She is the embodied spirit of wealth, as can be clearly seen in one of the best of Fitzgerald's early stories, "Winter Dreams." A rising young man named Dexter Green takes home the daughter of a millionaire for whom he used to be a caddy. She is Judy Jones, "a slender enamelled doll in cloth of gold: gold in a band at her head, gold in two slipper points at her dress's hem." The rising young man stops his coupé, Fitzgerald says, "in front of the great white bulk of the Mortimer Jones house, somnolent, gorgeous, drenched with the splendor of the damp moonlight. Its solidity startled him. The strong walls, the steel of the girders, the breadth and beam and pomp of it were there only to bring out the contrast with the young beauty beside him. It was sturdy to accentuate her slightness—as if to show what a breeze could be generated by a butterfly's wing." Butterflies used to be taken as symbols of the soul. The inference is clear that, holding Judy in his arms, Dexter is embracing the spirit of a great fortune.

Nicole Warren, the heroine of *Tender Is the Night,* is the spirit of an even greater fortune. Fitzgerald says of her:

> Nicole was the product of much ingenuity and toil. For her sake trains began their run at Chicago and traversed the round belly of the continent to California; chicle factories fumed and link belts grew link by link in factories; men mixed toothpaste in vats and drew mouthwash out of copper hogsheads; girls canned tomatoes quickly in August or worked rudely at the five-and-tens on Christmas Eve; half-breed Indians toiled on Brazilian coffee plantations and dreamers were muscled out of patent rights in new tractors—these were some of the people who gave a tithe to Nicole, and as the whole system swayed and thundered onward it lent a feverish bloom to such processes of hers as wholesale buying [of luxuries], like the flush of a fireman's face holding his post before a spreading blaze.

Sometimes Fitzgerald's heroines are candid, even brutal, about class relationships. "Let's start right," the heroine of "Winter Dreams" says to Dexter Green on the first evening they spend alone together. "Who are you?"

"I'm nobody," Dexter tells her, without adding that he had been her father's caddy. "My career is largely a matter of futures."

"Are you poor?"

"No," he says frankly, "I'm probably making more money than any man my age in the Northwest. I know that's an obnoxious remark, but you advised me to start right."

"There was a pause," Fitzgerald adds. "Then she smiled and the corners of her mouth drooped and an almost imperceptible sway brought her closer to him, looking up into his eyes." Money brings them together, but later they are separated by something undefined —a mere whim of Judy's, it seems on one's first reading of the story, though one comes to feel that the whim was based on her feeling that she should marry a man of her own caste. Dexter, as he goes East to earn a still larger income, is filled with regret for "the country of illusions, of youth, of the richness of life, where his winter dreams had flourished." It seems likely that Judy Jones, like Josephine Perry in a series of later stories, was a character suggested by Fitzgerald's memories of a debutante with whom he was desperately in love during his first years at Princeton; afterward she made a more sensible marriage and Fitzgerald, too, regretted his winter dreams. As for the general attitude toward the rich that began to be expressed in the story, it is perhaps connected with his experiences in 1919, when Zelda broke off their engagement because they couldn't hope to live on his salary as a junior copywriter. Later he said of the time:

> During a long summer of despair I wrote a novel instead of letters, so it came out all right; but it came out all right for a different person. The man with the jingle of money in his pocket who married the girl a year later would always cherish an abiding distrust, an animosity, toward the leisure class—not the conviction of a revolutionist but the smoldering hatred of a peasant.

His mixture of feelings toward the very rich, which included curiosity and admiration as well as distrust, is revealed in his treatment of a basic situation that reappears in many of his stories. Of course he presented other situations that were not directly concerned with the relationship between social classes. He wrote about the problem of adjusting oneself to life, which he thought was especially difficult in the case of self-indulgent American women. He wrote about the manners of flappers and slickers. He wrote engagingly about his own boyhood. He wrote about the attempt to recapture youthful dreams, about the patching-up of broken marriages, about the contrast between Northern and Southern manners, about Americans going to pieces in Europe, about the self-tortures of gifted alcoholics, and in much of his later work—as notably in *The Last Tycoon*—he would be expressing his admiration for supremely great technicians, such as brain surgeons and movie directors. But a great number of his stories, especially the early ones, start with the basic situation I have mentioned: a rising young man of the middle class in love with the daughter of a very rich family. (Sometimes the family is Southern, in which case it needn't be so rich, since a high social status can exist in the South without great wealth.)

From that beginning the story may take any one of several turns. The hero may marry the girl, but only after she loses her fortune or (as in "Presumption" and "'The Sensible Thing'") he gains an income greater than hers. He may lose the girl (as in "Winter Dreams") and always remember that she represented his early aspirations. In "The Bridal Party" he resigns himself to the loss after being forced to recognize that the rich man she married is stronger and more capable than himself. In "More Than Just a House" he learns that the girl is empty and selfish and ends by marrying her good sister; in "The Rubber Check" he marries Ellen Mortmain's quiet cousin. There is, however, still another development out of the Fitzgerald situation that comes closer to revealing his ambiguous feelings toward the very rich. To state it simply—too simply—the rising young man wins the rich girl and then is destroyed by her wealth or her relatives.

The plot is like that of "Young Lochinvar," but with a tragic ending—as if fair Ellen's armed kinsmen had overtaken the pair, or as if they had slain the hero by treachery. Fitzgerald used it for the first time in a fantasy, "The Diamond as Big as the Ritz," which he wrote in St. Paul in the winter of 1921–22. Like many other fantasies it reveals more of the author's mind than does his more realistic work. It deals with the adventures of a boy named John T. Unger (we might read "Hunger"), who was born in a town on the Mississippi called Hades, though it might also be called St. Paul. He is sent away to St. Midas', which is "the most expensive and most exclusive boys' preparatory school in the world," and there he meets a classmate named Percy Washington, who invites him to spend the summer at his home in the West. On the train Percy confides to him that his father is the richest man alive and owns a diamond bigger than the Ritz-Carlton Hotel (solid as opposed to fluid wealth).

The description of the Washington mansion, in its hidden valley that wasn't even shown on the maps of the U. S. Geodetic Survey, is fantasy mingled with burlesque; but then the familiar Fitzgerald note appears. John falls in love with Percy's younger sister, Kismine. After an idyllic summer Kismine tells him accidentally—she had meant to keep the secret—that he will very soon be murdered, like all the former guests of the Washingtons. "It was done very nicely,"

Kismine explains to him. "They were drugged while they were asleep—and their families were always told that they died of scarlet fever in Butte. . . . I shall probably have visitors too—I'll harden up to it. We can't let such an inevitable thing as death stand in the way of enjoying life while we have it. Think how lonesome it'd be out here if we never had *any*one. Why, father and mother have sacrificed some of their best friends just as we have."

Tom and Daisy Buchanan also sacrificed some of their best friends. "They were careless people, Tom and Daisy—they smashed up things and creatures and then retreated back into their money or their vast carelessness, or whatever it was that kept them together, and let other people clean up the mess they had made." "The Diamond as Big as the Ritz" can have a happy ending for the two lovers because it is fantasy; but the same plot reappears in *The Great Gatsby,* where it is surrounded by the real world of the 1920s and for the first time it is carried through to its logical conclusion.

3

There is a moment in any real author's career when he suddenly becomes capable of doing his best work. He has found a fable that expresses his central truth and everything falls into place around it, so that his whole experience of life is available for use in his fiction. Something like that happened to Fitzgerald when he invented the story of Jimmy Gatz, otherwise known as Jay Gatsby, and it explains the amazing richness and scope of a very short novel.

To put facts on record, *The Great Gatsby* is a book of about fifty thousand words, a small structure built of nine chapters like big blocks. The fifth chapter—Gatsby's meeting with Daisy Buchanan— is the center of the narrative, as is proper; the seventh chapter is the climax. Each chapter consists of one or more dramatic scenes, some- times with intervening passages of straight narration. The "scenic" method is one that Fitzgerald probably learned from Edith Whar- ton, who in turn learned it from Henry James; at any rate the book is technically in the Jamesian tradition (and Daisy Buchanan is named for James's heroine, Daisy Miller).

Part of the tradition is the device of having the story told by a single observer, who stands somewhat apart from the action and whose vision "frames" it for the reader. In this case the observer plays a special role. Although Nick Carraway doesn't save or ruin Gatsby, his personality in itself provides an essential comment on all the other characters. Nick stands for the older values that prevailed in the Middle West before the First World War. His family isn't tremendously rich, like the Buchanans, but it has a long established and sufficient fortune, so that Nick is the only person in the book who hasn't been corrupted by seeking or spending money. He is so certain of his own values that he hesitates to criticize others, but when he does pass judgment—on Gatsby, on Jordan Baker, on the Buchanans—he speaks as if for ages to come.

All the other characters belong to their own brief era of confused and dissolving standards, but they are affected by the era in different fashions. Each of them, we note on reading the book a second time, represents some particular variety of moral failure; Lionel Trilling says that they are "treated as if they were ideographs," a true observation; but the treatment does not detract from their reality as persons. Tom Buchanan is wealth brutalized by selfishness and arrogance; he looks for a mistress in the valley of ashes and finds an ignorant woman, Myrtle Wilson, whose raw vitality is like his own. Daisy Buchanan is the spirit of wealth and offers a continual promise "that she had done gay, exciting things just a while since and that there were gay, exciting things hovering in the next hour"; but it is a false promise, since at heart she is as self-centered as Tom and even colder. Jordan Baker apparently lives by the old standards, but she uses them only as a subterfuge. Aware of her own cowardice and dishonesty, she feels "safer on a plane where any divergence from a code would be thought impossible."

All these, except Myrtle Wilson, are East Egg people, that is, they are part of a community where wealth takes the form of solid possessions. Set against them are the West Egg people, whose wealth is fluid income that might cease overnight. The West Egg people, with Gatsby as their archetype and tragic hero, have worked furiously to rise in the world, but they will never reach East Egg for all the money they spend; at most they can sit at the water's edge and look across the bay at the green light that shines and promises at the end of the Buchanans' dock. The symbolism of place has a great part in Fitzgerald's novel, as has that of motorcars. The characters are visibly represented by the cars they drive: Nick has a conservative old Dodge, the Buchanans, too rich for ostentation, have an "easy-going blue coupé," while Gatsby's car is "a rich cream color, bright with nickel, swollen here and there in its monstrous length with triumphant hat-boxes and supper-boxes and tool-boxes, and terraced with a labyrinth of wind-shields that mirrored a dozen suns"—it is West Egg on wheels. When Daisy drives through the valley of ashes in Gatsby's car, she causes the two deaths that end the story.

The symbols are not synthetic or contrived, like those in so many recent novels; they are images that Fitzgerald instinctively found to represent his characters and their destiny. When he says, "Daisy took her face in her hands as if feeling its lovely shape," he is watching her act the charade of her self-love. When he says, "Tom would drift on forever seeking, a little wistfully, for the dramatic turbulence of some irrecoverable football game," he suggests the one appealing side of Tom's nature. He is so familiar with the characters and their background, so absorbed in their fate, that the book has an admirable unity of texture; we can open it to any page and find another of the touches that illuminate the story. We end by feeling that *Gatsby* has a double virtue. Except for *The Sun Also Rises* it is the best picture we possess of the age in which it was written and it also achieves a sort of moral permanence. Fitzgerald's story of the innocent murdered suitor for wealth is a compendious fable of the 1920s that will survive as a legend for other times.

MALCOLM COWLEY

THE
GREAT GATSBY

Then wear the gold hat, if that will move her;

  If you can bounce high, bounce for her too,

Till she cry "Lover, gold-hatted, high-bouncing lover,

  I must have you!"

—THOMAS PARKE D'INVILLIERS.

THE GREAT GATSBY

CHAPTER I

IN MY YOUNGER and more vulnerable years my father gave me some advice that I've been turning over in my mind ever since.

"Whenever you feel like criticizing any one," he told me, "just remember that all the people in this world haven't had the advantages that you've had."

He didn't say any more, but we've always been unusually communicative in a reserved way, and I understood that he meant a great deal more than that. In consequence, I'm inclined to reserve all judgments, a habit that has opened up many curious natures to me and also made me the victim of not a few veteran bores. The abnormal mind is quick to detect and attach itself to this quality when it appears in a normal person, and so it came about that in college I was unjustly accused of being a politician, because I was privy to the secret griefs of wild, unknown men. Most of the confidences were unsought—frequently I have feigned sleep, preoccupation, or a hostile levity when I realized by some unmistakable sign that an intimate revelation was quivering on the horizon; for the intimate revelations of young men, or at least the terms in which they express them, are usually plagiaristic and marred by obvious suppressions. Reserving judgments is a matter of infinite hope. I am still a little afraid of missing something if I forget that, as my father snobbishly suggested, and I snobbishly repeat, a sense of the fundamental decencies is parcelled out unequally at birth.

And, after boasting this way of my tolerance, I come to the admission that it has a limit. Conduct may be founded on the hard rock or the wet marshes, but after a certain point I don't care what it's founded on. When I came back from the East last autumn I felt that I wanted the world to be in uniform and at a sort of moral attention forever; I wanted no more riotous excursions with privileged glimpses into the human heart. Only Gatsby, the man who gives his name to this book, was exempt from my reaction—Gatsby, who represented everything for which I have an unaffected scorn.

If personality is an unbroken series of successful gestures, then there was something gorgeous about him, some heightened sensitivity to the promises of life, as if he were related to one of those intricate machines that register earthquakes ten thousand miles away. This responsiveness had nothing to do with that flabby impressionability which is dignified under the name of the "creative temperament"— it was an extraordinary gift for hope, a romantic readiness such as I have never found in any other person and which it is not likely I shall ever find again. No—Gatsby turned out all right at the end; it is what preyed on Gatsby, what foul dust floated in the wake of his dreams that temporarily closed out my interest in the abortive sorrows and short-winded elations of men.

My family have been prominent, well-to-do people in this Middle Western city for three generations. The Carraways are something of a clan, and we have a tradition that we're descended from the Dukes of Buccleuch, but the actual founder of my line was my grandfather's brother, who came here in fifty-one, sent a substitute to the Civil War, and started the wholesale hardware business that my father carries on to-day.

I never saw this great-uncle, but I'm supposed to look like him— with special reference to the rather hard-boiled painting that hangs in father's office. I graduated from New Haven in 1915, just a quarter of a century after my father, and a little later I participated in that delayed Teutonic migration known as the Great War. I enjoyed the counter-raid so thoroughly that I came back restless. Instead of being the warm centre of the world, the Middle West now seemed like the ragged edge of the universe—so I decided to go East and learn the bond business. Everybody I knew was in the bond business, so I supposed it could support one more single man. All my aunts and uncles talked it over as if they were choosing a prep school for me, and finally said, "Why—ye-es," with very grave, hesitant faces. Father agreed to finance me for a year, and after various delays I came East, permanently, I thought, in the spring of twenty-two.

The practical thing was to find rooms in the city, but it was a warm season, and I had just left a country of wide lawns and friendly trees, so when a young man at the office suggested that we take a house together in a commuting town, it sounded like a great idea. He found the house, a weatherbeaten cardboard bungalow at eighty a month, but at the last minute the firm ordered him to Washington, and I went out to the country alone. I had a dog—at least I had him for a few days until he ran away—and an old Dodge and a Finnish woman, who made my bed and cooked breakfast and muttered Finnish wisdom to herself over the electric stove.

It was lonely for a day or so until one morning some man, more recently arrived than I, stopped me on the road.

"How do you get to West Egg village?" he asked helplessly.

I told him. And as I walked on I was lonely no longer. I was a guide, a pathfinder, an original settler. He had casually conferred on me the freedom of the neighborhood.

And so with the sunshine and the great bursts of leaves growing on the trees, just as things grow in fast movies, I had that familiar conviction that life was beginning over again with the summer.

There was so much to read, for one thing, and so much fine health to be pulled down out of the young breath-giving air. I bought a dozen volumes on banking and credit and investment securities, and they stood on my shelf in red and gold like new money from the mint, promising to unfold the shining secrets that only Midas and Morgan and Mæcenas knew. And I had the high intention of reading many other books besides. I was rather literary in college— one year I wrote a series of very solemn and obvious editorials for the *Yale News*—and now I was going to bring back all such things into my life and become again that most limited of all specialists, the "well-rounded man." This isn't just an epigram—life is much more successfully looked at from a single window, after all.

It was a matter of chance that I should have rented a house in one of the strangest communities in North America. It was on that slender riotous island which extends itself due east of New York —and where there are, among other natural curiosities, two unusual formations of land. Twenty miles from the city a pair of enormous eggs, identical in contour and separated only by a courtesy bay, jut out into the most domesticated body of salt water in the Western hemisphere, the great wet barnyard of Long Island Sound. They are not perfect ovals—like the egg in the Columbus story, they are both crushed flat at the contact end—but their physical resemblance must be a source of perpetual confusion to the gulls that fly overhead. To the wingless a more arresting phenomenon is their dissimilarity in every particular except shape and size.

I lived at West Egg, the—well, the less fashionable of the two, though this is a most superficial tag to express the bizarre and not a little sinister contrast between them. My house was at the very tip of the egg, only fifty yards from the Sound, and squeezed between two huge places that rented for twelve or fifteen thousand a season. The one on my right was a colossal affair by any standard—it was a factual imitation of some Hôtel de Ville in Normandy, with a tower on one side, spanking new under a thin beard of raw ivy, and a marble swimming pool, and more than forty acres of lawn and garden. It was Gatsby's mansion. Or, rather, as I didn't know Mr. Gatsby, it was a mansion, inhabited by a gentleman of that name. My own house was an eyesore, but it was a small eyesore, and it had been overlooked, so I had a view of the water, a partial view of my neighbor's lawn, and the consoling proximity of millionaires—all for eighty dollars a month.

Across the courtesy bay the white palaces of fashionable East Egg glittered along the water, and the history of the summer really begins on the evening I drove over there to have dinner with the Tom Buchanans. Daisy was my second cousin once removed, and I'd known Tom in college. And just after the war I spent two days with them in Chicago.

Her husband, among various physical accomplishments, had been one of the most powerful ends that ever played football at New Haven—a national figure in a way, one of those men who reach such an acute limited excellence at twenty-one that everything afterward savors of anticlimax. His family were enormously wealthy—even in college his freedom with money was a matter for reproach—but now he'd left Chicago and come East in a fashion that rather took your breath away; for instance, he'd brought down a string of polo ponies from Lake Forest. It was hard to realize that a man in my own generation was wealthy enough to do that.

Why they came East I don't know. They had spent a year in France for no particular reason, and then drifted here and there unrestfully wherever people played polo and were rich together. This was a permanent move, said Daisy over the telephone, but

I didn't believe it—I had no sight into Daisy's heart, but I felt that Tom would drift on forever seeking, a little wistfully, for the dramatic turbulence of some irrecoverable football game.

And so it happened that on a warm windy evening I drove over to East Egg to see two old friends whom I scarcely knew at all. Their house was even more elaborate than I expected, a cheerful red-and-white Georgian Colonial mansion, overlooking the bay. The lawn started at the beach and ran toward the front door for a quarter of a mile, jumping over sun-dials and brick walks and burning gardens—finally when it reached the house drifting up the side in bright vines as though from the momentum of its run. The front was broken by a line of French windows, glowing now with reflected gold and wide open to the warm windy afternoon, and Tom Buchanan in riding clothes was standing with his legs apart on the front porch.

He had changed since his New Haven years. Now he was a sturdy straw-haired man of thirty with a rather hard mouth and a supercilious manner. Two shining arrogant eyes had established dominance over his face and gave him the appearance of always leaning aggressively forward. Not even the effeminate swank of his riding clothes could hide the enormous power of that body—he seemed to fill those glistening boots until he strained the top lacing, and you could see a great pack of muscle shifting when his shoulder moved under his thin coat. It was a body capable of enormous leverage—a cruel body.

His speaking voice, a gruff husky tenor, added to the impression of fractiousness he conveyed. There was a touch of paternal contempt in it, even toward people he liked—and there were men at New Haven who had hated his guts.

"Now, don't think my opinion on these matters is final," he seemed to say, "just because I'm stronger and more of a man than you are." We were in the same senior society, and while we were never intimate I always had the impression that he approved of me and wanted me to like him with some harsh, defiant wistfulness of his own.

We talked for a few minutes on the sunny porch.

"I've got a nice place here," he said, his eyes flashing about restlessly.

Turning me around by one arm, he moved a broad flat hand along the front vista, including in its sweep a sunken Italian garden, a half acre of deep, pungent roses, and a snub-nosed motor-boat that bumped the tide offshore.

"It belonged to Demaine, the oil man." He turned me around again, politely and abruptly. "We'll go inside."

We walked through a high hallway into a bright rosy-colored space, fragilely bound into the house by French windows at either end. The windows were ajar and gleaming white against the fresh grass outside that seemed to grow a little way into the house. A breeze blew through the room, blew curtains in at one end and out the other like pale flags, twisting them up toward the frosted wedding-cake of the ceiling, and then rippled over the wine-colored rug, making a shadow on it as wind does on the sea.

The only completely stationary object in the room was an enormous couch on which two young women were buoyed up as though upon an anchored balloon. They were both in white, and their dresses were rippling and fluttering as if they had just been blown back in after a short flight around the house. I must have stood for a few moments listening to the whip and snap of the curtains and the groan of a picture on the wall. Then there was a boom as Tom Buchanan shut the rear windows and the caught wind died out about the room, and the curtains and the rugs and the two young women ballooned slowly to the floor.

The younger of the two was a stranger to me. She was extended full length at her end of the divan, completely motionless, and with her chin raised a little, as if she were balancing something on it which was quite likely to fall. If she saw me out of the corner of her eyes she gave no hint of it—indeed, I was almost surprised into murmuring an apology for having disturbed her by coming in.

The other girl, Daisy, made an attempt to rise—she leaned slightly forward with a conscientious expression—then she laughed, an absurd, charming little laugh, and I laughed too and came forward into the room.

"I'm p-paralyzed with happiness."

She laughed again, as if she said something very witty, and held my hand for a moment, looking up into my face, promising that there was no one in the world she so much wanted to see. That was a way she had. She hinted in a murmur that the surname of the balancing girl was Baker. (I've heard it said that Daisy's murmur was only to make people lean toward her; an irrelevant criticism that made it no less charming.)

At any rate, Miss Baker's lips fluttered, she nodded at me almost imperceptibly, and then quickly tipped her head back again—the object she was balancing had obviously tottered a little and given her something of a fright. Again a sort of apology arose to my lips. Almost any exhibition of complete self-sufficiency draws a stunned tribute from me.

I looked back at my cousin, who began to ask me questions in her low, thrilling voice. It was the kind of voice that the ear follows up and down, as if each speech is an arrangement of notes that will never be played again. Her face was sad and lovely with bright things in it, bright eyes and a bright passionate mouth, but there was an excitement in her voice that men who had cared for her found difficult to forget: a singing compulsion, a whispered "Listen," a promise that she had done gay, exciting things just a while since and that there were gay, exciting things hovering in the next hour.

I told her how I had stopped off in Chicago for a day on my way East, and how a dozen people had sent their love through me.

"Do they miss me?" she cried ecstatically.

"The whole town is desolate. All the cars have the left rear wheel painted black as a mourning wreath, and there's a persistent wail all night along the north shore."

"How gorgeous! Let's go back, Tom. To-morrow!" Then she added irrelevantly: "You ought to see the baby."

"I'd like to."

"She's asleep. She's three years old. Haven't you ever seen her?"

"Never."

"Well, you ought to see her. She's——"

Tom Buchanan, who had been hovering restlessly about the room, stopped and rested his hand on my shoulder.

"What you doing, Nick?"

"I'm a bond man."

"Who with?"

I told him.

"Never heard of them," he remarked decisively.

This annoyed me.

"You will," I answered shortly. "You will if you stay in the East."

"Oh, I'll stay in the East, don't you worry," he said, glancing at Daisy and then back at me, as if he were alert for something more. "I'd be a God damned fool to live anywhere else."

At this point Miss Baker said: "Absolutely!" with such suddenness that I started—it was the first word she had uttered since I came into the room. Evidently it surprised her as much as it did me, for she yawned and with a series of rapid, deft movements stood up into the room.

"I'm stiff," she complained, "I've been lying on that sofa for as long as I can remember."

"Don't look at me," Daisy retorted, "I've been trying to get you to New York all afternoon."

"No, thanks," said Miss Baker to the four cocktails just in from the pantry, "I'm absolutely in training."

Her host looked at her incredulously.

"You are!" He took down his drink as if it were a drop in the bottom of a glass. "How you ever get anything done is beyond me."

I looked at Miss Baker, wondering what it was she "got done." I enjoyed looking at her. She was a slender, small-breasted girl, with an erect carriage, which she accentuated by throwing her body backward at the shoulders like a young cadet. Her gray sun-strained eyes looked back at me with polite reciprocal curiosity out of a wan, charming, discontented face. It occurred to me now that I had seen her, or a picture of her, somewhere before.

"You live in West Egg," she remarked contemptuously. "I know somebody there."

"I don't know a single——"

"You must know Gatsby."

"Gatsby?" demanded Daisy. "What Gatsby?"

Before I could reply that he was my neighbor dinner was announced; wedging his tense arm imperatively under mine, Tom Buchanan compelled me from the room as though he were moving a checker to another square.

Slenderly, languidly, their hands set lightly on their hips, the two young women preceded us out onto a rosy-colored porch, open toward the sunset, where four candles flickered on the table in the diminished wind.

"Why *candles*?" objected Daisy, frowning. She snapped them out with her fingers. "In two weeks it'll be the longest day in the year." She looked at us all radiantly. "Do you always watch for the longest day of the year and then miss it? I always watch for the longest day in the year and then miss it."

"We ought to plan something," yawned Miss Baker, sitting down at the table as if she were getting into bed.

"All right," said Daisy. "What'll we plan?" She turned to me helplessly: "What do people plan?"

Before I could answer her eyes fastened with an awed expression on her little finger.

"Look!" she complained; "I hurt it."

We all looked—the knuckle was black and blue.

"You did it, Tom," she said accusingly. "I know you didn't mean to, but you *did* do it. That's what I get for marrying a brute of a man, a great, big, hulking physical specimen of a——"

"I hate that word hulking," objected Tom crossly, "even in kidding."

"Hulking," insisted Daisy.

Sometimes she and Miss Baker talked at once, unobtrusively and with a bantering inconsequence that was never quite chatter, that was as cool as their white dresses and their impersonal eyes in the absence of all desire. They were here, and they accepted Tom and me, making only a polite pleasant effort to entertain or to be entertained. They knew that presently dinner would be over and a little later the evening, too, would be over and casually put away. It was sharply different from the West, where an evening was hurried from phase to phase toward its close, in a continually disappointed anticipation or else in sheer nervous dread of the moment itself.

"You make me feel uncivilized, Daisy," I confessed on my second glass of corky but rather impressive claret. "Can't you talk about crops or something?"

I meant nothing in particular by this remark, but it was taken up in an unexpected way.

"Civilization's going to pieces," broke out Tom violently. "I've gotten to be a terrible pessimist about things. Have you read 'The Rise of the Colored Empires' by this man Goddard?"

"Why, no," I answered, rather surprised by his tone.

"Well, it's a fine book, and everybody ought to read it. The idea is if we don't look out the white race will be—will be utterly submerged. It's all scientific stuff; it's been proved."

"Tom's getting very profound," said Daisy, with an expression of unthoughtful sadness. "He reads deep books with long words in them. What was that word we——"

"Well, these books are all scientific," insisted Tom, glancing at her impatiently. "This fellow has worked out the whole thing. It's up to us, who are the dominant race, to watch out or these other races will have control of things."

"We've got to beat them down," whispered Daisy, winking ferociously toward the fervent sun.

"You ought to live in California—" began Miss Baker, but Tom interrupted her by shifting heavily in his chair.

"This idea is that we're Nordics. I am, and you are, and you are, and—" After an infinitesimal hesitation he included Daisy with a slight nod, and she winked at me again. "—And we've produced all the things that go to make civilization—oh, science and art, and all that. Do you see?"

There was something pathetic in his concentration, as if his complacency, more acute than of old, was not enough to him any more. When, almost immediately, the telephone rang inside and the butler left the porch Daisy seized upon the momentary interruption and learned toward me.

"I'll tell you a family secret," she whispered enthusiastically. "It's about the butler's nose. Do you want to hear about the butler's nose?"

"That's why I came over to-night."

"Well, he wasn't always a butler; he used to be the silver polisher for some people in New York that had a silver service for two hundred people. He had to polish it from morning till night, until finally it began to affect his nose——"

"Things went from bad to worse," suggested Miss Baker.

"Yes. Things went from bad to worse, until finally he had to give up his position."

For a moment the last sunshine fell with romantic affection upon her glowing face; her voice compelled me forward breathlessly as I listened—then the glow faded, each light deserting her with lingering regret, like children leaving a pleasant street at dusk.

The butler came back and murmured something close to Tom's ear, whereupon Tom frowned, pushed back his chair, and without a word went inside. As if his absence quickened something within her, Daisy leaned forward again, her voice glowing and singing.

"I love to see you at my table, Nick. You remind me of a—of a rose, an absolute rose. Doesn't he?" She turned to Miss Baker for confirmation: "An absolute rose?"

This was untrue. I am not even faintly like a rose. She was only extemporizing, but a stirring warmth flowed from her, as if her heart was trying to come out to you concealed in one of those breathless, thrilling words. Then suddenly she threw her napkin on the table and excused herself and went into the house.

Miss Baker and I exchanged a short glance consciously devoid of meaning. I was about to speak when she sat up alertly and said "Sh!" in a warning voice. A subdued impassioned murmur was audible in the room beyond, and Miss Baker leaned forward unashamed, trying to hear. The murmur trembled on the verge of coherence, sank down, mounted excitedly, and then ceased altogether.

"This Mr. Gatsby you spoke of is my neighbor—" I said.

"Don't talk. I want to hear what happens."

"Is something happening?" I inquired innocently.

"You mean to say you don't know?" said Miss Baker, honestly surprised. "I thought everybody knew."

"I don't."

"Why—" she said hesitantly, "Tom's got some woman in New York."

"Got some woman?" I repeated blankly.

Miss Baker nodded.

"She might have the decency not to telephone him at dinner time. Don't you think?"

Almost before I had grasped her meaning there was the flutter of a dress and the crunch of leather boots, and Tom and Daisy were back at the table.

"It couldn't be helped!" cried Daisy with tense gayety.

She sat down, glanced searchingly at Miss Baker and then at me, and continued: "I looked outdoors for a minute, and it's very romantic outdoors. There's a bird on the lawn that I think must be a nightingale come over on the Cunard or White Star Line. He's singing away—" Her voice sang: "It's romantic, isn't it, Tom?"

"Very romantic," he said, and then miserably to me: "If it's light enough after dinner, I want to take you down to the stables."

The telephone rang inside, startlingly, and as Daisy shook her head decisively at Tom the subject of the stables, in fact all subjects, vanished into air. Among the broken fragments of the last five minutes at table I remember the candles being lit again, pointlessly, and I was conscious of wanting to look squarely at every one, and yet to avoid all eyes. I couldn't guess what Daisy and Tom were thinking, but I doubt if even Miss Baker, who seemed to have mastered a certain hardy scepticism, was able utterly to put this fifth guest's shrill metallic urgency out of mind. To a certain temperament the situation might have seemed intriguing—my own instinct was to telephone immediately for the police.

The horses, needless to say, were not mentioned again. Tom and Miss Baker, with several feet of twilight between them, strolled back into the library, as if to a vigil beside a perfectly tangible body, while, trying to look pleasantly interested and a little deaf, I followed Daisy around a chain of connecting verandas to the porch in front. In its deep gloom we sat down side by side on a wicker settee.

Daisy took her face in her hands as if feeling its lovely shape, and her eyes moved gradually out into the velvet dusk. I saw that turbulent emotions possessed her, so I asked what I thought would be some sedative questions about her little girl.

"We don't know each other very well, Nick," she said suddenly. "Even if we are cousins. You didn't come to my wedding."

"I wasn't back from the war."

"That's true." She hesitated. "Well, I've had a very bad time, Nick, and I'm pretty cynical about everything."

Evidently she had reason to be. I waited but she didn't say any more, and after a moment I returned rather feebly to the subject of her daughter.

"I suppose she talks, and—eats, and everything."

"Oh, yes." She looked at me absently. "Listen, Nick; let me tell you what I said when she was born. Would you like to hear?"

"Very much.

"It'll show you how I've gotten to feel about—things. Well, she was less than an hour old and Tom was God knows where. I woke up out of the ether with an utterly abandoned feeling, and asked the nurse right away if it was a boy or a girl. She told me it was a girl, and so I turned my head away and wept. 'All right,' I said, 'I'm glad it's a girl. And I hope she'll be a fool—that's the best thing a girl can be in this world, a beautiful little fool.'

"You see I think everything's terrible anyhow," she went on in a convinced way. "Everybody thinks so—the most advanced people. And I *know*. I've been everywhere and seen everything and done everything." Her eyes flashed around her in a defiant way, rather like Tom's, and she laughed with thrilling scorn. "Sophisticated—God, I'm sophisticated!"

The instant her voice broke off, ceasing to compel my attention, my belief, I felt the basic insincerity of what she had said. It made me uneasy, as though the whole evening had been a trick of some sort to exact a contributory emotion from me. I waited, and sure enough, in a moment she looked at me with an absolute smirk on her lovely face, as if she had asserted her membership in a rather distinguished secret society to which she and Tom belonged.

Inside, the crimson room bloomed with light. Tom and Miss Baker sat at either end of the long couch and she read aloud to him from *The Saturday Evening Post*—the words, murmurous and uninfected, running together in a soothing tune. The lamp-light, bright on his boots and dull on the autumn-leaf yellow of her hair, glinted along the paper as she turned a page with a flutter of slender muscles in her arms.

When we came in she held us silent for a moment with a lifted hand.

"To be continued," she said, tossing the magazine on the table, "in our very next issue."

Her body asserted itself with a restless movement of her knee, and she stood up.

"Ten o'clock," she remarked, apparently finding the time on the ceiling. "Time for this good girl to go to bed."

"Jordan's going to play in the tournament to-morrow," explained Daisy, "over at Westchester."

"Oh—you're *Jor*dan Baker."

I knew now why her face was familiar—its pleasing contemptuous expression had looked out at me from many rotogravure pictures of the sporting life at Asheville and Hot Springs and Palm Beach. I had heard some story of her too, a critical, unpleasant story, but what it was I had forgotten long ago.

"Good night," she said softly. "Wake me at eight, won't you?"

"If you'll get up."

"I will. Good night Mr. Carraway. See you anon."

"Of course you will," confirmed Daisy. "In fact, I think I'll arrange a marriage. Come over often, Nick, and I'll sort of—oh—fling you together. You know—lock you up accidentally in linen closets and push you out to sea in a boat, and all that sort of thing——"

"Good night," called Miss Baker from the stairs. "I haven't heard a word."

"She's a nice girl," said Tom after a moment. "They oughtn't to let her run around the country this way."

"Who oughtn't to?" inquired Daisy coldly.

"Her family."

"Her family is one aunt about a thousand years old. Besides, Nick's going to look after her, aren't you, Nick? She's going to spend lots of week-ends out here this summer. I think the home influence will be very good for her."

Daisy and Tom looked at each other for a moment in silence.

"Is she from New York?" I asked quickly.

"From Louisville. Our white girlhood was passed together there. Our beautiful white——"

"Did you give Nick a little heart-to-heart talk on the veranda?" demanded Tom suddenly.

"Did I?" She looked at me. "I can't seem to remember, but I think we talked about the Nordic race. Yes, I'm sure we did. It sort of crept up on us and first thing you know——"

"Don't believe everything you hear, Nick," he advised me.

I said lightly that I had heard nothing at all, and a few minutes later I got up to go home. They came to the door with me and stood side by side in a cheerful square of light. As I started my motor Daisy peremptorily called: "Wait!

"I forgot to ask you something, and it's important. We heard you were engaged to a girl out West."

"That's right," corroborated Tom kindly. "We heard that you were engaged."

"It's a libel. I'm too poor."

"But we heard it," insisted Daisy, surprising me by opening up again in a flower-like way. "We heard it from three people, so it must be true."

Of course I knew what they were referring to, but I wasn't even vaguely engaged. The fact that gossip had published the banns was one of the reasons I had come East. You can't stop going with an old friend on account of rumors, and on the other hand I had no intention of being rumored into marriage.

Their interest rather touched me and made them less remotely rich—nevertheless, I was confused and a little disgusted as I drove away. It seemed to me that the thing for Daisy to do was to rush out of the house, child in arms—but apparently there were no such intentions in her head. As for Tom, the fact that he "had some woman in New York" was really less surprising than that he had been depressed by a book. Something was making him nibble at the edge of stale ideas as if his sturdy physical egotism no longer nourished his peremptory heart.

Already it was deep summer on roadhouse roofs and in front of wayside garages, where new red gas-pumps sat out in pools of light, and when I reached my estate at West Egg I ran the car under its shed and sat for a while on an abandoned grass roller in the yard. The wind had blown off, leaving a loud, bright night, with wings beating in the trees and a persistent organ sound as the full bellows of the earth blew the frogs full of life. The silhouette of a moving cat wavered across the moonlight, and turning my head to watch it, I saw that I was not alone—fifty feet away a figure had emerged from the shadow of my neighbor's mansion and was standing with his hands in his pockets regarding the silver pepper of the stars. Something in his leisurely movements and the secure position of his feet upon the lawn suggested that it was Mr. Gatsby himself, come out to determine what share was his of our local heavens.

I decided to call to him. Miss Baker had mentioned him at dinner, and that would do for an introduction. But I didn't call to him, for he gave a sudden intimation that he was content to be alone—he stretched out his arms toward the dark water in a curious way, and, far as I was from him, I could have sworn he was trembling. Involuntarily I glanced seaward—and distinguished nothing except a single green light, minute and far away, that might have been the end of a dock. When I looked once more for Gatsby he had vanished, and I was alone again in the unquiet darkness.

CHAPTER II

ABOUT half way between West Egg and New York the motor road hastily joins the railroad and runs beside it for a quarter of a mile, so as to shrink away from a certain desolate area of land. This is a valley of ashes—a fantastic farm where ashes grow like wheat into ridges and hills and grotesque gardens; where ashes take the forms of houses and chimneys and rising smoke and, finally, with a transcendent effort, of men who move dimly and already crumbling through the powdery air. Occasionally a line of gray cars crawls along an invisible track, gives out a ghastly creak, and comes to rest, and immediately the ash-gray men swarm up with leaden spades and stir up an impenetrable cloud, which screens their obscure operations from your sight.

But above the gray land and the spasms of bleak dust which drift endlessly over it, you perceive, after a moment, the eyes of Doctor T. J. Eckleburg. The eyes of Doctor T. J. Eckleburg are blue and gigantic—their retinas are one yard high. They look out of no face, but, instead, from a pair of enormous yellow spectacles which pass over a non-existent nose. Evidently some wild wag of an oculist set them there to fatten his practice in the borough of Queens, and then sank down himself into eternal blindness, or forgot them and moved away. But his eyes, dimmed a little by many paintless days under sun and rain, brood on over the solemn dumping ground.

The valley of ashes is bounded on one side by a small foul river, and, when the drawbridge is up to let barges through, the passengers on waiting trains can stare at the dismal scene for as long as half an hour. There is always a halt there of at least a minute, and it was because of this that I first met Tom Buchanan's mistress.

The fact that he had one was insisted upon wherever he was known. His acquaintances resented the fact that he turned up in popular restaurants with her and, leaving her at a table, sauntered about, chatting with whomsoever he knew. Though I was curious to see her, I had no desire to meet her—but I did. I went up to New

York with Tom on the train one afternoon and when we stopped by the ashheaps he jumped to his feet and, taking hold of my elbow, literally forced me from the car.

"We're getting off," he insisted. "I want you to meet my girl."

I think he'd tanked up a good deal at luncheon, and his determination to have my company bordered on violence. The supercilious assumption was that on Sunday afternoon I had nothing better to do.

I followed him over a low whitewashed railroad fence, and we walked back a hundred yards along the road under Doctor Eckleburg's persistent stare. The only building in sight was a small block of yellow brick sitting on the edge of the waste land, a sort of compact Main Street ministering to it, and contiguous to absolutely nothing. One of the three shops it contained was for rent and another was an all-night restaurant, approached by a trail of ashes; the third was a garage—*Repairs.* GEORGE B. WILSON. *Cars bought and sold.*—and I followed Tom inside.

The interior was unprosperous and bare; the only car visible was the dust-covered wreck of a Ford which crouched in a dim corner. It had occurred to me that this shadow of a garage must be a blind, and that sumptuous and romantic apartments were concealed overhead, when the proprietor himself appeared in the door of an office, wiping his hands on a piece of waste. He was a blond, spiritless man, anæmic, and faintly handsome. When he saw us a damp gleam of hope sprang into his light blue eyes.

"Hello, Wilson, old man," said Tom, slapping him jovially on the shoulder. "How's business?"

"I can't complain," answered Wilson unconvincingly. "When are you going to sell me that car?"

"Next week; I've got my man working on it now."

"Works pretty slow, don't he?"

"No, he doesn't," said Tom coldly. "And if you feel that way about it, maybe I'd better sell it somewhere else after all."

"I don't mean that," explained Wilson quickly. "I just meant——"

His voice faded off and Tom glanced impatiently around the garage. Then I heard footsteps on a stairs, and in a moment the thickish figure of a woman blocked out the light from the office door. She was in the middle thirties, and faintly stout, but she carried her surplus flesh sensuously as some women can. Her face, above a spotted dress of dark blue crêpe-de-chine, contained no facet or gleam of beauty, but there was an immediately perceptible vitality about her as if the nerves of her body were continually smouldering. She smiled slowly and, walking through her husband as if he were a ghost, shook hands with Tom, looking him flush in the eye. Then she wet her lips, and without turning around spoke to her husband in a soft, coarse voice:

"Get some chairs, why don't you, so somebody can sit down."

"Oh, sure," agreed Wilson hurriedly, and went toward the little office mingling immediately with the cement color of the walls. A white ashen dust veiled his dark suit and his pale hair as it veiled everything in the vicinity—except his wife, who moved close to Tom.

"I want to see you," said Tom intently. "Get on the next train."

"All right."

"I'll meet you by the news-stand on the lower level."

She nodded and moved away from him just as George Wilson emerged with two chairs from his office door.

We waited for her down the road and out of sight. It was a few days before the Fourth of July, and a gray, scrawny Italian child was setting torpedoes in a row along the railroad track.

"Terrible place, isn't it," said Tom, exchanging a frown with Doctor Eckleburg.

"Awful."

"It does her good to get away."

"Doesn't her husband object?"

"Wilson? He thinks she goes to see her sister in New York. He's so dumb he doesn't know he's alive."

So Tom Buchanan and his girl and I went up together to New York—or not quite together, for Mrs. Wilson sat discreetly in another car. Tom deferred that much to the sensibilities of those East Eggers who might be on the train.

She had changed her dress to a brown figured muslin, which stretched tight over her rather wide hips as Tom helped her to the platform in New York. At the news-stand she bought a copy of *Town Tattle* and a moving-picture magazine, and in the station drug-store some cold cream and a small flask of perfume. Up-stairs, in the solemn echoing drive she let four taxicabs drive away before she selected a new one, lavender-colored with gray upholstery, and in this we slid out from the mass of the station into the glowing sunshine. But immediately she turned sharply from the window and, leaning forward, tapped on the front glass.

"I want to get one of those dogs," she said earnestly. "I want to get one for the apartment. They're nice to have—a dog."

We backed up to a gray old man who bore an absurd resemblance to John D. Rockefeller. In a basket swung from his neck cowered a dozen very recent puppies of an indeterminate breed.

"What kind are they?" asked Mrs. Wilson eagerly, as he came to the taxi-window.

"All kinds. What kind do you want, lady?"

"I'd like to get one of those police dogs; I don't suppose you got that kind?"

The man peered doubtfully into the basket, plunged in his hand and drew one up, wriggling, by the back of the neck.

"That's no police dog," said Tom.

"No, it's not exactly a police dog," said the man with disappointment in his voice. "It's more of an Airedale." He passed his hand over the brown washrag of a back. "Look at that coat. Some coat. That's a dog that'll never bother you with catching cold."

"I think it's cute," said Mrs. Wilson enthusiastically. "How much is it?"

"That dog?" He looked at it admiringly. "That dog will cost you ten dollars."

The Airedale—undoubtedly there was an Airedale concerned in it somewhere, though its feet were startlingly white—changed hands and settled down into Mrs. Wilson's lap, where she fondled the weatherproof coat with rapture.

"Is it a boy or a girl?" she asked delicately.

"That dog? That dog's a boy."

"It's a bitch," said Tom decisively. "Here's your money. Go and buy ten more dogs with it."

We drove over to Fifth Avenue, so warm and soft, almost pastoral, on the summer Sunday afternoon that I wouldn't have been surprised to see a great flock of white sheep turn the corner.

"Hold on," I said, "I have to leave you here."

"No, you don't," interposed Tom quickly. "Myrtle'll be hurt if you don't come up to the apartment. Won't you, Myrtle?"

"Come on," she urged. "I'll telephone my sister Catherine. She's said to be very beautiful by people who ought to know."

"Well, I'd like to, but——"

We went on, cutting back again over the Park toward the West Hundreds. At 158th Street the cab stopped at one slice in a long white cake of apartment-houses. Throwing a regal homecoming glance around the neighborhood, Mrs. Wilson gathered up her dog and her other purchases, and went haughtily in.

"I'm going to have the McKees come up," she announced as we rose in the elevator. "And, of course, I got to call up my sister, too."

The apartment was on the top floor—a small living-room, a small dining-room, a small bedroom, and a bath. The living-room was crowded to the doors with a set of tapestried furniture entirely too large for it, so that to move about was to stumble continually over scenes of ladies swinging in the gardens of Versailles. The only picture was an over-enlarged photograph, apparently a hen sitting on a blurred rock. Looked at from a distance, however, the hen resolved itself into a bonnet, and the countenance of a stout old lady beamed down into the room. Several old copies of *Town Tattle* lay on the table together with a copy of *Simon Called Peter,* and some of the small scandal magazines of Broadway. Mrs. Wilson was first concerned with the dog. A reluctant elevator-boy went for a box full of straw and some milk, to which he added on his own initiative a tin of large, hard dog-biscuits—one of which decomposed apathetically in the saucer of milk all afternoon. Meanwhile Tom brought out a bottle of whiskey from a locked bureau door.

I have been drunk just twice in my life, and the second time was that afternoon; so everything that happened has a dim, hazy cast over it, although until after eight o'clock the apartment was full of cheerful sun. Sitting on Tom's lap Mrs. Wilson called up several people on the telephone; then there were no cigarettes, and I went out to buy some at the drugstore on the corner. When I came back they had disappeared, so I sat down discreetly in the living-room and read a chapter of *Simon Called Peter*—either it was terrible stuff or the whiskey distorted things, because it didn't make any sense to me.

Just as Tom and Myrtle (after the first drink Mrs. Wilson and I called each other by our first names) reappeared, company commenced to arrive at the apartment-door.

The sister, Catherine, was a slender, worldly girl of about thirty, with a solid, sticky bob of red hair, and a complexion powdered milky white. Her eyebrows had been plucked and then drawn on again at a more rakish angle but the efforts of nature toward the restoration of the old alignment gave a blurred air to her face. When she moved about there was an incessant clicking as innumerable pottery bracelets jingled up and down upon her arms. She came in with such a proprietary haste, and looked around so possessively at the furniture that I wondered if she lived here. But when I asked her she laughed immoderately, repeated my question aloud, and told me she lived with a girl friend at a hotel.

Mr. McKee was a pale, feminine man from the flat below. He had just shaved, for there was a white spot of lather on his cheekbone, and he was most respectful in his greeting to every one in the room. He informed me that he was in the "artistic game," and I gathered later that he was a photographer and had made the dim enlargement of Mrs. Wilson's mother which hovered like an ectoplasm on the wall. His wife was shrill, languid, handsome, and horrible. She told me with pride that her husband had photographed her a hundred and twenty-seven times since they had been married.

Mrs. Wilson had changed her costume some time before, and was now attired in an elaborate afternoon dress of cream-colored chiffon, which gave out a continual rustle as she swept about the room. With the influence of the dress her personality had also undergone a change. The intense vitality that had been so remarkable in the garage was converted into impressive hauteur. Her laughter, her gestures, her assertions became more violently affected moment by moment, and as she expanded the room grew smaller around her, until she seemed to be revolving on a noisy, creaking pivot through the smoky air.

"My dear," she told her sister in a high, mincing shout, "most of these fellas will cheat you every time. All they think of is money. I had a woman up here last week to look at my feet, and when she gave me the bill you'd of thought she had my appendicitis out."

"What was the name of the woman?" asked Mrs. McKee.

"Mrs. Eberhardt. She goes around looking at people's feet in their own homes."

"I like your dress," remarked Mrs. McKee, "I think it's adorable."

Mrs. Wilson rejected the compliment by raising her eyebrow in disdain.

"It's just a crazy old thing," she said. "I just slip it on sometimes when I don't care what I look like."

"But it looks wonderful on you, if you know what I mean," pursued Mrs. McKee. "If Chester could only get you in that pose I think he could make something of it."

We all looked in silence at Mrs. Wilson, who removed a strand of hair from over her eyes and looked back at us with a brilliant smile. Mr. McKee regarded her intently with his head on one side, and then moved his hand back and forth slowly in front of his face.

"I should change the light," he said after a moment. "I'd like to bring out the modelling of the features. And I'd try to get hold of all the back hair."

"I wouldn't think of changing the light," cried Mrs. McKee. "I think it's——"

Her husband said "Sh!" and we all looked at the subject again, whereupon Tom Buchanan yawned audibly and got to his feet.

"You McKees have something to drink," he said. "Get some more ice and mineral water, Myrtle, before everybody goes to sleep."

"I told that boy about the ice." Myrtle raised her eyebrows in despair at the shiftlessness of the lower orders. "These people! You have to keep after them all the time."

She looked at me and laughed pointlessly. Then she flounced over to the dog, kissed it with ecstasy, and swept into the kitchen, implying that a dozen chefs awaited her orders there.

"I've done some nice things out on Long Island," asserted Mr. McKee.

Tom looked at him blankly.

"Two of them we have framed down-stairs."

"Two what?" demanded Tom.

"Two studies. One of them I call *Montauk Point—The Gulls,* and the other I call *Montauk Point—The Sea.*"

The sister Catherine sat down beside me on the couch.

"Do you live down on Long Island, too?" she inquired.

"I live at West Egg."

"Really? I was down there at a party about a month ago. At a man named Gatsby's. Do you know him?"

"I live next door to him."

"Well, they say he's a nephew or a cousin of Kaiser Wilhelm's That's where all his money comes from."

"Really?"

She nodded.

"I'm scared of him. I'd hate to have him get anything on me."

This absorbing information about my neighbor was interrupted by Mrs. McKee's pointing suddenly at Catherine:

"Chester, I think you could do something with *her,*" she broke out, but Mr. McKee only nodded in a bored way, and turned his attention to Tom.

"I'd like to do more work on Long Island, if I could get the entry. All I ask is that they should give me a start."

"Ask Myrtle," said Tom, breaking into a short shout of laughter as Mrs. Wilson entered with a tray. "She'll give you a letter of introduction, won't you, Myrtle?"

"Do what?" she asked, startled.

"You'll give McKee a letter of introduction to your husband, so he can do some studies of him." His lips moved silently for a moment as he invented. "*George B. Wilson at the Gasoline Pump,* or something like that."

Catherine leaned close to me and whispered in my ear:

"Neither of them can stand the person they're married to."

"Can't they?"

"Can't *stand* them." She looked at Myrtle and then at Tom. "What I say is, why go on living with them if they can't stand them? If I was them I'd get a divorce and get married to each other right away."

"Doesn't she like Wilson either?"

The answer to this was unexpected. It came from Myrtle, who had overheard the question, and it was violent and obscene.

"You see," cried Catherine triumphantly. She lowered her voice again. "It's really his wife that's keeping them apart. She's a Catholic, and they don't believe in divorce."

Daisy was not a Catholic, and I was a little shocked at the elaborateness of the lie.

"When they do get married," continued Catherine, "they're going West to live for a while until it blows over."

"It'd be more discreet to go to Europe."

"Oh, do you like Europe?" she exclaimed surprisingly. "I just got back from Monte Carlo."

"Really."

"Just last year. I went over there with another girl."

"Stay long?"

"No, we just went to Monte Carlo and back. We went by way of Marseilles. We had over twelve hundred dollars when we started, but we got gypped out of it all in two days in the private rooms. We had an awful time getting back, I can tell you. God, how I hated that town!"

The late afternoon sky bloomed in the window for a moment like the blue honey of the Mediterranean—then the shrill voice of Mrs. McKee called me back into the room.

"I almost made a mistake, too," she declared vigorously. "I almost married a little kike who'd been after me for years. I knew he was below me. Everybody kept saying to me: 'Lucille, that man's 'way below you!' But if I hadn't met Chester, he'd of got me sure."

"Yes, but listen," said Myrtle Wilson, nodding her head up and down, "at least you didn't marry him."

"I know I didn't."

"Well, I married him," said Myrtle, ambiguously. "And that's the difference between your case and mine."

"Why did you, Myrtle?" demanded Catherine. "Nobody forced you to."

Myrtle considered.

"I married him because I thought he was a gentleman," she said finally. "I thought he knew something about breeding, but he wasn't fit to lick my shoe."

"You were crazy about him for a while," said Catherine.

"Crazy about him!" cried Myrtle incredulously. "Who said I was crazy about him? I never was any more crazy about him than I was about that man there."

She pointed suddenly at me, and every one looked at me accusingly. I tried to show by my expression that I had played no part in her past.

"The only *crazy* I was was when I married him. I knew right away I made a mistake. He borrowed somebody's best suit to get married in, and never even told me about it, and the man came after it one day when he was out." She looked around to see who was listening. " 'Oh, is that your suit?' I said. 'This is the first I ever heard about it.' But I gave it to him and then I lay down and cried to beat the band all afternoon."

"She really ought to get away from him," resumed Catherine to me. "They've been living over that garage for eleven years. And Tom's the first sweetie she ever had."

The bottle of whiskey—a second one—was now in constant demand by all present, excepting Catherine, who "felt just as good on nothing at all." Tom rang for the janitor and sent him for some celebrated sandwiches, which were a complete supper in themselves. I wanted to get out and walk eastward toward the park through the soft twilight, but each time I tried to go I became entangled in some wild, strident argument which pulled me back, as if with ropes, into my chair. Yet high over the city our line of yellow windows must have contributed their share of human secrecy to the casual watcher in the darkening streets, and I was him too, looking up and wondering. I was within and without, simultaneously enchanted and repelled by the inexhaustible variety of life.

Myrtle pulled her chair close to mine, and suddenly her warm breath poured over me the story of her first meeting with Tom.

"It was on the two little seats facing each other that are always the last ones left on the train. I was going up to New York to see my sister and spend the night. He had on a dress suit and patent leather shoes, and I couldn't keep my eyes off him, but every time he looked at me I had to pretend to be looking at the advertisement over his head. When we came into the station he was next to me, and his white shirt-front pressed against my arm, and so I told him I'd have to call policeman, but he knew I lied. I was so excited that when I got into a taxi with him I didn't hardly know I wasn't getting into a subway train. All I kept thinking about, over and over, was 'You can't live forever; you can't live forever.' "

She turned to Mrs. McKee and the room rang full of her artificial laughter.

"My dear," she cried, "I'm going to give you this dress as soon as I'm through with it. I've got to get another one tomorrow. I'm going to make a list of all the things I've got to get. A massage and a wave, and a collar for the dog, and one of those cute little ash-trays where you touch a spring, and a wreath with a black silk bow for mother's grave that'll last all summer. I got to write down a list so I won't forget all the things I got to do."

It was nine o'clock—almost immediately afterward I looked at my watch and found it was ten. Mr. McKee was asleep on a chair with his fists clenched in his lap, like a photograph of a man of action. Taking out my handkerchief I wiped from his cheek the remains of the spot of dried lather that had worried me all the afternoon.

The little dog was sitting on the table looking with blind eyes through the smoke, and from time to time groaning faintly. People disappeared, reappeared, made plans to go somewhere, and then lost each other, searched for each other, found each other a few feet away. Some time toward midnight Tom Buchanan and Mrs. Wilson stood face to face, discussing in impassioned voices whether Mrs. Wilson had any right to mention Daisy's name.

"Daisy! Daisy! Daisy!" shouted Mrs. Wilson. "I'll say it whenever I want to! Daisy! Dai——"

Making a short deft movement, Tom Buchanan broke her nose with his open hand.

Then there were bloody towels upon the bathroom floor, and women's voices scolding, and high over the confusion a long broken wail of pain. Mr. McKee awoke from his doze and started in a daze toward the door. When he had gone halfway he turned around and stared at the scene—his wife and Catherine scolding and consoling as they stumbled here and there among the crowded furniture with articles of aid, and the despairing figure on the couch, bleeding fluently, and trying to spread a copy of *Town Tattle* over the tapestry scenes of Versailles. Then Mr. McKee turned and continued on out the door. Taking my hat from the chandelier, I followed.

"Come to lunch some day," he suggested, as we groaned down in the elevator.

"Where?"

"Anywhere."

"Keep your hands off the lever," snapped the elevator boy.

"I beg your pardon," said Mr. McKee with dignity, "I didn't know I was touching it."

"All right," I agreed, "I'll be glad to."

... I was standing beside his bed and he was sitting up between the sheets, clad in his underwear, with a great portfolio in his hands.

"Beauty and the Beast . . . Loneliness . . . Old Grocery Horse . . . Brook'n Bridge. . . . ."

Then I was lying half asleep in the cold lower level of the Pennsylvania Station, staring at the morning *Tribune,* and waiting for the four o'clock train.

CHAPTER III

THERE was music from my neighbor's house through the summer nights. In his blue gardens men and girls came and went like moths among the whisperings and the champagne and the stars. At high tide in the afternoon I watched his guests diving from the tower of his raft, or taking the sun on the hot sand of his beach while his two motor-boats slit the waters of the Sound, drawing aquaplanes over cataracts of foam. On week-ends his Rolls-Royce became an omnibus, bearing parties to and from the city between nine in the morning and long past midnight, while his station wagon scampered like a brisk yellow bug to meet all trains. And on Mondays eight servants, including an extra gardener, toiled all day with mops and scrubbing-brushes and hammers and garden-shears, repairing the ravages of the night before.

Every Friday five crates of oranges and lemons arrived from a fruiterer in New York—every Monday these same oranges and lemons left his back door in a pyramid of pulpless halves. There was a machine in the kitchen which could extract the juice of two hundred oranges in half an hour if a little button was pressed two hundred times by a butler's thumb.

At least once a fortnight a corps of caterers came down with several hundred feet of canvas and enough colored lights to make a Christmas tree of Gatsby's enormous garden. On buffet tables, garnished with glistening hors-d'œuvre, spiced baked hams crowded against salads of harlequin designs and pastry pigs and turkeys bewitched to a dark gold. In the main hall a bar with a real brass rail was set up, and stocked with gins and liquors and with cordials so long forgotten that most of his female guests were too young to know one from another.

By seven o'clock the orchestra has arrived, no thin five-piece affair, but a whole pitful of oboes and trombones and saxophones and viols and cornets and piccolos, and low and high drums. The last swimmers have come in from the beach now and are dressing

31

up-stairs; the cars from New York are parked five deep in the drive, and already the halls and salons and verandas are gaudy with primary colors, and hair shorn in strange new ways, and shawls beyond the dreams of Castile. The bar is in full swing, and floating rounds of cocktails permeate the garden outside, until the air is alive with chatter and laughter, and casual innuendo and introductions forgotten on the spot, and enthusiastic meetings between women who never knew each other's names.

The lights grow brighter as the earth lurches away from the sun, and now the orchestra is playing yellow cocktail music, and the opera of voices pitches a key higher. Laughter is easier minute by minute, spilled with prodigality, tipped out at a cheerful word. The groups change more swiftly, swell with new arrivals, dissolve and form in the same breath; already there are wanderers, confident girls who weave here and there among the stouter and more stable, become for a sharp, joyous moment the center of a group, and then, excited with triumph, glide on through the sea-change of faces and voices and color under the constantly changing light.

Suddenly one of these gypsies, in trembling opal, seizes a cocktail out of the air, dumps it down for courage and, moving her hands like Frisco, dances out alone on the canvas platform. A momentary hush; the orchestra leader varies his rhythm obligingly for her, and there is a burst of chatter as the erroneous news goes around that she is Gilda Gray's understudy from the *Follies*. The party has begun.

I believe that on the first night I went to Gatsby's house I was one of the few guests who had actually been invited. People were not invited—they went there. They got into automobiles which bore them out to Long Island, and somehow they ended up at Gatsby's door. Once there they were introduced by somebody who knew Gatsby, and after that they conducted themselves according to the rules of behavior associated with an amusement park. Sometimes they came and went without having met Gatsby at all, came for the party with a simplicity of heart that was its own ticket of admission.

I had been actually invited. A chauffeur in a uniform of robin's-egg blue crossed my lawn early that Saturday morning with a surprisingly formal note from his employer: the honor would be entirely Gatsby's, it said, if I would attend his "little party" that night. He had seen me several times, and had intended to call on me long before, but a peculiar combination of circumstances had prevented it—signed Jay Gatsby, in a majestic hand.

Dressed up in white flannels I went over to his lawn a little after seven, and wandered around rather ill at ease among swirls and eddies of people I didn't know—though here and there was a face I had noticed on the commuting train. I was immediately struck by the number of young Englishmen dotted about; all well dressed, all looking a little hungry, and all talking in low, earnest voices to solid and prosperous Americans. I was sure that they were selling something: bonds or insurance or automobiles. They were at least agonizingly aware of the easy money in the vicinity and convinced that it was theirs for a few words in the right key.

As soon as I arrived I made an attempt to find my host, but the two or three people of whom I asked his whereabouts stared at me in such an amazed way, and denied so vehemently any knowledge of his movements, that I slunk off in the direction of the cocktail table—the only place in the garden where a single man could linger without looking purposeless and alone.

I was on my way to get roaring drunk from sheer embarrassment when Jordan Baker came out of the house and stood at the head of the marble steps, leaning a little backward and looking with contemptuous interest down into the garden.

Welcome or not, I found it necessary to attach myself to some one before I should begin to address cordial remarks to the passers-by.

"Hello!" I roared, advancing toward her. My voice seemed unnaturally loud across the garden.

"I thought you might be here," she responded absently as I came up. "I remembered you lived next door to——"

She held my hand impersonally, as a promise that she'd take care of me in a minute, and gave ear to two girls in twin yellow dresses, who stopped at the foot of the steps.

"Hello!" they cried together. "Sorry you didn't win."

That was for the golf tournament. She had lost in the finals the week before.

"You don't know who we are," said one of the girls in yellow, "but we met you here about a month ago."

"You've dyed your hair since then," remarked Jordan, and I started, but the girls had moved casually on and her remark was addressed to the premature moon, produced like the supper, no doubt, out of a caterer's basket. With Jordan's slender golden arm resting in mine, we descended the steps and sauntered about the garden. A tray of cocktails floated at us through the twilight, and we sat down at a table with the two girls in yellow and three men, each one introduced to us as Mr. Mumble.

"Do you come to these parties often?" inquired Jordan of the girl beside her.

"The last one was the one I met you at," answered the girl, in an alert confident voice. She turned to her companion: "Wasn't it for you, Lucille?"

It was for Lucille, too.

"I like to come," Lucille said. "I never care what I do, so I always have a good time. When I was here last I tore my gown on a chair, and he asked me my name and address—inside of a week I got a package from Croirier's with a new evening gown in it."

"Did you keep it?" asked Jordan.

"Sure I did. I was going to wear it tonight, but it was too big in the bust and had to be altered. It was gas blue with lavender beads. Two hundred and sixty-five dollars."

"There's something funny about a fellow that'll do a thing like that," said the other girl eagerly. "He doesn't want any trouble with *any*body."

"Who doesn't?" I inquired.

"Gatsby. Somebody told me——"

The two girls and Jordan leaned together confidentially.

"Somebody told me they thought he killed a man once."

A thrill passed over all of us. The three Mr. Mumbles bent forward and listened eagerly.

"I don't think it's so much *that*," argued Lucille sceptically; "it's more that he was a German spy during the war."

One of the men nodded in confirmation.

"I heard that from a man who knew all about him, grew up with him in Germany," he assured us positively.

"Oh, no," said the first girl, "it couldn't be that, because he was in the American army during the war." As our credulity switched back to her she leaned forward with enthusiasm. "You look at him sometimes when he thinks nobody's looking at him. I'll bet he killed a man."

She narrowed her eyes and shivered. Lucille shivered. We all turned and looked around for Gatsby. It was testimony to the romantic speculation he inspired that there were whispers about him from those who had found little that it was necessary to whisper about in this world.

The first supper—there would be another one after midnight— was now being served, and Jordan invited me to join her own party, who were spread around a table on the other side of the garden. There were three married couples and Jordan's escort, a persistent undergraduate given to violent innuendo, and obviously under the impression that sooner or later Jordan was going to yield him up her person to a greater or lesser degree. Instead of rambling, this party had preserved a dignified homogeneity, and assumed to itself the function of representing the staid nobility of the country-side— East Egg condescending to West Egg, and carefully on guard against its spectroscopic gayety.

"Let's get out," whispered Jordan, after a somehow wasteful and inappropriate half-hour; "this is much too polite for me."

We got up, and she explained that we were going to find the host: I had never met him, she said, and it was making me uneasy. The undergraduate nodded in a cynical, melancholy way.

The bar, where we glanced first, was crowded, but Gatsby was not there. She couldn't find him from the top of the steps, and he wasn't on the veranda. On a chance we tried an important-looking door, and walked into a high Gothic library, panelled with carved English oak, and probably transported complete from some ruin overseas.

A stout, middle-aged man, with enormous owl-eyed spectacles, was sitting somewhat drunk on the edge of a great table, staring with unsteady concentration at the shelves of books. As we entered he wheeled excitedly around and examined Jordan from head to foot.

"What do you think?" he demanded impetuously.

"About what?"

He waved his hand toward the book-shelves.

"About that. As a matter of fact you needn't bother to ascertain. I ascertained. They're real."

"The books?"

He nodded.

"Absolutely real—have pages and everything. I thought they'd be a nice durable cardboard. Matter of fact, they're absolutely real. Pages and— Here! Lemme show you."

Taking our scepticism for granted, he rushed to the bookcases and returned with Volume One of the "Stoddard Lectures."

"See!" he cried triumphantly. "It's a bona-fide piece of printed matter. It fooled me. This fella's a regular Belasco. It's a triumph. What thoroughness! What realism! Knew when to stop, too—didn't cut the pages. But what do you want? What do you expect?"

He snatched the book from me and replaced it hastily on its shelf, muttering that if one brick was removed the whole library was liable to collapse.

"Who brought you?" he demanded. "Or did you just come? I was brought. Most people were brought."

Jordan looked at him alertly, cheerfully, without answering.

"I was brought by a woman named Roosevelt," he continued. "Mrs. Claude Roosevelt. Do you know her? I met her somewhere last night. I've been drunk for about a week now, and I thought it might sober me up to sit in a library."

"Has it?"

"A little bit, I think. I can't tell yet. I've only been here an hour. Did I tell you about the books? They're real. They're——"

"You told us."

We shook hands with him gravely and went back outdoors.

There was dancing now on the canvas in the garden; old men pushing young girls backward in eternal graceless circles, superior couples holding each other tortuously, fashionably, and keeping in the corners—and a great number of single girls dancing individualistically or relieving the orchestra for a moment of the burden of the banjo or the traps. By midnight the hilarity had increased. A celebrated tenor had sung in Italian, and a notorious contralto had sung in jazz, and between the numbers people were doing "stunts" all over the garden, while happy, vacuous bursts of laughter rose toward the summer sky. A pair of stage twins, who turned out to be the girls in yellow, did a baby act in costume, and champagne was served in glasses bigger than finger-bowls. The moon had risen higher, and floating in the Sound was a triangle of silver scales, trembling a little to the stiff, tinny drip of the banjoes on the lawn.

I was still with Jordan Baker. We were sitting at a table with a man of about my age and a rowdy little girl, who gave way upon the slightest provocation to uncontrollable laughter. I was enjoying myself now. I had taken two finger-bowls of champagne, and the scene had changed before my eyes into something significant, elemental, and profound.

At a lull in the entertainment the man looked at me and smiled.

"Your face is familiar," he said, politely. "Weren't you in the Third Divison during the war?"

"Why, yes. I was in the ninth machine-gun battalion."

"I was in the Seventh Infantry until June nineteen-eighteen. I knew I'd seen you somewhere before."

We talked for a moment about some wet, gray little villages in France. Evidently he lived in this vicinity, for he told me that he had just bought a hydroplane, and was going to try it out in the morning.

"Want to go with me, old sport? Just near the shore along the Sound."

"What time?"

"Any time that suits you best."

It was on the tip of my tongue to ask his name when Jordan looked around and smiled.

"Having a gay time now?" she inquired.

"Much better." I turned again to my new acquaintance. "This is an unusual party for me. I haven't even seen the host. I live over there—" I waved my hand at the invisible hedge in the distance, "and this man Gatsby sent over his chauffeur with an invitation."

For a moment he looked at me as if he failed to understand.

"I'm Gatsby," he said suddenly.

"What!" I exclaimed. "Oh, I beg your pardon."

"I thought you knew, old sport. I'm afraid I'm not a very good host."

He smiled understandingly—much more than understandingly. It was one of those rare smiles with a quality of eternal reassurance in it, that you may come across four or five times in life. It faced—or seemed to face—the whole external world for an instant, and then concentrated on *you* with an irresistible prejudice in your favor. It understood you just as far as you wanted to be understood, believed in you as you would like to believe in yourself, and assured you that it had precisely the impression of you that, at your best, you hoped to convey. Precisely at that point it vanished—and I was looking at an elegant young roughneck, a year or two over thirty, whose elaborate formality of speech just missed being absurd. Some time before he introduced himself I'd got a strong impression that he was picking his words with care.

Almost at the moment when Mr. Gatsby identified himself, a butler hurried toward him with the information that Chicago was calling him on the wire. He excused himself with a small bow that included each of us in turn.

"If you want anything just ask for it, old sport," he urged me. "Excuse me. I will rejoin you later."

When he was gone I turned immediately to Jordan—constrained to assure her of my surprise. I had expected that Mr. Gatsby would be a florid and corpulent person in his middle years.

"Who is he?" I demanded. "Do you know?"

"He's just a man named Gatsby."

"Where is he from, I mean? And what does he do?"

"Now *you're* started on the subject," she answered with a wan smile. "Well, he told me once he was an Oxford man."

A dim background started to take shape behind him, but at her next remark it faded away.

"However, I don't believe it."

"Why not?"

"I don't know," she insisted, "I just don't think he went there."

Something in her tone reminded me of the other girl's "I think he killed a man," and had the effect of stimulating my curiosity. I would have accepted without question the information that Gatsby sprang from the swamps of Louisiana or from the lower East Side of New York. That was comprehensible. But young men didn't—at least in my provincial inexperience I believed they didn't—drift coolly out of nowhere and buy a palace on Long Island Sound.

"Anyhow, he gives large parties," said Jordan, changing the subject with an urban distaste for the concrete. "And I like large parties. They're so intimate. At small parties there isn't any privacy."

There was the boom of a bass drum, and the voice of the orchestra leader rang out suddenly above the echolalia of the garden.

"Ladies and gentlemen," he cried. "At the request of Mr. Gatsby we are going to play for you Mr. Vladimir Tostoff's latest work, which attracted so much attention at Carnegie Hall last May. If you read the papers, you know there was a big sensation." He smiled with jovial condescension, and added: "Some sensation!" Whereupon everybody laughed.

"The piece is known," he concluded lustily, "as Vladimir Tostoff's *Jazz History of the World*."

The nature of Mr. Tostoff's composition eluded me, because just as it began my eyes fell on Gatsby, standing alone on the marble steps and looking from one group to another with approving eyes. His tanned skin was drawn attractively tight on his face and his short hair looked as though it were trimmed every day. I could see nothing sinister about him. I wondered if the fact that he was not drinking helped to set him off from his guests, for it seemed to me that he grew more correct as the fraternal hilarity increased. When the *Jazz History of the World* was over, girls were putting their heads on men's shoulders in a puppyish, convivial way, girls were swooning backward playfully into men's arms, even into groups, knowing that some one would arrest their falls—but no one swooned backward on Gatsby, and no French bob touched Gatsby's shoulder, and no singing quartets were formed with Gatsby's head for one link.

"I beg your pardon."

Gatsby's butler was suddenly standing beside us.

"Miss Baker?" he inquired. "I beg your pardon, but Mr. Gatsby would like to speak to you alone."

"With me?" she exclaimed in surprise.

"Yes, madame."

She got up slowly, raising her eyebrows at me in astonishment, and followed the butler toward the house. I noticed that she wore her evening-dress, all her dresses, like sports clothes—there was a jauntiness about her movements as if she had first learned to walk upon golf courses on clean, crisp mornings.

I was alone and it was almost two. For some time confused and intriguing sounds had issued from a long, many-windowed room which overhung the terrace. Eluding Jordan's undergraduate, who was now engaged in an obstetrical conversation with two chorus girls, and who implored me to join him, I went inside.

The large room was full of people. One of the girls in yellow was playing the piano, and beside her stood a tall, red-haired young lady from a famous chorus, engaged in song. She had drunk a quantity of champagne, and during the course of her song she had decided, ineptly, that everything was very, very sad—she was not only singing, she was weeping too. Whenever there was a pause in the song she filled it with gasping, broken sobs, and then took up the lyric in a quavering soprano. The tears coursed down her cheeks—not freely, however, for when they came into contact with her heavily beaded eyelashes they assumed an inky color, and pursued the rest of their way in slow black rivulets. A humorous suggestion was made that she sing the notes on her face, whereupon she threw up her hands, sank into a chair, and went off into a deep vinous sleep.

"She had a fight with a man who says he's her husband," explained a girl at my elbow.

I looked around. Most of the remaining women were now having fights with men said to be their husbands. Even Jordan's party, the quartet from East Egg, were rent asunder by dissension. One of the men was talking with curious intensity to a young actress, and his wife, after attempting to laugh at the situation in a dignified and indifferent way, broke down entirely and resorted to flank attacks—at intervals she appeared suddenly at his side like an angry diamond, and hissed: "You promised!" into his ear.

The reluctance to go home was not confined to wayward men. The hall was at present occupied by two deplorably sober men and their highly indignant wives. The wives were sympathizing with each other in slightly raised voices.

"Whenever he sees I'm having a good time he wants to go home."

"Never heard anything so selfish in my life."

"We're always the first ones to leave."

"So are we."

"Well, we're almost the last tonight," said one of the men sheepishly. "The orchestra left half an hour ago."

In spite of the wives' agreement that such malevolence was beyond credibility, the dispute ended in a short struggle, and both wives were lifted, kicking, into the night.

As I waited for my hat in the hall the door of the library opened and Jordan Baker and Gatsby came out together. He was saying some last word to her, but the eagerness in his manner tightened abruptly into formality as several people approached him to say good-by.

Jordan's party were calling impatiently to her from the porch, but she lingered for a moment to shake hands.

"I've just heard the most amazing thing," she whispered. "How long were we in there?"

"Why, about an hour."

"It was . . . simply amazing," she repeated abstractedly. "But I swore I wouldn't tell it and here I am tantalizing you." She yawned gracefully in my face. "Please come and see me. . . . Phone book. . . . Under the name of Mrs. Sigourney Howard. . . . My aunt. . . ." She was hurrying off as she talked—her brown hand waved a jaunty salute as she melted into her party at the door.

Rather ashamed that on my first appearance I had stayed so late, I joined the last of Gatsby's guests, who were clustered around him. I wanted to explain that I'd hunted for him early in the evening and to apologize for not having known him in the garden.

"Don't mention it," he enjoined me eagerly. "Don't give it another thought, old sport." The familiar expression held no more familiarity than the hand which reassuringly brushed my shoulder. "And don't forget we're going up in the hydroplane tomorrow morning, at nine o'clock."

Then the butler, behind his shoulder:

"Philadelphia wants you on the 'phone, sir."

"All right, in a minute. Tell them I'll be right there. . . . Good night."

"Good night."

"Good night." He smiled—and suddenly there seemed to be a pleasant significance in having been among the last to go, as if he had desired it all the time. "Good night, old sport. . . . Good night."

But as I walked down the steps I saw that the evening was not quite over. Fifty feet from the door a dozen headlights illuminated a bizarre and tumultuous scene. In the ditch beside the road, right side up, but violently shorn of one wheel, rested a new coupé which had left Gatsby's drive not two minutes before. The sharp jut of a wall accounted for the detachment of the wheel, which was now getting considerable attention from half a dozen curious chauffeurs. However, as they had left their cars blocking the road, a harsh, discordant din from those in the rear had been audible for some time, and added to the already violent confusion of the scene.

A man in a long duster had dismounted from the wreck and now stood in the middle of the road, looking from the car to the tire and from the tire to the observers in a pleasant, puzzled way.

"See!" he explained. "It went in the ditch."

The fact was infinitely astonishing to him, and I recognized first the unusual quality of wonder, and then the man—it was the late patron of Gatsby's library.

"How'd it happen?"

He shrugged his shoulders.

"I know nothing whatever about mechanics," he said decisively.

"But how did it happen? Did you run into the wall?"

"Don't ask me," said Owl Eyes, washing his hands of the whole matter. "I know very little about driving—next to nothing. It happened, and that's all I know."

"Well, if you're a poor driver you oughtn't to try driving at night."

"But I wasn't even trying," he explained indignantly, "I wasn't even trying."

An awed hush fell upon the bystanders.

"Do you want to commit suicide?"

"You're lucky it was just a wheel! A bad driver and not even trying!"

"You don't understand," explained the criminal. "I wasn't driving. There's another man in the car."

The shock that followed this declaration found voice in a sustained "Ah-h-h!" as the door of the coupé swung slowly open. The crowd—it was now a crowd—stepped back involuntarily, and when the door had opened wide there was a ghostly pause. Then, very gradually, part by part, a pale, dangling individual stepped out of the wreck, pawing tentatively at the ground with a large uncertain dancing shoe.

Blinded by the glare of the headlights and confused by the incessant groaning of the horns, the apparition stood swaying for a moment before he perceived the man in the duster.

"Wha's matter?" he inquired calmly. "Did we run outa gas?"

"Look!"

Half a dozen fingers pointed at the amputated wheel—he stared at it for a moment, and then looked upward as though he suspected that it had dropped from the sky.

"It came off," some one explained.

He nodded.

"At first I din' notice we'd stopped."

A pause. Then, taking a long breath and straightening his shoulders, he remarked in a determined voice:

"Wonder'ff tell me where there's a gas'line station?"

At least a dozen men, some of them a little better off than he was, explained to him that wheel and car were no longer joined by any physical bond.

"Back out," he suggested after a moment. "Put her in reverse."

"But the *wheel's* off!"

He hesitated.

"No harm in trying," he said.

The caterwauling horns had reached a crescendo and I turned away and cut across the lawn toward home. I glanced back once. A wafer of a moon was shining over Gatsby's house, making the night fine as before, and surviving the laughter and the sound of his still glowing garden. A sudden emptiness seemed to flow now from the windows and the great doors, endowing with complete isolation the figure of the host, who stood on the porch, his hand up in a formal gesture of farewell.

Reading over what I have written so far, I see I have given the impression that the events of three nights several weeks apart were all that absorbed me. On the contrary, they were merely casual events in a crowded summer, and, until much later, they absorbed me infinitely less than my personal affairs.

Most of the time I worked. In the early morning the sun threw my shadow westward as I hurried down the white chasms of lower New York to the Probity Trust. I knew the other clerks and young bond-salesmen by their first names, and lunched with them in dark, crowded restaurants on little pig sausages and mashed potatoes and coffee. I even had a short affair with a girl who lived in Jersey City and worked in the accounting department, but her brother began throwing mean looks in my direction, so when she went on her vacation in July I let it blow quietly away.

I took dinner usually at the Yale Club—for some reason it was the gloomiest event of my day—and then I went upstairs to the library and studied investments and securities for a conscientious hour. There were generally a few rioters around, but they never came into the library, so it was a good place to work. After that, if the night was mellow, I strolled down Madison Avenue past the old Murray Hill Hotel, and over 33d Street to the Pennsylvania Station.

I began to like New York, the racy, adventurous feel of it at night, and the satisfaction that the constant flicker of men and women and machines gives to the restless eye. I liked to walk up Fifth Avenue and pick out romantic women from the crowd and imagine that in a few minutes I was going to enter into their lives, and no one would ever know or disapprove. Sometimes, in my mind, I followed them to their apartments on the corners of hidden streets, and they turned and smiled back at me before they faded through a door into warm darkness. At the enchanted metropolitan twilight I felt a haunting loneliness sometimes, and felt it in others—poor young clerks who loitered in front of windows waiting until it was time for a solitary restaurant dinner—young clerks in the dusk, wasting the most poignant moments of night and life.

Again at eight o'clock, when the dark lanes of the Forties were five deep with throbbing taxicabs, bound for the theater district, I felt a sinking in my heart. Forms leaned together in the taxis as they waited, and voices sang, and there was laughter from unheard jokes, and lighted cigarettes outlined unintelligible gestures inside. Imagining that I, too, was hurrying toward gayety and sharing their intimate excitement, I wished them well.

For a while I lost sight of Jordan Baker, and then in midsummer I found her again. At first I was flattered to go places with her, because she was a golf champion, and everyone knew her name. Then it was something more. I wasn't actually in love, but I felt a sort of tender curiosity. The bored haughty face that she turned to the world concealed something—most affectations conceal something eventually, even though they don't in the beginning—and one day I found what it was. When we were on a house-party together up in Warwick, she left a borrowed car out in the rain with the top down, and then lied about it—and suddenly I remembered the story about her that had eluded me that night at Daisy's. At her first big golf tournament there was a row that nearly reached the newspapers —a suggestion that she had moved her ball from a bad lie in the semi-final round. The thing approached the proportions of a scandal—then died away. A caddy retracted his statement, and the only other witness admitted that he might have been mistaken. The incident and the name had remained together in my mind.

Jordan Baker instinctively avoided clever, shrewd men, and now I saw that this was because she felt safer on a plane where any divergence from a code would be thought impossible. She was incurably dishonest. She wasn't able to endure being at a disadvantage and, given this unwillingness, I suppose she had begun dealing in subterfuges when she was very young in order to keep that cool, insolent smile turned to the world and yet satisfy the demands of her hard, jaunty body.

It made no difference to me. Dishonesty in a woman is a thing you never blame deeply—I was casually sorry, and then I forgot. It was on that same house-party that we had a curious conversation about driving a car. It started because she passed so close to some workmen that our fender flicked a button on one man's coat.

"You're a rotten driver," I protested. "Either you ought to be more careful, or you oughtn't to drive at all."

"I am careful."

"No, you're not."

"Well, other people are," she said lightly.

"What's that got to do with it?"

"They'll keep out of my way," she insisted. "It takes two to make an accident."

"Suppose you met somebody just as careless as yourself."

"I hope I never will," she answered. "I hate careless people. That's why I like you."

Her gray, sun-strained eyes stared straight ahead, but she had deliberately shifted our relations, and for a moment I thought I loved her. But I am slow-thinking and full of interior rules that act as brakes on my desires, and I knew that first I had to get myself definitely out of that tangle back home. I'd been writing letters once a week and signing them: "Love, Nick," and all I could think of was how, when that certain girl played tennis, a faint mustache of perspiration appeared on her upper lip. Nevertheless there was a vague understanding that had to be tactfully broken off before I was free.

Every one suspects himself of at least one of the cardinal virtues, and this is mine: I am one of the few honest people that I have ever known.

CHAPTER IV

ON SUNDAY MORNING while church bells rang in the villages along-shore, the world and its mistress returned to Gatsby's house and twinkled hilariously on his lawn.

"He's a bootlegger," said the young ladies, moving somewhere between his cocktails and his flowers. "One time he killed a man who had found out that he was nephew to Von Hindenburg and second cousin to the devil. Reach me a rose, honey, and pour me a last drop into that there crystal glass."

Once I wrote down on the empty spaces of a timetable the names of those who came to Gatsby's house that summer. It is an old time-table now, disintegrating at its folds, and headed "This schedule in effect July 5th, 1922." But I can still read the gray names, and they will give you a better impression than my generalities of those who accepted Gatsby's hospitality and paid him the subtle tribute of knowing nothing whatever about him.

From East Egg, then, came the Chester Beckers and the Leeches, and a man named Bunsen, whom I knew at Yale, and Doctor Webster Civet, who was drowned last summer up in Maine. And the Hornbeams and the Willie Voltaires, and a whole clan named Blackbuck, who always gathered in a corner and flipped up their noses like goats at whosoever came near. And the Ismays and the Chrysties (or rather Hubert Auerbach and Mr. Chrystie's wife), and Edgar Beaver, whose hair, they say, turned cotton-white one winter afternoon for no good reason at all.

Clarence Endive was from East Egg, as I remember. He came only once, in white knickerbockers, and had a fight with a bum named Etty in the garden. From farther out on the Island came the Cheadles and the O. R. P. Schraeders, and the Stonewall Jackson Abrams of Georgia, and the Fishguards and the Ripley Snells. Snell was there three days before he went to the penitentiary, so drunk out on the gravel drive that Mrs. Ulysses Swett's automobile ran over

nand. The Dancies came, too, and S. B. Whitebait, who
vell over sixty, and Maurice A. Flink, and the Hammerheads,
..d Beluga the tobacco importer, and Beluga's girls.

From West Egg came the Poles and the Mulreadys and Cecil
Roebuck and Cecil Schoen and Gulick the State senator and New-
ton Orchid, who controlled Films Par Excellence, and Eckhaust
and Clyde Cohen and Don S. Schwartze (the son) and Arthur
McCarty, all connected with the movies in one way or another. And
the Catlips and the Bembergs and G. Earl Muldoon, brother to that
Muldoon who afterward strangled his wife. Da Fontano the pro-
moter came there, and Ed Legros and James B. ("Rot-Gut") Ferret
and the De Jongs and Ernest Lilly—they came to gamble, and when
Ferret wandered into the garden it meant he was cleaned out
and Associated Traction would have to fluctuate profitably next
day.

A man named Klipspringer was there so often and so long that
he became known as "the boarder"—I doubt if he had any other
home. Of theatrical people there were Gus Waize and Horace
O'Donavan and Lester Myer and George Duckweed and Francis
Bull. Also from New York were the Chromes and the Backhyssons
and the Dennickers and Russell Betty and the Corrigans and the
Kellehers and the Dewers and the Scullys and S. W. Belcher and
the Smirkes and the young Quinns, divorced now, and Henry L.
Palmetto, who killed himself by jumping in front of a subway train
in Times Square.

Benny McClenahan arrived always with four girls. They were
never quite the same ones in physical person, but they were so identical one with another that it inevitably seemed they had been there
before. I have forgotten their names—Jaqueline, I think, or else
Consuela, or Gloria or Judy or June, and their last names were either
the melodious names of flowers and months or the sterner ones of
the great American capitalists whose cousins, if pressed, they would
confess themselves to be.

In addition to all these I can remember that Faustina O'Brien
came there at least once and the Baedeker girls and young Brewer,
who had his nose shot off in the war, and Mr. Albrucksburger and
Miss Haag, his fiancée, and Ardita Fitz-Peters and Mr. P. Jewett,
once head of the American Legion, and Miss Claudia Hip, with a

man reputed to be her chauffeur, and a prince of something, whom we called Duke, and whose name, if I ever knew it, I have forgotten.

All these people came to Gatsby's house in the summer.

At nine o'clock, one morning late in July, Gatsby's gorgeous car lurched up the rocky drive to my door and gave out a burst of melody from its three-noted horn. It was the first time he had called on me, though I had gone to two of his parties, mounted in his hydroplane, and, at his urgent invitation, made frequent use of his beach.

"Good morning, old sport. You're having lunch with me today and I thought we'd ride up together."

He was balancing himself on the dashboard of his car with that resourcefulness of movement that is so peculiarly American—that comes, I suppose, with the absence of lifting work or rigid sitting in youth and, even more, with the formless grace of our nervous, sporadic games. This quality was continually breaking through his punctilious manner in the shape of restlessness. He was never quite still; there was always a tapping foot somewhere or the impatient opening and closing of a hand.

He saw me looking with admiration at his car.

"It's pretty, isn't it, old sport!" He jumped off to give me a better view. "Haven't you ever seen it before?"

I'd seen it. Everybody had seen it. It was a rich cream color, bright with nickel, swollen here and there in its monstrous length with triumphant hat-boxes and supper-boxes and tool-boxes, and terraced with a labyrinth of wind-shields that mirrored a dozen suns. Sitting down behind many layers of glass in a sort of green leather conservatory, we started to town.

I had talked with him perhaps six times in the past month and found, to my disappointment, that he had little to say. So my first impression, that he was a person of some undefined consequence, had gradually faded and he had become simply the proprietor of an elaborate road-house next door.

And then came that disconcerting ride. We hadn't reached West Egg Village before Gatsby began leaving his elegant sentences unfinished and slapping himself indecisively on the knee of his caramel-colored suit.

"Look here, old sport," he broke out surprisingly, "what's your opinion of me, anyhow?"

A little overwhelmed, I began the generalized evasions which that question deserves.

"Well, I'm going to tell you something about my life," he interrupted. "I don't want you to get a wrong idea of me from all these stories you hear."

So he was aware of the bizarre accusations that flavored conversation in his halls.

"I'll tell you God's truth." His right hand suddenly ordered divine retribution to stand by. "I am the son of some wealthy people in the Middle West—all dead now. I was brought up in America but educated at Oxford, because all my ancestors have been educated there for many years. It is a family tradition."

He looked at me sideways—and I knew why Jordan Baker had believed he was lying. He hurried the phrase "educated at Oxford," or swallowed it, or choked on it, as though it had bothered him before. And with this doubt, his whole statement fell to pieces, and I wondered if there wasn't something a little sinister about him, after all.

"What part of the Middle West?" I inquired casually.

"San Francisco."

"I see."

"My family all died and I came into a good deal of money."

His voice was solemn, as if the memory of that sudden extinction of a clan still haunted him. For a moment I suspected that he was pulling my leg, but a glance at him convinced me otherwise.

"After that I lived like a young rajah in all the capitals of Europe —Paris, Venice, Rome—collecting jewels, chiefly rubies, hunting big game, painting a little, things for myself only, and trying to forget something very sad that had happened to me long ago."

With an effort I managed to restrain my incredulous laughter. The very phrases were worn so threadbare that they evoked no image except that of a turbaned "character" leaking sawdust at every pore as he pursued a tiger through the Bois de Boulogne.

"Then came the war, old sport. It was a great relief, and I tried very hard to die, but I seemed to bear an enchanted life. I accepted a commission as first lieutenant when it began. In the Argonne

Forest I took two machine-gun detachments so far forward that there was a half mile gap on either side of us where the infantry couldn't advance. We stayed there two days and two nights, a hundred and thirty men with sixteen Lewis guns, and when the infantry came up at last they found the insignia of three German divisions among the piles of dead. I was promoted to be a major, and every Allied government gave me a decoration—even Montenegro, little Montenegro down on the Adriatic Sea!"

Little Montenegro! He lifted up the words and nodded at them—with his smile. The smile comprehended Montenegro's troubled history and sympathized with the brave struggles of the Montenegrin people. It appreciated fully the chain of national circumstances which had elicited this tribute from Montenegro's warm little heart. My incredulity was submerged in fascination now; it was like skimming hastily through a dozen magazines.

He reached in his pocket, and a piece of metal, slung on a ribbon, fell into my palm.

"That's the one from Montenegro."

To my astonishment, the thing had an authentic look. "Orderi de Danilo," ran the circular legend, "Montenegro, Nicolas Rex."

"Turn it."

"Major Jay Gatsby," I read, "For Valour Extraordinary."

"Here's another thing I always carry. A souvenir of Oxford days. It was taken in Trinity Quad—the man on my left is now the Earl of Doncaster."

It was a photograph of half a dozen young men in blazers loafing in an archway through which were visible a host of spires. There was Gatsby, looking a little, not much, younger—with a cricket bat in his hand.

Then it was all true. I saw the skins of tigers flaming in his palace on the Grand Canal; I saw him opening a chest of rubies to ease, with their crimson-lighted depths, the gnawings of his broken heart.

"I'm going to make a big request of you today," he said, pocketing his souvenirs with satisfaction, "so I thought you ought to know something about me. I didn't want you to think I was just some nobody. You see, I usually find myself among strangers because I drift here and there trying to forget the sad thing that happened to me." He hesitated. "You'll hear about it this afternoon."

"At lunch?"

"No, this afternoon. I happened to find out that you're taking Miss Baker to tea."

"Do you mean you're in love with Miss Baker?"

"No, old sport, I'm not. But Miss Baker has kindly consented to speak to you about this matter."

I hadn't the faintest idea what "this matter" was, but I was more annoyed than interested. I hadn't asked Jordan to tea in order to discuss Mr. Jay Gatsby. I was sure the request would be something utterly fantastic, and for a moment I was sorry I'd ever set foot upon his overpopulated lawn.

He wouldn't say another word. His correctness grew on him as we neared the city. We passed Port Roosevelt, where there was a glimpse of red-belted ocean-going ships, and sped along a cobbled slum lined with the dark, undeserted saloons of the faded-gilt nineteen-hundreds. Then the valley of ashes opened out on both sides of us, and I had a glimpse of Mrs. Wilson straining at the garage pump with panting vitality as we went by.

With fenders spread like wings we scattered light through half Astoria—only half, for as we twisted among the pillars of the elevated I heard the familiar "jug-jug-*spat*!" of a motorcycle, and a frantic policeman rode alongside.

"All right, old sport," called Gatsby. We slowed down. Taking a white card from his wallet, he waved it before the man's eyes.

"Right you are," agreed the policeman, tipping his cap. "Know you next time, Mr. Gatsby. Excuse *me*!"

"What was that?" I inquired. "The picture of Oxford?"

"I was able to do the commissioner a favor once, and he sends me a Christmas card every year."

Over the great bridge, with the sunlight through the girders making a constant flicker upon the moving cars, with the city rising up across the river in white heaps and sugar lumps all built with a wish out of non-olfactory money. The city seen from the Queensboro Bridge is always the city seen for the first time, in its first wild promise of all the mystery and the beauty in the world.

A dead man passed us in a hearse heaped with blooms, followed by two carriages with drawn blinds, and by more cheerful carriages for friends. The friends looked out at us with the tragic eyes and short upper lips of southeastern Europe, and I was glad that the sight of Gatsby's splendid car was included in their somber holiday. As we crossed Blackwell's Island a limousine passed us, driven by a white chauffeur, in which sat three modish negroes, two bucks and a girl. I laughed aloud as the yolks of their eyeballs rolled toward us in haughty rivalry.

"Anything can happen now that we've slid over this bridge," I thought; "anything at all. . . ."

Even Gatsby could happen, without any particular wonder.

Roaring noon. In a well-fanned Forty-second Street cellar I met Gatsby for lunch. Blinking away the brightness of the street outside, my eyes picked him out obscurely in the anteroom, talking to another man.

"Mr. Carraway, this is my friend Mr. Wolfsheim."

A small, flat-nosed Jew raised his large head and regarded me with two fine growths of hair which luxuriated in either nostril. After a moment I discovered his tiny eyes in the half-darkness.

"—So I took one look at him," said Mr. Wolfsheim, shaking my hand earnestly, "and what do you think I did?"

"What?" I inquired politely.

But evidently he was not addressing me, for he dropped my hand and covered Gatsby with his expressive nose.

"I handed the money to Katspaugh and I said: 'All right, Katspaugh, don't pay him a penny till he shuts his mouth.' He shut it then and there."

Gatsby took an arm of each of us and moved forward into the restaurant, whereupon Mr. Wolfsheim swallowed a new sentence he was starting and lapsed into a somnambulatory abstraction.

"Highballs?" asked the head waiter.

"This is a nice restaurant here," said Mr. Wolfsheim, looking at the Presbyterian nymphs on the ceiling. "But I like across the street better!"

"Yes, highballs," agreed Gatsby, and then to Mr. Wolfsheim: "It's too hot over there."

"Hot and small—yes," said Mr. Wolfsheim, "but full of memories."

"What place is that?" I asked.

"The old Metropole.

"The old Metropole," brooded Mr. Wolfsheim gloomily. "Filled with faces dead and gone. Filled with friends gone now forever. I can't forget so long as I live the night they shot Rosy Rosenthal there. It was six of us at the table, and Rosy had eat and drunk a lot all evening. When it was almost morning the waiter came up to him with a funny look and says somebody wants to speak to him outside. 'All right,' says Rosy, and begins to get up, and I pulled him down in his chair.

" 'Let the bastards come in here if they want you, Rosy, but don't you, so help me, move outside this room.'

"It was four o'clock in the morning then, and if we'd of raised the blinds we'd of seen daylight."

"Did he go?" I asked innocently.

"Sure he went." Mr. Wolfsheim's nose flashed at me indignantly. "He turned around in the door and says: 'Don't let that waiter take away my coffee!' Then he went out on the sidewalk, and they shot him three times in his full belly and drove away."

"Four of them were electrocuted," I said, remembering.

"Five, with Becker." His nostrils turned to me in an interested way. "I understand you're looking for a business gonnegtion."

The juxtaposition of these two remarks was startling. Gatsby answered for me:

"Oh, no," he exclaimed, "this isn't the man."

"No?" Mr. Wolfsheim seemed disappointed.

"This is just a friend. I told you we'd talk about that some other time."

"I beg your pardon," said Mr. Wolfsheim, "I had a wrong man."

A succulent hash arrived, and Mr. Wolfsheim, forgetting the more sentimental atmosphere of the old Metropole, began to eat with ferocious delicacy. His eyes, meanwhile, roved very slowly all around the room—he completed the arc by turning to inspect the people directly behind. I think that, except for my presence, he would have taken one short glance beneath our own table.

"Look here, old sport," said Gatsby leaning toward me, "I'm afraid i made you a little angry this morning in the car."

There was the smile again, but this time I held out against it.

"I don't like mysteries," I answered, "and I don't understand why you won't come out frankly and tell me what you want. Why has it all got to come through Miss Baker?"

"Oh, it's nothing underhand," he assured me. "Miss Baker's a great sportswoman, you know, and she'd never do anything that wasn't all right."

Suddenly he looked at his watch, jumped up, and hurried from the room, leaving me with Mr. Wolfsheim at the table.

"He has to telephone," said Mr. Wolfsheim, following him with his eyes. "Fine fellow, isn't he? Handsome to look at and a perfect gentleman."

"Yes."

"He's an Oggsford man."

"Oh!"

"He went to Oggsford College in England. You know Oggsford College?"

"I've heard of it."

"It's one of the most famous colleges in the world."

"Have you known Gatsby for a long time?" I inquired.

"Several years," he answered in a gratified way. "I made the pleasure of his acquaintance just after the war. But I knew I had discovered a man of fine breeding after I talked with him an hour. I said to myself: 'There's the kind of man you'd like to take home and introduce to your mother and sister.'" He paused. "I see you're looking at my cuff buttons."

I hadn't been looking at them, but I did now. They were composed of oddly familiar pieces of ivory.

"Finest specimens of human molars," he informed me.

"Well!" I inspected them. "That's a very interesting idea."

"Yeah." He flipped his sleeves up under his coat. "Yeah, Gatsby's very careful about women. He would never so much as look at a friend's wife."

When the subject of this instinctive trust returned to the table and sat down Mr. Wolfsheim drank his coffee with a jerk and got to his feet.

"I have enjoyed my lunch," he said, "and I'm going to run off from you two young men before I outstay my welcome."

"Don't hurry, Meyer," said Gatsby, without enthusiasm. Mr. Wolfsheim raised his hand in a sort of benediction.

"You're very polite, but I belong to another generation," he announced solemnly. "You sit here and discuss your sports and your young ladies and your—" He supplied an imaginary noun with another wave of his hand. "As for me, I am fifty years old, and I won't impose myself on you any longer."

As he shook hands and turned away his tragic nose was trembling. I wondered if I had said anything to offend him.

"He becomes very sentimental sometimes," explained Gatsby. "This is one of his sentimental days. He's quite a character around New York—a denizen of Broadway."

"Who is he, anyhow, an actor?"

"No."

"A dentist?"

"Meyer Wolfshiem? No, he's a gambler." Gatsby hesitated, then added coolly: "He's the man who fixed the World's Series back in 1919."

"Fixed the World's Series?" I repeated.

The idea staggered me. I remembered, of course, that the World's Series had been fixed in 1919, but if I had thought of it at all I would have thought of it as a thing that merely *happened,* the end of some inevitable chain. It never occurred to me that one man could start to play with the faith of fifty million people—with the single-mindedness of a burglar blowing a safe.

"How did he happen to do that?" I asked after a minute.

"He just saw the opportunity."

"Why isn't he in jail?"

"They can't get him, old sport. He's a smart man."

I insisted on paying the check. As the waiter brought my change I caught sight of Tom Buchanan across the crowded room.

"Come along with me for a minute," I said; "I've got to say hello to some one."

When he saw us Tom jumped up and took half a dozen steps in our direction.

"Where've you been?" he demanded eagerly. "Daisy's furious because you haven't called up."

"This is Mr. Gatsby, Mr. Buchanan."

They shook hands briefly, and a strained, unfamiliar look of embarrassment came over Gatsby's face.

"How've you been, anyhow?" demanded Tom of me. "How'd you happen to come up this far to eat?"

"I've been having lunch with Mr. Gatsby."

I turned toward Mr. Gatsby, but he was no longer there.

One October day in nineteen-seventeen——
(said Jordan Baker that afternoon, sitting up very straight on a straight chair in the tea-garden at the Plaza Hotel)
—I was walking along from one place to another, half on the sidewalks and half on the lawns. I was happier on the lawns because I had on shoes from England with rubber nobs on the soles that bit into the soft ground. I had on a new plaid skirt also that blew a little in the wind, and whenever this happened the red, white, and blue banners in front of all the houses stretched out stiff and said *tut-tut-tut-tut,* in a disapproving way.

The largest of the banners and the largest of the lawns belonged to Daisy Fay's house. She was just eighteen, two years older than me, and by far the most popular of all the young girls in Louisville. She dressed in white, and had a little white roadster, and all day long the telephone rang in her house and excited young officers from Camp Taylor demanded the privilege of monopolizing her that night. "Anyways, for an hour!"

When I came opposite her house that morning her white roadster was beside the curb, and she was sitting in it with a lieutenant I had never seen before. They were so engrossed in each other that she didn't see me until I was five feet away.

"Hello, Jordan," she called unexpectedly. "Please come here."

I was flattered that she wanted to speak to me, because of all the older girls I admired her most. She asked me if I was going to the Red Cross and make bandages. I was. Well, then, would I tell them that she couldn't come that day? The officer looked at Daisy while she was speaking, in a way that every young girl wants to be looked at some time, and because it seemed romantic to me I have remembered the incident ever since. His name was Jay Gatsby, and I didn't lay eyes on him again for over four years—even after I'd met him on Long Island I didn't realize it was the same man.

That was nineteen-seventeen. By the next year I had a few beaux myself, and I began to play in tournaments, so I didn't see Daisy very often. She went with a slightly older crowd—when she went with anyone at all. Wild rumors were circulating about her—how her mother had found her packing her bag one winter night to go to New York and say good-by to a soldier who was going overseas. She was effectually prevented, but she wasn't on speaking terms with her family for several weeks. After that she didn't play around with the soldiers any more, but only with a few flat-footed, short-sighted young men in town, who couldn't get into the army at all.

By the next autumn she was gay again, gay as ever. She had a début after the Armistice, and in February she was presumably engaged to a man from New Orleans. In June she married Tom Buchanan of Chicago, with more pomp and circumstance than Louisville ever knew before. He came down with a hundred people in four private cars, and hired a whole floor of the Muhlbach Hotel, and the day before the wedding he gave her a string of pearls valued at three hundred and fifty thousand dollars.

I was a bridesmaid. I came into her room half an hour before the bridal dinner, and found her lying on her bed as lovely as the June night in her flowered dress—and as drunk as a monkey. She had a bottle of Sauterne in one hand and a letter in the other.

" 'Gratulate me," she muttered. "Never had a drink before, but oh how I do enjoy it."

"What's the matter, Daisy?"

I was scared, I can tell you; I'd never seen a girl like that before.

"Here, deares'." She groped around in a waste-basket she had with her on the bed and pulled out the string of pearls. "Take 'em down-stairs and give 'em back to whoever they belong to. Tell 'em all Daisy's change' her mine. Say: 'Daisy's change' her mine!' "

She began to cry—she cried and cried. I rushed out and found her mother's maid, and we locked the door and got her into a cold bath. She wouldn't let go of the letter. She took it into the tub with her and squeezed it up into a wet ball, and only let me leave it in the soap-dish when she saw that it was coming to pieces like snow.

But she didn't say another word. We gave her spirits of ammonia and put ice on her forehead and hooked her back into her dress, and half an hour later, when we walked out of the room, the pearls were around her neck and the incident was over. Next day at five o'clock she married Tom Buchanan without so much as a shiver, and started off on a three months' trip to the South Seas.

I saw them in Santa Barbara when they came back, and I thought I'd never seen a girl so mad about her husband. If he left the room for a minute she'd look around uneasily, and say: "Where's Tom gone?" and wear the most abstracted expression until she saw him coming in the door. She used to sit on the sand with his head in her lap by the hour, rubbing her fingers over his eyes and looking at him with unfathomable delight. It was touching to see them together—it made you laugh in a hushed, fascinated way. That was in August. A week after I left Santa Barbara Tom ran into a wagon on the Ventura road one night, and ripped a front wheel off his car. The girl who was with him got into the papers, too, because her arm was broken—she was one of the chambermaids in the Santa Barbara Hotel.

The next April Daisy had her little girl, and they went to France for a year. I saw them one spring in Cannes, and later in Deauville, and then they came back to Chicago to settle down. Daisy was popular in Chicago, as you know. They moved with a fast crowd, all of them young and rich and wild, but she came out with an absolutely perfect reputation. Perhaps because she doesn't drink. It's a great advantage not to drink among hard-drinking people. You can hold your tongue, and, moreover, you can time any little irregularity of your own so that everybody else is so blind that they don't see or care. Perhaps Daisy never went in for amour at all—and yet there's something in that voice of hers. . . .

Well, about six weeks ago, she heard the name Gatsby for the first time in years. It was when I asked you—do you remember?— if you knew Gatsby in West Egg. After you had gone home she came into my room and woke me up, and said: "What Gatsby?" and when I described him—I was half asleep—she said in the strangest voice that it must be the man she used to know. It wasn't until then that I connected this Gatsby with the officer in her white car.

When Jordan Baker had finished telling all this we had left the Plaza for half an hour and were driving in a victoria through Central Park. The sun had gone down behind the tall apartments of the movie stars in the West Fifties, and the clear voices of little girls already gathered like crickets on the grass, rose through the hot twilight:

> "I'm the Sheik of Araby.
> Your love belongs to me.
> At night when you're asleep
> Into your tent I'll creep——"

"It was a strange coincidence," I said.

"But it wasn't a coincidence at all."

"Why not?"

"Gatsby bought that house so that Daisy would be just across the bay."

Then it had not been merely the stars to which he had aspired on that June night. He came alive to me, delivered suddenly from the womb of his purposeless splendor.

"He wants to know," continued Jordan, "if you'll invite Daisy to your house some afternoon and then let him come over."

The modesty of the demand shook me. He had waited five years and bought a mansion where he dispensed starlight to casual moths— so that he could "come over" some afternoon to a stranger's garden.

"Did I have to know all this before he could ask such a little thing?"

"He's afraid, he's waited so long. He thought you might be offended. You see, he's a regular tough underneath it all."

Something worried me.

"Why didn't he ask you to arrange a meeting?"

"He wants her to see his house," she explained. "And your house is right next door."

"Oh!"

"I think he half expected her to wander into one of his parties, some night," went on Jordan, "but she never did. Then he began asking people casually if they knew her, and I was the first one he found. It was that night he sent for me at his dance, and you should have heard the elaborate way he worked up to it. Of course, I immediately suggested a luncheon in New York—and I thought he'd go mad:

" 'I don't want to do anything out of the way!' he kept saying.
·I want to see her right next door.'

"When I said you were a particular friend of Tom's, he started
to abandon the whole idea. He doesn't know very much about Tom,
though he says he's read a Chicago paper for years just on the
chance of catching a glimpse of Daisy's name."

It was dark now, and as we dipped under a little bridge I put
my arm around Jordan's golden shoulder and drew her toward me
and asked her to dinner. Suddenly I wasn't thinking of Daisy and
Gatsby any more, but of this clean, hard, limited person, who dealt
in universal scepticism, and who leaned back jauntily just within
the circle of my arm. A phrase began to beat in my ears with a sort
of heady excitement: "There are only the pursued, the pursuing,
the busy, and the tired."

"And Daisy ought to have something in her life," murmured
Jordan to me.

"Does she want to see Gatsby?"

"She's not to know about it. Gatsby doesn't want her to know.
You're just supposed to invite her to tea."

We passed a barrier of dark trees, and then the façade of Fifty-
ninth Street, a block of delicate pale light, beamed down into the
park. Unlike Gatsby and Tom Buchanan, I had no girl whose disembodied face floated along the dark cornices and blinding signs,
and so I drew up the girl beside me, tightening my arms. Her wan,
scornful mouth smiled, and so I drew her up again closer, this time
to my face.

CHAPTER V

When I came home to West Egg that night I was afraid for a moment that my house was on fire. Two o'clock and the whole corner of the peninsula was blazing with light, which fell unreal on the shrubbery and made thin elongating glints upon the roadside wires. Turning a corner, I saw that it was Gatsby's house, lit from tower to cellar.

At first I thought it was another party, a wild rout that had resolved itself into "hide-and-go-seek" or "sardines-in-the-box" with all the house thrown open to the game. But there wasn't a sound. Only wind in the trees, which blew the wires and made the lights go off and on again as if the house had winked into the darkness. As my taxi groaned away I saw Gatsby walking toward me across his lawn.

"Your place looks like the World's Fair," I said.

"Does it?" He turned his eyes toward it absently. "I have been glancing into some of the rooms. Let's go to Coney Island, old sport. In my car."

"It's too late."

"Well, suppose we take a plunge in the swimming-pool? I haven't made use of it all summer."

"I've got to go to bed."

"All right."

He waited, looking at me with suppressed eagerness.

"I talked with Miss Baker," I said after a moment. "I'm going to call up Daisy tomorrow and invite her over here to tea."

"Oh, that's all right," he said carelessly. "I don't want to put you to any trouble."

"What day would suit you?"

"What day would suit *you*?" he corrected me quickly. "I don't want to put you to any trouble, you see."

"How about the day after tomorrow?"

He considered for a moment. Then, with reluctance:

"I want to get the grass cut," he said.

We both looked at the grass—there was a sharp line where my ragged lawn ended and the darker, well-kept expanse of his began. I suspected that he meant my grass.

"There's another little thing," he said uncertainly, and hesitated.

"Would you rather put it off for a few days?" I asked.

"Oh, it isn't about that. At least—" He fumbled with a series of beginnings. "Why, I thought—why, look here, old sport, you don't make much money, do you?"

"Not very much."

This seemed to reassure him and he continued more confidently.

"I thought you didn't if you'll pardon my—you see, I carry on a little business on the side, a sort of side line, you understand. And I thought that if you don't make very much— You're selling bonds, aren't you, old sport?"

"Trying to."

"Well, this would interest you. It wouldn't take up much of your time and you might pick up a nice bit of money. It happens to be a rather confidential sort of thing."

I realize now that under different circumstances that conversation might have been one of the crises of my life. But, because the offer was obviously and tactlessly for a service to be rendered, I had no choice except to cut him off there.

"I've got my hands full," I said. "I'm much obliged but I couldn't take on any more work."

"You wouldn't have to do any business with Wolfsheim." Evidently he thought that I was shying away from the "gonnegtion" mentioned at lunch, but I assured him he was wrong. He waited a moment longer, hoping I'd begin a conversation, but I was too absorbed to be responsive, so he went unwillingly home.

The evening had made me light-headed and happy; I think I walked into a deep sleep as I entered my front door. So I don't know whether or not Gatsby went to Coney Island, or for how many hours he "glanced into rooms" while his house blazed gaudily on. I called up Daisy from the office next morning, and invited her to come to tea.

"Don't bring Tom," I warned her.

"What?"

"Don't bring Tom."

"Who is 'Tom'?" she asked innocently.

The day agreed upon was pouring rain. At eleven o'clock a man in a raincoat, dragging a lawn-mower, tapped at my front door and said that Mr. Gatsby had sent him over to cut my grass. This reminded me that I had forgotten to tell my Finn to come back, so I drove into West Egg Village to search for her among soggy whitewashed alleys and to buy some cups and lemons and flowers.

The flowers were unnecessary, for at two o'clock a greenhouse arrived from Gatsby's, with innumerable receptacles to contain it. An hour later the front door opened nervously, and Gatsby, in a white flannel suit, silver shirt, and gold-colored tie, hurried in. He was pale, and there were dark signs of sleeplessness beneath his eyes.

"Is everything all right?" he asked immediately.

"The grass looks fine, if that's what you mean."

"What grass?" he inquired blankly. "Oh, the grass in the yard." He looked out the window at it, but, judging from his expression, I don't believe he saw a thing.

"Looks very good," he remarked vaguely. "One of the papers said they thought the rain would stop about four. I think it was *The Journal*. Have you got everything you need in the shape of— of tea?"

I took him into the pantry, where he looked a little reproachfully at the Finn. Together we scrutinized the twelve lemon cakes from the delicatessen shop.

"Will they do?" I asked

"Of course, of course! They're fine!" and he added hollowly, ". . . old sport."

The rain cooled about half-past three to a damp mist, through which occasional thin drops swam like dew. Gatsby looked with vacant eyes through a copy of Clay's *Economics,* starting at the Finnish tread that shook the kitchen floor, and peering toward the bleared windows from time to time as if a series of invisible but alarming happenings were taking place outside. Finally he got up and informed me, in an uncertain voice, that he was going home.

"Why's that?"

"Nobody's coming to tea. It's too late!" He looked at his watch as if there was some pressing demand on his time elsewhere. "I can't wait all day."

"Don't be silly; it's just two minutes to four."

He sat down miserably, as if I had pushed him, and simultaneously there was the sound of a motor turning into my lane. We both jumped up, and, a little harrowed myself, I went out into the yard.

Under the dripping bare lilac-trees a large open car was coming up the drive. It stopped. Daisy's face, tipped sideways beneath a three-cornered lavender hat, looked out at me with a bright ecstatic smile.

"Is this absolutely where you live, my dearest one?"

The exhilarating ripple of her voice was a wild tonic in the rain. I had to follow the sound of it for a moment, up and down, with my ear alone, before any words came through. A damp streak of hair lay like a dash of blue paint across her cheek, and her hand was wet with glistening drops as I took it to help her from the car.

"Are you in love with me," she said low in my ear, "or why did I have to come alone?"

"That's the secret of Castle Rackrent. Tell your chauffeur to go far away and spend an hour."

"Come back in an hour, Ferdie." Then in a grave murmur: "His name is Ferdie."

"Does the gasoline affect his nose?"

"I don't think so," she said innocently. "Why?"

We went in. To my overwhelming surprise the living-room was deserted.

"Well, that's funny," I exclaimed.

"What's funny?"

She turned her head as there was a light dignified knocking at the front door. I went out and opened it. Gatsby, pale as death, with his hands plunged like weights in his coat pockets, was standing in a puddle of water glaring tragically into my eyes.

With his hands still in his coat pockets he stalked by me into the hall, turned sharply as if he were on a wire, and disappeared into the living-room. It wasn't a bit funny. Aware of the loud beating of my own heart I pulled the door to against the increasing rain.

For half a minute there wasn't a sound. Then from the living-room I heard a sort of choking murmur and part of a laugh, followed by Daisy's voice on a clear artificial note:

"I certainly am awfully glad to see you again."

A pause; it endured horribly. I had nothing to do in the hall, so I went into the room.

Gatsby, his hands still in his pockets, was reclining against the mantelpiece in a strained counterfeit of perfect ease, even of boredom. His head leaned back so far that it rested against the face of a defunct mantelpiece clock, and from this position his distraught eyes stared down at Daisy, who was sitting, frightened but graceful, on the edge of a stiff chair.

"We've met before," muttered Gatsby. His eyes glanced momentarily at me, and his lips parted with an abortive attempt at a laugh. Luckily the clock took this moment to tilt dangerously at the pressure of his head, whereupon he turned and caught it with trembling fingers and set it back in place. Then he sat down, rigidly, his elbow on the arm of the sofa and his chin in his hand.

"I'm sorry about the clock," he said.

My own face had now assumed a deep tropical burn. I couldn't muster up a single commonplace out of the thousand in my head.

"It's an old clock," I told them idiotically.

I think we all believed for a moment that it had smashed in pieces on the floor.

"We haven't met for many years," said Daisy, her voice as matter-of-fact as it could ever be.

"Five years next November."

The automatic quality of Gatsby's answer set us all back at least another minute. I had them both on their feet with the desperate suggestion that they help me make tea in the kitchen when the demoniac Finn brought it in on a tray.

Amid the welcome confusion of cups and cakes a certain physical decency established itself. Gatsby got himself into a shadow and, while Daisy and I talked, looked conscientiously from one to the other of us with tense, unhappy eyes. However, as calmness wasn't an end in itself, I made an excuse at the first possible moment, and got to my feet.

"Where are you going?" demanded Gatsby in immediate alarm.

"I'll be back."

"I've got to speak to you about something before you go."

He followed me wildly into the kitchen, closed the door, and whispered: "Oh, God!" in a miserable way.

"What's the matter?"

"This is a terrible mistake," he said, shaking his head from side to side, "a terrible, terrible mistake."

"You're just embarrassed, that's all," and luckily I added: "Daisy's embarrassed too."

"She's embarrassed?" he repeated incredulously.

"Just as much as you are."

"Don't talk so loud."

"You're acting like a little boy," I broke out impatiently. "Not only that, but you're rude. Daisy's sitting in there all alone."

He raised his hand to stop my words, looked at me with unforgettable reproach, and, opening the door cautiously, went back into the other room.

I walked out the back way—just as Gatsby had when he had made his nervous circuit of the house half an hour before—and ran for a huge black knotted tree, whose massed leaves made a fabric against the rain. Once more it was pouring, and my irregular lawn, well-shaved by Gatsby's gardener, abounded in small muddy swamps and prehistoric marshes. There was nothing to look at from under the tree except Gatsby's enormous house, so I stared at it, like Kant at his church steeple, for half an hour. A brewer had built it early in the "period" craze a decade before, and there was a story that he'd agreed to pay five years' taxes on all the neighboring cottages if the owners would have their roofs thatched with straw. Perhaps their refusal took the heart out of his plan to Found a Family— he went into an immediate decline. His children sold his house with the black wreath still on the door. Americans, while occasionally willing to be serfs, have always been obstinate about being peasantry.

After half an hour, the sun shone again, and the grocer's automobile rounded Gatsby's drive with the raw material for his servants' dinner—I felt sure he wouldn't eat a spoonful. A maid began opening the upper windows of his house, appeared momentarily in each, and, leaning from a large central bay, spat meditatively into the garden. It was time I went back. While the rain continued it had seemed like the murmur of their voices, rising and swelling a little now and then with gusts of emotion. But in the new silence I felt that silence had fallen within the house too.

I went in—after making every possible noise in the kitchen, short of pushing over the stove—but I don't believe they heard a sound. They were sitting at either end of the couch, looking at each other as if some question had been asked, or was in the air, and every vestige of embarrassment was gone. Daisy's face was smeared with tears, and when I came in she jumped up and began wiping at it with her handkerchief before a mirror. But there was a change in Gatsby that was simply confounding. He literally glowed; without a word or a gesture of exultation a new well-being radiated from him and filled the little room.

"Oh, hello old sport," he said, as if he hadn't seen me for years. I thought for a moment he was going to shake hands.

"It's stopped raining."

"Has it?" When he realized what I was talking about, that there were twinkle-bells of sunshine in the room, he smiled like a weather man, like an ecstatic patron of recurrent light, and repeated the news to Daisy. "What do you think of that? It's stopped raining."

"I'm glad, Jay." Her throat, full of aching, grieving beauty, told only of her unexpected joy.

"I want you and Daisy to come over to my house," he said, "I'd like to show her around."

"You're sure you want me to come?"

"Absolutely, old sport."

Daisy went up-stairs to wash her face—too late I thought with humiliation of my towels—while Gatsby and I waited on the lawn.

"My house looks well, doesn't it?" he demanded. "See how the whole front of it catches the light."

I agreed that it was splendid.

"Yes." His eyes went over it, every arched door and square tower. "It took me just three years to earn the money that bought it."

"I thought you inherited your money."

"I did, old sport," he said automatically, "but I lost most of it in the big panic—the panic of the war."

I think he hardly knew what he was saying, for when I asked him what business he was in he answered: "That's my affair," before he realized that it wasn't an appropriate reply.

"Oh, I've been in several things," he corrected himself. "I was in the drug business and then I was in the oil business. But I'm not in either one now." He looked at me with more attention. "Do you mean you've been thinking over what I proposed the other night?"

Before I could answer, Daisy came out of the house and two rows of brass buttons on her dress gleamed in the sunlight.

"That huge place *there*?" she cried pointing.

"Do you like it?"

"I love it, but I don't see how you live there all alone."

"I keep it always full of interesting people, night and day. People who do interesting things. Celebrated people."

Instead of taking the short cut along the Sound we went down to the road and entered by the big postern. With enchanting murmurs Daisy admired this aspect or that of the feudal silhouette against the sky, admired the gardens, the sparkling odor of jonquils and the frothy odor of hawthorn and plum blossoms and the pale gold odor of kiss-me-at-the-gate. It was strange to reach the marble steps and find no stir of bright dresses in and out of the door, and hear no sound but bird voices in the trees.

And inside, as we wandered through Marie Antoinette music-rooms and Restoration salons, I felt that there were guests concealed behind every couch and table, under orders to be breathlessly silent until we had passed through. As Gatsby closed the door of "the Merton College Library" I could have sworn I heard the owl-eyed man break into ghostly laughter.

We went upstairs, through period bedrooms swathed in rose and lavender silk and vivid with new flowers, through dressing-rooms and poolrooms, and bathrooms, with sunken baths—intruding into one chamber where a dishevelled man in pajamas was doing liver exercises on the floor. It was Mr. Klipspringer, the "boarder." I had seen him wandering hungrily about the beach that morning. Finally we came to Gatsby's own apartment, a bedroom and a bath, and an Adam study, where we sat down and drank a glass of some Chartreuse he took from a cupboard in the wall.

He hadn't once ceased looking at Daisy, and I think he revalued everything in his house according to the measure of response it drew from her well-loved eyes. Sometimes, too, he stared around at his possessions in a dazed way, as though in her actual and astounding presence none of it was any longer real. Once he nearly toppled down a flight of stairs.

His bedroom was the simplest room of all—except where the dresser was garnished with a toilet set of pure dull gold. Daisy took the brush with delight, and smoothed her hair, whereupon Gatsby sat down and shaded his eyes and began to laugh.

"It's the funniest thing, old sport," he said hilariously. "I can't— when I try to——"

He had passed visibly through two states and was entering upon a third. After his embarrassment and his unreasoning joy he was consumed with wonder at her presence. He had been full of the idea so long, dreamed it right through to the end, waited with his teeth set, so to speak, at an inconceivable pitch of intensity. Now, in the reaction, he was running down like an overwound clock.

Recovering himself in a minute he opened for us two hulking patent cabinets which held his massed suits and dressing-gowns and ties, and his shirts, piled like bricks in stacks a dozen high.

"I've got a man in England who buys me clothes. He sends over a selection of things at the beginning of each season, spring and fall."

He took out a pile of shirts and began throwing them, one by one, before us, shirts of sheer linen and thick silk and fine flannel, which lost their folds as they fell and covered the table in many-colored disarray. While we admired he brought more and the soft rich heap mounted higher—shirts with stripes and scrolls and plaids in coral and apple-green and lavender and faint orange, with monograms of Indian blue. Suddenly, with a strained sound, Daisy bent her head into the shirts and began to cry stormily.

"They're such beautiful shirts," she sobbed, her voice muffled in the thick folds. "It makes me sad because I've never seen such— such beautiful shirts before."

After the house, we were to see the grounds and the swimming-pool, and the hydroplane and the mid-summer flowers—but outside Gatsby's window it began to rain again, so we stood in a row looking at the corrugated surface of the Sound.

"If it wasn't for the mist we could see your home across the bay," said Gatsby. "You always have a green light that burns all night at the end of your dock."

Daisy put her arm through his abruptly, but he seemed absorbed in what he had just said. Possibly it had occurred to him that the colossal significance of that light had now vanished forever. Compared to the great distance that had separated him from Daisy it had seemed very near to her, almost touching her. It had seemed as close as a star to the moon. Now it was again a green light on a dock. His count of enchanted objects had diminished by one.

I began to walk about the room, examining various indefinite objects in the half darkness. A large photograph of an elderly man in yaching costume attracted me, hung on the wall over his desk.

"Who's this?"

"That? That's Mr. Dan Cody, old sport."

The name sounded faintly familiar.

"He's dead now. He used to be my best friend years ago."

There was a small picture of Gatsby, also in yachting costume, on the bureau—Gatsby with his head thrown back defiantly—taken apparently when he was about eighteen.

"I adore it," exclaimed Daisy. "The pompadour! You never told me you had a pompadour—or a yacht."

"Look at this," said Gatsby quickly. "Here's a lot of clippings—about you."

They stood side by side examining it. I was going to ask to see the rubies when the phone rang, and Gatsby took up the receiver.

"Yes. . . . Well, I can't talk now. . . . I can't talk now, old sport. . . . I said a *small* town. . . . He must know what a small town is. . . . Well, he's no use to us if Detroit is his idea of a small town. . . ."

He rang off.

"Come here *quick*!" cried Daisy at the window.

The rain was still falling, but the darkness had parted in the west, and there was a pink and golden billow of foamy clouds above the sea.

"Look at that," she whispered, and then after a moment: "I'd like to just get one of those pink clouds and put you in it and push you around."

I tried to go then, but they wouldn't hear of it; perhaps my presence made them feel more satisfactorily alone.

"I know what we'll do," said Gatsby, "we'll have Klipspringer play the piano."

He went out of the room calling "Ewing!" and returned in a few minutes accompanied by an embarrassed, slightly worn young man, with shell-rimmed glasses and scanty blond hair. He was now decently clothed in a sport shirt, open at the neck, sneakers, and duck trousers of a nebulous hue.

"Did we interrupt your exercises?" inquired Daisy politely.

"I was asleep," cried Mr. Klipspringer, in a spasm of embarrassment. "That is, I'd *been* asleep. Then I got up. . . ."

"Klipspringer plays the piano," said Gatsby, cutting him off. "Don't you, Ewing, old sport?"

"I don't play well. I don't—I hardly play at all. I'm all out of prac——"

"We'll go downstairs," interrupted Gatsby. He flipped a switch. The gray windows disappeared as the house glowed full of light.

In the music-room Gatsby turned on a solitary lamp beside the piano. He lit Daisy's cigarette from a trembling match, and sat down with her on a couch far across the room, where there was no light save what the gleaming floor bounced in from the hall.

When Klipspringer had played *The Love Nest* he turned around on the bench and searched unhappily for Gatsby in the gloom.

"I'm all out of practice, you see. I told you I couldn't play. I'm all out of prac——"

"Don't talk so much, old sport," commanded Gatsby. "Play!"

> *"In the morning,*
> *In the evening,*
> *Ain't we got fun——"*

Outside the wind was loud and there was a faint flow of thunder along the Sound. All the lights were going on in West Egg now; the electric trains, men-carrying, were plunging home through the rain from New York. It was the hour of a profound human change, and excitement was generating on the air

> *"One thing's sure and nothing's surer*
> *The rich get richer and the poor get—children.*
> *In the meantime,*
> *In between time——"*

As I went over to say good-by I saw that the expression of bewilderment had come back into Gatsby's face, as though a faint doubt had occurred to him as to the quality of his present happiness. Almost five years! There must have been moments even that afternoon when Daisy tumbled short of his dreams—not through her own fault, but because of the colossal vitality of his illusion. It had gone beyond her, beyond everything. He had thrown himself into it with a creative passion, adding to it all the time, decking it out with every bright feather that drifted his way. No amount of fire or freshness can challenge what a man will store up in his ghostly heart.

As I watched him he adjusted himself a little, visibly. His hand took hold of hers, and as she said something low in his ear he turned toward her with a rush of emotion. I think that voice held him most, with its fluctuating, feverish warmth, because it couldn't be over-dreamed—that voice was a deathless song.

They had forgotten me, but Daisy glanced up and held out her hand; Gatsby didn't know me now at all. I looked once more at them and they looked back at me, remotely, possessed by intense life. Then I went out of the room and down the marble steps into the rain, leaving them there together.

CHAPTER VI

ABOUT this time an ambitious young reporter from New York arrived one morning at Gatsby's door and asked him if he had anything to say.

"Anything to say about what?" inquired Gatsby politely.

"Why—any statement to give out."

It transpired after a confused five minutes that the man had heard Gatsby's name around his office in a connection which he either wouldn't reveal or didn't fully understand. This was his day off and with laudable initiative he had hurried out "to see."

It was a random shot, and yet the reporter's instinct was right. Gatsby's notoriety, spread about by the hundreds who had accepted his hospitality and so become authorities upon his past, had increased all summer until he fell just short of being news. Contemporary legends such as the "underground pipe-line to Canada" attached themselves to him, and there was one persistent story that he didn't live in a house at all, but in a boat that looked like a house and was moved secretly up and down the Long Island shore. Just why these inventions were a source of satisfaction to James Gatz of North Dakota isn't easy to say.

James Gatz—that was really, or at least legally, his name. He had changed it at the age of seventeen and at the specific moment that witnessed the beginning of his career—when he saw Dan Cody's yacht drop anchor over the most insidious flat on Lake Superior. It was James Gatz who had been loafing along the beach that afternoon in a torn green jersey and a pair of canvas pants, but it was already Jay Gatsby who borrowed a rowboat, pulled out to the *Tuolomee,* and informed Cody that a wind might catch him and break him up in half an hour.

I suppose he'd had the name ready for a long time, even then. His parents were shiftless and unsuccessful farm people—his imagination had never really accepted them as his parents at all.

The truth was that Jay Gatsby of West Egg, Long Island, sprang from his Platonic conception of himself. He was a son of God—a phrase which, if it means anything, means just that—and he must be about His Father's business, the service of a vast, vulgar, and meretricious beauty. So he invented just the sort of Jay Gatsby that a seventeen-year-old boy would be likely to invent, and to this conception he was faithful to the end.

For over a year he had been beating his way along the south shore of Lake Superior as a clam-digger and a salmon-fisher or in any other capacity that brought him food and bed. His brown, hardening body lived naturally through the half-fierce, half-lazy work of the bracing days. He knew women early, and since they spoiled him he became contemptuous of them, of young virgins because they were ignorant, of the others because they were hysterical about things which in his overwhelming self-absorption he took for granted.

But his heart was in a constant, turbulent riot. The most grotesque and fantastic conceits haunted him in his bed at night. A universe of ineffable gaudiness spun itself out in his brain while the clock ticked on the wash-stand and the moon soaked with wet light his tangled clothes upon the floor. Each night he added to the pattern of his fancies until drowsiness closed down upon some vivid scene with an oblivious embrace. For a while these reveries provided an outlet for his imagination; they were a satisfactory hint of the unreality of reality, a promise that the rock of the world was founded securely on a fairy's wing.

An instinct toward his future glory had led him, some months before, to the small Lutheran college of St. Olaf's in southern Minnesota. He stayed there two weeks, dismayed at its ferocious indifference to the drums of his destiny, to destiny itself, and despising the janitor's work with which he was to pay his way through. Then he drifted back to Lake Superior, and he was still searching for something to do on the day that Dan Cody's yacht dropped anchor in the shallows alongshore.

Cody was fifty years old then, a product of the Nevada silver fields, of the Yukon, of every rush for metal since seventy-five. The transactions in Montana copper that made him many times a millionaire found him physically robust but on the verge of soft-mindedness, and, suspecting this, an infinite number of women tried to separate him from his money. The none too savory ramifications by which Ella Kaye, the newspaper woman, played Madame de Maintenon to his weakness and sent him to sea in a yacht, were common knowledge to the turgid sub or suppressed journalism of 1902. He had been coasting along all too hospitable shores for five years when he turned up as James Gatz's destiny in Little Girl Bay.

To young Gatz, resting on his oars and looking up at the railed deck, that yacht represented all the beauty and glamour in the world. I suppose he smiled at Cody—he had probably discovered that people liked him when he smiled. At any rate Cody asked him a few questions (one of them elicited the brand new name) and found that he was quick and extravagantly ambitious. A few days later he took him to Duluth and bought him a blue coat, six pairs of white duck trousers, and a yachting cap. And when the *Tuolomee* left for the West Indies and the Barbary Coast Gatsby left too.

He was employed in a vague personal capacity—while he remained with Cody he was in turn steward, mate, skipper, secretary, and even jailor, for Dan Cody sober knew what lavish doings Dan Cody drunk might soon be about, and he provided for such contingencies by reposing more and more trust in Gatsby. The arrangement lasted five years, during which the boat went three times around the Continent. It might have lasted indefinitely except for the fact that Ella Kaye came on board one night in Boston and a week later Dan Cody inhospitably died.

I remember the portrait of him up in Gatsby's bedroom, a gray, florid man with a hard, empty face—the pioneer debauchee, who during one phase of American life brought back to the Eastern seaboard the savage violence of the frontier brothel and saloon. It was indirectly due to Cody that Gatsby drank so little. Sometimes in the course of gay parties women used to rub champagne into his hair; for himself he formed the habit of letting liquor alone.

And it was from Cody that he inherited money—a legacy of twenty-five thousand dollars. He didn't get it. He never understood the legal device that was used against him, but what remained of the millions went intact to Ella Kaye. He was left with his singularly appropriate education; the vague contour of Jay Gatsby had filled out to the substantiality of a man.

He told me all this very much later, but I've put it down here with the idea of exploding those first wild rumors about his antecedents, which weren't even faintly true. Moreover he told it to me at a time of confusion, when I had reached the point of believing everything and nothing about him. So I take advantage of this short halt, while Gatsby, so to speak, caught his breath, to clear this set of misconceptions away.

It was a halt, too, in my association with his affairs. For several weeks I didn't see him or hear his voice on the phone—mostly I was in New York, trotting around with Jordan and trying to ingratiate myself with her senile aunt—but finally I went over to his house one Sunday afternoon. I hadn't been there two minutes when somebody brought Tom Buchanan in for a drink. I was startled, naturally, but the really surprising thing was that it hadn't happened before .

They were a party of three on horseback—Tom and a man named Sloane and a pretty woman in a brown riding-habit, who had been there previously.

"I'm delighted to see you," said Gatsby, standing on his porch. "I'm delighted that you dropped in."

As though they cared!

"Sit right down. Have a cigarette or a cigar." He walked around the room quickly, ringing bells. "I'll have something to drink for you in just a minute."

He was profoundly affected by the fact that Tom was there. But he would be uneasy anyhow until he had given them something, realizing in a vague way that that was all they came for. Mr. Sloane wanted nothing. A lemonade? No, thanks. A little champagne? Nothing at all, thanks. . . . I'm sorry——

"Did you have a nice ride?"

"Very good roads around here."

"I suppose the automobiles——"

"Yeah."

Moved by an irresistible impulse, Gatsby turned to Tom, who had accepted the introduction as a stranger.

"I believe we've met somewhere before, Mr. Buchanan."

"Oh, yes," said Tom, gruffly polite, but obviously not remembering. "So we did. I remember very well."

"About two weeks ago."

"That's right. You were with Nick here."

"I know your wife," continued Gatsby, almost aggressively.

"That so?"

Tom turned to me.

"You live near here, Nick?"

"Next door."

"That so?"

Mr. Sloane didn't enter into the conversation, but lounged back haughtily in his chair; the woman said nothing either—until unexpectedly, after two highballs, she became cordial.

"We'll all come over to your next party, Mr. Gatsby," she suggested. "What do you say?"

"Certainly; I'd be delighted to have you."

"Be ver' nice," said Mr. Sloane, without gratitude. "Well—think ought to be starting home."

"Please don't hurry," Gatsby urged them. He had control of himself now, and he wanted to see more of Tom. "Why don't you— why don't you stay for supper? I wouldn't be surprised if some other people dropped in from New York."

"You come to supper with *me*," said the lady enthusiastically. "Both of you."

This included me. Mr. Sloane got to his feet.

"Come along," he said—but to her only.

"I mean it," she insisted. "I'd love to have you. Lots of room."

Gatsby looked at me questioningly. He wanted to go, and he didn't see that Mr. Sloane had determined he shouldn't.

"I'm afraid I won't be able to," I said.

"Well, you come," she urged, concentrating on Gatsby.

Mr. Sloane murmured something close to her ear.

"We won't be late if we start now," she insisted aloud.

"I haven't got a horse," said Gatsby. "I used to ride in the army, but I've never bought a horse. I'll have to follow you in my car. Excuse me for just a minute."

The rest of us walked out on the porch, where Sloane and the lady began an impassioned conversation aside.

"My God, I believe the man's coming," said Tom. "Doesn't he know she doesn't want him?"

"She says she does want him."

"She has a big dinner party and he won't know a soul there." He frowned. "I wonder where in the devil he met Daisy. By God, I may be old-fashioned in my ideas, but women run around too much these days to suit me. They meet all kinds of crazy fish."

Suddenly Mr. Sloane and the lady walked down the steps and mounted their horses.

"Come on," said Mr. Sloane to Tom, "we're late. We've got to go." And then to me: "Tell him we couldn't wait, will you?"

Tom and I shook hands, the rest of us exchanged a cool nod, and they trotted quickly down the drive, disappearing under the August foliage just as Gatsby, with hat and light overcoat in hand, came out the front door.

Tom was evidently perturbed at Daisy's running around alone, for on the following Saturday night he came with her to Gatsby's party. Perhaps his presence gave the evening its peculiar quality of oppressiveness—it stands out in my memory from Gatsby's other parties that summer. There were the same people, or at least the same sort of people, the same profusion of champagne, the same many-colored, many-keyed commotion, but I felt an unpleasantness in the air, a pervading harshness that hadn't been there before. Or perhaps I had merely grown used to it, grown to accept West Egg as a world complete in itself, with its own standards and its own great figures, second to nothing because it had no consciousness of being so, and now I was looking at it again, through Daisy's eyes. It is invariably saddening to look through new eyes at things upon which you have expended your own powers of adjustment.

They arrived at twilight, and, as we strolled out among the sparkling hundreds, Daisy's voice was playing murmurous tricks in her throat.

"These things excite me *so*," she whispered. "If you want to kiss me any time during the evening, Nick, just let me know and I'll be glad to arrange it for you. Just mention my name. Or present a green card. I'm giving out green——"

"Look around," suggested Gatsby.

"I'm looking around. I'm having a marvellous——"

"You must see the faces of many people you've heard about."

Tom's arrogant eyes roamed the crowd.

"We don't go around very much," he said; "in fact, I was just thinking I don't know a soul here."

"Perhaps you know that lady," Gatsby indicated a gorgeous, scarcely human orchid of a woman who sat in state under a white-plum tree. Tom and Daisy stared, with that particularly unreal feeling that accompanies the recognition of a hitherto ghostly celebrity of the movies.

"She's lovely," said Daisy.

"The man bending over her is her director."

He took them ceremoniously from group to group:

"Mrs. Buchanan . . . and Mr. Buchanan—" After an instant's hesitation he added: "the polo player."

"Oh, no," objected Tom quickly, "not me."

But evidently the sound of it pleased Gatsby, for Tom remained "the polo player" for the rest of the evening.

"I've never met so many celebrities," Daisy exclaimed. "I liked that man—what was his name?—with the sort of blue nose."

Gatsby identified him, adding that he was a small producer.

"Well, I liked him anyhow."

"I'd a little rather not be the polo player," said Tom pleasantly, "I'd rather look at all these famous people in—in oblivion."

Daisy and Gatsby danced. I remember being surprised by his graceful, conservative fox-trot—I had never seen him dance before. Then they sauntered over to my house and sat on the steps for half an hour, while at her request I remained watchfully in the garden. "In case there's a fire or a flood," she explained, "or any act of God."

Tom appeared from his oblivion as we were sitting down to supper together. "Do you mind if I eat with some people over here?" he said. "A fellow's getting off some funny stuff."

"Go ahead," answered Daisy genially, "and if you want to take down any addresses here's my little gold pencil." . . . She looked around after a moment and told me the girl was "common but pretty," and I knew that except for the half-hour she'd been alone with Gatsby she wasn't having a good time.

We were at a particularly tipsy table. That was my fault—
Gatsby had been called to the phone, and I'd enjoyed these same
people only two weeks before. But what had amused me then turned
septic on the air now.

"How do you feel, Miss Baedeker?"

The girl addressed was trying, unsuccessfully, to slump against
my shoulder. At this inquiry she sat up and opened her eyes.

"Wha'?"

A massive and lethargic woman, who had been urging Daisy
to play golf with her at the local club to-morrow, spoke in Miss
Baedeker's defence:

"Oh, she's all right now. When she's had five or six cocktails
she always starts screaming like that. I tell her she ought to leave
it alone."

"I do leave it alone," affirmed the accused hollowly.

"We heard you yelling, so I said to Doc Civet here: 'There's somebody that needs your help, Doc.' "

"She's much obliged, I'm sure," said another friend, without
gratitude, "but you got her dress all wet when you stuck her head
in the pool."

"Anything I hate is to get my head stuck in a pool," mumbled
Miss Baedeker. "They almost drowned me once over in New
Jersey."

"Then you ought to leave it alone," countered Doctor Civet.

"Speak for yourself!" cried Miss Baedeker violently. "Your hand
shakes. I wouldn't let you operate on me!"

It was like that. Almost the last thing I remember was standing
with Daisy and watching the moving-picture director and his Star.
They were still under the white-plum tree and their faces were
touching except for a pale, thin ray of moonlight between. It
occurred to me that he had been very slowly bending toward her
all evening to attain this proximity, and even while I watched I
saw him stoop one ultimate degree and kiss at her cheek.

"I like her," said Daisy, "I think she's lovely."

But the rest offended her—and inarguably, because it wasn't
a gesture but an emotion. She was appalled by West Egg, this
unprecedented "place" that Broadway had begotten upon a Long
Island fishing village—appalled by its raw vigor that chafed under

the old euphemisms and by the too obtrusive fate that herded its inhabitants along a short-cut from nothing to nothing. She saw something awful in the very simplicity she failed to understand.

I sat on the front steps with them while they waited for their car. It was dark here in front; only the bright door sent ten square feet of light volleying out into the soft black morning. Sometimes a shadow moved against a dressing-room blind above, gave way to another shadow, an indefinite procession of shadows, that rouged and powdered in an invisible glass.

"Who is this Gatsby anyhow?" demanded Tom suddenly. "Some big bootlegger?"

"Where'd you hear that?" I inquired.

"I didn't hear it. I imagined it. A lot of these newly rich people are just big bootleggers, you know."

"Not Gatsby," I said shortly.

He was silent for a moment. The pebbles of the drive crunched under his feet.

"Well, he certainly must have strained himself to get this menagerie together."

A breeze stirred the gray haze of Daisy's fur collar.

"At least they're more interesting than the people we know," she said with an effort.

"You didn't look so interested."

"Well, I was."

Tom laughed and turned to me.

"Did you notice Daisy's face when that girl asked her to put her under a cold shower?"

Daisy began to sing with the music in a husky, rhythmic whisper, bringing out a meaning in each word that it had never had before and would never have again. When the melody rose, her voice broke up sweetly, following it, in a way contralto voices have, and each change tipped out a little of her warm human magic upon the air.

"Lots of people come who haven't been invited," she said suddenly. "That girl hadn't been invited. They simply force their way in and he's too polite to object."

"I'd like to know who he is and what he does," insisted Tom. "And I think I'll make a point of finding out."

"I can tell you right now," she answered. "He owned some drug-stores, a lot of drug-stores. He built them up himself."

The dilatory limousine came rolling up the drive.

"Good night, Nick," said Daisy.

Her glance left me and sought the lighted top of the steps, where *Three O'Clock in the Morning,* a neat, sad little waltz of that year, was drifting out the open door. After all, in the very casualness of Gatsby's party there were romantic possibilities totally absent from her world. What was it up there in the song that seemed to be calling her back inside? What would happen now in the dim, incalculable hours? Perhaps some unbelievable guest would arrive, a person infinitely rare and to be marvelled at, some authentically radiant young girl who with one fresh glance at Gatsby, one moment of magical encounter, would blot out those five years of unwavering devotion.

I stayed late that night, Gatsby asked me to wait until he was free, and I lingered in the garden until the inevitable swimming party had run up, chilled and exalted, from the black beach, until the lights were extinguished in the guest-rooms **overhead.** When he came down the steps at last the tanned skin was drawn unusually tight on his face, and his eyes were bright and tired.

"She didn't like it," he said immediately.

"Of course she did."

"She didn't like it," he insisted. "She didn't **have a good** time."

He was silent, and I guessed at his unutterable depression.

"I feel far away from her," he said. "It's hard to make her understand."

"You mean about the dance?"

"The dance?" He dismissed all the dances he had given with a snap of his fingers. "Old sport, the dance is unimportant."

He wanted nothing less of Daisy than that she should go to Tom and say: "I never loved you." After she had obliterated four years with that sentence they could decide upon the more practical measures to be taken. One of them was that, after she was free, they were to go back to Louisville and be married from her house—— just as if it were five years ago.

"And she doesn't understand," he said. "She used to be able to understand. We'd sit for hours——"

He broke off and began to walk up and down a desolate path of fruit rinds and discarded favors and crushed flowers.

"I wouldn't ask too much of her," I ventured. "You can't repeat the past."

"Can't repeat the past?" he cried incredulously. "Why of course you can!"

He looked around him wildly, as if the past were lurking here in the shadow of his house, just out of reach of his hand.

"I'm going to fix everything just the way it was before," he said, nodding determinedly. "She'll see."

He talked a lot about the past, and I gathered that he wanted to recover something, some idea of himself perhaps, that had gone into loving Daisy. His life had been confused and disordered since then, but if he could once return to a certain starting place and go over it all slowly, he could find out what that thing was. . . .

. . . One autumn night, five years before, they had been walking down the street when the leaves were falling, and they came to a place where there were no trees and the sidewalk was white with moonlight. They stopped here and turned toward each other. Now it was a cool night with that mysterious excitement in it which comes at the two changes of the year. The quiet lights in the houses were humming out into the darkness and there was a stir and bustle among the stars. Out of the corner of his eye Gatsby saw that the blocks of the sidewalks really formed a ladder and mounted to a secret place above the trees—he could climb to it, if he climbed alone, and once there he could suck on the pap of life, gulp down the incomparable milk of wonder.

His heart beat faster and faster as Daisy's white face came up to his own. He knew that when he kissed this girl, and forever wed his unutterable visions to her perishable breath, his mind would never romp again like the mind of God. So he waited, listening for a moment longer to the tuning-fork that had been struck upon a star. Then he kissed her. At his lips' touch she blossomed for him like a flower and the incarnation was complete.

Through all he said, even through his appalling sentimentality, I was reminded of something—an elusive rhythm, a fragment of lost words, that I had heard somewhere a long time ago. For a moment a phrase tried to take shape in my mouth and my lips parted like a dumb man's, as though there was more struggling upon them than a wisp of startled air. But they made no sound, and what I had almost remembered was uncommunicable forever.

CHAPTER VII

It was when curiosity about Gatsby was at its highest that the lights in his house failed to go on one Saturday night—and, as obscurely as it had begun, his career as Trimalchio was over. Only gradually did I become aware that the automobiles which turned expectantly into his drive stayed for just a minute and then drove sulkily away. Wondering if he were sick I went over to find out— an unfamiliar butler with a villainous face squinted at me suspiciously from the door.

"Is Mr. Gatsby sick?"

"Nope." After a pause he added "sir" in a dilatory, grudging way.

"I hadn't seen him around, and I was rather worried. Tell him Mr. Carraway came over."

"Who?" he demanded rudely.

"Carraway."

"Carraway. All right, I'll tell him."

Abruptly he slammed the door.

My Finn informed me that Gatsby had dismissed every servant in his house a week ago and replaced them with half a dozen others, who never went into West Egg Village to be bribed by the tradesmen, but ordered moderate supplies over the telephone. The grocery boy reported that the kitchen looked like a pigsty, and the general opinion in the village was that the new people weren't servants at all.

Next day Gatsby called me on the phone.

"Going away?" I inquired.

"No, old sport."

"I hear you fired all your servants."

"I wanted somebody who wouldn't gossip. Daisy comes over quite often—in the afternoons."

So the whole caravansary had fallen in like a card house at the disapproval in her eyes.

"They're some people Wolfsheim wanted to do something for. They're all brothers and sisters. They used to run a small hotel."

"I see."

He was calling up at Daisy's request—would I come to lunch at her house to-morrow? Miss Baker would be there. Half an hour later Daisy herself telephoned and seemed relieved to find that I was coming. Something was up. And yet I couldn't believe that they would choose this occasion for a scene—especially for the rather harrowing scene that Gatsby had outlined in the garden.

The next day was broiling, almost the last, certainly the warmest, of the summer. As my train emerged from the tunnel into sunlight, only the hot whistles of the National Biscuit Company broke the simmering hush at noon. The straw seats of the car hovered on the edge of combustion; the woman next to me perspired delicately for a while into her white shirtwaist, and then, as her newspaper dampened under her fingers, lapsed despairingly into deep heat with a desolate cry. Her pocket-book slapped to the floor.

"Oh, my!" she gasped.

I picked it up with a weary bend and handed it back to her, holding it at arm's length and by the extreme tip of the corners to indicate that I had no designs upon it—but every one near by, including the woman, suspected me just the same.

"Hot!" said the conductor to familiar faces. "Some weather! . . . Hot! . . . Hot! . . . Hot! . . . Is it hot enough for you? Is it hot? Is it . . . ?"

My commutation ticket came back to me with a dark stain from his hand. That any one should care in this heat whose flushed lips he kissed, whose head made damp the pajama pocket over his heart!

. . . Through the hall of the Buchanans' house blew a faint wind, carrying the sound of the telephone bell out to Gatsby and me as we waited at the door.

"The master's body!" roared the butler into the mouthpiece. "I'm sorry, madame, but we can't furnish it—it's far too hot to touch this noon!"

What he really said was: "Yes . . . Yes . . . I'll see."

He set down the receiver and came toward us, glistening slightly, to take our stiff straw hats.

"Madame expects you in the salon!" he cried, needlessly indicating the direction. In this heat every extra gesture was an affront to the common store of life.

The room, shadowed well with awnings, was dark and cool.
Daisy and Jordan lay upon an enormous couch, like silver idols
weighing down their own white dresses against the singing breeze
of the fans.

"We can't move," they said together.

Jordan's fingers, powdered white over their tan, rested for a
moment in mine.

"And Mr. Thomas Buchanan, the athlete?" I inquired.

Simultaneously I heard his voice, gruff, muffled, husky, at the
hall telephone.

Gatsby stood in the centre of the crimson carpet and gazed
around with fascinated eyes. Daisy watched him and laughed, her
sweet, exciting laugh; a tiny gust of powder rose from her bosom
into the air.

"The rumor is," whispered Jordan, "that that's Tom's girl on
the telephone."

We were silent. The voice in the hall rose high with annoyance:
"Very well, then, I won't sell you the car at all. . . . I'm under
no obligations to you at all . . . and as for your bothering me
about it at lunch time, I won't stand that at all!"

"Holding down the receiver," said Daisy cynically.

"No, he's not," I assured her. "It's a bona-fide deal. I happen
to know about it."

Tom flung open the door, blocked out its space for a moment
with his thick body, and hurried into the room.

"Mr. Gatsby!" He put out his broad, flat hand with well-con-
cealed dislike. "I'm glad to see you, sir. . . . Nick. . . ."

"Make us a cold drink," cried Daisy.

As he left the room again she got up and went over to Gatsby
and pulled his face down, kissing him on the mouth.

"You know I love you," she murmured.

"You forget there's a lady present," said Jordan.

Daisy looked around doubtfully.

"You kiss Nick too."

"What a low, vulgar girl!"

"I don't care!" cried Daisy, and began to clog on the brick fire-
place. Then she remembered the heat and sat down guiltily on the

couch just as a freshly laundered nurse leading a little girl came into the room.

"Bles-sed pre-cious," she crooned, holding out her arms. "Come to your own mother that loves you."

The child, relinquished by the nurse, rushed across the room and rooted shyly into her mother's dress.

The bles-sed pre-cious! Did mother get powder on your old yellowy hair? Stand up now, and say—How-de-do."

Gatsby and I in turn leaned down and took the small reluctant hand. Afterward he kept looking at the child with surprise. I don't think he had ever really believed in its existence before.

"I got dressed before luncheon," said the child, turning eagerly to Daisy.

"That's because your mother wanted to show you off." Her face bent into the single wrinkle of the small white neck. "You dream, you. You absolute little dream."

"Yes," admitted the child calmly. "Aunt Jordan's got on a white dress too."

"How do you like mother's friends?" Daisy turned her around so that she faced Gatsby. "Do you think they're pretty?"

"Where's Daddy?"

"She doesn't look like her father," explained Daisy. "She looks like me. She's got my hair and shape of the face."

Daisy sat back upon the couch. The nurse took a step forward and held out her hand.

"Come, Pammy."

"Good-by, sweetheart!"

With a reluctant backward glance the well-disciplined child held to her nurse's hand and was pulled out the door, just as Tom came back, preceding four gin rickeys that clicked full of ice.

Gatsby took up his drink.

"They certainly look cool," he said, with visible tension.

We drank in long, greedy swallows.

"I read somewhere that the sun's getting hotter every year," said Tom genially. "It seems that pretty soon the earth's going to fall into the sun—or wait a minute—it's just the opposite—the sun's getting colder every year."

"Come outside," he suggested to Gatsby, "I'd like you to have a look at the place."

I went with them out to the veranda. On the green Sound, stagnant in the heat, one small sail crawled slowly toward the fresher sea. Gatsby's eyes followed it momentarily; he raised his hand and pointed across the bay.

"I'm right across from you."

"So you are."

Our eyes lifted over the rose-beds and the hot lawn and the weedy refuse of the dog-days alongshore. Slowly the white wings of the boat moved against the blue cool limit of the sky. Ahead lay the scalloped ocean and the abounding blessed isles.

"There's sport for you," said Tom, nodding. "I'd like to be out there with him for about an hour."

We had luncheon in the dining-room, darkened too against the heat, and drank down nervous gayety with the cold ale.

"What'll we do with ourselves this afternoon?" cried Daisy, "and the day after that, and the next thirty years?"

"Don't be morbid," Jordan said. "Life starts all over again when it gets crisp in the fall."

"But it's so hot," insisted Daisy, on the verge of tears, "and everything's so confused. Let's all go to town!"

Her voice struggled on through the heat, beating against it, molding its senselessness into forms.

"I've heard of making a garage out of a stable," Tom was saying to Gatsby, "but I'm the first man who ever made a stable out of a garage."

"Who wants to go to town?" demanded Daisy insistently. Gatsby's eyes floated toward her. "Ah," she cried, "you look so cool."

Their eyes met, and they stared together at each other, alone in space. With an effort she glanced down at the table.

"You always look so cool," she repeated.

She had told him that she loved him, and Tom Buchanan saw. He was astounded. His mouth opened a little, and he looked at Gatsby, and then back at Daisy as if he had just recognized her as some one he knew a long time ago.

"You resemble the advertisement of the man," she went on innocently. "You know the advertisement of the man——"

"All right," broke in Tom quickly, "I'm perfectly willing to go to town. Come on—we're all going to town."

He got up, his eyes still flashing between Gatsby and his wife. No one moved.

"Come on!" His temper cracked a little. "What's the matter, anyhow? If we're going to town, let's start."

His hand, trembling with his effort at self-control, bore to his lips the last of his glass of ale. Daisy's voice got us to our feet and out on to the blazing gravel drive.

"Are we just going to go?" she objected. "Like this? Aren't we going to let any one smoke a cigarette first?"

"Everybody smoked all through lunch."

"Oh, let's have fun," she begged him. "It's too hot to fuss."

He didn't answer.

"Have it your own way," she said. "Come on, Jordan."

They went upstairs to get ready while we three men stood there shuffling the hot pebbles with our feet. A silver curve of the moon hovered already in the western sky. Gatsby started to speak, changed his mind, but not before Tom wheeled and faced him expectantly.

"Have you got your stables here?" asked Gatsby with an effort.

"About a quarter of a mile down the road."

"Oh."

A pause.

"I don't see the idea of going to town," broke out Tom savagely. "Women get these notions in their heads——"

"Shall we take anything to drink?" called Daisy from an upper window.

"I'll get some whiskey," answered Tom. He went inside.

Gatsby turned to me rigidly:

"I can't say anything in his house, old sport."

"She's got an indiscreet voice," I remarked. "It's full of—" I hesitated.

"Her voice is full of money," he said suddenly.

That was it. I'd never understood before. It was full of money—that was the inexhaustible charm that rose and fell in it, the jingle of it, the cymbals' song of it. . . . High in a white palace the king's daughter, the golden girl. . . .

Tom came out of the house wrapping a quart bottle in a towel, followed by Daisy and Jordan wearing small tight hats of metallic cloth and carrying light capes over their arms.

"Shall we all go in my car?" suggested Gatsby. He felt the hot, green leather of the seat. "I ought to have left it in the shade."

"Is it standard shift?" demanded Tom.

"Yes."

"Well, you take my coupé and let me drive your car to town."

The suggestion was distasteful to Gatsby.

"I don't think there's much gas," he objected.

"Plenty of gas," said Tom boisterously. He looked at the gauge. "And if it runs out I can stop at a drug-store. You can buy anything at a drug-store nowadays."

A pause followed this apparently pointless remark. Daisy looked at Tom frowning, and an indefinable expression, at once definitely unfamiliar and vaguely recognizable, as if I had only heard it described in words, passed over Gatsby's face.

"Come on, Daisy," said Tom, pressing her with his hand toward Gatsby's car. "I'll take you in this circus wagon."

He opened the door, but she moved out from the circle of his arm.

"You take Nick and Jordan. We'll follow you in the coupé."

She walked close to Gatsby, touching his coat with her hand. Jordan and Tom and I got into the front seat of Gatsby's car, Tom pushed the unfamiliar gears tentatively, and we shot off into the oppressive heat, leaving them out of sight behind.

"Did you see that?" demanded Tom.

"See what?"

He looked at me keenly, realizing that Jordan and I must have known all along.

"You think I'm pretty dumb, don't you?" he suggested. "Perhaps I am, but I have a—almost a second sight, sometimes, that tells me what to do. Maybe you don't believe that, but science——"

He paused. The immediate contingency overtook him, pulled him back from the edge of the theoretical abyss.

"I've made a small investigation of this fellow," he continued. "I could have gone deeper if I'd known——"

"Do you mean you've been to a medium?" inquired Jordan humorously.

"What?" Confused, he stared at us as we laughed. "A medium?"

"About Gatsby."

"About Gatsby! No, I haven't. I said I'd been making a small investigation of his past."

"And you found he was an Oxford man," said Jordan helpfully.

"An Oxford man!" He was incredulous. "Like hell he is! He wears a pink suit."

"Nevertheless he's an Oxford man."

"Oxford, New Mexico," snorted Tom contemptuously, "or something like that."

"Listen, Tom. If you're such a snob, why did you invite him to lunch?" demanded Jordan crossly.

"Daisy invited him; she knew him before we were married— God knows where!"

We were all irritable now with the fading ale, and aware of it we drove for a while in silence. Then as Doctor T. J. Eckleburg's faded eyes came into sight down the road, I remembered Gatsby's caution about gasoline.

"We've got enough to get us to town," said Tom.

"But there's a garage right here," objected Jordan. "I don't want to get stalled in this baking heat."

Tom threw on both brakes impatiently, and we slid to an abrupt dusty spot under Wilson's sign. After a moment the proprietor emerged from the interior of his establishment and gazed hollow-eyed at the car.

"Let's have some gas!" cried Tom roughly. "What do you think we stopped for—to admire the view?"

"I'm sick," said Wilson without moving. "Been sick all day."

"What's the matter?"

"I'm all run down."

"Well, shall I help myself?" Tom demanded. "You sounded well enough on the phone."

With an effort Wilson left the shade and support of the doorway and, breathing hard, unscrewed the cap of the tank. In the sunlight his face was green.

"I didn't mean to interrupt your lunch," he said. "But I need money pretty bad, and I was wondering what you were going to do with your old car."

"How do you like this one?" inquired Tom. "I bought it last week."

"It's a nice yellow one," said Wilson, as he strained at the handle.

"Like to buy it?"

"Big chance," Wilson smiled faintly. "No, but I could make some money on the other."

"What do you want money for, all of a sudden?"

"I've been here too long. I want to get away. My wife and I want to go West."

"Your wife does," exclaimed Tom, startled.

"She's been talking about it for ten years." He rested for a moment against the pump, shading his eyes. "And now she's going whether she wants to or not. I'm going to get her away."

The coupé flashed by us with a flurry of dust and the flash of a waving hand.

"What do I owe you?" demanded Tom harshly.

"I just got wised up to something funny the last two days," remarked Wilson. "That's why I want to get away. That's why I been bothering you about the car."

"What do I owe you?"

"Dollar twenty."

The relentless beating heat was beginning to confuse me and I had a bad moment there before I realized that so far his suspicions hadn't alighted on Tom. He had discovered that Myrtle had some sort of life apart from him in another world, and the shock had made him physically sick. I stared at him and then at Tom, who had made a parallel discovery less than an hour before—and it occurred to me that there was no difference between men, in intelligence or race, so profound as the difference between the sick and the well. Wilson was so sick that he looked guilty, unforgivably guilty —as if he had just got some poor girl with child.

"I'll let you have that car," said Tom. "I'll send it over to-morrow afternoon."

That locality was always vaguely disquieting, even in the broad glare of afternoon, and now I turned my head as though I had been warned of something behind. Over the ashheaps the giant eyes of Doctor T. J. Eckleburg kept their vigil, but I perceived, after a moment, that the other eyes were regarding us less than twenty feet away.

In one of the windows over the garage the curtains had been moved aside a little, and Myrtle Wilson was peering down at the car. So engrossed was she that she had no consciousness of being observed, and one emotion after another crept into her face like objects into a slowly developing picture. Her expression was curiously familiar—it was an expression I had often seen on women's faces, but on Myrtle Wilson's face it seemed purposeless and inexplicable until I realized that her eyes, wide with jealous terror, were fixed not on Tom, but on Jordan Baker, whom she took to be his wife.

There is no confusion like the confusion of a simple mind, and as we drove away Tom was feeling the hot whips of panic. His wife and his mistress, until an hour ago secure and inviolate, were slipping precipitately from his control. Instinct made him step on the accelerator with the double purpose of overtaking Daisy and leaving Wilson behind, and we sped along toward Astoria at fifty miles an hour, until, among the spidery girders of the elevated, we came in sight of the easy-going blue coupé.

"Those big movies around Fiftieth Street are cool," suggested Jordan. "I love New York on summer afternoons when every one's away. There's something very sensuous about it—overripe, as if all sorts of funny fruits were going to fall into your hands."

The word "sensuous" had the effect of further disquieting Tom, but before he could invent a protest the coupé came to a stop, and Daisy signalled us to draw up alongside.

"Where are we going?" she cried.

"How about the movies?"

"It's so hot," she complained. "You go. We'll ride around and meet you after." With an effort her wit rose faintly, "We'll meet you on some corner. I'll be the man smoking two cigarettes."

"We can't argue about it here," Tom said impatiently, as a truck gave out a cursing whistle behind us. "You follow me to the south side of Central Park, in front of the Plaza."

Several times he turned his head and looked back for their car, and if the traffic delayed them he slowed up until they came into sight. I think he was afraid they would dart down a side street and out of his life forever.

But they didn't. And we all took the less explicable step of engaging the parlor of a suite in the Plaza Hotel.

The prolonged and tumultuous argument that ended by herding us into that room eludes me, though I have a sharp physical memory that, in the course of it, my underwear kept climbing like a damp snake around my legs and intermittent beads of sweat raced cool across my back. The notion originated with Daisy's suggestion that we hire five bathrooms and take cold baths, and then assumed more tangible form as "a place to have a mint julep." Each of us said over and over that it was a "crazy idea"—we all talked at once to a baffled clerk and thought, or pretended to think, that we were being very funny . . .

The room was large and stifling, and, though it was already four o'clock, opening the windows admitted only a gust of hot shrubbery from the Park. Daisy went to the mirror and stood with her back to us, fixing her hair.

"It's a swell suite," whispered Jordan respectfully, and every one laughed.

"Open another window," commanded Daisy, without turning around.

"There aren't any more."

"Well, we'd better telephone for an axe——"

"The thing to do is to forget about the heat," said Tom impatiently. "You make it ten times worse by crabbing about it."

He unrolled the bottle of whiskey from the towel and put it on the table.

"Why not let her alone, old sport?" remarked Gatsby. "You're the one that wanted to come to town."

There was a moment of silence. The telephone book slipped from its nail and splashed to the floor, whereupon Jordan whispered, "Excuse me"—but this time no one laughed.

"I'll pick it up," I offered.

"I've got it." Gatsby examined the parted string, muttered "Hum!" in an interested way, and tossed the book on a chair.

"That's a great expression of yours, isn't it?" said Tom sharply.

"What is?"

"All this 'old sport' business. Where'd you pick that up?"

"Now see here, Tom," said Daisy, turning around from the mirror, "if you're going to make personal remarks I won't stay here a minute. Call up and order some ice for the mint julep."

As Tom took up the receiver the compressed heat exploded into sound and we were listening to the portentous chords of Mendelssohn's Wedding March from the ballroom below.

"Imagine marrying anybody in this heat!" cried Jordan dismally.

"Still—I was married in the middle of June," Daisy remembered, "Louisville in June! Somebody fainted. Who was it fainted, Tom?"

"Biloxi," he answered shortly.

"A man named Biloxi. 'Blocks' Biloxi, and he made boxes—that's a fact—and he was from Biloxi, Mississippi."

"They carried him into my house," appended Jordan, "because we lived just two doors from the church. And he stayed three weeks, until Daddy told him he had to get out. The day after he left Daddy died." After a moment she added as if she might have sounded irreverent, "There wasn't any connection."

"I used to know a Bill Biloxi from Memphis," I remarked.

"That was his cousin. I knew his whole family history before he left. He gave me an aluminum putter that I use today."

The music had died down as the ceremony began and now a long cheer floated in at the window, followed by intermittent cries of "Yea—ea—ea!" and finally by a burst of jazz as the dancing began.

"We're getting old," said Daisy. "If we were young we'd rise and dance."

"Remember Biloxi," Jordan warned her. "Where'd you know him, Tom?"

"Biloxi?" He concentrated with an effort. "I didn't know him. He was a friend of Daisy's."

"He was not," she denied. "I'd never seen him before. He came down in the private car."

"Well, he said he knew you. He said he was raised in Louisville. Asa Bird brought him around at the last minute and asked if we had room for him."

Jordan smiled. "He was probably bumming his way home. He told me he was president of your class at Yale."

Tom and I looked at each other blankly.

"Biloxi?"

"First place, we didn't have any president——"

Gatsby's foot beat a short, restless tattoo and Tom eyed him suddenly.

"By the way, Mr. Gatsby, I understand you're an Oxford man."

"Not exactly."

"Oh, yes, I understand you went to Oxford."

"Yes—I went there."

A pause. Then Tom's voice incredulous and insulting:

"You must have gone there about the time Biloxi went to New Haven."

Another pause. A waiter knocked and came in with crushed mint and ice, but the silence was unbroken by his "thank you" and the soft closing of the door. This tremendous detail was to be cleared up at last.

"I told you I went there," said Gatsby.

"I heard you, but I'd like to know when."

"It was in nineteen-nineteen. I only stayed five months. That's why I can't really call myself an Oxford man."

Tom glanced around to see if we mirrored his unbelief. But we were all looking at Gatsby.

"It was an opportunity they gave to some of the officers after the Armistice," he continued. "We could go to any of the universities in England or France."

I wanted to get up and slap him on the back. I had one of those renewals of complete faith in him that I'd experienced before.

Daisy rose, smiling faintly, and went to the table.

"Open the whiskey, Tom," she ordered, "and I'll make you a mint julep. Then you won't seem so stupid to yourself. . . . Look at the mint!"

"Wait a minute," snapped Tom, "I want to ask Mr. Gatsby one more question."

"Go on," Gatsby said politely.

"What kind of a row are you trying to cause in my house anyhow?"

They were out in the open at last and Gatsby was content.

"He isn't causing a row," Daisy looked desperately from one to the other. "You're causing a row. Please have a little self-control."

"Self-control!" repeated Tom incredulously. "I suppose the latest thing is to sit back and let Mr. Nobody from Nowhere make love to your wife. Well, if that's the idea you can count me out. . . . Nowadays people begin by sneering at family life and family institutions, and next they'll throw everything overboard and have intermarriage between black and white."

Flushed with his impassioned gibberish, he saw himself standing alone on the last barrier of civilization.

"We're all white here," murmured Jordan.

"I know I'm not very popular. I don't give big parties. I suppose you've got to make your house into a pigsty in order to have any friends—in the modern world."

Angry as I was, as we all were, I was tempted to laugh whenever he opened his mouth. The transition from libertine to prig was so complete.

"I've got something to tell *you*, old sport—" began Gatsby. But Daisy guessed at his intention.

"Please don't!" she interrupted helplessly. "Please let's all go home. Why don't we all go home?"

"That's a good idea." I got up. "Come on, Tom. Nobody wants a drink."

"I want to know what Mr. Gatsby has to tell me."

"Your wife doesn't love you," said Gatsby. "She's never loved you. She loves me."

"You must be crazy!" exclaimed Tom automatically.

Gatsby sprang to his feet, vivid with excitement.

"She never loved you, do you hear?" he cried. "She only married you because I was poor and she was tired of waiting for me. It was a terrible mistake, but in her heart she never loved any one except me!"

At this point Jordan and I tried to go, but Tom and Gatsby insisted with competitive firmness that we remain—as though neither of them had anything to conceal and it would be a privilege to partake vicariously of their emotions.

"Sit down, Daisy," Tom's voice groped unsuccessfully for the paternal note. "What's been going on? I want to hear all about it."

"I told you what's been going on," said Gatsby. "Going on for five years—and you didn't know."

Tom turned to Daisy sharply.

"You've been seeing this fellow for five years?"

"Not seeing," said Gatsby. "No, we couldn't meet. But both of us loved each other all that time, old sport, and you didn't know. I used to laugh sometimes"—but there was no laughter in his eyes—"to think that you didn't know."

"Oh—that's all." Tom tapped his thick fingers together like a clergyman and leaned back in his chair.

"You're crazy!" he exploded. "I can't speak about what happened five years ago because I didn't know Daisy then—and I'll be damned if I see how you got within a mile of her unless you brought the groceries to the back door. But all the rest of that's a God damned lie. Daisy loved me when she married me and she loves me now."

"No," said Gatsby, shaking his head.

"She does, though. The trouble is that sometimes she gets foolish ideas in her head and doesn't know what she's doing." He nodded sagely. "And what's more I love Daisy too. Once in a while I go off on a spree and make a fool of myself, but I always come back, and in my heart I love her all the time."

"You're revolting," said Daisy. She turned to me, and her voice, dropping an octave lower, filled the room with thrilling scorn: "Do you know why we left Chicago? I'm surprised that they didn't treat you to the story of that little spree."

Gatsby walked over and stood beside her.

"Daisy, that's all over now," he said earnestly. "It doesn't matter any more. Just tell him the truth—that you never loved him—and it's all wiped out forever."

She looked at him blindly. "Why—how could I love him—possibly?"

"You never loved him."

She hesitated. Her eyes fell on Jordan and me with a sort of appeal, as though she realized at last what she was doing—and as though she had never, all along, intended doing anything at all. But it was done now. It was too late.

"I never loved him," she said, with perceptible reluctance.

"Not at Kapiolani?" demanded Tom suddenly.

"No."

From the ballroom beneath, muffled and suffocating chords were drifting up on hot waves of air.

"Not that day I carried you down from the Punch Bowl to keep your shoes dry?" There was a husky tenderness in his tone. . . . "Daisy?"

"Please don't." Her voice was cold, but the rancor was gone from it. She looked at Gatsby. "There, Jay," she said—but her hand as she tried to light a cigarette was trembling. Suddenly she threw the cigarette and the burning match on the carpet.

"Oh, you want too much!" she cried to Gatsby. "I love you now —isn't that enough? I can't help what's past." She began to sob helplessly. "I did love him once—but I loved you too."

Gatsby's eyes opened and closed.

"You loved me *too*?" he repeated.

"Even that's a lie," said Tom savagely. "She didn't know you were alive. Why—there're things between Daisy and me that you'll never know, things that neither of us can ever forget."

The words seemed to bite physically into Gatsby.

"I want to speak to Daisy alone," he insisted. "She's all excited now——"

"Even alone I can't say I never loved Tom," she admitted in a pitiful voice. "It wouldn't be true."

"Of course it wouldn't," agreed Tom.

She turned to her husband.

"As if it mattered to you," she said.

"Of course it matters. I'm going to take better care of you from now on."

"You don't understand," said Gatsby, with a touch of panic. "You're not going to take care of her any more."

"I'm not?" Tom opened his eyes wide and laughed. He could afford to control himself now. "Why's that?"

"Daisy's leaving you."

"Nonsense."

"I am, though," she said with a visible effort.

"She's not leaving me!" Tom's words suddenly leaned down over Gatsby. "Certainly not for a common swindler who'd have to steal the ring he put on her finger."

"I won't stand this!" cried Daisy. "Oh, please let's get out."

"Who are you, anyhow?" broke out Tom. "You're one of that bunch that hangs around with Meyer Wolfsheim—that much I happen to know. I've made a little investigation into your affairs—and I'll carry it further to-morrow."

"You can suit yourself about that, old sport," said Gatsby steadily.

"I found out what your 'drug-stores' were." He turned to us and spoke rapidly. "He and this Wolfsheim bought up a lot of side-street drug-stores here and in Chicago and sold grain alcohol over the counter. That's one of his little stunts. I picked him for a bootlegger the first time I saw him, and I wasn't far wrong."

"What about it?" said Gatsby politely. "I guess your friend Walter Chase wasn't too proud to come in on it."

"And you left him in the lurch, didn't you? You let him go to jail for a month over in New Jersey. God! You ought to hear Walter on the subject of *you*."

"He came to us dead broke. He was very glad to pick up some money, old sport."

"Don't you call me 'old sport'!" cried Tom. Gatsby said nothing. "Walter could have you up on the betting laws too, but Wolfsheim scared him into shutting his mouth."

That unfamiliar yet recognizable look was back again in Gatsby's face.

"That drug-store business was just small change," continued Tom slowly, "but you've got something on now that Walter's afraid to tell me about."

I glanced at Daisy, who was staring terrified between Gatsby and her husband, and at Jordan, who had begun to balance an invisible but absorbing object on the tip of her chin. Then I turned back to Gatsby—and was startled at his expression. He looked—and this is said in all contempt for the babbled slander of his garden—as if he had "killed a man." For a moment the set of his face could be described in just that fantastic way.

It passed, and he began to talk excitedly to Daisy, denying everything, defending his name against accusations that had not been made. But with every word she was drawing further and further into herself, so he gave that up, and only the dead dream fought on as the afternoon slipped away, trying to touch what was no longer tangible, struggling unhappily, undespairingly, toward that lost voice across the room.

The voice begged again to go.

"*Please,* Tom! I can't stand this any more."

Her frightened eyes told that whatever intentions, whatever courage she had had, were definitely gone.

"You two start on home, Daisy," said Tom. "In Mr. Gatsby's car."

She looked at Tom, alarmed now, but he insisted with magnanimous scorn.

"Go on. He won't annoy you. I think he realizes that his presumptuous little flirtation is over."

They were gone, without a word, snapped out, made accidental isolated, like ghosts, even from our pity.

After a moment Tom got up and began wrapping the unopened bottle of whiskey in the towel.

"Want any of this stuff? Jordan? . . . Nick?"

I didn't answer.

"Nick?" He asked again.

"What?"

"Want any?"

"No . . . I just remembered that today's my birthday."

I was thirty. Before me stretched the portentous, menacing road of a new decade.

It was seven o'clock when we got into the coupé with him and started for Long Island. Tom talked incessantly, exulting and laughing, but his voice was as remote from Jordan and me as the foreign clamor on the sidewalk or the tumult of the elevated overhead. Human sympathy has its limits, and we were content to let all their tragic arguments fade with the city lights behind. Thirty—the promise of a decade of loneliness, a thinning list of single men to know, a thinning brief-case of enthusiasm, thinning hair. But there was Jordan beside me, who, unlike Daisy, was too wise ever to carry well-forgotten dreams from age to age. As we passed over the dark bridge her wan face fell lazily against my coat's shoulder and the formidable stroke of thirty died away with the reassuring pressure of her hand.

So we drove on toward death through the cooling twilight.

The young Greek, Michaelis, who ran the coffee joint beside the ashheaps was the principal witness at the inquest. He had slept through the heat until after five, when he strolled over to the garage, and found George Wilson sick in his office—really sick, pale as his own pale hair and shaking all over. Michaelis advised him to go to bed, but Wilson refused, saying that he'd miss a lot of business if he did. While his neighbor was trying to persuade him a violent racket broke out overhead.

"I've got my wife locked in up there," explained Wilson calmly. "She's going to stay there till the day after to-morrow, and then we're going to move away."

Michaelis was astonished; they had been neighbors for four years, and Wilson had never seemed faintly capable of such a statement. Generally he was one of these worn-out men: when he wasn't working, he sat on a chair in the doorway and stared at the people and the cars that passed along the road. When any one spoke to him he invariably laughed in an agreeable, colorless way. He was his wife's man and not his own.

So naturally Michaelis tried to find out what had happened, but Wilson wouldn't say a word—instead he began to throw curious, suspicious glances at his visitor and ask him what he'd been doing at certain times on certain days. Just as the latter was getting uneasy, some workmen came past the door bound for his restaurant, and Michaelis took the opportunity to get away, intending to come back later. But he didn't. He supposed he forgot to, that's all. When he came outside again, a little after seven, he was reminded of the conversation because he heard Mrs. Wilson's voice, loud and scolding, down-stairs in the garage.

"Beat me!" he heard her cry. "Throw me down and beat me, you dirty little coward!"

A moment later she rushed out into the dusk, waving her hands and shouting—before he could move from his door the business was over.

The "death car" as the newspapers called it, didn't stop; it came out of the gathering darkness, wavered tragically for a moment, and then disappeared around the next bend. Michaelis wasn't even sure of its color—he told the first policeman that it was light green. The other car, the one going toward New York, came to rest a hundred yards beyond, and its driver hurried back to where Myrtle Wilson, her life violently extinguished, knelt in the road and mingled her thick dark blood with the dust.

Michaelis and this man reached her first, but when they had torn open her shirtwaist, still damp with perspiration, they saw that her left breast was swinging loose like a flap, and there was no need to listen for the heart beneath. The mouth was wide open and ripped at the corners, as though she had choked a little in giving up the tremendous vitality she had stored so long.

We saw the three or four automobiles and the crowd when we were still some distance away.

"Wreck!" said Tom. "That's good. Wilson'll have a little business at last."

He slowed down, but still without any intention of stopping, until, as we came nearer, the hushed, intent faces of the people at the garage door made him automatically put on the brakes.

"We'll take a look," he said doubtfully, "just a look."

I became aware now of a hollow, wailing sound which issued incessantly from the garage, a sound which as we got out of the coupé and walked toward the door resolved itself into the words "Oh, my God!" uttered over and over in a gasping moan.

"There's some bad trouble here," said Tom excitedly.

He reached up on tiptoes and peered over a circle of heads into the garage, which was lit only by a yellow light in a swinging wire basket overhead. Then he made a harsh sound in his throat, and with a violent thrusting movement of his powerful arms pushed his way through.

The circle closed up again with a running murmur of expostulation; it was a minute before I could see anything at all. Then new arrivals deranged the line, and Jordan and I were pushed suddenly inside.

Myrtle Wilson's body, wrapped in a blanket, and then in another blanket, as though she suffered from a chill in the hot night, lay on a work-table by the wall, and Tom, with his back to us, was bending over it, motionless. Next to him stood a motorcycle policeman taking down names with much sweat and correction in a little book. At first I couldn't find the source of the high, groaning words that echoed clamorously through the bare garage—then I saw Wilson standing on the raised threshold of his office, swaying back and forth and holding to the doorposts with both hands. Some man was talking to him in a low voice and attempting, from time to time, to lay a hand on his shoulder, but Wilson neither heard nor saw. His eyes would drop slowly from the swinging light to the laden table by the wall, and then jerk back to the light again, and he gave out incessantly his high, horrible call:

"Oh, my Ga-od! Oh, my Ga-od! Oh, Ga-od! Oh, my Ga-od!"

Presently Tom lifted his head with a jerk and, after staring around the garage with glazed eyes, addressed a mumbled incoherent remark to the policeman.

"M-a-y—" the policeman was saying, "—o——"

"No, r—" corrected the man, "M-a-v-r-o——"

"Listen to me!" muttered Tom fiercely.

"r" said the policeman, "o— "

"g——"

"g—" He looked up as Tom's broad hand fell sharply on his shoulder. "What you want, fella?"

"What happened?—that's what I want to know."

"Auto hit her. Ins'antly killed."

"Instantly killed," repeated Tom, staring.

"She ran out ina road. Son-of-a-bitch didn't even stopus car."

"There was two cars," said Michaelis, "one comin', one goin', see?"

"Going where?" asked the policeman keenly.

"One goin' each way. Well, she"—his hand rose toward the blankets but stopped half way and fell to his side—"she ran out there an' the one comin' from N'York knock right into her, goin' thirty or forty miles an hour."

"What's the name of this place here?" demanded the officer.

"Hasn't got any name."

A pale well-dressed negro stepped near.

"It was a yellow car," he said, "big yellow car. New."

"See the accident?" asked the policeman.

"No, but the car passed me down the road, going faster'n forty Going fifty, sixty."

"Come here and let's have your name. Look out now. I want to get his name."

Some words of this conversation must have reached Wilson, swaying in the office door, for suddenly a new theme found voice among his gasping cries:

"You don't have to tell me what kind of car it was! I know what kind of car it was!"

Watching Tom, I saw the wad of muscle back of his shoulder tighten under his coat. He walked quickly over to Wilson and, standing in front of him, seized him firmly by the upper arms.

"You've got to pull yourself together," he said with soothing gruffness.

Wilson's eyes fell upon Tom; he started up on his tiptoes and then would have collapsed to his knees had not Tom held him upright.

"Listen," said Tom, shaking him a little. "I just got here a minute ago, from New York. I was bringing you that coupé we've been talking about. That yellow car I was driving this afternoon wasn't mine—do you hear? I haven't seen it all afternoon."

Only the negro and I were near enough to hear what he said, but the policeman caught something in the tone and looked over with truculent eyes.

"What's all that?" he demanded.

"I'm a friend of his." Tom turned his head but kept his hands firm on Wilson's body. "He says he knows the car that did it. . . . It was a yellow car."

Some dim impulse moved the policeman to look suspiciously at Tom.

"And what color's your car?"

"It's a blue car, a coupé."

"We've come straight from New York," I said.

Some one who had been driving a little behind us confirmed this, and the policeman turned away.

"Now, if you'll let me have that name again correct——"

Picking up Wilson like a doll, Tom carried him into the office, set him down in a chair, and came back.

"If somebody'll come here and sit with him," he snapped authoritatively. He watched while the two men standing closest glanced at each other and went unwillingly into the room. Then Tom shut the door on them and came down the single step, his eyes avoiding the table. As he passed close to me he whispered: "Let's get out."

Self-consciously, with his authoritative arms breaking the way, we pushed through the still gathering crowd, passing a hurried doctor, case in hand, who had been sent for in wild hope half an hour ago.

Tom drove slowly until we were beyond the bend—then his foot came down hard, and the coupé raced along through the night. In a little while I heard a low husky sob, and saw that the tears were overflowing down his face.

"The God damned coward!" he whimpered. "He didn't even stop his car."

The Buchanans' house floated suddenly toward us through the dark rustling trees. Tom stopped beside the porch and looked up at the second floor, where two windows bloomed with light among the vines.

"Daisy's home," he said. As we got out of the car he glanced at me and frowned slightly.

"I ought to have dropped you in West Egg, Nick. There's nothing we can do to-night."

A change had come over him, and he spoke gravely, and with decision. As we walked across the moonlight gravel to the porch he disposed of the situation in a few brisk phrases.

"I'll telephone for a taxi to take you home, and while you're waiting you and Jordan better go in the kitchen and have them get you some supper—if you want any." He opened the door. "Come in."

"No, thanks. But I'd be glad if you'd order me the taxi. I'll wait outside."

Jordan put her hand on my arm.

"Won't you come in, Nick?"

"No, thanks."

I was feeling a little sick and I wanted to be alone. But Jordan lingered for a moment more.

"It's only half-past nine," she said.

I'd be damned if I'd go in; I'd had enough of all of them for one day, and suddenly that included Jordan too. She must have seen something of this in my expression, for she turned abruptly away and ran up the porch steps into the house. I sat down for a few minutes with my head in my hands, until I heard the phone taken up inside and the butler's voice calling a taxi. Then I walked slowly down the drive away from the house, intending to wait by the gate.

I hadn't gone twenty yards when I heard my name and Gatsby stepped from between two bushes into the path. I must have felt pretty weird by that time, because I could think of nothing except the luminosity of his pink suit under the moon.

"What are you doing?" I inquired.

"Just standing here, old sport."

Somehow, that seemed a despicable occupation. For all I knew he was going to rob the house in a moment; I wouldn't have been surprised to see sinister faces, the faces of "Wolfsheim's people," behind him in the dark shrubbery.

"Did you see any trouble on the road?" he asked after a minute.

"Yes."

He hesitated.

"Was she killed?"

"Yes."

"I thought so; I told Daisy I thought so. It's better that the shock should all come at once. She stood it pretty well."

He spoke as if Daisy's reaction was the only thing that mattered.

"I got to West Egg by a side road," he went on, "and left the car in my garage. I don't think anybody saw us, but of course I can't be sure."

I disliked him so much by this time that I didn't find it necessary to tell him he was wrong.

"Who was the woman?" he inquired.

"Her name was Wilson. Her husband owns the garage. How the devil did it happen?"

"Well, I tried to swing the wheel—" He broke off, and suddenly I guessed at the truth.

"Was Daisy driving?"

"Yes," he said after a moment, "but of course I'll say I was. You see, when we left New York she was very nervous and she thought it would steady her to drive—and this woman rushed out at us just as we were passing a car coming the other way. It all happened in a minute, but it seemed to me that she wanted to speak to us, thought we were somebody she knew. Well, first Daisy turned away from the woman toward the other car, and then she lost her nerve and turned back. The second my hand reached the wheel I felt the shock —it must have killed her instantly."

"It ripped her open——"

"Don't tell me, old sport." He winced. "Anyhow—Daisy stepped on it. I tried to make her stop, but she couldn't, so I pulled on the emergency brake. Then she fell over into my lap and I drove on.

"She'll be all right tomorrow," he said presently. "I'm just going to wait here and see if he tries to bother her about that unpleasantness this afternoon. She's locked herself into her room, and if he tries any brutality she's going to turn the light out and on again."

"He won't touch her," I said. "He's not thinking about her."

"I don't trust him, old sport."

"How long are you going to wait?"

"All night, if necessary. Anyhow, till they all go to bed."

A new point of view occurred to me. Suppose Tom found out that Daisy had been driving. He might think he saw a connection in it— he might think anything. I looked at the house; there were two or three bright windows downstairs and the pink glow from Daisy's room on the second floor.

"You wait here," I said. "I'll see if there's any sign of a commotion."

I walked back along the border of the lawn, traversed the gravel softly, and tiptoed up the veranda steps. The drawing-room curtains were open, and I saw that the room was empty. Crossing the porch where we had dined that June night three months before, I came to a small rectangle of light which I guessed was the pantry window. The blind was drawn, but I found a rift at the sill.

Daisy and Tom were sitting opposite each other at the kitchen table, with a plate of cold fried chicken between them, and two bottles of ale. He was talking intently across the table at her, and in his earnestness his hand had fallen upon and covered her own. Once in a while she looked up at him and nodded in agreement.

They weren't happy, and neither of them had touched the chicken or the ale—and yet they weren't unhappy either. There was an unmistakable air of natural intimacy about the picture, and anybody would have said that they were conspiring together.

As I tiptoed from the porch I heard my taxi feeling its way along the dark road toward the house. Gatsby was waiting where I had left him in the drive.

"Is it all quiet up there?" he asked anxiously.

"Yes, it's all quiet." I hesitated. "You'd better come home and get some sleep."

He shook his head.

"I want to wait here till Daisy goes to bed. Good night, old sport."

He put his hands in his coat pockets and turned back eagerly to his scrutiny of the house, as though my presence marred the sacredness of the vigil. So I walked away and left him standing there in the moonlight—watching over nothing.

CHAPTER VIII

I COULDN'T sleep all night; a fog-horn was groaning incessantly on the Sound, and I tossed half-sick between grotesque reality and savage, frightening dreams. Toward dawn I heard a taxi go up Gatsby's drive, and immediately I jumped out of bed and began to dress—I felt that I had something to tell him, something to warn him about, and morning would be too late.

Crossing his lawn, I saw that his front door was still open and he was leaning against a table in the hall, heavy with dejection or sleep.

"Nothing happened," he said wanly. "I waited, and about four o'clock she came to the window and stood there for a minute and then turned out the light."

His house had never seemed so enormous to me as it did that night when we hunted through the great rooms for cigarettes. We pushed aside curtains that were like pavilions, and felt over innumerable feet of dark wall for electric light switches—once I tumbled with a sort of splash upon the keys of a ghostly piano. There was an inexplicable amount of dust everywhere, and the rooms were musty, as though they hadn't been aired for many days. I found the humidor on an unfamiliar table, with two stale, dry cigarettes inside. Throwing open the French windows of the drawing-room, we sat smoking out into the darkness.

"You ought to go away," I said. "It's pretty certain they'll trace your car."

"Go away *now*, old sport?"

"Go to Atlantic City for a week, or up to Montreal."

He wouldn't consider it. He couldn't possibly leave Daisy until he knew what she was going to do. He was clutching at some last hope and I couldn't bear to shake him free.

It was this night that he told me the strange story of his youth with Dan Cody—told it to me because "Jay Gatsby" had broken up like glass against Tom's hard malice, and the long secret extravaganza was played out. I think that he would have acknowledged anything now, without reserve, but he wanted to talk about Daisy.

She was the first "nice" girl he had ever known. In various un-revealed capacities he had come in contact with such people, but always with indiscernible barbed wire between. He found her ex-citingly desirable. He went to her house, at first with other officers from Camp Taylor, then alone. It amazed him—he had never been in such a beautiful house before. But what gave it an air of breathless intensity was that Daisy lived there—it was as casual a thing to her as his tent out at camp was to him. There was a ripe mystery about it, a hint of bedrooms upstairs more beautiful and cool than other bedrooms, of gay and radiant activities taking place through its cor-·ridors, and of romances that were not musty and laid away already in lavender, but fresh and breathing and redolent of this year's shining motor-cars and of dances whose flowers were scarcely withered. It excited him, too, that many men had already loved Daisy—it increased her value in his eyes. He felt their presence all about the house, pervading the air with the shades and echoes of still vibrant emotions.

But he knew that he was in Daisy's house by a colossal accident. However glorious might be his future as Jay Gatsby, he was at present a penniless young man without a past, and at any moment the invisible cloak of his uniform might slip from his shoulders. So he made the most of his time. He took what he could get, raven-ously and unscrupulously—eventually he took Daisy one still October night, took her because he had no real right to touch her hand.

He might have despised himself, for he had certainly taken her under false pretenses. I don't mean that he had traded on his phan-tom millions, but he had deliberately given Daisy a sense of security; he let her believe that he was a person from much the same stratum as herself—that he was fully able to take care of her. As a matter of fact, he had no such facilities—he had no comfortable family stand-ing behind him, and he was liable at the whim of an impersonal gov-ernment to be blown anywhere about the world.

But he didn't despise himself and it didn't turn out as he had imagined. He had intended, probably, to take what he could and go —but now he found that he had committed himself to the following of a grail. He knew that Daisy was extraordinary, but he didn't real-ize just how extraordinary a "nice" girl could be. She vanished into her rich house, into her rich, full life, leaving Gatsby—nothing. He felt married to her, that was all.

When they met again, two days later, it was Gatsby who was breathless, who was, somehow, betrayed. Her porch was bright with the bought luxury of star-shine; the wicker of the settee squeaked fashionably as she turned toward him and he kissed her curious and lovely mouth. She had caught a cold, and it made her voice huskier and more charming than ever, and Gatsby was overwhelmingly aware of the youth and mystery that wealth imprisons and preserves, of the freshness of many clothes, and of Daisy, gleaming like silver, safe and proud above the hot struggles of the poor.

"I can't describe to you how surprised I was to find out I loved her, old sport. I even hoped for a while that she'd throw me over, but she didn't, because she was in love with me too. She thought I knew a lot because I knew different things from her . . . Well, there I was, 'way off my ambitions, getting deeper in love every minute, and all of a sudden I didn't care. What was the use of doing great things if I could have a better time telling her what I was going to do?"

On the last afternoon before he went abroad, he sat with Daisy in his arms for a long, silent time. It was a cold fall day, with fire in the room and her cheeks flushed. Now and then she moved and he changed his arm a little, and once he kissed her dark shining hair. The afternoon had made them tranquil for a while, as if to give them a deep memory for the long parting the next day promised. They had never been closer in their month of love, nor communicated more profoundly one with another, than when she brushed silent lips against his coat's shoulder or when he touched the end of her fingers, gently, as though she were asleep.

He did extraordinarily well in the war. He was a captain before he went to the front, and following the Argonne battles he got his majority and the command of the divisional machine-guns. After the Armistice he tried frantically to get home, but some complication or misunderstanding sent him to Oxford instead. He was worried now—there was a quality of nervous despair in Daisy's letters. She didn't see why he couldn't come. She was feeling the pressure of the world outside, and she wanted to see him and feel his presence beside her and be reassured that she was doing the right thing after all.

For Daisy was young and her artificial world was redolent of orchids and pleasant, cheerful snobbery and orchestras which set the rhythm of the year, summing up the sadness and suggestiveness of life in new tunes. All night the saxophones wailed the hopeless comment of the *Beale Street Blues* while a hundred pairs of golden and silver slippers shuffled the shining dust. At the gray tea hour there were always rooms that throbbed incessantly with this low, sweet fever, while fresh faces drifted here and there like rose petals blown by the sad horns around the floor.

Through this twilight universe Daisy began to move again with the season; suddenly she was again keeping half a dozen dates a day with half a dozen men, and drowsing asleep at dawn with the beads and chiffon of an evening dress tangled among dying orchids on the floor beside her bed. And all the time something within her was crying for a decision. She wanted her life shaped now, immediately —and the decision must be made by some force—of love, of money, of unquestionable practicality—that was close at hand.

That force took shape in the middle of spring with the arrival of Tom Buchanan. There was a wholesome bulkiness about his person and his position, and Daisy was flattered. Doubtless there was a certain struggle and a certain relief. The letter reached Gatsby while he was still at Oxford.

It was dawn now on Long Island and we went about opening the rest of the windows downstairs, filling the house with gray-turning, gold-turning light. The shadow of a tree fell abruptly across the dew and ghostly birds began to sing among the blue leaves. There was a slow, pleasant movement in the air, scarcely a wind, promising a cool, lovely day.

"I don't think she ever loved him," Gatsby turned around from a window and looked at me challengingly. "You must remember, old sport, she was very excited this afternoon. He told her those things in a way that frightened her—that made it look as if I was some kind of cheap sharper. And the result was she hardly knew what she was saying."

He sat down gloomily.

"Of course she might have loved him just for a minute, when they were first married—and loved me more even then, do you see?"

Suddenly he came out with a curious remark.

"In any case," he said, "it was just personal."

What could you make of that, except to suspect some intensity in his conception of the affair that couldn't be measured?

He came back from France when Tom and Daisy were still on their wedding trip, and made a miserable but irresistible journey to Louisville on the last of his army pay. He stayed there a week, walking the streets where their footsteps had clicked together through the November night and revisiting the out-of-the-way places to which they had driven in her white car. Just as Daisy's house had always seemed to him more mysterious and gay than other houses, so his idea of the city itself, even though she was gone from it, was pervaded with a melancholy beauty.

He left, feeling that if he had searched harder, he might have found her—that he was leaving her behind. The day-coach—he was penniless now—was hot. He went out to the open vestibule and sat down on a folding-chair, and the station slid away and the backs of unfamiliar buildings moved by. Then out into the spring fields, where a yellow trolley raced them for a minute with people in it who might once have seen the pale magic of her face along the casual street.

The track curved and now it was going away from the sun, which, as it sank lower, seemed to spread itself in benediction over the vanishing city where she had drawn her breath. He stretched out his hand desperately as if to snatch only a wisp of air, to save a fragment of the spot that she had made lovely for him. But it was all going by too fast now for his blurred eyes and he knew that he had lost that part of it, the freshest and the best, forever.

It was nine o'clock when we finished breakfast and went out on the porch. The night had made a sharp difference in the weather and there was an autumn flavor in the air. The gardener, the last one of Gatsby's former servants, came to the foot of the steps.

"I'm going to drain the pool today, Mr. Gatsby. Leaves'll start falling pretty soon, and then there's always trouble with the pipes."

"Don't do it to-day," Gatsby answered. He turned to me apologetically. "You know, old sport, I've never used that pool all summer?"

I looked at my watch and stood up.

"Twelve minutes to my train."

I didn't want to go to the city. I wasn't worth a decent stroke of work, but it was more than that—I didn't want to leave Gatsby. I missed that train, and then another, before I could get myself away.

"I'll call you up," I said finally.

"Do, old sport."

"I'll call you about noon."

We walked slowly down the steps.

"I suppose Daisy'll call too." He looked at me anxiously, as if he hoped I'd corroborate this.

"I suppose so."

"Well, good-by."

We shook hands and I started away. Just before I reached the hedge I remembered something and turned around.

"They're a rotten crowd," I shouted across the lawn. "You're worth the whole damn bunch put together."

I've always been glad I said that. It was the only compliment I ever gave him, because I disapproved of him from beginning to end. First he nodded politely, and then his face broke into that radiant and understanding smile, as if we'd been in ecstatic cahoots on that fact all the time. His gorgeous pink rag of a suit made a bright spot of color against the white steps, and I thought of the night when I first came to his ancestral home, three months before. The lawn and drive had been crowded with the faces of those who guessed at his corruption—and he had stood on those steps, concealing his incorruptible dream, as he waved them good-by.

I thanked him for his hospitality. We were always thanking him for that—I and the others.

"Good-by," I called. "I enjoyed breakfast, Gatsby."

Up in the city, I tried for a while to list the quotations on an interminable amount of stock, then I fell asleep in my swivel-chair. Just before noon the phone woke me, and I started up with sweat breaking out on my forehead. It was Jordan Baker; she often called me up at this hour because the uncertainty of her own movements between hotels and clubs and private houses made her hard to find in any other way. Usually her voice came over the wire as something fresh and cool, as if a divot from a green golf-links had come sailing in at the office window, but this morning it seemed harsh and dry.

"I've left Daisy's house," she said. "I'm at Hempstead, and I'm going down to Southampton this afternoon."

Probably it had been tactful to leave Daisy's house, but the act annoyed me, and her next remark made me rigid.

"You weren't so nice to me last night."

"How could it have mattered then?"

Silence for a moment. Then:

"However—I want to see you."

"I want to see you, too."

"Suppose I don't go to Southampton, and come into town this afternoon?"

"No—I don't think this afternoon."

"Very well."

"It's impossible this afternoon. Various——"

We talked like that for a while, and then abruptly we weren't talking any longer. I don't know which of us hung up with a sharp click, but I know I didn't care. I couldn't have talked to her across a tea-table that day if I never talked to her again in this world.

I called Gatsby's house a few minutes later, but the line was busy. I tried four times; finally an exasperated central told me the wire was being kept open for long distance from Detroit. Taking out my time-table, I drew a small circle around the three-fifty train. Then I leaned back in my chair and tried to think. It was just noon.

When I passed the ashheaps on the train that morning I had crossed deliberately to the other side of the car. I supposed there'd be a curious crowd around there all day with little boys searching for dark spots in the dust, and some garrulous man telling over and over what had happened, until it became less and less real even to him and he could tell it no longer, and Myrtle Wilson's tragic achievement was forgotten. Now I want to go back a little and tell what happened at the garage after we left there the night before.

They had difficulty in locating the sister, Catherine. She must have broken her rule against drinking that night, for when she arrived she was stupid with liquor and unable to understand that the ambulance had already gone to Flushing. When they convinced her of this, she immediately fainted, as if that was the intolerable part of the affair. Some one, kind or curious, took her in his car and drove her in the wake of her sister's body.

Until long after midnight a changing crowd lapped up against the front of the garage, while George Wilson rocked himself back and forth on the couch inside. For a while the door of the office was open, and every one who came into the garage glanced irresistibly through it. Finally some one said it was a shame, and closed the door. Michaelis and several other men were with him; first, four or five men, later two or three men. Still later Michaelis had to ask the last stranger to wait there fifteen minutes longer, while he went back to his own place and made a pot of coffee. After that, he stayed there alone with Wilson until dawn.

About three o'clock the quality of Wilson's incoherent muttering changed—he grew quieter and began to talk about the yellow car. He announced that he had a way of finding out whom the yellow car belonged to, and then he blurted out that a couple of months ago his wife had come from the city with her face bruised and her nose swollen.

But when he heard himself say this, he flinched and began to cry "Oh, my God!" again in his groaning voice. Michaelis made a clumsy attempt to distract him.

"How long have you been married, George? Come on there, try and sit still a minute and aswer my question. How long have you been married?"

"Twelve years."

"Ever had any children? Come on, George, sit still—I asked you a question. Did you ever have any children?"

The hard brown beetles kept thudding against the dull light, and whenever Michaelis heard a car go tearing along the road outside it sounded to him like the car that hadn't stopped a few hours before. He didn't like to go into the garage, because the work bench was stained where the body had been lying, so he moved uncomfortably around the office—he knew every object in it before morning—and from time to time sat down beside Wilson trying to keep him more quiet.

"Have you got a church you go to sometimes, George? Maybe even if you haven't been there for a long time? Maybe I could call up the church and get a priest to come over and he could talk to you, see?"

"Don't belong to any."

"You ought to have a church, George, for times like this. You must have gone to church once. Didn't you get married in a church? Listen, George, listen to me. Didn't you get married in a church?"

"That was a long time ago."

The effort of answering broke the rhythm of his rocking—for a moment he was silent. Then the same half-knowing, half-bewildered look came back into his faded eyes.

"Look in the drawer there," he said, pointing at the desk.

"Which drawer?"

"That drawer—that one."

Michaelis opened the drawer nearest his hand. There was nothing in it but a small, expensive dog-leash, made of leather and braided silver. It was apparently new.

"This?" he inquired, holding it up.

Wilson stared and nodded.

"I found it yesterday afternoon. She tried to tell me about it, but I knew it was something funny."

"You mean your wife bought it?"

"She had it wrapped in tissue paper on her bureau."

Michaelis didn't see anything odd in that, and he gave Wilson a dozen reasons why his wife might have bought the dog-leash. But conceivably Wilson had heard some of these same explanations before, from Myrtle, because he began saying "Oh, my God!" again in a whisper—his comforter left several explanations in the air.

"Then he killed her," said Wilson. His mouth dropped open suddenly.

"Who did?"

"I have a way of finding out."

"You're morbid, George," said his friend. "This has been a strain to you and you don't know what you're saying. You'd better try and sit quiet till morning."

"He murdered her."

"It was an accident, George."

Wilson shook his head. His eyes narrowed and his mouth widened slightly with the ghost of a superior "Hm!"

"I know," he said definitely, "I'm one of these trusting fellas and I don't think any harm to *no*body, but when I get to know a thing I know it. It was the man in that car. She ran out to speak to him and he wouldn't stop."

Michaelis had seen this too, but it hadn't occurred to him that there was any special significance in it. He believed that Mrs. Wilson had been running away from her husband, rather than trying to stop any particular car.

"How could she of been like that?"

"She's a deep one," said Wilson, as if that answered the question. "Ah-h-h——"

He began to rock again, and Michaelis stood twisting the leash in his hand.

"Maybe you got some friend that I could telephone for, George?"

This was a forlorn hope—he was almost sure that Wilson had no friend: there was not enough of him for his wife. He was glad a little later when he noticed a change in the room, a blue quickening by the window, and realized that dawn wasn't far off. About five o'clock it was blue enough outside to snap off the light.

Wilson's glazed eyes turned out to the ashheaps, where small gray clouds took on fantastic shapes and scurried here and there in the faint dawn wind.

"I spoke to her," he muttered, after a long silence. "I told her she might fool me but she couldn't fool God. I took her to the window"—with an effort he got up and walked to the rear window and leaned with his face pressed against it—"and I said 'God knows what you've been doing, everything you've been doing. You may fool me, but you can't fool God!'"

Standing behind him, Michaelis saw with a shock that he was looking at the eyes of Doctor T. J. Eckleburg, which had just emerged, pale and enormous, from the dissolving night.

"God sees everything," repeated Wilson.

"That's an advertisement," Michaelis assured him. Something made him turn away from the window and look back into the room. But Wilson stood there a long time, his face close to the window pane, nodding into the twilight.

By six o'clock Michaelis was worn out, and grateful for the sound of a car stopping outside. It was one of the watchers of the night before who had promised to come back, so he cooked breakfast for three, which he and the other man ate together. Wilson was quieter now, and Michaelis went home to sleep; when he awoke four hours later and hurried back to the garage, Wilson was gone.

His movements—he was on foot all the time—were afterward traced to Port Roosevelt and then to Gad's Hill, where he bought a sandwich that he didn't eat, and a cup of coffee. He must have been tired and walking slowly, for he didn't reach Gad's Hill until noon. Thus far there was no difficulty in accounting for his time—there were boys who had seen a man "acting sort of crazy," and motorists at whom he stared oddly from the side of the road. Then for three hours he disappeared from view. The police, on the strength of what he said to Michaelis, that he "had a way of finding out," supposed that he spent that time going from garage to garage thereabout, inquiring for a yellow car. On the other hand, no garage man who had seen him ever came forward, and perhaps he had an easier, surer way of finding out what he wanted to know. By half-past two he was in West Egg, where he asked some one the way to Gatsby's house. So by that time he knew Gatsby's name.

At two o'clock Gatsby put on his bathing-suit and left word with the butler that if any one phoned word was to be brought to him at the pool. He stopped at the garage for a pneumatic mattress that had amused his guests during the summer, and the chauffeur helped him pump it up. Then he gave instructions that the open car wasn't to be taken out under any circumstances—and this was strange, because the front right fender needed repair.

Gatsby shouldered the mattress and started for the pool. Once he stopped and shifted it a little, and the chauffeur asked him if he needed help, but he shook his head and in a moment disappeared among the yellowing trees.

No telephone message arrived, but the butler went without his sleep and waited for it until four o'clock—until long after there was any one to give it to if it came. I have an idea that Gatsby himself didn't believe it would come, and perhaps he no longer cared. If that was true he must have felt that he had lost the old warm world, paid a high price for living too long with a single dream. He must have looked up at an unfamiliar sky through frightening leaves and shivered as he found what a grotesque thing a rose is and how raw the sunlight was upon the scarcely created grass. A new world, material without being real, where poor ghosts, breathing dreams like air, drifted fortuitously about . . . like that ashen, fantastic figure gliding toward him through the amorphous trees.

The chauffeur—he was one of Wolfsheim's protégés—heard the shots—afterward he could only say that he hadn't thought anything much about them. I drove from the station directly to Gatsby's house and my rushing anxiously up the front steps was the first thing that alarmed any one. But they knew then, I firmly believe. With scarcely a word said, four of us, the chauffeur, butler, gardener, and I, hurried down to the pool.

There was a faint, barely perceptible movement of the water as the fresh flow from one end urged its way toward the drain at the other. With little ripples that were hardly the shadows of waves, the laden mattress moved irregularly down the pool. A small gust of wind that scarcely corrugated the surface was enough to disturb its accidental course with its accidental burden. The touch of a cluster of leaves revolved it slowly, tracing, like the leg of transit, a thin red circle in the water.

It was after we started with Gatsby toward the house that the gardener saw Wilson's body a little way off in the grass, and the holocaust was complete.

CHAPTER IX

AFTER TWO YEARS I remember the rest of that day, and that night and the next day, only as an endless drill of police and photographers and newspaper men in and out of Gatsby's front door. A rope stretched across the main gate and a policeman by it kept out the curious, but little boys soon discovered that they could enter through my yard, and there were always a few of them clustered open-mouthed about the pool. Some one with a positive manner, perhaps a detective, used the expression "madman" as he bent over Wilson's body that afternoon, and the adventitious authority of his voice set the key for the newspaper reports next morning.

Most of those reports were a nightmare—grotesque, circumstantial, eager, and untrue. When Michaelis's testimony at the inquest brought to light Wilson's suspicions of his wife I thought the whole tale would shortly be served up in racy pasquinade—but Catherine, who might have said anything, didn't say a word. She showed a surprising amount of character about it too—looked at the coroner with determined eyes under that corrected brow of hers, and swore that her sister had never seen Gatsby, that her sister was completely happy with her husband, that her sister had been into no mischief whatever. She convinced herself of it, and cried into her handkerchief, as if the very suggestion was more than she could endure. So Wilson was reduced to a man "deranged by grief" in order that the case might remain in its simplest form. And it rested there.

But all this part of it seemed remote and unessential. I found myself on Gatsby's side, and alone. From the moment I telephoned news of the catastrophe to West Egg village, every surmise about him, and every practical question, was referred to me. At first I was surprised and confused; then, as he lay in his house and didn't move or breathe or speak, hour upon hour, it grew upon me that I was responsible, because no one else was interested—interested, I mean, with that intense personal interest to which every one has some vague right at the end.

I called up Daisy half an hour after we found him, called her instinctively and without hesitation. But she and Tom had gone away
early that afternoon, and taken baggage with them.

"Left no address?"

"No."

"Say when they'd be back?"

"No."

"Any idea where they are? How I could reach them?"

"I don't know. Can't say."

I wanted to get somebody for him. I wanted to go into the room
where he lay and reassure him: "I'll get somebody for you, Gatsby.
Don't worry. Just trust me and I'll get somebody for you——"

Meyer Wolfsheim's name wasn't in the phone book. The butler
gave me his office address on Broadway, and I called Information,
but by the time I had the number it was long after five, and no one
answered the phone.

"Will you ring again?"

"I've rung them three times."

"It's very important."

"Sorry. I'm afraid no one's there."

I went back to the drawing-room and thought for an instant tnat
they were chance visitors, all these official people who suddenly filled
it. But, as they drew back the sheet and looked at Gatsby with
unmoved eyes, his protest continued in my brain:

"Look here, old sport, you've got to get somebody for me. You've
got to try hard. I can't go through this alone."

Some one started to ask me questions, but I broke away and going
upstairs looked hastily through the unlocked parts of his desk—he'd
never told me definitely that his parents were dead. But there was
nothing—only the picture of Dan Cody, a token of forgotten violence, staring down from the wall.

Next morning I sent the butler to New York with a letter to
Wolfsheim, which asked for information and urged him to come out
on the next train. That request seemed superfluous when I wrote it.
I was sure he'd start when he saw the newspapers, just as I was sure
there'd be a wire from Daisy before noon—but neither a wire nor
Mr. Wolfsheim arrived; no one arrived except more police and
photographers and newspaper men. When the butler brought back

Wolfsheim's answer I began to have a feeling of defiance, of scorn, ful solidarity between Gatsby and me against them all.

Dear Mr. Carraway. This has been one of the most terrible shocks of my life to me I hardly can believe it that it is true at all. Such a mad act as that man did should make us all think. I cannot come down now as I am tied up in some very important business and cannot get mixed up in this thing now. If there is anything I can do a little later let me know in a letter by Edgar. I hardly know where I am when I hear about a thing like this and am completely knocked down and out.

Yours truly

MEYER WOLFSHEIM

and then hasty addenda beneath:

Let me know about the funeral etc do not know his family at all.

When the phone rang that afternoon and Long Distance said Chicago was calling I thought this would be Daisy at last. But the connection came through as a man's voice, very thin and far away.

"This is Slagle speaking . . ."

"Yes?" The name was unfamiliar.

"Hell of a note, isn't it? Get my wire?"

"There haven't been any wires."

"Young Parke's in trouble," he said rapidly. "They picked him up when he handed the bonds over the counter. They got a circular from New York giving 'em the numbers just five minutes before. What d'you know about that, hey? You never can tell in these hick towns——"

"Hello!" I interrupted breathlessly. "Look here—this isn't Mr. Gatsby. Mr. Gatsby's dead."

There was a long silence on the other end of the wire, followed by an exclamation . . . then a quick squawk as the connection was broken.

I think it was on the third day that a telegram signed Henry C. Gatz arrived from a town in Minnesota. It said only that the sender was leaving immediately and to postpone the funeral until he came.

It was Gatsby's father, a solemn old man, very helpless and dismayed, bundled up in a long cheap ulster against the warm September day. His eyes leaked continuously with excitement, and when I took the bag and umbrella from his hands he began to pull so incessantly at his sparse gray beard that I had difficulty in getting off his coat. He was on the point of collapse, so I took him into the music room and made him sit down while I sent for something to eat. But he wouldn't eat, and the glass of milk spilled from his trembling hand.

"I saw it in the Chicago newspaper," he said. "It was all in the Chicago newspaper. I started right away."

"I didn't know how to reach you."

His eyes, seeing nothing, moved ceaselessly about the room.

"It was a madman," he said. "He must have been mad."

"Wouldn't you like some coffee?" I urged him.

"I don't want anything. I'm all right now, Mr——"

"Carraway."

"Well, I'm all right now. Where have they got Jimmy?"

I took him into the drawing-room, where his son lay, and left him there. Some little boys had come up on the steps and were looking into the hall; when I told them who had arrived, they went reluctantly away.

After a little while Mr. Gatz opened the door and came out, his mouth ajar, his face flushed slightly, his eyes leaking isolated and unpunctual tears. He had reached an age where death no longer has the quality of ghastly surprise, and when he looked around him now for the first time and saw the height and splendor of the hall and the great rooms opening out from it into other rooms, his grief began to be mixed with an awed pride. I helped him to a bedroom upstairs; while he took off his coat and vest I told him that all arrangements had been deferred until he came.

"I didn't know what you'd want, Mr. Gatsby——"

"Gatz is my name."

"—Mr. Gatz. I thought you might want to take the body West."

He shook his head.

"Jimmy always liked it better down East. He rose up to his position in the East. Were you a friend of my boy's, Mr. ——?"

"We were close friends."

"He had a big future before him, you know. He was only a young man, but he had a lot of brain power here."

He touched his head impressively, and I nodded.

"If he'd of lived, he'd of been a great man. A man like James J. Hill. He'd of helped build up the country."

"That's true," I said, uncomfortably.

He fumbled at the embroidered coverlet, trying to take it from the bed, and lay down stiffly—was instantly asleep.

That night an obviously frightened person called up, and demanded to know who I was before he would give his name.

"This is Mr. Carraway," I said.

"Oh!" He sounded relieved. "This is Klipspringer."

I was relieved too, for that seemed to promise another friend at Gatsby's grave. I didn't want it to be in the papers and draw a sightseeing crowd, so I'd been calling up a few people myself. They were hard to find.

"The funeral's tomorrow," I said. "Three o'clock, here at the house. I wish you'd tell anybody who'd be interested."

"Oh, I will," he broke out hastily. "Of course I'm not likely to see anybody, but if I do."

His tone made me suspicious.

"Of course you'll be there yourself."

"Well, I'll certainly try. What I called up about is——"

"Wait a minute," I interrupted. "How about saying you'll come?"

"Well, the fact is—the truth of the matter is that I'm staying with some people up here in Greenwich, and they rather expect me to be with them tomorrow. In fact, there's a sort of picnic or something. Of course I'll do my very best to get away."

I ejaculated an unrestrained "Huh!" and he must have heard me, for he went on nervously:

"What I called up about was a pair of shoes I left there. I wonder if it'd be too much trouble to have the butler send them on. You see, they're tennis shoes, and I'm sort of helpless without them. My address is care of B. F.——"

I didn't hear the rest of the name, because I hung up the receiver.

After that I felt a certain shame for Gatsby—one gentleman to whom I telephoned implied that he had got what he deserved. However, that was my fault, for he was one of those who used to sneer most bitterly at Gatsby on the courage of Gatsby's liquor, and I should have known better than to call him.

The morning of the funeral I went up to New York to see Meyer Wolfsheim; I couldn't seem to reach him any other way. The door that I pushed open, on the advice of an elevator boy, was marked "The Swastika Holding Company," and at first there didn't seem to be any one inside. But when I'd shouted "hello" several times in vain, an argument broke out behind a partition, and presently a lovely Jewess appeared at an interior door and scrutinized me with black hostile eyes.

"Nobody's in," she said. "Mr. Wolfsheim's gone to Chicago."

The first part of this was obviously untrue, for some one had begun to whistle "The Rosary," tunelessly, inside.

"Please say that Mr. Carraway wants to see him."

"I can't get him back from Chicago, can I?"

At this moment a voice, unmistakably Wolfsheim's, called "Stella!" from the other side of the door.

"Leave your name on the desk," she said quickly. "I'll give it to him when he gets back."

"But I know he's there."

She took a step toward me and began to slide her hands indignantly up and down her hips.

"You young men think you can force your way in here any time," she scolded. "We're getting sickantired of it. When I say he's in Chicago, he's in Chicago."

I mentioned Gatsby.

"Oh-h!" She looked at me over again. "Will you just— What was your name?"

She vanished. In a moment Meyer Wolfsheim stood solemnly in the doorway, holding out both hands. He drew me into his office, remarking in a reverent voice that it was a sad time for all of us, and offered me a cigar.

"My memory goes back to when first I met him," he said. "A young major just out of the army and covered over with medals he got in the war. He was so hard up he had to keep on wearing his uniform because he couldn't buy some regular clothes. First time I saw him was when he come into Winebrenner's poolroom at Forty-third Street and asked for a job. He hadn't eat anything for a couple of days. 'Come on have some lunch with me,' I said. He ate more than four dollars' worth of food in half an hour."

"Did you start him in business?" I inquired.

"Start him! I made him."

"Oh."

"I raised him up out of nothing, right out of the gutter. I saw right away he was a fine-appearing, gentlemanly young man, and when he told me he was an Oggsford I knew I could use him good. I got him to join up in the American Legion and he used to stand high there. Right off he did some work for a client of mine up to Albany. We were so thick like that in everything"—he held up two bulbous fingers—"always together."

I wondered if this partnership had included the World's Series transaction in 1919.

"Now he's dead," I said after a moment. "You were his closest friend, so I know you'll want to come to his funeral this afternoon."

"I'd like to come."

"Well, come then."

The hair in his nostrils quivered slightly, and as he shook his head his eyes filled with tears.

"I can't do it—I can't get mixed up in it," he said.

"There's nothing to get mixed up in. It's all over now."

"When a man gets killed I never like to get mixed up in it in any way. I keep out. When I was a young man it was different—if a friend of mine died, no matter how, I stuck with them to the end. You may think that's sentimental, but I mean it—to the bitter end."

I saw that for some reason of his own he was determined not to come, so I stood up.

"Are you a college man?" he inquired suddenly.

For a moment I thought he was going to suggest a "gonnegtion," but he only nodded and shook my hand.

"Let us learn to show our friendship for a man when he is alive and not after he is dead," he suggested. "After that, my own rule is to let everything alone."

When I left his office the sky had turned dark and I got back to West Egg in a drizzle. After changing my clothes I went next door and found Mr. Gatz walking up and down excitedly in the hall. His pride in his son and in his son's possessions was continually increasing and now he had something to show me.

"Jimmy sent me this picture." He took out his wallet with trembling fingers. "Look there."

It was a photograph of the house, cracked in the corners and dirty with many hands. He pointed out every detail to me eagerly. "Look there!" and then sought admiration from my eyes. He had shown it so often that I think it was more real to him now than the house itself.

"Jimmy sent it to me. I think it's a very pretty picture. It shows up well."

"Very well. Had you seen him lately?"

"He come out to see me two years ago and bought me the house I live in now. Of course we was broke up when he run off from home, but I see now there was a reason for it. He knew he had a big future in front of him. And ever since he made a success he was very generous with me."

He seemed reluctant to put away the picture, held it for another minute, lingeringly, before my eyes. Then he returned the wallet and pulled from his pocket a ragged old copy of a book called *Hopalong Cassidy*.

"Look here, this is a book he had when he was a boy. It just shows you."

He opened it at the back cover and turned it around for me to see. On the last fly-leaf was printed the word SCHEDULE, and the date September 12, 1906. And underneath:

Rise from bed .... 6.00   A. M.
Dumbbell exercise and wall-scaling................... 6.15–6.30   "
Study electricity, etc............................. 7.15–8.15   "
Work .... 8.30–4.30 P. M.
Baseball and sports................................ 4.30–5.00   "
Practice elocution, poise and how to attain it.......... 5.00–6.00   "
Study needed inventions........................... 7.00–9.00   "

GENERAL RESOLVES

No wasting time at Shafters or [a name, indecipherable]
No more smokeing or chewing.
Bath every other day
Read one improving book or magazine per week
Save $5.00 [crossed out] $3.00 per week
Be better to parents

"I come across this book by accident," said the old man. "It just shows you, don't it?"

"Jimmy was bound to get ahead. He always had some resolves like this or something. Do you notice what he's got about improving his mind? He was always great for that. He told me I et like a hog once, and I beat him for it."

He was reluctant to close the book, reading each item aloud and then looking eagerly at me. I think he rather expected me to copy down the list for my own use.

A little before three the Lutheran minister arrived from Flushing, and I began to look involuntarily out the windows for other cars. So did Gatsby's father. And as the time passed and the servants came in and stood waiting in the hall, his eyes began to blink anxiously, and he spoke of the rain in a worried, uncertain way. The minister glanced several times at his watch, so I took him aside and asked him to wait for half an hour. But it wasn't any use. Nobody came.

About five o'clock our procession of three cars reached the cemetery and stopped in a thick drizzle beside the gate—first a motor hearse, horribly black and wet, then Mr. Gatz and the minister and I in the limousine, and a little later four or five servants and the postman from West Egg, in Gatsby's station wagon, all wet to the skin. As we started through the gate into the cemetery I heard a car stop and then the sound of some one splashing after us over the soggy ground. I looked around. It was the man with owl-eyed glasses whom I had found marvelling over Gatsby's books in the library one night three months before.

I'd never seen him since then. I don't know how he knew about the funeral, or even his name. The rain poured down his thick glasses, and he took them off and wiped them to see the protecting canvas unrolled from Gatsby's grave.

I tried to think about Gatsby then for a moment, but he was already too far away, and I could only remember, without resentment, that Daisy hadn't sent a message or a flower. Dimly I heard some one murmur "Blessed are the dead that the rain falls on," and then the owl-eyed man said "Amen to that," in a brave voice.

We straggled down quickly through the rain to the cars. Owl-eyes spoke to me by the gate.

"I couldn't get to the house," he remarked.

"Neither could anybody else."

"Go on!" He started. "Why, my God! they used to go there by the hundreds."

He took off his glasses and wiped them again, outside and in.

"The poor son-of-a-bitch," he said.

One of my most vivid memories is of coming back West from prep school and later from college at Christmas time. Those who went farther than Chicago would gather in the old dim Union Station at six o'clock of a December evening, with a few Chicago friends, already caught up into their own holiday gayeties, to bid them a hasty good-by. I remember the fur coats of the girls returning from Miss This-or-That's and the chatter of frozen breath and the hands waving overhead as we caught sight of old acquaintances, and the matchings of invitations: "Are you going to the Ordways'? the Herseys'? the Schultzes'?" and the long green tickets clasped tight in our gloved hands. And last the murky yellow cars of the Chicago, Milwaukee & St. Paul railroad looking cheerful as Christmas itself on the tracks beside the gate.

When we pulled out into the winter night and the real snow, our snow, began to stretch out beside us and twinkle against the windows, and the dim lights of small Wisconsin stations moved by, a sharp wild brace came suddenly into the air. We drew in deep breaths of it as we walked back from dinner through the cold vestibules, unutterably aware of our identity with this country for one strange hour, before we melted indistinguishably into it again.

That's my Middle West—not the wheat or the prairies or the lost Swede towns, but the thrilling returning trains of my youth, and the street lamps and sleigh bells in the frosty dark and the shadows of holly wreaths thrown by lighted windows on the snow. I am part of that, a little solemn with the feel of those long winters, a little complacent from growing up in the Carraway house in a city where dwellings are still called through decades by a family's name. I see now that this has been a story of the West, after all—Tom and Gatsby, Daisy and Jordan and I, were all Westerners, and perhaps we possessed some deficiency in common which made us subtly unadaptable to Eastern life.

Even when the East excited me most, even when I was most keenly aware of its superiority to the bored, sprawling, swollen towns beyond the Ohio, with their interminable inquisitions which spared only the children and the very old—even then it had always for me a quality of distortion. West Egg, especially, still figures in my more fantastic dreams. I see it as a night scene by El Greco: a hundred houses, at once conventional and grotesque, crouching under a sullen, overhanging sky and a lustreless moon. In the foreground four solemn men in dress suits are walking along the sidewalk with a stretcher on which lies a drunken woman in a white evening dress. Her hand, which dangles over the side, sparkles cold with jewels. Gravely the men turn in at a house—the wrong house. But no one knows the woman's name, and no one cares.

After Gatsby's death the East was haunted for me like that, distorted beyond my eyes' power of correction. So when the blue smoke of brittle leaves was in the air and the wind blew the wet laundry stiff on the line I decided to come back home.

There was one thing to be done before I left, an awkward, unpleasant thing that perhaps had better have been let alone. But I wanted to leave things in order and not just trust that obliging and indifferent sea to sweep my refuse away. I saw Jordan Baker and talked over and around what had happened to us together, and what had happened afterward to me, and she lay perfectly still, listening, in a big chair.

She was dressed to play golf, and I remember thinking she looked like a good illustration, her chin raised a little jauntily, her hair the color of an autumn leaf, her face the same brown tint as the fingerless glove on her knee. When I had finished she told me without comment that she was engaged to another man. I doubted that, though there were several she could have married at a nod of her head, but I pretended to be surprised. For just a minute I wondered if I wasn't making a mistake, then I thought it all over again quickly and got up to say good-by.

"Nevertheless you did throw me over," said Jordan suddenly. "You threw me over on the telephone. I don't give a damn about you now, but it was a new experience for me, and I felt a little dizzy for a while."

We shook hands.

"Oh, and do you remember"—she added—"a conversation we had once about driving a car?"

"Why—not exactly."

"You said a bad driver was only safe until she met another bad driver? Well, I met another bad driver, didn't I? I mean it was careless of me to make such a wrong guess. I thought you were rather an honest, straightforward person. I thought it was your secret pride."

"I'm thirty," I said. "I'm five years too old to lie to myself and call it honor."

She didn't answer. Angry, and half in love with her, and tremendously sorry, I turned away.

One afternoon late in October I saw Tom Buchanan. He was walking ahead of me along Fifth Avenue in his alert, aggressive way, his hands out a little from his body as if to fight off interference, his head moving sharply here and there, adapting itself to his restless eyes. Just as I slowed up to avoid overtaking him he stopped and began frowning into the windows of a jewelry store. Suddenly he saw me and walked back, holding out his hand.

"What's the matter, Nick? Do you object to shaking hands with me?"

"Yes. You know what I think of you."

"You're crazy, Nick," he said quickly. "Crazy as hell. I don't know what's the matter with you."

"Tom," I inquired, "what did you say to Wilson that afternoon?"

He stared at me without a word, and I knew I had guessed right about those missing hours. I started to turn away, but he took a step after me and grabbed my arm.

"I told him the truth," he said. "He came to the door while we were getting ready to leave, and when I sent down word that we weren't in he tried to force his way upstairs. He was crazy enough to kill me if I hadn't told him who owned the car. His hand was on a revolver in his pocket every minute he was in the house——" He broke off defiantly. "What if I did tell him? That fellow had it coming to him. He threw dust into your eyes just like he did in Daisy's, but he was a tough one. He ran over Myrtle like you'd run over a dog and never even stopped his car."

There was nothing I could say, except the one unutterable fact that it wasn't true.

"And if you think I didn't have my share of suffering—look here, when I went to give up that flat and saw that damn box of dog biscuits sitting there on the sideboard, I sat down and cried like a baby. By God it was awful——"

I couldn't forgive him or like him, but I saw that what he had done was, to him, entirely justified. It was all very careless and confused. They were careless people, Tom and Daisy—they smashed up things and creatures and then retreated back into their money or their vast carelessness, or whatever it was that kept them together, and let other people clean up the mess they had made. . . .

I shook hands with him; it seemed silly not to, for I felt suddenly as though I were talking to a child. Then he went into the jewelry store to buy a pearl necklace—or perhaps only a pair of cuff buttons—rid of my provincial squeamishness forever.

Gatsby's house was still empty when I left—the grass on his lawn had grown as long as mine. One of the taxi drivers in the village never took a fare past the entrance gate without stopping for a minute and pointing inside; perhaps it was he who drove Daisy and Gatsby over to East Egg the night of the accident, and perhaps he had made a story about it all his own. I didn't want to hear it and I avoided him when I got off the train.

I spent my Saturday nights in New York, because those gleaming, dazzling parties of his were with me so vividly that I could still hear the music and the laughter, faint and incessant, from his garden, and the cars going up and down his drive. One night I did hear a material car there, and saw its lights stop at his front steps. But I didn't investigate. Probably it was some final guest who had been away at the ends of the earth and didn't know that the party was over.

On the last night, with my trunk packed and my car sold to the grocer, I went over and looked at that huge incoherent failure of a house once more. On the white steps an obscene word, scrawled by some boy with a piece of brick, stood out clearly in the moonlight, and I erased it, drawing my shoe raspingly along the stone. Then I wandered down to the beach and sprawled out on the sand.

Most of the big shore places were closed now and there were hardly any lights except the shadowy, moving glow of a ferryboat across the Sound. And as the moon rose higher the inessential houses began to melt away until gradually I became aware of the old island here that flowered once for Dutch sailors' eyes—a fresh, green breast of the new world. Its vanished trees, the trees that had made way for Gatsby's house, had once pandered in whispers to the last and greatest of all human dreams; for a transitory enchanted moment man must have held his breath in the presence of this continent, compelled into an æsthetic contemplation he neither understood nor desired, face to face for the last time in history with something commensurate to his capacity for wonder.

And as I sat there brooding on the old, unknown world, I thought of Gatsby's wonder when he first picked out the green light at the end of Daisy's dock. He had come a long way to this blue lawn, and his dream must have seemed so close that he could hardly fail to grasp it. He did not know that it was already behind him, somewhere back in that vast obscurity beyond the city, where the dark fields of the republic rolled on under the night.

Gatsby believed in the green light, the orgiastic future that year by year recedes before us. It eluded us then, but that's no matter—tomorrow we will run faster, stretch out our arms farther. . . . And one fine morning——

So we beat on, boats against the current, borne back ceaselessly into the past.

TENDER
IS THE NIGHT

INTRODUCTION

TO THE END OF his life Fitzgerald was puzzled by the comparative failure of *Tender Is the Night,* after the years he spent on it and his efforts to make it the best American novel of his time. He had started it when he was living on the Riviera in the late summer of 1925. At first he had worked in bursts and had put aside the manuscript for months at a time while he wrote his profitable stories for the *Saturday Evening Post;* but early in 1932 he had found a more ambitious plan for it and had gone into debt to work on it steadily until the last chapters were written and the last deletions made in proof. He had watched it grow from a short dramatic novel like *The Great Gatsby* to a long psychological or philosophical novel on the model of *Vanity Fair,* and then, as he omitted scene after scene, he had watched it diminish again to a medium-length novel, but one in which he was sure that the overtones of the longer book remained. Nine years of his life had gone into the writing and into the story itself. Reading closely one could find in it the bedazzlement of his first summer at the Cap d'Antibes—for he could picture himself as Rosemary Hoyt in the novel, besides playing the part of Dick Diver; then his feelings about money and about the different levels of American society; then his struggle with alcoholism and his worries about becoming an emotional bankrupt; then his wife's illness and everything he learned from the Swiss and American doctors who diagnosed her case; then the bitter wisdom he gained from experience and couldn't put back into it, but only into his stories; then darker things as well, his sense of guilt, his fear of disaster that became a longing for disaster—it was all in the book, in different layers, like the nine buried cities of Troy.

When another writer went to see him at Rodgers Forge, near Baltimore, in the spring of 1933, Fitzgerald took the visitor to his study and showed him a pile of manuscript nearly a foot high. "There's my new novel," he said. "I've written four hundred thousand words and thrown away three-fourths of it. Now I only have fifteen thousand left to write and——" He stood there with a glass in his hand, then suddenly burst out, "It's good, good, good. When it's published people will say that it's good, good, good."

Tender was published in the spring of 1934 and people said nothing of the sort. It dealt with fashionable life in the 1920s at a time when most readers wanted to forget that they had ever been concerned with frivolities; the new fashion was for novels about destitution and revolt. The book had some friendly and even admiring notices, but most reviewers implied that it belonged to the bad old days before the crash; they dismissed it as having a "clever and brilliant surface" without being "wise and mature." Nor was it a popular success as compared with Fitzgerald's first three novels, which had been easier to write; in the first season it sold twelve thousand copies, or less than one-fourth as much as *This Side of Paradise*. In the following seasons the sale dwindled and stopped.

Fitzgerald didn't blame the public or the critics. It was one of the conditions of the game he played with life to accept the rules as they were written; if he lost point and set after playing his hardest, that was due to some mistake in strategy to be corrected in the future. He began looking in a puzzled fashion for the mistake in *Tender Is the Night*. There must have been an error in presentation that had kept his readers from grasping the richness and force of his material; for a time he suspected that it might merely be the lack of something that corresponded to stage directions at the beginning of each scene. In 1936 the book was being considered for republication by the Modern Library. The new edition, if it appeared, would have to be printed from the plates of the first edition in order to reduce the manufacturing costs, but Fitzgerald begged for the privilege of making some minor changes. These, he said in a letter to Bennett Cerf, "would include in several cases sudden stops and part headings which would be to some extent explanatory; certain pages would have to be inserted bearing merely headings. . . .

"I know what printing costs are," he added humbly. "There will be no pushing over of paragraphs or disorganization of the present set-up except in the aforesaid inserted pages. I don't want to change anything in the book but sometimes by a single word change one can throw a new emphasis or give a new value to the exact same scene or setting."

The new edition didn't appear and *Tender* seemed to be forgotten, although it really wasn't; it stayed in people's minds like a regret or an unanswered question. "A strange thing is that in retrospect his *Tender Is the Night* gets better and better," Ernest Hemingway told Maxwell Perkins, of Scribners, who was the editor of both novelists. In scores of midnight arguments that I remember, other writers ended by finding that they had the same feeling about the book. Fitzgerald continued to brood about it. In December 1938, when he was in Hollywood and was drawing near the end of his contract with Metro-Goldwyn-Mayer, he wrote to Perkins suggesting that three of his novels might be reprinted in one volume. *This Side of Paradise* would appear with a glossary that Fitzgerald planned to make of its absurdities and inaccuracies. *Gatsby* would be unchanged except for some corrections in the text. "But I am especially concerned about *Tender,*" he added, "—that book is not dead. The *depth* of its appeal exists—I meet people constantly who have the same exclusive attachment to it as others had to *Gatsby* and *Paradise,* people who identified themselves with Dick Diver. Its great fault is that the *true* beginning—the young psychiatrist in Switzerland—is tucked away in the middle of the book."

The first edition of the novel had opened with the visit to the Cap d'Antibes of a young moving-picture actress, Rosemary Hoyt, and her meeting with the circle that surrounded the Richard Divers. It was the summer of 1925 and Antibes was enjoying its days of quiet glory. Rosemary had been entranced with the Divers and their friends, had fallen in love with Dick in a pleasantly hopeless fashion, and had become aware that there was some mystery about his wife. Then, on pages 151–212, the story had gone back to wartime Switzerland in order to explain the mystery by telling about Doctor Diver's courtship and marriage. Fitzgerald now proposed to rearrange the book in chronological order. "If pages 151–212 were taken from their present place and put at the start," he said in his letter to Perkins, "the improvement in appeal would be enormous."

It must have been about the same time that Fitzgerald made an entry in his notebook, outlining the changed order and dividing the novel into five books instead of three. The entry reads:

Analysis of *Tender:*
    I Case History 151–212 61 pps. (change moon) p. 212
    II Rosemary's Angle 3–104 101 pps. P. 3
    III Casualties 104–148, 213–224 55 pps. (−2) (120 & 121)
    IV Escape 225–306 82 pps.
    V The Way Home 306–408 103 pps. (−8) (332–341)

I haven't been able to find the moon that was to be changed in Book I; perhaps Fitzgerald gave some special meaning to the word, and in any case it doesn't occur on 212. That was of course the last page of "Case History" and it had to be revised in order to prepare the reader for 3, which was the first page of Book II and also needed minor revisions. The page numbers in parenthesis— (120 & 121), (332–341)—were passages that the author planned to omit. All these changes were made in Fitzgerald's personal copy of *Tender Is the Night,* which is now in the manuscript room of the Princeton University Library. In that copy the pages are cut loose from the binding and rearranged as suggested in the notebook; but Fitzgerald had some afterthoughts while working over them. Pages 207–212, instead of being the last chapter of Book I, are now the beginning of Book II. The necessary small revisions are made on pages 3 and 212. Book III, the one he thought of as "Casualties," begins on 74, with the Divers' visit to the battlefield of the Somme —and it is a good beginning, too, since it sets the tone for what will follow. There are many small changes and corrections in the text, especially at the beginning of Book I. On the inside front cover Fitzgerald has written in pencil:
"This is the *final version* of the book as I would like it."
The words "final version" are underlined, but they have to be taken as a statement of intention rather than as an accomplished fact. It is clear that Fitzgerald had other changes in mind besides his rearrangement of the narrative and the minor revisions already mentioned: he also planned to correct the text from beginning to end. One can see what he intended to do if one reads the first two chapters of the Princeton copy. There he has caught some of his

errors in spelling proper names, has revised the punctuation to make it more logical, has sharpened a number of phrases, and has omitted others. Small as the changes are, they make the style smoother and remove the reader's occasional suspicion that the author had hesitated over a word or had failed to hear a name correctly. Near the end of Chapter II there is a pencilled asterisk and a note in Fitzgerald's handwriting: "This is my mark to say that I have made final corrections up to this point." Beyond the mark are a few other corrections but only of errors that happened to catch his eye.

It is too late now to make the changes in phrasing that, as he said, "can throw a new emphasis or give a new value to the exact same scene or setting." It is not too late, however, to correct the mistakes in spelling and punctuation, and sometimes in grammar and chronology, that disfigure the first edition of *Tender*. On this mechanical level the book was full of errors; in fact, a combination of circumstances was required to get so many of them into one published volume. Fitzgerald had a fine ear for words, but a weak eye for them; he was possibly the worst speller who ever failed to graduate from Princeton. His punctuation was impulsive and his grammar more instinctive than reasoned. Maxwell Perkins, his editor, was better in all these departments, but had an aristocratic disregard for details so long as a book was right in its feeling for life. Since Fitzgerald was regarded as one of his special authors, the manuscript was never copy-edited by others. The author received the proofs while his wife was critically ill. He worked over them for weeks, making extensive changes and omitting long passages, but he was in no state to notice his own errors of detail. Scores of them slipped into the first edition and, though they were unimportant if taken separately, I suspect that they had a cumulative effect on readers and ended by distracting their attention, like flaws in a window through which they were looking at the countryside. That the novel continued to be read in spite of the flaws was evidence of its lasting emotion and vitality.

Now that it is being reissued with Fitzgerald's changes I have tried to give it the sort of proofreading that the first edition failed to receive. I used dictionaries and Baedekers and consulted several of the author's friends; two or three of them had made their own lists of errors in the text. For a long time I hesitated over the two passages that Fitzgerald had marked for omission. One was the episode of the American newspaper vendor, on pages 120–121 of the first edition, and I ended by feeling that the pages could be dropped without much loss (although the newspaper vendor reappears on page 399 and once again serves as a herald of disaster). A longer omission was the Divers' visit to Mary Minghetti on pages 332–341. That change was not so easy to make, because it would have required an explanation in a later chapter of how the former Mary North had become very rich and a papal countess; besides, the episode is good in itself and that was a further reason for retaining it. Except in this instance I have tried to follow Fitzgerald's wishes at all points and to provide, so far as possible, the permanent text of a book that will continue to be read for a long time.

The question remains whether the final version as Fitzgerald would like it is also the best version of the novel. I was slow to make up my mind about it, perhaps out of affection for the book in its earlier form. The beginning of the first edition, with the Divers seen and admired through the innocent eyes of Rosemary Hoyt, is effective by any standards. Some of the effectiveness is lost in the new arrangement, where the reader already knows the truth about the Divers before Rosemary meets them. There is a mystery-story element in the earlier draft: something has passed between Nicole Diver and Mrs. McKisco that is shocking enough to cause a duel, and we read on to learn what Nicole has done or said. There is also the suggestion of a psychoanalytical case study: it is as if we were listening behind the analyst's door while his two patients, Nicole and Dick, help him to penetrate slowly beneath their glittering surfaces. But the mystery story ends when Rosemary discovers—on page 148 of the first edition—what Violet McKisco had seen in the bathroom at Villa Diana. The psychoanalytical case study is finished by page 212, when the reader has all the pertinent information about the past life of the Divers; but meanwhile half of the novel is still to come. The early critics of *Tender* were right when they said that it broke in two after Rosemary left the scene and that the first part failed to prepare us for what would follow. By rearranging the story in chronological order Fitzgerald tied it together. He sacrificed a brilliant beginning and all the element of mystery, but there is no escaping the judgment that he ended with a better constructed and more effective novel.

One fault of the earlier version was its uncertainty of focus. We weren't quite sure in reading it whether the author had intended to write about a whole group of Americans on the Riviera—that is, to make the book a social study with a collective hero—or whether he had intended to write a psychological novel about the glory and decline of Richard Diver as a person. Simply by changing the order of the story and starting with Diver as a young doctor in Zurich, Fitzgerald answered our hesitation. We are certain in reading the final version that the novel is psychological, that it is about Dick Diver, and that its social meanings are obtained by extension or synecdoche. Dick is the part that stands for the whole. He stands for other Americans on the Riviera, he stands for all the smart men who played too close to the line, he even stands for the age that was ending with the Wall Street crash, but first he stands for himself. The other characters are grouped around him in their subordinate roles: Rosemary sets in operation the forces waiting to destroy him, Abe North announces his fate, and Tommy Barban is his stronger and less talented successor. From beginning to end Dick is the center of the novel.

All this corresponds to the plan that Fitzgerald made early in 1932, after working for years on other plans and putting them aside. At first he had intended to write a short novel about a young man named Francis Melarky, a movie technician who visited the Riviera with his possessive mother. He met the Seth Pipers, a couple much like the Divers; he fell in love with the wife, followed them to Paris, went on a round of parties, and lost control of himself. The last chapters of this early draft are missing—if Fitzgerald ever wrote them—but it seems that Melarky was to kill his mother in a fit of rage, run away from the police, and then meet his own death —just how we aren't certain. In later versions of the story Melarky was somewhat less the central figure, while Abe Grant (later Abe North) and Seth Piper moved into the foreground. Then, at the beginning of 1932, Fitzgerald drew up the outline of a more ambitious book. "The novel should do this," he said in a memorandum to himself that was written at the time: "Show a man who is a natural idealist, a spoiled priest, giving in for various causes to the ideas of the haute bourgeoisie, and in his rise to the top of the social world losing his idealism, his talent and turning to drink and dissipation. Background one in which the leisure class is at their truly most brilliant and glamorous. . . ." In finishing the book Fitzgerald changed and deepened and complicated his picture of Dick Diver, but his statement of purpose is still the best short definition of the finished novel. His final revision brings the book even closer to the plan made in 1932.

It has to be said that Fitzgerald could never have revised *Tender* into the perfect novel that existed as an ideal in his mind. He had worked too long over it and his plans for it had changed too often, just as the author himself had changed in the years since his first summer on the Riviera. To make it all of a piece he would have had to start over from the beginning and invent a wholly new series of episodes, instead of trying to salvage as much as possible from the earlier versions. No matter how often he threw his material back into the melting pot, some of it would prove refractory to heat and would keep its former shape when poured into the new mould. The scenes written for Francis Melarky, then reassigned to Rosemary or Dick, would retain some marks of their origin. The whole Rosemary episode, being rewritten from the oldest chapters of the book, would be a little out of key with the story of Dick Diver as witnessed by himself and by his wife. But a novel has to be judged for what it gives us, not for its defects in execution, and *Tender* gives us an honesty of feeling, a complexity of life, that we miss in many books admired for being nearly perfect in form.

Moreover, in Fitzgerald's final revision it has a symmetry that we do not often find in long psychological novels. All the themes introduced in the first book are resolved in the last, and both books are written in the same key. In the first book young Doctor Diver is like Grant in his general store in Galena, waiting "to be called to an intricate destiny"; meanwhile he helps another psychiatrist with the case of Nicole Warren, a beautiful heiress suffering from schizophrenia, and learns that the Warrens have planned to buy a young doctor for her to marry. In the last book he finishes her cure, realizes that the Warrens have indeed purchased and used him—"That's what he was educated for," Nicole's sister says—and is left

biding his time, "again like Grant in Galena," but with the difference that his one great adventure has ended. The Rosemary section of the novel no longer misleads our expectations; coming in
the middle it simply adds fullness and relief to the story.

Although the new beginning is less brilliant than the older one,
it prepares us for the end and helps us to appreciate the last section
of the novel as we had probably failed to do on our first reading.
That is the principal virtue of Fitzgerald's new arrangement. When
I read *Tender* in 1934 it seemed to me as to many others that the
Rosemary section was the best part of it. The writing there was
of a type too seldom encountered in serious American fiction. It
was not an attempt to analyze social values, show their falseness,
tear them down—that is a necessary attempt at all times when values
have become perverted, but it requires no special imaginative vitality
and Fitzgerald was doing something more difficult: he was trying
to discover and even create values in a society where they had
seemed to be lacking. Rosemary with her special type of innocence
offered the right point of view from which to reveal the grace and
manners and apparent moral superiority of the Diver clan. The
high point of her experience—and of the reader's—was the dinner
at Villa Diana, when "The table seemed to have risen a little toward
the sky like a mechanical dancing platform, giving the people
around it a sense of being alone with each other in the dark universe, nourished by its only food, warmed by its only lights." Then
came the underside of the Divers' little world, as revealed in Abe
North's self-destructiveness and in what Violet McKisco had seen
in the bathroom at Villa Diana, and everything that followed seemed
a long anticlimax or at best the end of a different story.

Coming back to the novel long afterward and reading it in the
new arrangement I had a different impression. The Rosemary section had its old charm and something new as well, for it now
seemed the evocation of an age first condemned, then forgotten, and
finally recalled with pleasure in the midst of harsher events; but the
writing seemed to be on a lower level of intensity than the story of
the hero's decay as told in the last section of the novel. That becomes the truly memorable passage: not Dick as the "organizer of
private gaiety, curator of a richly incrusted happiness"; not Dick
creating his group of friends and making them seem incredibly dis-

tinguished—"so bright a unit that Rosemary felt an impatient disregard for all who were not at their table"; but another Dick who has lost command of himself and deteriorates before our eyes in a strict progression from scene to scene. At this point Fitzgerald was right when he stopped telling the story from Dick's point of view and allowed us merely to guess at the hero's thoughts. Dick fades like a friend who is withdrawing into a private world or sinking to another level of society and, in spite of knowing so much about him, we are never quite certain of the reasons for his decline. Perhaps, as Fitzgerald first planned, it was the standards of the leisure class that corrupted him; perhaps it was the strain of curing a psychotic wife, who gains strength as he loses it by a mysterious transfer of vitality; perhaps it was a form of emotional exhaustion, a giving of himself so generously that he went beyond his resources, "like a man overdrawing at his bank," as Fitzgerald would later say of his own crack-up; or perhaps it was something far back in his childhood that could only be discovered by deep analysis—we can argue about the causes as we can argue about the decline of a once-intimate friend, without coming to any fixed conclusion; but the point is that we always believe in Dick and in his progress in a circle from obscurity to obscurity. With our last glimpse of him swaying a little as he stands on a high terrace and makes a papal cross over the beach that he had found and peopled and that has now rejected him, his fate is accomplished and the circle closed.

MALCOLM COWLEY

Already with thee! tender is the night,

.   .   .   .

But here there is no light,
Save what from heaven is with the breezes blown
Through verdurous glooms and winding mossy ways.

—ODE TO A NIGHTINGALE.

BOOK I

CASE HISTORY
1917~1919

TENDER IS THE NIGHT

CHAPTER I

IN THE SPRING OF 1917, when Doctor Richard Diver first arrived in Zurich, he was twenty-six years old, a fine age for a man, indeed the very acme of bachelorhood. Even in war-time days it was a fine age for Dick, who was already too valuable, too much of a capital investment, to be shot off in a gun. Years later it seemed to him that even in this sanctuary he did not escape lightly, but about that he never fully made up his mind—in 1917 he laughed at the idea, saying apologetically that the war didn't touch him at all. Instructions from his local board were that he was to complete his studies in Zurich and take a degree as he had planned.

Switzerland was an island, washed on one side by the waves of thunder around Gorizia and on another by the cataracts along the Somme and the Aisne. For once there seemed more intriguing strangers than sick ones in the cantons, but that had to be guessed at—the men who whispered in the little cafés of Berne and Geneva were as likely to be diamond salesmen or commercial travellers. However, no one had missed the long trains of blinded or one-legged men, or dying trunks, that crossed each other between the bright lakes of Constance and Neuchâtel. In the beer-halls and shop-windows were bright posters presenting the Swiss defending their frontiers in 1914—with inspiring ferocity young men and old men glared down from the mountains at phantom French and Germans; the purpose was to assure the Swiss heart that it had shared the contagious glory of those days. As the massacre continued the posters withered away, and no country was more surprised than its sister republic when the United States bungled its way into the war.

Doctor Diver had seen around the edges of the war by that time: he was an Oxford Rhodes Scholar from Connecticut in 1914. He returned home for a final year at Johns Hopkins, and took his degree. In 1916 he managed to get to Vienna under the impression

3

that, if he did not make haste, the great Freud would eventually succumb to an airplane bomb. Even then Vienna was old with death, but Dick managed to get enough coal and oil to sit in his room in the Damenstiftgasse and write the pamphlets that he later destroyed, but that, rewritten, were the backbone of the book he published in Zurich in 1920.

Most of us have a favorite, a heroic period in our lives and that was Dick Diver's. For one thing he had no idea that he was charming, that the affection he gave and inspired was anything unusual among healthy people. In his last year at New Haven someone referred to him as "lucky Dick"—the name lingered in his head.

"Lucky Dick, you big stiff," he would whisper to himself, walking around the last sticks of flame in his room. "You hit it, my boy. Nobody knew it was there before you came along."

At the beginning of 1917, when it was becoming difficult to find coal, Dick burned for fuel almost a hundred textbooks that he had accumulated; but only, as he laid each one on the fire, with an assurance chuckling inside him that he was himself a digest of what was within the book, that he could brief it five years from now, if it deserved to be briefed. This went on at any odd hour, if necessary, with a floor rug over his shoulders, with the fine quiet of the scholar which is nearest of all things to heavenly peace—but which, as will presently be told, had to end.

For its temporary continuance he thanked his body that had done the flying rings at New Haven, and now swam in the winter Danube. With Elkins, second secretary at the Embassy, he shared an apartment, and there were two nice girl visitors—which was that and not too much of it, nor too much of the Embassy either. His contact with Ed Elkins aroused in him a first faint doubt as to the quality of his mental processes; he could not feel that they were profoundly different from the thinking of Elkins—Elkins, who would name you all the quarterbacks at New Haven for thirty years.

"—And Lucky Dick can't be one of these clever men; he must be less intact, even faintly destroyed. If life won't do it for him it's not a substitute to get a disease, or a broken heart, or an inferiority complex, though it'd be nice to build out some broken side till it was better than the original structure."

He mocked at his reasoning, calling it specious and "American"

—his criterion of uncerebral phrase-making was that it was American. He knew, though, that the price of his intactness was incompleteness.

"The best I can wish you, my child," so said the Fairy Blackstick in Thackeray's *The Rose and the Ring,* "is a little misfortune."

In some moods he griped at his own reasoning: Could I help it that Pete Livingstone sat in the locker-room Tap Day when everybody looked all over hell for him? And I got an election when otherwise I wouldn't have got Elihu, knowing so few men. He was good and right and I ought to have sat in the locker-room instead. Maybe I would, if I'd thought I had a chance at an election. But Mercer kept coming to my room all those weeks. I guess I knew I had a chance all right, all right. But it would have served me right if I'd swallowed my pin in the shower and set up a conflict.

After the lectures at the university he used to argue this point with a young Rumanian intellectual who reassured him: "There's no evidence that Goethe ever had a 'conflict' in the modern sense, or a man like Jung, for instance. You're not a romantic philosopher —you're a scientist. Memory, force, character—especially good sense. That's going to be your trouble—judgment about yourself. Once I knew a man who worked two years on the brain of an armadillo, with the idea that he would sooner or later know more about the brain of an armadillo than anyone. I kept arguing with him that he was not really pushing out the extension of the human range— it was too arbitrary. And sure enough, when he sent his work to the medical journal they refused it—they had just accepted a thesis by another man on the same subject. No good sense."

Dick got up to Zurich on fewer Achilles' heels than would be required to equip a centipede, but with plenty—the illusions of eternal strength and health, and of the essential goodness of people— they were the illusions of a nation, the lies of generations of frontier mothers who had to croon falsely that there were no wolves outside the cabin door. After he took his degree, he received his orders to join a neurological unit forming in Bar-sur-Aube. In France, to his disgust, the work was executive rather than practical. In compensation he found time to complete the short textbook and assemble the material for his next venture. He returned to Zurich in the spring of 1919 discharged.

The foregoing has the ring of a biography, without the satisfaction of knowing that the hero, like Grant, lolling in his general store in Galena, is ready to be called to an intricate destiny. Best to be reassuring—Dick Diver's moment now began.

CHAPTER II

IT WAS A DAMP April day, with long diagonal clouds over the Albishorn and water inert in the low places. Zurich is not unlike an American city. Missing something ever since his arrival two days before, Dick perceived that it was the sense he had had in finite French lanes that there was nothing more. In Zurich there was a lot besides Zurich—the roofs upled the eyes to tinkling cow pastures, which in turn modified hilltops further up—so life was a perpendicular starting off to a postcard heaven. The Alpine lands, home of the toy and the funicular, the merry-go-round and the thin chime, were not a being *here,* as in France, with French vines growing over one's feet on the ground.

In Salzburg once Dick had felt the superimposed quality of a bought and borrowed century of music; once in the laboratories of the university in Zurich, delicately poking at the cortex of a brain, he had felt like a toy-maker rather than like the tornado who had hurried through the old red buildings of Hopkins, two years before, unstayed by the irony of the gigantic Christ in the entrance hall.

Yet he had decided to remain another two years in Zurich, for he did not underestimate the value of toy-making, of infinite precision, of infinite patience.

Today he went out to see Franz Gregorovius at Dohmler's clinic on the Zurichsee. Franz, resident pathologist at the clinic, a Vaudois by birth, a few years older than Dick, met him at the tram stop. He had a dark and magnificent aspect of Cagliostro about him, contrasted with holy eyes; he was the third of the Gregoroviuses—his grandfather had instructed Kraepelin when psychiatry was just emerging from the darkness of all time. In personality he was proud, fiery, and sheeplike—he fancied himself as a hypnotist. Though the original genius of the family had grown a little tired, Franz would without doubt become a fine clinician.

7

On the way to the clinic he said: "Tell me of your experiences in the war. Are you changed like the rest? You are still a carrot top. You have the same unaging American face."

"I didn't see any of the war," Dick said. "You must have gathered that from my letters, Franz."

"That doesn't matter—we have some shell-shocks who merely heard an air raid from a distance. We have a few who merely read newspapers."

"It sounds like nonsense to me."

"Maybe it is, Dick. But, we're a rich person's clinic—we don't use the word nonsense. Frankly, did you come down to see me or to see that girl?"

They looked sideways at each other; Franz smiled enigmatically.

"Naturally I saw all the first letters," he said in his official basso. "When the change began, delicacy prevented me from opening any more. Really it had become your case."

"Then she's well?" Dick demanded.

"Perfectly well. I have charge of her, in fact I have charge of the majority of the English and American patients. They call me Doctor Gregory."

"Let me explain about that girl," Dick said. "I only saw her one time, that's a fact. When I came out to say good-by to you just before I went over to France. It was the first time I put on my uniform and I felt very bogus in it—went around saluting privates and all that."

"Why didn't you wear it today?"

"Hey! I've been discharged three weeks. Here's the way I happened to see that girl. When I left you I walked down toward that building of yours on the lake to get my bicycle——"

"Toward the Cedars?"

"—a wonderful night, you know, moon over that mountain——"

"The Krenzegg."

"—I caught up with a nurse and a young girl. I didn't think the girl was a patient; I asked the nurse about tram times and we walked along. The girl was about the prettiest thing I ever saw."

"She still is."

"She'd never seen an American uniform and we talked, and I didn't think anything about it." He broke off, recognizing a familiar perspective, and then resumed: "Except, Franz, I'm not as hard-boiled as you are—yet; when I see a beautiful shell like that I can't help feeling a regret about what's inside it. That was absolutely all—till the letters began to come."

"It was the best thing that could have happened to her," said Franz dramatically, "a transference of the most fortuitous kind. That's why I came down to meet you on a very busy day. I want you to come into my office and talk a long time before you see her. In fact, I sent her into Zurich to do errands." His voice was tense with enthusiasm. "In fact, I sent her without a nurse, with a less stable patient. I'm intensely proud of this case, which I handled, with your accidental assistance."

The car had followed the shore of the Zurichsee into a fertile region of pasture farms and low hills, steepled with châlets. The sun swam out into a blue sea of sky and suddenly it was a Swiss valley at its best—pleasant sounds and murmurs and a good fresh smell of health and cheer.

Professor Dohmler's plant consisted of three old buildings and a pair of new ones, between a slight plateau and the shore of the lake. At its founding, ten years before, it had been the first modern clinic for mental illness; at a casual glance no layman would recognize it as a refuge for the broken, the incomplete, the menacing, of this world, though two buildings were surrounded with vine-softened walls of a deceptive height. Outside, some men raked straw in the sunshine; here and there, as one rode into the grounds, the car passed the white flag of a nurse waving beside a patient on a path.

After conducting Dick to his office, Franz excused himself for half an hour. Left alone Dick wandered about the room and tried to reconstruct Franz from the litter of his desk, from his books and the books of and by his father and grandfather; from the Swiss piety of a huge claret-colored photo of the former on the wall. There was smoke in the room. Pushing open a French window, Dick let in a cone of sunshine. Suddenly his thoughts swung to the patient, the girl.

He had received about fifty letters from her written over a period of eight months. The first was apologetic, explaining that she had heard from America how girls wrote to soldiers whom they did not know. She had obtained the name and address from Doctor Gregory

and she hoped he would not mind if she sometimes sent word
to wish him well, etc., etc.

So far it was easy to recognize the tone—from *Daddy-Long-Legs*
and *Molly Make-Believe,* sprightly and sentimental epistolary col-
lections enjoying a vogue in the States. But there the resemblance
ended.

The letters were divided into two classes, of which the first class,
up to about the armistice, was of a marked pathological turn, and
of which the second class, running from there up to the present,
was entirely normal and displayed a richly maturing nature. For
these latter letters Dick had come to wait eagerly in the last dull
months at Bar-sur-Aube—yet even from the first letters he had
pieced together more than Franz would have guessed of the story.

MON CAPITAINE:

I thought when I saw you in your uniform you were so handsome.
Then I thought Je m'en fiche French too and German. You thought
I was pretty too but I've had that before and a long time I've stood it.
If you come here again with that attitude base and criminal and not
even faintly what I had been taught to associate with the rôle of gentle-
man then heaven help you. However, you seem quieter than the others,

[page] 2—

all soft like a big cat. I have only gotten to like boys who are rather
sissies. Are you a sissy? There were some somewhere.

Excuse all this, it is the third letter I have written you and will send
immediately or will never send. I've thought a lot about moonlight too,
and there are many witnesses I could find if I could only be out of here.

3—

They said you were a doctor, but so long as you are a cat it is different. My head aches so, so excuse this walking there like an ordinary
with a white cat will explain, I think. I can speak three languages, four
with English, and am sure I could be useful interpreting if you arrange
such thing in France I'm sure I could control everything with the belts
all bound around everybody like it was Wednesday. It is now Saturday

4—

and you are far away, perhaps killed.

Come back to me some day, for I will be here always on this green hill. Unless they will let me write my father, whom I loved dearly. Excuse this. I am not myself today. I will write when I feel better.

Cheerio

NICOLE WARREN.

Excuse all this.

CAPTAIN DIVER:

I know introspection is not good for a highly nervous state like mine, but I would like you to know where I stand. Last year or whenever it was in Chicago when I got so I couldn't speak to servants or walk in the street I kept waiting for someone to tell me. It was the duty of someone who understood. The blind must be led. Only no one would tell me everything—they would just tell me half and I was already too muddled to put two and two together. One man was nice—he was a French officer and he understood. He gave me a flower and said it was

[page] 2—

"plus petite et moins entendue." We were friends. Then he took it away. I grew sicker and there was no one to explain to me. They had a song about Joan of Arc that they used to sing at me but that was just mean—it would just make me cry, for there was nothing the matter with my head then. They kept making reference to sports, too, but I didn't care by that time. So there was that day I went walking on Michigan Boulevard on and on for miles and finally they followed me in an

3—

automobile, but I wouldn't get in. Finally they pulled me in and there were nurses. After that time I began to realize it all, because I could feel what was happening in others. So you see how I stand. And what good can it be for me to stay here with the doctors harping constantly on the things I was here to get over. So today I have written my father to come

4—

and take me away. I am glad you are so interested in examining people and sending them back. It must be so much fun.

And again, from another letter:

You might pass up your next examination and write me a letter. They just sent me some phonograph records in case I should forget my lesson and I broke them all so the nurse won't speak to me. They were in

English, so that the nurses would not understand. One doctor in Chicago said I was bluffing, but what he really meant was that I was a twin six and he had never seen one before. But I was very busy being mad then, so I didn't care what he said, when I am very busy being mad I don't usually care what they say, not if I were a million girls.

You told me that night you'd teach me to play. Well, I think love

[page] 2—

is all there is or should be. Anyhow I am glad your interest in examinations keeps you busy.

Tout à vous,

NICOLE WARREN.

There were other letters among whose helpless cæsuras lurked darker rhythms.

DEAR CAPTAIN DIVER:

I write to you because there is no one else to whom I can turn and it seems to me if this farcicle situation is apparent to one as sick as me it should be apparent to you. The mental trouble is all over and besides that I am completely broken and humiliated, if that was what they wanted. My family have shamefully neglected me, there's no use asking them for help or pity. I have had enough and it is simply ruining my

[page] 2—

health and wasting my time pretending that what is the matter with my head is curable.

Here I am in what appears to be a semi-insane-asylum, all because nobody saw fit to tell me the truth about anything. If I had only known what was going on like I know now I could have stood it I guess for I am pretty strong, but those who should have, did not see fit to en-

3—

lighten me. And now, when I know and have paid such a price for knowing, they sit there with their dogs lives and say I should believe what I did believe. Especially one does but I know now.

I am lonesome all the time far away from friends and family across the Atlantic I roam all over the place in a half daze. If you could get

4—

me a position as interpreter (I know French and German like a native,

fair Italian and a little Spanish) or in the Red Cross Ambulance or as
a train nurse, though I would have to train you would prove a great
blessing.

And again:

Since you will not accept my explanation of what is the matter you
could at least explain to me what you think, because you have a kind
cat's face, and not that funny look that seems to be so fashionable here.
Dr. Gregory gave me a snapshot of you, not as handsome as you are
in your uniform, but younger looking.

MON CAPITAINE:

It was fine to have your postcard. I am so glad you take such interest
in disqualifying nurses—oh, I understood your note very well indeed.
Only I thought from the moment I met you that you were different.

DEAR CAPITAINE:

I think one thing today and another tomorrow. That is really all that's
the matter with me, except a crazy defiance and a lack of proportion.
I would gladly welcome any alienist you might suggest. Here they lie
in their bath tubs and sing Play in Your Own Backyard as if I had my
backyard to play in or any hope which I can find by looking either

[page] 2—

backward or forward. They tried it again in the candy store again
and I almost hit the man with the weight, but they held me.
I am not going to write you any more. I am too unstable.

And then a month with no letters. And then suddenly the change.

—I am slowly coming back to life. . . .
—Today the flowers and the clouds. . . .
—The war is over and I scarcely knew there was a war. . . .
—How kind you have been! You must be very wise behind your face
like a white cat, except you don't look like that in the picture Dr.
Gregory gave me. . . .
—Today I went to Zurich, how strange a feeling to see a city again.
—Today we went to Berne, it was so nice with the clocks.
—Today we climbed high enough to find asphodel and edelweiss. . . .

After that the letters were fewer, but he answered them all. There
was one:

I wish someone were in love with me like boys were ages ago before I was sick. I suppose it will be years, though, before I could think of anything like that.

But when Dick's answer was delayed for any reason, there was a fluttering burst of worry—like a worry of a lover: "Perhaps I have bored you," and "Afraid I have presumed," and "I keep thinking at night you have been sick."

In actuality Dick was sick with the flu. When he recovered, all except the formal part of his correspondence was sacrificed to the consequent fatigue, and shortly afterward the memory of her became overlaid by the vivid presence of a Wisconsin telephone girl at headquarters in Bar-sur-Aube. She was red-lipped like a poster, and known obscenely in the messes as "The Switchboard."

Franz came back into his office feeling self-important. Dick thought he would probably be a fine clinician, for the sonorous or staccato cadences by which he disciplined nurse or patient came not from his nervous system, but from a tremendous and harmless vanity. His true emotions were more ordered and kept to himself.

"Now about the girl, Dick," he said. "Of course, I want to find out about you and tell you about myself, but first about the girl, because I have been waiting to tell you about it so long."

He searched for and found a sheaf of papers in a filing cabinet, but after shuffling through them he found they were in his way and put them on his desk. Instead he told Dick the story.

CHAPTER III

ABOUT A YEAR AND a half before, Doctor Dohmler had some vague correspondence with an American gentleman living in Lausanne, a Mr. Devereux Warren, of the Warren family of Chicago. A meeting was arranged and one day Mr. Warren arrived at the clinic with his daughter Nicole, a girl of sixteen. She was obviously not well and the nurse who was with her took her to walk about the grounds while Mr. Warren had his consultation.

Warren was a strikingly handsome man looking less than forty. He was a fine American type in every way, tall, broad, well-made —"un homme très chic," as Doctor Dohmler described him to Franz. His large gray eyes were sun-veined from rowing on Lake Geneva, and he had that special air about him of having known the best of this world. The conversation was in German, for it developed that he had been educated in Göttingen. He was nervous and obviously very moved by his errand.

"Doctor Dohmler, my daughter isn't right in the head. I've had lots of specialists and nurses for her and she's taken a couple of rest cures, but the thing has grown too big for me and I've been strongly recommended to come to you."

"Very well," said Doctor Dohmler. "Suppose you start at the beginning and tell me everything."

"There isn't any beginning, at least there isn't any insanity in the family that I know of, on either side. Nicole's mother died when she was twelve and I've sort of been father and mother both to her, with the help of governesses—father and mother both to her."

He was very moved as he said this. Doctor Dohmler saw that there were tears in the corners of his eyes and noticed for the first time that there was whiskey on his breath.

"As a child she was a darling thing—everybody was crazy about her, everybody that came in contact with her. She was smart as a

15

whip and happy as the day is long. She liked to read or draw or dance or play the piano—anything. I used to hear my wife say she was the only one of our children who never cried at night. I've got an older girl, too, and there was a boy that died, but Nicole was —Nicole was—Nicole——"

He broke off and Doctor Dohmler helped him.

"She was a perfectly normal, bright, happy child."

"Perfectly."

Doctor Dohmler waited. Mr. Warren shook his head, blew a long sigh, glanced quickly at Doctor Dohmler and then at the floor again.

"About eight months ago, or maybe it was six months ago or maybe ten—I try to figure but I can't remember exactly where we were when she began to do funny things—crazy things. Her sister was the first one to say anything to me about it—because Nicole was always the same to me," he added rather hastily, as if someone had accused him of being to blame, "—the same loving little girl. The first thing was about a valet."

"Oh, yes," said Doctor Dohmler, nodding his venerable head, as if, like Sherlock Holmes, he had expected a valet and only a valet to be introduced at this point.

"I had a valet—been with me for years—Swiss, by the way." He looked up for Doctor Dohmler's patriotic approval. "And she got some crazy idea about him. She thought he was making up to her —of course, at the time I believed her and I let him go, but I know now it was all nonsense."

"What did she claim he had done?"

"That was the first thing—the doctors couldn't pin her down. She just looked at them as if they ought to know what he'd done. But she certainly meant he'd made some kind of indecent advances to her—she didn't leave us in any doubt of that."

"I see."

"Of course, I've read about women getting lonesome and thinking there's a man under the bed and all that, but why should Nicole get such an idea? She could have all the young men she wanted. We were in Lake Forest—that's a summer place near Chicago where we have a place—and she was out all day playing golf or tennis with boys. And some of them pretty gone on her at that."

All the time Warren was talking to the dried old package of

Doctor Dohmler, one section of the latter's mind kept thinking intermittently of Chicago. Once in his youth he could have gone to Chicago as fellow and docent at the university, and perhaps become rich there and owned his own clinic instead of being only a minor shareholder in a clinic. When he had thought of what he considered his own thin knowledge spread over that whole area, over all those wheat fields, those endless prairies, he had decided against it. But he had read about Chicago in those days, about the great feudal families of Armour, Palmer, Field, Crane, Warren, Swift, and McCormick and many others, and since that time not a few patients had come to him from that stratum of Chicago and New York.

"She got worse," continued Warren. "She had a fit or something —the things she said got crazier and crazier. Her sister wrote some of them down—" He handed a much-folded piece of paper to the doctor. "Almost always about men going to attack her, men she knew or men on the street, anybody——"

He told of their alarm and distress, of the horrors families go through under such circumstances, of the ineffectual efforts they had made in America, finally of the faith in a change of scene that had made him run the submarine blockade and bring his daughter to Switzerland.

"—on a United States cruiser," he specified with a touch of hauteur. "It was possible for me to arrange that, by a stroke of luck. And, may I add," he smiled apologetically, "that as they say: money is no object."

"Certainly not," agreed Dohmler dryly.

He was wondering why and about what the man was lying to him. Or, if he was wrong about that, what was ᴛhe falsity that pervaded the whole room, the handsome figure in tweeds sprawling in his chair with a sportsman's ease? That was a tragedy out there, in the February day, the young bird with wings crushed somehow, and inside here it was all too thin, thin and wrong.

"I would like—to talk to her—a few minutes now," said Doctor Dohmler, going into English as if it would bring him closer to Warren.

Afterward when Warren had left his daughter and returned to Lausanne, and several days had passed, the doctor and Franz entered upon Nicole's card:

Diagnostic: Schizophrénie. Phase aiguë en décroissance. La peur des hommes est un symptôme de la maladie, et n'est point constitutionnelle. . . . Le pronostic doit rester réservé.*

And then they waited with increasing interest as the days passed for Mr. Warren's promised second visit.

It was slow in coming. After a fortnight Doctor Dohmler wrote. Confronted with further silence he committed what was for those days "une folie," and telephoned to the Grand Hotel at Vevey. He learned from Mr. Warren's valet that he was at the moment packing to sail for America. But reminded that the forty francs Swiss for the call would show up on the clinic books, the blood of the Tuileries Guard rose to Doctor Dohmler's aid and Mr. Warren was got to the phone.

"It is—absolutely necessary—that you come. Your daughter's health —all depends. I can take no responsibility."

"But look here, Doctor, that's just what you're for. I have a hurry call to go home!"

Doctor Dohmler had never yet spoken to anyone so far away, but he dispatched his ultimatum so firmly into the phone that the agonized American at the other end yielded. Half an hour after this second arrival on the Zurichsee, Warren had broken down, his fine shoulders shaking with awful sobs inside his easy-fitting coat, his eyes redder than the very sun on Lake Geneva, and they had the awful story.

"It just happened," he said hoarsely. "I don't know—I don't know.

"After her mother died when she was little she used to come into my bed every morning, sometimes she'd sleep in my bed. I was sorry for the little thing. Oh, after that, whenever we went places in an automobile or a train we used to hold hands. She used to sing to me. We used to say, 'Now let's not pay any attention to anybody else this afternoon—let's just have each other—for this morning you're mine.'" A broken sarcasm came into his voice. "People used to say what a wonderful father and daughter we were—they used to wipe their eyes. We were just like lovers—and then all at once we were lovers—and ten minutes after it happened I could have shot myself

*Diagnosis: Divided Personality. Acute and down-hill phase of the illness. The fear of men is a symptom of the illness and is not at all constitutional. . . . The prognosis must be reserved.

—except I guess I'm such a God-damned degenerate I didn't have the nerve to do it."

"Then what?" said Doctor Dohmler, thinking again of Chicago and of a mild pale gentleman with a pince-nez who had looked him over in Zurich thirty years before. "Did this thing go on?"

"Oh, no! She almost—she seemed to freeze up right away. She'd just say, 'Never mind, never mind, Daddy. It doesn't matter. Never mind.'"

"There were no consequences?"

"No." He gave one short convulsive sob and blew his nose several times. "Except now there're plenty of consequences."

As the story concluded Dohmler sat back in the focal armchair of the middle class and said to himself sharply, "Peasant!"—it was one of the few absolute worldly judgments that he had permitted himself for twenty years. Then he said:

"I would like for you to go to a hotel in Zurich and spend the night and come see me in the morning."

"And then what?"

Doctor Dohmler spread his hands wide enough to carry a young pig.

"Chicago," he suggested.

CHAPTER IV

"THEN WE KNEW WHERE we stood," said Franz. "Dohmler told Warren we would take the case if he would agree to keep away from his daughter indefinitely, with an absolute minimum of five years. After Warren's first collapse, he seemed chiefly concerned as to whether the story would ever leak back to America.

"We mapped out a routine for her and waited. The prognosis was bad—as you know, the percentage of cures, even so-called social cures, is very low at that age."

"These first letters looked bad," agreed Dick.

"Very bad—very typical. I hesitated about letting the first one get out of the clinic. Then I thought it will be good for Dick to know we're carrying on here. It was generous of you to answer them."

Dick sighed. "She was such a pretty thing—she enclosed a lot of snapshots of herself. And for a month there I didn't have anything to do. All I said in my letters was 'Be a good girl and mind the doctors.'"

"That was enough—it gave her somebody to think of outside. For a while she didn't have anybody—only one sister that she doesn't seem very close to. Besides, reading her letters helped us here—they were a measure of her condition."

"I'm glad."

"You see now what happened? She felt complicity—that's neither here nor there, except as we want to revalue her ultimate stability and strength of character. First came this shock. Then she went off to a boarding-school and heard the girls talking—so from sheer self-protection she developed the idea that she had had no complicity —and from there it was easy to slide into a phantom world where all men, the more you liked them and trusted them, the more evil——"

"Did she ever go into the—horror directly?"

"No, and as a matter of fact when she began to seem normal, about October, we were in a predicament. If she had been thirty years old we would have let her make her own adjustment, but she was so young we were afraid she might harden with it all twisted inside her. So Doctor Dohmler said to her frankly, 'Your duty now is to yourself. This doesn't by any account mean the end of anything for you—your life is just at its beginning,' and so forth and so forth. She really has an excellent mind, so he gave her a little Freud to read, not too much, and she was very interested. In fact, we've made rather a pet of her around here. But she is reticent," he added; he hesitated: "We have wondered if in her recent letters to you which she mailed herself from Zurich, she has said anything that would be illuminating about her state of mind and her plans for the future."

Dick considered.

"Yes and no—I'll bring the letters out here if you want. She seems hopeful and normally hungry for life—even rather romantic. Sometimes she speaks of 'the past' as people speak who have been in prison. But you never know whether they refer to the crime or the imprisonment or the whole experience. After all I'm only a sort of stuffed figure in her life."

"Of course, I understand your position exactly, and I express our gratitude once again. That was why I wanted to see you before you see her."

Dick laughed.

"You think she's going to make a flying leap at my person?"

"No, not that. But I want to ask you to go very gently. You are attractive to women, Dick."

"Then God help me! Well, I'll be gentle and repulsive—I'll chew garlic whenever I'm going to see her and wear a stubble beard. I'll drive her to cover."

"Not garlic!" said Franz, taking him seriously. "You don't want to compromise your career. But you're partly joking."

"—and I can limp a little. And there's no real bathtub where I'm living, anyhow."

"You're entirely joking," Franz relaxed—or rather assumed the posture of one relaxed. "Now tell me about yourself and your plans."

"I've only got one, Franz, and that's to be a good psychologist—maybe to be the greatest one that ever lived."

Franz laughed pleasantly, but he saw that this time Dick wasn't joking.

"That's very good—and very American," he said. "It's more difficult for us." He got up and went to the French window. "I stand here and I see Zurich—there is the steeple of the Gross-Münster. In its vault my grandfather is buried. Across the bridge from it lies my ancestor Lavater, who would not be buried in any church. Nearby is the statue of another ancestor, Heinrich Pestalozzi, and one of Doctor Alfred Escher. And over everything there is always Zwingli—I am continually confronted with a pantheon of heroes."

"Yes, I see." Dick got up. "I was only talking big. Everything's just starting over. Most of the Americans in France are frantic to get home, but not me—I draw military pay all the rest of the year if I only attend lectures at the university. How's that for a government on the grand scale that knows its future great men? Then I'm going home for a month and see my father. Then I'm coming back—I've been offered a job."

"Where?"

"Your rivals—Gisler's clinic at Interlaken."

"Don't touch it," Franz advised him. "They've had a dozen young men there in a year. Gisler's a manic-depressive himself, his wife and her lover run the clinic—of course, you understand that's confidential."

"How about your old scheme for America?" asked Dick lightly. "We were going to New York and start an up-to-date establishment for billionaires."

"That was students' talk."

Dick dined with Franz and his bride and a small dog with a smell of burning rubber, in their cottage on the edge of the grounds. He felt vaguely oppressed, not by the atmosphere of modest retrenchment, nor by Frau Gregorovius, who might have been prophesied, but by the sudden contracting of horizon, to which Franz seemed so reconciled. For him the boundaries of asceticism were differently marked—he could see it as a means to an end, even as a carrying on with a glory it would itself supply, but it was hard to think of deliberately cutting life down to the scale of an inherited suit. The domestic gestures of Franz and his wife as they turned in a cramped space lacked grace and adventure. The post-war months in France, and the lavish liquidations taking place under the ægis of American splendor, had affected Dick's outlook. Also, men and women had made much of him, and perhaps what had brought him back to the center of the great Swiss watch was an intuition that this was not too good for a serious man.

He made Kaethe Gregorovius feel charming, meanwhile becoming increasingly restless at the all-pervading cauliflower—simultaneously hating himself, too, for this incipience of he knew not what superficiality.

"God, am I like the rest after all?"—so he used to think starting awake at night—"Am I like the rest?"

This was poor material for a socialist but good material for those who do much of the world's rarest work. The truth was that for some months he had been going through that partitioning of the things of youth wherein it is decided whether or not to die for what one no longer believes. In the dead white hours in Zurich staring into a stranger's pantry across the upshine of a street-lamp, he used to think that he wanted to be good, he wanted to be kind, he wanted to be brave and wise, but it was all pretty difficult. He wanted to be loved, too, if he could fit it in.

CHAPTER V

THE VERANDA OF THE central building was illuminated from open French windows, save where the black shadows of stripling walls and the fantastic shadows of iron chairs slithered down into a gladiolus bed. From the figures that shuffled between the rooms Miss Warren emerged first in glimpses and then sharply when she saw him; as she crossed the threshold her face caught the room's last light and brought it outside with her. She walked to a rhythm —all that week there had been singing in her ears, summer songs of ardent skies and wild shade, and with his arrival the singing had become so loud she could have joined in with it.

"How do you do, Captain," she said, unfastening her eyes from his with difficulty, as though they had become entangled. "Shall we sit out here?" She stood still, her glance moving about for a moment. "It's summer practically."

A woman had followed her out, a dumpy woman in a shawl, and Nicole presented Dick: "Señora ——"

Franz excused himself and Dick grouped three chairs together.

"The lovely night," the Señora said.

"Muy bella," agreed Nicole; then to Dick, "Are you here for a long time?"

"I'm in Zurich for a long time, if that's what you mean."

"This is really the first night of real spring," the Señora suggested.

"To stay?"

"At least till July."

"I'm leaving in June."

"June is a lovely month here," the Señora commented. "You should stay for June and then leave in July when it gets really too hot."

"You're going where?" Dick asked Nicole.

"Somewhere with my sister—somewhere exciting, I hope, because

24

I've lost so much time. But perhaps they'll think I ought to go to a quiet place at first—perhaps Como. Why don't you come to Como?"

"Ah, Como—" began the Señora.

Within the building a trio broke into Suppé's "Light Cavalry." Nicole took advantage of this to stand up and the impression of her youth and beauty grew on Dick until it welled up inside him in a compact paroxysm of emotion. She smiled, a moving childish smile that was like all the lost youth in the world.

"The music's too loud to talk against—suppose we walk around. Buenas noches, Señora."

"G't night—g't night."

They went down two steps to the path, where, in a moment, a shadow cut across it—she took his arm.

"I have some phonograph records my sister sent me from America," she said. "Next time you come here I'll play them for you—I know a place to put the phonograph where no one can hear."

"That'll be nice."

"Do you know 'Hindustan'?" she asked wistfully. "I'd never heard it before, but I like it. And I've got 'Why Do They Call Them Babies?' and 'I'm Glad I Can Make You Cry.' I suppose you've danced to all those tunes in Paris?"

"I haven't been to Paris."

Her cream-colored dress, alternately blue or gray as they walked, and her very blonde hair, dazzled Dick—whenever he turned toward her she was smiling a little, her face lighting up like an angel's when they came into the range of a roadside arc. She thanked him for everything, rather as if he had taken her to some party, and as Dick became less and less certain of his relation to her, her confidence increased—there was that excitement about her that seemed to reflect all the excitement of the world.

"I'm not under any restraint at all," she said. "I'll play you two good tunes called 'Wait Till the Cows Come Home' and 'Good-by, Alexander.'"

He was late the next time, a week later, and Nicole was waiting for him at a point in the path which he would pass walking from Franz's house. Her hair, drawn back of her ears, brushed her shoulders in such a way that the face seemed to have just emerged from

it, as if this were the exact moment when she was coming from
a wood into clear moonlight. The unknown yielded her up; Dick
wished she had no background, that she was just a girl lost with no
address save the night from which she had come. They went to the
cache where she had left the phonograph, turned a corner by the
workshop, climbed a rock, and sat down behind a low wall, facing
miles and miles of rolling night.

They were in America now; even Franz with his conception of
Dick as an irresistible Lothario would never have guessed that they
had gone so far away. They were so sorry, dear; they went down to
meet each other in a taxi, honey; they had preferences in smiles and
had met in Hindustan, and shortly afterward they must have quarrelled, for nobody knew and nobody seemed to care—yet finally one
of them had gone and left the other crying, only to feel blue, to
feel sad.

The thin tunes, holding lost times and future hopes in liaison,
twisted upon the Valais night. In the lulls of the phonograph a
cricket held the scene together with a single note. By and by Nicole
stopped playing the machine and sang to him.

> *"Lay a silver dollar*
> *On the ground*
> *And watch it roll*
> *Because it's round——"*

On the pure parting of her lips no breath hovered. Dick stood
up suddenly.

"What's the matter, you don't like it?"

"Of course I do."

"Our cook at home taught it to me:

> *"A woman never knows*
> *What a good man she's got*
> *Till after she turns him down——"*

"You like it?"

She smiled at him, making sure that the smile gathered up everything inside her, and directed it toward him, making him a profound promise of herself for so little, for the beat of a response, the

assurance of a complementary vibration in him. Minute by minute the sweetness drained down into her out of the willow trees, out of the dark world.

She stood up and, stumbling over the phonograph, was momentarily against him, leaning into the hollow of his rounded shoulder —then apart.

"I've got one more record.—Have you heard 'So Long, Letty'? I suppose you have."

"Honestly, you don't understand—I haven't heard a thing."

Nor known, nor smelt, nor tasted, he might have added; only hot-cheeked girls in hot secret rooms. The young maidens he had known at New Haven in 1914 kissed men, saying "There!" hands at the man's chest to push him away. Now there was this scarcely saved waif of disaster bringing him the essence of a continent. . . .

CHAPTER VI

IT WAS MAY WHEN he next found her. The luncheon in Zurich was a council of caution; obviously the logic of his life tended away from the girl; yet when a stranger stared at her from a nearby table, male eyes burning disturbingly like an uncharted light, he turned to the man with an urbane version of intimidation and broke the regard.

"He was just a peeper," he explained cheerfully. "He was just looking at your clothes. Why do you have so many different clothes?"

"Sister says we're very rich," she offered humbly. "Since Grandmother is dead."

"I forgive you."

He was enough older than Nicole to take pleasure in her youthful vanities and delights, the way she paused fractionally in front of the hall mirror on leaving the restaurant, so that the incorruptible quicksilver could give her back to herself. He delighted in her stretching out her hands to new octaves now that she found herself beautiful and rich. He tried honestly to divorce her from any obsessions that he had stitched her together—glad to see her build up happiness and confidence apart from him; the difficulty was that, eventually, Nicole brought everything to his feet, gifts of sacrificial ambrosia, of worshipping myrtle.

The first week of summer found Dick re-established in Zurich. He had arranged his pamphlets and what work he had done in the army into a pattern from which he intended to make his revision of "A Psychology for Psychiatrists." He thought he had a publisher; he had established contact with a poor student who would iron out his errors in German. Franz considered it a rash business, but one day at luncheon Dick pointed out the disarming modesty of the theme.

28

"This is stuff I'll never know so well again," he insisted. "I have a hunch it's a thing that only fails to be basic because it's never had material recognition. The weakness of this profession is its attraction for the man a little crippled and broken. Within the walls of the profession he compensates by tending toward the clinical, the 'practical'—he has won his battle without a struggle.

"On the contrary, you are a good man, Franz, because fate selected you for your profession before you were born. You better thank God you had no 'bent'—I got to be a psychiatrist because there was a girl at St. Hilda's in Oxford that went to the same lectures. Maybe I'm getting trite but I don't want to let my current ideas slide away with a few dozen glasses of beer."

"All right," Franz answered. "You are an American. You can do this without professional harm. I do not like these generalities. Soon you will be writing little books called 'Deep Thoughts for the Layman,' so simplified that they are positively guaranteed not to cause thinking. If my father were alive he would look at you and grunt, Dick. He would take his napkin and fold it so, and hold his napkin ring, this very one"—he held it up, a boar's head was carved in the brown wood—"and he would say, 'Well, my impression is—' then he would look at you and think suddenly, 'What is the use?' then he would stop and grunt again; then we would be at the end of dinner."

"I am alone today," said Dick testily. "But I may not be alone tomorrow. After that I'll fold up my napkin like your father and grunt."

Franz waited a moment.

"How about our patient?" he asked.

"I don't know."

"Well, you should know about her by now."

"I like her. She's attractive. What do you want me to do—take her up in the edelweiss?"

"No, I thought since you go in for scientific books you might have an idea."

"—devote my life to her?"

Franz called his wife in the kitchen: "Du lieber Gott! Bitte, bringe Dick noch ein Glas Bier."

"I don't want any more if I've got to see Dohmler."

"We think it's best to have a program. Four weeks have passed away—apparently the girl is in love with you. That's not our business if we were in the world, but here in the clinic we have a stake in the matter."

"I'll do whatever Doctor Dohmler says," Dick agreed.

But he had little faith that Dohmler would throw much light on the matter; he himself was the incalculable element involved. By no conscious volition of his own, the thing had drifted into his hands. It reminded him of a scene in his childhood when everyone in the house was looking for the lost key to the silver closet, Dick knowing he had hid it under the handkerchiefs in his mother's top drawer; at that time he had experienced a philosophical detachment, and this was repeated now when he and Franz went together to Professor Dohmler's office.

The professor, his face beautiful under straight whiskers, like a vine-overgrown veranda of some fine old house, disarmed him. Dick knew some individuals with more talent, but no person of a class qualitatively superior to Dohmler.

—Six months later he thought the same way when he saw Dohmler dead, the light out on the veranda, the vines of his whiskers tickling his stiff white collar, the many battles that had swayed before the chink-like eyes stilled forever under the frail delicate lids——

". . . Good day, sir." He stood formally, thrown back to the army.

Professor Dohmler interlaced his tranquil fingers. Franz spoke in terms half of liaison officer, half of secretary, till his senior cut through him in mid-sentence.

"We have gone a certain way," he said mildly. "It's you, Doctor Diver, who can best help us now."

Routed out, Dick confessed: "I'm not so straight on it myself."

"I have nothing to do with your personal reactions," said Dohmler. "But I have much to do with the fact that this so-called 'transference' "—he darted a short ironic look at Franz, which the latter returned in kind—"must be terminated. Miss Nicole does well indeed, but she is in no condition to survive what she might interpret as a tragedy."

Again Franz began to speak, but Doctor Dohmler motioned him silent.

"I realize that your position has been difficult."

"Yes, it has."

Now the professor sat back and laughed, saying on the last syllable of his laughter, with his sharp little gray eyes shining through: "Perhaps you have got sentimentally involved yourself."

Aware that he was being drawn on, Dick, too, laughed.

"She's a pretty girl—anybody responds to that to a certain extent. I have no intention——"

Again Franz tried to speak—again Dohmler stopped him with a question directed pointedly at Dick. "Have you thought of going away?"

"I can't go away."

Doctor Dohmler turned to Franz: "Then we can send Miss Warren away."

"As you think best, Professor Dohmler," Dick conceded. "It's certainly a situation."

Professor Dohmler raised himself like a legless man mounting a pair of crutches.

"But it is a professional situation," he cried quietly.

He sighed himself back into his chair, waiting for the reverberating thunder to die out about the room. Dick saw that Dohmler had reached his climax, and he was not sure that he himself had survived it. When the thunder had diminished Franz managed to get his word in.

"Doctor Diver is a man of fine character," he said. "I feel he only has to appreciate the situation in order to deal correctly with it. In my opinion Dick can co-operate right here, without anyone going away."

"How do you feel about that?" Professor Dohmler asked Dick.

Dick felt churlish in the face of the situation; at the same time he realized in the silence after Dohmler's pronouncement that the state of inanimation could not be indefinitely prolonged; suddenly he spilled everything.

"I'm half in love with her—the question of marrying her has passed through my mind."

"Tch! Tch!" uttered Franz.

"Wait." Dohmler warned him. Franz refused to wait: "What! And devote half your life to being doctor and nurse and all—never!

I know what these cases are. One time in twenty it's finished in the first push—better never see her again!"

"What do you think?" Dohmler asked Dick.

"Of course Franz is right."

CHAPTER VII

IT WAS LATE AFTERNOON when they wound up the discussion as to what Dick should do: he must be most kind and yet eliminate himself. When the doctors stood up at last, Dick's eyes fell outside the window to where a light rain was falling—Nicole was waiting, expectant, somewhere in that rain. When presently he went out, buttoning his oil-skin at the throat, pulling down the brim of his hat, he came upon her immediately under the roof of the main entrance.

"I know a new place we can go," she said. "When I was ill I didn't mind sitting inside with the others in the evening—what they said seemed like everything else. Naturally now I see them as ill and it's—it's——"

"You'll be leaving soon."

"Oh, soon. My sister, Beth, but she's always been called Baby, she's coming in a few weeks to take me somewhere; after that I'll be back here for a last month."

"The older sister?"

"Oh, quite a bit older. She's twenty-four—she's very English. She lives in London with my father's sister. She was engaged to an Englishman but he was killed—I never saw him."

Her face, ivory gold against the blurred sunset that strove through the rain, had a promise Dick had never seen before: the high cheekbones, the faintly wan quality, cool rather than feverish, was reminiscent of the frame of a promising colt—a creature whose life did not promise to be only a projection of youth upon a grayer screen, but instead, a true growing; the face would be handsome in middle life; it would be handsome in old age: the essential structure and the economy were there.

"What are you looking at?"

"I was just thinking that you're going to be rather happy."

Nicole was frightened: "Am I? All right—things couldn't be worse than they have been."

In the covered woodshed to which she had led him, she sat cross-legged upon her golf shoes, her burberry wound about her and her cheeks stung alive by the damp air. Gravely she returned his gaze, taking in his somewhat proud carriage that never quite yielded to the wooden post against which he leaned; she looked into his face that always tried to discipline itself into molds of attentive serious-ness, after excursions into joys and mockeries of its own. That part of him which seemed to fit his reddish Irish coloring she knew least; she was afraid of it, yet more anxious to explore—this was his more masculine side: the other part, the trained part, the consideration in the polite eyes, she expropriated without question, as most women did.

"At least this institution has been good for languages," said Nicole. "I've spoken French with two doctors, and German with the nurses, and Italian, or something like it, with a couple of scrub-women and one of the patients, and I've picked up a lot of Spanish from another."

"That's fine."

He tried to arrange an attitude, but no logic seemed forthcoming.

"—Music too. Hope you didn't think I was only interested in ragtime. I practise every day—the last few months I've been taking a course in Zurich on the history of music. In fact is was all that kept me going at times—music and the drawing." She leaned sud-denly and twisted a loose strip from the sole of her shoe, and then looked up. "I'd like to draw you just the way you are now."

It made him sad when she brought out her accomplishments for his approval.

"I envy you. At present I don't seem to be interested in anything except my work."

"Oh, I think that's fine for a man," she said quickly. "But for a girl I think she ought to have lots of minor accomplishments and pass them on to her children."

"I suppose so," said Dick with deliberated indifference.

Nicole sat quiet. Dick wished she would speak so that he could play the easy rôle of wet blanket, but now she sat quiet.

"You're all well," he said. "Try to forget the past; don't overdo things for a year or so. Go back to America and be a débutante and fall in love—and be happy."

"I couldn't fall in love." Her injured shoe scraped a cocoon of must from the log on which she sat.

"Sure you can," Dick insisted. "Not for a year, maybe, but sooner or later." Then he added brutally: "You can have a perfectly normal life with a houseful of beautiful descendants. The very fact that you could make a complete comeback at your age proves that the precipitating factors were pretty near everything. Young woman, you'll be pulling your weight long after your friends are carried off screaming."

—But there was a look of pain in her eyes as she took the rough dose, the harsh reminder.

"I know I wouldn't be fit to marry anyone for a long time," she said humbly.

Dick was too upset to say any more. He looked out into the grain field trying to recover his hard brassy attitude.

"You'll be all right—everybody here believes in you. Why, Doctor Gregory is so proud of you that he'll probably——"

"I hate Doctor Gregory."

"Well, you shouldn't."

Nicole's world had fallen to pieces, but it was only a flimsy and scarcely created world; beneath it her emotions and instincts fought on. Was it an hour ago she had waited by the entrance, wearing her hope like a corsage at her belt?

. . . Dress stay crisp for him, button stay put, bloom narcissus—air stay still and sweet.

"It will be nice to have fun again," she fumbled on. For a moment she entertained a desperate idea of telling him how rich she was, what big houses she lived in, that really she was a valuable property—for a moment she made herself into her grandfather, Sid Warren, the horse-trader. But she survived the temptation to confuse all values and shut these matters into their Victorian side-chambers—even though there was no home left to her, save emptiness and pain.

"I have to go back to the clinic. It's not raining now."

Dick walked beside her, feeling her unhappiness, and wanting to drink the rain that touched her cheek.

"I have some new records," she said. "I can hardly wait to play them. Do you know——"

After supper that evening, Dick thought, he would finish the break; also he wanted to kick Franz's bottom for having partially introduced him to such a sordid business. He waited in the hall. His eyes followed a beret, not wet with waiting like Nicole's beret, but covering a skull recently operated on. Beneath it human eyes peered, found him and came over:

"Bonjour, Docteur."

"Bonjour, Monsieur."

"Il fait beau temps."

"Oui, merveilleux."

"Vous êtes ici maintenant?"

"Non, pour la journée seulement."

"Ah, bon. Alors—au revoir, Monsieur."

Glad at having survived another contact, the wretch in the beret moved away. Dick waited. Presently a nurse came downstairs and delivered him a message.

"Miss Warren asks to be excused, Doctor. She wants to lie down. She wants to have dinner upstairs tonight."

The nurse hung on his response, half expecting him to imply that Miss Warren's attitude was pathological.

"Oh, I see. Well—" He rearranged the flow of his own saliva, the pulse of his heart. "I hope she feels better. Thanks."

He was puzzled and discontent. At any rate it freed him.

Leaving a note for Franz begging off from supper, he walked through the countryside to the tram station. As he reached the platform, with spring twilight gilding the rails and the glass in the slot machines, he began to feel that the station, the hospital, was hovering between being centripetal and centrifugal. He felt frightened. He was glad when the substantial cobblestones of Zurich clicked once more under his shoes.

He expected to hear from Nicole next day, but there was no word. Wondering if she was ill, he called the clinic and talked to Franz.

"She came downstairs to luncheon yesterday and today," said Franz. "She seemed a little abstracted and in the clouds. How did it go off?"

Dick tried to plunge over the Alpine crevasse between the sexes.

"We didn't get to it—at least I didn't think we did. I tried to be distant, but I didn't think enough happened to change her attitude if it ever went deep."

Perhaps his vanity had been hurt that there was no coup de grâce to administer.

"From some things she said to her nurse I'm inclined to think she understood."

"All right."

"It was the best thing that could have happened. She doesn't seem over-agitated—only a little in the clouds."

"All right, then."

"Dick, come soon and see me."

CHAPTER VIII

DURING THE NEXT WEEKS Dick experienced a vast dissatisfaction. The pathological origin and mechanistic defeat of the affair left a flat and metallic taste. Nicole's emotions had been used unfairly—what if they turned out to have been his own? Necessarily he must absent himself from felicity a while—in dreams he saw her walking on the clinic path swinging her wide straw hat.

One time he saw her in person; as he walked past the Palace Hotel, a magnificent Rolls curved into the half-moon entrance. Small within its gigantic proportions, and buoyed up by the power of a hundred superfluous horses, sat Nicole and a young woman who he assumed was her sister. Nicole saw him and momentarily her lips parted in an expression of fright. Dick shifted his hat and passed, yet for a moment the air around him was loud with the circlings of all the goblins on the Gross-Münster. He tried to write the matter out of his mind in a memorandum that went into detail as to the solemn régime before her; the possibilities of another "push" of the malady under the stresses which the world would inevitably supply—in all a memorandum that would have been convincing to anyone save to him who had written it.

The total value of this effort was to make him realize once more how far his emotions were involved; thenceforth he resolutely provided antidotes. One was the telephone girl from Bar-sur-Aube, now touring Europe from Nice to Coblenz, in a desperate roundup of the men she had known in her never-to-be-equalled holiday; another was the making of arrangements to get home on a government transport in August; a third was a consequent intensification of work on his proofs for the book that this autumn was to be presented to the German-speaking world of psychiatry.

Dick had outgrown the book; he wanted now to do more spade

38

work; if he got an exchange fellowship he could count on plenty of routine.

Meanwhile he had projected a new work: *An Attempt at a Uniform and Pragmatic Classification of the Neuroses and Psychoses, Based on an Examination of Fifteen Hundred Pre-Kraepelin and Post-Kraepelin Cases as they would be Diagnosed in the Terminology of the Different Contemporary Schools*—and another sonorous paragraph—*Together with a Chronology of Such Subdivisions of Opinion as Have Arisen Independently.*

This title would look monumental in German.*

Going into Montreux Dick pedalled slowly, gaping at the Dent du Midi whenever possible, and blinded by glimpses of the lake through the alleys of the shore hotels. He was conscious of the groups of English, emergent after four years and walking with detective-story suspicion in their eyes, as though they were about to be assaulted in this questionable country by German trainbands. There were building and awakening everywhere on this mound of débris formed by a mountain torrent. At Berne and at Lausanne on the way south, Dick had been eagerly asked if there would be Americans this year —"By August, if not in June?"

He wore leather shorts, an army shirt, mountain shoes. In his knapsack were a cotton suit and a change of underwear. At the Glion funicular he checked his bicycle and took a small beer on the terrace of the station buffet, meanwhile watching the little bug crawl down the eighty-degree slope of the hill. His ear was full of dried blood from La Tour de Pelz, where he had sprinted under the impression that he was a spoiled athlete. He asked for alcohol and cleared up the exterior while the funicular slid down into port. He saw his bicycle embarked, slung his knapsack into the lower compartment of the car, and followed it in.

Mountain-climbing cars are built on a slant similar to the angle of a hat-brim of a man who doesn't want to be recognized. As water

*Ein Versuch die Neurosen und Psychosen gleichmässig und pragmatisch zu klassifizieren auf Grund der Untersuchung von fünfzehn hundert pre-Kraepelin und post-Kraepelin Fällen wie sie diagnostiziert sein würden in der Terminologie von den verschiedenen Schulen der Gegenwart—and another sonorous paragraph—Zusammen mit einer Chronologie solcher Subdivisionen der Meinung welche unabhängig entstanden sind.

gushed from the chamber under the car, Dick was impressed with the ingenuity of the whole idea—a complementary car was now taking on mountain water at the top and would pull the lightened car up by gravity, as soon as the brakes were released. It must have been a great inspiration. In the seat across, a couple of British were discussing the cable itself.

"The ones made in England always last five or six years. Two years ago the Germans underbid us, and how long do you think their cable lasted?"

"How long?"

"A year and ten months. Then the Swiss sold it to the Italians. They don't have rigid inspections of cables."

"I can see it would be a terrible thing for Switzerland if a cable broke."

The conductor shut a door; he telephoned his confrere among the undulati, and with a jerk the car was pulled upward, heading for a pinpoint on an emerald hill above. After it cleared the low roofs, the skies of Vaud, Valais, Swiss Savoy, and Geneva spread around the passengers in cyclorama. On the centre of the lake, cooled by the piercing current of the Rhône, lay the true centre of the Western World. Upon it floated swans like boats and boats like swans, both lost in the nothingness of the heartless beauty. It was a bright day, with sun glittering on the grass beach below and the white courts of the Kursaal. The figures on the courts threw no shadows.

When Chillon and the island palace of Salagnon came into view Dick turned his eyes inward. The funicular was above the highest houses of the shore; on both sides a tangle of foliage and flowers culminated at intervals in masses of color. It was a rail-side garden, and in the car was a sign: *Défense de cueillir les fleurs.*

Though one must not pick flowers on the way up, the blossoms trailed in as they passed—Dorothy Perkins roses dragged patiently through each compartment, slowly waggling with the motion of the funicular, letting go at the last to swing back to their rosy cluster. Again and again these branches went through the car.

In the compartment above and in front of Dick's, a group of English were standing up and exclaiming upon the backdrop of sky, when suddenly there was a confusion among them—they parted to give passage to a couple of young people who made apologies and scrambled over into the rear compartment of the funicular—Dick's compartment. The young man was a Latin with the eyes of a stuffed deer; the girl was Nicole.

The two climbers gasped momentarily from their efforts; as they settled into seats, laughing and crowding the English to the corners, Nicole said, "Hel*lo*." She was lovely to look at; immediately Dick saw that something was different; in a second he realized it was her fine-spun hair, bobbed like Irene Castle's and fluffed into curls. She wore a sweater of powder blue and a white tennis skirt—she was the first morning in May and every taint of the clinic was departed.

"Plunk!" she gasped. "Whoo-oo, that guard. They'll arrest us at the next stop. Doctor Diver, the Conte de Marmora."

"Gee-imminy!" She felt her new hair, panting. "Sister bought first-class tickets—it's a matter of principle with her." She and Marmora exchanged glances and shouted: "Then we found that first class is the hearse part behind the chauffeur—shut in with curtains for a rainy day, so you can't see anything. But Sister's very dignified—" Again Nicole and Marmora laughed with young intimacy.

"Where you bound?" asked Dick.

"Caux. You, too?" Nicole looked at his costume. "That your bicycle they got up in front?"

"Yes. I'm going to coast down Monday."

"With me on your handle-bars? I mean, really—will you? I can't think of more fun."

"But I will carry you down in my arms," Marmora protested intensely. "I will roller-skate you—or I will throw you and you will fall slowly like a feather."

The delight in Nicole's face—to be a feather again instead of a plummet, to float and not to drag. She was a carnival to watch—at times primly coy, posing, grimacing and gesturing—sometimes the shadow fell and the dignity of old suffering flowed down into her finger tips. Dick wished himself away from her, fearing that he was a reminder of a world well left behind. He resolved to go to the other hotel.

When the funicular came to rest those new to it stirred in suspension between the blues of two heavens. It was merely for a mysterious exchange between the conductor of the car going up and the conductor of the car coming down. Then up and up over a forest path and a gorge—then again up a hill that became solid with narcissus, from passengers to sky. The people in Montreux playing tennis in the lakeside courts were pinpoints now. Something new was in the air; freshness—freshness embodying itself in music as the car slid into Glion and they heard the orchestra in the hotel garden.

When they changed to the mountain train the music was drowned by the rushing water released from the hydraulic chamber. Almost overhead was Caux, where the thousand windows of a hotel burned in the late sun.

But the approach was different—a leather-lunged engine pushed the passengers round and round in a corkscrew, mounting, rising; they chugged through low-level clouds and for a moment Dick lost Nicole's face in the spray of the slanting donkey-engine; they skirted a lost streak of wind with the hotel growing in size at each spiral, until with a vast surprise they were there, on top of the sunshine.

In the confusion of arrival, as Dick slung his knapsack and started forward on the platform to get his bicycle, Nicole was beside him.

"Aren't you at our hotel?" she asked.

"I'm economizing."

"Will you come down and have dinner?" Some confusion with baggage ensued. "This is my sister—Doctor Diver from Zurich."

Dick bowed to a young woman of twenty-four, tall and confident. She was both formidable and vulnerable, he decided, remembering other women with flower-like mouths grooved for bits.

"I'll drop in after dinner," Dick promised. "First I must get acclimated."

He wheeled off his bicycle, feeling Nicole's eyes following him, feeling her helpless first love, feeling it twist around inside him. He went three hundred yards up the slope to the other hotel, he engaged a room and found himself washing without a memory of the intervening ten minutes, only a sort of drunken flush pierced with voices, unimportant voices that did not know how much he was loved.

CHAPTER IX

THEY WERE WAITING FOR him and incomplete without him. He was still the incalculable element; Miss Warren and the young Italian wore their anticipation as obviously as Nicole. The salon of the hotel, a room of fabled acoustics, was stripped for dancing, but there was a small gallery of English-women of a certain age, with neckbands, dyed hair, and faces powdered pinkish gray; and of American women of a certain age, with snowy-white transformations, black dresses, and lips of cherry red. Miss Warren and Marmora were at a corner table. Nicole was diagonally across from them forty yards away, and as Dick arrived he heard her voice:

"Can you hear me? I'm speaking naturally."

"Perfectly."

"Hello, Doctor Diver."

"What's this?"

"You realize the people in the centre of the floor can't hear what I say, but you can?"

"A waiter told us about it," said Miss Warren. "Corner to corner —it's like wireless."

It was exciting up on the mountain, like a ship at sea. Presently Marmora's parents joined them. They treated the Warrens with respect—Dick gathered that their fortunes had something to do with a bank in Milan that had something to do with the Warren fortunes. But Baby Warren wanted to talk to Dick, wanted to talk to him with the impetus that sent her out vagrantly toward all new men, as though she were on an inelastic tether and considered that she might as well get to the end of it as soon as possible. She crossed and recrossed her knees frequently in the manner of tall restless virgins.

"—Nicole told me that you took part care of her, and had a lot to do with her getting well. What I can't understand is what *we're*

43

supposed to do—they were so indefinite at the sanitarium; they only told me she ought to be natural and gay. I knew the Marmoras were up here so I asked Tino to meet us at the funicular. And you see what happens—the very first thing Nicole has him crawling over the sides of the car as if they were both insane——"

"That was absolutely normal," Dick laughed. "I'd call it a good sign. They were showing off for each other."

"But how can *I* tell? Before I knew it, almost in front of my eyes, she had her hair cut off, in Zurich, because of a picture in *Vanity Fair.*"

"That's all right. She's a schizoid—a permanent eccentric. You can't change that."

"What is it?"

"Just what I said—an eccentric."

"Well, how can any one tell what's eccentric and what's crazy?"

"Nothing is going to be crazy—Nicole is all fresh and happy, you needn't be afraid."

Baby shifted her knees about—she was a compendium of all the discontented women who had loved Byron a hundred years before, yet, in spite of the tragic affair with the Guards officer, there was something wooden and onanistic about her.

"I don't mind the responsibility," she declared, "but I'm in the air. We've never had anything like this in the family before—we know Nicole had some shock and my opinion is it was about a boy, but we don't really know. Father says he would have shot him if he could have found out."

The orchestra was playing "Poor Butterfly"; young Marmora was dancing with his mother. It was a tune new enough to them all. Listening, and watching Nicole's shoulders as she chattered to the elder Marmora, whose hair was dashed with white like a piano keyboard, Dick thought of the shoulders of a violin, and then he thought of the dishonor, the secret. Oh, butterfly—the moments pass into hours——

"Actually *I* have a plan," Baby continued with apologetic hardness. "It may seem absolutely impractical to you but they say Nicole will need to be looked after for a few years. I don't know whether you know Chicago or not——"

"I don't."

"Well, there's a North Side and a South Side and they're very much separated. The North Side is chic and all that, and we've always lived over there, at least for many years, but lots of old families, old Chicago families, if you know what I mean, still live on the South Side. The University is there. I mean it's stuffy to some people, but anyhow it's different from the North Side. I don't know whether you understand."

He nodded. With some concentration he had been able to follow her.

"Now of course we have lots of connections there—Father controls certain chairs and fellowships and so forth at the University, and I thought if we took Nicole home and threw her with that crowd—you see she's quite musical and speaks all these languages—what could be better in her condition than if she fell in love with some good doctor——"

A burst of hilarity surged up in Dick, the Warrens were going to buy Nicole a doctor—You got a nice doctor you can let us use? There was no use worrying about Nicole when they were in the position of being able to buy her a nice young doctor, the paint scarcely dry on him.

"But how about the doctor?" he said automatically.

"There must be many who'd jump at the chance."

The dancers were back, but Baby whispered quickly:

"This is the sort of thing I mean. Now where is Nicole—she's gone off somewhere. Is she upstairs in her room? What am *I* supposed to do? I never know whether it's something innocent or whether I ought to go find her."

"Perhaps she just wants to be by herself—people living alone get used to loneliness." Seeing that Miss Warren was not listening he stopped. "I'll take a look around."

For a moment all the outdoors shut in with mist was like spring with the curtains drawn. Life was gathered near the hotel. Dick passed some cellar windows where bus boys sat on bunks and played cards over a litre of Spanish wine. As he approached the promenade, the stars began to come through the white crests of the high Alps. On the horseshoe walk overlooking the lake Nicole was the figure motionless between two lamp stands, and he approached silently across the grass. She turned to him with an expression of:

"Here *you* are," and for a moment he was sorry he had come.

"Your sister wondered."

"Oh!" She was accustomed to being watched. With an effort she explained herself: "Sometimes I get a little—it gets a little too much. I've lived so quietly. Tonight that music was too much. It made me want to cry——"

"I understand."

"This has been an awfully exciting day."

"I know."

"I don't want to do anything anti-social—I've caused everybody enough trouble. But tonight I wanted to get away."

It occurred to Dick suddenly, as it might occur to a dying man that he had forgotten to tell where his will was, that Nicole had been "re-educated" by Dohmler and the ghostly generations behind him; it occurred to him also that there would be so much she would have to be told. But having recorded this wisdom within himself, he yielded to the insistent face-value of the situation and said:

"You're a nice person—just keep using your own judgment about yourself."

"You like me?"

"Of course."

"Would you—" They were strolling along toward the dim end of the horseshoe, two hundred yards ahead. "If I hadn't been sick would you—I mean, would I have been the sort of girl you might have—oh, slush, you know what I mean."

He was in for it now, possessed by a vast irrationality. She was so near that he felt his breathing change, but again his training came to his aid in a boy's laugh and a trite remark.

"You're teasing yourself, my dear. Once I knew a man who fell in love with his nurse—" The anecdote rambled on, punctuated by their footsteps. Suddenly Nicole interrupted in succinct Chicago-ese: "Bull!"

"That's a very vulgar expression."

"What about it?" she flared up. "You don't think I've got any common sense—before I was sick I didn't have any, but I have now. And if I don't know you're the most attractive man I ever met you must think I'm still crazy. It's my hard luck, all right—but don't pretend I don't *know*—I know everything about you and me."

Dick was at an additional disadvantage. He remembered the statement of the elder Miss Warren as to the young doctors that could be purchased in the intellectual stockyards of the South Side of Chicago, and he hardened for a moment. "You're a fetching kid, but I couldn't fall in love."

"You won't give me a chance."

"*What!*"

The impertinence, the right to invade implied, astounded him. Short of anarchy he could not think of any chance that Nicole Warren deserved.

"Give me a chance now."

The voice fell low, sank into her breast and stretched the tight bodice over her heart as she came up close. He felt the young lips, her body sighing in relief against the arm growing stronger to hold her. There were now no more plans than if Dick had arbitrarily made some indissoluble mixture, with atoms joined and inseparable; you could throw it all out but never again could they fit back into atomic scale. As he held her and tasted her, and as she curved in further and further toward him, with her own lips, new to herself, drowned and engulfed in love, yet solaced and triumphant, he was thankful to have an existence at all, if only as a reflection in her wet eyes.

"My God," he gasped, "you're fun to kiss."

That was talk, but Nicole had a better hold on him now and she held it; she turned coquette and walked away, leaving him as suspended as in the funicular of the afternoon. She felt: There, that'll show him, how conceited; how he could do with me; oh, wasn't it wonderful! I've got him, he's mine. Now in the sequence came flight, but it was also so sweet and new that she dawdled, wanting to draw all of it in.

She shivered suddenly. Two thousand feet below she saw the necklace and bracelet of lights that were Montreux and Vevey, beyond them a dim pendant of Lausanne. From down there somewhere ascended a faint sound of dance music. Nicole was up in her head now, cool as cool, trying to collate the sentimentalities of her childhood, as deliberate as a man getting drunk after battle. But she was still afraid of Dick, who stood near her leaning, characteristically, against the iron fence that rimmed the horseshoe; and this prompted her to say: "I can remember how I stood waiting for you in the garden—holding all myself in my arms like a basket of flowers. It was that to me anyhow—I thought I was sweet—waiting to hand that basket to you."

He breathed over her shoulder and turned her insistently about; she kissed him several times, her face getting big every time she came close, her hands holding him by the shoulders.

"It's raining hard."

Suddenly there was a booming from the wine slopes across the lake; cannons were shooting at hail-bearing clouds in order to break them. The lights of the promenade went off, went on again. Then the storm came swiftly, first falling from the heavens, then doubly falling in torrents from the mountains and washing loud down the roads and stone ditches; with it came a dark, frightening sky and savage filaments of lightning and world-splitting thunder, while ragged, destroying clouds fled along past the hotel. Mountains and lake disappeared—the hotel crouched amid tumult, chaos, and darkness.

By this time Dick and Nicole had reached the vestibule, where Baby Warren and the three Marmoras were anxiously awaiting them. It was exciting coming out of the wet fog, with the doors banging, to stand and laugh and quiver with emotion, wind in their ears and rain on their clothes. Now in the ballroom the orchestra was playing a Strauss waltz, high and confusing.

. . . For Doctor Diver to marry a mental patient? How did it happen? Where did it begin?

"Won't you come back after you've changed?" Baby Warren asked after a close scrutiny.

"I haven't got any change, except some shorts."

As he trudged up to his hotel in a borrowed raincoat he kept laughing derisively in his throat.

"*Big* chance—oh, yes. My God!—they decided to buy a doctor? Well, they better stick to whoever they've got in Chicago." Revolted by his harshness he made amends to Nicole, remembering that nothing had ever felt so young as her lips, remembering rain like tears shed for him that lay upon her softly shining porcelain cheeks . . . The silence of the storm ceasing woke him about three o'clock and he went to the window. Her beauty climbed the rolling slope, it came into the room, rustling ghost-like through the curtains. . . . He climbed two thousand meters to Rocher de Naye the following morning, amused by the fact that his conductor of the day before was using his day off to climb also.

Then Dick descended all the way to Montreux for a swim, got back to his hotel in time for dinner. Two notes awaited him.

"I'm not ashamed about last night—it was the nicest thing that ever happened to me and even if I never saw you again, Mon Capitaine, I would be glad it happened."

That was disarming enough—the heavy shade of Dohmler retreated as Dick opened the second envelope:

DEAR DOCTOR DIVER: I phoned but you were out. I wonder if I may ask you a great big favor. Unforeseen circumstances call me back to Paris, and I find I can make better time by way of Lausanne. Can you let Nicole ride as far as Zurich with you, since you are going back Monday? and drop her at the sanitarium? Is this too much to ask?

Sincerely,

BETH EVAN WARREN.

Dick was furious—Miss Warren had known he had a bicycle with him; yet she had so phrased her note that it was impossible to refuse. Throw us together! Sweet propinquity and the Warren money!

He was wrong; Baby Warren had no such intentions. She had looked Dick over with worldly eyes, she had measured him with the warped rule of an Anglophile and found him wanting—in spite of the fact that she found him toothsome. But for her he was too "intellectual" and she pigeonholed him with a shabby-snobby crowd she had once known in London—he put himself out too much to be really of the correct stuff. She could not see how he could be made into her idea of an aristocrat.

In addition to that he was stubborn—she had seen him leave her conversation and get down behind his eyes in that odd way that people did, half a dozen times. She had not liked Nicole's free and easy manner as a child and now she was sensibly habituated to thinking of her as a "gone coon"; and anyhow Doctor Diver was not the sort of medical man she could envisage in the family.

She only wanted to use him innocently as a convenience.

But her request had the effect that Dick assumed she desired. A ride in a train can be a terrible, heavy-hearted or comic thing; it can be a trial flight; it can be a prefiguration of another journey, just as a given day with a friend can be long, from the taste of hurry in the morning up to the realization of both being hungry and taking food together. Then comes the afternoon with the journey fading and dying, but quickening again at the end. Dick was sad to see Nicole's meagre joy; yet it was a relief for her, going back to the only home she knew. They made no love that day, but when he left her outside the sad door on the Zurichsee and she turned and looked at him he knew her problem was one they had together for good now.

BOOK II

ROSEMARY'S ANGLE
1919 - 1925

CHAPTER I

IN ZURICH IN SEPTEMBER Doctor Diver had tea with Baby Warren.

"I think it's ill advised," she said, "I'm not sure I truly understand your motives."

"Don't let's be unpleasant."

"After all I'm Nicole's sister."

"That doesn't give you the right to be unpleasant." It irritated Dick that he knew so much that he could not tell her. "Nicole's rich, but that doesn't make me an adventurer."

"That's just it," complained Baby stubbornly. "Nicole's rich."

"Just how much money has she got?" he asked.

She started; and with a silent laugh he continued, "You see how silly this is? I'd rather talk to some man in your family——"

"Everything's been left to me," she persisted. "It isn't we think you're an adventurer. We don't know who you are."

"I'm a doctor of medicine," he said. "My father is a clergyman, now retired. We lived in Buffalo and my past is open to investigation. I went to New Haven; after that I was a Rhodes scholar. My great-grandfather was Governor of North Carolina and I'm a direct descendant of Mad Anthony Wayne."

"Who was Mad Anthony Wayne?" Baby asked suspiciously.

"Mad Anthony Wayne?"

"I think there's enough madness in this affair."

He shook his head hopelessly, just as Nicole came out on the hotel terrace and looked around for them.

"He was too mad to leave as much money as Marshall Field," he said.

"That's all very well——"

Baby was right and she knew it. Face to face, her father would have it on almost any clergyman. They were an American ducal family without a title—the very name written in a hotel register, signed to an introduction, used in a difficult situation, caused a psychological metamorphosis in people, and in return this change had crystallized her own sense of position. She knew these facts from the English, who had known them for more than two hundred years. But she did not know that twice Dick had come close to flinging the marriage in her face. All that saved it this time was Nicole finding their table and glowing away, white and fresh and new in the September afternoon.

How do you do, lawyer. We're going to Como tomorrow for a week and then back to Zurich. That's why I wanted you and sister to settle this, because it doesn't matter to us how much I'm allowed. We're going to live very quietly in Zurich for two years and Dick has enough to take care of us. No, Baby, I'm more practical than you think— It's only for clothes and things I'll need it. . . . Why, that's more than—can the estate really afford to give me all that? I know I'll never manage to spend it. Do you have that much? Why do you have more—is it because I'm supposed to be incompetent? All right, let my share pile up then. . . . No, Dick refuses to have anything whatever to do with it. I'll have to feel bloated for us both. . . . Baby, you have no more idea of what Dick is like than, than— Now where do I sign? Oh, I'm sorry.

. . . Isn't it funny and lonely being together, Dick. No place to go except close. Shall we just love and love? Ah, but I love the most, and I can tell when you're away from me, even a little. I think it's wonderful to be just like everybody else, to reach out and find you all warm beside me in the bed.

. . . If you will kindly call my husband at the hospital. Yes, the little book is selling everywhere—they want it published in six languages. I was to do the French translation but I'm tired these days—I'm afraid of falling, I'm so heavy and clumsy—like a broken roly-poly that can't stand up straight. The cold stethoscope against my heart and my strongest feeling "Je m'en fiche de tout."—Oh, that poor woman in the hospital with the blue baby, much better dead. Isn't it fine there are three of us now?

. . . That seems unreasonable, Dick—we have every reason for taking the bigger apartment. Why should we penalize ourselves just because there's more Warren money than Diver money? Oh, thank you, cameriere, but we've changed our minds. This English clergy-man tells us that your wine here in Orvieto is excellent. It doesn't travel? That must be why we have never heard of it, because we love wine.

The lakes are sunk in the brown clay and the slopes have all the creases of a belly. The photographer gave us the picture of me, my hair limp over the rail on the boat to Capri. "Good-by, Blue Grotto," sang the boatman, "come again soo-oon." And afterward tracing down the hot sinister shin of the Italian boot with the wind soughing around those eerie castles, the dead watching from up on those hills.

. . . This ship is nice, with our heels hitting the deck together. This is the blowy corner and each time we turn it I slant forward against the wind and pull my coat together without losing step with Dick. We are chanting nonsense:

> "Oh—oh—oh—oh—
> Other flamingoes than me,
> Oh—oh—oh—oh
> Other flamingoes than me——"

Life is fun with Dick—the people in deck chairs look at us, and a woman is trying to hear what we are singing. Dick is tired of singing it, so go on alone, Dick. You will walk differently alone, dear, through a thicker atmosphere, forcing your way through the shadows of chairs, through the dripping smoke of the funnels. You will feel your own reflection sliding along the eyes of those who look at you. You are no longer insulated; but I suppose you must touch life in order to spring from it.

Sitting on the stanchion of this life-boat I look seaward and let my hair blow and shine. I am motionless against the sky and the boat is made to carry my form onward into the blue obscurity of the future, I am Pallas Athene carved reverently on the front of a galley. The waters are lapping in the public toilets and the agate green foliage of spray changes and complains about the stern.

. . . We travelled a lot that year—from Woolloomooloo Bay to Biskra. On the edge of the Sahara we ran into a plague of locusts and the chauffeur explained kindly that they were bumble-bees. The sky was low at night, full of the presence of a strange and watchful God. Oh, the poor little naked Ouled Naïl; the night was noisy with drums from Senegal and flutes and whining camels, and the natives pattering about in shoes made of old automobile tires.

But I was gone again by that time—trains and beaches they were all one. That was why he took me travelling, but after my second child, my little girl Topsy, was born everything got dark again.

. . . If I could get word to my husband who has seen fit to desert me here, to leave me in the hands of incompetents. You tell me my baby is black—that's farcical, that's very cheap. We went to Africa merely to see Timgad, since my principal interest in life is archæology. I am tired of knowing nothing and being reminded of it all the time.

. . . When I get well I want to be a fine person like you, Dick— I would study medicine except it's too late. We must spend my money and have a house—I'm tired of apartments and waiting for you. You're bored with Zurich and you can't find time for writing here and you say that it's a confession of weakness for a scientist not to write. And I'll look over the whole field of knowledge and pick out something and really know about it, so I'll have it to hang on to if I go to pieces again. You'll help me, Dick, so I won't feel so guilty. We'll live near a warm beach where we can be brown and young together.

. . . This is going to be Dick's work house. Oh, the idea came to us both at the same moment. We had passed Tarmes a dozen times and we rode up here and found the houses empty, except two stables. When we bought we acted through a Frenchman, but the navy sent spies up here in no time when they found that Americans had bought part of a hill village. They looked for cannons all through the building material, and finally Baby had to twitch wires for us at the Affaires Étrangères in Paris.

No one comes to the Riviera in summer, so we expect to have a few guests and to work. There are some French people here— Mistinguette last week, surprised to find the hotel open, and Picasso and the man who wrote *Pas sur la Bouche*.

. . . Dick, why did you register Mr. and Mrs. Diver instead of Doctor and Mrs. Diver? I just wondered—it just floated through my mind.—You've taught me that work is everything and I believe you. You used to say a man knows things and when he stops knowing things he's like anybody else, and the thing is to get power before he stops knowing things. If you want to turn things topsy-turvy, all right, but must your Nicole follow you walking on her hands, darling?

. . . Abe North says I am silent. Since I was well the first time I talked a lot to Dick late at night, both of us sitting up in bed and lighting cigarettes, then diving down afterward out of the blue dawn and into the pillows, to keep the light from our eyes. Sometimes I sing, and play with the animals, and I have a few friends too—Mary, for instance. When Mary and I talk neither of us listens to the other. Talk is men. When I talk I say to myself that I am probably Dick. Already I have even been my son, remembering how wise and slow he is. Sometimes I am Doctor Dohmler and one time I may even be an aspect of you, Tommy Barban. Tommy is in love with me, I think, but gently, reassuringly. Enough, though, so that he and Dick have begun to disapprove of each other. All in all, everything has never gone better. I am among friends who like me. I am here on this tranquil beach near my home above the Mediterranean with my husband and two children and our dear friends. Everything is all right—if I can finish translating this damn recipe for chicken à la Maryland into French. My toes feel warm in the sand.

"Yes, I'll look. More new people—oh, that girl—yes. Who did you say she looked like? . . . No, I haven't, we don't get much chance to see the new American pictures over here. Rosemary who? Well, we're getting very fashionable for July—seems very peculiar to me."

CHAPTER II

On the shore of the French Riviera, about half way between Marseilles and the Italian border, stood a large, proud, rose-colored hotel. Deferential palms cooled its flushed façade, and before it stretched a short dazzling beach. Now it has become a summer resort of notable and fashionable people; in 1925 it·was almost deserted after its English clientele went north in April; only the cupolas of a dozen old villas rotted like water lilies among the massed pines between Gausse's Hôtel des Étrangers and Cannes, five miles away.

The hotel and its bright tan prayer rug of a beach were one. In the early morning the distant image of Cannes, the pink and cream of old fortifications, the purple Alp that bounded Italy, were cast across the water and lay quavering in the ripples and rings sent up by sea-plants through the clear shallows. Before eight a man had come down to the beach in a blue bathrobe and with much preliminary application to his person of the chilly water, and much grunting and loud breathing, had floundered a minute in the sea. When he had gone, beach and bay were quiet for an hour. Merchantmen crawled westward on the horizon; bus boys shouted in the hotel court; the dew dried upon the pines. In another hour the horns of motors began to blow down from the winding road along the low range of the Maures, which separates the littoral from true Provençal France.

A mile from the sea, where pines give way to dusty poplars, is an isolated railroad stop, whence this June morning in 1925 a victoria brought a woman and her daughter down to Gausse's hotel. The mother's face was of a fading prettiness that would soon be patted with broken veins; her expression was both tranquil and aware in a pleasant way. However, one's eyes moved on quickly to her daughter, who had magic in her pink palms and her cheeks lit to a lovely flame, like the thrilling flush of children after their cold baths in the evening. Her fine high forehead sloped gently up to where her hair, bordering it like an armorial shield, burst into lovelocks and waves and curlicues of ash blonde and gold. Her eyes were bright, big, clear, wet, and shining, the color of her cheeks was real, breaking close to the surface from the strong young pump of her heart. Her body hovered delicately on the last edge of childhood—she was almost eighteen, nearly complete, but the dew was still on her.

As sea and sky appeared below them in a thin, hot line the mother said:

"Something tells me we're not going to like this place."

"I want to go home anyhow," the girl answered.

They both spoke cheerfully, but were obviously without direction and bored by the fact—moreover, just any direction would not do. They wanted high excitement, not from the necessity of stimulating jaded nerves, but with the avidity of prize-winning schoolchildren who deserved their vacations.

"We'll stay three days and then go home. I'll wire right away for steamer tickets."

At the hotel the girl made the reservation in idiomatic but rather flat French, like something remembered. When they were installed on the ground floor she walked into the glare of the French windows and out a few steps onto the stone veranda that ran the length of the hotel. When she walked she carried herself like a balletdancer, not slumped down on her hips but held up in the small of her back. Out there the hot light clipped close her shadow and she retreated—it was too bright to see. Fifty yards away the Mediterranean yielded up its pigments, moment by moment, to the brutal sunshine; below the balustrade a faded Buick cooked on the hotel drive.

Indeed, of all the region only the beach stirred with activity. Three British nannies sat knitting the slow pattern of Victorian England, the pattern of the forties, the sixties, and the eighties, into sweaters and socks, to the tune of gossip as formalized as incantation; closer to the sea a dozen persons kept house under striped umbrellas, while their dozen children pursued unintimidated fish through the shallows or lay naked and glistening with cocoanut oil out in the sun.

As Rosemary came onto the beach a boy of twelve ran past her and dashed into the sea with exultant cries. Feeling the impactive scrutiny of strange faces, she took off her bathrobe and followed. She floated face down for a few yards and, finding it shallow, staggered to her feet and plodded forward, dragging slim legs like weights against the resistance of the water. When it was about breast high, she glanced back toward shore: a bald man in a monocle and a pair of tights, his tufted chest thrown out, his brash navel sucked in, was regarding her attentively. As Rosemary returned the gaze the man dislodged the monocle, which went into hiding amid the facetious whiskers of his chest, and poured himself a glass of something from a bottle in his hand.

Rosemary laid her face on the water and swam a choppy little four-beat crawl out to the raft. The water reached up for her, pulled her down tenderly out of the heat, seeped in her hair and ran into the corners of her body. She turned round and round in it, embracing it, wallowing in it. Reaching the raft she was out of breath, but a tanned woman with very white teeth looked down at her, and Rosemary, suddenly conscious of the raw whiteness of her own body, turned on her back and drifted toward shore. The hairy man holding the bottle spoke to her as she came out.

"I say—they have sharks out behind the raft." He was of indeterminate nationality, but spoke English with a slow Oxford drawl. "Yesterday they devoured two British sailors from the flotte at Golfe Juan."

"Heavens!" exclaimed Rosemary.

"They come in for the refuse from the flotte."

Glazing his eyes to indicate that he had spoken only in order to warn her, he minced off two steps and poured himself another drink.

Not unpleasantly self-conscious, since there had been a slight sway of attention toward her during this conversation, Rosemary looked for a place to sit. Obviously each family possessed the strip of sand immediately in front of its umbrella; besides there was much visiting and talking back and forth—the atmosphere of a community upon which it would be presumptuous to intrude. Farther up, where the beach was strewn with pebbles and dead sea-weed, sat a group with flesh as white as her own. They lay under small hand-parasols instead of beach umbrellas and were obviously less indigenous to the place. Between the dark people and the light, Rosemary found room and spread out her peignoir on the sand.

Lying so, she first heard their voices and felt their feet skirt her body and their shapes pass between the sun and herself. The breath of an inquisitive dog blew warm and nervous on her neck; she could feel her skin broiling a little in the heat and hear the small exhausted wa-*waa* of the expiring waves. Presently her ear distinguished individual voices and she became aware that someone referred to scornfully as "that North guy" had kidnapped a waiter from a café in Cannes last night in order to saw him in two. The sponsor of the story was a white-haired woman in full evening dress, obviously a relic of the previous evening, for a tiara still clung to her head and a discouraged orchid expired from her shoulder. Rosemary, forming a vague antipathy to her and her companions, turned away.

Nearest her, on the other side, a young woman lay under a roof of umbrellas making out a list of things from a book open on the sand. Her bathing suit was pulled off her shoulders and her back, a ruddy, orange brown, set off by a string of creamy pearls, shone in the sun. Her face was hard and lovely and pitiful. Her eyes met Rosemary's but did not see her. Beyond her was a fine man in a jockey cap and red-striped tights; then the woman Rosemary had seen on the raft, who looked back at her, seeing her; then a man with a long face and a golden, leonine head, with blue tights and no hat, talking very seriously to an unmistakably Latin young man in black tights, both of them picking at little pieces of sea-weed in the sand. She thought they were mostly Americans, but something made them unlike the Americans she had known of late.

After a while she realized that the man in the jockey cap was giving a quiet little performance for this group; he moved gravely about with a rake, ostensibly removing gravel and meanwhile developing some esoteric burlesque held in suspension by his grave face. Its faintest ramification had become hilarious, until whatever he said released a burst of laughter. Even those who, like herself, were too far away to hear, sent out antennæ of attention until the only person on the beach not caught up in it was the young woman with the string of pearls. Perhaps from modesty of possession, she responded to each salvo of amusement by bending closer over her list.

The man of the monocle and bottle spoke suddenly out of the sky above Rosemary.

"You are a ripping swimmer."

She demurred.

"Jolly good. My name is Campion. Here is a lady who says she saw you in Sorrento last week and knows who you are and would so like to meet you."

Glancing around with concealed annoyance Rosemary saw the untanned people were waiting. Reluctantly she got up and went over to them.

"Mrs. Abrams—Mrs. McKisco—Mr. McKisco—Mr. Dumphry——"

"We know who you are," spoke up the woman in evening dress. "You're Rosemary Hoyt and I recognized you in Sorrento and asked the hotel clerk and we all think you're perfectly marvellous and we want to know why you're not back in America making another marvellous moving picture."

They made a superfluous gesture of moving over for her. The woman who had recognized her was not a Jewess, despite her name. She was one of those elderly "good sports" preserved by an imperviousness to experience and a good digestion into another generation.

"We wanted to warn you about getting burned the first day," she continued cheerily, "because *your* skin is important, but there seems to be so darn much formality on this beach that we didn't know whether you'd mind."

CHAPTER III

"WE THOUGHT MAYBE YOU were in the plot," said Mrs. McKisco. She was a shabby-eyed, pretty young woman with a disheartening intensity. "We don't know who's in the plot and who isn't. One man my husband had been particularly nice to turned out to be a chief character—practically the assistant hero."

"The plot?" inquired Rosemary, half understanding. "Is there a plot?"

"My dear, we don't *know*," said Mrs. Abrams, with a convulsive, stout woman's chuckle. "We're not in it. We're the gallery."

Mr. Dumphry, a tow-headed, effeminate young man, remarked: "Mama Abrams is a plot in herself," and Campion shook his monocle at him, saying: "Now, Royal, don't be too ghastly for words." Rosemary looked at them all uncomfortably, wishing her mother had come down here with her. She did not like these people, especially in her immediate comparison of them with those who had interested her at the other end of the beach. Her mother's modest but compact social gift got them out of unwelcome situations swiftly and firmly. But Rosemary had been a celebrity for only six months, and sometimes the French manners of her early adolescence and the democratic manners of America, these latter superimposed, made a certain confusion and let her in for just such things.

Mr. McKisco, a scrawny, freckle-and-red man of thirty, did not find the topic of the "plot" amusing. He had been staring at the sea; now after a swift glance at his wife he turned to Rosemary and demanded aggressively:

"Been here long?"

"Only a day."

"Oh."

Evidently feeling that the subject had been thoroughly changed, he looked in turn at the others.

"Going to stay all summer?" asked Mrs. McKisco, innocently. "If you do you can watch the plot unfold."

"For God's sake, Violet, drop the subject!" exploded her husband. "Get a new joke, for God's sake!"

Mrs. McKisco swayed toward Mrs. Abrams and breathed audibly: "He's nervous."

"I'm not nervous," disagreed McKisco. "It just happens I'm not nervous at all."

He was burning visibly—a grayish flush had spread over his face, dissolving all his expressions into a vast ineffectuality. Suddenly remotely conscious of his condition he got up to go in the water. He was followed by his wife, and seizing the opportunity Rosemary waded after them.

Mr. McKisco drew a long breath, flung himself into the shallows, and began a stiff-armed batting of the Mediterranean, obviously intended to suggest a crawl. His breath exhausted he arose and looked around with an expression of surprise that he was still in sight of shore.

"I haven't learned to breathe yet. I never quite understood how they breathed." He looked at Rosemary inquiringly.

"I think you breathe out under water," she explained. "And every fourth beat you roll your head over for air."

"The breathing's the hardest part for me. Shall we go to the raft?"

The man with the leonine head lay stretched out upon the raft, which tipped back and forth with the motion of the water. As Mrs. McKisco reached for it a sudden tilt struck her arm up roughly, whereupon the man started up and pulled her on board.

"I was afraid it hit you." His voice was slow and shy; he had one of the saddest faces Rosemary had ever seen, the high cheek-bones of an Indian, a long upper lip, and enormous deep-set dark golden eyes. He had spoken out of the side of his mouth, as if he hoped his words would reach Mrs. McKisco by a circuitous and unobstrusive route; in a minute he had shoved off into the water and his long body lay motionless toward shore.

Rosemary and Mrs. McKisco watched him. When he had exhausted his momentum he abruptly bent double, his thin thighs rose above the surface, and he disappeared totally, leaving scarcely a fleck of foam behind.

"He's a good swimmer," Rosemary said.

Mrs. McKisco's answer came with surprising violence.

"Well, he's a rotten musician." She turned to her husband, who after two unsuccessful attempts had managed to climb on the raft and, having attained his balance, was trying to make some kind of compensatory flourish, achieving only an extra stagger. "I was just saying that Abe North may be a good swimmer but he's a rotten musician."

"Yes," agreed McKisco, grudgingly. Obviously he had created his wife's world, and allowed her few liberties in it.

"Antheil's my man." Mrs. McKisco turned challengingly to Rosemary," Antheil and Joyce. I don't suppose you ever hear much about those sort of people in Hollywood, but my husband wrote the first criticism of *Ulysses* that ever appeared in America."

"I wish I had a cigarette," said McKisco calmly. "That's more important to me just now."

"He's got insides—don't you think so, Albert?"

Her voice faded off suddenly. The woman of the pearls had joined her two children in the water, and now Abe North came up under one of them like a volcanic island, raising him on his shoulders. The child yelled with fear and delight and the woman watched with a lovely peace, without a smile.

"Is that his wife?" Rosemary asked.

"No, that's Mrs. Diver. They're not at the hotel." Her eyes, photographic, did not move from the woman's face. After a moment she turned vehemently to Rosemary.

"Have you been abroad before?"

"Yes—I went to school in Paris."

"Oh! Well, then, you probably know that if you want to enjoy yourself here the thing is to get to know some real French families. What do these people get out of it?" She pointed her left shoulder toward shore. "They just stick around with each other in little cliques. Of course, we had letters of introduction and met all the best French artists and writers in Paris. That made it very nice."

"I should think so."

"My husband is finishing his first novel, you see."

Rosemary said: "Oh, he is?" She was not thinking anything special, except wondering whether her mother had got to sleep in this heat.

"It's on the idea of *Ulysses*," continued Mrs. McKisco. "Only instead of taking twenty-four hours my husband takes a hundred years. He takes a decayed old French aristocrat and puts him in contrast with the mechanical age——"

"Oh, for God's sake, Violet, don't go telling everybody the idea," protested McKisco. "I don't want it to get all around before the book's published."

Rosemary swam back to the shore, where she threw her peignoir over her already sore shoulders and lay down again in the sun. The man with the jockey cap was now going from umbrella to umbrella, carrying a bottle and little glasses in his hands; presently he and his friends grew livelier and closer together and now they were all under a single assemblage of umbrellas—she gathered that someone was leaving and that this was a last drink on the beach. Even the children knew that excitement was generating under the umbrella and turned toward it—and it seemed to Rosemary that it all came from the man in the jockey cap.

Noon dominated sea and sky—even the white line of Cannes, five miles off, had faded to a mirage of what was fresh and cool; a robin-breasted sailing boat pulled in behind it a strand from the outer, darker sea. It seemed that there was no life anywhere in all this expanse of coast except under the filtered sunlight of those umbrellas, where something went on amid the color and the murmur.

Campion walked near her, stood a few feet away and Rosemary closed her eyes, pretending to be asleep; then she half-opened them and watched two dim, blurred pillars that were legs. The man tried to edge his way into a sand-colored cloud, but the cloud floated off into the vast hot sky. Rosemary fell really asleep.

She awoke drenched with sweat to find the beach deserted save for the man in the jockey cap, who was folding a last umbrella. As Rosemary lay blinking, he walked nearer and said:

"I was going to wake you before I left. It's not good to get too burned right away."

"Thank you." Rosemary looked down at her crimson legs. "Heavens!"

She laughed cheerfully, inviting him to talk, but Dick Diver was already carrying a tent and a beach umbrella up to a waiting car, so she went into the water to wash off the sweat. He came back and gathering up a rake, a shovel, and a sieve, stowed them in a crevice of a rock. He glanced up and down the beach to see if he had left anything.

"Do you know what time it is?" Rosemary asked.

"It's about half-past one."

They faced the seascape together momentarily.

"It's not a bad time," said Dick Diver. "It's not one of the worst times of the day."

He looked at her and for a moment she lived in the bright blue worlds of his eyes, eagerly and confidently. Then he shouldered his last piece of junk and went up to his car, and Rosemary came out of the water, shook out her peignoir, and walked up to the hotel.

CHAPTER IV

IT WAS ALMOST TWO when they went into the dining-room. Back and forth over the deserted tables a heavy pattern of beams and shadows swayed with the motion of the pines outside. Two waiters, piling plates and talking loud Italian, fell silent when they came in and brought them a tired version of the table d'hôte luncheon.

"I fell in love on the beach," said Rosemary.

"Who with?"

"First with a whole lot of people who looked nice. Then with one man."

"Did you talk to him?"

"Just a little. Very handsome. With reddish hair." She was eating, ravenously. "He's married, though—it's usually the way."

Her mother was her best friend and had put every last possibility into the guiding of her, not so rare a thing in the theatrical profession, but rather special in that Mrs. Elsie Speers was not recompensing herself for a defeat of her own. She had no personal bitterness or resentments about life—twice satisfactorily married and twice widowed, her cheerful stoicism had each time deepened. Her first husband, Rosemary's father, had been an army doctor and her second a cavalry officer, and they both left something to her that she tried to present intact to Rosemary. By not sparing Rosemary she had made her hard—by not sparing her own labor and devotion she had cultivated an idealism in Rosemary, which at present was directed toward herself and saw the world through her eyes. So that while Rosemary Hoyt was a "simple" child she was protected by a double sheath of her mother's armor and her own—she had a mature distrust of the trivial, the facile, and the vulgar. However, with Rosemary's sudden success in pictures, Mrs. Speers felt it was time that she was spiritually weaned; it would please rather than pain her

68

if this somewhat bouncing, breathless, and exigent idealism would focus on something except herself.

"Then you like it here?" she asked.

"It might be fun if we knew those people. There were some other people, but they weren't nice. They recognized me—no matter where we go everybody's seen *Daddy's Girl*."

Mrs. Speers waited for the glow of egotism to subside; then she said in a matter-of-fact way: "That reminds me, when are you going to see Earl Brady?"

"I thought we might go this afternoon—if you're rested."

"You go—I'm not going."

"We'll wait till tomorrow then."

"I want you to go alone. It's only a short way—it isn't as if you didn't speak French."

"Mother—aren't there some things I don't have to do?"

"Oh, well then, go later—but some day before we leave."

"All right, Mother."

After lunch they were both overwhelmed by the sudden flatness that comes over American travellers in quiet foreign places. No stimuli worked upon them, no voices called them from without, no fragments of their own thoughts came suddenly from the minds of others, and missing the clamor of Empire they felt that life was not continuing here.

"Let's only stay three days, Mother," Rosemary said when they were back in their rooms. Outside a light wind blew the heat around, straining it through the trees and sending little hot gusts through the shutters.

"How about the man you fell in love with on the beach?"

"I don't love anybody but you, Mother darling."

Rosemary stopped in the lobby and spoke to Gausse père about trains. The concierge, lounging in light-brown khaki by the desk, stared at her rigidly, then suddenly remembered the manners of his métier. She took the bus and rode with a pair of obsequious waiters to the station, embarrassed by their deferential silence, wanting to urge them: "Go on, talk, enjoy yourselves. It doesn't bother me."

The first-class compartment was stifling; the vivid advertising cards of the railroad companies—the Pont du Gard at Arles, the

Ampitheatre at Orange, winter sports at Chamonix—were fresher than the long motionless sea outside. Unlike American trains that were absorbed in an intense destiny of their own and scornful of people on another world less swift and breathless, this train was part of the country through which it passed. Its breath stirred the dust from the palm leaves, the cinders mingled with the dry dung in the gardens. Rosemary was sure she could lean from the window and pull flowers with her hand.

A dozen cabbies slept in their hacks outside the Cannes station. Over on the promenade the Casino, the smart shops, and the great hotels turned blank iron masks to the summer sea. It was unbelievable that there could ever have been a "season," and Rosemary, half in the grip of fashion, became a little self-conscious, as though she were displaying an unhealthy taste for the moribund; as though people were wondering why she was here in the lull between the gaiety of last winter and next winter, while up north the true world thundered by.

As she came out of a drug store with a bottle of cocoanut oil, a woman, whom she recognized as Mrs. Diver, crossed her path with arms full of sofa cushions and went to a car parked down the street. A long, low black dog barked at her, a dozing chauffeur woke with a start. She sat in the car, her lovely face set, controlled, her eyes brave and watchful, looking straight ahead toward nothing. Her dress was bright red and her brown legs were bare. She had thick, dark, gold hair like a chow's.

With half an hour to wait for her train Rosemary sat down in the Café des Alliées on the Croisette, where the trees made a green twilight over the tables and an orchestra wooed an imaginary public of cosmopolites with the Nice Carnival Song and last year's American tune. She had bought *Le Temps* and the *Saturday Evening Post* for her mother, and as she drank her citronade she opened the latter at the memoirs of a Russian princess, finding the dim conventions of the nineties realer and nearer than the headlines of the French paper. It was the same feeling that had oppressed her at the hotel—accustomed to seeing the starkest grotesqueries of a continent heavily underlined as comedy or tragedy, untrained to the task of separating out the essential for herself, she now began to feel that

French life was empty and stale. This feeling was surcharged by listening to the sad tunes of the orchestra, reminiscent of the melancholy music played for acrobats in vaudeville. She was glad to go back to Gausse's hotel.

Her shoulders were too burned to swim with the next day, so she and her mother hired a car—after much haggling, for Rosemary had formed her valuations of money in France—and drove along the Riviera, the delta of many rivers. The chauffeur, a Russian czar of the period of Ivan the Terrible, was a self-appointed guide, and the resplendent names—Cannes, Nice, Monte Carlo—began to glow through their torpid camouflage, whispering of old kings come here to dine or die, of rajahs tossing Buddhas' eyes to English ballerinas, of Russian princes turning the weeks into Baltic twilights in the lost caviare days. Most of all, there was the scent of the Russians along the coast—their closed book shops and grocery stores. Eleven years before, when the season ended in April, the doors of the Orthodox Church had been locked, and the sweet champagnes they favored had been put away until their return. "We'll be back next season," they said, but this was premature, for they were never coming back any more.

It was pleasant to drive back to the hotel in the late afternoon, above a sea as mysteriously colored as the agates and cornelians of childhood, green as green milk, blue as laundry water, wine dark. It was pleasant to pass people eating outside their doors, and to hear the fierce mechanical pianos behind the vines of country estaminets. When they turned off the Corniche d'Or and down to Gausse's hotel through the darkening banks of trees, set one behind another in many greens, the moon already hovered over the ruins of the aqueducts.

Somewhere in the hills behind the hotel there was a dance, and Rosemary listened to the music through the ghostly moonshine of her mosquito net, realizing that there was gaiety too somewhere about, and she thought of the nice people on the beach. She thought she might meet them in the morning, but they obviously formed a self-sufficient little group, and once their umbrellas, bamboo rugs, dogs, and children were set out in place that part of the plage was literally fenced in. She resolved in any case not to spend her last two mornings with the other ones.

CHAPTER V

THE MATTER WAS SOLVED for her. The McKiscos were not yet there and she had scarcely spread her peignoir when two men—the man with the jockey cap and the tall blond man given to sawing waiters in two—left the group and came down toward her.

"Good morning," said Dick Diver. He broke down. "Look—sunburn or no sunburn, why did you stay away yesterday? We worried about you."

She sat up and her happy little laugh welcomed their intrusion.

"We wondered," Dick Diver said, "if you wouldn't come over this morning. We go in, we take food and drink, so it's a substantial invitation.

He seemed kind and charming—his voice promised that he would take care of her, and that a little later he would open up whole new worlds for her, unroll an endless succession of magnificent possibilities. He managed the introduction so that her name wasn't mentioned and then let her know easily that everyone knew who she was but was respecting the completeness of her private life—a courtesy that Rosemary had not met with save from professional people since her success.

Nicole Diver, her brown back hanging from her pearls, was looking through a recipe book for chicken Maryland. She was about twenty-four, Rosemary guessed—her face could have been described in terms of conventional prettiness, but the effect was that it had been made first on the heroic scale with strong structure and marking, as if the features and vividness of brow and coloring, everything we associate with temperament and character, had been molded with a Rodinesque intention, and then chiselled away in the direction of prettiness to a point where a single slip would have irreparably diminished its force and quality. With the mouth the sculptor had taken desperate chances—it was the cupid's bow of a magazine cover, yet it shared the distinction of the rest.

"Are you here for a long time?" Nicole asked. Her voice was low, almost harsh.

Suddenly Rosemary let the possibility enter her mind that they might stay another week.

"Not very long," she answered vaguely. "We've been abroad a long time—we landed in Sicily in March and we've been slowly working our way north. I got pneumonia making a picture last January and I've been recuperating."

"Mercy! How did that happen?"

"Well, it was from swimming." Rosemary was rather reluctant at embarking upon personal revelations. "One day I happened to have the grippe and didn't know it, and they were taking a scene where I dove into a canal in Venice. It was a very expensive set, so I had to dive and dive and dive all morning. Mother had a doctor right there, but it was no use—I got pneumonia." She changed the subject determinedly before they could speak. "Do you like it here —this place?"

"They have to like it," said Abe North slowly. "They invented it." He turned his noble head slowly so that his eyes rested with tenderness and affection on the two Divers.

"Oh, did you?"

"This is only the second season that the hotel's been open in summer," Nicole explained. "We persuaded Gausse to keep on a cook and a garçon and a chasseur—it paid its way and this year it's doing even better."

"But you're not in the hotel."

"We built a house, up at Tarmes."

"The theory is," said Dick, arranging an umbrella to clip a square of sunlight off Rosemary's shoulder, "that all the northern places, like Deauville, were picked out by Russians and English, who don't mind the cold, while half of us Americans come from tropical climates—that's why we're beginning to come here."

The young man of Latin aspect had been turning the pages of the Paris edition of the *New York Herald*.

"Well, what nationality are these people?" he demanded, suddenly, and read with a slight French intonation, " 'Registered at the Hotel Palace at Vevey are Mr. Pandely Vlasco, Mme. Bonneasse' —I don't exaggerate—'Corinna Medonca, Mme. Pasche, Seraphim

Tullio, Maria Amalia Roto Mais, Moises Teubel, Mme. Paragoris, Apostle Alexandre, Yolanda Yosfuglu and Geneveva de Momus!' She attracts me most—Geneveva de Momus. Almost worth running up to Vevey to take a look at Geneveva de Momus."

He stood up with sudden restlessness, stretching himself with one sharp movement. He was a few years younger than Diver or North. He was tall and his body was hard but overspare, save for the bunched force gathered in his shoulders and upper arms. At first glance he seemed conventionally handsome, but there was a faint disgust always in his face which marred the full fierce lustre of his brown eyes. Yet one remembered them afterward, when one had forgotten the inability of the mouth to endure boredom and the young forehead with its furrows of fretful and unprofitable pain.

"We found some fine ones in the news of Americans last week," said Nicole. "Mrs. Evelyn Oyster and—what were the others?"

"There was Mr. S. Flesh," said Diver, getting up also. He took his rake and began to work seriously at getting small stones out of the sand.

"Oh, yes—S. Flesh—doesn't he give you the creeps?"

It was quiet alone with Nicole—Rosemary found it even quieter than with her mother. Abe North and Barban, the Frenchman, were talking about Morocco, and Nicole having copied her recipe picked up a piece of sewing. Rosemary examined their appurtenances—four large parasols that made a canopy of shade, a portable bath house for dressing, a pneumatic rubber horse, new things that Rosemary had never seen, from the first burst of luxury manufacturing after the war, and probably in the hands of the first of purchasers. She had gathered that they were fashionable people, but though her mother had brought her up to beware of such people as drones, she did not feel that way here. Even in their absolute immobility, complete as that of the morning, she felt a purpose, a working over something, a direction, an act of creation different from any she had known. Her immature mind made no speculations upon the nature of their relation to each other, she was only concerned with their attitude toward herself—but she perceived the web of some pleasant interrelation, which she expressed with the thought that they seemed to have a very good time.

She looked in turn at the three men, temporarily expropriating them. All three were personable in different ways: all were of a special gentleness that she felt was part of their lives, past and future, not circumstanced by events, not at all like the company manners of actors, and she detected also a far-reaching delicacy that was different from the rough and ready good fellowship of directors, who represented the intellectuals in her life. Actors and directors —those were the only men she had ever known, those and the heterogeneous, indistinguishable mass of college boys, interested only in love at first sight, whom she had met at the Yale prom last fall.

These three were different. Barban was less civilized, more skeptical and scoffing; his manners were formal, even perfunctory. Abe North had, under his shyness, a desperate humor that amused but puzzled her. Her serious nature distrusted its ability to make a supreme impression on him.

But Dick Diver—he was all complete there. Silently she admired him. His complexion was reddish and weather-burned, so was his short hair—a light growth of it rolled down his arms and hands. His eyes were of a bright, hard blue. His nose was somewhat pointed and there was never any doubt at whom he was looking or talking —and this is a flattering attention, for who looks at us?—glances fall upon us, curious or uninterested, nothing more. His voice, with some faint Irish melody running through it, wooed the world, yet she felt the layer of hardness in him, of self-control and of self-discipline, her own virtues. Oh, she chose him, and Nicole lifting her head saw her choose him, heard the little sigh at the fact that he was already possessed.

Toward noon the McKiscos, Mrs. Abrams, Mr. Dumphry, and Señor Campion came on the beach. They had brought a new umbrella that they set up with side glances toward the Divers, and crept under with satisfied expressions—all save Mr. McKisco, who remained derisively without. In his raking Dick had passed near them and now he returned to the umbrellas.

"The two young men are reading the Book of Etiquette together," he said in a low voice.

"Planning to mix wit de quality," said Abe.

Mary North, the very tanned young woman whom Rosemary had

encountered the first day on the raft, came in from swimming and said with a smile that was a rakish gleam:

"So Mr. and Mrs. Neverquiver have arrived."

"They're this man's friends," Nicole reminded her, indicating Abe. "Why doesn't he go and speak to them? Don't you think they're attractive?"

"I think they're very attractive," Abe agreed. "I just don't think they're attractive, that's all."

"Well, I *have* felt there were too many people on the beach this summer," Nicole admitted. "*Our* beach that Dick made out of a pebble pile." She considered, and then lowering her voice out of the range of the trio of nannies who sat back under another umbrella, "Still they're preferable to those British last summer who kept shouting about: 'Isn't the sea blue? Isn't the sky white? Isn't little Nellie's nose red?'"

Rosemary thought she would not like to have Nicole for an enemy.

"But you didn't see the fight," Nicole continued. "The day before you came, the married man, the one with the name that sounds like a substitute for gasoline or butter——"

"McKisco?"

"Yes—well they were having words and she tossed some sand in his face. So naturally he sat on top of her and rubbed her face in the sand. We were—electrified. I wanted Dick to interfere."

"I think," said Dick Diver, staring down abstractedly at the straw mat, "that I'll go over and invite them to dinner."

"No, you won't," Nicole told him quickly.

"I think it would be a very good thing. They're here—let's adjust ourselves."

"We're very well adjusted," she insisted, laughing. "I'm not going to have *my* nose rubbed in the sand. I'm a mean, hard woman," she explained to Rosemary, and then raising her voice, "Children, put on your bathing suits!"

Rosemary felt that this swim would become the typical one of her life, the one that would always pop up in her memory at the mention of swimming. Simultaneously the whole party moved toward the water, super-ready from the long, forced inaction, passing from the heat to the cool with the gourmandise of a tingling curry eaten with chilled white wine. The Divers' day was spaced like the day of the older civilizations to yield the utmost from the materials at hand, and to give all the transitions their full value, and she did not know that there would be another transition presently from the utter absorption of the swim to the garrulity of the Provencal lunch hour. But again she had the sense that Dick was taking care of her, and she delighted in responding to the eventual movement as if it had been an order.

Nicole handed her husband the curious garment on which she had been working. He went into the dressing tent and inspired a commotion by appearing in a moment clad in transparent black lace drawers. Close inspection revealed that actually they were lined with flesh-colored cloth.

"Well, if that isn't a pansy's trick!" exclaimed Mr. McKisco contemptuously—then turning quickly to Mr. Dumphry and Mr. Campion he added, "Oh, I beg your pardon."

Rosemary bubbled with delight at the trunks. Her naïveté responded whole-heartedly to the expensive simplicity of the Divers, unaware of its complexity and its lack of innocence, unaware that it was all a selection of quality rather than quantity from the run of the world's bazaar; and that the simplicity of behavior also, the nursery-like peace and good will, the emphasis on the simpler virtues, was part of a desperate bargain with the gods and had been attained through struggles she could not have guessed at. At that moment the Divers represented externally the exact furthermost evolution of a class, so that most people seemed awkward beside them—in reality a qualitative change had already set in that was not at all apparent to Rosemary.

She stood with them as they took sherry and ate crackers. Dick Diver looked at her with cold blue eyes; his kind, strong mouth said thoughtfully and deliberately:

"You're the only girl I've seen for a long time that actually did look like something blooming."

In her mother's lap afterward Rosemary cried and cried.

"I love him, Mother. I'm desperately in love with him—I never knew I could feel that way about anybody. And he's married and I like her too—it's just hopeless. Oh, I love him so!"

"I'm curious to meet him."

"She invited us to dinner Friday."

"If you're in love it ought to make you happy. You ought to laugh."

Rosemary looked up and gave a beautiful little shiver of her face and laughed. Her mother always had a great influence on her.

CHAPTER VI

Rosemary went to Monte Carlo feeling nearly as sulky as it was possible for her to be. She rode up the rugged hill to La Turbie, to an old Gaumont lot in process of reconstruction, and as she stood by the grilled entrance waiting for an answer to the message on her card, she might have been looking into Hollywood. The bizarre débris of some recent picture, a decayed street scene in India, a great cardboard whale, a monstrous tree bearing cherries large as basket-balls, bloomed there by exotic dispensation, autochthonous as the pale amaranth, mimosa, cork oak, or dwarfed pine. There were a quick-lunch shack and two barnlike stages and, everywhere about the lot, groups of waiting, hopeful, painted faces.

After ten minutes a young man with hair the color of canary feathers hurried down to the gate.

"Come in, Miss Hoyt. Mr. Brady's on the set, but he's very anxious to see you. I'm sorry you were kept waiting, but you know some of these French dames are worse about pushing themselves in——"

The studio manager opened a small door in the blank wall of stage building and with sudden glad familiarity Rosemary followed him into half darkness. Here and there figures spotted the twilight, turning up ashen faces to her like souls in purgatory watching the passage of a mortal through. There were whispers and soft voices and, apparently from afar, the gentle tremolo of a small organ. Turning the corner made by some flats, they came upon the white crackling glow of a stage, where a French actor—his shirt-front, collar, and cuffs tinted a brilliant pink—and an American actress stood motionless face to face. They stared at each other with dogged eyes, as though they had been in the same position for hours; and still for a long time nothing happened, no one moved. A bank of lights went off with a savage hiss, went on again; the plaintive tap of a hammer begged admission to nowhere in the distance; a blue face appeared among the blinding lights above, called something unintelligible into the upper blackness. Then the silence was broken by a voice in front of Rosemary.

"Baby, you don't take off the stockings, you can spoil ten more pairs. That dress is fifteen pounds."

Stepping backward the speaker ran against Rosemary, whereupon the studio manager said, "Hey, Earl—Miss Hoyt."

They were meeting for the first time. Brady was quick and strenuous. As he took her hand she saw him look her over from head to foot, a gesture she recognized and one that made her feel at home, but gave her always a faint feeling of superiority to whoever made it. If her person was property she could exercise whatever advantage was inherent in its ownership.

"I thought you'd be along any day now," Brady said, in a voice that was just a little too compelling for private life, and that trailed with it a faintly defiant cockney accent. "Have a good trip?"

"Yes, but we're glad to be going home."

"No-o-o!" he protested. "Stay awhile—I want to talk to you. Let me tell you that was some picture of yours—that *Daddy's Girl*. I saw it in Paris. I wired the coast right away to see if you were signed."

"I just had—I'm sorry."

"God, what a picture!"

Not wanting to smile in silly agreement Rosemary frowned.

"Nobody wants to be thought of forever for just one picture," she said.

"Sure—that's right. What're your plans?"

"Mother thought I needed a rest. When I get back we'll probably either sign up with First National or keep on with Famous."

"Who's we?"

"My mother. She decides business matters. I couldn't do without her."

Again he looked her over completely and, as he did, something in Rosemary went out to him. It was not liking, not at all the spontaneous admiration she had felt for the man on the beach this morning. It was a click. He desired her and, so far as her virginal emotions went, she contemplated a surrender with equanimity. Yet

she knew she would forget him half an hour after she left him—
like an actor kissed in a picture.

"Where are you staying?" Brady asked. "Oh, yes, at Gausse's.
Well, my plans are made for this year, too, but that letter I wrote
you still stands. Rather make a picture with you than any girl since
Connie Talmadge was a kid."

"I feel the same way. Why don't you come back to Hollywood?"

"I can't stand the damn place. I'm fine here. Wait till after this
shot and I'll show you around."

Walking onto the set he began to talk to the French actor in
a low, quiet voice.

Five minutes passed—Brady talked on, while from time to time
the Frenchman shifted his feet and nodded. Abruptly, Brady broke
off, calling something to the lights that startled them into a humming glare. Los Angeles was loud about Rosemary now. Unap-
palled she moved once more through the city of thin partitions,
wanting to be back there. But she did not want to see Brady in the
mood she sensed he would be in after he had finished and she left
the lot with a spell still upon her. The Mediterranean world was
less silent now that she knew the studio was there. She liked the
people on the streets and bought herself a pair of espadrilles on
the way to the train.

Her mother was pleased that she had done so accurately what
she was told to do, but she still wanted to launch her out and
away. Mrs. Speers was fresh in appearance but she was tired;
deathbeds make people tired indeed and she had watched beside
a couple.

CHAPTER VII

FEELING GOOD FROM THE rosy wine at lunch, Nicole Diver folded her arms high enough for the artificial camellia on her shoulder to touch her cheek, and went out into her lovely grassless garden. The garden was bounded on one side by the house, from which it flowed and into which it ran, on two sides by the old village, and on the last by the cliff falling by ledges to the sea.

Along the walls on the village side all was dusty, the wriggling vines, the lemon and eucalyptus trees, the casual wheelbarrow, left only a moment since, but already grown into the path, atrophied and faintly rotten. Nicole was invariably somewhat surprised that, by turning in the other direction past a bed of peonies, she walked into an area so green and cool that the leaves and petals were curled with tender damp.

Knotted at her throat she wore a lilac scarf that even in the achromatic sunshine cast its color up to her face and down around her moving feet in a lilac shadow. Her face was hard, almost stern, save for the soft gleam of piteous doubt that looked from her green eyes. Her once fair hair had darkened, but she was lovelier now at twenty-four than she had been at eighteen, when her hair was brighter than she.

Following a walk marked by an intangible mist of bloom that followed the white border stones, she came to a space overlooking the sea where there were lanterns asleep in the fig trees and a big table and wicker chairs and a great market umbrella from Siena, all gathered about an enormous pine, the biggest tree in the garden. She paused there a moment, looking absently at a growth of nasturtiums and iris tangled at its foot, as though sprung from a careless handful of seeds, listening to the plaints and accusations of some nursery squabble in the house. When this died away on the summer air, she walked on, between kaleidoscopic peonies massed in pink

82

clouds, black and brown tulips and fragile mauve-stemmed roses, transparent like sugar flowers in a confectioner's window—until, as if the scherzo of color could reach no further intensity, it broke off suddenly in mid-air, and moist steps went down to a level five feet below.

Here there was a well with the boarding around it dank and slippery even on the brightest days. She went up the stairs on the other side and into the vegetable garden; she walked rather quickly; she liked to be active, though at times she gave an impression of repose that was at once static and evocative. This was because she knew few words and believed in none, and in the world she was rather silent, contributing just her share of urbane humor with a precision that approached meagreness. But at the moment when strangers tended to grow uncomfortable in the presence of this economy she would seize the topic and rush off with it, feverishly surprised with herself—then bring it back and relinquish it abruptly, almost timidly, like an obedient retriever, having been adequate and something more.

As she stood in the fuzzy green light of the vegetable garden, Dick crossed the path ahead of her going to his work house. Nicole waited silently till he had passed; then she went on through lines of prospective salads to a little menagerie where pigeons and rabbits and a parrot made a medley of insolent noises at her. Descending to another ledge she reached a low, curved wall and looked down seven hundred feet to the Mediterranean Sea.

She stood in the ancient hill village of Tarmes. The villa and its grounds were made out of a row of peasant dwellings that abutted on the cliff—five small houses had been combined to make the house and four destroyed to make the garden. The exterior walls were untouched, so that from the road far below it was indistinguishable from the violet gray mass of the town.

For a moment Nicole stood looking down at the Mediterranean, but there was nothing to do with that, even with her tireless hands. Presently Dick came out of his one-room house carrying a telescope and looked east toward Cannes. In a moment Nicole swam into his field of vision, whereupon he disappeared into his house and came out with a megaphone. He had many light mechanical devices.

"Nicole," he shouted, "I forgot to tell you that as a final apostolic gesture I invited Mrs. Abrams, the woman with the white hair."

"I suspected it. It's an outrage."

The ease with which her reply reached him seemed to belittle his megaphone, so she raised her voice and called, "Can you hear me?"

"Yes." He lowered the megaphone and then raised it stubbornly. "I'm going to invite some more people too. I'm going to invite the two young men."

"All right," she agreed placidly.

"I want to give a really *bad* party. I mean it. I want to give a party where there's a brawl and seductions and people going home with their feelings hurt and women passed out in the cabinet de toilette. You wait and see."

He went back into his house and Nicole saw that one of his most characteristic moods was upon him, the excitement that swept everyone up into it and was inevitably followed by his own form of melancholy, which he never displayed but at which she guessed. This excitement about things reached an intensity out of proportion to their importance, generating a really extraordinary virtuosity with people. Save among a few of the tough-minded and perennially suspicious, he had the power of arousing a fascinating and un-critical love. The reaction came when he realized the waste and extravagance involved. He sometimes looked back with awe at the carnivals of affection he had given, as a general might gaze upon a massacre he had ordered to satisfy an impersonal blood lust.

But to be included in Dick Diver's world for a while was a remarkable experience: people believed he made special reservations about them, recognizing the proud uniqueness of their destinies. He won everyone quickly with an exquisite consideration and a polite-ness that moved so fast and intuitively that it could be examined only in its effect. Then, without caution, lest the first bloom of the relation wither, he opened the gate to his amusing world. So long as they subscribed to it completely, their happiness was his pre-occupation, but at the first flicker of doubt as to its all-inclusiveness he evaporated before their eyes, leaving little communicable memory of what he had said or done.

At eighty-thirty that evening he came out to meet his first guests, his coat carried rather ceremoniously, rather promisingly, in his hand, like a toreador's cape. It was characteristic that after greeting

Rosemary and her mother he waited for them to speak first, as if to allow them the reassurance of their own voices in new surroundings.

Under the spell of the climb to Tarmes and the fresher air, Rosemary and her mother looked about appreciatively. Just as the personal qualities of extraordinary people can make themselves plain in an unaccustomed change of expression, so the intensely calculated perfection of Villa Diana transpired all at once through such minute failures as the chance apparition of a maid in the background or the perversity of a cork. While the first guests arrived bringing with them the excitement of the night, the domestic activity of the day receded past them gently, symbolized by the Diver children and their governess still at supper on the terrace.

"What a beautiful garden!" Mrs. Speers exclaimed.

"Nicole's garden," said Dick. "She won't let it alone—she nags it all the time, worries about its diseases. Any day now I expect to have her come down with Powdery Mildew or Fly Speck, or Late Blight." He pointed his forefinger decisively at Rosemary, saying with a lightness seeming to conceal a paternal interest, "I'm going to save your reason—I'm going to give you a hat to wear on the beach."

He turned them from the garden to the terrace, where he poured a cocktail. Earl Brady arrived and discovered Rosemary with surprise. His manner was softer than at the studio, as if his differentness had been put on at the gate, and Rosemary, comparing him instantly with Dick Diver, swung sharply toward the latter. In comparison Earl Brady seemed faintly gross, faintly ill-bred; once more, though, she felt an electric response to his person.

He spoke familiarly to the children, who were getting up from their outdoor supper.

"Hello, Lanier, how about a song? Will you and Topsy sing me a song?"

"What shall we sing?" agreed the little boy, with the odd chanting accent of American children brought up in France.

"That song about 'Mon Ami Pierrot.' "

Brother and sister stood side by side without self-consciousness and their voices soared sweet and shrill upon the evening air.

> *"Au clair de la lune,*
> *Mon ami Pierrot,*
> *Prête-moi ta plume*
> *Pour écrire un mot.*
> *Ma chandelle est morte,*
> *Je n'ai plus de feu,*
> *Ouvre-moi ta porte,*
> *Pour l'amour de Dieu."*

The singing ceased and the children, their faces aglow with the late sunshine, stood smiling calmly at their success. Rosemary was thinking that the Villa Diana was the centre of the world. On such a stage some memorable thing was sure to happen. She lighted up higher as the gate tinkled open and the rest of the guests arrived in a body. The McKiscos, Mrs. Abrams, Mr. Dumphry, and Mr. Campion came up to the terrace.

Rosemary had a sharp feeling of disappointment—she looked quickly at Dick, as though to ask an explanation of this incongruous mingling. But there was nothing unusual in his expression. He greeted his new guests with a proud bearing and an obvious deference to their infinite and unknown possibilities. She believed in him so much that presently she accepted the rightness of the McKiscos' presence as if she had expected to meet them all long.

"I've met you in Paris," McKisco said to Abe North, who with his wife had arrived on their heels, "in fact I've met you twice."

"Yes, I remember," Abe said.

"Then where was it?" demanded McKisco, not content to let well enough alone.

"Why, I think—" Abe got tired of the game, "I can't remember."

The interchange filled a pause and Rosemary's instinct was that something tactful should be said by somebody, but Dick made no attempt to break up the grouping formed by these late arrivals, not even to disarm Mrs. McKisco of her air of supercilious amusement. He did not solve this social problem because he knew it was not of importance at the moment and would solve itself. He was saving his newness for a larger effort, waiting a more significant moment for his guests to be conscious of a good time.

Rosemary stood beside Tommy Barban. He was in a particularly

scornful mood and there seemed to be some special stimulus working upon him. He was leaving in the morning.

"Going home?"

"Home? I have no home. I am going to a war."

"What war?"

"What war? Any war. I haven't seen a paper lately but I suppose there's a war—there always is."

"Don't you care what you fight for?"

"Not at all—so long as I'm well treated. When I'm in a rut I
come to see the Divers, because then I know that in a few weeks
I'll want to go to war."

Rosemary stiffened.

"You like the Divers," she reminded him.

"Of course—especially her—but they make me want to go to
war."

She considered this, to no avail. The Divers made her want to
stay near them forever.

"You're half American," she said, as if that should solve the
problem.

"Also I'm half French, and I was educated in England and since
I was eighteen I've worn the uniforms of eight countries. But I
hope I did not give you the impression that I am not fond of the
Divers—I am, especially of Nicole."

"How could anyone help it?" she said simply.

She felt far from him. The undertone of his words repelled her
and she withdrew her adoration for the Divers from the profanity
of his bitterness. She was glad he was not next to her at dinner
and she was still thinking of his words "especially her" as they
moved toward the table in the garden.

For a moment now she was beside Dick Diver on the path.
Alongside his hard, neat brightness everything faded into the surety
that he knew everything. For a year, which was forever, she had
had money and a certain celebrity and contact with the celebrated,
and these latter had presented themselves merely as powerful en-
largements of the people with whom the doctor's widow and her
daughter had associated in a hôtel-pension in Paris. Rosemary was
a romantic and her career had not provided many satisfactory oppor-
tunities on that score. Her mother, with the idea of a career for

Rosemary, would not tolerate any such spurious substitutes as the excitations available on all sides, and indeed Rosemary was already beyond that—she was In the movies but not at all At them. So when she had seen approval of Dick Diver in her mother's face it meant that he was "the real thing"; it meant permission to go as far as she could.

"I was watching you," he said, and she knew he meant it. "We've grown very fond of you."

"I fell in love with you the first time I saw you," she said quietly.

He pretended not to have heard, as if the compliment were purely formal.

"New friends," he said, as if it were an important point, "can often have a better time together than old friends."

With that remark, which she did not understand precisely, she found herself at the table, picked out by slowly emerging lights against the dark dusk. A chord of delight struck inside her when she saw that Dick had taken her mother on his right hand; for herself she was between Luis Campion and Brady.

Surcharged with her emotion she turned to Brady with the intention of confiding in him, but at her first mention of Dick a hard-boiled sparkle in his eyes gave her to understand that he refused the fatherly office. In turn she was equally firm when he tried to monopolize her hand, so they talked shop, or rather she listened while he talked shop, her polite eyes never leaving his face; but her mind was so definitely elsewhere that she felt he must guess the fact. Intermittently she caught the gist of his sentences and supplied the rest from her subconscious, as one picks up the striking of a clock in the middle with only the rhythm of the first uncounted strokes lingering in the mind.

CHAPTER VIII

In a pause Rosemary looked away and up the table, where Nicole sat between Tommy Barban and Abe North, her chow's hair foaming and frothing in the candlelight. Rosemary listened, caught sharply by the rich clipped voice in infrequent speech:

"The poor man," Nicole exclaimed. "Why did you want to saw him in two?"

"Naturally I wanted to see what was inside a waiter. Wouldn't you like to know what was inside a waiter?"

"Old menus," suggested Nicole with a short laugh. "Pieces of broken china and tips and pencil stubs."

"Exactly—but the thing was to prove it scientifically. And of course doing it with that musical saw would have eliminated any sordidness."

"Did you intend to play the saw while you performed the operation?" Tommy inquired.

"We didn't get quite that far. We were alarmed by the screams. We thought he might rupture something."

"All sounds very peculiar to me," said Nicole. "Any musician that'll use another musician's saw to——"

They had been at table half an hour and a perceptible change had set in—person by person had given up something, a preoccupation, an anxiety, a suspicion, and now they were only their best selves and the Divers' guests. Not to have been friendly and interested would have seemed to reflect on the Divers, so now they were all trying and, seeing this, Rosemary liked everyone—except McKisco, who had contrived to be the unassimilated member of the party. This was less from ill will than from his determination to sustain with wine the good spirits he had enjoyed on his arrival. Lying back in his place between Earl Brady, to whom he had addressed several withering remarks about the movies, and Mrs.

Abrams, to whom he said nothing, he stared at Dick Diver with an expression of devastating irony, the effect being occasionally interrupted by his attempts to engage Dick in a cater-cornered conversation across the table.

"Aren't you a friend of Van Buren Denby?" he would say.

"I don't believe I know him."

"I thought you were a friend of his," he persisted irritably.

When the subject of Mr. Denby fell of its own weight, he essayed other equally irrelevant themes, but each time the very deference of Dick's attention seemed to paralyze him, and after a moment's stark pause the conversation that he had interrupted would go on without him. He tried breaking into other dialogues, but it was like continually shaking hands with a glove from which the hand had been withdrawn—so finally, with a resigned air of being among children, he devoted his attention entirely to the champagne.

Rosemary's glance moved at intervals around the table, eager for the others' enjoyment, as if they were her future stepchildren. A gracious table light, emanating from a bowl of spicy pinks, fell upon Mrs. Abrams' face, cooked to a turn in Veuve Cliquot, full of vigor, tolerance, adolescent good will; next to her sat Mr. Royal Dumphry, his girl's comeliness less startling in the pleasure world of evening; then Violet McKisco, whose prettiness had been piped to the surface of her, so that she ceased her struggle to make tangible to herself her shadowy position as the wife of an arriviste who had not arrived.

Then came Dick, with his arms full of the slack he had taken up from others, deeply merged in his own party.

Then her mother, forever perfect.

Then Barban, talking to her mother with an urbane fluency that made Rosemary like him again. Then Nicole. Rosemary saw her suddenly in a new way and found her one of the most beautiful people she had ever known. Her face, the face of a saint, a viking madonna, shone through the faint motes that snowed across the candlelight, drew down its flush from the wine-colored lanterns in the pine. She was still as still.

Abe North was talking to her about his moral code: "Of course I've got one," he insisted, "—a man can't live without a moral code. Mine is that I'm against the burning of witches. Whenever they burn a witch I get all hot under the collar." Rosemary knew from

Brady that he was a musician who, after a brilliant and precocious start, had composed nothing for seven years.

Next was Campion, managing somehow to restrain his most blatant effeminacy, and even to visit upon those near him a certain disinterested motherliness. Then Mary North with a face so merry that it was impossible not to smile back into the white mirrors of her teeth—the whole area around her parted lips was a lovely little circle of delight.

Finally Brady, whose heartiness became, moment by moment, a social thing instead of a crude assertion and reassertion of his own mental health, and his preservation of it by a detachment from the frailties of others.

Rosemary, as dewy with belief as a child from one of Mrs. Burnett's vicious tracts, had a conviction of homecoming, of a return from the derisive and salacious improvisations of the frontier. There were fireflies riding on the dark air and a dog baying on some low and far-away ledge of the cliff. The table seemed to have risen a little toward the sky like a mechanical dancing platform, giving the people around it a sense of being alone with each other in the dark universe, nourished by its only food, warmed by its only lights. And, as if a curious hushed laugh from Mrs. McKisco were a signal that such a detachment from the world had been attained, the two Divers began suddenly to warm and glow and expand, as if to make up to their guests, already so subtly assured of their importance, so flattered with politeness, for anything they might still miss from that country well left behind. Just for a moment they seemed to speak to everyone at the table, singly and together, assuring them of their friendliness, their affection. And for a moment the faces turned up toward them were like the faces of poor children at a Christmas tree. Then abruptly the table broke up—the moment when the guests had been daringly lifted above conviviality into the rarer atmosphere of sentiment was over before it could be irreverently breathed, before they had half realized it was there.

But the diffused magic of the hot sweet South had withdrawn into them—the soft-pawed night and the ghostly wash of the Mediterranean far below—the magic left these things aand melted into the two Divers and became part of them. Rosemary watched Nicole pressing upon her mother a yellow evening bag she had admired, saying, "I think things ought to belong to the people that like them"—and then sweeping into it all the yellow articles she could find, a pencil, a lipstick, a little notebook, "because they all go together."

Nicole disappeared and presently Rosemary noticed that Dick was no longer there; the guests distributed themselves in the garden or drifted in toward the terrace.

"Do you want," Violet McKisco asked Rosemary, "to go to the bathroom?"

Not at that precise moment.

"I want," insisted Mrs. McKisco, "to go to the bathroom." As a frank outspoken woman she walked toward the house, dragging her secret after her, while Rosemary looked after with reprobation. Earl Brady proposed that they walk down to the sea wall, but she felt that this was her time to have a share of Dick Diver when he reappeared, so she stalled, listening to McKisco quarrel with Barban.

"Why do you want to fight the Soviets?" McKisco said. "The greatest experiment ever made by humanity? And the Riff? It seems to me it would be more heroic to fight on the just side."

"How do you find out which it is?" asked Barban dryly.

"Why—usually everybody intelligent knows."

"Are you a Communist?"

"I'm a Socialist," said McKisco, "I sympathize with Russia."

"Well, I'm a soldier," Barban answered pleasantly. "My business is to kill people. I fought against the Riff because I am a European, and I have fought the Communists because they want to take my property from me."

"Of all the narrow-minded excuses." McKisco looked around to establish a derisive liaison with someone else, but without success. He had no idea what he was up against in Barban, neither of the simplicity of the other man's bag of ideas nor of the complexity of his training. McKisco knew what ideas were, and as his mind grew he was able to recognize and sort an increasing number of them —but faced by a man whom he considered "dumb," one in whom he found no ideas he could recognize as such, and yet to whom he could not feel personally superior, he jumped at the conclusion that Barban was the end product of an archaic world and, as such, worthless. McKisco's contacts with the princely classes in America had impressed upon him their uncertain and fumbling snobbery, their delight in ignorance, and their deliberate rudeness, all lifted from the English with no regard paid to factors that make English philistinism and rudeness purposeful, and applied in a land where a little knowledge and civility buy more than they do anywhere else —an attitude which reached its apogee in the "Harvard manner" of about 1900. He thought that this Barban was of that type, and being drunk rashly forgot that he was in awe of him.

Feeling vaguely ashamed for McKisco, Rosemary waited, placid but inwardly on fire, for Dick Diver's return. From her chair at the deserted table with Barban, McKisco, and Abe she looked up along the path edged with shadowy myrtle and fern to the stone terrace and, falling in love with her mother's profile against a lighted door, was about to go there when Mrs. McKisco came hurrying down from the house.

She exuded excitement. In the very silence with which she pulled out a chair and sat down, her eyes staring, her mouth working a little, they all recognized a person crop-full of news, and her husband's "What's the matter, Vi?" came naturally, as all eyes turned toward her.

"My dear—" she said at large, and then addressed Rosemary, "my dear—it's nothing. I really can't say a word."

"You're among friends," said Abe.

"Well, upstairs I came upon a scene, my dears——'

Shaking her head cryptically she broke off just in time, for Tommy arose and addressed her politely but sharply:

"It's inadvisable to comment on what goes on in this house.'

CHAPTER IX

Violet breathed loud and hard once and with an effort brought another expression into her face.

Dick came finally and with a sure instinct he separated Barban and the McKiscos and became excessively ignorant and inquisitive about literature with McKisco—thus giving the latter the moment of superiority which he required. The others helped him carry lamps up—who would not be pleased at carrying lamps helpfully through the darkness? Rosemary helped, meanwhile responding patiently to Royal Dumphry's inexhaustible curiosity about Hollywood.

Now—she was thinking—I've earned a time alone with him. He must know that because his laws are like the laws Mother taught me.

Rosemary was right—presently he detached her from the company on the terrace and they were alone together, borne away from the house toward the seaside wall with what were less steps than irregularly spaced intervals, through some of which she was pulled, through others blown.

They looked out over the Mediterranean. Far below, the last excursion boat from the Iles de Lérins floated across the bay like a Fourth-of-July balloon footloose in the heavens. Between the black isles it floated, softly parting the dark tide.

"I understand why you speak as you do of your mother," he said. "Her attitude toward you is very fine, I think. She has a sort of wisdom that's rare in America."

"Mother is perfect," she prayed.

"I was talking to her about a plan I have—she told me that how long you both stayed in France depended on you."

On *you*, Rosemary all but said aloud.

"So since things are over down here——"

"Over?" she inquired.

"Well, this is over—this part of the summer is over. Last week Nicole's sister left, tomorrow Tommy Barban leaves, Monday Abe and Mary North are leaving. Maybe we'll have more fun this summer, but this particular fun is over. I want it to die violently instead of fading out sentimentally—that's why I gave this party. What I'm coming to is—Nicole and I are going up to Paris to see Abe North off for America—I wonder if you'd like to go with us."

"What did Mother say?"

"She seemed to think it would be fine. She doesn't want to go herself. She wants you to go alone."

"I haven't seen Paris since I've been grown," said Rosemary. "I'd love to see it with you."

"That's nice of you." Did she imagine that his voice was suddenly metallic? "Of course we've been excited about you from the moment you came on the beach. That vitality, we were sure it was professional—especially Nicole was. It'd never use itself up on any one person or group."

Her instinct cried out to her that he was passing her along slowly toward Nicole and she put her own brakes on, saying with an equal hardness:

"I wanted to know all of you too—especially you. I told you I fell in love with you the first time I saw you."

She was right going at it that way. But the space between heaven and earth had cooled his mind, destroyed the impulsiveness that had led him to bring her here, and made him aware of the too obvious appeal, the struggle with an unrehearsed scene and unfamiliar words.

He tried now to make her want to go back to the house and it was difficult, and he did not quite want to lose her. She felt only the draft blowing as he joked with her good-humoredly.

"You don't know what you want. You go and ask your mother what you want."

She was stricken. She touched him, feeling the smooth cloth of his dark coat like a chasuble. She seemed about to fall to her knees —from that position she delivered her last shot.

"I think you're the most wonderful person I ever met—except my mother."

"You have romantic eyes."

His laughter swept them on up toward the terrace where he delivered her to Nicole.

Too soon it had become time to go and the Divers helped them all to go quickly. In the Divers' big Isotta there would be Tommy Barban and his baggage—he was spending the night at the hotel to catch an early train—with Mrs. Abrams, the McKiscos, and Campion. Earl Brady was going to drop Rosemary and her mother on his way to Monte Carlo, and Royal Dumphry rode with them because the Divers' car was crowded. Down in the garden lanterns still glowed over the table where they had dined, as the Divers stood side by side in the gate, Nicole blooming away and filling the night with graciousness, and Dick bidding good-bye to everyone by name. To Rosemary it seemed very poignant to drive away and leave them in their house. Again she wondered what Mrs. McKisco had seen in the bathroom.

CHAPTER X

IT WAS A LIMPID black night, hung as in a basket from a single dull star. The horn of the car ahead was muffled by the resistance of the thick air. Brady's chauffeur drove slowly; the tail-light of the other car appeared from time to time at turnings—then not at all. But after ten minutes it came into sight again, drawn up at the side of the road. Brady's chauffeur slowed up behind, but immediately it began to roll forward slowly and they passed it. In the instant they passed it they heard a blur of voices from behind the reticence of the limousine and saw that the Divers' chauffeur was grinning. Then they went on, going fast through the alternating banks of darkness and thin night, descending at last in a series of roller-coaster swoops, to the great bulk of Gausse's hotel.

Rosemary dozed for three hours and then lay awake, suspended in the moonshine. Cloaked by the erotic darkness she exhausted the future quickly, with all the eventualities that might lead up to a kiss, but with the kiss itself as blurred as a kiss in pictures. She changed position in bed deliberately, the first sign of insomnia she had ever had, and tried to think with her mother's mind about the question. In this process she was often acute beyond her experience, with remembered things from old conversations that had gone into her half-heard.

Rosemary had been brought up with the idea of work. Mrs. Speers had spent the slim leavings of the men who had widowed her on her daughter's education, and when she blossomed out at sixteen with that extraordinary hair, had rushed her to Aix-les-Bains and marched her unannounced into the suite of an American producer who was recuperating there. When the producer went to New York they went too. Thus Rosemary had passed her entrance examinations. With the ensuing success and the promise of comparative stability that followed, Mrs. Speers had felt free to tacitly imply tonight:

"You were brought up to work—not especially to marry. Now you've found your first nut to crack and it's a good nut—go ahead and put whatever happens down to experience. Wound yourself or him—whatever happens it can't spoil you, because economically you're a boy, not a girl."

Rosemary had never done much thinking, save about the illimitability of her mother's perfections, so this final severance of the umbilical cord disturbed her sleep. A false dawn sent the sky pressing through the tall French windows, and getting up she walked out on the terrace, warm to her bare feet. There were secret noises in the air, an insistent bird achieved an ill-natured triumph with regularity in the trees above the tennis court; footfalls followed a round drive in the rear of the hotel, taking their tone in turn from the dust road, the crushed-stone walk, the cement steps, and then reversing the process in going away. Beyond the inky sea and far up that high, black shadow of a hill lived the Divers. She thought of them both together, heard them still singing faintly a song like rising smoke, like a hymn, very remote in time and far away. Their children slept, their gate was shut for the night.

She went inside and, dressing in a light gown and espadrilles, went out her window again and along the continuous terrace toward the front door, going fast since she found that other private rooms, exuding sleep, gave upon it. She stopped at the sight of a figure seated on the wide white stairway of the formal entrance—then she saw that it was Luis Campion and that he was weeping.

He was weeping hard and quietly and shaking in the same parts as a weeping woman. A scene in a rôle she had played last year swept over her irresistibly and advancing she touched him on the shoulder. He gave a little yelp before he recognized her.

"What is it?" Her eyes were level and kind and not slanted into him with hard curiosity. "Can I help you?"

"Nobody can help me. I knew it. I have only myself to blame. It's always the same."

He looked at her to see.

"No," he decided. "When you're older you'll know what people who love suffer. The agony. It's better to be cold and young than to love. It's happened to me before but never like this—so accidental —just when everything was going well."

His face was repulsive in the quickening light. Not by a flicker of her personality, a movement of the smallest muscle, did she betray her sudden disgust with whatever it was. But Campion's sensitivity realized it and he changed the subject rather suddenly.

"Abe North is around here somewhere."

"Why, he's staying at the Divers'!"

"Yes, but he's up—don't you know what happened?"

A shutter opened suddenly in a room two stories above and an English voice spat distinctly:

"*Will you kaindlay stup tucking!*"

Rosemary and Luis Campion went humbly down the steps and to a bench beside the road to the beach.

"Then you have no idea what's happened? My dear, the most extraordinary thing—" He was warming up now, hanging on to his revelation. "I've never seen a thing come so suddenly—I have always avoided violent people—they upset me so I sometimes have to go to bed for days."

He looked at her triumphantly. She had no idea what he was talking about.

"My dear," he burst forth, leaning toward her with his whole body as he touched her on the upper leg, to show it was no mere irresponsible venture of his hand—he was so sure of himself. "There's going to be a duel."

"Wh-at?"

"A duel with—we don't know what yet."

"Who's going to duel?"

"I'll tell you from the beginning." He drew a long breath and then said, as if it were rather to her discredit but he wouldn't hold it against her, "Of course, you were in the other automobile. Well, in a way you were lucky—I lost at least two years of my life, it came so suddenly."

"What came?" she demanded.

"I don't know what began it. First she began to talk——"

"Who?"

"Violet McKisco." He lowered his voice as if there were people under the bench. "But don't mention the Divers, because he made threats against anybody who mentioned it."

"Who did?"

"Tommy Barban, so don't you say I so much as mentioned them. None of us ever found out anyhow what it was Violet had to say because he kept interrupting her, and then her husband got into it and now, my dear, we have the duel. This morning—at five o'clock—in an hour." He sighed, suddenly thinking of his own griefs. "I almost wish it were I. I might as well be killed now I have nothing to live for." He broke off and rocked to and fro with sorrow.

Again the iron shutter parted above and the same British voice said:

"*Rilly, this must stup immejitly.*"

Simultaneously Abe North, looking somewhat distracted, came out of the hotel and perceived them against the sky, white over the sea. Rosemary shook her head warningly before he could speak and they moved another bench further down the road. Rosemary saw that Abe was a little tight.

"What are *you* doing up?" he demanded.

"I just got up." She started to laugh, but remembering the voice above she restrained herself.

"Plagued by the nightingale," Abe suggested, and repeated, "probably plagued by the nightingale. Has this sewing-circle member told you what happened?"

Campion said with dignity:

"I only know what I heard with my own ears."

He got up and walked swiftly away; Abe sat down beside Rosemary.

"Why did you treat him so badly?"

"Did I?" he asked surprised. "He's been weeping around here all morning."

"Well, maybe he's sad about something."

"Maybe he is."

"What about a duel? Who's going to duel? I thought there was something strange in that car. Is it true?"

"It certainly is cuckoo, but it seems to be true."

CHAPTER XI

THE TROUBLE BEGAN AT the time Earl Brady's car passed the Divers' car stopped on the road—Abe's account melted impersonally into the thronged night—Violet McKisco was telling Mrs. Abrams something she had found out about the Divers—she had gone upstairs in their house and she had come upon something there which had made a great impression on her. But Tommy is a watch-dog about the Divers. As a matter of fact she is inspiring and formidable—but it's a mutual thing, and the fact of The Divers together is more important to their friends than many of them realize. Of course it's done at a certain sacrifice—sometimes they seem just rather charming figures in a ballet, and worth just the attention you give a ballet, but it's more than that—you'd have to know the story. Anyhow Tommy is one of those men that Dick's passed along to Nicole and when Mrs. McKisco kept hinting at her story, he called them on it. He said:

"Mrs. Kisco, please don't talk further about Mrs. Diver."

"I wasn't talking to you," she objected.

"I think it's better to leave them out."

"Are they so sacred?"

"Leave them out. Talk about something else."

He was sitting on one of the two little seats beside Campion. Campion told me the story.

"Well, you're pretty high-handed," Violet came back.

You know how conversations are in cars late at night, some people murmuring and some not caring, giving up after the party, or bored or asleep. Well, none of them knew just what happened until the car stopped and Barban cried in a voice that shook everybody, a voice for cavalry:

"Do you want to step out here—we're only a mile from the hotel and you can walk it or I'll drag you there. *You've got to shut up and shut your wife up!*"

"You're a bully," said McKisco. "You know you're stronger muscularly than I am. But I'm not afraid of you—what they ought to have is the code duello——"

There's where he made his mistake, because Tommy, being French, leaned over and clapped him one, and then the chauffeur drove on. That was where you passed them. Then the women began. That was still the state of things when the car got to the hotel.

Tommy telephoned some man in Cannes to act as second and McKisco said he wasn't going to be seconded by Campion, who wasn't crazy for the job anyhow, so he telephoned me not to say anything but to come right down. Violet McKisco collapsed and Mrs. Abrams took her to her room and gave her a bromide, whereupon she fell comfortably asleep on the bed. When I got there I tried to argue with Tommy, but he wouldn't accept anything short of an apology and McKisco rather spunkily wouldn't give it.

When Abe had finished Rosemary asked thoughtfully:

"Do the Divers know it was about them?"

"No—and they're not ever going to know they had anything to do with it. That damn Campion had no business talking to you about it, but since he did—I told the chauffeur I'd get out the old musical saw if he opened his mouth about it. This fight's between two men—what Tommy needs is a good war."

"I hope the Divers don't find out," Rosemary said.

Abe peered at his watch.

"I've got to go up and see McKisco—do you want to come?—he feels sort of friendless. I bet he hasn't slept."

Rosemary had a vision of the desperate vigil that high-strung, badly organized man had probably kept. After a moment balanced between pity and repugnance she agreed and, full of morning energy, bounced upstairs beside Abe.

McKisco was sitting on his bed with his alcoholic combativeness vanished, in spite of the glass of champagne in his hand. He seemed very puny and cross and white. Evidently he had been writing and drinking all night. He stared confusedly at Abe and Rosemary and asked:

"Is it time?"

"No, not for half an hour."

The table was covered with papers, which he assembled with some difficulty into a long letter; the writing on the last pages was very large and illegible. In the delicate light of electric lamps fading, he scrawled his name at the bottom, crammed it into an envelope and handed it to Abe. "For my wife."

"You better souse your head in cold water," Abe suggested.

"You think I'd better?" inquired McKisco doubtfully. "I don't want to get too sober."

"Well, you look terrible now."

Obediently McKisco went into the bathroom.

"I'm leaving everything in an awful mess," he called. "I don't know how Violet will get back to America. I don't carry any insurance. I never got around to it."

"Don't talk nonsense, you'll be right here eating breakfast in an hour."

"Sure, I know." He came back with his hair wet and looked at Rosemary as if he saw her for the first time. Suddenly tears stood in his eyes. "I never have finished my novel. That's what makes me so sore. You don't like me," he said to Rosemary, "but that can't be helped. I'm primarily a literary man." He made a vague discouraged sound and shook his head helplessly. "I've made lots of mistakes in my life—many of them. But I've been one of the most prominent—in some ways——"

He gave this up and puffed at a dead cigarette.

"I do like you," said Rosemary, "but I don't think you ought to fight a duel."

"Yeah, I should have tried to beat him up, but it's done now. I've let myself be drawn into something that I had no right to be. I have a very violent temper—" He looked closely at Abe as if he expected the statement to be challenged. Then with an aghast laugh he raised the cold cigarette butt toward his mouth. His breathing quickened.

"The trouble was I suggested the duel—if Violet had only kept her mouth shut I could have fixed it. Of course even now I can just leave, or sit back and laugh at the whole thing—but I don't think Violet would ever respect me again."

"Yes, she would," said Rosemary. "She'd respect you more."

"No—you don't know Violet. She's very hard when she gets an advantage over you. We've been married twelve years, we had a little girl seven years old and she died and after that you know how it is. We both played around on the side a little, nothing serious but drifting apart—she called me a coward out there to-night."

Troubled, Rosemary didn't answer.

"Well, we'll see there's as little damage done as possible," said Abe. He opened the leather case. "These are Barban's duelling pistols—I borrowed them so you could get familiar with them. He carries them in his suitcase." He weighed one of the archaic weapons in his hand. Rosemary gave an exclamation of uneasiness and McKisco looked at the pistols anxiously.

"Well—it isn't as if we were going to stand up and pot each other with forty-fives," he said.

"I don't know," said Abe cruelly; "the idea is you can sight better along a long barrel."

"How about distance?" asked McKisco.

"I've inquired about that. If one or the other party has to be definitely eliminated they make it eight paces, if they're just good and sore it's twenty paces, and if it's only to vindicate their honor it's forty paces. His second agreed with me to make it forty."

"That's good."

"There's a wonderful duel in a novel of Pushkin's," recollected Abe. "Each man stood on the edge of a precipice, so if he was hit at all he was done for."

This seemed very remote and academic to McKisco, who stared at him and said, "What?"

"Do you want to take a quick dip and freshen up?"

"No—no, I couldn't swim." He sighed. "I don't see what it's all about," he said helplessly. "I don't see why I'm doing it."

It was the first thing he had ever done in his life. Actually he was one of those for whom the sensual world does not exist, and faced with a concrete fact he brought to it a vast surprise.

"We might as well be going," said Abe, seeing him fail a little.

"All right." He drank off a stiff drink of brandy, put the flask in his pocket, and said with almost a savage air: "What'll happen if I kill him—will they throw me in jail?"

"I'll run you over the Italian border."

He glanced at Rosemary—and then said apologetically to Abe:

"Before we start there's one thing I'd like to see you about alone."

"I hope neither of you gets hurt," Rosemary said. "I think it's very foolish and you ought to try to stop it."

CHAPTER XII

She found Campion downstairs in the deserted lobby.

"I saw you go upstairs," he said excitedly. "Is he all right? When is the duel going to be?"

"I don't know." She resented his speaking of it as a circus, with McKisco as the tragic clown.

"Will you go with me?" he demanded, with the air of having seats. "I've hired the hotel car."

"I don't want to go."

"Why not? I imagine it'll take years off my life, but I wouldn't miss it for worlds. We could watch it from quite far away."

"Why don't you get Mr. Dumphry to go with you?"

His monocle fell out, with no whiskers to hide in. He drew himself up.

"I never want to see him again."

"Well, I'm afraid I can't go. Mother wouldn't like it."

As Rosemary entered her room Mrs. Speers stirred sleepily and called to her:

"Where've you been?"

"I just couldn't sleep. You go back to sleep, Mother."

"Come in my room." Hearing her sit up in bed, Rosemary went in and told her what had happened.

"Why don't you go and see it?" Mrs. Speers suggested. "You needn't go up close and you might be able to help afterwards."

Rosemary did not like the picture of herself looking on and she demurred, but Mrs. Speers' consciousness was still clogged with sleep and she was reminded of night calls to death and calamity when she was the wife of a doctor. "I like you to go places and do things on your own initiative without me—you did much harder things for Rainy's publicity stunts."

Still Rosemary did not see why she should go, but she obeyed the sure, clear voice that had sent her into the stage entrance of the Odéon in Paris when she was twelve and greeted her when she came out again.

She thought she was reprieved when from the steps she saw Abe and McKisco drive away—but after a moment the hotel car came around the corner. Squealing delightedly Luis Campion pulled her in beside him.

"I hid there because they might not let us come. I've got my movie camera, you see."

She laughed helplessly. He was so terrible that he was no longer terrible, only dehumanized.

"I wonder why Mrs. McKisco didn't like the Divers?" she said. "They were very nice to her."

"Oh, it wasn't that. It was something she saw. We never did find exactly what it was because of Barban."

"Then that wasn't what made you so sad."

"Oh, no," he said, his voice breaking, "that was something else that happened when we got back to the hotel. But now I don't care—I wash my hands of it completely."

They followed the other car east along the shore past Juan les Pins, where the skeleton of the new Casino was rising. It was past four and under a blue-gray sky the first fishing boats were creaking out into a glaucous sea. Then they turned off the main road and into the back country.

"It's the golf course," cried Campion. "I'm sure that's where it's going to be."

He was right. When Abe's car pulled up ahead of them the east was crayoned red and yellow, promising a sultry day. Ordering the hotel car into a grove of pines Rosemary and Campion kept in the shadow of a wood and skirted the bleached fairway where Abe and McKisco were walking up and down, the latter raising his head at intervals like a rabbit scenting. Presently there were moving figures over by a farther tee and the watchers made out Barban and his French second, who carried the box of pistols under his arm.

Somewhat appalled, McKisco slipped behind Abe and took a long swallow of brandy. He walked on choking and would have marched directly up into the other party, but Abe stopped him and went forward to talk to the Frenchman. The sun was over the horizon.

Campion grabbed Rosemary's arm.

"I can't stand it," he squeaked, almost voiceless. "It's too much. This will cost me——"

"Let go," Rosemary said peremptorily. She breathed a frantic prayer in French.

The principals faced each other, Barban with the sleeve rolled up from his arm. His eyes gleamed restlessly in the sun, but his motion was deliberate as he wiped his palm on the seam of his trousers. McKisco, reckless with brandy, pursed his lips in a whistle and pointed his long nose about nonchalantly, until Abe stepped forward with a handkerchief in his hand. The French second stood with his face turned away. Rosemary caught her breath in terrible pity and gritted her teeth with hatred for Barban; then:

"One—two—three!" Abe counted in a strained voice.

They fired at the same moment. McKisco swayed but recovered himself. Both shots had missed.

"Now, that's enough!" cried Abe.

The duellists walked in, and everyone looked at Barban inquiringly.

"I declare myself unsatisfied."

"What? Sure you're satisfied," said Abe impatiently. "You just don't know it."

"Your man refuses another shot?"

"You're damn right, Tommy. You insisted on this and my client went through with it."

Tommy laughed scornfully.

"The distance was ridiculous," he said. "I'm not accustomed to such farces—your man must remember he's not now in America."

"No use cracking at America," said Abe rather sharply. And then, in a more conciliatory tone, "This has gone far enough, Tommy." They parleyed briskly for a moment—then Barban nodded and bowed coldly to his late antagonist.

"No shake hand?" suggested the French doctor.

"They already know each other," said Abe.

He turned to McKisco.

"Come on, let's get out."

As they strode off, McKisco, in exultation, gripped his arm.

"Wait a minute!" Abe said. "Tommy wants his pistol back. He might need it again."

McKisco handed it over.

"To hell with him," he said in a tough voice. "Tell him he can——"

"Shall I tell him you want another shot?"

"Well, I did it," cried McKisco, as they went along. "And I did it pretty well, didn't I? I wasn't yellow."

"You were pretty drunk," said Abe bluntly.

"No, I wasn't."

"All right, then, you weren't."

"Why would it make any difference if I had a drink or so?"

As his confidence mounted he looked resentfully at Abe.

"What difference does that make?" he repeated.

"If you can't see it, there's no use going into it."

"Don't you know everybody was drunk all the time during the war?"

"Well, let's forget it."

But the episode was not quite over. There were urgent footsteps in the heather behind them and the doctor drew up alongside.

"Pardon, Messieurs," he panted. "Voulez-vous régler mes honoraires? Naturellement c'est pour soins médicaux seulement. M. Barban n'a qu'un billet de mille et ne peut pas les régler et l'autre a laissé son porte-monnaie chez lui."

"Trust a Frenchman to think of that," said Abe, and then to the doctor. "Combien?"

"Let me pay this," said McKisco.

"No, I've got it. We were all in about the same danger."

Abe paid the doctor while McKisco suddenly turned into the bushes and was sick there. Then, paler than before, he strutted on with Abe toward the car through the now rosy morning.

Campion lay gasping on his back in the shrubbery, the only casualty of the duel, while Rosemary suddenly hysterical with laughter kept kicking at him with her espadrille. She did this persistently until she roused him—the only matter of importance to her now was that a few hours later on the beach she would see the person whom she still referred to in her mind as "the Divers."

CHAPTER XIII

THEY WERE AT VOISINS waiting for Nicole, six of them, Rosemary, the Norths, Dick Diver and two young French musicians. They were looking over the other patrons of the restaurant to see if they had repose—Dick said no American men had any repose, except himself, and they were seeking an example to confront him with. Things looked black for them—not a man had come into the restaurant for ten minutes without raising his hand to his face.

"We ought never to have given up waxed mustaches," said Abe. "Nevertheless Dick isn't the *only* man with repose——"

"Oh, yes, I am."

"—but he may be the only sober man with repose."

A well-dressed American had come in with two women, who swooped and fluttered unself-consciously around a table. Suddenly he perceived that he was being watched—whereupon his hand rose spasmodically and arranged a phantom bulge in his necktie. In another unseated party a man endlessly patted his shaven cheek with his palm, and his companion mechanically raised and lowered the stub of a cold cigar. The luckier ones fingered eyeglasses and facial hair, the unequipped stroked blank mouths, or even pulled desperately at the lobes of their ears.

A well-known general came in and Abe, counting on the man's first year at West Point—that year during which no cadet can resign and from which none ever recovers—made a bet with Dick of five dollars.

His hands hanging naturally at his sides, the general waited to be seated. Once his arms swung suddenly backward like a jumper's and Dick said, "Ah!" supposing he had lost control, but the general recovered and they breathed again—the agony was nearly over, the garcon was pulling out his chair.

With a touch of fury the conqueror shot up his hand and scratched his gray immaculate head.

"You see," said Dick smugly, "I'm the only one."

Rosemary was quite sure of it and Dick, realizing that he never had a better audience, made the group into so bright a unit that Rosemary felt an impatient disregard for all who were not at their table. They had been two days in Paris, but actually they were still under the beach umbrella. When, as at the ball of the Corps des Pages the night before, the surroundings seemed formidable to Rosemary, who had yet to attend a Mayfair party in Hollywood, Dick would bring the scene within range by greeting a few people, a sort of selection—the Divers seemed to have a large acquaintance, but it was always as if the person had not seen them for a long, long time and was utterly bowled over, "Why, where do you *keep* yourselves?"—and then re-create the unity of his own party by destroying the outsiders softly but permanently with an ironic coup de grâce. Presently Rosemary seemed to have known those people herself in some deplorable past, and then got on to them, rejected them, discarded them.

Their own party was overwhelmingly American and sometimes scarcely American at all. It was themselves he gave back to them, blurred by the compromises of how many years.

Into the dark, smoky restaurant, smelling of the rich raw foods on the buffet, slid Nicole's sky-blue suit like a stray segment of the weather outside. Seeing from their eyes how beautiful she was, she thanked them with a smile of radiant appreciation. They were all very nice people for a while, very courteous and all that. Then they grew tired of it and they were funny and bitter, and finally they made a lot of plans. They laughed at things that they would not remember clearly afterward—laughed a lot and the men drank three bottles of wine. The trio of women at the table were representative of the enormous flux of American life. Nicole was the granddaughter of a self-made American capitalist and the granddaughter of a count of the house of Lippe-Weissenfeld. Mary North was the daughter of a journeyman paper-hanger and a descendant of President Tyler. Rosemary was from the middle of the middle class, catapulted by her mother to the uncharted heights of Hollywood. Their point of resemblance to each other, and their difference from so many American women, lay in the fact that they were all happy to exist in a man's world—they preserved their individuality through men and not by opposition to them. They would all three have made alternatively good courtesans or good wives, not by the accident of birth but through the greater accident of finding their man or not finding him.

So Rosemary found it a pleasant party, that luncheon, nicer in that there were only seven people, about the limit of a good party. Perhaps, too, the fact that she was new to their world acted as a sort of catalytic agent to precipitate out all their old reservations about one another. After the table broke up, a waiter directed Rosemary back into the dark hinterland of all French restaurants, where she looked up a phone number by a dim orange bulb and called Franco-American Films. Sure, they had a print of *Daddy's Girl*—it was out for the moment, but they would run it off later in the week for her at 341 Rue des Saintes Anges—ask for Mr. Crowder.

The semi-booth gave on the vestiaire and as Rosemary hung up the receiver she heard two low voices not five feet from her on the other side of a row of coats.

"—So you love me?"

"Oh, *do* I!"

It was Nicole—Rosemary hesitated in the door of the booth—then she heard Dick say:

"I want you terribly—let's go to the hotel now." Nicole gave a little gasping sigh. For a moment the words conveyed nothing at all to Rosemary—but the tone did. The vast secretiveness of it vibrated to herself.

"I want you."

"I'll be at the hotel at four."

Rosemary stood breathless as the voices moved away. She was at first even astonished—she had seen them in their relation to each other as people without personal exigencies—as something cooler. Now a strong current of emotion flowed through her, profound and unidentified. She did not know whether she was attracted or repelled, but only that she was deeply moved. It made her feel very alone as she went back into the restaurant, but it was touching to look in upon, and the passionate gratitude of Nicole's "Oh, *do* I!" echoed in her mind. The particular mood of the passage she had witnessed lay ahead of her; but however far she was from it her stomach told her it was all right—she had none of the aversion she had felt in the playing of certain love scenes in pictures.

Being far away from it she nevertheless irrevocably participated in it now, and shopping with Nicole she was much more conscious of the assignation than Nicole herself. She looked at Nicole in a new way, estimating her attractions. Certainly she was the most attractive woman Rosemary had ever met—with her hardness, her devotions and loyalties, and a certain elusiveness, which Rosemary, thinking now through her mother's middle-class mind, associated with her attitude about money. Rosemary spent money she had earned—she was here in Europe because she had gone in the pool six times that January day with her temperature roving from 99° in the early morning to 103°, when her mother stopped it.

With Nicole's help Rosemary bought two dresses and two hats and four pairs of shoes with her money. Nicole bought from a great list that ran two pages, and bought the things in the windows besides. Everything she liked that she couldn't possibly use herself, she bought as a present for a friend. She bought colored beads, folding beach cushions, artificial flowers, honey, a guest bed, bags, scarfs, love birds, miniatures for a doll's house, and three yards of some new cloth the color of prawns. She bought a dozen bathing suits, a rubber alligator, a travelling chess set of gold and ivory, big linen handkerchiefs for Abe, two chamois leather jackets of kingfisher blue and burning bush from Hermes—bought all these things not a bit like a high-class courtesan buying underwear and jewels, which were after all professional equipment and insurance, but with an entirely different point of view. Nicole was the product of much ingenuity and toil. For her sake trains began their run at Chicago and traversed the round belly of the continent to California; chicle factories fumed and link belts grew link by link in factories; men mixed toothpaste in vats and drew mouthwash out of copper hogsheads; girls canned tomatoes quickly in August or worked rudely at the Five-and-Tens on Christmas Eve; half-breed Indians toiled on Brazilian coffee plantations and dreamers were muscled out of patent rights in new tractors—these were some of the people who gave a tithe to Nicole and, as the whole system swayed and thundered onward, it lent a feverish bloom to such processes of hers as wholesale buying, like the flush of a fireman's face holding his post before a spreading blaze. She illustrated very simple principles, containing in herself her own doom, but illustrated them so accurately that there was grace in the procedure, and presently Rosemary would try to imitate it.

It was almost four. Nicole stood in a shop with a love bird on her shoulder, and had one of her infrequent outbursts of speech.

"Well, what if you hadn't gone in that pool that day—I sometimes wonder about such things. Just before the war we were in Berlin—I was twelve, it was just before Mother died. My sister was going to a court ball and she had three of the royal princes on her dance card, all arranged by a chamberlain and everything. Half an hour before she was going to start she had a side ache and a high fever. The doctor said it was appendicitis and she ought to be operated on. But Mother had her plans made, so Baby went to the ball and danced till two with an ice pack strapped on under her evening dress. She was operated on at seven o'clock next morning."

It was good to be hard, then; all nice people were hard on themselves. But it was four o'clock and Rosemary kept thinking of Dick waiting for Nicole now at the hotel. She must go there, she must not make him wait for her. She kept thinking, "Why don't you go?" and then suddenly, "Or let me go if you don't want to." But Nicole went to one more place to buy corsages for them both and sent one to Mary North. Only then she seemed to remember and with sudden abstraction she signalled for a taxi.

"Good-bye," said Nicole. "We had fun, didn't we?"

"Loads of fun," said Rosemary.

It was more difficult than she thought and her whole self protested as Nicole drove away.

BOOK III

CASUALTIES
1925

CHAPTER I

DICK TURNED THE CORNER of the traverse and continued along the trench walking on the duckboard. He came to a periscope, looked through it a moment, then he got up on the step and peered over the parapet. In front of him beneath a dingy sky was Beaumont-Hamel; to his left the tragic hill of Thiepval. Dick stared at them through his field glasses, his throat straining with sadness.

He went on along the trench and found the others waiting for him in the next traverse. He was full of excitement and he wanted to communicate it to them, to make them understand about this, though actually Abe North had seen battle service and he had not.

"This land here cost twenty lives a foot that summer," he said to Rosemary. She looked out obediently at the rather bare green plain with its low trees of six years' growth. If Dick had added that they were now being shelled she would have believed him that afternoon. Her love had reached a point where now at last she was beginning to be unhappy, to be desperate. She didn't know what to do—she wanted to talk to her mother.

"There are lots of people dead since and we'll all be dead soon," said Abe consolingly.

Rosemary waited tensely for Dick to continue.

"See that little stream—we could walk to it in two minutes. It took the British a month to walk to it—a whole empire walking very slowly, dying in front and pushing forward behind. And another empire walked very slowly backward a few inches a day, leaving the dead like a million bloody rugs. No European will ever do that again in this generation."

"Why, they've only just quit over in Turkey," said Abe. "And in Morocco——"

"That's different. This western-front business couldn't be done again, not for a long time. The young men think they could do it but they couldn't. They could fight the first Marne again but not this. This took religion and years of plenty and tremendous sureties and the exact relation that existed between the classes. The Russians and Italians weren't any good on this front. You had to have a whole-souled sentimental equipment going back further than you could remember. You had to remember Christmas, and postcards of the Crown Prince and his fiancée, and little cafés in Valence and beer gardens in Unter den Linden and weddings at the mairie, and going to the Derby, and your grandfather's whiskers."

"General Grant invented this kind of battle at Petersburg in sixty-five."

"No, he didn't—he just invented mass butchery. This kind of battle was invented by Lewis Carroll and Jules Verne and whoever wrote *Undine,* and country deacons bowling and marraines in Marseilles and girls seduced in the back lanes of Württemberg and Westphalia. Why, this was a love battle—there was a century of middle-class love spent here. This was the last love battle."

"You want to hand over this battle to D. H. Lawrence," said Abe.

"All my beautiful lovely safe world blew itself up here with a great gust of high explosive love," Dick mourned persistently. "Isn't that true, Rosemary?"

"I don't know," she answered with a grave face. "You know everything."

They dropped behind the others. Suddenly a shower of earth gobs and pebbles came down on them and Abe yelled from the next traverse:

"The war spirit's getting into me again. I have a hundred years of Ohio love behind me and I'm going to bomb out this trench." His head popped up over the embankment. "You're dead—don't you know the rules? That was a grenade."

Rosemary laughed and Dick picked up a retaliatory handful of stones and then put them down.

"I couldn't kid here," he said rather apologetically. "The silver cord is cut and the golden bowl is broken and all that, but an old romantic like me can't do anything about it."

"I'm romantic too."

They came out of the neat restored trench, and faced a memorial to the Newfoundland dead. Reading the inscription Rosemary burst into sudden tears. Like most women she liked to be told how she should feel, and she liked Dick's telling her which things were ludicrous and which things were sad. But most of all she wanted him to know how she loved him, now that the fact was upsetting everything, now that she was walking over the battle-field in a thrilling dream.

After that they got in their car and started back toward Amiens. A thin warm rain was falling on the new scrubby woods and underbrush and they passed great funeral pyres of sorted duds, shells, bombs, grenades, and equipment, helmets, bayonets, gun stocks, and rotten leather, abandoned seven years in the ground. And suddenly around a bend the white caps of a great sea of graves. Dick asked the chauffeur to stop.

"There's that girl—and she still has her wreath."

They watched as he got out and went over to the girl, who stood uncertainly by the gate with a wreath in her hand. Her taxi waited. She was a red-haired girl from Tennessee whom they had met on the train this morning, come from Knoxville to lay a memorial on her brother's grave. There were tears of vexation on her face.

"The War Department must have given me the wrong number," she whimpered. "It had another name on it. I been lookin' for it since two o'clock, and there's so many graves."

"Then if I were you I'd just lay it on any grave without looking at the name," Dick advised her.

"You reckon that's what I ought to do?"

"I think that's what he'd have wanted you to do."

It was growing dark and the rain was coming down harder. She left the wreath on the first grave inside the gate, and accepted Dick's suggestion that she dismiss her taxicab and ride back to Amiens with them.

Rosemary shed tears again when she heard of the mishap—altogether it had been a watery day, but she felt that she had learned something, though exactly what it was she did not know. Later she remembered all the hours of the afternoon as happy—one of those uneventful times that seem at the moment only a link between past and future pleasure, but turn out to have been the pleasure itself.

Amiens was an echoing purple town, still sad with the war, as some railroad stations were: the Gare du Nord and Waterloo station in London. In the day-time one is deflated by such towns, with their little trolley cars of twenty years ago crossing the great gray cobble-stoned squares in front of the cathedral, and the very weather seems to have a quality of the past, faded weather like that of old photographs. But after dark all that is most satisfactory in French life swims back into the picture—the sprightly tarts, the men arguing with a hundred Voilàs in the cafés, the couples drifting, head to head, toward the satisfactory inexpensiveness of nowhere. Waiting for the train they sat in a big arcade, tall enough to release the smoke and chatter and music upward, and obligingly the orchestra launched into "Yes, We Have No Bananas"—they clapped, because the leader looked so pleased with himself. The Tennessee girl forgot her sorrow and enjoyed herself, even began flirtations of tropical eye-rollings and pawings, with Dick and Abe. They teased her gently.

Then, leaving infinitesimal sections of Württembergers, Prussian Guards, Chasseurs Alpins, Manchester mill hands and Old Etonians to pursue their eternal dissolution under the warm rain, they took the train for Paris. They ate sandwiches of mortadelle sausage and bel paese cheese made up in the station restaurant, and drank Beaujolais. Nicole was abstracted, biting her lip restlessly and reading over the guidebooks to the battle-field that Dick had brought along—indeed, he had made a quick study of the whole affair, simplifying it always until it bore a faint resemblance to one of his own parties.

CHAPTER II

WHEN THEY REACHED PARIS Nicole was too tired to go on to the grand illumination at the Decorative Arts Exposition as they had planned. They left her at the Hôtel Roi George and, as she disappeared between the intersecting planes made by lobby lights of the glass doors, Rosemary's oppression lifted. Nicole was a force —not necessarily well disposed or predictable like her mother, an incalculable force. Rosemary was somewhat afraid of her.

At eleven she sat with Dick and the Norths at a houseboat café just opened on the Seine. The river shimmered with lights from the bridges and cradled many cold moons. On Sundays sometimes when Rosemary and her mother had lived in Paris they had taken the little steamer up to Suresnes and talked about plans for the future. They had little money, but Mrs. Speers was so sure of Rosemary's beauty and had implanted in her so much ambition that she was willing to gamble the money on "advantages"; Rosemary in turn was to repay her mother when she got her start. . . .

Since reaching Paris Abe North had had a thin vinous fur over him; his eyes were bloodshot from sun and wine. Rosemary realized for the first time that he was always stopping in places to get a drink, and she wondered how Mary North liked it. Mary was quiet, so quiet save for her frequent laughter that Rosemary had learned little about her. She liked the straight dark hair brushed back until it met some sort of natural cascade that took care of it —from time to time it eased with a jaunty slant over the corner of her temple until it was almost in her eye, then she tossed her head and caused it to fall sleek into place once more.

"We'll turn in early tonight, Abe, after this drink." Mary's voice was light, but it held a little flicker of anxiety. "You don't want to be poured on the boat."

"It's pretty late now," Dick said. "We'd all better go."

The noble dignity of Abe's face took on a certain stubbornness and he remarked with determination:

"Oh, no." He paused gravely. "Oh, no, not yet. We'll have another bottle of champagne."

"No more for me," said Dick.

"It's Rosemary I'm thinking of. She's a natural alcoholic—keeps a bottle of gin in the bathroom and all that—her mother told me."

He emptied what was left of the first bottle into Rosemary's glass. She had made herself quite sick the first day in Paris with quarts of lemonade; after that she had taken nothing with them, but now she raised the champagne and drank at it.

"But what's this?" exclaimed Dick. "You told me you didn't drink."

"I didn't say I was never going to."

"What about your mother?"

"I'm just going to drink this one glass." She felt some necessity for it. Dick drank, not too much, but he drank, and perhaps it would bring her closer to him, be a part of the equipment for what she had to do. She drank it quickly, choked, and then said, "Besides, yesterday was my birthday—I was eighteen."

"Why didn't you tell us?" they said indignantly.

"I knew you'd make a fuss over it and go to a lot of trouble." She finished the champagne. "So this is the celebration."

"It most certainly is not," Dick assured her. "The dinner tomorrow night is your birthday party and don't forget it. Eighteen—why that's a terribly important age."

"I used to think until you're eighteen nothing matters," said Mary.

"That's right," Abe agreed. "And afterward it's the same way."

"Abe feels that nothing matters till he gets on the boat," said Mary. "This time he really has got everything planned out when he gets to New York." She spoke as if she were tired of saying things that no longer had a meaning for her, as if in reality the course that she and her husband followed, or failed to follow, had become merely an intention.

"He'll be writing music in America and I'll be working at singing in Munich, so when we get together again there'll be nothing we can't do."

"That's wonderful," agreed Rosemary, feeling the champagne.

"Meanwhile, another touch of champagne for Rosemary. Then she'll be more able to rationalize the acts of her lymphatic glands. They only begin to function at eighteen."

Dick laughed indulgently at Abe, whom he loved, and in whom he had long lost hope: "That's medically incorrect and we're going." Catching the faint patronage Abe said lightly:

"Something tells me I'll have a new score on Broadway long before you've finished your scientific treatise."

"I hope so," said Dick evenly. "I hope so. I may even abandon what you call my 'scientific treatise.'"

"Oh, Dick!" Mary's voice was startled, was shocked. Rosemary had never before seen Dick's face utterly expressionless; she felt that this announcement was something momentous and she was inclined to exclaim with Mary, "Oh, Dick!"

But suddenly Dick laughed again, added to his remark "—abandon it for another one," and got up from the table.

"But Dick, sit down. I want to know——"

"I'll tell you some time. Good night, Abe. Good night, Mary."

"Good night, dear Dick." Mary smiled as if she were going to be perfectly happy sitting there on the almost deserted boat. She was a brave, hopeful woman and she was following her husband somewhere, changing herself to this kind of person or that, without being able to lead him a step out of his path, and sometimes realizing with discouragement how deep in him the guarded secret of her direction lay. And yet an air of luck clung about her, as if she were a sort of token.

CHAPTER III

"WHAT IS IT YOU are giving up?" demanded Rosemary, facing Dick earnestly in the taxi.

"Nothing of importance."

"Are you a scientist?"

"I'm a doctor of medicine."

"Oh-h!" She smiled delightedly. "My father was a doctor too. Then why don't you—" she stopped.

"There's no mystery. I didn't disgrace myself at the height of my career and hide away on the Riviera. I'm just not practising. You can't tell, I'll probably practise again some day."

Rosemary put up her face quietly to be kissed. He looked at her for a moment as if he didn't understand. Then holding her in the hollow of his arm he rubbed his cheek against her cheek's softness, and then looked down at her for another long moment.

"Such a lovely child," he said gravely.

She smiled up at him, her hands playing conventionally with the lapels of his coat. "I'm in love with you and Nicole. Actually that's my secret—I can't even talk about you to anybody because I don't want any more people to know how wonderful you are. Honestly —I love you and Nicole—I do."

—So many times he had heard this—even the formula was the same.

Suddenly she came toward him, her youth vanishing as she passed inside the focus of his eyes and he had kissed her breathlessly as if she were any age at all. Then she lay back against his arm and sighed.

"I've decided to give you up," she said.

Dick started—had he said anything to imply that she possessed any part of him?

"But that's very mean," he managed to say lightly, "just when I was getting interested."

"I've loved you so—" As if it had been for years. She was weeping a little now. "I've loved you so-o-o."

Then he should have laughed, but he heard himself saying, "Not only are you beautiful but you are somehow on the grand scale. Everything you do, like pretending to be in love or pretending to be shy, gets across."

In the dark cave of the taxi, fragrant with the perfume Rosemary had bought with Nicole, she came close again, clinging to him. He kissed her without enjoying it. He knew that there was passion there, but there was no shadow of it in her eyes or on her mouth; there was a faint spray of champagne on her breath. She clung nearer desperately and once more he kissed her and was chilled by the innocence of her kiss, by the glance that at the moment of contact looked beyond him out into the darkness of the night, the darkness of the world. She did not know yet that splendor is something in the heart; at the moment when she realized that and melted into the passion of the universe he could take her without question or regret.

Her room in the hotel was diagonally across from theirs and nearer the elevator. When they reached the door she said suddenly:

"I know you don't love me—I don't expect it. But you said I should have told you about my birthday. Well, I did, and now for my birthday present I want you to come into my room a minute while I tell you something. Just one minute."

They went in and he closed the door, and Rosemary stood close to him, not touching him. The night had drawn the color from her face—she was pale as pale now, she was a white carnation left after a dance.

"When you smile—" He had recovered his paternal attitude, perhaps because of Nicole's silent proximity, "I always think I'll see a gap where you've lost some baby teeth."

But he was too late—she came close up against him with a forlorn whisper.

"Take me."

"Take you where?"

Astonishment froze him rigid.

"Go on," she whispered. "Oh, please go on, whatever they do. I don't care if I don't like it—I never expected to—I've always hated to think about it but now I don't. I want you to."

She was astonished at herself—she had never imagined she could talk like that. She was calling on things she had read, seen, dreamed through a decade of convent hours. Suddenly she knew too that it was one of her greatest rôles and she flung herself into it more passionately.

"This is not as it should be," Dick deliberated. "Isn't it just the champagne? Let's more or less forget it."

"Oh, no, *now*. I want you to do it now, take me, show me, I'm absolutely yours and I want to be."

"For one thing, have you thought how much it would hurt Nicole?"

"She won't know—this won't have anything to do with her."

He continued kindly.

"Then there's the fact that I love Nicole."

"But you can love more than just one person, can't you? Like I love mother and I love you—more. I love you more now."

"—the fourth place you're not in love with me but you might be afterward, and that would begin your life with a terrible mess."

"No, I promise I'll never see you again. I'll get mother and go to America right away."

He dismissed this. He was remembering too vividly the youth and freshness of her lips. He took another tone.

"You're just in that mood."

"Oh, please, I don't care even if I had a baby. I could go into Mexico like a girl at the studio. Oh, this is so different from anything I ever thought—I used to hate it when they kissed me seriously." He saw she was still under the impression that it must happen. "Some of them had great big teeth, but you're all different and beautiful. I want you to do it."

"I believe you think people just kiss some way and you want me to kiss you."

"Oh, don't tease me—I'm not a baby. I know you're not in love with me." She was suddenly humble and quiet. "I didn't expect that much. I know I must seem just nothing to you."

"Nonsense. But you seem young to me." His thoughts added, "—there'd be so much to teach you."

Rosemary waited, breathing eagerly till Dick said: "And lastly things aren't arranged so that this could be as you want."

Her face drooped with dismay and disappointment and Dick said automatically, "We'll have to simply—" He stopped himself, followed her to the bed, sat down beside her while she wept. He was suddenly confused, not about the ethics of the matter, for the impossibility of it was sheerly indicated from all angles, but simply confused, and for a moment his usual grace, the tensile strength of his balance, was absent.

"I knew you wouldn't," she sobbed. "It was just a forlorn hope." He stood up.

"Good night, child. This is a damn shame. Let's drop it out of the picture." He gave her two lines of hospital patter to go to sleep on. "So many people are going to love you and it might be nice to meet your first love all intact, emotionally too. That's an old-fashioned idea, isn't it?" She looked up at him as he took a step toward the door; she looked at him without the slightest idea as to what was in his head, she saw him take another step in slow motion, turn and look at her again, and she wanted for a moment to hold him and devour him, wanted his mouth, his ears, his coat collar, wanted to surround him and engulf him; she saw his hand fall on the doorknob. Then she gave up and sank back on the bed. When the door closed she got up and went to the mirror, where she began brushing her hair, sniffling a little. One hundred and fifty strokes Rosemary gave it, as usual, then a hundred and fifty more. She brushed it until her arm ached, then she changed arms and went on brushing.

CHAPTER IV

SHE WOKE UP COOLED and shamed. The sight of her beauty in the mirror did not reassure her but only awakened the ache of yesterday; and a letter, forwarded by her mother, from the boy who had taken her to the Yale prom last fall, which announced his presence in Paris, was no help—all that seemed far away. She emerged from her room for the ordeal of meeting the Divers weighted with a double trouble. But it was hidden by a sheath as impermeable as Nicole's when they met and went together to a series of fittings. It was consoling, though, when Nicole remarked, apropos of a distraught saleswoman: "Most people think everybody feels about them much more violently than they actually do—they think other people's opinions of them swing through great arcs of approval or disapproval." Yesterday in her expansiveness Rosemary would have resented that remark—today in her desire to minimize what had happened she welcomed it eagerly. She admired Nicole for her beauty and her wisdom, and also for the first time in her life she was jealous. Just before leaving Gausse's hotel her mother had said in that casual tone, which Rosemary knew concealed her most significant opinions, that Nicole was a great beauty, with the frank implication that Rosemary was not. This did not bother Rosemary, who had only recently been allowed to learn that she was even personable; so that her prettiness never seemed exactly her own but rather an acquirement, like her French. Nevertheless, in the taxi she looked at Nicole, matching herself against her. There were all the potentialities for romantic love in that lovely body and in the delicate mouth, sometimes tight, sometimes expectantly half open to the world. Nicole had been a beauty as a young girl and she would be a beauty later when her skin stretched tight over her high cheek-bones—the essential structure was there. She had been white-Saxon-blonde, but she was more beautiful now that her hair had darkened than when it had been like a cloud and more beautiful than she.

"We lived there." Rosemary suddenly pointed to a building in the Rue des Saints-Pères.

"That's strange. Because when I was twelve mother and Baby and I once spent a winter there," and she pointed to a hotel directly across the street. The two dingy fronts stared at them, gray echoes of girlhood.

"We'd just built our Lake Forest house and we were economizing," Nicole continued. "At least Baby and I and the governess economized and Mother travelled."

"We were economizing too," said Rosemary, realizing that the word meant different things to them.

"Mother always spoke of it very carefully as a small hotel—" Nicole gave her quick magnetic little laugh, "—I mean instead of saying a 'cheap' hotel. If any swanky friends asked us our address we'd never say, 'We're in a dingy little hole over in the apache quarter where we're glad of running water'—we'd say, 'We're in a small hotel.' As if all the big ones were too noisy and vulgar for us. Of course the friends always saw through us and told everyone about it, but Mother always said it showed we knew our way around Europe. She did, of course: she was born a German citizen. But her mother was American, and she was brought up in Chicago, and she was more American than European."

They were meeting the others in two minutes, and Rosemary reconstructed herself once more as they got out of the taxi in the Rue Guynemer, across from the Luxembourg Gardens. They were lunching in the Norths' already dismantled apartment high above the green mass of leaves. The day seemed different to Rosemary from the day before. When she saw him face to face their eyes met and brushed like birds' wings. After that everything was all right, everything was wonderful, she knew that he was beginning to fall in love with her. She felt wildly happy, felt the warm sap of emotion being pumped through her body. A cool, clear confidence deepened and sang in her. She scarcely looked at Dick but she knew everything was all right.

After luncheon the Divers and the Norths and Rosemary went to the Franco-American Films. They were joined by Collis Clay, her

young man from New Haven, to whom she had telephoned. He
was a Georgian, with the peculiarly regular, even stencilled ideas
of Southerners who are educated in the North. Last winter she had
thought him attractive—once they held hands in an automobile
going from New Haven to New York; now he no longer existed
for her.

In the projection room she sat between Collis Clay and Dick
while the mechanic mounted the reels of *Daddy's Girl* and a French
executive fluttered about her trying to talk American slang. "Yes,
boy," he said when there was trouble with the projector, "I have
not any benenas." Then the lights went out, there was the sudden
click and a flickering noise and she was alone with Dick at last.
They looked at each other in the half darkness.

"Dear Rosemary," he murmured. Their shoulders touched. Nicole
stirred restlessly at the end of the row and Abe coughed convul-
sively and blew his nose; then they all settled down and the picture ran.

There she was—the school girl of a year ago, hair down her back
and rippling out stiffly like the solid hair of a tanagra figure; there
she was—*so* young and innocent—the product of her mother's loving care; there she was—embodying all the immaturity of the race,
cutting a new cardboard paper doll to pass before its empty harlot's
mind. She remembered how she had felt in that dress, especially
fresh and new under the fresh young silk.

Daddy's girl. Was it a 'itty-bitty bravekins and did it suffer?
Ooo-ooo-tweet, de tweetest thing, wasn't she dest too tweet? Before
her tiny fist the forces of lust and corruption rolled away; nay, the
very march of destiny stopped; inevitably became evitable; syllogism,
dialectic, all rationality fell away. Women would forget the dirty
dishes at home and weep; even within the picture one woman wept
so long that she almost stole the film away from Rosemary. She
wept all over a set that cost a fortune, in a Duncan Phyfe dining-
room, in an airport, and during a yacht-race that was only used in
two flashes, in a subway, and finally in a bathroom. But Rosemary
triumphed—her fineness of character, her courage and steadfastness
intruded upon by the vulgarity of the world, and Rosemary showing what it took with a face that had not yet become mask-like;
yet it was actually so moving that the emotions of the whole row

of people went out to her at intervals during the picture. There was a break once and the light went on and after the chatter of applause Dick said to her sincerely: "I'm simply astounded. You're going to be one of the best actresses on the stage.

Then back to *Daddy's Girl:* happier days now, and a lovely shot of Rosemary and her parent united at the last in a father complex so apparent that Dick winced for all psychologists at the vicious sentimentality. The screen vanished, the lights went on, the moment had come.

"I've arranged one other thing," announced Rosemary to the company at large, "I've arranged a test for Dick."

"A what?"

"A screen test, they'll take one now."

There was an awful silence—then an irrepressible chortle from the Norths. Rosemary watched Dick comprehend what she meant, his face moving first in an Irish way; simultaneously she realized that she had made some mistake in the playing of her trump and still she did not suspect that the card was at fault.

"I don't want a test," said Dick firmly; then, seeing the situation as a whole, he continued lightly, "Rosemary, I'm disappointed. The pictures make a fine career for a woman—but my God, they can't photograph me. I'm an old scientist all wrapped up in his private life."

Nicole and Mary urged him ironically to seize the opportunity; they teased him, both faintly annoyed at not having been asked for a sitting. But Dick closed the subject with a somewhat tart discussion of actors: "The strongest guard is placed at the gateway to nothing," he said. "Maybe because the condition of emptiness is too shameful to be divulged."

In the taxi with Dick and Collis Clay—they were dropping Collis, and Dick was taking Rosemary to a tea from which Nicole and the Norths had resigned in order to do the things Abe had left undone till the last—in the taxi Rosemary reproached him.

"I thought if the test turned out to be good I could take it to California with me. And then maybe if they liked it you'd come out and be my leading man in a picture."

He was overwhelmed. "It was a darn sweet thought, but I'd rather look at *you*. You were about the nicest sight I ever looked at."

"That's a great picture," said Collis. "I've seen it four times. I know one boy at New Haven who's seen it a dozen times—he went all the way to Hartford to see it one time. And when I brought Rosemary up to New Haven he was so shy he wouldn't meet her. Can you beat that? This little girl knocks them cold."

Dick and Rosemary looked at each other, wanting to be alone, but Collis failed to understand.

"I'll drop you where you're going," he suggested. "I'm staying at the Lutetia."

"We'll drop you," said Dick.

"It'll be easier for me to drop you. No trouble at all."

"I think it will be better if we drop you."

"But—" began Collis; he grasped the situation at last and began discussing with Rosemary when he would see her again.

Finally he was gone, with the shadowy unimportance but the offensive bulk of the third party. The car stopped unexpectedly, unsatisfactorily, at the address Dick had given. He drew a long breath.

"Shall we go in?"

"I don't care," Rosemary said. "I'll do anything you want."

He considered.

"I almost have to go in—she wants to buy some pictures from a friend of mine who needs the money."

Rosemary smoothed the brief expressive disarray of her hair.

"We'll stay just five minutes," he decided. "You're not going to like these people."

She assumed that they were dull and stereotyped people, or gross and drunken people, or tiresome, insistent people, or any of the sorts of people that the Divers avoided. She was entirely unprepared for the impression that the scene made on her.

CHAPTER V

It was a house hewn from the frame of Cardinal de Retz's palace in the Rue Monsieur, but once inside the door there was nothing of the past, nor of any present that Rosemary knew. The outer shell, the masonry, seemed rather to enclose the future, so that it was an electric-like shock, a definite nervous experience, perverted as a breakfast of oatmeal and hashish, to cross that threshold, if it could be so called, into the long hall of blue steel, silver-gilt, and the myriad facets of many oddly bevelled mirrors. The effect was unlike that of any part of the Decorative Arts Exhibition—for there were people *in* it, not in front of it. Rosemary had the detached false-and-exalted feeling of being on a set and she guessed that everyone else present had that feeling too.

There were about thirty people, mostly women, and all fashioned by Louisa M. Alcott or Madame de Ségur; and they functioned on this set as cautiously, as precisely, as does a human hand picking up jagged broken glass. Neither individually nor as a crowd could they be said to dominate the environment, as one comes to dominate a work of art he may possess, no matter how esoteric. No one knew what this room meant because it was evolving into something else, becoming everything a room was not; to exist in it was as difficult as walking on a highly polished moving stairway, and no one could succeed at all save with the qualities of a hand moving among broken glass—which qualities limited and defined the majority of those present.

These were of two sorts. There were the Americans and English, who had been dissipating all spring and summer, so that now everything they did had a purely nervous inspiration. They were very quiet and lethargic at certain hours and then they exploded into sudden quarrels and breakdowns and seductions. The other class, who might be called the exploiters, was formed by the sponges, who were sober, serious people by comparison, with a purpose in life and no time for fooling. These kept their balance best in that environment, and what tone there was, beyond the apartment's novel organization of light values, came from them.

The Frankenstein took down Dick and Rosemary at a gulp—it separated them immediately and Rosemary suddenly discovered herself to be an insincere little person, living all in the upper registers of her throat and wishing the director would come. There was, however, such a wild beating of wings in the room that she did not feel her position was more incongruous than anyone else's. In addition, her training told and after a series of semi-military turns, shifts, and marches she found herself presumably talking to a neat, slick girl with a lovely boy's face, but actually absorbed by a conversation taking place on a sort of gun-metal ladder diagonally opposite her and four feet away.

There was a trio of young women sitting on the bench. They were all tall and slender with small heads groomed like manikins' heads, and as they talked the heads waved gracefully above their dark tailored suits, rather like long-stemmed flowers and rather like cobras' hoods.

"Oh, they give a good show," said one of them, in a deep rich voice. "Practically the best show in Paris—I'd be the last one to deny that. But after all—" She sighed. "Those phrases he uses over and over—'Oldest inhabitant gnawed by rodents.' You laugh once."

"I prefer people whose lives have more corrugated surfaces," said the second, "and I don't like her."

"I've never really been able to get very excited about them, or their entourage either. Why, for example, the entirely liquid Mr. North?"

"He's out," said the first girl. "But you must admit that the party in question can be one of the most charming human beings you have ever met."

It was the first hint Rosemary had had that they were talking about the Divers, and her body grew tense with indignation. But the girl talking to her, in the starched blue shirt with the bright blue eyes and the red cheeks and the very gray suit, a poster of a girl, had begun to play up. Desperately she kept sweeping things from between them, afraid that Rosemary couldn't see her, sweeping them away until presently there was not so much as a veil of brittle humor hiding the girl, and with distaste Rosemary saw her plain.

"Couldn't you have lunch, or maybe dinner, or lunch the day after?" begged the girl. Rosemary looked about for Dick, finding him with the hostess, to whom he had been talking since they came in. Their eyes met and he nodded slightly, and simultaneously the three cobra women noticed her; their long necks darted toward her and they fixed finely critical glances upon her. She looked back at them defiantly, acknowledging that she had heard what they said. Then she threw off her exigent vis-à-vis with a polite but clipped parting that she had just learned from Dick, and went over to join him. The hostess—she was another tall rich American girl, promenading insouciantly upon the national prosperity—was asking Dick innumerable questions about Gausse's hotel, to which she evidently wanted to come, and battering persistently against his reluctance. Rosemary's presence reminded her that she had been recalcitrant as a hostess and glancing about she said: "Have you met anyone amusing, have you met Mr. ——" Her eyes groped for a male who might interest Rosemary, but Dick said they must go. They left immediately, moving over the brief threshold of the future to the sudden past of the stone façade without.

"Wasn't it terrible?" he said.

"Terrible," she echoed obediently.

"Rosemary?"

She murmured, "What?" in an awed voice.

"I feel terribly about this."

She was shaken with audibly painful sobs. "Have you got a handkerchief?" she faltered. But there was little time to cry, and lovers now they fell ravenously on the quick seconds, while outside the taxi windows the green and cream twilight faded, and the fire-red, gas-blue, ghost-green signs began to shine smokily through the tranquil rain. It was nearly six, the streets were in movement, the bistros gleamed, the Place de la Concorde moved by in pink majesty as the cab turned north.

They looked at each other at last, murmuring names that were a spell. Softly the two names lingered on the air, died away more slowly than other words, other names, slower than music in the mind.

"I don't know what came over me last night," Rosemary said.

"That glass of champagne? I've never done anything like that before."

"You simply said you loved me."

"I do love you—I can't change that." It was time for Rosemary to cry, so she cried a little in her handkerchief.

"I'm afraid I'm in love with you," said Dick, "and that's not the best thing that could happen."

Again the names—then they lurched together as if the taxi had swung them. Her breasts crushed flat against him, her mouth was all new and warm, owned in common. They stopped thinking with an almost painful relief, stopped seeing; they only breathed and sought each other. They were both in the gray gentle world of a mild hangover of fatigue, when the nerves relax in bunches like piano strings and crackle suddenly like wicker chairs. Nerves so raw and tender must surely join other nerves, lips to lips, breast to breast.

They were still in the happier stage of love. They were full of brave illusions about each other, tremendous illusions, so that the communion of self with self seemed to be on a plane where no other human relations mattered. They both seemed to have arrived there with an extraordinary innocence, as though a series of pure accidents had driven them together, so many accidents that at last they were forced to conclude that they were for each other. They had arrived with clean hands, or so it seemed, after no traffic with the merely curious and clandestine.

But for Dick that portion of the road was short; the turning came before they reached the hotel.

"There's nothing to do about it," he said, with a feeling of panic. "I'm in love with you but it doesn't change what I said last night."

"That doesn't matter now. I just wanted to make you love me—if you love me everything's all right."

"Unfortunately I do. But Nicole mustn't know—she mustn't suspect even faintly. Nicole and I have got to go on together. In a way that's more important than just wanting to go on."

"Kiss me once more."

He kissed her, but momentarily he had left her.

"Nicole mustn't suffer—she loves me and I love her—you understand that."

She did understand; it was the sort of thing she understood well, not hurting people. She knew the Divers loved each other because it had been her primary assumption. She had thought, however, that it was a rather cooled relation, and actually rather like the love of herself and her mother. When people have so much for outsiders didn't it indicate a lack of inner intensity?

"And I mean love," he said, guessing her thoughts. "Active love —it's more complicated than I can tell you. It was responsible for that crazy duel."

"How did you know about the duel? I thought we were to keep it from you."

"Do you think Abe can keep a secret?" He spoke with incisive irony. "Tell a secret over the radio, publish it in a tabloid, but never tell it to a man who drinks more than three or four a day."

She laughed in agreement, staying close to him.

"So you understand my relations with Nicole are complicated. She's not very strong—she looks strong but she isn't. And this makes rather a mess."

"Oh, say that later! But kiss me now—love me now. I'll love you and never let Nicole see."

"You darling."

They reached the hotel and Rosemary walked a little behind him, to admire him, to adore him. His step was alert as if he had just come from some great doings and was hurrying on toward others. Organizer of private gaiety, curator of a richly incrusted happiness. His hat was a perfect hat and he carried a heavy stick and yellow gloves. She thought what a good time they would all have being with him tonight.

They walked upstairs—five flights. At the first landing they stopped and kissed; she was careful on the next landing, on the third more careful still. On the next—there were two more—she stopped half way and kissed him fleetingly good-bye. At his urgency she walked down with him to the one below for a minute—and then up and up. Finally it was good-bye, with their hands stretching to touch along the diagonal of the banister and then the fingers slipping apart. Dick went back downstairs to make some arrangements for the evening. Rosemary ran to her room and wrote a letter to her mother; she was conscience-stricken because she did not miss her mother at all.

CHAPTER VI

ALTHOUGH THE DIVERS WERE honestly apathetic to organized fashion, they were nevertheless too acute to abandon its contemporaneous rhythm and beat—Dick's parties were all concerned with excitement, and a chance breath of fresh night air was the more precious for being experienced in the intervals of the excitement.

The party that night moved with the speed of a slapstick comedy. They were twelve, they were sixteen, they were quartets in separate motors bound on a quick odyssey over Paris. Everything had been foreseen. People joined them as if by magic, accompanied them as specialists, almost guides, through a phase of the evening, dropped out and were succeeded by other people, so that it appeared as if the freshness of each one had been husbanded for them all day. Rosemary appreciated how different it was from any party in Hollywood, no matter how splendid in scale. There was, among many diversions, the car of the Shah of Persia. Where Dick had commandeered this vehicle, what bribery was employed, these were facts of irrelevance. Rosemary accepted it as merely a new facet of the fabulous, which for two years had filled her life. The car had been built on a special chassis in America. Its wheels were of silver, so was the radiator. The inside of the body was inlaid with innumerable brilliants, which would be replaced with true gems by the court jeweller when the car arrived in Teheran the following week. There was only one real seat in back, because the Shah must ride alone, so they took turns riding in it and sitting on the marten fur that covered the floor.

But always there was Dick. Rosemary assured the image of her mother, ever carried with her, that never, never had she known anyone so nice, so thoroughly nice as Dick was that night. She compared him with the two Englishmen, whom Abe addressed conscientiously as "Major Hengist and Mr. Horsa," and with the heir to a Scandinavian throne and the novelist just back from Russia, and with Abe, who was desperate and witty, and with Collis Clay, who joined them somewhere and stayed along—and felt there was no comparison. The enthusiasm, the selflessness, behind the whole performance ravished her; the technic of moving many varied types, each as immobile, as dependent on supplies of attention as an infantry battalion is dependent on rations, appeared so effortless that he still had pieces of his own most personal self for everyone.

—Afterward she remembered the times when she had felt the happiest. The first time was when she and Dick danced together and she felt her beauty sparkling bright against his tall, strong form as they floated, hovering like people in an amusing dream—he turned her here and there with such a delicacy of suggestion that she was like a bright bouquet, a piece of precious cloth being displayed before fifty eyes. There was a moment when they were not dancing at all, simply clinging together. Sometime in the early morning they were alone, and her damp powdery young body came up close to him in a crush of tired cloth, and stayed there, crushed against a background of other people's hats and wraps. . . .

The time she laughed most was later, when six of them, the best of them, noblest relics of the evening, stood in the dusky front lobby of the Ritz telling the night concierge that General Pershing was outside and wanted caviare and champagne. "He brooks no delay. Every man, every gun is at his service." Frantic waiters emerged from nowhere, a table was set in the lobby, and Abe came in representing General Pershing while they stood up and mumbled remembered fragments of war songs at him. In the waiters' injured reaction to this anti-climax they found themselves neglected, so they built a waiter trap—a huge and fantastic device constructed of all the furniture in the lobby and functioning like one of the bizarre machines of a Goldberg cartoon. Abe shook his head doubtfully at it.

"Perhaps it would be better to steal a musical saw and——"

"That's enough," Mary interrupted. "When Abe begins bringing up that it's time to go home." Anxiously she confided to Rosemary:

"I've got to get Abe home. His boat train leaves at eleven. It's so important—I feel the whole future depends on his catching it, but whenever I argue with him he does the exact opposite."

"I'll try and persuade him," offered Rosemary.

"Would you?" Mary said doubtfully. "Maybe you could."

Then Dick came up to Rosemary:

"Nicole and I are going home and we thought you'd want to go with us."

Her face was pale with fatigue in the false dawn. Two wan dark spots in her cheek marked where the color was by day.

"I can't," she said. "I promised Mary North to stay along with them—or Abe'll never go to bed. Maybe you could do something."

"Don't you know you can't do anything about people?" he advised her. "If Abe was my room-mate in college, tight for the first time, it'd be different. Now there's nothing to do."

"Well, I've got to stay. He says he'll go to bed if we only come to the Halles with him," she said, almost defiantly.

He kissed the inside of her elbow quickly.

"Don't let Rosemary go home alone," Nicole called to Mary as they left. "We feel responsible to her mother."

—Later Rosemary and the Norths and a manufacturer of dolls' voices from Newark and the ubiquitous Collis and a big splendidly dressed oil Indian named George T. Horseprotection were riding along on top of thousands of carrots in a market wagon. The earth in the carrot beards was fragrant and sweet in the darkness, and Rosemary was so high up in the load that she could hardly see the others in the long shadow between infrequent street lamps. Their voices came from far off, as if they were having experiences different from hers, different and far away, for she was with Dick in her heart, sorry she had come with the Norths, wishing she was at the hotel and Dick asleep across the hall, or that he was here beside her with the warm darkness streaming down.

"Don't come up," she called to Collis, "the carrots will all roll." She threw one at Abe, who was sitting beside the driver, stiffly like an old man. . . .

Later she was homeward bound at last in broad daylight, with the pigeons already breaking over Saint-Sulpice. All of them began to laugh spontaneously, because they knew it was still last night while the people in the streets had the delusion that it was bright hot morning.

"At last I've been on a wild party," thought Rosemary, "but it's no fun when Dick isn't there."

She felt a little betrayed and sad, but presently a moving object came into sight. It was a huge horse-chestnut tree in full bloom bound for the Champs-Élysées, strapped now into a long truck and simply shaking with laughter—like a lovely person in an undignified position yet confident none the less of being lovely. Looking at it with fascination Rosemary identified herself with it, and laughed cheerfully with it, and everything all at once seemed gorgeous.

CHAPTER VII

ABE LEFT FROM THE Gare Saint-Lazare at eleven—he stood alone under the fouled glass dome, relic of the seventies, era of the Crystal Palace; his hands, of that vague gray color that only twenty-four hours can produce, were in his coat pockets to conceal the trembling fingers. With his hat removed it was plain that only the top layer of his hair was brushed back; the lower levels were pointed resolutely sidewise. He was scarcely recognizable as the man who had swum at Gausse's beach a fortnight ago.

He was early; he looked from left to right with his eyes only; it would have taken nervous forces out of his control to use any other part of his body. New-looking baggage went past him; presently prospective passengers with dark little bodies were calling: "Jew-uls-*Hoo-oo!*" in dark piercing voices.

At the minute when he wondered whether or not he had time for a drink at the buffet, and began clutching at the soggy wad of thousand-franc notes in his pocket, one end of his pendulous glance came to rest upon the apparition of Nicole at the stairhead. He watched her—she was self-revelatory in her little expressions as people seem to someone waiting for them, who as yet is himself unobserved. She was frowning, thinking of her children, less gloating over them than merely animally counting them—a cat checking her cubs with a paw.

When she saw Abe, the mood passed out of her face; the glow of the morning skylight was sad, and Abe made a gloomy figure with dark circles that showed through the crimson tan under his eyes. They sat down on a bench.

"I came because you asked me," said Nicole defensively. Abe seemed to have forgotten why he had asked her and Nicole was quite content to look at the travellers passing by.

"That's going to be the belle of your boat—that one with all the men to say good-bye—you see why she bought that dress?" Nicole talked faster and faster. "You see why nobody else would buy it except the belle of the world cruise? See? No? Wake up! That's a story dress—that extra material tells a story and somebody on a world cruise would be lonesome enough to want to hear it."

She bit close her last words; she had talked too much for her; and Abe found it difficult to gather from her serious set face that she had spoken at all. With an effort he drew himself up to a posture that looked as if he were standing up while he was sitting down.

"The afternoon you took me to that funny ball—you know, St. Genevieve's—" he began.

"I remember. It was fun, wasn't it?"

"No fun for me. I haven't had fun seeing you this time. I'm tired of you both, but it doesn't show because you're even more tired of me—you know what I mean. If I had any enthusiasm, I'd go on to new people."

There was a rough nap on Nicole's velvet gloves as she slapped him back:

"Seems rather foolish to be unpleasant, Abe. Anyhow you don't mean that. I can't see why you've given up about everything."

Abe considered, trying hard not to cough or blow his nose.

"I suppose I got bored; and then it was such a long way to go back in order to get anywhere."

Often a man can play the helpless child in front of a woman, but he can almost never bring it off when he feels most like a helpless child.

"No excuse for it," Nicole said crisply.

Abe was feeling worse every minute—he could think of nothing but disagreeable and sheerly nervous remarks. Nicole thought that the correct attitude for her was to sit staring straight ahead, hands in her lap. For a while there was no communication between them —each was racing away from the other, breathing only insofar as there was blue space ahead, a sky not seen by the other. Unlike lovers they possessed no past; unlike man and wife, they possessed no future; yet up to this morning Nicole had liked Abe better than anyone except Dick—and he had been heavy, belly-frightened, with love for her for years.

"Tired of women's worlds," he spoke up suddenly.

"Then why don't you make a world of your own?"

"Tired of friends. The thing is to have sycophants."

Nicole tried to force the minute hand around on the station clock, but, "You agree?" he demanded.

"I am a woman and my business is to hold things together."

"My business is to tear them apart."

"When you get drunk you don't tear anything apart except yourself," she said, cold now, and frightened and unconfident. The station was filling but no one she knew came. After a moment her eyes fell gratefully on a tall girl with straw hair like a helmet, who was dropping letters in the mail slot.

"A girl I have to speak to, Abe. Abe, wake up! You fool!"

Patiently Abe followed her with his eyes. The woman turned in a startled way to greet Nicole, and Abe recognized her as someone he had seen around Paris. He took advantage of Nicole's absence to cough hard and retchingly into his handkerchief and to blow his nose loud. The morning was warmer and his underwear was soaked with sweat. His fingers trembled so violently that it took four matches to light a cigarette; it seemed absolutely necessary to make his way into the buffet for a drink, but immediately Nicole returned.

"That was a mistake," she said with frosty humor. "After begging me to come and see her, she gave me a good snubbing. She looked at me as if I were rotted." Excited, she did a little laugh, as with two fingers high in the scales. "Let people come to you."

Abe recovered from a cigarette cough and remarked:

"Trouble is when you're sober you don't want to see anybody, and when you're tight nobody wants to see you."

"Who, me?" Nicole laughed again; for some reason the late encounter had cheered her.

"No—me."

"Speak for yourself. I like people, a lot of people—I like——"

Rosemary and Mary North came in sight, walking slowly and searching for Abe, and Nicole burst forth grossly with "Hey! Hi! Hey!" and laughed and waved the package of handkerchiefs she had bought for Abe.

They stood in an uncomfortable little group weighted down by Abe's gigantic presence: he lay athwart them like the wreck of a galleon, dominating with his presence his own weakness and self-indulgence, his narrowness and bitterness. All of them were conscious of the solemn dignity that flowed from him, of his achievement, fragmentary, suggestive, and surpassed. But they were frightened at his survivant will, once a will to live, now become a will to die.

Dick Diver came and brought with him a fine glowing surface on which the three women sprang like monkeys with cries of relief, perching on his shoulders, on the beautiful crown of his hat or the gold head of his cane. Now, for a moment, they could disregard the spectacle of Abe's gigantic obscenity. Dick saw the situation quickly and grasped it quietly. He pulled them out of themselves into the station, making plain its wonders. Nearby, some Americans were saying good-bye in voices that mimicked the cadence of water running into a large old bathtub. Standing in the station, with Paris in back of them, it seemed as if they were vicariously leaning a little over the ocean, already undergoing a sea-change, a shifting about of atoms to form the essential molecule of a new people.

So the well-to-do Americans poured through the station onto the platforms with frank new facees, intelligent, considerate, thoughtless, thought-for. An occasional English face among them seemed sharp and emergent. When there were enough Americans on the platform the first impression of their immaculacy and their money began to fade into a vague racial dusk that hindered and blinded both them and their observers.

Nicole seized Dick's arm, crying, "Look!" Dick turned in time to see what took place in half a minute. At a Pullman entrance two cars off, a vivid scene detached itself from the tenor of many farewells. The young woman with the helmet-like hair to whom Nicole had spoken made an odd dodging little run away from the man to whom she was talking and plunged a frantic hand into her purse; then the sound of two revolver shots cracked the narrow air of the platform. Simultaneously the engine whistled sharply and the train began to move, momentarily dwarfing the shots in significance. Abe waved again from his window, oblivious to what had happened. But before the crowd closed in, the others had seen the shots take effect, seen the target sit down upon the platform.

Only after a hundred years did the train stop; Nicole, Mary, and

Rosemary waited on the outskirts while Dick fought his way through. It was five minutes before he found them again—by this time the crowd had split into two sections, following, respectively, the man on a stretcher and the girl walking pale and firm between distraught gendarmes.

"It was Maria Wallis," Dick said hurriedly. "The man she shot was an Englishman—they had an awful time finding out who, because she shot him through his identification card." They were walking quickly from the train, swayed along with the crowd. "I found out what poste de police they're taking her to so I'll go there——"

"But her sister lives in Paris," Nicole objected. "Why not phone her? Seems very peculiar nobody thought of that. She's married to a Frenchman, and he can do more than we can."

Dick hesitated, shook his head, and started off.

"Wait!" Nicole cried after him. "That's foolish—how can you do any good—with your French?"

"At least I'll see they don't do anything outrageous to her."

"They're certainly going to hold on to her," Nicole assured him briskly. "She *did* shoot the man. The best thing is to phone right away to Laura—she can do more than we can."

Dick was unconvinced—also he was showing off for Rosemary.

"You wait," said Nicole firmly, and hurried off to a telephone booth.

"When Nicole takes things into her hands," he said with affectionate irony, "there is nothing more to be done."

He saw Rosemary for the first time that morning. They exchanged glances, trying to recognize the emotions of the day before. For a moment each seemed unreal to the other—then the slow warm hum of love began again.

"You like to help everybody, don't you?" Rosemary said.

"I only pretend to."

"Mother likes to help everybody—of course she can't help as many people as you do." She sighed. "Sometimes I think I'm the most selfish person in the world."

For the first time the mention of her mother annoyed rather than amused Dick. He wanted to sweep away her mother, remove the whole affair from the nursery footing upon which Rosemary persistently established it. But he realized that this impulse was a loss of control—what would become of Rosemary's urge toward him if, for even a moment, he relaxed? He saw, not without panic, that the affair was sliding to rest; it could not stand still, it must go on or go back; for the first time it occurred to him that Rosemary had her hand on the lever more authoritatively than he.

Before he had thought out a course of procedure, Nicole returned.

"I found Laura. It was the first news she had and her voice kept fading away and then getting loud again—as if she was fainting and then pulling herself together. She said she knew something was going to happen this morning."

"Maria ought to be with Diaghilev," said Dick in a gentle tone, in order to bring them back to quietude. "She has a nice sense of décor—not to say rhythm. Will any of us ever see a train pulling out without hearing a few shots?"

They bumped down the wide steel steps. "I'm sorry for the poor man," Nicole said. "Course that's why she talked so strange to me —she was getting ready to open fire."

She laughed, Rosemary laughed too, but they were both horrified, and both of them deeply wanted Dick to make a moral comment on the matter and not leave it to them. This wish was not entirely conscious, especially on the part of Rosemary, who was accustomed to having shell fragments of such events shriek past her head. But a totality of shock had piled up in her too. For the moment, Dick was too shaken by the impetus of his newly recognized emotion to resolve things into the pattern of the holiday, so the women, missing something, lapsed into a vague unhappiness.

Then, as if nothing had happened, the lives of the Divers and their friends flowed out into the street.

However, everything had happened—Abe's departure and Mary's impending departure for Salzburg this afternoon had ended the time in Paris. Or perhaps the shots, the concussions that had finished God knew what dark matter, had terminated it. The shots had entered into all their lives: echoes of violence followed them out onto the pavement, where two porters held a post-mortem beside them as they waited for a taxi.

"Tu as vu le revolver? Il était très petit, vraie perle—un jouet."

"Mais assez puissant!" said the other porter sagely. "Tu as vu sa chemise? Assez de sang pour se croire à la guerre."

CHAPTER VIII

In the square, as they came out, a suspended mass of gasoline exhaust cooked slowly in the July sun. It was a terrible thing—unlike pure heat it held no promise of rural escape but suggested only roads choked with the same foul asthma. During their luncheon, outdoors, across from the Luxembourg Gardens, Rosemary had cramps and felt fretful and full of impatient lassitude—it was the foretaste of this that had inspired her self-accusation of selfishness in the station.

Dick had no suspicion of the sharpness of the change; he was profoundly unhappy and the subsequent increase of egotism tended momentarily to blind him to what was going on round about him, and deprive him of the long ground-swell of imagination that he counted on for his judgments.

After Mary North left them, accompanied by the Italian singing teacher who had joined them for coffee and was taking her to her train, Rosemary, too, stood up, bound for an engagement at her studio: "meet some officials."

"And oh—" she proposed "—if Collis Clay, that Southern boy—if he comes while you are still sitting here, just tell him I couldn't wait; tell him to call me tomorrow."

Too insouciant, in reaction from the late disturbance, she had assumed the privileges of a child—the result being to remind the Divers of their exclusive love for their own children. Rosemary was sharply rebuked in a short passage between the women: "You'd better leave the message with a waiter," Nicole's voice was stern and unmodulated, "we're leaving immediately."

Rosemary got it, took it without resentment.

"I'll let it go then. Good-bye, you darlings."

Dick asked for the check; the Divers relaxed, chewing tentatively on toothpicks.

"Well—" they said together.

He saw a flash of unhappiness on her mouth, so brief that only he would have noticed, and he could pretend not to have seen. What did Nicole think? Rosemary was one of a dozen people he had "worked over" in the past years: these had included a French circus clown, Abe and Mary North, a pair of dancers, a writer, a painter, a comedienne from the Grand Guignol, a half-crazy pederast from the Russian Ballet, a promising tenor they had staked to a year in Milan. Nicole well knew how seriously these people interpreted his interest and enthusiasm; but she realized also that, except while their children were being born, Dick had not spent a night apart from her since their marriage. On the other hand, there was a pleasingness about him that simply had to be used—those who possessed that pleasingness had to keep their hands in, and go along attaching people that they had no use to make of.

Now Dick hardened himself and let minutes pass without making any gesture of confidence, any representation of constantly renewed surprise that they were one together.

Collis Clay out of the South edged a passage between the closely packed tables and greeted the Divers cavalierly. Such salutations always astonished Dick—acquaintances saying "Hi!" to them, or speaking only to one of them. He felt so intensely about people that in moments of apathy he preferred to remain concealed; that one could parade a casualness into his presence was a challenge to the key on which he lived.

Collis, unaware that he was without a wedding garment, heralded his arrival with: "I reckon I'm late—the beyed has flown." Dick had to wrench something out of himself before he could forgive him for not having first complimented Nicole.

She left almost immediately and he sat with Collis, finishing the last of his wine. He rather liked Collis—he was "post-war"; less difficult than most of the Southerners he had known at New Haven a decade previously. Dick listened with amusement to the conversation that accompanied the slow, profound stuffing of a pipe. In the early afternoon children and nurses were trekking into the Luxembourg Gardens; it was the first time in months that Dick had let this part of the day out of his hands.

Suddenly his blood ran cold as he realized the content of Collis's confidential monologue.

"—she's not so cold as you'd probably think. I admit I thought she was cold for a long time. But she got into a jam with a friend of mine going from New York to Chicago at Easter—a boy named Hillis she thought was pretty nutsey at New Haven—she had a compartment with a cousin of mine but she and Hillis wanted to be alone, so in the afternoon my cousin came and played cards in our compartment. Well, after about two hours we went back and there was Rosemary and Bill Hillis standing in the vestibule arguing with the 'conductor—Rosemary white as a sheet. Seems they locked the door and pulled down the blinds and I guess there was some heavy stuff going on when the conductor came for the tickets and knocked on the door. They thought it was us kidding them and wouldn't let him in at first, and when they did he was plenty sore. He asked Hillis if that was his compartment and whether he and Rosemary were married that they locked the door, and Hillis lost his temper trying to explain there was nothing wrong. He said the conductor had insulted Rosemary and he wanted him to fight, but that conductor could have made trouble—and believe me I had an awful time smoothing it over."

With every detail imagined, with even envy for the pair's community of misfortune in the vestibule, Dick felt a change taking place within him. Only the image of a third person, even a vanished one, entering into his relation with Rosemary was needed to throw him off his balance and send through him waves of pain, misery, desire, desperation. The vividly pictured hand on Rosemary's cheek, the quicker breath, the white excitement of the event viewed from outside, the inviolable secret warmth within.

—Do you mind if I pull down the curtain?

—Please do. It's too light in here.

Collis Clay was now speaking about fraternity politics at New Haven, in the same tone, with the same emphasis. Dick had gathered that he was in love with Rosemary in some curious way Dick could not have understood. The affair with Hillis seemed to have made no emotional impression on Collis save to give him the joyful conviction that Rosemary was "human."

"Bones got a wonderful crowd," he said. "We all did, as a matter of fact. New Haven's so big now the sad thing is the men we have to leave out."

—Do you mind if I pull down the curtain?

—Please do. It's too light in here.

. . . Dick went over Paris to his bank. Writing a check, he looked along the row of men at the desks, deciding to which one he would present it for an O. K. As he wrote he engrossed himself in the material act, examining meticulously the pen, writing laboriously upon the high glass-topped desk. Once he raised glazed eyes to look toward the mail department, then glazed his spirit again by concentration upon the objects he dealt with.

Still he failed to decide to whom the check should be presented, which man in the line would guess least of the unhappy predicament in which he found himself and, also, which one would be least likely to talk. There was Perrin, the suave New Yorker, who had asked him to luncheons at the American Club, there was Casasus, the Spaniard, with whom he usually discussed a mutual friend in spite of the fact that the friend had passed out of his life a dozen years before; there was Muchhause, who always asked him whether he wanted to draw upon his wife's money or his own.

As he entered the amount on the stub, and drew two lines under it, he decided to go to Pierce, who was young and for whom he would have to put on only a small show. It was often easier to give a show than to watch one.

He went to the mail desk first. As the woman who served him pushed up with her bosom a piece of paper that had nearly escaped the desk, he thought how differently women use their bodies from men. He took his letters aside to open. There was a bill for seventeen psychiatric books from a German concern, a bill from Brentano's, a letter from Buffalo from his father, in a handwriting that year by year became more indecipherable; there was a card from Tommy Barban post-marked Fez and bearing a facetious communication; there were letters from doctors in Zurich, both in German; a disputed bill from a plasterer in Cannes; a bill from a furniture maker; a letter from the publisher of a medical journal in Baltimore, miscellaneous announcements, and an invitation to a showing of pictures by an incipient artist; also there were three letters for Nicole, and a letter for Rosemary sent in his care.

—Do you mind if I pull down the curtain?

He went toward Pierce, but he was engaged with a woman, and

Dick saw with his heels that he would have to present his check to Casasus at the next desk, who was free.

"How are you, Diver?" Casasus was genial. He stood up, his mustache spreading with his smile. "We were talking about Featherstone the other day and I thought of you—he's out in California now."

Dick widened his eyes and bent forward a little.

"In California?"

"That's what I heard."

Dick held the check poised; to focus the attention of Casasus upon it he looked toward Pierce's desk, holding the latter for a moment in a friendly eye-play conditioned by an old joke of three years before, when Pierce had been involved with a Lithuanian countess. Pierce played up with a grin until Casasus had authorized the check and had no further recourse to detain Dick, whom he liked, than to stand up holding his pince-nez and repeat, "Yes, he's in California."

Meanwhile Dick had seen that Perrin, at the head of the line of desks, was in conversation with the heavyweight champion of the world; from a sidesweep of Perrin's eye Dick saw that he was considering calling him over and introducing him, but that he finally decided against it.

Cutting across the social mood of Casasus with the intensity he had accumulated at the glass desk—which is to say he looked hard at the check, studying it, and then fixed his eyes on grave problems beyond the first marble pillar to the right of the banker's head and made a business of shifting the cane, hat, and letters he carried —he said good-bye and went out. He had long ago purchased the doorman; his taxi sprang to the curb.

"I want to go to the Films Par Excellence Studio—it's on a little street in Passy. Go to the Muette. I'll direct you from there."

He was rendered so uncertain by the events of the last forty-eight hours that he was not even sure of what he wanted to do; he paid off the taxi at the Muette and walked in the direction of the studio, crossing to the opposite side of the street before he came to the building. Dignified in his fine clothes, with their fine accessories, he was yet swayed and driven as an animal. Dignity could come only with an overthrowing of his past, of the effort of the last six years. He went briskly around the block with the fatuousness of one of Tarkington's adolescents, hurrying at the blind places lest he miss Rosemary's coming out of the studio. It was a melancholy neighborhood. Next door to the place he saw a sign: "100,000 Chemises." The shirts filled the window, piled, cravated, stuffed, or draped with shoddy grace on the showcase floor: "100,000 Chemises"—count them! On either side he read: "Papeterie," "Pâtisserie," "Solde," "Réclame"—and Constance Talmadge in "Déjeuner de Soleil," and farther away there were more sombre announcements: "Vêtements Ecclésiastiques," "Déclaration de Décès" and "Pompes Funèbres." Life and death.

He knew that what he was now doing marked a turning point in his life—it was out of line with everything that had preceded it, even out of line with what effect he might hope to produce upon Rosemary. Rosemary saw him always as a model of correctness—his presence walking around this block was an intrusion. But Dick's necessity of behaving as he did was a projection of some submerged reality: he was compelled to walk there, or stand there, his shirt-sleeve fitting his wrist and his coat sleeve encasing his shirt-sleeve like a sleeve valve, his collar moulded plastically to his neck, his red hair cut exactly, his hand holding his small brief-case like a dandy—just as another man once found it necessary to stand in front of a church in Ferrara, in sackcloth and ashes. Dick was paying some tribute to things unforgotten, unshriven, unexpurgated.

CHAPTER IX

AFTER THREE-QUARTERS OF AN hour it became apparent that Rosemary either had escaped on one of his early circuits of the block or else had left before he came into the neighborhood. He went into the bistro on the corner, bought a lead disk, and, squeezed in an alcove between the kitchen and the foul toilet, he called the Roi George. He recognized Cheyne-Stokes tendencies in his respiration—but like everything the symptom served only to turn him in toward his emotion. He gave the number of the hotel; then stood holding the phone and staring into the café; after a long while a strange little voice said hello.

"This is Dick—I had to call you."

A pause from her—then bravely, and in key with his emotion: "I'm glad you did."

"I came to meet you at your studio—I'm out in Passy across the way from it. I thought maybe we'd ride around through the Bois."

"Oh, I only stayed there a minute! I'm so sorry." A silence.

"Rosemary."

"Yes, Dick."

"Look, I'm in an extraordinary condition about you. When a child can disturb a middle-aged gent—things get difficult."

"You're not middle-aged, Dick—you're the youngest person in the world."

"Rosemary?" Silence while he stared at a shelf that held the humbler poisons of France—bottles of Otard, Rhum St. James, Marie Brizard, Punch Orangeade, Fernet Branca, Cherry Rocher, and Armagnac.

"Are you alone?"

—*Do you mind if I pull down the curtain?*

"Who do you think I'd be with?"

"That's the state I'm in. I'd like to be with you now."

Silence, then a sigh and an answer. "I wish you were with me now."

There was the hotel room where she lay behind a telephone number, and little gusts of music wailed around her—

> *"And two—for tea.*
> *And me for you,*
> *And you for me*
> *Alow-own."*

There was the remembered dust of powder over her tan—when he kissed her face it was damp around the corners of her hair; there was the flash of a white face under his own, the arc of a shoulder.

"It's impossible," he said to himself. In a minute he was out in the street marching along toward the Muette, or away from it, his small brief-case still in his hand, his gold-headed stick held at a sword-like angle.

Rosemary returned to her desk and finished a letter to her mother.

"—I only saw him for a little while but I thought he was wonderful looking. I fell in love with him (Of course I Do Love Dick Best but you know what I mean). He really is going to direct the picture and is leaving immediately for Hollywood, and I think we ought to leave, too. Collis Clay has been here. I like him all right but have not seen much of him because of the Divers, who really are divine, about the Nicest People I ever Knew. I am feeling not very well today and am taking the Medicine, though see No need for it I'm not even Going to Try to tell you All that's Happened until I see You!!! So when you get this letter *wire, wire, wire!* Are you coming north or shall I come south with the Divers?"

At six Dick called Nicole.

"Have you any special plans?" he asked. "Would you like to do something quiet—dinner at the hotel and then a play?"

"Would you? I'll do whatever you want. I phoned Rosemary a while ago and she's having dinner in her room. I think this upset all of us, don't you?"

"It didn't upset me," he objected. "Darling, unless you're physically tired let's do something. Otherwise we'll get south and spend a week wondering why we didn't see Boucher. It's better than brooding——"

This was a blunder and Nicole took him up sharply.

"Brooding about what?"

"About Maria Wallis."

She agreed to go to a play. It was a tradition between them that they should never be too tired for anything, and they found it made the days better on the whole and put the evenings more in order. When, inevitably, their spirits flagged they shifted the blame to the weariness and fatigue of others. Before they went out, as fine-looking a couple as could be found in Paris, they knocked softly at Rosemary's door. There was no answer; judging that she was asleep they walked into a warm strident Paris night, snatching a vermouth and bitters in the shadow by Fouquet's bar.

CHAPTER X

Nicole awoke late, murmuring something back into her dream before she parted her long lashes tangled with sleep. Dick's bed was empty—only after a minute did she realize that she had been awakened by a knock at their salon door.

"Entrez!" she called, but there was no answer, and after a moment she slipped on a dressing-gown and went to open it. A sergent de ville confronted her courteously and stepped inside the door.

"Mr. Afghan North—is he here?"

"What? No—he's gone to America."

"When did he leave, Madame?"

"Yesterday morning."

He shook his head and waved his forefinger at her in a quicker rhythm.

"He was in Paris last night. He is registered here but his room is not occupied. They told me I had better ask at this room."

"Sounds very peculiar to me—we saw him off yesterday morning on the boat train."

"Be that as it may, he has been seen here this morning. Even his carte d'identité has been seen. And there you are."

"We know nothing about it," she proclaimed in amazement.

He considered. He was an ill-smelling, handsome man.

"You were not with him at all last night?"

"But no."

"We have arrested a Negro. We are convinced we have at last arrested the correct Negro."

"I assure you that I haven't an idea what you're talking about. If it's the Mr. Abraham North, the one we know, well, if he was in Paris last night we weren't aware of it."

The man nodded, sucked his upper lip, convinced but disappointed.

"What happened?" Nicole demanded.

He showed his palms, puffing out his closed mouth. He had begun to find her attractive and his eyes flickered at her.

"What do you wish, Madame? A summer affair. Mr. Afghan North was robbed and he made a complaint. We have arrested the miscreant. Mr. Afghan should come to identify him and make the proper charges."

Nicole pulled her dressing-gown closer around her and dismissed him briskly. Mystified she took a bath and dressed. By this time it was after ten and she called Rosemary, but got no answer—then she phoned the hotel office and found that Abe had indeed registered, at six-thirty this morning. His room, however, was still unoccupied. Hoping for a word from Dick she waited in the parlor of the suite; just as she had given up and decided to go out, the office called and announced:

"Meestaire Crawshow, un nègre."

"On what business?" she demanded.

"He says he knows you and the doctaire. He says there is a Meestaire Freeman into prison that is a friend of all the world. He says there is injustice and he wishes to see Meestaire North before he himself is arrested."

"We know nothing about it." Nicole disclaimed the whole business with a vehement clap of the receiver. Abe's bizarre reappearance made it plain to her how fatigued she was with his dissipation. Dismissing him from her mind she went out, ran into Rosemary at the dressmaker's, and shopped with her for artificial flowers and all-colored strings of colored beads on the Rue de Rivoli. She helped Rosemary choose a diamond for her mother, and some scarfs and novel cigarette cases to take home to business associates in California. For her son she bought Greek and Roman soldiers, a whole army of them, costing more than a thousand francs. Once again they spent their money in different ways, and again Rosemary admired Nicole's method of spending. Nicole was sure that the money she spent was hers—Rosemary still thought her money was miraculously lent to her and she must consequently be very careful of it.

It was fun spending money in the sunlight of the foreign city, with healthy bodies under them that sent streams of color up to their faces; with arms and hands, legs and ankles that they stretched out confidently, reaching or stepping with the confidence of women lovely to men.

When they got back to the hotel and found Dick, all bright and new in the morning, both of them had a moment of complete childish joy.

He had just received a garbled telephone call from Abe, who, so it appeared, had spent the forenoon in hiding.

"It was one of the most extraordinary telephone conversations I've ever held."

Dick had talked not only to Abe but to a dozen others. On the phone these supernumeraries had been typically introduced as: "—man wants to talk to you is in the teput dome, well he says he was in it—what is it?

"Hey, somebody, shut up—anyhow, he was in some shandel-scandal and he kaa *possibly* go home. My own *personal* is that—my personal is he's had a—" Gulps sounded and thereafter what the party had, rested with the unknown.

The phone yielded up a supplementary offer:

"I thought it would appeal to you anyhow as a psychologist." The vague personality who corresponded to this statement was eventually hung on to the phone; in the sequence he failed to appeal to Dick as a psychologist or indeed as anything else. Abe's conversation flowed on as follows:

"Hello."

"Well?"

"Well, hello."

"Who are you?"

"Well." There were interpolated snorts of laughter.

"Well, I'll put somebody else on the line."

Sometimes Dick could hear Abe's voice, accompanied by scuf-flings, droppings of the receiver, far-away fragments such as, "No, I don't, Mr. North. . . ." Then a pert decided voice had said: "If you are a friend of Mr. North you will come down and take him away."

Abe cut in, solemn and ponderous, beating it all down with an overtone of earth-bound determination.

"Dick, I've launched a race riot in Montmartre. I'm going over and get Freeman out of jail. If a Negro from Copenhagen that makes shoe polish—hello, can you hear me—well, look, if anybody comes there—" Once again the receiver was a chorus of innumerable melodies.

"Why are you back in Paris?" Dick demanded.

"I got as far as Évreux, and I decided to take a plane back so I could compare it with St. Sulpice. I mean I don't intend to bring St. Sulpice back to Paris. I don't even mean Baroque! I meant St. Germain. For God's sake, wait a minute and I'll put the chasseur on the wire."

"For God's sake, don't."

"Listen—did Mary get off all right?"

"Yes."

"Dick, I want you to talk with a man I met here this morning, the son of a naval officer that's been to every doctor in Europe. Let me tell you about him——"

Dick had rung off at this point—perhaps that was a piece of ingratitude, for he needed grist for the grinding activity of his mind.

"Abe used to be so nice," Nicole told Rosemary. "So nice. Long ago—when Dick and I were first married. If you had known him then. He'd come to stay with us for weeks and weeks and we scarcely knew he was in the house. Sometimes he'd play—sometimes he'd be in the library with a muted piano, making love to it by the hour—Dick, do you remember that maid? She thought he was a ghost and sometimes Abe used to meet her in the hall and moo at her, and it cost us a whole tea service once—but we didn't care."

So much fun—so long ago. Rosemary envied them their fun, imagining a life of leisure unlike her own. She knew little of leisure, but she had the respect for it of those who have never had it. She thought of it as a resting, without realizing that the Divers were as far from relaxing as she was herself.

"What did this to him?" she asked. "Why does he have to drink?"

Nicole shook her head right and left, disclaiming responsibility for the matter: "So many smart men go to pieces nowadays."

"And when haven't they?" Dick asked. "Smart men play close to the line because they have to—some of them can't stand it, so they quit."

"It must lie deeper than that." Nicole clung to her conversation; also she was irritated that Dick should contradict her before Rosemary. "Artists like—well, like Fernand don't seem to have to wallow in alcohol. Why is it just Americans who dissipate?"

There were so many answers to this question that Dick decided to leave it in the air, to buzz victoriously in Nicole's ears. He had become intensely critical of her. Though he thought she was the most attractive human creature he had ever seen, though he got from her everything he needed, he scented battle from afar, and subconsciously he had been hardening and arming himself, hour by hour. He was not given to self-indulgence and he felt comparatively graceless at this moment of indulging himself, blinding his eyes with the hope that Nicole guessed at only an emotional excitement about Rosemary. He was not sure—last night at the theatre she had referred pointedly to Rosemary as a child.

The trio lunched downstairs in an atmosphere of carpets and padded waiters, who did not march at the stomping quick-step of those men who brought good food to the tables at which they had recently dined. Here there were families of Americans staring around at families of Americans and trying to make conversation with one another.

There was a party at the next table that they could not account for. It consisted of an expansive, somewhat secretarial, would-you-mind-repeating young man, and a score of women. The women were neither young nor old nor of any particular social class; yet the party gave the impression of a unit, held more closely together, for example, than a group of wives stalling through a professional congress of their husbands. Certainly it was more of a unit than any conceivable tourist party.

An instinct made Dick suck back the grave derision that formed on his tongue; he asked the waiter to find out who they were.

"Those are the gold-star muzzers," explained the waiter.

Aloud and in low voices they exclaimed. Rosemary's eyes filled with tears.

"Probably the young ones are the wives," said Nicole.

Over his wine Dick looked at them again; in their happy faces, the dignity that surrounded and pervaded the party, he perceived all the maturity of an older America. For a while the sobered women who had come to mourn for their dead, for something they could not repair, made the room beautiful. Momentarily, he sat again on his father's knee, riding with Mosby while the old loyalties and devotions fought on around him. Almost with an effort he turned back to his two women at the table and faced the whole new world in which he believed.

—Do you mind if I pull down the curtain?

CHAPTER XI

ABE NORTH WAS STILL in the Ritz bar, where he had been since nine in the morning. When he arrived seeking sanctuary the windows were open and great beams were busy at pulling up the dust from smoky carpets and cushions. Chasseurs tore through the corridors, liberated and disembodied, moving for the moment in pure space. The sit-down bar for women, across from the bar proper, seemed very small—it was hard to imagine what throngs it could accommodate in the afternoon.

The famous Paul, the concessionnaire, had not arrived, but Claude, who was checking stock, broke off his work with no improper surprise to make Abe a pick-me-up. Abe sat on a bench against a wall. After two drinks he began to feel better—so much better that he mounted to the barber's shop and was shaved. When he returned to the bar Paul had arrived—in his custom-built motor, from which he had disembarked correctly at the Boulevard des Capucines. Paul liked Abe and came over to talk.

"I was supposed to ship home this morning," Abe said. "I mean yesterday morning, or whatever this is."

"Why din you?" asked Paul.

Abe considered, and happened finally to a reason: "I was reading a serial in *Liberty* and the next installment was due here in Paris—so if I'd sailed I'd have missed it—then I never would have read it."

"It must be a very good story."

"It's a terr-r-rible story."

Paul arose chuckling and paused, leaning on the back of a chair:

"If you really want to get off, Mr. North, there are friends of yours going tomorrow on the *France*—Mister what is this name—and Slim Pearson. Mister—I'll think of it—tall with a new beard."

"Yardly," Abe supplied.

"Mr. Yardly. They're both going on the *France*."

163

He was on his way to his duties, but Abe tried to detain him: "If I didn't have to go by way of Cherbourg. The baggage went that way."

"Get your baggage in New York," said Paul, receding.

The logic of the suggestion fitted gradually into Abe's pitch—he grew rather enthusiastic about being cared for, or rather about prolonging his state of irresponsibility.

Other clients had meanwhile drifted in to the bar: first came a huge Dane whom Abe had somewhere encountered. The Dane took a seat across the room, and Abe guessed he would be there all the day, drinking, lunching, talking, or reading newspapers. He felt a desire to outstay him. At eleven the college boys began to drop in, stepping gingerly lest they tear one another bag from bag. It was about then he had the chasseur telephone to the Divers; by the time he was in touch with them he was in touch also with other friends and his hunch was to put them all on different phones at once—the result was somewhat general. From time to time his mind reverted to the fact that he ought to go over and get Freeman out of jail, but he shook off all facts as parts of the nightmare.

By one o'clock the bar was jammed; amidst the consequent mixture of voices the staff of waiters functioned, pinning down their clients to the facts of drink and money.

"That makes two stingers . . . and one more . . . two martinis and one . . . nothing for you, Mr. Quarterly . . . that makes three rounds. That makes seventy-five francs, Mr. Quarterly. Mr. Schaeffer said he had this—you had the last . . . I can only do what you say . . . thanks vera-much."

In the confusion Abe had lost his seat; now he stood gently swaying and talking to some of the people with whom he had involved himself. A terrier ran a leash around his legs, but Abe managed to extricate himself without upsetting and became the recipient of profuse apologies. Presently he was invited to lunch, but declined. It was almost Briglith, he explained, and there was something he had to do at Briglith. A little later, with the exquisite manners of the alcoholic that are like the manners of a prisoner or a family servant, he said good-bye to an acquaintance and, turning around, discovered that the bar's great moment was over as precipitately as it had begun.

Across from him the Dane and his companions had ordered luncheon. Abe did likewise but scarcely touched it. Afterward he just sat, happy to live in the past. The drink made past happy things contemporary with the present, as if they were still going on, contemporary even with the future, as if they were about to happen again.

At four the chasseur approached him:

"You wish to see a colored fellow of the name Jules Peterson?"

"God! How did he find me?"

"I didn't tell him you were present."

"Who did?" Abe fell over his glasses but recovered himself.

"Says he's already been around to all the American bars and hotels."

"Tell him I'm not here—" As the chasseur turned away Abe asked: "Can he come in here?"

"I'll find out."

Receiving the question Paul glanced over his shoulder; he shook his head, then seeing Abe he came over.

"I'm sorry; I can't allow it."

Abe got himself up with an effort and went out to the Rue Cambon.

CHAPTER XII

WITH HIS MINIATURE LEATHER brief-case in his hand Richard Diver walked from the seventh arrondissement—where he left a note for Maria Wallis signed "Dicole," the word with which he and Nicole had signed communications in the first days of love—to his shirt-makers, where the clerks made a fuss over him out of proportion to the money he spent. He was ashamed at promising so much to these poor Englishmen, with his fine manners, his air of having the key to security, ashamed of making a tailor shift an inch of silk on his arm Afterward he went to the bar of the Crillon and drank a small coffee and two fingers of gin.

As he entered the hotel the halls had seemed unnaturally bright; when he left he realized that it was because it had already turned dark outside. It was a windy four-o'clock night, with the leaves on the Champs-Élysées singing and failing, thin and wild. Dick turned down the Rue de Rivoli, walking two squares under the arcades to his bank, where there was mail. Then he took a taxi and started up the Champs-Élysées through the first patter of rain, sitting alone with his love.

Back at two o'clock in the Roi George corridor the beauty of Nicole had been to the beauty of Rosemary as the beauty of Leonardo's girl was to that of the girl of an illustrator. Dick moved on through the rain, demoniac and frightened, the passions of many men inside him and nothing simple that he could see.

Rosemary opened her door full of emotions no one else knew of. She was now what is sometimes called a "little wild thing"— by twenty-four full hours she was not yet unified and she was absorbed in playing around with chaos, as if her destiny were a picture puzzle—counting benefits, counting hopes, telling off Dick, Nicole, her mother, the director she met yesterday, like stops on a string of beads.

When Dick knocked she had just dressed and had been watching the rain, thinking of some poem, and of full gutters in Beverly Hills. When she opened the door she saw him as something fixed and godlike as he had always been, as older people are to younger, rigid and unmalleable. Dick saw her with an inevitable sense of disappointment. It took him a moment to respond to the unguarded sweetness of her smile, her body calculated to a millimeter to suggest a bud yet guarantee a flower. He was conscious of the print of her wet foot on a rug through the bathroom door.

"Miss Television," he said with a lightness he did not feel. He put his gloves, his brief-case on the dressing-table, his stick against the wall. His chin dominated the lines of pain around his mouth, forcing them up into his forehead and the corner of his eyes, like fear that cannot be shown in public.

"Come and sit on my lap close to me," he said softly, "and let me see about your lovely mouth."

She came over and sat there and while the dripping slowed down outside—drip—dri-i-ip, she laid her lips to the beautiful cold image she had created.

Presently she kissed him several times in the mouth. He had never seen anything so dazzling as the quality of her skin, and since sometimes beauty gives back the images of one's best thoughts, he thought of his responsibility about Nicole, and of the responsibility of her being two doors down across the corridor.

"The rain's over," he said. "Do you see the sun on the slate?"

Rosemary stood up and leaned down and said her most sincere thing to him:

"Oh, we're such *actors*—you and I."

She went to her dresser and the moment that she laid her comb flat against her hair there was a slow persistent knocking at the door.

They were shocked motionless; the knock was repeated insistently, and in the sudden realization that the door was not locked Rosemary finished her hair with one stroke, nodded at Dick, who had quickly jerked the wrinkles out of the bed where they had been sitting, and started for the door. Dick said in quite a natural voice, not too loud:

"—so if you don't feel up to going out, I'll tell Nicole and we'll have a very quiet last evening."

The precautions were needless, for the situation of the parties outside the door was so harassed as to preclude any but the most fleeting judgments on matters not pertinent to themselves. Standing there was Abe, aged by several months in the last twenty-four hours, and a very frightened, concerned colored man, whom Abe introduced as Mr. Peterson of Stockholm.

"He's in a terrible situation and it's my fault," said Abe. "We need some good advice."

"Come in our rooms," said Dick.

Abe insisted that Rosemary come too and they crossed the hall to the Divers' suite. Jules Peterson, a small, respectable Negro, on the suave model that heels the Republican party in the border states, followed.

It appeared that the latter had been a legal witness to the early-morning dispute in Montparnasse; he had accompanied Abe to the police station and supported his assertion that a thousand-franc note had been seized out of his hand by a Negro, whose identification was one of the points of the case. Abe and Jules Peterson, accompanied by an agent of police, returned to the bistro and too hastily identified as the criminal a Negro who, so it was established after an hour, had only entered the place after Abe left. The police had further complicated the situation by arresting the prominent Negro restaurateur, Freeman, who had drifted through the alcoholic fog at a very early stage and then vanished. The true culprit, whose case, as reported by his friends, was that he had merely commandeered a fifty-franc note to pay for drinks that Abe had ordered, had only recently and in a somewhat sinister rôle, reappeared upon the scene.

In brief, Abe had succeeded in the space of an hour in entangling himself with the personal lives, consciences, and emotions of one Afro-European and three Afro-Americans inhabiting the Latin Quarter. The disentanglement was not even faintly in sight and the day had passed in an atmosphere of unfamiliar Negro faces bobbing up in unexpected places and around unexpected corners, and insistent Negro voices on the phone.

In person, Abe had succeeded in evading all of them, save Jules

Peterson. Peterson was rather in the position of the friendly Indian who had helped a white. The Negroes who suffered from the betrayal were not so much after Abe as after Peterson, and Peterson was very much after what protection he might get from Abe.

Up in Stockholm Peterson had failed as a small manufacturer of shoe polish and now possessed only his formula and sufficient trade tools to fill a small box; however, his new protector had promised in the early hours to set him up in business in Versailles. Abe's former chauffeur was a shoemaker there and Abe had handed Peterson two hundred francs on account.

Rosemary listened with distaste to this rigmarole; to appreciate its grotesquerie required a more robust sense of humor than hers. The little man with his portable manufactory, his insincere eyes that, from time to time, rolled white semi-circles of panic into view; the figure of Abe, his face as blurred as the gaunt fine lines of it would permit—all this was as remote from her as sickness.

"I ask only a chance in life," said Peterson with the sort of precise yet distorted intonation peculiar to colonial countries. "My methods are simple, my formula is so good that I was drove away from Stockholm, ruined, because I did not care to dispose of it."

Dick regarded him politely—interest formed, dissolved, he turned to Abe.

"You go to some hotel and go to bed. After you're all straight Mr. Peterson will come and see you."

"But don't you appreciate the mess that Peterson's in?" Abe protested.

"I shall wait in the hall," said Mr. Peterson with delicacy. "It is perhaps hard to discuss my problems in front of me."

He withdrew after a short travesty of a French bow; Abe pulled himself to his feet with the deliberation of a locomotive.

"I don't seem highly popular today."

"Popular but not probable," Dick told him. "My advice is to leave this hotel—by way of the bar, if you want. Go to the Chambord, or if you'll need a lot of service, go over to the Majestic."

"Could I annoy you for a drink?"

"There's not a thing up here," Dick lied.

Resignedly Abe shook hands with Rosemary; he composed his

face slowly, holding her hand a long time and forming sentences that did not emerge.

"You are the most—one of the most——"

She was sorry, and rather revolted at his dirty hands, but she laughed in a well-bred way, as though it were nothing unusual to her to watch a man walking in a slow dream. Often people display a curious respect for a man drunk, rather like the respect of simple races for the insane. Respect rather than fear. There is something awe-inspiring in one who has lost all inhibitions, who will do anything. Of course we make him pay afterward for his moment of superiority, his moment of impressiveness. Abe turned to Dick with a last appeal.

"If I go to a hotel and get all steamed and curry-combed, and sleep awhile, and fight off these Senegalese—could I come and spend the evening by the fireside?"

Dick nodded at him, less in agreement than in mockery, and said: "You have a high opinion of your current capacities."

"I bet if Nicole was here she'd let me come back."

"All right." Dick went to a trunk tray and brought a box to the central table; inside were innumerable cardboard letters.

"You can come if you want to play anagrams."

Abe eyed the contents of the box with physical revulsion, as though he had been asked to eat them like oats.

"What are anagrams? Haven't I had enough strange——"

"It's a quiet game. You spell words with them—any word except alcohol."

"I bet you can spell alcohol," Abe plunged his hand among the counters. "Can I come back if I can spell alcohol?"

"You can come back if you want to play anagrams."

Abe shook his head resignedly.

"If you're in that frame of mind there's no use—I'd just be in the way." He waved his finger reproachfully at Dick. "But remember what George the Third said, that if Grant was drunk he wished he would bite the other generals."

With a last desperate glance at Rosemary from the golden corners of his eyes, he went out. To his relief Peterson was no longer in the corridor. Feeling lost and homeless he went back to ask Paul the name of that boat.

CHAPTER XIII

WHEN HE HAD TOTTERED out, Dick and Rosemary embraced fleetingly. There was a dust of Paris over both of them through which they scented each other: the rubber guard on Dick's fountain pen, the faintest odor of warmth from Rosemary's neck and shoulders. For another half-minute Dick clung to the situation; Rosemary was first to return to reality.

"I must go, youngster," she said.

They blinked at each other across a widening space, and Rosemary made an exit that she had learned young, and on which no director had ever tried to improve.

She opened the door of her room and went directly to her desk, where she had suddenly remembered leaving her wristwatch. It was there; slipping it on she glanced down at the daily letter to her mother, finishing the last sentence in her mind. Then, rather gradually, she realized without turning about that she was not alone in the room.

In an inhabited room there are refracting objects only half noticed: varnished wood, more or less polished brass, silver, and ivory, and beyond these a thousand conveyors of light and shadow so mild that one scarcely thinks of them as that, the tops of picture-frames, the edges of pencils or ash-trays, of crystal or china ornaments; the totality of this refraction—appealing to equally subtle reflexes of the vision as well as to those associational fragments in the sub-conscious that we seem to hang on to, as a glass-fitter keeps the irregularly shaped pieces that may do some time—this fact might account for what Rosemary afterward mystically described as "realizing" that there was someone in the room, before she could determine it. But when she did realize it she turned swift in a sort of ballet step and saw that a dead Negro was stretched upon her bed.

As she cried "aaouu!" and her still unfastened wristwatch banged against the desk she had the preposterous idea that it was Abe North. Then she dashed for the door and across the hall.

Dick was straightening up; he had examined the gloves worn that day and thrown them into a pile of soiled gloves in a corner of a trunk. He had hung up coat and vest and spread his shirt on another hanger—a trick of his own. "You'll wear a shirt that's a little dirty where you won't wear a mussed shirt." Nicole had come in and was dumping one of Abe's extraordinary ash-trays into the wastebasket when Rosemary tore into the room.

"*Dick! Dick!* Come and see!"

Dick jogged across the hall into her room. He knelt to Peterson's heart, and felt the pulse—the body was warm, the face, harassed and indirect in life, was gross and bitter in death; the box of materials was held under one arm, but the shoe that dangled over the bedside was bare of polish and its sole was worn through. By French law Dick had no right to touch the body, but he moved the arm a little to see something—there was a stain on the green coverlet, there would be faint blood on the blanket beneath.

Dick closed the door and stood thinking; he heard cautious steps in the corridor and then Nicole calling him by name. Opening the door he whispered: "Bring the couverture and top blankets from one of our beds—don't let any one see you." Then, noticing the strained look on her face, he added quickly, "Look here, you mustn't get upset over this—it's only some nigger scrap."

"I want it to be over."

The body, as Dick lifted it, was light and ill-nourished. He held it so that further hemorrhages from the wound would flow into the man's clothes. Laying it beside the bed he stripped off the coverlet and top blanket and then opening the door an inch, listened— there was a clank of dishes down the hall followed by a loud patronizing "Mer*ci* Madame," but the waiter went in the other direction, toward the service stairway. Quickly Dick and Nicole exchanged bundles across the corridor; after spreading this covering on Rosemary's bed, Dick stood sweating in the warm twilight, considering. Certain points had become apparent to him in the moment following his examination of the body; first, that Abe's first hostile Indian had tracked the friendly Indian and discovered him in the corridor and, when the latter had taken desperate refuge in Rosemary's room, had hunted down and slain him; second, that if the situation were allowed to develop naturally, no power on earth could keep the smear off Rosemary—the paint was scarcely dry on the Arbuckle case. Her contract was contingent upon an obligation to continue rigidly and unexceptionally as Daddy's Girl.

Automatically Dick made the old motion of turning up his sleeves, though he wore a sleeveless undershirt, and bent over the body. Getting a purchase on the shoulders of the coat he kicked open the door with his heel, and dragged the body quickly into a plausible position in the corridor. He came back into Rosemary's room and smoothed back the grain of the plush floor rug. Then he went to the phone in his suite and called the manager-owner of the hotel.

"McBeth?—it's Doctor Diver speaking—something very important. Are we on a more or less private line?"

It was good that he had made the extra effort which had firmly entrenched him with Mr. McBeth. Here was one use for all the pleasingness that Dick had expended over a large area he would never retrace.

"Going out of the suite we came on a dead Negro . . . in the hall . . . no, no, he's a civilian. Wait a minute now—I knew you didn't want any guests to blunder on the body so I'm phoning you. Of course I must ask you to keep my name out of it. I don't want any French red tape just because I discovered the man."

What exquisite consideration for the hotel! Only because Mr. McBeth, with his own eyes, had seen these traits in Doctor Diver two nights before, could he credit the story without question.

In a minute Mr. McBeth arrived and in another minute he was joined by a gendarme. In the interval he found time to whisper to Dick, "You can be sure the name of any guest will be protected. I'm only too grateful to you for your pains."

Mr. McBeth took an immediate step that may only be imagined, but that influenced the gendarme so as to make him pull his mustaches in a frenzy of uneasiness and greed. He made perfunctory notes and sent a telephone call to his post. Meanwhile with a celerity that Jules Peterson, as a business man, would have quite understood, the remains were carried into another apartment of one of the most fashionable hotels in the world.

Dick went back to his salon.

"What *hap*pened?" cried Rosemary. "Do all the Americans in Paris just shoot at each other all the time?"

"This seems to be the open season," he answered. "Where's Nicole?"

"I think she's in the bathroom."

She adored him for saving her—disasters that could have attended upon the event had passed in prophecy through her mind; and she had listened in wild worship to his strong, sure, polite voice making it all right. But before she reached him in a sway of soul and body his attention focussed on something else: he went into the bedroom and toward the bathroom. And now Rosemary, too, could hear, louder and louder, a verbal inhumanity that penetrated the keyholes and the cracks in the door, swept into the suite and in the shape of horror took form again.

With the idea that Nicole had fallen in the bathroom and hurt herself, Rosemary followed Dick. That was not the condition of affairs at which she stared before Dick shouldered her back and brusquely blocked her view.

Nicole knelt beside the tub swaying sidewise and sidewise. "It's you!" she cried, "—it's you come to intrude on the only privacy I have in the world—with your spread with red blood on it. I'll wear it for you—I'm not ashamed, though it was such a pity. On All Fools Day we had a party on the Zurichsee, and all the fools were there, and I wanted to come dressed in a spread but they wouldn't let me——"

"Control yourself!"

"—so I sat in the bathroom and they brought me a domino and said wear that. I did. What else could I do?"

"Control yourself, Nicole!"

"I never expected you to love me—it was too late—only don't come in the bathroom, the only place I can go for privacy, dragging spreads with red blood on them and asking me to fix them."

"Control yourself. Get up——"

Rosemary, back in the salon, heard the bathroom door bang, and stood trembling: now she knew what Violet McKisco had seen in the bathroom at Villa Diana. She answered the ringing phone and almost cried with relief when she found it was Collis Clay, who had traced her to the Divers' apartment. She asked him to come up while she got her hat, because she was afraid to go into her room alone.

CHAPTER XIV

Doctor Richard Diver and Mrs. Elsie Speers sat in the Café des Alliées in August, under cool and dusty trees. The sparkle of the mica was dulled by the baked ground, and a few gusts of mistral from down the coast seeped through the Esterel and rocked the fishing boats in the harbor, pointing the masts here and there at a featureless sky.

"I had a letter this morning," said Mrs. Speers "What a terrible time you all must have had with those Negroes! But Rosemary said you were perfectly wonderful to her."

"Rosemary ought to have a service stripe. It was pretty harrowing—the only person it didn't disturb was Abe North. He flew off to Havre—he probably doesn't know about it yet."

"I'm sorry Mrs. Diver was upset," she said carefully.

Rosemary had written from Paris:

"Nicole seemed Out of her Mind. I didn't want to come South with them because I felt Dick had enough on his hands."

"She's all right now." He spoke almost impatiently. "So you're leaving tomorrow. When will you sail?"

"Right away."

"My God, it's awful to have you go."

"We're glad we came here. We've had a good time, thanks to you. You're the first man Rosemary ever cared for."

Another gust of wind strained around the porphyry hills of la Napoule. There was a hint in the air that the earth was hurrying on toward other weather; the lush midsummer moment outside of time was already over.

"Rosemary's had crushes, but sooner or later she always turned the man over to me"—Mrs. Speers laughed—"for dissection."

"So I was spared."

"There was nothing I could have done. She was in love with you before I ever saw you. I told her to go ahead."

He saw that no provision had been made for him, or for Nicole, in Mrs. Speers' plans—and he saw that her amorality sprang from the conditions of her own withdrawal. It was her right, the pension on which her own emotions had retired. Women are necessarily capable of almost anything in their struggle for survival and can scarcely be convicted of such man-made crimes as "cruelty." So long as the shuffle of love and pain went on within proper walls Mrs. Speers could view it with as much detachment and humor as a eunuch. She had not even allowed for the possibility of Rosemary's being damaged—or was she certain that she couldn't be?

"If what you say is true I don't think it did her any harm." He was keeping up to the end the pretense that he could still think objectively about Rosemary. "She's over it already. Still—so many of the important times in life begin by seeming incidental."

"This wasn't incidental," Mrs. Speers insisted. "You were the first man—you're an ideal to her. In every letter she says that."

"She's so polite."

"You and Rosemary are the politest people I've ever known, but she means this."

"My politeness is a trick of the heart."

This was partly true. From his father Dick had learned the somewhat conscious good manners of the young Southerner coming north after the Civil War. Often he used them, and just as often he despised them because they were not a protest against how unpleasant selfishness was, but against how unpleasant it looked.

"I'm in love with Rosemary," he told her suddenly. "It's a kind of self-indulgence saying that to you."

It seemed very strange and official to him, as if the very tables and chairs in the Café des Alliées would remember it forever. Already he felt her absence from these skies: on the beach he could only remember the sun-torn flesh of her shoulder; at Tarmes he crushed out her footprints as he crossed the garden; and now the orchestra launching into the "Nice Carnival Song," an echo of last year's vanished gaieties, started the little dance that went on all about her. In a hundred hours she had come to possess all the world's dark magic; the blinding belladonna, the caffeine converting physical into nervous energy, the mandragora that imposes harmony.

With an effort he once more accepted the fiction that he shared Mrs. Speers' detachment.

"You and Rosemary aren't really alike," he said. "The wisdom she got from you is all molded up into her persona, into the mask she faces the world with. She doesn't think; her real depths are Irish and romantic and illogical."

Mrs. Speers knew too that Rosemary, for all her delicate surface, was a young mustang, perceptibly by Captain Doctor Hoyt, U. S. A. Cross-sectioned, Rosemary would have displayed an enormous heart, liver and soul, all crammed close together under the lovely shell.

Saying good-bye, Dick was aware of Elsie Speers' full charm, aware that she meant rather more to him than merely a last unwillingly relinquished fragment of Rosemary. He could possibly have made up Rosemary; he could never have made up her mother. If the cloak, spurs, and brilliants in which Rosemary had walked off were things with which he had endowed her, it was nice in contrast to watch her mother's grace, knowing it was surely something he had not evoked. She had an air of seeming to wait, as if for a man to get through with something more important than herself, a battle or an operation, during which he must not be hurried or interfered with. When the man had finished she would be waiting, without fret or impatience, somewhere on a high stool, turning the pages of a newspaper.

"Good-bye—and I want you both to remember always how fond of you Nicole and I have grown."

Back at the Villa Diana, he went to his workroom and opened the shutters, closed against the mid-day glare. On his two long tables, in ordered confusion, lay the materials of his book. Volume I, concerned with Classification, had achieved some success in a small subsidized edition. He was negotiating for its reissue. Volume II was to be a great amplification of his first little book, *A Psychology for Psychiatrists*. Like so many men he had found that he had only one or two ideas—that his little collection of pamphlets now in its fiftieth German edition contained the germ of all he would ever think or know.

But he was currently uneasy about the whole thing. He resented the wasted years at New Haven, but mostly he felt a discrepancy between the growing luxury in which the Divers lived and the need for display that apparently went along with it. Remembering his Rumanian friend's story, about the man who had worked for years on the brain of an armadillo, he suspected that patient Germans were sitting close to the libraries of Berlin and Vienna callously anticipating him. He had about decided to brief the work in its present condition and publish it in an undocumented volume of a hundred thousand words as an introduction to more scholarly volumes to follow.

He confirmed this decision walking around the rays of late afternoon in his workroom. With the new plan he could be through by spring. It seemed to him that when a man with his energy was pursued for a year by increasing doubts, it indicated some fault in the plan.

He laid the bars of gilded metal that he used as paperweights along the sheaves of notes. He swept up, for no servant was allowed in here, treated his washroom sketchily with Bon Ami, repaired a screen, and sent off an order to a publishing house in Zurich. Then he drank an ounce of gin with twice as much water.

He saw Nicole in the garden. Presently he must encounter her and the prospect gave him a leaden feeling. Before her he must keep up a perfect front, now and tomorrow, next week and next year. All night in Paris he had held her in his arms while she slept light under the luminol; in the early morning he broke in upon her confusion before it could form, with words of tenderness and protection, and she slept again with his face against the warm scent of her hair. Before she woke he had arranged everything at the phone in the next room. Rosemary was to move to another hotel. She was to be Daddy's Girl and even to give up saying good-bye to them. The proprietor of the hotel, Mr. McBeth, was to be the three Chinese monkeys. Packing amid the piled boxes and tissue paper of many purchases, Dick and Nicole left for the Riviera at noon.

Then there was a reaction. As they settled down in the wagon-lit Dick saw that Nicole was waiting for it, and it came quickly and desperately, before the train was out of the ceinture—his only instinct was to step off while the train was still going slow, rush back and see where Rosemary was, what she was doing. He opened a book and bent his pince-nez upon it, aware that Nicole was watching him from her pillow across the compartment. Unable to read, he pretended to be tired and shut his eyes, but she was still watching him and, though still she was half asleep from the hangover of the drug, she was relieved and almost happy that he was hers again.

It was worse with his eyes shut, for it gave a rhythm of finding and losing, finding and losing; but so as not to appear restless he lay like that until noon. At luncheon things were better—it was always a fine meal; a thousand lunches in inns and restaurants, wagon-lits, buffets, and airplanes were a mighty collation to have taken together. The familiar hurry of the train waiters, the little bottles of wine and mineral water, the excellent food of the Paris-Lyons-Méditerranée gave them the illusion that everything was the same as before, but it was almost the first trip he had ever taken with Nicole that was a going away rather than a going toward. He drank a whole bottle of wine save for Nicole's single glass; they talked about the house and the children. But once back in the compartment a silence fell over them like the silence in the restaurant across from the Luxembourg. Receding from a grief, it seems necessary to retrace the same steps that brought us there. An unfamiliar impatience settled on Dick; suddenly Nicole said:

"It seemed too bad to leave Rosemary like that—do you suppose she'll be all right?"

"Of course. She could take care of herself anywhere—" Lest this belittle Nicole's ability to do likewise, he added, "After all, she's an actress, and even though her mother's in the background she *has* to look out for herself."

"She's very attractive."

"She's an infant."

"She's attractive, though."

They talked aimlessly back and forth, each speaking for the other.

"She's not as intelligent as I thought," Dick offered.

"She's quite smart."

"Not very, though—there's a persistent aroma of the nursery."

"She's very—very pretty," Nicole said in a detached, emphatic way, "and I thought she was very good in the picture."

"She was well directed. Thinking it over, it wasn't very individual."

"I thought it was. I can see how she'd be very attractive to men." His heart twisted. To what men? How many men?

—Do you mind if I pull down the curtain?

—Please do, it's too light in here.

Where now? And with whom?

"In a few years she'll look ten years older than you."

"On the contrary. I sketched her one night on a theatre program, I think she'll last."

They were both restless in the night. In a day or two Dick would try to banish the ghost of Rosemary before it became walled up with them, but for the moment he had no force to do it. Sometimes it is harder to deprive oneself of a pain than of a pleasure, and the memory so possessed him that for the moment there was nothing to do but to pretend. This was more difficult because he was currently annoyed with Nicole, who, after all these years, should recognize symptoms of strain in herself and guard against them. Twice within a fortnight she had broken up: there had been the night of the dinner at Tarmes, when he had found her in her bedroom dissolved in crazy laughter telling Mrs. McKisco she could not go into the bathroom because the key was thrown down the well. Mrs. McKisco was astonished and resentful, baffled and yet in a way comprehending. Dick had not been particularly alarmed then, for afterward Nicole was repentant. She called at Gausse's hotel but the McKiscos were gone.

The collapse in Paris was another matter, adding significance to the first one. It prophesied possibly a new cycle, a new pousse of the malady. Having gone through unprofessional agonies during her long relapse following the birth of Topsy, their second child, he had hardened himself about her, making a cleavage between Nicole sick and Nicole well. This made it difficult now to distinguish between his self-protective professional detachment and some new coldness in his heart. As an indifference cherished, or left to atrophy, becomes an emptiness, to this extent he had learned to become empty of Nicole, serving her against his will with negations and emotional neglect. One writes of scars healed, a loose parallel to the pathology of the skin, but there is no such thing in the life of an individual. There are open wounds, shrunk sometimes to the size of a pin-prick, but wounds still. The marks of suffering are more comparable to the loss of a finger, or of the sight of an eye. We may not miss them, either, for one minute in a year, but if we should there is nothing to be done about it.

CHAPTER XV

He found Nicole in the garden with her arms folded high on her shoulders. She looked at him with straight gray eyes, with a child's searching wonder.

"I went to Cannes," he said. "I ran into Mrs. Speers. She's leaving tomorrow. She wanted to come up and say good-bye to you, but I slew the idea."

"I'm sorry. I'd like to have seen her. I like her."

"Who else do you think I saw—Bartholomew Tailor."

"You didn't."

"I couldn't have missed that face of his, the old experienced weasel. He was looking over the ground for Ciro's menagerie—they'll all be down next year. I suspected Mrs. Abrams was a sort of outpost."

"And Baby was outraged the first summer we came here."

"They don't really give a damn where they are, so I don't see why they don't stay and freeze in Deauville."

"Can't we start rumors about cholera or something?"

"I told Bartholomew that some categories died off like flies here—I told him the life of a suck was as short as the life of a machine-gunner in the war."

"You didn't."

"No, I didn't," he admitted. "He was very pleasant. It was a beautiful sight, he and I shaking hands there on the boulevard. The meeting of Sigmund Freud and Ward McAllister."

Dick didn't want to talk—he wanted to be alone so that his thoughts about work and the future would overpower his thoughts of love and today. Nicole knew about it, but only darkly and tragically, hating him a little in an animal way, yet wanting to rub against his shoulder.

"The darling," Dick said lightly.

He went into the house, forgetting something he wanted to do there, and then remembering it was the piano. He sat down whistling and played by ear:

"Just picture you upon my knee
With tea for two and two for tea
And me for you and you for me——"

Through the melody flowed a sudden realization that Nicole, hearing it, would guess quickly at a nostalgia for the past fortnight. He broke off with a casual chord and left the piano.

It was hard to know where to go. He glanced about the house that Nicole had made, that Nicole's grandfather had paid for. He owned only his work house and the ground on which it stood. Out of three thousand a year and what dribbled in from his publications he paid for his clothes and personal expenses, for cellar charges, and for Lanier's education, so far confined to a nurse's wage. Never had a move been contemplated without Dick's figuring his share. Living rather ascetically, travelling third-class when he was alone, with the cheapest wine, and good care of his clothes, and penalizing himself for any extravagances, he maintained a qualified financial independence. After a certain point, though, it was difficult—again and again it was necessary to decide together as to the uses to which Nicole's money should be put. Naturally Nicole, wanting to own him, wanting him to stand still forever, encouraged any slackness on his part, and in multiplying ways he was constantly inundated by a trickling of goods and money. The inception of the idea of the cliff villa, which they had elaborated as a fantasy one day, was a typical example of the forces divorcing them from the first simple arrangements in Zurich.

"Wouldn't it be fun if—" it had been; and then, "Won't it be fun when——"

It was not so much fun. His work became confused with Nicole's problems; in addition, her income had increased so fast of late that it seemed to belittle his work. Also, for the purpose of her cure, he had for many years pretended to a rigid domesticity from which he was drifting away, and the pretense became more arduous in this effortless immobility, in which he was inevitably subjected to microscopic examination. When Dick could no longer play what he wanted to play on the piano, it was an indication that life was being refined down to a point. He stayed in the big room a long time, listening to the buzz of the electric clock, listening to time.

BOOK IV

ESCAPE
1925-1929

CHAPTER I

IN NOVEMBER THE WAVES grew black and dashed over the sea wall onto the shore road, such summer life as had survived disappeared, and the beaches were melancholy and desolate under the mistral and rain. Gausse's hotel was closed for repairs and enlargement and the scaffolding of the summer casino at Juan les Pins grew larger and more formidable. Going into Cannes or Nice, Dick and Nicole met new people—members of orchestras, restaurateurs, horticultural enthusiasts, shipbuilders—for Dick had bought an old dinghy—and members of the Syndicat d'Initiative. They knew their servants well and gave thought to the children's education. In December Nicole seemed well-knit again; when a month had passed without tension, without the tight mouth, the unmotivated smile, the unfathomable remark, they went to the Swiss Alps for the Christmas holidays.

With his cap, Dick slapped the snow from his dark blue ski-suit before going inside. The great hall, its floor pockmarked by two decades of hobnails, was cleared for the tea dance and four-score young Americans, domiciled in schools near Gstaad, bounced about to the frolic of "Don't Bring Lulu," or exploded violently with the first percussions of the Charleston. It was a colony of the young, simple, and expensive—the Sturmtruppen of the rich were at St. Moritz. Baby Warren felt that she had made a gesture of renunciation in joining the Divers here.

Dick picked out the two sisters easily across the delicately haunted, soft-swaying room—they were poster-like, formidable in their snow costumes, Nicole's of cerulean blue, Baby's of brick red. The young Englishman was talking to them; but they were paying no attention, lulled to the staring point by the adolescent dance.

Nicole's snow-warm face lighted up further as she saw Dick. "Where is he?"

"He missed the train—I'm meeting him later." Dick sat down,

swinging a heavy boot over his knee. "You two look very striking together. Every once in a while I forget we're in the same party and get a big shock at seeing you."

Baby was a tall, fine-looking woman, deeply engaged in being just over thirty. Symptomatically she had pulled two men with her from London, one scarcely down from Cambridge, one old and hard with Victorian lecheries. Baby had certain spinster's characteristics—she was alien from touch, she started if she was touched suddenly, and such lingering touches as kisses and embraces slipped directly through the flesh into the forefront of her consciousness. She made few gestures with her trunk, her body proper—instead, she stamped her foot and tossed her head in almost an old-fashioned way. She relished the foretaste of death, prefigured by the catastrophes of friends; persistently she clung to the idea of Nicole's tragic destiny.

Baby's younger Englishman had been chaperoning the women down appropriate inclines and harrowing them on the bob-run. Dick, having turned an ankle in a too ambitious telemark, loafed gratefully about the nursery slope with the children or drank kvass with a Russian doctor at the hotel.

"Please be happy, Dick," Nicole urged him. "Why don't you meet some of these ickle durls and dance with them in the afternoon?"

"What would I say to them?"

Her low, almost harsh voice rose a few notes, simulating a plaintive coquetry: "Say, 'Ickle durl, oo is de pwettiest sing.' What do you think you say?"

"I don't like ickle durls. They smell of castile soap and peppermint. When I dance with them, I feel as if I'm pushing a baby carriage."

It was a dangerous subject—he was careful, to the point of self-consciousness, to stare far over the heads of young maidens.

"There's a lot of business," said Baby. "First place, there's news from home—the property we used to call the station property. The railroads only bought the centre of it at first. Now they've bought the rest, and it belonged to Mother. It's a question of investing the money."

Pretending to be repelled by this gross turn in the conversation, the Englishman made for a girl on the floor. Following him for an instant with the uncertain eyes of an American girl in the grip of a lifelong Anglophilia, Baby continued defiantly:

"It's a lot of money. It's three hundred thousand apiece. I keep an eye on my own investments, but Nicole doesn't know anything about securities, and I don't suppose you do either."

"I've got to meet the train," Dick said evasively.

Outside he inhaled damp snowflakes that he could no longer see against the darkening sky. Three children sledding past shouted a warning in some strange language; he heard them yell at the next bend and a little farther on he heard sleigh-bells coming up the hill in the dark. The holiday station glittered with expectancy, boys and girls waiting for new boys and girls, and by the time the train arrived Dick had caught the rhythm and pretended to Franz Gregorovius that he was clipping off a half-hour from an endless roll of pleasures. But Franz had some intensity of purpose at the moment that fought through any superimposition of mood on Dick's part. "I may get up to Zurich for a day," Dick had written, "or you can manage to come to Lausanne." Franz had managed to come all the way to Gstaad.

He was forty. Upon his healthy maturity reposed a set of pleasant official manners, but he was most at home in a somewhat stuffy safety from which he could despise the broken rich whom he re-educated. His scientific heredity might have bequeathed him a wider world, but he seemed to have deliberately chosen the standpoint of an humbler class, a choice typified by his selection of a wife. At the hotel Baby Warren made a quick examination of him and, failing to find any of the hall-marks she respected, the subtler virtues or courtesies by which the privileged classes recognized one another, treated him thereafter with her second manner. Nicole was always a little afraid of him. Dick liked him, as he liked his friends, without reservations.

For the evening they were sliding down the hill into the village, on those little sleds which serve the same purpose as gondolas do in Venice. Their destination was a hotel with an old-fashioned Swiss taproom, wooden and resounding, a room of clocks, kegs, steins, and antlers. Many parties at long tables blurred into one great party and ate fondue—a peculiarly indigestible form of Welsh rarebit, mitigated by hot spiced wine.

It was jolly in the big room; the younger Englishman remarked it and Dick conceded that there was no other word. With the pert heady wine he relaxed and pretended that the world was all put together again by the gray-haired men of the golden nineties who shouted old glees at the piano, by the young voices and the bright costumes toned into the room by the swirling smoke. For a moment he felt that they were in a ship with landfall just ahead; in the faces of all the girls was the same innocent expectation of the possibilities inherent in the situation and the night. He looked to see if that special girl was there and got an impression that she was at the table behind them—then he forgot her and invented a rigmarole and tried to make his party have a good time.

"I must talk to you," said Franz in English. "I have only two days to spend here."

"I suspected you had something on your mind."

"I have a plan that is—so marvellous." His hand fell upon Dick's knee. "I have a plan that will be the making of us two."

"Well?"

"Dick—there is a clinic we could have together—the old clinic of Braun on the Zugersee. The plant is all modern except for a few points. He is sick—he wants to go up in Austria, to die probably. It is a chance that is just insuperable. You and me—what a pair! Now don't say anything yet until I finish."

From the yellow glint in Baby's eyes, Dick saw she was listening.

"We must undertake it together. It would not bind you too tight —it would give you a base, a laboratory, a centre. You could stay in residence say no more than half the year, when the weather is fine. In winter you could go to France or America and write your texts fresh from clinical experience." He lowered his voice. "And for the convalescence in your family, there are the atmosphere and regularity of the clinic at hand." Dick's expression did not encourage this note, so Franz dropped it with the punctuation of his tongue leaving his lip quickly. "We could be partners, I the executive manager, you the theoretician, the brilliant consultant and all that. I know myself—I know I have no genius and you have. But, in my way, I am thought very capable; I am utterly competent at the most modern clinical methods. Sometimes for months I have served as the practical head of the old clinic. The professor says this plan is excellent, he advises me to go ahead. He says he is going to live forever and work up to the last minute."

Dick formed imaginary pictures of the prospect as a preliminary to any exercise of judgment.

"What's the financial angle?" he asked.

Franz threw up his chin, his eyebrows, the transient wrinkles of his forehead, his hands, his elbows, his shoulders; he strained up the muscles of his legs, so that the cloth of his trousers bulged, pushed up his heart into his throat and his voice into the roof of his mouth.

"There we have it! Money!" he bewailed. "I have little money. The price in American money is two hundred thousand dollars. The innovation—ary—" he tasted the coinage doubtfully, "—steps that you will agree are necessary will cost twenty thousand dollars American. But the clinic is a gold mine—I tell you, I have seen the books. For an investment of two hundred and twenty thousand dollars we have an assured income of——"

Baby's curiosity was such that Dick brought her into the conversation.

"In your experience, Baby," he demanded, "have you found that when a European wants to see an American *very* pressingly it is invariably something concerned with money?"

"What is it?" she said innocently.

"This young Privat-dozent thinks that he and I ought to launch into big business and try to attract nervous breakdowns from America."

Worried, Franz stared at Baby as Dick continued:

"But who are we, Franz? You bear a big name and I've written two textbooks. Is that enough to attract anybody? And I haven't got that much money—I haven't got a tenth of it." Franz smiled cynically. "Honestly I haven't. Nicole and Baby are rich as Crœsus, but I haven't managed to get my hands on any of it yet."

They were all listening now—Dick wondered if the girl at the table behind was listening too. The idea attracted him. He decided to let Baby speak for him, as one often lets women raise their voices over issues that are not in their hands. Baby became suddenly her grandfather, cool and experimental.

"I think it's a suggestion you ought to consider, Dick. I don't know what Doctor Gregory was saying—but it seems to me——"

Behind him the girl had leaned forward into a smoke ring and was picking up something from the floor. Nicole's face fitted into his own across the table—her beauty, tentatively nesting and posing, flowed into his love, ever braced to protect it.

"Consider it, Dick," Franz urged excitedly. "When one writes on psychiatry, one should have actual clinical contacts. Jung writes, Bleuler writes, Freud writes, Forel writes, Adler writes—also they are in constant contact with mental disorder."

"Dick has me," laughed Nicole. "I should think that'd be enough mental disorder for one man."

"That's different," said Franz cautiously.

Baby was thinking that if Nicole lived beside a clinic she would always feel quite safe about her.

"We must think it over carefully," she said.

Though amused at her insolence, Dick did not encourage it.

"The decision concerns me, Baby," he said gently. "It's nice of you to want to buy me a clinic."

Realizing she had meddled, Baby withdrew hurriedly:

"Of course, it's entirely your affair."

"A thing as important as this will take weeks to decide. I wonder how I like the picture of Nicole and me anchored to Zurich—" He turned to Franz, anticipating, "—I know. Zurich has a gashouse and running water and electric light—I lived there three years."

"I will leave you to think it over," said Franz. "I am confident——"

One hundred pairs of five-pound boots had begun to clump toward the door, and they joined the press. Outside in the crisp moonlight, Dick saw the girl tying her sled to one of the sleighs ahead. They piled into their own sleigh and at the crisp-cracking whips the horses strained, breasting the dark air. Past them figures ran and scrambled, the younger ones shoving each other from sleds and runners, landing in the soft snow, then panting after the horses to drop exhausted on a sled or wail that they were abandoned. On either side the fields were beneficently tranquil; the space through which the cavalcade moved was high and limitless. In the country there was less noise, as though they were all listening atavistically for wolves in the wide snow.

In Saanen they poured into the municipal dance, crowded with cow herders, hotel servants, shopkeepers, ski teachers, guides, tourists, peasants. To come into the warm enclosed place after the pantheistic animal feeling without was to reassume some absurd and impressive knightly name, as thunderous as spurred boots in war, as football cleats on the cement of a locker-room floor. There was conventional yodelling, and the familiar rhythm of it separated Dick from what he had first found romantic in the scene. At first he thought it was because he had hounded the girl out of his consciousness; then it came to him under the form of what Baby had said: "We must think it over carefully—" and the unsaid lines back of that: "We own you, and you'll admit it sooner or later. It is absurd to keep up the pretense of independence."

It had been years since Dick had bottled up malice against a creature—since freshman year at New Haven, when he had come upon a popular essay about "mental hygiene." Now he lost his temper at Baby and simultaneously tried to coop it up within him, resenting her cold rich insolence. It would be hundreds of years before any emergent Amazons would ever grasp the fact that a man is vulnerable only in his pride, but delicate as Humpty Dumpty once that is meddled with—though some of them paid the fact a cautious lip-service. Doctor Diver's profession of sorting the broken shells of another sort of egg had given him a dread of breakage. But:

"There's too much good manners," he said on the way back to Gstaad in the smooth sleigh.

"Well, I think that's nice," said Baby.

"No, it isn't," he insisted to the anonymous bundle of fur. "Good manners are an admission that everybody is so tender that they have to be handled with gloves. Now, human respect—you don't call a man a coward or a liar lightly, but if you spend your life sparing people's feelings and feeding their vanity, you get so you can't distinguish what *should* be respected in them."

"I think Americans take their manners rather seriously," said the elder Englishman.

"I guess so," said Dick. "My father had the kind of manners he inherited from the days when you shot first and apologized afterward. Men armed—why, you Europeans haven't carried arms in civil life since the beginning of the eighteenth century——"

"Not actually, perhaps——"

"Not actually. Not really."

"Dick, you've always had such beautiful manners," said Baby conciliatingly.

The women were regarding him across the zoo of robes with some alarm. The younger Englishman did not understand—he was one of the kind who were always jumping around cornices and balconies, as if they thought they were in the rigging of a ship—and filled the ride to the hotel with a preposterous story about a boxing match with his best friend, in which they loved and bruised each other for an hour, always with great reserve. Dick became facetious.

"So every time he hit you you considered him an even better friend?"

"I respected him more."

"It's the premise I don't understand. You and your best friend scrap about a trivial matter——"

"If you don't understand, I can't explain it to you," said the young Englishman coldly.

—This is what I'll get if I begin saying what I think, Dick said to himself.

He was ashamed at baiting the man, relizing that the absurdity of the story rested in the immaturity of the attitude combined with the sophisticated method of its narration.

The carnival spirit was strong and they went with the crowd into the grill, where a Tunisian barman manipulated the illumination in a counterpoint, whose other melody was the moon off the ice rink staring in the big windows. In that light, Dick found the girl devitalized and uninteresting. He turned from her to enjoy the darkness, the cigarette points going green and silver when the lights shone red, the band of white that fell across the dancers as the door to the bar was opened and closed.

"Now tell me, Franz," he demanded, "do you think after sitting up all night drinking beer, you can go back and convince your patients that you have any character? Don't you think they'll see you're a gastropath?"

"I'm going to bed," Nicole announced. Dick accompanied her to the door of the elevator.

"I'd come with you, but I must show Franz that I'm not intended for a clinician."

Nicole walked into the elevator.

"Baby has lots of common sense," she said meditatively.

"Baby is one of——"

The door slashed shut. Facing a mechanical hum, Dick finished the sentence in his mind, "—Baby is a trivial, selfish woman."

But two days later, sleighing to the station with Franz, Dick admitted that he thought favorably upon the matter.

"We're beginning to turn in a circle," he admitted. "Living on this scale, there's an unavoidable series of strains, and Nicole doesn't survive them. The pastoral quality down on the summer Riviera is all changing anyhow—next year they'll have a Season."

They passed the crisp green rinks where Wiener waltzes blared and the colors of many mountain schools flashed against the pale-blue skies.

"—I hope we'll be able to do it, Franz. There's nobody I'd rather try it with than you——"

Good-bye, Gstaad! Good-bye, fresh faces, cold sweet flowers, flakes in the darkness. Good-bye, Gstaad, good-bye!

CHAPTER II

ONE JULY MORNING DICK awoke at five after a long dream of war, walked to the window and stared out at the Zugersee. His dream had begun in sombre majesty; navy-blue uniforms crossed a dark plaza behind bands playing the second movement of Prokofiev's *Love for Three Oranges*. Presently there were fire engines, symbols of disaster, and a ghastly uprising of the mutilated in a dressing station. He turned on his bed-lamp and made a thorough note of it, ending with the half-ironic phrase: "Non-combatant's shell-shock."

As he sat on the side of his bed he felt the room, the house, and the night as empty. In the next room Nicole muttered something desolate and he felt sorry for whatever loneliness she was feeling in her sleep. For him time stood still and then every few years accelerated in a rush, like the quick rewind of a film, but for Nicole the years slipped away by clock and calendar and birthday, with the added poignance of her perishable beauty.

Even this past year and a half on the Zugersee seemed wasted time for her, the seasons marked only by the workmen on the road turning pink in May, brown in July, black in September, white again in Spring. She had come out of her first illness alive with new hopes, expecting so much, yet deprived of any subsistence except Dick, bringing up children she could only pretend gently to love, guided orphans. The people she liked, rebels mostly, disturbed her and were bad for her—she sought in them the vitality that had made them independent or creative or rugged, sought in vain—for their secrets were buried deep in childhood struggles they had forgotten. They were more interested in Nicole's exterior harmony and charm, the other face of her illness. She led a lonely life owning Dick, who did not want to be owned.

Many times he had tried unsuccessfully to let go his hold on her. They had many fine times together, fine talks between the loves of the white nights, but always when he turned away from her into himself he left her holding Nothing in her hands and staring at it, calling it many names, but knowing it was only the hope that he would come back soon.

He scrunched his pillow hard, lay down, and put the back of his neck against it as a Japanese does to slow the circulation, and slept again for a time. Later, while he shaved, Nicole awoke and marched around, giving abrupt, succinct orders to children and servants. Lanier came in to watch his father shave—living beside a psychiatric clinic he had developed an extraordinary confidence in and admiration for his father, together with an exaggerated indifference toward most other adults; the patients appeared to him either in their odd aspects, or else as devitalized, over-correct creatures without personality. He was a handsome, promising boy and Dick devoted much time to him, in the relationship of a sympathetic but exacting officer and a respectful enlisted man.

"Why," Lanier asked, "do you always leave a little lather on the top of your hair when you shave?"

Cautiously Dick parted soapy lips: "I have never been able to find out. I've often wondered. I think it's because I get the first finger soapy when I make the line of my side-burn, but how it gets up on top of my head I don't know."

"I'm going to watch it all tomorrow."

"That's your only question before breakfast."

"I don't really call it a question."

"That's one on you."

Half an hour later Dick started up to the administration building. He was thirty-seven—still declining a beard he yet had a more medical aura about him than he had worn upon the Riviera. For eighteen months now he had lived at the clinic, certainly one of the best-appointed in Europe. Like Dohmler's it was of the modern type—no longer a single dark and sinister building, but a small, scattered, yet deceitfully integrated village. Dick and Nicole had added much in the domain of taste, so that the plant was a thing of beauty, visited by every psychologist passing through Zurich. With the addition of a caddy house it might very well have been a country club. The Eglantine and the Beeches, houses for those sunk into eternal darkness, were screened by little copses from the main building, camouflaged strong-points. Behind was a large truck farm, worked partly by the patients. The workshops for ego-therapy were three, placed under a single roof, and there Doctor Diver began his morning's inspection. The carpentry shop, full of sunlight, exuded the sweetness of sawdust, of a lost age of wood; always half a dozen men were there, hammering, planing, buzzing—silent men, who lifted solemn eyes from their work as he passed through. Himself a good carpenter, he discussed with them the efficiency of some tools for a moment in a quiet, personal, interested voice. Adjoining was the book-bindery, adapted to the most mobile patients, who were not always, however, those who had the greatest chance for recovery. The last chamber was devoted to bead-work, weaving, and work in brass. The faces of the patients here wore the expression of one who has just sighed profoundly, dismissing something insoluble—but their sighs only marked the beginning of another ceaseless round of ratiocination, not in a line as with normal people but in the same circle. Round, round, and round. Around forever. But the bright colors of the stuffs they worked with gave strangers a momentary illusion that all was well, as in a kindergarten. These patients brightened as Doctor Diver came in. Most of them liked him better than they liked Doctor Gregorovius. Those who had once lived in the great world invariably liked him better. There were a few who thought he neglected them, or that he was not simple, or that he posed. Their responses were not dissimilar to those that Dick evoked in non-professional life, but here they were warped and distorted.

One Englishwoman spoke to him always about a subject which she considered her own.

"Have we got music tonight?"

"I don't know," he answered. "I haven't seen Doctor Lladislau. How did you enjoy the music that Mrs. Sachs and Mr. Longstreet gave us last night?"

"It was so-so."

"I thought it was fine—especially the Chopin."

"I thought it was so-so."

"When are you going to play for us yourself?"

She shrugged her shoulders, as pleased at this question as she had been for several years.

"Some time. But I only play so-so."

They knew that she did not play at all—she had had two sisters who were brilliant musicians, but she had never been able to learn the notes when they had been young together.

From the workshops Dick went to visit the Eglantine and the Beeches. Exteriorly these houses were as cheerful as the others; Nicole had designed the decoration and the furniture on a necessary base of concealed grills and bars and immovable furniture. She had worked with so much imagination—the inventive quality, which she lacked, being supplied by the problem itself—that no instructed visitor would have dreamed that the light, graceful filigree work at a window was a strong, unyielding end of a tether, that the pieces reflecting modern tubular tendencies were stancher than the massive creations of the Edwardians—even the flowers lay in iron fingers and every casual ornament and fixture was as necessary as a girder in a skyscraper. Her tireless eyes had made each room yield up its greatest usefulness. Complimented, she referred to herself brusquely as a master plumber.

For those whose compasses were not depolarized there seemed many odd things in these houses. Doctor Diver was often amused in the Eglantine, the men's building—here there was a strange little exhibitionist who thought that if he could walk unclothed and unmolested from the Etoile to the Place de la Concorde he would solve many things—and, perhaps, Dick thought, he was quite right.

His most interesting case was in the main building. The patient was a woman of thirty who had been in the clinic six months; she was an American painter who had lived long in Paris. They had no very satisfactory history of her. A cousin had happened upon her all mad and gone, and after an unsatisfactory interlude at one of the whoopee cures that fringed the city, dedicated largely to tourist victims of drug and drink, he had managed to get her to Switzerland. On her admittance she had been exceptionally pretty—now she was a living, agonizing sore. All blood tests had failed to give a positive reaction and the trouble was unsatisfactorily catalogued as nervous eczema. For two months she had lain under it, as if imprisoned in the Iron Maiden. She was coherent, even brilliant, within the limits of her special hallucinations.

She was particularly his patient. During spells of over-excitement he was the only doctor who could "do anything with her." Several weeks ago, on one of many nights that she had passed in sleepless torture, Franz had succeeded in hypnotizing her into a few hours of needed rest, but he had never again succeeded. Hypnosis was a tool that Dick distrusted and seldom used, for he knew that he could not always summon up the mood in himself—he had once tried it on Nicole and she had scornfully laughed at him.

The woman in Room Twenty could not see him when he came in—the area about her eyes was too tightly swollen. She spoke in a strong, rich, deep, thrilling voice.

"How long will this last? Is it going to be forever?"

"It's not going to be very long now. Doctor Lladislau tells me there are whole areas cleared up."

"If I knew what I had done to deserve this I could accept it with equanimity."

"It isn't wise to be mystical about it—we recognize it as a nervous phenomenon. It's related to the blush—when you were a girl, did you blush easily?"

She lay with her face turned to the ceiling.

"I have found nothing to blush for since I cut my wisdom teeth."

"Haven't you committed your share of petty sins and mistakes?"

"I have nothing to reproach myself with."

"You're very fortunate."

The woman thought a moment; her voice came up through her bandaged face afflicted with subterranean melodies:

"I'm sharing the fate of the women of my time who challenged men to battle."

"To your vast surprise it was just like all battles," he answered, adopting her formal diction.

"Just like all battles." She thought this over. "You pick a set-up, or else win a Pyrrhic victory, or you're wrecked and ruined—you're a ghostly echo from a broken wall."

"You are neither wrecked nor ruined," he told her. "Are you quite sure you've been in a real battle?"

"Look at me!" she cried furiously.

"You've suffered, but many women suffered before they mistook themselves for men." It was becoming an argument and he retreated. "In any case you mustn't confuse a single failure with a final defeat."

She sneered, "Beautiful words," and the phrase transpiring up through the crust of pain humbled him.

"We would like to go into the true reasons that brought you here—" he began, but she interrupted.

"I am here as a symbol of something. I thought perhaps you would know what it was."

"You are sick," he said mechanically.

"Then what was it I had almost found?"

"A greater sickness."

"That's all?"

"That's all." With disgust he heard himself lying, but here and now the vastness of the subject could only be compressed into a lie. "Outside of that there's only confusion and chaos. I won't lecture to you—we have too acute a realization of your physical suffering. But it's only by meeting the problems of every day, no matter how trifling and boring they seem, that you can make things drop back into place again. After that—perhaps you'll be able again to examine——"

He had slowed up to avoid the inevitable end of his thought: "—the frontiers of consciousness." The frontiers that artists must explore were not for her, ever. She was fine-spun, inbred—eventually she might find rest in some quiet mysticism. Exploration was for those with a measure of peasant blood, those with big thighs and thick ankles who could take punishment as they took bread and salt, on every inch of flesh and spirit.

—Not for you, he almost said. It's too tough a game for you.

Yet in the awful majesty of her pain he went out to her unreservedly, almost sexually. He wanted to gather her up in his arms, as he so often had Nicole, and cherish even her mistakes, so deeply were they part of her. The orange light through the drawn blind, the sarcophagus of her figure on the bed, the spot of face, the voice searching the vacuity of her illness and finding only remote abstractions.

As he arose the tears fled lava-like into her bandages.

"That is for something," she whispered. "Something must come out of it."

He stooped and kissed her forehead.

"We must all try to be good," he said.

Leaving her room he sent the nurse in to her. There were other patients to see: an American girl of fifteen who had been brought up on the basis that childhood was intended to be all fun—his visit was provoked by the fact that she had just hacked off all her hair with nail scissors. There was nothing much to be done for her—a family history of neurosis and nothing stable in her past to build on. The father, normal and conscientious himself, had tried to protect a nervous brood from life's troubles and had succeeded merely in preventing them from developing powers of adjustment to life's inevitable surprises. There was little that Dick could say: "Helen, when you're in doubt you must ask a nurse, you must learn to take advice. Promise me you will."

What was a promise with the head sick? He looked in upon a frail exile from the Caucasus buckled securely in a sort of hammock, which in turn was submerged in a warm medical bath, and upon the three daughters of a Portuguese general who slid almost imperceptibly toward paresis. He went into the room next to them and told a collapsed psychiatrist that he was better, always better, and the man tried to read his face for conviction, since he hung on the real world only through such reassurance as he could find in the resonance, or lack of it, in Doctor Diver's voice. After that Dick discharged a shiftless orderly and by then it was the lunch hour.

CHAPTER III

MEALS WITH THE PATIENTS were a chore he approached with apathy. The gathering, which of course did not include residents at the Eglantine or the Beeches, was conventional enough at first sight, but over it brooded always a heavy melancholy. Such doctors as were present kept up a conversation, but most of the patients, as if exhausted by their morning's endeavor or depressed by the company, spoke little and ate looking into their plates.

Luncheon over, Dick returned to his villa. Nicole was in the salon wearing a strange expression.

"Read that," she said.

He opened the letter. It was from a woman recently discharged, though with skepticism on the part of the faculty. It accused him in no uncertain terms of having seduced her daughter, who had been at her mother's side during the crucial stage of the illness. It presumed that Mrs. Diver would be glad to have this information and learn what her husband was "really like."

Dick read the letter again. Though it was couched in clear and concise English he recognized it as the letter of a maniac. Upon a single occasion he had let the girl, a flirtatious little brunette, ride into Zurich with him, at her request, and in the evening had brought her back to the clinic. In an idle, almost indulgent way, he kissed her. Later, she tried to carry the affair further, but he was not interested and subsequently, probably consequently, the girl had come to dislike him, and had taken her mother away.

"This letter is deranged," he said. "I had no relations of any kind with that girl. I didn't even like her."

"Yes, I've tried thinking that," said Nicole.

"Surely you don't believe it?"

"I've been sitting here."

He sank his voice to a reproachful note and sat beside her.

"This is absurd. This is a letter from a mental patient."

"I was a mental patient."

He stood up and spoke more authoritatively.

"Suppose we don't have any nonsense, Nicole. Go and round up the children and we'll start."

In the car, with Dick driving, they followed the little promontories of the lake, catching the burn of light and water in the windshield, tunnelling through cascades of evergreen. It was Dick's car, a Renault so dwarfish that they all stuck out of it except the children, between whom Mademoiselle towered mast-like in the rear seat. They knew every kilometer of the road—where they would smell the pine needles and the black stove smoke. A high sun with a face traced on it beat fierce on the straw hats of the children.

Nicole was silent; Dick was uneasy at her straight hard gaze. Often he felt lonely with her, and frequently she tired him with the short floods of personal revelations that she reserved exclusively for him, "I'm like this—I'm more like that," but this afternoon he would have been glad had she rattled on in staccato for a while and given him glimpses of her thoughts. The situation was always most threatening when she backed up into herself and closed the doors behind her.

At Zug Mademoiselle got out and left them. The Divers approached the Agiri Fair through a menagerie of mammoth steamrollers that made way for them. Dick parked the car and, as Nicole looked at him without moving, he said: "Come on, darl." Her lips drew apart into a sudden awful smile and his belly quailed, but as if he hadn't seen it he repeated: "Come on. So the children can get out."

"Oh, I'll come all right," she answered, tearing the words from some story spinning itself out inside her, too fast for him to grasp. "Don't worry about that. I'll come——"

"Then come."

She turned from him as he walked beside her, but the smile still flickered across her face, derisive and remote. Only when Lanier spoke to her several times did she manage to fix her attention upon an object, a Punch-and-Judy show, and to orient herself by anchoring to it.

Dick tried to think what to do. The dualism in his views of her —that of the husband, that of the psychiatrist—was increasingly paralyzing his faculties. In these nine years she had several times carried him over the line with her, disarming him by exciting emotional pity or by a flow of wit, fantastic and dissociated, so that only after the episode did he realize, with the consciousness of his own relaxation from tension, that she had succeeded in getting a point against his better judgment.

A discussion with Topsy about the guignol—as to whether the Punch was the same Punch they had seen last year in Cannes—having been settled, the family walked along again between the booths under the open sky. The women's bonnets, perching over velvet vests, the bright, spreading skirts of many cantons, seemed demure against the blue and orange paint of the wagons and displays. There was the sound of a whining, tinkling hootchy-kootchy show.

Nicole began to run very suddenly, so suddenly that for a moment Dick did not miss her. Far ahead he saw her yellow dress twisting through the crowd, an ochre stitch along the edge of reality and unreality, and he started after her. Secretly she ran and secretly he followed. As the hot afternoon went shrill and terrible with her flight he had forgotten the children; then he wheeled and ran back to them, drawing them this way and that by their arms, his eyes jumping from booth to booth.

"Madame," he cried to a young woman behind a white lottery wheel, "Est-ce que je peux laisser ces petits avec vous deux minutes? C'est très urgent—je vous donnerai dix francs."

"Mais oui."

He headed the children into the booth. "Alors—restez avec cette gentille dame."

"Oui, Dick."

He darted off again but he had lost her; he circled the merry-go-round, keeping up with it till he realized he was running beside it, staring always at the same horse. He elbowed through the crowd in the buvette; then remembering a predilection of Nicole's he snatched up an edge of a fortune-teller's tent and peered within. A droning voice greeted him: "La septième fille d'une septième fille née sur les rives du Nil—entrez, Monsieur——"

Dropping the flap he ran along toward where the plaisance terminated at the lake and a small ferris wheel revolved slowly against the sky. There he found her.

She was alone in what was momentarily the top boat of the wheel and, as it descended, he saw that she was laughing hilariously; he slunk back in the crowd, which, at the wheel's next revolution, spotted the intensity of Nicole's hysteria.

"Regardez-moi ça!"

"Regarde donc cette Anglaise!"

Down she dropped again—this time the wheel and its music were slowing and a dozen people were around her car, all of them impelled by the quality of her laughter to smile in sympathetic idiocy. But when Nicole saw Dick her laughter died—she made a gesture of slipping by and away from him, but he caught her arm and held it as they walked away.

"Why did you lose control of yourself like that?"

"You know very well why."

"No, I don't."

"That's just preposterous—let me loose—that's an insult to my intelligence. Don't you think I saw that girl look at you—that little dark girl. Oh, this is farcical—a child, not more than fifteen. Don't you think I saw?"

"Stop here a minute and quiet down."

They sat at a table, her eyes in a profundity of suspicion, her hand moving across her line of sight as if it were obstructed. "I want a drink—I want a brandy."

"You can't have brandy—you can have a bock if you want it."

"Why can't I have a brandy?"

"We won't go into that. Listen to me—this business about a girl is a delusion, do you understand that word?"

"It's always a delusion when I see what you don't want me to see."

He had a sense of guilt, as in one of those nightmares where we are accused of a crime which we recognize as something undeniably experienced, but which upon waking we realize we have not committed. His eyes wavered from hers.

"I left the children with a gypsy woman in a booth. We ought to get them."

"Who do you think you are?" she demanded. "Svengali?"

Fifteen minutes ago they had been a family. Now as she was crushed into a corner by his unwilling shoulder, he saw them all, child and man, as a perilous accident.

"We're going home."

"Home!" she roared in a voice so abandoned that its louder tones wavered and cracked. "And sit and think that we're all rotting and the children's ashes are rotting in every box I open? That filth!"

Almost with relief he saw that her words sterilized her, and Nicole, sensitized down to the corium of the skin, saw the withdrawal in his face. Her own face softened and she begged, "Help me, help me, Dick!"

A wave of agony went over him. It was awful that such a fine tower should not be erected, only suspended, suspended from him. Up to a point that was right: men were for that, beam and idea, girder and logarithm; but somehow Dick and Nicole had become one and equal, not opposite and complementary; she was Dick too, the drought in the marrow of his bones. He could not watch her disintegrations without participating in them. His intuition rilled out of him as tenderness and compassion—he could only take the characteristically modern course, to interpose. He would get a nurse from Zurich, to take her over tonight.

"You *can* help me."

Her sweet bullying pulled him forward off his feet. "You've helped me before—you can help me now."

"I can only help you the same old way."

"Someone can help me."

"Maybe so. You can help yourself most. Let's find the children."

There were numerous lottery booths with white wheels. Dick was startled when he inquired at the first and encountered blank disavowals. Evil-eyed, Nicole stood apart, denying the children, resenting them as part of a downright world she sought to make amorphous. Presently Dick found them, surrounded by women who were examining them with delight like fine goods, and by peasant children staring.

"Merci, Monsieur, et Monsieur est trop généreux. C'était un plaisir, M'sieur, Dame. Au revoir, mes petits."

They started back with a hot sorrow streaming down upon them; the car was weighted with their mutual apprehension and anguish, and the children's mouths were grave with disappointment. Grief presented itself in its terrible, dark unfamiliar color. Somewhere around Zug, Nicole, with a convulsive effort, reiterated a remark she had made before about a misty yellow house set back from the road that looked like a painting not yet dry, but it was just an attempt to catch at a rope that was playing out too swiftly.

Dick tried to rest. The struggle would come presently at home and he might have to sit a long time restating the universe for her. A schizophrenic is well named as a split personality—Nicole was alternately a person to whom nothing need be explained and one to whom nothing *could* be explained. It was necessary to treat her with active and affirmative insistence, keeping the road to reality always open, making the road to escape harder going. But the brilliance, the versatility of madness is akin to the resourcefulness of water seeping through, over, and around a dike. It requires the united front of many people to work against it. He felt it necessary that this time Nicole cure herself; he wanted to wait until she remembered the other times and revolted from them. In a tired way, he planned that they would again resume the régime relaxed two years before.

He had turned up a hill that made a short cut to the clinic and now, as he stepped on the accelerator for a short straightaway run parallel to the hillside, the car swerved violently left, swerved right, tipped on two wheels and, as Dick, with Nicole's voice screaming in his ear, crushed down the mad hand clutching the steering wheel, righted itself, swerved once more and shot off the road; it tore through low underbrush, tipped again and settled slowly at an angle of ninety degrees against a tree.

The children were screaming and Nicole was screaming and cursing and trying to tear at Dick's face. Thinking first of the list of the car and unable to estimate it Dick bent away Nicole's arm, climbed over the top side and lifted out the children; then he saw the car was in a stable position. Before doing anything else he stood there shaking and panting.

"You—!" he cried.

She was laughing hilariously, unashamed, unafraid, unconcerned. No one coming on the scene would have imagined that she had caused it; she laughed as after some mild escape of childhood.

"You were scared, weren't you?" she accused him. "You wanted to live!"

She spoke with such force that in his shocked state Dick wondered if he had been frightened for himself—but the strained faces of the children, looking from parent to parent, made him want to grind her grinning mask into jelly.

Directly above them, half a kilometer by the winding road but only a hundred yards climbing, was an inn; one of its wings showed through the wooded hill.

"Take Topsy's hand," he said to Lanier, "like that, tight, and climb up that hill—see the little path? When you get to the inn tell them, 'La voiture Divare est cassée.' Someone must come right down."

Lanier, not sure what had happened, but suspecting the dark and unprecedented, asked:

"What will you do, Dick?"

"We'll stay here with the car."

Neither of them looked at their mother as they started off. "Be careful crossing the road up there! Look both ways!" Dick shouted after them.

He and Nicole looked at each other directly, their eyes like blazing windows across a court of the same house. Then she took out a compact, looked in its mirror, and smoothed back the temple hair. Dick watched the children climbing for a moment until they disappeared among the pines halfway up; then he walked around the car to see the damage and plan how to get it back on the road. In the dirt he could race the rocking course they had pursued for over a hundred feet; he was filled with a violent disgust that was not like anger.

In a few minutes the proprietor of the inn came running down.

"My God!" he exclaimed. "How did it happen, were you going fast? What luck! Except for that tree you'd have rolled down hill."

Taking advantage of Émile's reality, the wide black apron, the sweat upon the rolls of his face, Dick signalled to Nicole in a matter-of-fact way to let him help her from the car; whereupon she jumped over the lower side, lost her balance on the slope, fell to her knees, and got up again. As she watched the men trying to move the car her expression became defiant. Welcoming even that mood Dick said:

"Go and wait with the children, Nicole."

Only after she had gone did he remember that she had wanted cognac, and that there was cognac available up there—he told Émile never mind about the car; they would wait for the chauffeur and the big car to pull it up onto the road. Together they hurried up to the inn.

CHAPTER IV

"I WANT TO GO away," he told Franz. "For a month or so, for as long as I can."

"Why not, Dick? That was our original arrangement—it was you who insisted on staying. If you and Nicole——"

"I don't want to go away with Nicole. I want to go away alone. This last thing knocked me sideways—if I get two hours' sleep in twenty-four, it's one of Zwingli's miracles."

"You wish a real leave of abstinence?"

"The word is 'absence.' Look here: if I go to Berlin to the Psychiatric Congress could you manage to keep the peace? For three month's she's been all right and she likes her nurse. My God, you're the only human being in this world I can ask this of."

Franz grunted, considering whether or not he could be trusted to think always of his partner's interest.

In Zurich the next week Dick drove to the airport and took the big plane for Munich. Soaring and roaring into the blue he felt numb, realizing how tired he was. A vast persuasive quiet stole over him and he abandoned sickness to the sick, sound to the motors, direction to the pilot. He had no intention of attending so much as a single session of the congress—he could imagine it well enough, new pamphlets by Bleuler and the elder Forel that he could much better digest at home, the paper by the American who cured dementia præcox by pulling out his patients' teeth or cauterizing their tonsils, the half-derisive respect with which this idea would be greeted, for no more reason than that America was such a rich and powerful country. The other delegates from America—red-headed Schwartz with his saint's face and his infinite patience in straddling two worlds, as well as dozens of commercial alienists with hang-dog faces, who would be present partly to increase their standing, and hence their reach for the big plums of criminal practice, partly to master novel sophistries that they could weave into their stock in trade, to the infinite confusion of all values. There would be cynical Latins and some man of Freud's from Vienna. Articulate among them would be the great Jung, bland, super-vigorous, on his rounds between the forests of anthropology and the neuroses of schoolboys. At first there would be an American cast to the congress, almost Rotarian in its forms and ceremonies, then the closer-knit European vitality would fight through, and finally the Americans would play their trump card, the announcement of colossal gifts and endowments, of great new plants and training schools, and in the presence of the figures the Europeans would blanch and walk timidly. But he would not be there to see.

They skirted the Vorarlberg Alps, and Dick felt a pastoral delight in watching the villages. There were always four or five in sight, each one gathered around a church. It was simple looking at the earth from far off, simple as playing grim games with dolls and soldiers. This was the way statesmen and commanders and all retired people looked at things. Anyhow, it was a good draft of relief.

An Englishman spoke to him from across the aisle, but he found something antipathetic in the English lately. England was like a rich man after a disastrous orgy who makes up to the household by chatting with them individually, when it is obvious to them that he is only trying to get back his self-respect in order to usurp his former power.

Dick had with him what magazines were available on the station quays: the *Century*, the *Motion Picture*, *L'Illustration*, and *Fliegende Blätter*, but it was more fun to descend in his imagination into the villages and shake hands with the rural characters. He sat in the churches as he sat in his father's church in Buffalo, amid the starchy must of Sunday clothes. He listened to the wisdom of the Near East, was Crucified, Died, and was Buried in the cheerful church, and once more worried between five or ten cents for the collection plate, because of the girl who sat in the pew behind.

The Englishman suddenly borrowed his magazines with a little small change of conversation, and Dick, glad to see them go, thought of the voyage ahead of him. Wolf-like under his sheep's clothing

of long-staple Australian wool, he considered the world of pleasure
—the incorruptible Mediterranean with sweet old dirt caked in the
olive trees, the peasant girl near Savona with a face as green and
rose as the color of an illuminated missal. He would take her in
his hands and snatch her across the border . . .

. . . but there he deserted her—he must press on toward the Isles
of Greece, the cloudy waters of unfamiliar ports, the lost girl on
shore, the moon of popular songs. A part of Dick's mind was made
up of the tawdry souvenirs of his boyhood. Yet in that somewhat
littered Five-and-Ten, he had managed to keep alive the low painful fire of intelligence.

CHAPTER V

Tommy Barban was a ruler, Tommy was a hero—Dick happened upon him in the Marienplatz in Munich, in one of those cafés where small gamblers diced on "tapestry" mats. The air was full of politics and the slap of cards.

Tommy was at a table laughing his martial laugh: "Um-buh—ha-ha! Um-buh—ha-ha!" As a rule, he drank little; courage was his game and his companions were always a little afraid of him. Recently an eighth of the area of his skull had been removed by a Warsaw surgeon and was knitting under his hair, and the weakest person in the café could have killed him with a flip of a knotted napkin.

"—this is Prince Chillichev—" a battered, powder-gray Russian of fifty, "—and Mr. McKibben—and Mr. Hannan—" the latter was a lively ball of black eyes and hair, a clown; and he said immediately to Dick:

"The first thing before we shake hands—what do you mean by fooling around with my aunt?"

"Why, I——"

"You heard me. What are you doing here in Munich anyhow?"

"Um-bah—ha-ha!" laughed Tommy.

"Haven't you got aunts of your own? Why don't you fool with them?"

Dick laughed, whereupon the man shifted his attack:

"Now let's not have any more talk about aunts. How do I know you didn't make up the whole thing? Here you are a complete stranger with an acquaintance of less than half an hour, and you come up to me with a cock-and-bull story about your aunts. How do I know what you have concealed about you?"

Tommy laughed again, then he said good-naturedly, but firmly, "That enough, Carly. Sit down, Dick—how're you? How's Nicole?" He did not like any man very much or feel men's presence with

213

much intensity—he was all relaxed for combat; as a fine athlete playing secondary defense in any sport is really resting much of the time, while a lesser man only pretends to rest and is at a continual and self-destroying nervous tension.

Hannan, not entirely suppressed, moved to an adjoining piano and, with recurring resentment on his face whenever he looked at Dick, played chords, from time to time muttering, "Your aunts," and, in a dying cadence, "I didn't say aunts anyhow. I said pants."

"Well, how're you?" repeated Tommy. "You don't look so—" he fought for a word, "—so jaunty as you used to, so spruce, you know what I mean."

The remark sounded too much like one of those irritating accusations of waning vitality and Dick was about to retort by commenting on the extraordinary suits worn by Tommy and Prince Chillichev, suits of a cut and pattern fantastic enough to have sauntered down Beale Street on a Sunday—when an explanation was forthcoming.

"I see you are regarding our clothes," said the Prince. "We have just come out of Russia."

"These were made in Poland by the court tailor," said Tommy. "That's a fact—Pilsudski's own tailor."

"You've been touring?" Dick asked.

They laughed, the Prince inordinately clapping Tommy on the back.

"Yes, we have been touring. That's it, touring. We have made the Grand Tour of all the Russias. In state."

Dick waited for an explanation. It came from Mr. McKibben in two words:

"They escaped."

"Have you been prisoners in Russia?"

"It was I," explained Prince Chillichev, his dead yellow eyes staring at Dick. "Not a prisoner but in hiding."

"Did you have much trouble getting out?"

"Some trouble. We left three Red Guards dead at the border. Tommy left two—" He held up two fingers like a Frenchman—"I left one."

"That's the part I don't understand," said Mr. McKibben. "Why they should have objected to your leaving."

Hannan turned from the piano and said, winking at the others: "Mac thinks a Marxian is somebody who went to St. Mark's school."

It was an escape story in the best tradition—an aristocrat hiding nine years with a former servant and working in a government bakery; the eighteen-year-old daughter in Paris who knew Tommy Barban. . . . During the narrative Dick decided that this parched papier-mâché relic of the past was scarcely worth the lives of three young men. The question arose as to whether Tommy and Chillichev had been frightened.

"When I was cold," Tommy said. "I always get scared when I'm cold. During the war I was always frightened when I was cold."

McKibben stood up.

"I must leave. Tomorrow morning I'm going to Innsbruck by car with my wife and children—and the governess."

"I'm going there tomorrow, too," said Dick.

"Oh, are you?" exclaimed McKibben. "Why not come with us? It's a big Packard and there's only my wife and my children and myself—and the governess——"

"I can't possibly——"

"Of course she's not really a governess," McKibben concluded, looking rather pathetically at Dick. "As a matter of fact my wife knows your sister-in-law, Baby Warren."

But Dick was not to be drawn into a blind contract.

"I've promised to travel with two men."

"Oh," McKibben's face fell. "Well, I'll say good-bye." He unscrewed two blooded wire-hairs from a nearby table and lingered; Dick pictured the jammed Packard pounding toward Innsbruck with the McKibbens and their children and their baggage and yapping dogs—and the governess.

"The paper says they know the man who killed him," said Tommy. "But his cousins did not want it in the papers, because it happened in a speakeasy. What do you think of that?"

"It's what's known as family pride."

Hannan played a loud chord on the piano to attract attention to himself.

"I don't believe his first stuff holds up," he said. "Even barring the Europeans there are a dozen Americans can do what North did."

It was the first indication Dick had had that they were talking about Abe North.

"The only difference is that Abe did it first," said Tommy.

"I don't agree," persisted Hannan. "He got the reputation for being a good musician because he drank so much that his friends had to explain him away somehow——"

"What's this about Abe North? What about him? Is he in a jam?"

"Didn't you read the *Herald* this morning?"

"No."

"He's dead. He was beaten to death in a speakeasy in New York. He just managed to crawl home to the Racquet Club to die——"

"*Abe North?*"

"Yes, sure, they——"

"*Abe North?*" Dick stood up. "Are you sure he's dead?"

Hannan turned around to McKibben: "It wasn't the Racquet Club he crawled to—it was the Harvard Club. I'm sure he didn't belong to the Racquet."

"The paper said so," McKibben insisted.

"It must have been a mistake. I'm quite sure."

"*Beaten to death in a speakeasy.*"

"But I happen to know most of the members of the Racquet Club," said Hannan. "It *must* have been the Harvard Club."

Dick got up, Tommy too. Prince Chillichev started out of a wan study of nothing, perhaps of his chances of ever getting out of Russia, a study that had occupied him so long that it was doubtful if he could give it up immediately, and joined them in leaving.

"*Abe North beaten to death.*"

On the way to the hotel, a journey of which Dick was scarcely aware, Tommy said:

"We're waiting for a tailor to finish some suits so we can get to Paris. I'm going into stock-broking and they wouldn't take me if I showed up like this. Everybody in your country is making millions. Are you really leaving tomorrow? We can't even have dinner with you. It seems the Prince had an old girl in Munich. He called her up but she'd been dead five years and we're having dinner with the two daughters."

The Prince nodded.

"Perhaps I could have arranged for Doctor Diver."

"No, no," said Dick hastily.

He slept deep and awoke to a slow mournful march passing his window. It was a long column of men in uniform, wearing the familiar helmet of 1914, thick men in frock coats and silk hats, burghers, aristocrats, plain men. It was a society of veterans going to lay wreaths on the tombs of the dead. The column marched slowly with a sort of swagger for a lost magnificence, a past effort, a forgotten sorrow. The faces were only formally sad, but Dick's lungs burst for a moment with regret for Abe's death, and his own youth of ten years ago.

CHAPTER VI

HE REACHED INNSBRUCK AT dusk, sent his bags up to a hotel and walked into town. In the sunset the Emperor Maximilian knelt in prayer above his bronze mourners; a quartet of Jesuit novices paced and read in the university garden. The marble souvenirs of old sieges, marriages, anniversaries, faded quickly when the sun was down, and he had Erbsen-suppe with Würstchen cut up in it, drank four seidels of Pilsner and refused a formidable dessert known as Kaiser-schmarren.

Despite the overhanging mountains Switzerland was far away, Nicole was far away. Walking in the garden later when it was quite dark he thought about her with detachment, loving her for her best self. He remembered once when the grass was damp and she came to him on hurried feet, her thin slippers drenched with dew. She stood upon his shoes nestling close and held up her face, showing it as a book open at a page.

"Think how you love me," she whispered. "I don't ask you to love me always like this, but I ask you to remember. Somewhere inside me there'll always be the person I am tonight."

But Dick had come away for his soul's sake, and he began thinking about that. He had lost himself—he could not tell the hour when, or the day or the week, the month or the year. Once he had cut through things, solving the most complicated equations as the simplest problems of his simplest patients. Between the time he found Nicole flowering under a stone on the Zürichsee and the moment of his meeting with Rosemary the spear had been blunted.

Watching his father's struggles in poor parishes had wedded a desire for money to an essentially unacquisitive nature. It was not a healthy necessity for security—he had never felt more sure of himself, more thoroughly his own man, than at the time of his marriage to Nicole. Yet he had been swallowed up like a gigolo and had somehow permitted his arsenal to be locked up in the Warren safety-deposit vaults.

"There should have been a settlement in the Continental style; but it isn't over yet. I've wasted nine years teaching the rich the A B C's of human decency, but I'm not done. I've got too many unplayed trumps in my hand."

He loitered among the fallow rose bushes and the beds of damp sweet indistinguishable fern. It was warm for October, but cool enough to wear a heavy tweed coat buttoned by a little elastic tape at the neck. A figure detached itself from the black shape of a tree and he knew it was the woman whom he had passed in the lobby coming out. He was in love with every pretty woman he saw now, their forms at a distance, their shadows on a wall.

Her back was toward him as she faced the lights of the town. He scratched a match that she must have heard, but she remained motionless.

—Was it an invitation? Or an indication of obliviousness? He had long been outside of the world of simple desires and their fulfillments, and he was inept and uncertain. For all he knew there might be some code among the wanderers of obscure spas by which they found each other quickly.

—Perhaps the next gesture was his. Strange children should smile at each other and say, "Let's play."

He moved closer, the shadow moved sideways. Possibly he would be snubbed like the scapegrace drummers he had heard of in youth. His heart beat loud in contact with the unprobed, undissected, unanalyzed, unaccounted for. Suddenly he turned away and, as he did, the girl, too, broke the black frieze she made with the foliage, rounded a bench at a moderate but determined pace and took the path back to the hotel.

With a guide and two other men, Dick started up the Birkkar-spitze next morning. It was a fine feeling once they were above the cowbells of the highest pastures—Dick looked forward to the night in the shack, enjoying his own fatigue, enjoying the captaincy of the guide, feeling a delight in his own anonymity. But at mid-day the weather changed to black sleet and hail and mountain thunder. Dick and one of the other climbers wanted to go on, but the guide refused. Regretfully they struggled back to Innsbruck to start again tomorrow.

After dinner and a bottle of heavy local wine in the deserted dining-room, he felt excited, without knowing why, until he began thinking of the garden. He had passed the girl in the lobby before supper and this time she had looked at him and approved of him, but it kept worrying him: Why? When I could have had a good share of the pretty women of my time for the asking, why start that now? With a wraith, with a fragment of my desire? Why?

His imagination pushed ahead—the old asceticism, the actual unfamiliarity, triumphed: God, I might as well go back to the Riviera and sleep with Janice Caricamento or the Wilburhazy girl. To belittle all these years with something cheap and easy?

He was still excited, though, and he turned from the veranda and went up to his room to think. Being alone in body and spirit begets loneliness, and loneliness begets more loneliness.

Upstairs he walked around thinking of the matter and laying out his climbing clothes advantageously on the faint heater; he again encountered Nicole's telegram, still unopened, with which diurnally she accompanied his itinerary. He had delayed opening it before supper—perhaps because of the garden. It was a cablegram from Buffalo, forwarded through Zurich.

"Your father died peacefully tonight.   HOLMES."

He felt a sharp wince at the shock, a gathering of the forces of resistance; then it rolled through his loins and stomach and throat.

He read the message again. He sat down on the bed, breathing and staring; thinking first the old, selfish child's thought that comes with the death of a parent, how will it affect me now that this earliest and strongest of protections is gone?

The atavism passed and he walked the room still, stopping from time to time to look at the telegram. Holmes was formally his father's curate but actually, and for a decade, rector of the church. How did he die? Of old age—he was seventy-five. He had lived a long time.

Dick felt sad that he had died alone—he had survived his wife, and his brothers and sisters; there were cousins in Virginia, but they were poor and not able to come North, and Holmes had had to sign the telegram. Dick loved his father—again and again he referred judgments to what his father would probably have thought or done. Dick was born several months after the death of two young sisters and his father, guessing what would be the effect on Dick's mother, had saved him from a spoiling by becoming his moral guide. He was of tired stock yet he raised himself to that effort.

In the summer father and son walked downtown together to have their shoes shined—Dick in his starched duck sailor suit, his father always in beautifully cut clerical clothes—and the father was very proud of his handsome little boy. He told Dick all he knew about life, not much but most of it true, simple things, matters of behavior that came within his clergyman's range. "Once in a strange town when I was first ordained, I went into a crowded room and was confused as to who was my hostess. Several people I knew came toward me, but I disregarded them because I had seen a gray-haired woman sitting by a window far across the room. I went over to her and introduced myself. After that I made many friends in that town."

His father had done that from a good heart—his father had been sure of what he was, with a deep pride of the two proud widows who had raised him to believe that nothing could be superior to "good instincts," honor, courtesy, and courage.

The father always considered that his wife's small fortune belonged to his son, and in college and in medical school sent him a check for all the income four times a year. He was one of those about whom it was said with smug finality in the gilded age: "Very much the gentleman, but not much get-up-and-go about him."

. . . Dick sent down for a newspaper. Still pacing to and from the telegram open on his bureau, he chose a ship to go to America. Then he put in a call for Nicole in Zurich, remembering so many things as he waited, and wishing he had always been as good as he had intended to be.

CHAPTER VII

For an hour, tied up with his profound reaction to his father's death, the magnificent façade of the homeland, the harbor of New York, seemed all sad and glorious to Dick, but once ashore the feeling vanished, nor did he find it again in the streets or the hotels or the trains that bore him first to Buffalo, and then south to Virginia with his father's body. Only as the local train shambled into the low-forested clayland of Westmoreland County did he feel once more identified with his surroundings; at the station he saw a star he knew, and a cold moon bright over Chesapeake Bay; he heard the rasping wheels of buckboards turning, the lovely fatuous voices, the sound of sluggish primeval rivers flowing softly under soft Indian names.

Next day at the churchyard his father was laid among a hundred Divers, Dorseys, and Hunters. It was very friendly leaving him there with all his relations around him. Flowers were scattered on the brown unsettled earth. Dick had no more ties here now and did not believe he would come back. He knelt on the hard soil. These dead, he knew them all, their weather-beaten faces with blue flashing eyes, the spare violent bodies, the souls made of new earth in the forest-heavy darkness of the seventeenth century.

"Good-bye, my father—good-bye, all my fathers."

On the long-roofed steamship piers one is in a country that is no longer here and not yet there. The hazy yellow vault is full of echoing shouts. There are the rumble of trucks and the clump of trunks, the strident chatter of cranes, the first salt smell of the sea. One hurries through, even though there's time; the past, the continent, is behind; the future is the glowing mouth in the side of the ship; the dim, turbulent alley is too confusedly the present.

Up the gangplank and the vision of the world adjusts itself, narrows. One is a citizen of a commonwealth smaller than Andorra, no longer sure of anything. The men at the purser's desk are as oddly shaped as the cabins; disdainful are the eyes of voyagers and their friends. Next the loud mournful whistles, the portentous vibration and the boat, the human idea, is in motion. The pier and its faces slide by and for a moment the boat is a piece accidentally split off from them; the faces become remote, voiceless, the pier is one of many blurs along the water-front. The harbor flows swiftly toward the sea.

With it flowed Albert McKisco, labelled by the newspapers as the steamer's most precious cargo. McKisco was having a vogue. His novels were pastiches of the work of the best people of his time, a feat not to be disparaged, and in addition he possessed a gift for softening and debasing what he borrowed, so that many readers were charmed by the ease with which they could follow him. Success had improved him and humbled him. He was no fool about his capacities—he realized that he possessed more vitality than many men of superior talent, and he was resolved to enjoy the success he had earned. "I've done nothing yet," he would say. "I don't think I've got any real genius. But if I keep trying I may write a good book." Fine dives have been made from flimsier spring-boards. The innumerable snubs of the past were forgotten. Indeed, his success was founded psychologically upon his duel with Tommy Barban, upon the basis of which, as it withered in his memory, he had created, afresh, a new self-respect.

Spotting Dick Diver the second day out, he eyed him tentatively, then introduced himself in a friendly way and sat down. Dick laid aside his reading and, after the few minutes that it took to realize the change in McKisco, the disappearance of the man's annoying sense of inferiority, found himself pleased to talk to him. McKisco was "well-informed" on a range of subjects wider than Goethe's—it was interesting to listen to the innumerable facile combinations that he referred to as his opinions. They struck up an acquaintance and Dick had several meals with them. The McKiscos had been invited to sit at the captain's table, but with nascent snobbery they told Dick that they "couldn't stand that bunch."

Violet was very grand now, decked out by the grand couturiers, charmed about the little discoveries that well-bred girls make in their teens. She could, indeed, have learned them from her mother in Boise but her soul was born dismally in the small movie houses of Idaho, and she had had no time for her mother. Now she "belonged" —together with several million other people—and she was happy, though her husband still shushed her when she grew violently naïve.

The McKiscos got off at Gibraltar. Next evening in Naples Dick picked up a lost and miserable family of two girls and their mother in the bus from the hotel to the station. He had seen them on the ship. An overwhelming desire to help, or to be admired, came over him: he showed them fragments of gaiety; tentatively he bought them wine, with pleasure saw them begin to regain their proper egotism. He pretended they were this and that and, falling in with his own plot, drank too much to sustain the illusion, and all this time the women thought only that this was a windfall from heaven. He withdrew from them as the night waned and the train rocked and snorted at Cassino and Frosinone. Early in the morning, after weird American partings in the station at Rome, Dick went to the Hotel Quirinal, somewhat exhausted.

At the desk he suddenly stared and upped his head. As if a drink were acting on him, warming the lining of his stomach, throwing a flush up into his brain, he saw the person he had come to see, the person for whom he had made the Mediterranean crossing.

Simultaneously Rosemary saw him, acknowledging him before placing him; she looked back startled and, leaving the girl she was with, she hurried over. Holding himself erect, holding his breath, Dick turned to her. As she came across the lobby, her beauty all groomed like a young horse dosed with Black-seed oil and hoofs varnished, shocked him awake; but it all came too quick for him to do anything except conceal his fatigue as best he could. To meet her starry-eyed confidence he mustered an insincere pantomime implying, "You *would* turn up here—of all the people in the world."

Her gloved hands closed over his on the desk; "Dick—we're making *The Grandeur that was Rome*—at least we think we are; we may quit any day."

He looked at her hard, trying to make her a little self-conscious, so that she would observe less closely his unshaven face, his crumpled and slept-in collar. Fortunately she was in a hurry.

"We begin early because the mists rise at eleven—phone me at two."

In his room Dick collected his faculties. He left a call for noon, stripped off his clothes and dove literally into a heavy sleep.

He slept over the phone call but awoke at one, refreshed. Unpacking his bag, he sent out suits and laundry. He shaved, lay for half an hour in a warm bath and had breakfast. The sun had dipped into the Via Nazionale and he let it through the portières with a jingling of old brass rings. Waiting for a suit to be pressed, he read the *Corriere della Sera* and learned about "una novella di Sainclair Lewis *Wall Street* nella quale autore analizza la vita sociale di una piccola città Americana." Then he tried to think about Rosemary.

At first he thought nothing. She was young and magnetic, but so was Topsy. He guessed that she had had lovers and had loved them in the last four years. Well, you never knew exactly how much space you occupied in people's lives. Yet from this fog his affection emerged—the best contacts are when one knows the obstacles and still wants to preserve a relation. The past drifted back and he wanted to hold her eloquent giving-of-herself in its precious shell, till he enclosed it, till it no longer existed outside him. He tried to collect all that might attract her—it was less than it had been four years ago. Eighteen might look at thirty-four through a rising mist of adolescence; but twenty-two would see thirty-eight with discerning clarity. Moreover, Dick had been at an emotional peak at the time of the previous encounter; since then there had been a lesion of enthusiasm.

When the valet returned he put on a white shirt and collar and a black tie with a pearl; the cords of his reading glasses passed through another pearl of the same size that swung a casual inch below. After sleep, his face had resumed the ruddy brown of many Riviera summers, and to limber himself up he stood on his hands on a chair until his fountain pen and coins fell out. At three he called Rosemary and was bidden to come up. Momentarily dizzy from his acrobatics, he stopped in the bar for a gin-and-tonic.

"Hi, Doctor Diver!"

Only because of Rosemary's presence in the hotel did Dick place the man immediately as Collis Clay. He had his old confidence and an air of prosperity and big sudden jowls.

"Do you know Rosemary's here?" Collis asked.

"I ran into her."

"I was in Florence and I heard she was here, so I came down last week. You'd never know Mama's little girl." He modified the remark, "I mean she was so carefully brought up and now she's a woman of the world—if you know what I mean. Believe me, has she got some of these Roman boys tied up in bags! And how!"

"You studying in Florence?"

"Me? Sure, I'm studying architecture there. I go back Sunday— I'm staying for the races."

With difficulty Dick restrained him from adding the drink to the account he carried in the bar, like a stock-market report.

CHAPTER VIII

WHEN DICK GOT OUT of the elevator he followed a tortuous corridor and turned at length toward a distant voice outside a lighted door. Rosemary was in black pajamas; a luncheon table was still in the room; she was having coffee.

"You're still beautiful," he said. "A little more beautiful than ever."

"Do you want coffee, youngster?"

"I'm sorry I was so unpresentable this morning."

"You didn't look well—you all right now? Want coffee?"

"No, thanks."

"You're fine again, I was scared this morning. Mother's coming over next month, if the company stays. She always asks me if I've seen you over here, as if she thought we were living next door. Mother always liked you—she always felt you were someone I ought to know."

"Well, I'm glad she still thinks of me."

"Oh, she does," Rosemary reassured him. "A very great deal."

"I've seen you here and there in pictures," said Dick. "Once I had *Daddy's Girl* run off just for myself."

"I have a good part in this one if it isn't cut."

She crossed behind him, touching his shoulder as she passed. She phoned for the table to be taken away and settled in a big chair.

"I was just a little girl when I met you, Dick. Now I'm a woman."

"I want to hear everything about you."

"How is Nicole—and Lanier and Topsy?"

"They're fine. They often speak of you——"

The phone rang. While she answered it Dick examined two novels—one by Edna Ferber, one by Albert McKisco. The waiter came for the table; bereft of its presence Rosemary seemed more alone in her black pajamas.

227

". . . I have a caller. . . . No, not very well. I've got to go to the costumer's for a long fitting. . . . No, not now. . . ."

As though with the disappearance of the table she felt released, Rosemary smiled at Dick—that smile as if they two together had managed to get rid of all the trouble in the world and were now at peace in their own heaven.

"That's done," she said. "Do you realize I've spent the last hour getting ready for you?"

But again the phone called her. Dick got up to change his hat from the bed to the luggage stand, and in alarm Rosemary put her hand over the mouthpiece of the phone. "You're not going!"

"No."

When the communication was over he tried to drag the afternoon together, saying: "I expect some nourishment from people now."

"Me too," Rosemary agreed. "The man that just phoned me once knew a second cousin of mine. Imagine calling anybody up for a reason like that!"

Now she lowered the lights for love. Why else should she want to shut off his view of her? He sent his words to her like letters, as though they left him some time before they reached her.

"Hard to sit here and be close to you, and not kiss you." Then they kissed passionately in the centre of the floor. She pressed against him, and went back to her chair.

It could not go on being merely pleasant in the room. Forward or backward; when the phone rang once more he strolled into the bedchamber and lay down on her bed, opening Albert McKisco's novel. Presently Rosemary came in and sat beside him.

"You have the longest eyelashes," she remarked.

"We are now back at the Junior Prom. Among those present are Miss Rosemary Hoyt, the eyelash fancier——"

She kissed him and he pulled her down so that they lay side by side, and then they kissed till they were both breathless. Her breathing was young and eager and exciting. Her lips were faintly chapped but soft in the corners.

When they were still limbs and feet and clothes, struggles of his arms and back, and her throat and breasts, she whispered, "No, not now—those things are rhythmic."

Disciplined he crushed his passion into a corner of his mind, but bearing up her fragility on his arm until she was poised half a foot above him, he said lightly:

"Darling—that doesn't matter."

Her face had changed with his looking up at it; there was the eternal moonlight in it.

"That would be poetic justice if it should be you," she said. She twisted away from him, walked to the mirror, and boxed her disarranged hair with her hands. Presently she drew a chair close to the bed and stroked his cheek.

"Tell me the truth about you," he demanded.

"I always have."

"In a way—but nothing hangs together."

They both laughed, but he pursued.

"Are you actually a virgin?"

"No-o-o!" she sang. "I've slept with six hundred and forty men —if that's the answer you want."

"It's none of my business."

"Do you want me for a case in psychology?"

"Looking at you as a perfectly normal girl of twenty-two, living in the year nineteen twenty-nine, I guess you've taken a few shots at love."

"It's all been—abortive," she said.

Dick couldn't believe her. He could not decide whether she was deliberately building a barrier between them or whether this was intended to make an eventual surrender more significant.

"Let's go walk in the Pincio," he suggested.

He shook himself straight in his clothes and smoothed his hair. A moment had come and somehow passed. For three years Dick had been the ideal by which Rosemary measured other men and inevitably his stature had increased to heroic size. She did not want him to be like other men, yet here were the same exigent demands, as if he wanted to take some of herself away, carry it off in his pocket.

Walking on the greensward between cherubs and philosophers, fauns and falling water, she took his arm snugly, settling into it with a series of little readjustments, as if she wanted it to be right because it was going to be there forever. She plucked a twig and broke it, but she found no spring in it. Suddenly seeing what she wanted in Dick's face she took his gloved hand and kissed it. Then she cavorted childishly for him until he smiled and she laughed and they began having a good time.

"I can't go out with you tonight, darling, because I promised some people a long time ago. But if you'll get up early I'll take you out to the set tomorrow."

He dined alone at the hotel, went to bed early, and met Rosemary in the lobby at half-past six. Beside him in the car she glowed away fresh and new in the morning sunshine. They went out through the Porta San Sebastiano and along the Appian Way until they came to the huge set of the forum, larger than the forum itself. Rosemary turned him over to a man who led him about the great props: the arches and tiers of seats and the sanded arena. She was working on a stage which represented a guardroom for Christian prisoners, and presently they went there and watched Nicotera, one of many hopeful Valentinos, strut and pose before a dozen female "captives," their eyes melancholy and startling with mascara.

Rosemary appeared in a knee-length tunic.

"Watch this," she whispered to Dick. "I want your opinion. Everybody that's seen the rushes says——"

"What are the rushes?"

"When they run off what they took the day before. They say it's the first thing I've had sex appeal in."

"I don't notice it."

"You wouldn't! But I have."

Nicotera in his leopard skin talked attentively to Rosemary while the electrician discussed something with the director, meanwhile leaning on him. Finally the director pushed his hand off roughly and wiped a sweating forehead, and Dick's guide remarked: "He's on the hop again, and how!"

"Who?" asked Dick, but before the man could answer the director walked swiftly over to them.

"Who's on the hop—you're on the hop yourself." He spoke vehemently to Dick, as if to a jury. "When he's on the hop he always thinks everybody else is, and how!" He glared at the guide a moment longer, then he clapped his hands: "All right—everybody on the set."

It was like visiting a great turbulent family. An actress approached

Dick and talked to him for five minutes under the impression that he was an actor recently arrived from London. Discovering her mistake she scuttled away in panic. The majority of the company felt either sharply superior or sharply inferior to the world outside, but the former feeling prevailed. They were people of bravery and industry; they were risen to a position of prominence in a nation that for a decade had wanted only to be entertained.

The session ended as the light grew misty—a fine light for painters, but, for the camera, not to be compared with the clear California air. Nicotera followed Rosemary to the car and whispered something to her—she looked at him without smiling as she said good-bye.

Dick and Rosemary had luncheon at the Castelli dei Cæsari, a splendid restaurant in a high-terraced villa overlooking the ruined forum of an undetermined period of the decadence. Rosemary took a cocktail and a little wine, and Dick took enough so that his feeling of dissatisfaction left him. Afterward they drove back to the hotel, all flushed and happy, in a sort of exalted quiet. She wanted to be taken and she was, and what had begun with a childish infatuation on a beach was accomplished at last.

CHAPTER IX

Rosemary had another dinner date, a birthday party for a member of the company. Dick ran into Collis Clay in the lobby, but he wanted to dine alone and pretended an engagement at the Excelsior. He drank a cocktail with Collis and his vague dissatisfaction crystallized as impatience—he no longer had an excuse for playing truant to the clinic. This was less an infatuation than a romantic memory. Nicole was his girl—too often he was sick at heart about her, yet she was his girl. Time with Rosemary was self-indulgence—time with Collis was nothing plus nothing.

In the doorway of the Excelsior he ran into Baby Warren. Her large beautiful eyes, looking precisely like marbles, stared at him with surprise and curiosity. "I thought you were in America, Dick! Is Nicole with you?"

"I came back by way of Naples."

The black band on his arm reminded her to say: "I'm so sorry to hear of your trouble."

Inevitably they dined together.

"Tell me about everything," she demanded.

Dick gave her a version of the facts, and Baby frowned. She found it necessary to blame someone for the catastrophe in her sister's life.

"Do you think Doctor Dohmler took the right course with her from the first?"

"There's not much variety in treatment any more—of course you try to find the right personality to handle a particular case."

"Dick, I don't pretend to advise you or to know much about it, but don't you think a change might be good for her—to get out of that atmosphere of sickness and live in the world like other people?"

"But you were keen for the clinic," he reminded her. "You told me you'd never feel really safe about her——"

"That was when you were leading that hermit's life on the Riviera, up on a hill way off from anybody. I didn't mean to go back to that life. I meant, for instance, London. The English are the best-balanced race in the world."

"They are not," he disagreed.

"They are. I know them, you see. I meant it might be nice for you to take a house in London for the spring season—I know a dove of a house in Talbot Square you could get, furnished. I mean, living with sane, well-balanced English people."

She would have gone on to tell him all the old propaganda stories of 1914 if he had not laughed and said:

"I've been reading a book by Michael Arlen and if that's——"

She ruined Michael Arlen with a wave of her salad spoon.

"He only writes about degenerates. I mean the worth-while English."

As she thus dismissed her friends they were replaced in Dick's mind only by a picture of the alien, unresponsive faces that peopled the small hotels of Europe.

"Of course it's none of my business," Baby repeated, as a preliminary to a further plunge, "but to leave her alone in an atmosphere like that——"

"I went to America because my father died."

"I understand that, I told you how sorry I was." She fiddled with the glass grapes on her necklace. "But there's so *much* money now. Plenty for everything, and it ought to be used to get Nicole well."

"For one thing I can't see myself in London."

"Why not? I should think you could work there as well as anywhere else."

He sat back and looked at her. If she had ever suspected the rotted old truth, the real reason for Nicole's illness, she had certainly determined to deny it to herself, shoving it back in a dusty closet like one of the paintings she bought by mistake.

They continued the conversation in the Ulpia, where Collis Clay came over to their table and sat down, and a gifted guitar player thrummed and rumbled "Suona Fanfara Mia" in the cellar piled with wine casks.

"It's possible that I was the wrong person for Nicole," Dick said. "Still, she would probably have married someone of my type, someone she thought she could rely on—indefinitely."

"You think she'd be happier with somebody else?" Baby thought aloud suddenly. "Of course it could be arranged."

Only as she saw Dick bend forward with helpless laughter did she realize the preposterousness of her remark.

"Oh, you understand," she assured him. "Don't think for a moment that we're not grateful for all you've done. And we know you've had a hard time——"

"For God's sake," he protested. "If I didn't love Nicole it might be different."

"But you do love Nicole?" she demanded in alarm.

Collis was catching up with the conversation now and Dick switched it quickly: "Suppose we talk about something else—about you, for instance. Why don't you get married? We heard you were engaged to Lord Paley, the cousin of the——"

"Oh, no." She became coy and elusive. "That was last year."

"Why don't you marry?" Dick insisted stubbornly.

"I don't know. One of the men I loved was killed in the war, and the other one threw me over."

"Tell me about it. Tell me about your private life, Baby, and your opinions. You never do—we always talk about Nicole."

"Both of them were Englishmen. I don't think there's any higher type in the world than a first-rate Englishman, do you? If there is I haven't met him. This man—oh, it's a long story. I hate long stories, don't you?"

"And how!" said Collis.

"Why, no—I like them if they're good."

"That's something you do so well, Dick. You can keep a party moving by just a little sentence or a saying here and there. I think that's a wonderful talent."

"It's a trick," he said gently. That made three of her opinions he disagreed with.

"Of course I like formality—I like things to be just so, and on the grand scale. I know you probably don't, but you must admit it's a sign of solidity in me."

Dick did not even bother to dissent from this.

"Of course I know people say, Baby Warren is racing around over Europe, chasing one novelty after another, and missing the best things in life, but I think on the contrary that I'm one of the few people who really go after the best things. I've known the most interesting people of my time." Her voice blurred with the tinny drumming of another guitar number, but she called over it, "I've made very few big mistakes——"

"—Only the very big ones, Baby."

She had caught something facetious in his eye and she changed the subject. It seemed impossible for them to hold anything in common. But he admired something in her, and he deposited her at the Excelsior with a series of compliments that left her shimmering.

Rosemary insisted on treating Dick to lunch next day. They went to a little *trattoria* kept by an Italian who had worked in America, and ate ham and eggs and waffles. Afterward they went to the hotel. Dick's discovery that he was not in love with her, nor she with him, had added to rather than diminished his passion for her. Now that he knew he would not enter further into her life, she became the strange woman for him. He supposed many men meant no more than that when they said they were in love—not a wild submergence of soul, a dipping of all colors into an obscuring dye, such as his love for Nicole had been. Certain thoughts about Nicole, that she should die, sink into mental darkness, love another man, made him physically sick.

Nicotera was in Rosemary's sitting-room, chattering about a professional matter. When Rosemary gave him his cue to go, he left with humorous protests and a rather insolent wink at Dick. As usual the phone clamored and Rosemary was engaged at it for ten minutes to Dick's increasing impatience.

"Let's go up to my room," he suggested, and she agreed.

She lay across his knees on a big sofa; he ran his fingers through the lovely forelocks of her hair.

"Let me be curious about you again?" he asked.

"What do you want to know?"

"About men. I'm curious, not to say prurient."

"You mean how long after I met you?"

"Or before."

"Oh, no." She was shocked. "There was nothing before. You were the first man I cared about. You're still the only man I really care about." She considered. "It was about a year, I think."

"Who was it?"

"Oh, a man."

He closed in on her evasion.

"I'll bet I can tell you about it: the first affair was unsatisfactory and after that there was a long gap. The second was better, but you hadn't been in love with the man in the first place. The third was all right——"

Torturing himself he ran on. "Then you had one real affair that fell of its own weight, and by that time you were getting afraid that you wouldn't have anything to give to the man you finally loved." He felt increasingly Victorian. "Afterward there were half a dozen just episodic affairs, right up to the present. Is that close?"

She laughed between amusement and tears.

"It's about as wrong as it could be," she said, to Dick's relief. "But some day I'm going to find somebody and love him and love him and never let him go."

Now his phone rang and Dick recognized Nicotera's voice, asking for Rosemary. He put his palm over the transmitter.

"Do you want to talk to him?"

She went to the phone and jabbered in a rapid Italian Dick could not understand.

"This telephoning takes time," he said. "It's after four and I have an engagement at five. You better go play with Signor Nicotera."

"Don't be silly."

"Then I think that while I'm here you ought to count him out."

"It's difficult." She was suddenly crying. "Dick, I do love you, never anybody like you. But what have you got for me?"

"What has Nicotera got for anybody?"

"That's different."

—Because youth called to youth.

"He's a spic!" he said. He was frantic with jealousy, he didn't want to be hurt again.

"He's only a baby," she said, sniffing. "You know I'm yours first."

In reaction he put his arms about her but she relaxed wearily backward; he held her like that for a moment as in the end of an adagio, her eyes closed, her hair falling straight back like that of a girl drowned.

"Dick, let me go. I never felt so mixed up in my life."

He was a gruff red bird and instinctively she drew away from him as his unjustified jealousy began to snow over the qualities of consideration and understanding with which she felt at home.

"I want to know the truth," he said.

"Yes, then. We're a lot together, he wants to marry me, but I don't want to. What of it? What do you expect me to do? You never asked me to marry you. Do you want me to play around forever with halfwits like Collis Clay?"

"You were with Nicotera last night?"

"That's none of your business," she sobbed. "Excuse me, Dick, it is your business. You and Mother are the only two people in the world I care about."

"How about Nicotera?"

"How do I know?"

She had achieved the elusiveness that gives hidden significance to the least significant remarks.

"Is it like you felt toward me in Paris?"

"I feel comfortable and happy when I'm with you. In Paris it was different. But you never know how you once felt. Do you?"

He got up and began collecting his evening clothes—if he had to bring all the bitterness and hatred of the world into his heart, he was not going to be in love with her again.

"I don't care about Nicotera!" she declared. "But I've got to go to Livorno with the company tomorrow. Oh, why did this have to happen?" There was a new flood of tears. "It's such a shame. Why did you come here? Why couldn't we just have the memory anyhow? I feel as if I'd quarrelled with Mother."

As he began to dress, she got up and went to the door.

"I won't go to the party tonight." It was her last effort. "I'll stay with you. I don't want to go anyhow."

The tide began to flow again, but he retreated from it.

"I'll be in my room," she said. "Good-bye, Dick."

"Good-bye."

"Oh, such a shame, such a shame. Oh, such a shame. What's it all about anyhow?"

"I've wondered for a long time."

"But why bring it to me?"

"I guess I'm the Black Death," he said slowly. "I don't seem to bring people happiness any more."

CHAPTER X

THERE WERE FIVE PEOPLE in the Quirinal bar after dinner, a high-class Italian frail who sat on a stool making persistent conversation against the bartender's bored "Si . . . Si . . . Si," a light, snobbish Egyptian who was lonely but chary of the woman, and the two Americans.

Dick was always vividly conscious of his surroundings, while Collis Clay lived vaguely, the sharpest impressions dissolving upon a recording apparatus that had early atrophied, so the former talked and the latter listened, like a man sitting in a breeze.

Dick, worn away by the events of the afternoon, was taking it out on the inhabitants of Italy. He looked around the bar as if he hoped an Italian had heard him and would resent his words.

"This afternoon I had tea with my sister-in-law at the Excelsior. We got the last table and two men came up and looked around for a table and couldn't find one. So one of them came up to us and said, 'Isn't this table reserved for the Princess Orsini?' and I said, 'There was no sign on it,' and he said: 'But I think it's reserved for the Princess Orsini.' I couldn't even answer him."

"What'd he do?"

"He retired." Dick switched around in his chair. "I don't like these people. The other day I left Rosemary for two minutes in front of a store and an officer started walking up and down in front of her, tipping his hat."

"I don't know," said Collis after a moment. "I'd rather be here than up in Paris with somebody picking your pocket every minute."

He had been enjoying himself, and he held out against anything that threatened to dull his pleasure.

"I don't know," he persisted. "I don't mind it here."

Dick evoked the picture that the few days had imprinted on his mind, and stared at it. The walk toward the American Express past the odorous confectioneries of the Via Nazionale, through the foul

tunnel up to the Spanish Steps, where his spirit soared before the
flower stalls and the house where Keats had died. He cared only
about people; he was scarcely conscious of places except for their
weather, until they had been invested with color by tangible events.
Rome was the end of his dream of Rosemary.

A bell-boy came in and gave him a note.

"*I did not go to the party,*" it said. "*I am in my room. We leave
for Livorno early in the morning.*"

Dick handed the note and a tip to the boy.

"Tell Miss Hoyt you couldn't find me." Turning to Collis he
suggested the Bonbonieri.

They inspected the tart at the bar, granting her the minimum of
interest exacted by her profession, and she stared back with bright
boldness; they went through the deserted lobby oppressed by dra-
peries holding Victorian dust in stuffy folds, and they nodded at the
night concierge, who returned the gesture with the bitter servility
peculiar to night servants. Then in a taxi they rode along cheerless
streets through a dank November night. There were no women
in the streets, only pale men with dark coats buttoned to the neck,
who stood in groups beside shoulders of cold stone.

"My God!" Dick sighed.

"What's a matter?"

"I was thinking of that man this afternoon: 'This table is reserved
for the Princess Orsini.' Do you know what these old Roman
families are? They're bandits, they're the ones who got possession
of the temples and palaces after Rome went to pieces and preyed
on the people."

"I like Rome," insisted Collis. "Why won't you try the races?"

"I don't like races."

"But all the women turn out——"

"I know I wouldn't like anything here. I like France, where
everybody thinks he's Napoleon—down here everybody thinks he's
Christ."

At the Bonbonieri they descended to a panelled cabaret, hopelessly
impermanent amid the cold stone. A listless band played a tango
and a dozen couples covered the wide floor with those elaborate and
dainty steps so offensive to the American eye. A surplus of waiters
precluded the stir and bustle that even a few busy men can create;

over the scene as its form of animation brooded an air of waiting
for something—the dance, the night, the balance of forces which
kept it stable—to cease. It assured the impressionable guest that
whatever he was seeking he would not find it here.

This was plain as plain to Dick. He looked around, hoping his
eye would catch on something, so that spirit instead of imagination
could carry on for an hour. But there was nothing and after a moment he turned back to Collis. He had told Collis some of his
current notions, and he was bored with his audience's short memory and lack of response. After half an hour of Collis he felt a distinct lesion of his own vitality.

They drank a bottle of Italian mousseux and Dick became pale
and somewhat noisy. He called the orchestra leader over to their
table; this was a Bahama Negro, conceited and unpleasant, and in
a few minutes there was a row.

"You asked me to sit down."

"All right. And I gave you fifty lire, didn't I?"

"All right. All right. All right."

"All right, I gave you fifty lire, didn't I? Then you came up and
asked me to put some more in the horn."

"You asked me to sit down, didn't you? Didn't you?"

"I asked you to sit down but I gave you fifty lire, didn't I?"

"All right. All right."

The Negro got up sourly and went away, leaving Dick in a still
more evil humor. But he saw a girl smiling at him from across the
room and immediately the pale Roman shapes around him receded
into decent, humble perspective. She was a young English girl, with
blond hair and a healthy, pretty English face and she smiled at
him again with an invitation he understood, that denied the flesh
even in the act of tendering it.

"There's a quick trick or else I don't know bridge," said Collis.

Dick got up and walked to her across the room.

"Won't you dance?"

The middle-aged Englishman with whom she was sitting said,
almost apologetically: "I'm going out soon."

Sobered by excitement Dick danced. He found in the girl a suggestion of all the pleasanter English things; the story of safe gardens ringed around by the sea was implicit in her bright voice

and, as he leaned back to look at her, he meant what he said to her so sincerely that his voice trembled. When her current escort should leave, she promised to come and sit with them. The Englishman accepted her return with repeated apologies and smiles.

Back at his table Dick ordered another bottle of spumante.

"She looks like somebody in the movies," he said. "I can't think who." He glanced impatiently over his shoulder. "Wonder what's keeping her?"

"I'd like to get in the movies," said Collis thoughtfully. "I'm supposed to go into my father's business but it doesn't appeal to me much. Sit in an office in Atlanta for twenty years——"

His voice resisted the pressure of materialistic civilization.

"Too good for it?" suggested Dick.

"No, I don't mean that."

"Yes, you do."

"How do you know what I mean? Why don't you practise as a doctor, if you like to work so much?"

Dick had made them both wretched by this time, but simultaneously they had become vague with drink and in a moment they forgot; Collis left, and they shook hands warmly.

"Think it over," said Dick sagely.

"Think what over?"

"You know." It had been something about Collis going into his father's business—good sound advice.

Clay walked off into space. Dick finished his bottle and then danced with the English girl again, conquering his unwilling body with bold revolutions and stern determined marches down the floor. The most remarkable thing suddenly happened. He was dancing with the girl, the music stopped—and she had disappeared.

"Have you seen her?"

"Seen who?"

"The girl I was dancing with. Su'nly disappeared. Must be in the building."

"No! No! That's the ladies' room."

He stood up by the bar. There were two other men there, but he could think of no way of starting a conversation. He could have told them all about Rome and the violent origins of the Colonna and Gaetani families, but he realized that as a beginning that would be somewhat abrupt. A row of Yenci dolls on the cigar counter fell suddenly to the floor; there was a subsequent confusion and he had a sense of having been the cause of it, so he went back to the cabaret and drank a cup of black coffee. Collis was gone and the English girl was gone and there seemed nothing to do but go back to the hotel and lie down with his black heart. He paid his check and got his hat and coat.

There was dirty water in the gutters and between the rough cobblestones; a marshy vapor from the Campagna, a sweat of exhausted cultures tainted the morning air. A quartet of taxi-drivers, their little eyes bobbing in dark pouches, surrounded him. One who leaned insistently in his face he pushed harshly away.

"Quanto a Hotel Quirinal?"

"Cento lire."

Six dollars. He shook his head and offered thirty lire, which was twice the day-time fare, but they shrugged their shoulders as one pair, and moved off.

"Trente-cinque lire e mancie," he said firmly.

"Cento lire."

He broke into English.

"To go half a mile? You'll take me for forty lire."

"Oh, no."

He was very tired. He pulled open the door of a cab and got in.

"Hotel Quirinal!" he said to the driver who stood obstinately outside the window. "Wipe that sneer off your face and take me to the Quirinal."

"Ah, no."

Dick got out. By the door of the Bonbonieri someone was arguing with the taxi-drivers, someone who now tried to explain their attitude to Dick; again one of the men pressed close, insisting and gesticulating, and Dick shoved him away.

"I want to go the Quirinal Hotel."

"He says wan huner lire," explained the interpreter.

"I understand. I'll give him fif'y lire. Go on away." This last to the insistent man who had edged up once more. The man looked at him and spat contemptuously.

The passionate impatience of the week leaped up in Dick and clothed itself like a flash in violence, the honorable, the traditional resource of his land; he stepped forward and clapped the man's face.

They surged about him, threatening, waving their arms, trying ineffectually to close in on him—with his back against the wall Dick hit out clumsily, laughing a little, and for a few minutes the mock fight, an affair of foiled rushes and padded, glancing blows, swayed back and forth in front of the door. Then Dick tripped and fell; he was hurt somewhere but he struggled up again, wrestling in arms that suddenly broke apart. There was a new voice and a new argument but he leaned against the wall, panting and furious at the indignity of his position. He saw there was no sympathy for him, but he was unable to believe that he was wrong.

They were going to the police station and settle it there. His hat was retrieved and handed to him, and with someone holding his arm lightly he strode around the corner with the taxi-men and entered a bare barrack where carabinieri lounged under a single dim light.

At a desk sat a captain, to whom the officious individual who had stopped the battle spoke at length in Italian, at times pointing at Dick and letting himself be interrupted by the taxi-men, who delivered short bursts of invective and denunciation. The captain began to nod impatiently. He held up his hand and the hydra-headed address, with a few parting exclamations, died away. Then he turned to Dick.

"Spick Italiano?" he asked.

"No."

"Spick Français?"

"Oui," said Dick, glowering.

"Alors. Écoute. Va au Quirinal. Espèce d'endormi. Écoute: vous êtes saoul. Payez ce que le chauffeur demande. Comprenez-vous?"

Diver shook his head.

"Non, je ne veux pas."

"*Come?*"

"Je paierai quarante lires. C'est bien assez."

The captain stood up.

"Écoute!" he cried portentously, "Vous êtes saoul. Vous avez battu le chauffeur. Comme ci, comme ça." He struck the air excitedly with right hand and left. "C'est bon que je vous donne la liberté. Payez ce qu'il a dit—cento lire. Va au Quirinal."

Raging with humiliation, Dick stared back at him.

"All right." He turned blindly to the door—before him, leering and nodding, was the man who had brought him to the police station. "I'll go home," he shouted, "but first I'll fix this baby."

He walked past the staring carabinieri and up to the grinning face, hit it with a smashing left beside the jaw. The man dropped to the floor.

For a moment he stood over him in savage triumph—but even as a first pang of doubt shot through him the world reeled; he was clubbed down, and fists and boots beat on him in a savage tattoo. He felt his nose break like a shingle and his eyes jerk as if they had snapped back on a rubber band into his head. A rib splintered under a stamping heel. Momentarily he lost consciousness, regained it as he was raised to a sitting position and his wrists jerked together with handcuffs. He struggled automatically. The plainclothes lieutenant whom he had knocked down stood dabbing his jaw with a handkerchief and looking into it for blood; he came over to Dick, poised himself, drew back his arm and smashed him to the floor.

When Doctor Diver lay quite still a pail of water was sloshed over him. One of his eyes opened dimly as he was being dragged along by the wrists through a bloody haze, and he made out the human and ghastly face of one of the taxi-drivers.

"Go to the Excelsior Hotel," he cried faintly. "Tell Miss Warren. Two hundred lire! Miss Warren. Due centi lire! Oh, you dirty— you God——"

Still he was dragged along through the bloody haze, choking and sobbing, over vague irregular surfaces into some small place where he was dropped upon a stone floor. The men went out, a door clanged, he was alone.

CHAPTER XI

UNTIL ONE O'CLOCK BABY WARREN lay in bed, reading one of Marion Crawford's curiously inanimate Roman stories; then she went to a window and looked down into the street. Across from the hotel two carabinieri, grotesque in swaddling capes and harlequin hats, swung voluminously from this side and that, like mains'ls coming about, and watching them she thought of the guards' officer who had stared at her so intensely at lunch. He had possessed the arrogance of a tall member of a short race, with no obligation save to be tall. Had he come up to her and said: "Let's go along, you and I," she would have answered: "Why not?"—at least it seemed so now, for she was still disembodied by an unfamiliar background.

Her thoughts drifted back slowly through the guardsman to the two carabinieri, to Dick—she got into bed and turned out the light.

A little before four she was awakened by a brusque knocking.

"Yes—what is it?"

"It's the concierge, Madame."

She pulled on her kimono and faced him sleepily.

"Your friend name Deever he's in a trouble. He had trouble with the police, and they have him in the jail. He sent a taxi up to tell, the driver says that he promised him two hundred lire." He paused cautiously for this to be approved. "The driver says Mr. Deever in the bad trouble. He had a fight with the police and is terribly bad hurt."

"I'll be right down."

She dressed to an accompaniment of anxious heartbeats and ten minutes later stepped out of the elevator into the dark lobby. The chauffeur who brought the message was gone; the concierge hailed another one and told him the location of the jail. As they rode, the darkness lifted and thinned outside and Baby's nerves, scarcely

245

awake, cringed faintly at the unstable balance between night and day. She began to race against the day; sometimes on the broad avenues she gained, but whenever the thing that was pushing up paused for a moment, gusts of wind blew here and there impatiently and the slow creep of light began once more. The cab went past a loud fountain splashing in a voluminous shadow, turned into an alley so curved that the buildings were warped and strained following it, bumped and rattled over cobblestones, and stopped with a jerk where two sentry boxes were bright against a wall of green damp. Suddenly from the violet darkness of an archway came Dick's voice, shouting and screaming.

"Are there any English? Are there any Americans? Are there any English? Are there any—oh, my God! You dirty Wops!"

His voice died away and she heard a dull sound of beating on the door. Then the voice began again.

"Are there any Americans? Are there any English?"

Following the voice she ran through the arch into a court, whirled about in momentary confusion, and located the small guardroom whence the cries came. Two carabinieri started to their feet, but Baby brushed past them to the door of the cell.

"Dick!" she called. "What's the trouble?"

"They've put out my eye," he cried. "They handcuffed me and then they beat me, the goddamn—the——"

Flashing around Baby took a step toward the two carabinieri.

"What have you done to him?" she whispered so fiercely that they flinched before her gathering fury.

"Non capisco inglese."

In French she execrated them; her wild, confident rage filled the room, enveloped them until they shrank and wriggled from the garments of blame with which she invested them. "Do something! Do something!"

"We can do nothing until we are ordered."

"Bene. *Bay-nay! Bene!*"

Once more Baby let her passion scorch around them until they sweated out apologies for their impotence, looking at each other with the sense that something had after all gone terribly wrong. Baby went to the cell door, leaned against it, almost caressing it, as if that could make Dick feel her presence and power, and cried:

"I'm going to the Embassy, I'll be back." Throwing a last glance of infinite menace at the carabinieri she ran out.

She drove to the American Embassy, where she paid off the taxi-driver upon his insistence. It was still dark when she ran up the steps and pressed the bell. She had pressed it three times before a sleepy English porter opened the door to her.

"I want to see someone," she said. "Anyone—but right away."

"No one's awake, Madame. We don't open until nine o'clock."

Impatiently she waved the hour away.

"This is important. A man—an American has been terribly beaten. He's in an Italian jail."

"No one's awake now. At nine o'clock——"

"I can't wait. They've put out a man's eye—my brother-in-law, and they won't let him out of jail. I must talk to someone—can't you see? Are you crazy? Are you an idiot, you stand there with that look in your face?"

"Hime unable to do anything, Madame."

"You've got to wake someone up!" She seized him by the shoulders and jerked him violently. "It's a matter of life and death. If you won't wake someone a terrible thing will happen to you——"

"Kindly don't lay hands on me, Madame."

From above and behind the porter floated down a weary Groton voice.

"What is it there?"

The porter answered with relief.

"It's a lady, sir, and she has shook me." He had stepped back to speak and Baby pushed forward into the hall. On an upper landing, just aroused from sleep and wrapped in a white embroidered Persian robe, stood a singular young man. His face was of a monstrous and unnatural pink, vivid yet dead, and over his mouth was fastened what appeared to be a gag. When he saw Baby he moved his head back into a shadow.

"What is it?" he repeated.

Baby told him, in her agitation edging forward to the stairs. In the course of her story she realized that the gag was in reality a mustache bandage and that the man's face was covered with pink cold cream, but the fact fitted quietly into the nightmare. The thing to do, she cried passionately, was for him to come to the jail with her at once and get Dick out.

"It's a bad business," he said.

"Yes," she agreed conciliatingly. "Yes?"

"This trying to fight the police." A note of personal affront crept into his voice. "I'm afraid there's nothing to be done until nine o'clock."

"Till nine o'clock," she repeated aghast. "But you can do something, certainly! You can come to the jail with me and see that they don't hurt him any more."

"We aren't permitted to do anything like that. The Consulate handles these things. The Consulate will be open at nine."

His face, constrained to impassivity by the binding strap, infuriated Baby.

"I can't wait until nine. My brother-in-law says they've put his eye out—he's seriously hurt! I have to get to him. I have to find a doctor." She let herself go and began to cry angrily as she talked, for she knew that he would respond to her agitation rather than her words. "You've got to do something about this. It's your business to protect American citizens in trouble."

But he was of the Eastern seaboard and too hard for her. Shaking his head patiently at her failure to understand his position he drew the Persian robe closer about him and came down a few steps.

"Write down the address of the Consulate for this lady," he said to the porter, "and look up Doctor Colazzo's address and telephone number and write that down too." He turned to Baby, with the expression of an exasperated Christ. "My dear lady, the diplomatic corps represents the Government of the United States to the Government of Italy. It has nothing to do with the protection of citizens, except under specific instructions from the State Department. Your brother-in-law has broken the laws of this country and has been put in jail, just as an Italian might be put in jail in New York. The only people who can let him go are the Italian courts and if your brother-in-law has a case you can get aid and advice from the Consulate, which protects the rights of American citizens. The Consulate does not open until nine o'clock. Even if it were my brother I couldn't do anything——"

"Can you phone the Consulate?" she broke in.

"We can't interfere with the Consulate. When the Consul gets there at nine——"

"Can you give me his home address?"

After a fractional pause the man shook his head. He took the memorandum from the porter and gave it to her.

"Now I'll ask you to excuse me."

He had maneuvered her to the door: for an instant the violet dawn fell shrilly upon his pink mask and upon the linen sack that supported his mustache; then Baby was standing on the front steps alone. She had been in the embassy ten minutes.

The piazza on which it faced was empty save for an old man gathering cigarette butts with a spiked stick. Baby caught a taxi presently and went to the Consulate, but there was no one there save a trio of wretched women scrubbing the stairs. She could not make them understand that she wanted the Consul's home address —in a sudden resurgence of anxiety she rushed out and told the chauffeur to take her to the jail. He did not know where it was, but by the use of the words *sempre diretto, destra* and *sinistra* she maneuvered him to its approximate locality, where she dismounted and explored a labyrinth of familiar alleys. But the buildings and the alleys all looked alike. Emerging from one trail into the Piazza di Spagna she saw the American Express Company and her heart lifted at the word "American" on the sign. There was a light in the window and hurrying across the square she tried the door, but it was locked and inside the clock stood at seven. Then she thought of Collis Clay.

She remembered the name of his hotel, a stuffy villa sealed in red plush across from the Excelsior. The woman on duty at the office was not disposed to help her—she had no authority to disturb Mr. Clay and refused to let Miss Warren go up to his room alone; convinced finally that this was not an affair of passion she accompanied her.

Collis lay naked upon his bed. He had come in tight and, awakening, it took him some moments to realize his nudity. He atoned for it by an excess of modesty. Taking his clothes into the bathroom he dressed in haste, muttering to himself, "Gosh. She certainly musta got a good look at me." After some telephoning he and Baby found the jail and went to it.

The cell door was open and Dick was slumped on a chair in the guardroom. The carabiniere had washed some of the blood from his face, brushed him, and set his hat concealingly upon his head. Baby stood in the doorway trembling.

"Mr. Clay will stay with you," she said. "I want to get the Consul and a doctor."

"All right."

"Just stay quiet."

"All right."

"I'll be back."

She drove to the Consulate; it was after eight now, and she was permitted to sit in the anteroom. Toward nine the Consul came in and Baby, hysterical with impotence and exhaustion, repeated her story. The Consul was disturbed. He warned her against getting into brawls in strange cities, but he was chiefly concerned that she should wait outside—with despair she read in his elderly eye that he wanted to be mixed up as little as possible in this catastrophe. Waiting on his action she passed the minutes by phoning a doctor to go to Dick. There were other people in the anteroom and several were admitted to the Consul's office. After half an hour she chose the moment of someone's coming out and pushed past the secretary into the room.

"This is outrageous! An American has been beaten half to death and thrown into prison and you make no move to help."

"Just a minute, Mrs.——"

"I've waited long enough. You come right down to the jail and get him out!"

"Mrs.——"

"We're people of considerable standing in America—" Her mouth hardened as she continued. "If it wasn't for the scandal we can—I shall see that your indifference to this matter is reported in the proper quarter. If my brother-in-law were a British citizen he'd have been free hours ago, but you're more concerned with what the police will think than about what you're here for."

"Mrs.——"

"You put on your hat and come with me right away."

The mention of his hat alarmed the Consul, who began to clean his spectacles hurriedly and to ruffle his papers. This proved of no avail: the American Woman, aroused, stood over him; the clean-sweeping irrational temper that had broken the moral back of a race and made a nursery out of a continent, was too much for him. He rang for the vice-consul—Baby had won.

Dick sat in the sunshine that fell profusely through the guard-room window. Collis was with him and two carabinieri, and they were waiting for something to happen. With the narrowed vision of his one eye Dick could see the carabinieri; they were Tuscan peasants with short upper lips and he found it difficult to associate them with the brutality of last night. He sent one of them to fetch him a glass of beer.

The beer made him light-headed and the episode was momentarily illumined by a ray of sardonic humor. Collis was under the impression that the English girl had something to do with the catastrophe, but Dick was sure she had disappeared long before it happened. Collis was still absorbed by the fact that Miss Warren had found him naked on his bed.

Dick's rage had retreated into him a little and he felt a vast criminal irresponsibility. What had happened to him was so awful that nothing could make any difference unless he could choke it to death, and, as this was unlikely, he was hopeless. He would be a different person henceforward, and in his raw state he had bizarre feelings of what the new self would be. The matter had about it the impersonal quality of an act of God. No mature Aryan is able to profit by a humiliation; when he forgives, it has become part of his life, he has identified himself with the thing which has humiliated him—an upshot that in this case was impossible.

When Collis spoke of retribution, Dick shook his head and was silent. A lieutenant of carabinieri, pressed, burnished, vital, came into the room like three men and the guards jumped to attention. He seized the empty beer bottle and directed a stream of scolding at his men. The new spirit was in him, and the first thing was to get the beer bottle out of the guardroom. Dick looked at Collis and laughed.

The vice-consul, an overworked young man named Swanson, arrived, and they started to the court; Collis and Swanson on either side of Dick and the two carabinieri close behind. It was a yellow, hazy morning; the squares and arcades were crowded and Dick, pulling his hat low over his head, walked fast, setting the pace, until one of the short-legged carabinieri ran alongside and protested. Swanson arranged matters.

"I've disgraced you, haven't I?" said Dick jovially.

"You're liable to get killed fighting Italians," replied Swanson sheepishly. "They'll probably let you go this time, but if you were an Italian you'd get a couple of months in prison. And how!"

"Have you ever been in prison?"

Swanson laughed.

"I like him," announced Dick to Clay. "He's a very likeable young man and he gives people excellent advice, but I'll bet he's been to jail himself. Probably spent weeks at a time in jail."

Swanson laughed.

"I mean you want to be careful. You don't know how these people are."

"Oh, I know how they are," broke out Dick, irritably. "They're god damn stinkers." He turned around to the carabinieri: "Did you get that?"

"I'm leaving you here," Swanson said quickly. "I told your sister-in-law I would—our lawyer will meet you upstairs in the court-room. You want to be careful."

"Good-bye." Dick shook hands politely. "Thank you very much. I feel you have a future——"

With another smile Swanson hurried away, resuming his official expression of disapproval.

Now they came into a courtyard on all four sides of which outer stairways mounted to the chambers above. As they crossed the flags a groaning, hissing, booing sound went up from the loiterers in the courtyard, voices full of fury and scorn. Dick stared about.

"What's that?" he demanded, aghast.

One of the carabinieri spoke to a group of men and the sound died away.

They came into the courtroom. A shabby Italian lawyer from the Consulate spoke at length to the judge while Dick and Collis waited aside. Someone who knew English turned from the window that gave on the yard and explained the sound that had accompanied their passage through. A native of Frascati had raped and slain a five-year-old child and was to be brought in that morning—the crowd had assumed it was Dick.

In a few minutes the lawyer told Dick that he was freed—the court considered him punished enough.

"Enough!" Dick cried. "Punished for what?"

"Come along," said Collis. "You can't do anything now."

"But what did I do, except get into a fight with some taxi men?"

"They claim you went up to a detective as if you were going to shake hands with him and hit him——"

"That's not true! I told him I was going to hit him—I didn't know he was a detective."

"You better go along," urged the lawyer.

"Come along." Collis took his arm and they descended the steps.

"I want to make a speech," Dick cried. "I want to explain to these people how I raped a five-year-old girl. Maybe I did——"

"Come along."

Baby was waiting with a doctor in a taxi-cab. Dick did not want to look at her and he disliked the doctor, whose stern manner revealed him as one of that least palatable of European types, the Latin moralist. Dick summed up his conception of the disaster, but no one had much to say. In his room in the Quirinal the doctor washed off the rest of the blood and the oily sweat, set his nose, his fractured ribs and fingers, disinfected the smaller wounds and put a hopeful dressing on the eye. Dick asked for a quarter of a grain of morphine, for he was still wide awake and full of nervous energy. With the morphine he fell asleep; the doctor and Collis left and Baby waited with him until a woman could arrive from the English nursing home. It had been a hard night but she had the satisfaction of feeling that, whatever Dick's previous record was, they now possessed a moral superiority over him for as long as he proved of any use.

BOOK V

THE WAY HOME
1929 - 1930

CHAPTER I

Frau Kaethe Gregorovius overtook her husband on the path of their villa.

"How was Nicole?" she asked mildly; but she spoke out of breath, giving away the fact that she had held the question in her mind during her run.

Franz looked at her in surprise.

"Nicole's not sick. What makes you ask, dearest one?"

"You see her so much—I thought she must be sick."

"We will talk of this in the house."

Kaethe agreed meekly. His study was over in the administration building and the children were with their tutor in the living-room; they went up to the bedroom.

"Excuse me, Franz," said Kaethe before he could speak. "Excuse me, dear, I had no right to say that. I know my obligations and I am proud of them. But there is a bad feeling between Nicole and me."

"Birds in their little nests agree," Franz thundered. Finding the tone inappropriate to the sentiment he repeated his command in the spaced and considered rhythm with which his old master, Doctor Dohmler, could cast significance on the tritest platitude. "Birds—in—their—nests—*agree!*"

"I realize that. You haven't seen me fail in courtesy toward Nicole."

"I see you failing in common sense. Nicole is half a patient—she will possibly remain something of a patient all her life. In the absence of Dick I am responsible." He hesitated; sometimes as a quiet joke he tried to keep news from Kaethe. "There was a telegram from Rome this morning. Dick has had grippe and is starting home tomorrow."

Relieved, Kaethe pursued her course in a less personal tone:

"I think Nicole is less sick than anyone thinks—she only cherishes her illness as an instrument of power. She ought to be in the cinema, like your Norma Talmadge—that's where all American women would be happy."

"Are you jealous of Norma Talmadge, on a film?"

257

"I don't like Americans. They're selfish, *selfish*!"

"You like Dick?"

"I like him," she admitted. "He's different, he thinks of others."

—And so does Norma Talmadge, Franz said to himself. Norma Talmadge must be a fine, noble woman beyond her loveliness. They must compel her to play foolish rôles; Norma Talmadge must be a woman whom it would be a great privilege to know.

Kaethe had forgotten about Norman Talmadge, a vivid shadow that she had fretted bitterly upon one night as they were driving home from the movies in Zurich.

"—Dick married Nicole for her money," she said. "That was his weakness—you hinted as much yourself one night."

"You're being malicious."

"I shouldn't have said that," she retracted. "We must all live together like birds, as you say. But it's difficult when Nicole acts as —when Nicole pulls herself back a little, as if she were holding her breath—as if I *smelt* bad!"

Kaethe had touched a material truth. She did most of her work herself and, frugal, she bought few clothes. An American shop-girl, laundering two changes of underwear every night, would have noticed a hint of yesterday's reawakened sweat about Kaethe's person, less a smell than an ammoniacal reminder of the eternity of toil and decay. To Franz this was as natural as the thick dark scent of Kaethe's hair, and he would have missed it equally; but to Nicole, born hating the smell of a nurse's fingers dressing her, it was an offense only to be endured.

"And the children," Kaethe continued. "She doesn't like them to play with our children—" but Franz had heard enough:

"Hold your tongue—that kind of talk can hurt me professionally, since we owe this clinic to Nicole's money. Let us have lunch."

Kaethe realized that her outburst had been ill-advised, but Franz's last remark reminded her that other Americans had money, and a week later she put her dislike of Nicole into new words.

The occasion was the dinner they tendered the Divers upon Dick's return. Hardly had their footfalls ceased on the path when she shut the door and said to Franz:

"Did you see around his eyes? He's been on a debauch."

"Go gently," Franz requested. "Dick told me about that as soon as he came home. He was boxing on the trans-Atlantic trip.

The American passengers box a lot on these trans-Atlantic ships."

"I believe that?" she scoffed. "It hurts him to move one of his arms and he has an unhealed scar on his temple—you can see where the hair's been cut away."

Franz had not noticed these details.

"But what?" Kaethe demanded. "Do you think that sort of thing does the clinic any good? The liquor I smelt on him tonight, and several other times since he's been back."

She slowed her voice to fit the gravity of what she was about to say: "Dick is no longer a serious man."

Franz rocked his shoulders up the stairs, shaking off her persistence. In their bedroom he turned on her.

"He is most certainly a serious man and a brilliant man. Of all the men who have recently taken their degrees in neuropathology in Zurich, Dick has been regarded as the most brilliant—more brilliant than I could ever be."

"For shame!"

"It's the truth—the shame would be not to admit it. I turn to Dick when cases are highly involved. His publications are still standard in their line—go into any medical library and ask. Most students think he's an Englishman—they don't believe that such thoroughness could come out of America." He groaned domestically, taking his pajamas from under the pillow, "I can't understand why you talk this way, Kaethe—I thought you liked him."

"For shame!" Kaethe said. "You're the solid one, you do the work. It's a case of hare and tortoise—and in my opinion the hare's race is almost done."

"Tch! Tch!"

"Very well, then. It's true."

With his open hand he pushed down air briskly.

"Stop!"

The upshot was that they had exchanged viewpoints like debaters. Kaethe admitted to herself that she had been too hard on Dick, whom she admired and of whom she stood in awe, who had been so appreciative and understanding of herself. As for Franz, once Kaethe's idea had had time to sink in, he never after believed that Dick was a serious person. And as time went on he convinced himself that he had never thought so.

CHAPTER II

DICK TOLD NICOLE AN expurgated version of the catastrophe in Rome—in his version he had gone philanthropically to the rescue of a drunken friend. He could trust Baby Warren to hold her tongue, since he had painted the disastrous effect of the truth upon Nicole. All this, however, was a low hurdle compared with the lingering effect of the episode upon him.

In reaction he took himself for an intensified beating in his work, so that Franz, trying to break with him, could find no basis on which to begin a disagreement. No friendship worth the name was ever destroyed in an hour without some painful flesh being torn —so Franz let himself believe with ever-increasing conviction that Dick travelled intellectually and emotionally at such rate of speed that the vibrations jarred him; this was a contrast that had previously been considered a virtue in their relation. So, for the shoddiness of needs, are shoes made out of last year's hide.

Yet it was May before Franz found an opportunity to insert the first wedge. Dick came into his office white and tired one noon and sat down, saying:

"Well, she's gone."

"She's dead?"

"The heart quit."

Dick sat exhausted in the chair nearest the door. During three nights he had remained with the scabbed anonymous woman-artist he had come to love, formally to portion out the adrenalin, but really to throw as much wan light as he could into the darkness ahead.

Half appreciating his feeling, Franz travelled quickly over an opinion:

"It was neuro-syphilis. All the Wassermans we took won't tell me differently. The spinal fluid——"

"Never mind," said Dick. "Oh, God, never mind! If she cared enough about her secret to take it away with her, let it go at that."

"You better lay off for a day."

"Don't worry, I'm going to."

Franz had his wedge; looking up from the telegram that he was writing to the woman's brother he inquired: "Or do you want to take a little trip?"

"Not now."

"I don't mean a vacation. There's a case in Lausanne. I've been on the phone with a Chilean all morning——"

"She was so damn brave," said Dick. "And it took her so long." Franz shook his head sympathetically and Dick got himself together. "Excuse me for interrupting you."

"This is just a change. The situation is a father's problem with his son—the father can't get the son up here. He wants somebody to come down there."

"What is it? Alcoholism? Homosexuality? When you say Lausanne——"

"A little of everything."

"I'll go down. Is there any money in it?"

"Quite a lot, I'd say. Count on staying two or three days, and get the boy up here if he needs to be watched. In any case take your time, take your ease; combine business with pleasure."

After two hours' train sleep Dick felt renewed, and he approached the interview with Señor Pardo y Ciudad Real in good spirits.

These interviews were much of a type. Often the sheer hysteria of the family representative was as interesting psychologically as the condition of the patient. This one was no exception: Señor Pardo y Ciudad Real, a handsome iron-gray Spaniard, noble of carriage, with all the appurtenances of wealth and power, raged up and down his suite in the Hôtel des Trois Mondes and told the story of his son with no more self-control than a drunken woman.

"I am at the end of my invention. My son is corrupt. He was corrupt at Harrow, he was corrupt at King's College, Cambridge. He's incorrigibly corrupt. Now that there is this drinking it is more and more obvious how he is, and there is continual scandal. I have tried everything—I worked out a plan with a doctor friend of mine, sent them together for a tour of Spain. Every evening Francisco had an injection of cantharides and then the two went together to a reputable bordello—for a week or so it seemed to work but the result was nothing. Finally last week in this very room, rather in that bathroom"—he pointed at it, "—I made Francisco strip to the waist and lashed him with a whip——"

Exhausted with his emotion he sat down and Dick spoke:

"That was foolish—the trip to Spain was futile also—" He struggled against an upsurging hilarity—that any reputable medical man should have lent himself to such an amateurish experiment! "—Señor, I must tell you that in these cases we can promise nothing. In the case of the drinking we can often accomplish something—with proper co-operation. The first thing is to see the boy and get enough of his confidence to find whether he has any insight into the matter."

—The boy, with whom he sat on the terrace, was about twenty, handsome and alert.

"I'd like to know your attitude," Dick said. "Do you feel that the situation is getting worse? And do you want to do anything about it?"

"I suppose I do," said Francisco, "I am very unhappy."

"Do you think it's from the drinking or from the abnormality?"

"I think the drinking is caused by the other." He was serious for a while—suddenly an irrepressible facetiousness broke through and he laughed, saying, "It's hopeless. At King's I was known as the Queen of Chile. That trip to Spain—all it did was to make me nauseated by the sight of a woman."

Dick caught him up sharply.

"If you're happy in this mess, then I can't help you and I'm wasting my time."

"No, let's talk—I despise most of the others so." There was some manliness in the boy, perverted now into an active resistance to his father. But he had the typically roguish look in his eyes that homosexuals assume in discussing the subject.

"It's a hole-and-corner business at best," Dick told him. "You'll spend your life on it, and its consequences, and you won't have time or energy for any other decent or social act. If you want to face the world you'll have to begin by controlling your sensuality —and, first of all, the drinking that provokes it——"

He talked automatically, having abandoned the case ten minutes before. They talked pleasantly through another hour about the boy's home in Chile and about his ambitions. It was as close as Dick had ever come to comprehending such a character from any but the pathological angle—he gathered that this very charm made it possible for Francisco to perpetrate his outrages and, for Dick, charm always had an independent existence, whether it was the mad gallantry of the wretch who had died in the clinic this morning, or the courageous grace which this lost young man brought to a drab old story. Dick tried to dissect it into pieces small enough to store away, realizing that the totality of a life may be different in quality from its segments, and also that life during one's late thirties seemed capable of being observed only in segments. His love for Nicole and Rosemary, his friendship with Abe North, with Tommy Barban in the broken universe of the war's ending—in such contacts the personalities had seemed to press up so close to him that he became the personality itself; there seemed some necessity of taking all or nothing; it was as if for the remainder of his life he was condemned to carry with him the egos of certain people, early met and early loved, and to be only as complete as they were complete themselves. There was some element of loneliness involved—so easy to be loved —so hard to love.

As he sat on the veranda with young Francisco, a ghost of the past swam into his ken. A tall, singularly swaying male detached himself from the shrubbery and approached Dick and Francisco with feeble resolution. For a moment he formed such an apologetic part of the vibrant landscape that Dick scarcely remarked him— then Dick was on his feet, shaking hands with an abstracted air, thinking, "My God, I've stirred up a nest!" and trying to recollect the man's name.

"This is Doctor Diver, isn't it?"

"Well, well—Mr. Dumphry, isn't it?"

"Royal Dumphry. I had the pleasure of having dinner one night in that lovely garden of yours."

"Of course." Trying to dampen Mr. Dumphry's enthusiasm, Dick went into impersonal chronology. "It was in nineteen—twenty-four —or twenty-five——"

He had remained standing, but Royal Dumphry, shy as he had seemed at first, was no laggard with his pick and spade; he spoke to Francisco in a flip, intimate manner, but the latter, ashamed of him, joined Dick in trying to freeze him away.

"Doctor Diver—one thing I want to say before you go. I've never forgotten that evening in your garden—how nice you and your wife were. To me it's one of the finest memories in my life, one of the happiest ones. I've always thought of it as the most civilized gathering of people that I have ever known."

Dick continued a crab-like retreat toward the nearest door of the hotel.

"I'm glad you remembered it so pleasantly. Now I've got to see——"

"I understand," Royal Dumphry pursued sympathetically. "I hear he's dying."

"Who's dying?"

"Perhaps I shouldn't have said that—but we have the same physician."

Dick paused, regarding him in astonishment. "Who're you talking about?"

"Why, your wife's father—perhaps I——"

"My *what?*"

"I suppose—you mean I'm the first person——"

"You mean my wife's father is here, in Lausanne."

"Why, I thought you knew—I thought that was why you were here."

"What doctor is taking care of him?"

Dick scrawled the name in a notebook, excused himself, and hurried to a telephone booth.

It was convenient for Doctor Dangeu to see Doctor Diver at his house immediately.

Doctor Dangeu was a young Génevois; for a moment he was afraid that he was going to lose a profitable patient, but, when Dick reassured him, he divulged the fact that Mr. Warren was indeed dying.

"He is only fifty but the liver has stopped restoring itself; the precipitating factor is alcoholism."

"Doesn't respond?"

"The man can take nothing except liquids—I give him three days, or at most, a week."

"Does his elder daughter, Miss Warren, know his condition?"

"By his own wish no one knows except the man-servant. It was only this morning I felt I had to tell him—he took it excitedly, although he has been in a very religious and resigned mood from the beginning of his illness."

Dick considered: "Well—" he decided slowly, "in any case I'll take care of the family angle. But I imagine they would want a consultation."

"As you like."

"I know I speak for them when I ask you to call in one of the best-known medical men around the lake—Herbrugge, from Geneva."

"I was thinking of Herbrugge."

"Meanwhile I'm here for a day at least and I'll keep in touch with you."

That evening Dick went to Señor Pardo y Ciudad Real and they talked.

"We have large estates in Chile—" said the old man. "My son could well be taking care of them. Or I can get him in any one of a dozen enterprises in Paris—" He shook his head and paced across the windows against a spring rain so cheerful that it didn't even drive the swans to cover. "My only son! Can't you take him with you?"

The Spaniard knelt suddenly at Dick's feet.

"Can't you cure my only son? I believe in you—you can take him with you, cure him."

"It's impossible to commit a person on such grounds. I wouldn't if I could."

The Spaniard got up from his knees.

"I have been hasty—I have been driven——"

Descending to the lobby Dick met Doctor Dangeu in the elevator.

"I was about to call your room," the latter said. "Can we speak out on the terrace?"

"Is Mr. Warren dead?" Dick demanded.

"He is the same—the consultation is in the morning. Meanwhile he wants to see his daughter—your wife—with the greatest fervor. It seems there was some quarrel——"

"I know all about that."

The doctors looked at each other, thinking.

"Why don't you talk to him before you make up your mind?" Dangeu suggested. "His death will be graceful—merely a weakening and sinking."

With an effort Dick consented.

"All right."

The suite in which Devereux Warren was gracefully weakening and sinking was of the same size as that of the Señor Pardo y Ciudad Real—throughout this hotel there were many chambers where rich ruins, fugitives from justice, claimants to the thrones of mediatized principalities, lived on the derivatives of opium or barbitol listening eternally, as to an inescapable radio, to the coarse melodies of old sins. This corner of Europe does not so much draw people as accept them without inconvenient questions. Routes cross here —people bound for private sanitariums or tuberculosis resorts in the mountains, people who are no longer persona grata in France or Italy.

The suite was darkened. A nun with a holy face was nursing the man whose emaciated fingers stirred a rosary on the white sheet. He was still handsome and his voice summoned up a thick burr of individuality as he spoke to Dick, after Dangeu had left them together.

"We get a lot of understanding at the end of life. Only now, Doctor Diver, do I realize what it was all about."

Dick waited.

"I've been a bad man. You must know how little right I have to see Nicole again, yet a Bigger Man than either of us says to forgive and to pity." The rosary slipped from his weak hands and slid off the smooth bed covers. Dick picked it up for him. "If I could see Nicole for ten minutes I would go happy out of the world."

"It's not a decision I can make for myself," said Dick. "Nicole is not strong." He made his decision but pretended to hesitate. "I can put it up to my professional associate."

"What your associate says goes with me—very well, Doctor. Let me tell you my debt to you is so large——"

Dick stood up quickly.

"I'll let you know the result through Doctor Dangeu."

In his room he called the clinic on the Zugersee. After a long time Kaethe answered from her own house.

"I want to get in touch with Franz."

"Franz is up on the mountain. I'm going up myself—is it something I can tell him, Dick?"

"It's about Nicole—her father is dying here in Lausanne. Tell Franz that, to show him it's important; and ask him to phone me from up there."

"I will."

"Tell him I'll be in my room here at the hotel from three to five, and again from seven to eight, and after that to page me in the dining-room."

In plotting these hours he forgot to add that Nicole was not to be told; when he remembered it he was talking into a dead telephone. Certainly Kaethe should realize.

. . . Kaethe had no exact intention of telling Nicole about the call when she rode up the deserted hill of mountain wildflowers and secret winds, where the patients were taken to ski in winter and to climb in spring. Getting off the train she saw Nicole shepherding the children through some organized romp. Approaching, she drew her arm gently along Nicole's shoulder, saying: "You are clever with children—you must teach them more about swimming in the summer."

In the play they had grown hot, and Nicole's reflex in drawing away from Kaethe's arm was automatic to the point of rudeness. Kaethe's hand fell awkwardly into space, and then she too reacted, verbally, and deplorably.

"Did you think I was going to embrace you?" she demanded sharply. "It was only about Dick, I talked on the phone to him and I was sorry——"

"Is anything the matter with Dick?"

Kaethe suddenly realized her error, but she had taken a tactless course and there was no choice but to answer as Nicole pursued her with reiterated questions: ". . . then *why* were you sorry?"

"Nothing about Dick. I must talk to Franz."

"It *is* about Dick."

There was terror in her face and collaborating alarm in the faces of the Diver children, near at hand. Kaethe collapsed with: "Your father is ill in Lausanne—Dick wants to talk to Franz about it."

"Is he very sick?" Nicole demanded—just as Franz came up with his hearty hospital manner. Gratefully Kaethe passed the remnant of the buck to him, but the damage was done.

"I'm going to Lausanne," announced Nicole.

"One minute," said Franz. "I'm not sure it's advisable. I must first talk on the phone to Dick."

"Then I'll miss the train down," Nicole protested, "and then I'll miss the three o'clock from Zurich. If my father is dying I must—" She left this in the air, afraid to formulate it. "I *must* go. I'll have to run for the train." She was running even as she spoke toward the sequence of flat cars that crowned the bare hill with bursting steam and sound. Over her shoulder she called back, "If you phone Dick tell him I'm coming, Franz!"

. . . Dick was in his own room in the hotel reading the *New York Herald* when the swallow-like nun rushed in—simultaneously the phone rang.

"Is he dead?" Dick demanded of the nun, hopefully.

"Monsieur, il est parti—he has gone away."

"*Comment?*"

"Il est parti—his man and his baggage have gone away too!"

It was incredible. A man in that condition to arise and depart.

Dick answered the phone-call from Franz. "You shouldn't have told Nicole," he protested.

"Kaethe told her, very unwisely."

"I suppose it was my fault. Never tell a thing to a woman till it's done. However, I'll meet Nicole . . . say, Franz, the craziest thing has happened down here—the old boy took up his bed and walked. . . ."

"At what? What did you say?"

"I say he walked, old Warren—he walked!"

"But why not?"

"He was supposed to be dying of general collapse . . . he got up and walked away, back to Chicago, I guess. . . . I don't know, the nurse is here now. . . . I don't know, Franz—I've just heard about it. . . . Call me later."

He spent the better part of two hours tracing Warren's movements. The patient had found an opportunity between the change of day and night nurses to resort to the bar, where he had gulped down four whiskeys; he paid his hotel bill with a thousand-dollar note, instructing the desk that the change should be sent after him, and departed, presumably for America. A last-minute dash by Dick and Dangeu to overtake him at the station resulted only in Dick's failing to meet Nicole; when they did meet in the lobby of the hotel she seemed suddenly tired, and there was a tight purse to her lips that disquieted him.

"How's father?" she demanded.

"He's much better. He seemed to have a good deal of reserve energy after all." He hesitated, breaking it to her easy. "In fact, he got up and went away."

Wanting a drink, for the chase had occupied the dinner hour, he led her, puzzled, toward the grill, and continued as they occupied two leather easy-chairs and ordered a high-ball and a glass of beer: "The man who was taking care of him made a wrong prognosis or something—wait a minute, I've hardly had time to think the thing out myself."

"He's *gone?*"

"He got the evening train for Paris."

They sat silent. From Nicole flowed a vast tragic apathy.

"It was instinct," Dick said, finally. "He was really dying, but he tried to get a resumption of rhythm—he's not the first person that ever walked off his death-bed—like an old clock—you know, you shake it and somehow from sheer habit it gets going again. Now your father——"

"Oh, don't tell me," she said.

"His principal fuel was fear," he continued. "He got afraid, and off he went. He'll probably live till ninety——"

"Please don't tell me any more," she said. "Please don't—I couldn't stand any more."

"All right. The little devil I came down to see is hopeless. We may as well go back tomorrow."

"I don't see why you have to—come in contact with all this," she burst forth.

"Oh, don't you? Sometimes I don't either."

She put her hand on his.

"Oh, I'm sorry I said that, Dick."

Someone had brought a phonograph into the bar and they sat listening to "The Wedding of the Painted Doll."

CHAPTER III

ONE MORNING A WEEK later, stopping at the desk for his mail, Dick became aware of some extra commotion outside: Patient Von Cohn Morris was going away. His parents, Australians, were putting his baggage vehemently into a large limousine, and beside them stood Doctor Lladislau protesting with ineffectual attitudes against the violent gesturings of Morris, senior. The young man was regarding his embarkation with aloof cynicism as Doctor Diver approached.

"Isn't this a little sudden, Mr. Morris?"

Mr. Morris started as he saw Dick—his florid face and the large checks on his suit seemed to turn off and on like electric lights. He approached Dick as though to strike him.

"High time we left, we and those who have come with us," he began, and paused for breath. "It is high time, Doctor Diver. High time."

"Will you come into my office?" Dick suggested.

"Not I! I'll talk to you, but I'm washing my hands of you and your place."

"I'm sorry about that."

He shook his finger at Dick. "I was just telling this doctor here. We've wasted our time and our money."

Doctor Lladislau stirred in a feeble negative, signalling up a vague Slavic evasiveness. Dick had never liked Lladislau. He managed to walk the excited Australian along the path in the direction of his office, trying to persuade him to enter; but the man shook his head.

"It's *you*, Doctor Diver, *you*, the very man. I went to Doctor Lladislau because you were not to be found, Doctor Diver, and because Doctor Gregorovius is not expected until the nightfall, and I would not wait. No, sir! I would not wait a minute after my son told me the truth."

He came up menacingly to Dick, who kept his hands loose enough to drop him if it seemed necessary. "My son is here for alcoholism, and he told us he smelt liquor on your breath. Yes, sir!" He made a quick, apparently unsuccessful sniff. "Not once, but twice Von Cohn says he has smelt liquor on your breath. I and my lady have never touched a drop of it in our lives. We hand Von Cohn to you to be cured, and within a month he twice smells liquor on your breath! What kind of cure is that there?"

Dick hesitated; Mr. Morris was quite capable of making a scene on the clinic drive.

"After all, Mr. Morris, some people are not going to give up what they regard as food because of your son——"

"But you're a doctor, man!" cried Morris furiously. "When the workmen drink their beer that's bad cess to them—but you're here supposing to cure——"

"This has gone too far. Your son came to us because of kleptomania."

"What was behind it?" The man was almost shrieking. "Drink—black drink. Do you know what color black is? It's black! My own uncle was hung by the neck because of it, you hear! My son comes to a sanitarium, and a doctor reeks of it!"

"I must ask you to leave."

"You *ask* me! We *are* leaving!"

"If you could be a little temperate we could tell you the results of the treatment to date. Naturally, since you feel as you do, we would not want your son as a patient——"

"You dare to use the word temperate to me?"

Dick called to Doctor Lladislau and, as he approached, said: "Will you represent us in saying good-bye to the patient and to his family?"

He bowed slightly to Morris and went into his office, and stood rigid for a moment just inside the door. He watched until they drove away, the gross parents, the bland, degenerate offspring: it was easy to prophesy the family's swing around Europe, bullying their betters with hard ignorance and hard money. But the question that absorbed Dick after the disappearance of the caravan was to what extent he had provoked this. He drank claret with each meal, took a night-cap, generally in the form of hot rum, and sometimes he tippled with gin in the afternoons—gin was the most difficult to detect on the breath. He was averaging a half-pint of alcohol a day, too much for his system to burn up.

Dismissing a tendency to justify himself, he sat down at his desk and wrote out, like a prescription, a régime that would cut his liquor in half. Doctors, chauffeurs, and Protestant clergymen could never smell of liquor, as could painters, brokers, cavalry leaders; Dick blamed himself only for indiscretion. But the matter was by no means clarified half an hour later when Franz, revivified by an Alpine fortnight, rolled up the drive, so eager to resume work that he was plunged in it before he reached his office. Dick met him there.

"How was Mount Everest?"

"We could very well have done Mount Everest the rate we were doing. We thought of it. How goes it all? How is my Kaethe, how is your Nicole?"

"All goes smooth domestically. But my God, Franz, we had a rotten scene this morning."

"How? What was it?"

Dick walked around the room while Franz got in touch with his villa by telephone. After the family exchange was over, Dick said: "The Morris boy was taken away—there was a row."

Franz's buoyant face fell.

"I knew he'd left. I met Lladislau on the veranda."

"What did Lladislau say?"

"Just that young Morris had gone—that you'd tell me about it. What about it?"

"The usual incoherent reasons."

"He was a devil, that boy."

"He was a case for anesthesia," Dick agreed. "Anyhow, the father had beaten Lladislau into a colonial subject by the time I came along. What about Lladislau? Do we keep him? I say no—he's not much of a man, he can't seem to cope with anything." Dick hesitated on the verge of the truth, swung away to give himself space within which to recapitulate. Franz perched on the edge of a desk, still in his linen duster and travelling gloves. Dick said:

"One of the remarks the boy made to his father was that your distinguished collaborator was a drunkard. The man is a fanatic, and the descendant seems to have caught traces of vin-du-pays on me."

Franz sat down, musing on his lower lip. "You can tell me at length," he said finally.

"Why not now?" Dick suggested. "You must know I'm the last man to abuse liquor." His eyes and Franz's glinted on each other, pair on pair. "Lladislau let the man get so worked up that I was on the defensive. It might have happened in front of patients, and you can imagine how hard it could be to defend yourself in a situation like that!"

Franz took off his gloves and coat. He went to the door and told the secretary, "Don't disturb us." Coming back into the room he flung himself at the long table and fooled with his mail, reasoning as little as is characteristic of people in such postures, rather summoning up a suitable mask for what he had to say.

"Dick, I know well that you are a temperate, well-balanced man, even though we do not entirely agree on the subject of alcohol. But a time has come—Dick, I must say frankly that I have been aware several times that you have had a drink when it was not the moment to have one. There is some reason. Why not try another leave of abstinence?"

"Absence," Dick corrected him automatically. "It's no solution for me to go away."

They were both chafed, Franz at having his return marred and blurred.

"Sometimes you don't use your common sense, Dick."

"I never understood what common sense meant applied to complicated problems—unless it means that a general practitioner can perform a better operation than a specialist."

He was seized by an overwhelming disgust for the situation. To explain, to patch—these were not natural functions at their age—better to continue with the cracked echo of an old truth in the ears.

"This is no go," he said suddenly.

"Well, that's occurred to me," Franz admitted. "Your heart isn't in this project any more, Dick."

"I know. I want to leave—we could strike some arrangement about taking Nicole's money out gradually."

"I have thought about that too, Dick—I have seen this coming.

I am able to arrange other backing, and it will be possible to take all your money out by the end of the year."

Dick had not intended to come to a decision so quickly, nor was he prepared for Franz's so ready acquiescence in the break, yet he was relieved. Not without desperation he had long felt the ethics of his profession dissolving into a lifeless mass.

CHAPTER IV

THE DIVERS WOULD RETURN to the Riviera, which was home. The Villa Diana had been rented again for the summer, so they divided the intervening time between German spas and French cathedral towns, where they were always happy for a few days. Dick wrote a little with no particular method; it was one of those parts of life that are an awaiting; not upon Nicole's health, which seemed to thrive on travel, nor upon work, but simply an awaiting. The factor that gave purposefulness to the period was the children.

Dick's interest in them increased with their ages, now seven and nine. He managed to reach them over the heads of employees on the principle that both the forcing of children and the fear of forcing them were inadequate substitutes for the long, careful watchfulness, the checking and balancing and reckoning of accounts, to the end that there should be no slip below a certain level of duty. He came to know them much better than Nicole did, and in expansive moods over the wines of several countries he talked and played with them at length. They had that wistful charm, almost sadness, peculiar to children who have learned early not to cry or laugh with abandon; they were apparently moved to no extremes of emotion, but were content with a simple regimen and the simple pleasures allowed them. They lived on the even tenor found advisable in the experience of old families of the Western world, brought up rather than brought out. Dick thought, for example, that nothing was more conducive to the development of observation than compulsory silence.

Lanier was an unpredictable boy with an inhuman curiosity. "Well, how many Pomeranians would it take to lick a lion, father?" was typical of the questions with which he harassed Dick. Topsy was easier. She was seven and very fair and exquisitely made like Nicole, and in the past Dick had worried about that. Lately she had become as robust as any American child. He was satisfied with them both, but conveyed the fact to them only in a tacit way. They were not let off breaches of good conduct—"Either one learns politeness at home," Dick said, "or the world teaches it to you with a whip and you may get hurt in the process. What do I care whether Topsy 'adores' me or not? I'm not bringing her up to be my wife."

Another element that distinguished this summer and autumn for the Divers was a plenitude of money. Owing to the sale of their interest in the clinic, and to developments in America, there was now so much that the mere spending of it, the care of goods, was an absorption in itself. The style in which they travelled seemed fabulous.

Regard them, for example, as the train slows up at Boyen, where they are to spend a fortnight visiting. The shifting from the wagon-lit has begun at the Italian frontier. The governess's maid and Madame Diver's maid have come up from second class to help with the baggage and the dogs. Mlle. Bellois will superintend the hand-luggage, leaving the Sealyhams to one maid and the pair of Pekinese to the other. It is not necessarily poverty of spirit that makes a woman surround herself with life—it can be a superabundance of interest and, except during her flashes of illness, Nicole was capable of being curator of it all. Presently from the van would be unloaded four wardrobe trunks, a shoe trunk, three hat trunks and two hat boxes, a chest of servants' trunks, a portable filing-cabinet, a medicine case, a spirit-lamp container, a picnic set, four tennis rackets in presses and cases, a phonograph, a typewriter. Distributed among the spaces reserved for family and entourage were two dozen supplementary grips, satchels, and packages, each one numbered, down to the tag on the cane case. Thus, all of it could be checked up in two minutes on any station platform, some for storage, some for accompaniment from the "light trip list" or the "heavy trip list," constantly revised and carried on metal-edged plaques in Nicole's purse. She had devised the system as a child when travelling with her failing mother. It was equivalent to the system of a regimental supply officer who must think of the bellies and equipment of three thousand men.

The Divers flocked from the train into the early-gathered twilight of the valley. The village people watched the debarkation with an awe akin to that which followed the Italian pilgrimages of Lord Byron a century before. Their hostess was the Contessa di Minghetti, lately Mary North. The journey that had begun in a room over the shop of a paperhanger in Newark had ended in an extraordinary marriage.

"Conte di Minghetti" was merely a papal title; the wealth of Mary's husband flowed from his being ruler-owner of manganese deposits in southwestern Asia. He was not quite light enough to travel in a pullman south of Mason-Dixon; he was of the Kabyle-Berber-Sabæan-Hindu strain that belts across north Africa and Asia, more sympathetic to the European than the mongrel faces of the ports.

When these princely households, one of the East, one of the West, faced each other on the station platform, the splendor of the Divers seemed pioneer simplicity by comparison. Their hosts were accompanied by an Italian major-domo carrying a staff, by a quartet of turbaned retainers on motorcycles, and by two half-veiled females who stood respectfully a little behind Mary and salaamed at Nicole, making her jump with the gesture.

To Mary as well as to the Divers the greeting was faintly comic; Mary gave an apologetic, belittling giggle; yet her voice, as she introduced her husband by his Asiatic title, flew proud and high.

In their rooms as they dressed for dinner, Dick and Nicole grimaced at each other in an awed way: such rich as want to be thought democratic pretend in private to be swept off their feet by swank.

"Little Mary North knows what she wants," Dick muttered through his shaving cream. "Abe educated her, and now she's married to a Buddha. If Europe ever goes Bolshevik she'll turn up as the bride of Stalin."

Nicole looked around from her dressing-case. "Watch your tongue, Dick, will you?" But she laughed. "They're very swell. The warships all fire at them or salute them or something. Mary rides in the royal bus in London."

"All right," he agreed. As he heard Nicole at the door asking for pins, he called, "I wonder if I could have some whiskey; I feel the mountain air."

"She'll see to it," presently Nicole called through the bathroom door. "It was one of those women who were at the station. She has her veil off."

"What did Mary tell you about life?" he asked.

"She didn't say so much. She was interested in high life—she asked me a lot of questions about my genealogy and all that sort of thing, as if I knew anything about it. But it seems the bridegroom has two very tan children by another marriage—one of them ill with some Asiatic thing they can't diagnose. I've got to warn the children. Sounds very peculiar to me. Mary will see how we'd feel about it." She stood worrying a minute.

"She'll understand," Dick reassured her. "Probably the child's in bed."

At dinner Dick talked to Hosain, who had been at an English public school. Hosain wanted to know about stocks and about Hollywood, and Dick, whipping up his imagination with champagne, told him preposterous tales.

"Billions?" Hosain demanded.

"Trillions," Dick assured him.

"I didn't truly realize——"

"Well, perhaps millions," Dick conceded. "Every hotel guest is assigned a harem—or what amounts to a harem."

"Other than the actors and directors?"

"Every hotel guest—even travelling salesmen. Why, they tried to send me up a dozen candidates, but Nicole wouldn't stand for it."

Nicole reproved him when they were in their room alone. "Why so many highballs? Why did you use your word spic in front of him?"

"Excuse me, I meant smoke. The tongue slipped."

"Dick, this isn't faintly like you."

"Excuse me again. I'm not much like myself any more."

That night Dick opened a bathroom window, giving on a narrow and tubular court of the château, gray as rats but echoing at the moment to plaintive and peculiar music, sad as a flute. Two men were chanting in an Eastern language or dialect full of k's and l's —he leaned out but he could not see them; there was obviously a religious significance in the sounds, and tired and emotionless he let them pray for him too, but what for, save that he should not lose himself in his increasing melancholy, he did not know.

Next day, over a thinly wooded hillside, they shot scrawny birds, distant poor relations to the partridge. It was done in a vague imitation of the English manner, with a corps of inexperienced beaters whom Dick managed to miss by firing only directly overhead.

On their return Lanier was waiting in their suite.

"Father, you said tell you immediately if we were near the sick boy."

Nicole whirled about, immediately on guard.

"—so, Mother," Lanier continued, turning to her, "the boy takes a bath every evening and tonight he took his bath just before mine and I had to take mine in his water, and it was dirty."

"What? Now what?"

"I saw them take Tony out of it, and then they called me into it and the water was dirty."

"But—did you take it?"

"Yes, Mother."

"Heavens!" she exclaimed to Dick.

He demanded: "Why didn't Lucienne draw your bath?"

"Lucienne can't. It's a funny heater—it reached out of itself and burned her arm last night and she's afraid of it, so one of those two women——"

"You go in this bathroom and take a bath now."

"Don't say *I* told you," said Lanier from the doorway.

Dick went in and sprinkled the tub with sulphur; closing the door he said to Nicole:

"Either we speak to Mary or we'd better get out."

She agreed and he continued: "People think their children are constitutionally cleaner than other people's, and their diseases are less contagious."

Dick came in and helped himself from the decanter, chewing a biscuit savagely in the rhythm of the pouring water in the bathroom.

"Tell Lucienne that she's got to learn about the heater—" he suggested. At that moment the Asiatic woman came in person to the door.

"El Contessa——"

Dick beckoned her inside and closed the door.

"Is the little sick boy better?" he inquired pleasantly.

"Better, yes, but he still has the eruptions frequently."

"That's too bad—I'm very sorry. But you see our children mustn't be bathed in his water. That's out of the question—I'm sure your mistress would be furious if she had known you had done a thing like that."

"I?" She seemed thunderstruck. "Why, I merely saw your maid had difficulty with the heater—I told her about it and started the water."

"But with a sick person you must empty the bathwater entirely out, and clean the tub."

"I?"

Chokingly the woman drew a long breath, uttered a convulsed sob and rushed from the room.

"She mustn't get up on western civilization at our expense," he said grimly.

At dinner that night he decided that it must inevitably be a truncated visit: about his own country Hosain seemed to have observed only that there were many mountains and some goats and herders of goats. He was a reserved young man—to draw him out would have required the sincere effort that Dick now reserved for his family. Soon after dinner Hosain left Mary and the Divers to themselves, but the old unity was split—between them lay the restless social fields that Mary was about to conquer. Dick was relieved when, at nine-thirty, Mary received and read a note and got up.

"You'll have to excuse me. My husband is leaving on a short trip—and I must be with him."

Next morning, hard on the heels of the servant bringing coffee, Mary entered their room. She was dressed and they were not dressed, and she had the air of having been up for some time. Her face was toughened with quiet jerky fury.

"What is this story about Lanier having been bathed in a dirty bath?"

Dick began to protest, but she cut through:

"*What* is this story that you commanded my husband's sister to clean Lanier's tub?"

She remained on her feet staring at them, as they sat impotent as idols in their beds, weighed by their trays. Together they exclaimed: "His *sister!*"

"That you ordered one of his sisters to clean out a tub!"

"We didn't—" their voices rang together saying the same thing, "—I spoke to the native servant——"

"You spoke to Hosain's sister."

Dick could only say: "I supposed they were two maids."

"You were told they were Himadoun."

"What?" Dick got out of bed and into a robe.

"I explained it to you at the piano night before last. Don't tell me you were too merry to understand."

"Was that what you said? I didn't hear the beginning. I didn't connect the—we didn't make any connection, Mary. Well, all we can do is see her and apologize."

"See her and apologize! I explained to you that when the oldest member of the family—when the oldest one marries, well, the two oldest sisters consecrate themselves to being Himadoun, to being his wife's ladies-in-waiting."

"Was that why Hosain left the house last night?"

Mary hesitated; then nodded.

"He had to—they all left. His honor makes it necessary."

Now both the Divers were up and dressing; Mary went on:

"And what's all that about the bathwater. As if a thing like that could happen in this house! We'll ask Lanier about it."

Dick sat on the bedside indicating in a private gesture to Nicole that she should take over. Meanwhile Mary went to the door and spoke to an attendant in Italian.

"Wait a minute," Nicole said. "I won't have that."

"You accused us," answered Mary, in a tone she had never used to Nicole before. "Now I have a right to see."

"I won't have the child brought in." Nicole threw on her clothes as though they were chain mail.

"That's all right," said Dick. "Bring Lanier in. We'll settle this bathtub matter—fact or myth."

Lanier, half clothed mentally and physically, gazed at the angered faces of the adults.

"Listen, Lanier," Mary demanded, "how did you come to think you were bathed in water that had been used before?"

"Speak up," Dick added.

"It was just dirty, that was all."

"Couldn't you hear the new water running, from your room, next door?"

Lanier admitted the possibility but reiterated his point—the water was dirty. He was a little awed; he tried to see ahead:

"It couldn't have been running, because——"

They pinned him down.

"Why not?"

He stood in his little kimono arousing the sympathy of his parents and further arousing Mary's impatience—then he said:

"The water was dirty, it was full of soap-suds."

"When you're not sure what you're saying—" Mary began, but Nicole interrupted.

"Stop it, Mary. If there were dirty suds in the water it was logical to think it was dirty. His father told him to come——"

"There couldn't have been dirty suds in the water."

Lanier looked reproachfully at his father, who had betrayed him. Nicole turned him about by the shoulders and sent him out of the room; Dick broke the tensity with a laugh.

Then, as if the sound recalled the past, the old friendship, Mary guessed how far away from them she had gone and said in a mollifying tone: "It's always like that with children."

Her uneasiness grew as she remembered the past. "You'd be silly to go—Hosain wanted to make this trip anyhow. After all, you're my guests and you just blundered into the thing." But Dick, made more angry by this obliqueness and the use of the word blunder, turned away and began arranging his effects, saying:

"It's too bad about the young women. I'd like to apologize to the one who came in here."

"If you'd only listened on the piano seat!"

"But you've gotten so damned dull, Mary. I listened as long as I could."

"Be quiet!" Nicole advised him.

"I return his compliment," said Mary bitterly. "Good-bye, Nicole." She went out.

After all that there was no question of her coming to see them off; the major-domo arranged the departure. Dick left formal notes for Hosain and the sisters. There was nothing to do except to go, but all of them, especially Lanier, felt bad about it.

"I insist," insisted Lanier on the train, "that it was dirty bath-water."

"That'll do," his father said. "You better forget it—unless you want me to divorce you. Did you know there was a new law in France that you can divorce a child?"

Lanier roared with delight and the Divers were unified again—Dick wondered how many more times it could be done.

CHAPTER V

NICOLE WENT TO THE window and bent over the sill to take a look at the rising altercation on the terrace; the April sun shone pink on the saintly face of Augustine, the cook, and blue on the butcher's knife she waved in her drunken hand. She had been with them since their return to Villa Diana in February.

Because of an obstruction of an awning she could see only Dick's head and his hand holding one of his heavy canes with a bronze knob on it. The knife and the cane, menacing each other, were like tripos and short sword in a gladiatorial combat. Dick's words reached her first:

"—care how much kitchen wine you drink but when I find you digging into a bottle of Chablis Mouton——"

"You talk about drinking!" Augustine cried, flourishing her sabre. "You drink—all the time!"

Nicole called over the awning: "What's the matter, Dick?" and he answered in English:

"The old girl has been polishing off the vintage wines. I'm firing her—at least I'm trying to."

"Heavens! Well, don't let her reach you with that knife."

Augustine shook her knife up at Nicole. Her old mouth was made of two small intersecting cherries.

"I would like to say, Madame, if you knew that your husband drinks over at his Bastide comparatively as a day-laborer——"

"Shut up and get out!" interrupted Nicole. "We'll get the gendarmes."

"*You'll* get the gendarmes! With my brother in the corps! You —a disgusting American?"

In English Dick called up to Nicole:

"Get the children away from the house till I settle this."

"—disgusting Americans who come here and drink up our finest wines," screamed Augustine with the voice of the commune.

Dick mastered a firmer tone.

"You must leave now! I'll pay you what we owe you."

"Very sure you'll pay me! And let me tell you—" she came close and waved the knife so furiously that Dick raised his stick, whereupon she rushed into the kitchen and returned with the carving knife reinforced by a hatchet.

The situation was not prepossessing. Augustine was a strong woman and could be disarmed only at the risk of serious results to herself—and severe legal complications which were the lot of one who molested a French citizen. Trying a bluff Dick called up to Nicole:

"Phone the poste de police." Then to Augustine, indicating her armament, "This means arrest for you."

"Ha-*ha!*" she laughed demoniacally; nevertheless she came no nearer. Nicole phoned the police, but was answered with what was almost an echo of Augustine's laugh. She heard mumbles and passings of the word around—the connection was suddenly broken.

Returning to the window she called down to Dick: "Give her something extra!"

"If I could get to that phone!" As this seemed impracticable, Dick capitulated. For fifty francs, increased to a hundred as he succumbed to the idea of getting her out hastily, Augustine yielded her fortress, covering the retreat with stormy grenades of "Salaud!" She would leave only when her nephew could come for her baggage. Waiting cautiously in the neighborhood of the kitchen Dick heard a cork pop, but he yielded the point. There was no further trouble. When the nephew arrived, all apologetic, Augustine bade Dick a cheerful convivial good-bye and called up, "Au revoir, Madame! Bonne chance!" to Nicole's window.

The Divers went to Nice and dined on a bouillabaisse, which is a stew of rock fish and small lobsters highly seasoned with saffron, and a bottle of cold Chablis. He expressed pity for Augustine.

"I'm not sorry a bit," said Nicole.

"I'm sorry—and yet I wish I'd shoved her over the cliff."

There was little they dared talk about in these days; seldom did they find the right word when it counted, it arrived always a moment too late when one could not reach the other any more. Tonight Augustine's outburst had shaken them from their separate reveries; with the burn and chill of the spiced broth and the parching wine they talked.

"We can't go on like this?" Nicole suggested. "Or can we?—what do you think?" Startled that for the moment Dick did not deny it, she continued, "Some of the time I think it's my fault—I've ruined you."

"So I'm ruined, am I?" he inquired pleasantly.

"I didn't mean that. But you used to want to create things—now you seem to want to smash them up."

She trembled at criticizing him in these broad terms, but his enlarging silence frightened her even more. She guessed that something was developing behind the silence, behind the hard, blue eyes, the almost unnatural interest in the children. Uncharacteristic bursts of temper surprised her—he would suddenly unroll a long scroll of contempt for some person, race, class, way of life, way of thinking. It was as though an incalculable story was telling itself inside him, about which she could only guess in the moments when it broke through the surface.

"After all, what do you get out of this?" she demanded.

"Knowing you're stronger every day. Knowing that your illness follows the law of diminishing returns."

His voice came to her from far off, as though he were speaking of something remote and academic; her alarm made her exclaim, "Dick!" and she thrust her hand forward to his across the table. A reflex pulled Dick's hand back and he added: "There's the whole situation to think of, isn't there? There's not just you." He covered her hand with his and said in the old pleasant voice of a conspirator for pleasure, mischief, profit, and delight:

"See that boat out there?"

It was the motor yacht of T. F. Golding lying placid among the little swells of the Nicean bay, constantly bound upon a romantic voyage that was not dependent upon actual motion. "We'll go out there now and ask the people on board what's the matter with them. We'll find out if they're happy."

"We hardly know him," Nicole objected.

"He urged us. Besides, Baby knows him—she practically married him, doesn't she—didn't she?"

When they put out from the port in a hired launch it was already summer dusk and lights were breaking out in spasms along the rigging of the *Margin*. As they drew up alongside, Nicole's doubts reasserted themselves.

"He's having a party——"

"It's only a radio," he guessed.

They were hailed—a huge white-haired man in a white suit looked down at them, calling:

"Do I recognize the Divers?"

"Boat ahoy, *Margin!*"

Their boat moved under the companionway; as they mounted Golding doubled his huge frame to give Nicole a hand.

"Just in time for dinner."

A small orchestra was plaing astern:

> *"I'm yours for the asking,*
> *But till then you can't ask me to behave——"*

And as Golding's cyclonic arms blew them aft without touching them, Nicole was sorrier they had come, and more impatient at Dick. Having taken up an attitude of aloofness from the gay people here, at the time when Dick's work and her health were incompatible with going about, they had a reputation as refusers. Riviera replacements during the ensuing years interpreted this as a vague unpopularity. Nevertheless, having taken such a stand, Nicole felt it should not be cheaply compromised for a momentary self-indulgence.

As they passed through the principal salon they saw ahead of them figures that seemed to dance in the half light of the circular stern. This was an illusion made by the enchantment of the music, the unfamiliar lighting, and the surrounding presence of water. Actually, save for some busy stewards, the guests loafed on a wide divan that followed the curve of the deck. There were a white, a red, a blurred dress and the laundered chests of several men, of whom one, detaching and identifying himself, brought from Nicole a rare little cry of delight.

"Tommy!"

Brushing aside the Gallicism of his formal dip at her hand, Nicole pressed her face against his. They sat, or rather lay down together, on the Antoninian bench. His handsome face was so dark as to have lost the pleasantness of deep tan, without attaining the blue beauty of Negroes—it was just worn leather. The foreignness of his depigmentation by unknown suns, his nourishment by strange soils, his tongue awkward with the curl of many dialects, his reactions attuned to odd alarms—these things fascinated and rested Nicole; in the moment of meeting she lay on his bosom, spiritually, going out and out. . . . Then self-preservation reasserted itself and, retiring to her own world, she spoke lightly.

"You look just like all the adventurers in the movies—but why do you have to stay away so long?"

Tommy Barban looked at her, uncomprehending but alert; the pupils of his eyes flashed.

"Five years," she continued, in throaty mimicry of nothing. *"Much* too long. Couldn't you only slaughter a certain number of creatures and then come back, and breathe our air for a while?"

In her cherished presence Tommy Europeanized himself quickly.

"Mais pour nous autres héros il faut du temps, Nicole. Nous ne pouvons pas faire de petits exercices d'héroisme—il faut faire les grandes compositions."

"Talk English to me, Tommy."

"Parlez français avec moi, Nicole."

"But the meanings are different. In French you can be heroic and gallant with dignity, and you know it. But in English you can't be heroic and gallant without being a little absurd, and you know that too. That gives me an advantage."

"But after all—" He chuckled suddenly. "Even in English I'm brave, heroic, and all that."

She pretended to be groggy with wonderment, but he was not abashed.

"I only know what I see in the cinema," he said.

"Is it all like the movies?"

"The movies aren't so bad. Now this Ronald Colman—have you seen his pictures about the Bataillon d'Afrique? They're not bad at all."

"Very well, whenever I go to the movies I'll know you're going through just that sort of thing at that moment."

As she spoke, Nicole was aware of a small, pale, pretty young woman with lovely metallic hair, almost green in the deck lights, who had been sitting on the other side of Tommy and might have been part either of their conversation or of the one next to them. She had obviously had a monopoly of Tommy, for now she abandoned hope of his attention with what was once called ill grace, and petulantly crossed the crescent of the deck.

"After all, I am a hero," Tommy said calmly, only half joking. "I have ferocious courage, *us*ually, something like a lion, something like a drunken man."

Nicole waited until the echo of his boast had died away in his mind—she knew he had probably never made such a statement before. Then she looked among the strangers and found, as usual, the fierce neurotics pretending calm, liking the country only in horror of the city, of the sound of their own voices which had set the tone and pitch. She asked:

"Who is the woman in white?"

"The one who was beside me? Lady Caroline Sibley-Biers." They listened for a moment to her voice across the way:

"The man's a scoundrel, but he's a cat of the stripe. We sat up all night playing two-handed chemin-de-fer, and he owes me a mille Swiss."

Tommy laughed and said: "She is now the wickedest woman in London—whenever I come back to Europe there is a new crop of the wickedest women from London. She's the very latest—though I believe there is now one other who's considered almost as wicked."

Nicole glanced again at the woman across the deck. She was fragile, tubercular—it was incredible that such narrow shoulders, such puny arms could bear aloft the pennon of decadence, last ensign of the fading empire. Her resemblance was rather to one of John Held's flat-chested flappers than to the hierarchy of tall languid blondes who had posed for painters and novelists since before the war.

Golding approached, fighting down the resonance of his huge bulk, which transmitted his will as through a gargantuan amplifier, and Nicole, still reluctant, yielded to his reiterated points: that the *Margin* was starting for Cannes immediately after dinner; that they could always pack in some caviare and champagne, even though they had dined; that in any case Dick was now on the phone, telling their chauffeur in Nice to drive their car back to Cannes and leave it in front of the Café des Alliées, where the Divers could retrieve it.

They moved into the dining salon and Dick was placed next to Lady Caroline. Nicole saw that his usually ruddy face was drained of blood; he talked in a dogmatic voice, of which only snatches reached Nicole:

". . . It's all right for you English, you're doing a dance of death. . . . Sepoys in the ruined fort, I mean Sepoys at the gate and gaiety in the fort and all that. The green hat, the crushed hat, no future."

Lady Caroline answered him in short sentences spotted with the terminal "What?" the double-edged "Quite!" the depressing "Cheerio!" that always had a connotation of imminent peril, but Dick appeared oblivious to the warning signals. Suddenly he made a particularly vehement pronouncement, the purport of which eluded Nicole, but she saw the young woman turn dark and sinewy, and heard her answer sharply:

"After all a chep's a chep and a chum's a chum."

Again he had offended someone—couldn't he hold his tongue a little longer? How long? To death then.

At the piano, a fair-haired young Scotsman from the orchestra (entitled by its drum "The Ragtime College Jazzes of Edinboro") had begun singing in a Danny Deever monotone, accompanying himself with low chords on the piano. He pronounced his words with great precision, as though they impressed him almost intolerably:

> "There was a young lady from hell,
> Who jumped at the sound of a bell,
> Because she was bad—bad—bad,
> She jumped at the sound of a bell,
> From hell (BOOMBOOM)
> From hell (TOOTTOOT)
> There was a young lady from hell——"

"What is all this?" whispered Tommy to Nicole.

The girl on the other side of him supplied the answer:

"Caroline Sibley-Biers wrote the words. He wrote the music."

"Quelle enfantillage!" Tommy murmured as the next verse began, hinting at the jumpy lady's further predilections. "On dirait qu'il récite Racine!"

On the surface at least, Lady Caroline was paying no attention to the performance of her work. Glancing at her again Nicole found herself impressed, neither with the character nor the personality, but with the sheer strength derived from an attitude; Nicole thought that she was formidable, and she was confirmed in this point of view as the party rose from table. Dick remained in his seat wearing an odd expression; then he crashed into words with a harsh ineptness.

"I don't like innuendo in these deafening English whispers."

Already half-way out of the room Lady Caroline turned and walked back to him; she spoke in a low clipped voice purposely audible to the whole company.

"You came to me asking for it—disparaging my countrymen, disparaging my friend, Mary Minghetti. I simply said you were observed associating with a questionable crowd in Lausanne. Is that a deafening whisper? Or does it simply deafen *you?*"

"It's still not loud enough," said Dick, a little too late. "So I am actually a notorious——"

Golding crushed out the phrase with his voice, saying "What! What!" and moved his guests on out, with the threat of his powerful body. Turning the corner of the door Nicole saw that Dick was still sitting at the table. She was furious at the woman for her preposterous statement, equally furious at Dick for having brought them there, for having become fuddled, for having untipped the capped barbs of his irony, for having come off humiliated. She was a little more annoyed because she knew that her taking possession of Tommy Barban on their arrival had first irritated the Englishwoman.

A moment later she saw Dick standing in the gangway, apparently in complete control of himself as he talked with Golding; then for half an hour she did not see him anywhere about the deck and she broke out of an intricate Malay game, played with string and coffee beans, and said to Tommy:

"I've got to find Dick."

Since dinner the yacht had been in motion westward. The fine night streamed away on either side, the Diesel engines pounded softly, there was a spring wind that blew Nicole's hair abruptly when she reached the bow, and she had a sharp lessening of anxiety when she saw Dick standing in the angle by the flagstaff. His voice was serene as he recognized her.

"It's a nice night."

"I was worried."

"Oh, you were worried?"

"Oh, don't talk that way. It would give me so much pleasure to think of a little something I could do for you, Dick."

He turned away from her, toward the veil of starlight over Africa.

"I believe that's true, Nicole. And sometimes I believe that the littler it was, the more pleasure it would give you."

"Don't talk like that—don't say such things."

His face, wan in the light that the white spray caught and tossed back to the brilliant sky, had none of the lines of annoyance she had expected. It was even detached; his eyes focussed upon her gradually as upon a chessman to be moved; in the same slow manner he caught her wrist and drew her near.

"You ruined me, did you?" he inquired blandly. "Then we're both ruined. So——"

Cold in terror she put her other wrist into his grip. All right, she would go with him—again she felt the beauty of the night vividly in one moment of complete response and abnegation—all right, then——

—but now she was unexpectedly free and Dick turned his back, sighing, "Tch! tch!"

Tears streamed down Nicole's face. In a moment she heard someone approaching; it was Tommy.

"You found him! Nicole thought maybe you jumped overboard, Dick," he said, "because that little English poule slanged you."

"It'd be a good setting to jump overboard," said Dick mildly.

"Wouldn't it?" agreed Nicole hastily. "Let's borrow life-preservers and jump over. I think we should do something spectacular. I feel that all our lives have been too restrained."

Tommy sniffed from one to the other, trying to breathe in the situation with the night. "We'll go ask the Lady Beer-and-Ale what to do—she should know the latest things. And we should memorize her song 'There was a young lady from l'enfer.' I shall translate it and make a fortune from its success at the Casino."

"Are you rich, Tommy?" Dick asked him, as they retraced the length of the boat.

"Not as things go now. I got tired of the brokerage business and went away. But I have good stocks in the hands of friends who are holding them for me. All goes well."

"Dick's getting rich," Nicole said. In reaction her voice had begun to tremble.

On the after deck Golding had fanned three pairs of dancers into action with his colossal paws. Nicole and Tommy joined them and Tommy remarked: "Dick seems to be drinking."

"Only moderately," she said loyally.

"There are those who can drink and those who can't. Obviously Dick can't. You ought to tell him not to."

"I!" she exclaimed in amazement. "*I* tell Dick what he should do or shouldn't do!"

But in a reticent way Dick was still vague and sleepy when they reached the pier at Cannes. Golding buoyed him down into the launch of the *Margin,* whereupon Lady Caroline shifted her place conspicuously. On the dock he bowed good-bye with exaggerated formality, and for a moment he seemed about to speed her with a salty epigram, but the bone of Tommy's arm went into the soft part of his and they walked to the Divers' car.

"I'll drive you home," Tommy suggested.

"Don't bother—we can get a cab."

"I'd like to, if you can put me up."

On the back seat of the car Dick remained quiescent until the yellow monolith of Golfe Juan was passed, and then the constant carnival at Juan les Pins, where the night was musical and strident in many languages. When the car turned up the hill toward Tarmes, he sat up suddenly, prompted by the tilt of the vehicle and delivered a peroration:

"A charming representative of the—" he stumbled momentarily, "—a firm of—bring me Brains addled à l'Anglaise." Then he went into an appeased sleep, belching now and then contentedly into the soft warm darkness.

CHAPTER VI

NEXT MORNING DICK CAME early into Nicole's room. "I waited till I heard you up. Needless to say I feel badly about the evening—but how about no post-mortems?"

"I'm agreed," she answered coolly, carrying her face to the mirror. "Tommy drove us home? Or did I dream it?"

"You know he did."

"Seems probable," he admitted, "since I just heard him coughing. I think I'll call on him."

She was glad when he left her, for almost the first time in her life—his awful faculty of being right seemed to have deserted him at last.

Tommy was stirring in his bed, waking for café au lait.

"Feel all right?" Dick asked.

When Tommy complained of a sore throat he seized at a professional attitude.

"Better have a gargle or something."

"You have one?"

"Oddly enough I haven't—probably Nicole has."

"Don't disturb her."

"She's up."

"How is she?"

Dick turned around slowly. "Did you expect her to be dead because I was tight?" His tone was pleasant. "Nicole is now made of—of Georgia pine, which is the hardest wood known, except lignum vitæ from New Zealand——"

Nicole, going downstairs, heard the end of the conversation. She knew, as she had always known, that Tommy loved her; she knew he had come to dislike Dick, and that Dick had realized it before he did, and would react in some positive way to the man's lonely passion. This thought was succeeded by a moment of sheerly feminine satisfaction. She leaned over her children's breakfast table and

294

told off instructions to the governess, while upstairs two men were concerned about her.

Later in the garden she was happy; she did not want anything to happen, but only for the situation to remain in suspension as the two men tossed her from one mind to another; she had not existed for a long time, even as a ball.

"Nice, Rabbits, isn't it— Or is it? Hey, Rabbit—hey you! Is it nice?—hey? Or does it sound very peculiar to you?"

The rabbit, after an experience of practically nothing else and cabbage leaves, agreed after a few tentative shiftings of the nose.

Nicole went on through her garden routine. She left the flowers she cut in designated spots to be brought to the house later by the gardener. Reaching the sea wall she fell into a communicative mood and no one to communicate with; so she stopped and deliberated. She was somewhat shocked at the idea of being interested in another man—but other women have lovers—why not me? In the fine spring morning the inhibitions of the male world disappeared and she reasoned as gaily as a flower, while the wind blew her hair until her head moved with it. Other women have had lovers—the same forces that last night had made her yield to Dick up to the point of death, now kept her head nodding to the wind, content and happy with the logic of, Why shouldn't I?

She sat upon the low wall and looked down upon the sea. But from another sea, the wide swell of fantasy, she had fished out something tangible to lay beside the rest of her loot. If she need not, in her spirit, be forever one with Dick as he had appeared last night, she must be something in addition, not just an image on his mind, condemned to endless parades around the circumference of a medal.

Nicole had chosen this part of the wall on which to sit because the cliff shaded to a slanting meadow with a cultivated vegetable garden. Through a cluster of boughs she saw two men carrying rakes and spades and talking in a counterpoint of Niçois and Provençal. Attracted by their words and gestures she caught the sense:

"I laid her down here."

"I took her behind the vines there."

"She doesn't care—neither does he. It was that sacred dog. Well, I laid her down here——"

"You got the rake?"

"You got it yourself, you clown."

"Well, I don't care where you laid her down. Until that night I never even felt a woman's breast against my chest since I married —twelve years ago. And now you tell me——"

"But listen about the dog——"

Nicole watched them through the boughs; it seemed all right what they were saying—one thing was good for one person, another for another. Yet it was a man's world she had overheard; going back to the house she became doubtful again.

Dick and Tommy were on the terrace. She walked through them and into the house, brought out a sketch pad and began a head of Tommy.

"Hands never idle—distaff flying," Dick said lightly. How could he talk so trivially with the blood still drained down from his cheeks so that the auburn lather of beard showed red as his eyes? She turned to Tommy, saying:

"I can always do something. I used to have a nice active little Polynesian ape and juggle him around for hours till people began to make the most dismal rough jokes——"

She kept her eyes resolutely away from Dick. Presently he excused himself and went inside. She saw him pour himself two glasses of water, and she hardened further.

"Nicole—" Tommy began, but interrupted himself to clear the harshness from his throat.

"I'm going to get you some special camphor rub," she suggested. "It's American—Dick believes in it. I'll be just a minute."

"I must go, really."

Dick came out and sat down. "Believes in what?"

When she returned with the jar neither of the men had moved, though she gathered they had had some sort of excited conversation about nothing.

The chauffeur was at the door, with a bag containing Tommy's clothes of the night before. The sight of Tommy in clothes borrowed from Dick moved her sadly, falsely, as though Tommy were not able to afford such clothes.

"When you get to the hotel rub this into your throat and chest and then inhale it," she said.

"Say, there," Dick murmured as Tommy went down the steps,

"don't give Tommy the whole jar—it has to be ordered from Paris —it's out of stock down here."

Tommy came back within hearing and the three of them stood in the sunshine, Tommy squarely before the car, so that it seemed by leaning forward he would tip it upon his back.

Nicole stepped down to the path.

"Now catch it," she advised him. "It's extremely rare."

She heard Dick grow silent at her side; she took a step off from him and waved as the car drove off with Tommy and the special camphor rub. Then she turned to take her own medicine.

"There was no necessity for that gesture," Dick said. "There are four of us here—and for years whenever there's a cough——"

They looked at each other.

"We can always get another jar—" then she lost her nerve and presently followed him upstairs, where he lay down on his own bed and said nothing.

"Do you want lunch to be brought up to you?" she asked.

He nodded and continued to lie quiescent, staring at the ceiling. Doubtfully she went to give the order. Upstairs again she looked into his room—the blue eyes, like searchlights, played on a dark sky. She stood a minute in the doorway, aware of the sin she had committed against him, half afraid to come in. . . . She put out her hand as if to rub his head, but he turned away like a suspicious animal. Nicole could stand the situation no longer; in a kitchen-maid's panic she ran downstairs, afraid of what the stricken man above would feed on while she must still continue her dry suckling at his lean chest.

In a week Nicole forgot her flash about Tommy—she had not much memory for people and forgot them easily. But in the first hot blast of June she heard he was in Nice. He wrote a little note to them both—and she opened it under the parasol, together with other mail they had brought from the house. After reading it she tossed it over to Dick, and in exchange he threw a telegram into the lap of her beach pajamas:

"Dears will be at Gausses tomorrow unfortunately without mother am counting on seeing you.   ROSEMARY."

"I'll be glad to see her," said Nicole, grimly.

CHAPTER VII

BUT SHE WENT TO the beach with Dick next morning with a renewal of her apprehension that Dick was contriving at some desperate solution. Since the evening on Golding's yacht she had sensed what was going on. So delicately balanced was she between an old foothold that had always guaranteed her security, and the imminence of a leap from which she must alight changed in the very chemistry of blood and muscle, that she did not dare bring the matter into the true forefront of consciousness. The figures of Dick and herself, mutating, undefined, appeared as spooks caught up into a fantastic dance. For months every word had seemed to have an overtone of some other meaning, soon to be resolved under circumstances that Dick would determine. Though this state of mind was perhaps more hopeful—the long years of sheer being had had an enlivening effect on the parts of her nature that early illness had killed and that Dick had not reached, through no fault of his but simply because no one nature can extend entirely inside another—it was still disquieting. The most unhappy aspect of their relations was Dick's growing indifference, at present expressed by too much drinking. Nicole did not know whether she was to be crushed or spared—Dick's voice, throbbing with insincerity, confused the issue; she couldn't guess how he was going to behave next upon the tortuously slow unrolling of the carpet, nor what would happen at the end, at the moment of the leap.

For what might occur thereafter she had no anxiety—she suspected that that would be the lifting of a burden, an unblinding of eyes. Nicole had been designed for change, for flight, with money as fins and wings. The new state of things would be no more than if a racing chassis, concealed for years under the body of a family limousine, should be stripped to its original self. Nicole could feel the fresh breeze already—it was the wrench she feared, and the dark manner of its coming.

The Diver, went out on the beach with her white suit and his white trunks very white against the color of their bodies. Nicole saw Dick peer about for the children among the confused shapes and shadows of many umbrellas, and as his mind temporarily left her, ceasing to grip her, she looked at him with detachment and decided that he was seeking his children, not protectively but for protection. Probably it was the beach he feared, like a deposed ruler secretly visiting an old court. She had come to hate his world with its delicate jokes and politenesses, forgetting that for many years it was the only world open to her. Let him look at it—his beach, perverted now to the tastes of the tasteless; he could search it for a day and find no stone of the Chinese wall he had once erected around it, no footprint of an old friend.

For a moment Nicole was sorry it was so; remembering the glass he had raked out of the old trash heap, remembering the sailor trunks and sweaters they had bought in a Nice back street—garments that afterward ran through a vogue in silk among the Paris couturiers—remembering the simple little French girls climbing on the breakwaters crying "Dites donc! Dites donc!" like birds, and the ritual of the morning time, the quiet restful extraversion toward sea and sun—many inventions of his, buried deeper than the sand under the span of so few years. . . . Now the swimming place was a "club," though, like the international society it represented, it would be hard to say who was not admitted.

Nicole hardened again as Dick knelt on the straw mat and looked about for Rosemary. Her eyes followed his, searching among the new paraphernalia, the trapezes over the water, the swinging rings, the portable bathhouses, the floating towers, the searchlights from last night's fêtes, the modernistic buffet, white with a hackneyed motif of endless handlebars.

The water was almost the last place he looked for Rosemary, because few people swam any more in that blue paradise, children and one exhibitionistic valet who punctuated the morning with spectacular dives from a fifty-foot rock—most of Gausse's guests stripped the concealing pajamas from their flabbiness only for a short hangover dip at one o'clock.

"There she is," Nicole remarked.

She watched Dick's eyes following Rosemary's track from raft to raft; but the sigh that rocked out of her bosom was something left over from five years ago.

"Let's swim out and speak to Rosemary," he suggested.

"You go."

"We'll both go." She struggled a moment against his pronouncement, but eventually they swam out together, tracing Rosemary by the school of little fish who followed her, taking their dazzle from her, the shining spoon of a trout hook.

Nicole stayed in the water while Dick hoisted himself up beside Rosemary and the two sat dripping and talking, exactly as if they had never loved or touched each other. Rosemary was beautiful— her youth was a shock to Nicole, who rejoiced, however, that the young girl was less slender by a hairline than herself. Nicole swam around in little rings listening to Rosemary, who was acting amusement, joy, and expectation—more confident than she had been five years ago.

"I miss Mother so, but she's meeting me in Paris, Monday."

"Five years ago you came here," said Dick. "And what a funny little thing you were, in one of those hotel peignoirs!"

"How you remember things! You always did—and always the nice things."

Nicole saw the old game of flattery beginning again and she dove under water, coming up again to hear:

"I'm going to pretend it's five years ago and I'm a girl of eighteen again. You could always make me feel some you know, kind of, you know, kind of happy way—you and Nicole. I feel as if you're still on the beach there, under one of those umbrellas—the nicest people I'd ever known, maybe ever will."

Swimming away, Nicole saw that the cloud of Dick's heart-sickness had lifted a little as he began to play with Rosemary, bringing out his old expertness with people, a tarnished object of art; she guessed that with a drink or so he would have done his stunts on the swinging rings for her, fumbling through stunts he had once done with ease. She noticed that this summer, for the first time, he avoided high diving.

Later, as she dodged her way from raft to raft, Dick overtook her.

"Some of Rosemary's friends have a speed boat, the one out there. Do you want to aquaplane? I think it would be amusing."

Remembering that once he could stand on his hands on a chair at the end of a board, she indulged him as she might have indulged Lanier. Summer before last on the Zugersee they had played at that pleasant water game, and Dick had lifted a two-hundred-pound man from the board onto his shoulders and stood up. But women marry all their husbands' talents and naturally, afterward, are not so impressed with them as they may keep up the pretense of being. Nicole had not even pretended to be impressed, though she had said "Yes" to him, and "Yes, I think so too."

She knew, though, that he was somewhat tired, that it was only the closeness of Rosemary's exciting youth that prompted the impending effort—she had seen him draw the same inspiration from the new bodies of her children and she wondered coldly if he would make a spectacle of himself. The Divers were older than the others in the boat—the young people were polite, deferential, but Nicole felt an undercurrent of "Who are these Numbers anyhow?" and she missed Dick's easy talent of taking control of situations and making them all right—he had concentrated on what he was going to try to do.

The motor throttled down two hundred yards from shore and one of the young men dove flat over the edge. He swam at the aimless twisting board, steadied it, climbed slowly to his knees on it—then got on his feet as the boat accelerated. Leaning back he swung his light vehicle ponderously from side to side in slow, breathless arcs that rode the trailing side-swell at the end of each swing. In the direct wake of the boat he let go his rope, balanced for a moment, then back-flipped into the water, disappearing like a statue of glory, and reappearing as an insignificant head while the boat made the circle back to him.

Nicole refused her turn; then Rosemary rode the board neatly and conservatively, with facetious cheers from her admirers. Three of them scrambled egotistically for the honor of pulling her into the boat, managing, among them, to bruise her knee and hip against the side.

"Now you, Doctor," said the Mexican at the wheel.

Dick and the last young man dove over the side and swam to

the board. Dick was going to try his lifting trick and Nicole began to watch with smiling scorn. This physical showing-off for Rosemary irritated her most of all.

When the men had ridden long enough to find their balance, Dick knelt, and putting the back of his neck in the other man's crotch, found the rope through his legs, and slowly began to rise.

The people in the boat, watching closely, saw that he was having difficulties. He was on one knee; the trick was to straighten all the way up in the same motion with which he left his kneeling position. He rested for a moment, then his face contracted as he put his heart into the strain, and lifted.

The board was narrow, the man, though weighing less than a hundred and fifty, was awkward with his weight and grabbed clumsily at Dick's head. When, with a last wrenching effort of his back, Dick stood upright, the board slid sidewise and the pair toppled into the sea.

In the boat Rosemary exclaimed: "Wonderful! They almost had it."

But as they came back to the swimmers Nicole watched for a sight of Dick's face. It was full of annoyance as she expected, because he had done the thing with ease only two years ago.

The second time he was more careful. He rose a little, testing the balance of his burden, settled down again on his knee; then, grunting "Alley oop!" began to rise—but before he could really straighten out, his legs suddenly buckled and he shoved the board away with his feet to avoid being struck as they fell off.

This time when the *Baby Gar* came back it was apparent to all the passengers that he was angry.

"Do you mind if I try that once more?" he called, treading water. "We almost had it then."

"Sure. Go ahead."

To Nicole he looked white-around-the-gills, and she cautioned him:

"Don't you think that's enough for now?"

He didn't answer. The first partner had had plenty and was hauled over the side, the Mexican driving the motor boat obligingly took his place.

He was heavier than the first man. As the boat gathered motion,

Dick rested for a moment, belly-down on the board. Then he got beneath the man and took the rope, and his muscles flexed as he tried to rise.

He could not rise. Nicole saw him shift his position and strain upward again, but at the instant when the weight of his partner was full upon his shoulders he became immovable. He tried again—lifting an inch, two inches—Nicole felt the sweat glands of her forehead open as she strained with him—then he was simply holding his ground, then he collapsed back down on his knees with a smack, and they went over, Dick's head barely missing a kick of the board.

"Hurry back!" Nicole called to the driver; even as she spoke she saw him slide under water and she gave a little cry; but he came up again and turned on his back, and the Mexican swam near to help. It seemed forever till the boat reached them, but when they came alongside at last and Nicole saw Dick floating exhausted and expressionless, alone with the water and the sky, her panic changed suddenly to contempt.

"We'll help you up, Doctor. . . . Get his foot . . . all right . . . now altogether. . . ."

Dick sat panting and looking at nothing.

"I knew you shouldn't have tried it," Nicole could not help saying.

"He'd tired himself the first two times," said the Mexican.

"It was a foolish thing," Nicole insisted. Rosemary tactfully said nothing.

After a minute Dick got his breath, panting, "I couldn't have lifted a paper doll that time."

An explosive little laugh relieved the tension caused by his failure. They were all attentive to Dick as he disembarked at the dock. But Nicole was annoyed—everything he did annoyed her now.

She sat with Rosemary under an umbrella while Dick went to the buffet for a drink. He returned presently with some sherry for them.

"The first drink I ever had was with you," Rosemary said, and with a spurt of enthusiasm she added, "Oh, I'm so glad to see you and *know* you're all right. I was worried—" Her sentence broke as she changed direction "that maybe you wouldn't be."

"Did you hear I'd gone into a process of deterioration?"

"Oh, no. I simply—just heard you'd changed. And I'm glad to see with my own eyes it isn't true."

"It is true," Dick answered, sitting down with them. "The change came a long way back—but at first it didn't show. The manner remains intact for some time after the morale cracks."

"Do you practise on the Riviera?" Rosemary demanded hastily.

"It'd be a good ground to find likely specimens." He nodded here and there at the people milling about in the golden sand. "Great candidates. Notice our old friend, Mrs. Abrams, playing duchess to Mary North's queen? Don't get jealous about it—think of Mrs. Abrams's long climb up the back stairs of the Ritz on her hands and knees and all the carpet dust she had to inhale."

Rosemary interrupted him. "But is that really Mary North?" She was regarding a woman sauntering in their direction, followed by a small group who behaved as if they were accustomed to being looked at. When they were ten feet away, Mary's glance flickered fractionally over the Divers, one of those unfortunate glances that indicate to the glanced-upon that they have been observed but are to be overlooked, the sort of glance that neither the Divers nor Rosemary Hoyt had ever permitted themselves to throw at anyone in their lives. Dick was amused when Mary perceived Rosemary, changed her plans, and came over. She spoke to Nicole with pleasant heartiness, nodded unsmilingly to Dick as if he were somewhat contagious—whereupon he bowed in ironic respect—as she greeted Rosemary.

"I heard you were here. For how long?"

"Until tomorrow," Rosemary answered.

She, too, saw how Mary had walked through the Divers to talk to her, and a sense of obligation kept her unenthusiastic. No, she could not dine tonight.

Mary turned to Nicole, her manner indicating affection blended with pity.

"How are the children?" she asked.

They came up at the moment, and Nicole gave ear to a request that she overrule the governess on a swimming point.

"No," Dick answered for her. "What Mademoiselle says must go."

Agreeing that one must support delegated authority, Nicole refused their request, whereupon Mary—who in the manner of an Anita Loos heroine had dealings only with Faits Accomplis, who indeed could not have house-broken a French poodle puppy—regarded Dick as though he were guilty of a most flagrant bullying. Dick, chafed by the tiresome performance, inquired with mock solicitude:

"How are your children—and their aunts?"

Mary did not answer; she left them, first draping a sympathetic hand over Lanier's reluctant head. After she had gone Dick said: "When I think of the time I spent working over her."

"I like her," said Nicole.

Dick's bitterness had surprised Rosemary, who had thought of him as all-forgiving, all-comprehending. Suddenly she recalled what it was she had heard about him. In conversation with some State Department people on the boat—Europeanized Americans who had reached a position where they could scarcely have been said to belong to any nation at all, at least not to any great power, though perhaps to a Balkan-like state composed of similar citizens—the name of the ubiquitously renowned Baby Warren had occurred and it was remarked that Baby's younger sister had thrown herself away on a dissipated doctor. "He's not received anywhere any more," the woman said.

The phrase disturbed Rosemary. She could not place the Divers as living in any relation to society where such a fact, if fact it was, could have any meaning, yet the hint of a hostile and organized public opinion rang in her ears. "He's not received anywhere any more." She pictured Dick climbing the steps of a mansion, presenting cards, and being told by a butler: "We're not receiving you any more"; then proceeding down an avenue only to be told the same thing by the countless other butlers of countless Ambassadors, Ministers, Chargés d'Affaires. . . .

Nicole wondered how she could get away. She guessed that Dick, stung into alertness, would grow charming and would make Rosemary respond to him. Sure enough, in a moment his voice managed to qualify everything unpleasant he had said:

"Mary's all right—she's done very well. But it's hard to go on liking people who don't like you."

Rosemary, falling into line, swayed toward Dick and crooned:

"Oh, you're so nice. I can't imagine anybody not forgiving you anything, no matter what you did to them." Then feeling that her exuberance had transgressed on Nicole's rights, she looked at the sand exactly between them: "I wanted to ask you both what you thought of my latest pictures—if you saw them."

Nicole said nothing, having seen one of them and thought little about it.

"It'll take a few minutes to tell you," Dick said, "Let's suppose that Nicole says to you that Lanier is ill. What do you do in life? What does anyone do? They *act*—face, voice, words—the face shows sorrow, the voice shows shock, the words show sympathy."

"Yes—I understand."

"But, in the theatre, no. In the theatre all the best comédiennes have built up their reputations by bur*les*quing the correct emotional responses—fear and love and sympathy."

"I see." Yet she did not quite see.

Losing the thread of it, Nicole's impatience increased as Dick continued:

"The danger to an actress is in responding. Again, let's suppose that somebody told you, 'Your lover is dead.' In life you'd probably go to pieces. But on the stage you're trying to entertain—the audience can do the 'responding' for themselves. First the actress has lines to follow, then she has to get the audience's attention back on herself, away from the murdered Chinese or whatever the thing is. So she must do something unexpected. If the audience thinks the character is hard she goes soft on them—if they think she's soft she goes hard. You go all *out* of character—you understand?"

"I don't quite," admitted Rosemary. "How do you mean out of character?"

"You do the unexpected thing until you've maneuvered the audience back from the objective fact to yourself. *Then* you slide into character again."

Nicole could stand no more. She stood up sharply, making no attempt to conceal her impatience. Rosemary, who had been for a few minutes half-conscious of this, turned in a conciliatory way to Topsy.

"Would you like to be an actress when you grow up? I think you'd make a fine actress."

Nicole stared at her deliberately and in her grandfather's voice said, slow and distinct:

"It's absolutely *out* to put such ideas in the heads of other people's children. Remember, we may have quite different plans for them." She turned sharply to Dick. "I'm going to take the car home. I'll send Michelle for you and the children."

"You haven't driven for months," he protested.

"I haven't forgotten how."

Without a glance at Rosemary, whose face was "responding" violently, Nicole left the umbrella.

In the bathhouse, she changed to pajamas, her expression still hard as a plaque. But as she turned into the road of arched pines and the atmosphere changed—with a squirrel's flight on a branch, a wind nudging at the leaves, a cock splitting distant air, with a creep of sunlight transpiring through the immobility—then the voices of the beach receded. Nicole relaxed and felt new and happy; her thoughts were clear as good bells—she had a sense of being cured and in a new way. Her ego began blooming like a great rich rose as she scrambled back along the labyrinths in which she had wandered for years. She hated the beach, resented the places where she had played planet to Dick's sun.

"Why, I'm almost complete," she thought. "I'm practically standing alone, without him." And like a happy child, wanting the completion as soon as possible, and knowing vaguely that Dick had planned for her to have it, she lay on her bed as soon as she got home and wrote Tommy Barban in Nice a short provocative letter.

But that was for the daytime—toward evening, with the inevitable diminution of nervous energy, her spirits flagged and the arrows flew a little in the twilight. She was afraid of what was in Dick's mind; again she felt that a plan underlay his current actions and she was afraid of his plans—they worked well and they had an all-inclusive logic about them which Nicole was not able to command. She had somehow given over the thinking to him, and in his absences her every action seemed automatically governed by what he would like, so that now she felt inadequate to match her intentions against his. Yet think she must; she knew at last the number on the dreadful door of fantasy, the threshold to the escape that was no escape; she knew that for her the greatest sin now and in the future was to delude herself. It had been a long lesson but she had learned it. Either you think—or else others have to think for you and take power from you, pervert and discipline your natural tastes, civilize and sterilize you.

They had a tranquil supper with Dick drinking much beer and being cheerful with the children in the dusky room. Afterward he played some Schubert songs and some new jazz from America that Nicole hummed in her harsh, sweet contralto over his shoulder.

> *"Thank y' father-r*
> *Thank y' mother-r*
> *Thanks for meetingup with one another——"*

"I don't like that one," Dick said, starting to turn the page.

"Oh, play it!" she exclaimed. "Am I going through the rest of life flinching at the word 'father'?"

> *"—Thank the horse that pulled the buggy that night!*
> *Thank you both for being justabit tight——"*

Later they sat with the children on the Moorish roof and watched the fireworks of two casinos, far apart, far down on the shore. It was lonely and sad to be so empty-hearted toward each other.

Next morning, back from shopping in Cannes, Nicole found a note saying that Dick had taken the small car and gone up into Provence for a few days by himself. Even as she read it the phone rang—it was Tommy Barban from Monte Carlo, saying that he had received her letter and was driving over. She felt her lips' warmth in the receiver as she welcomed his coming.

CHAPTER VIII

She bathed and anointed herself and covered her body with a layer of powder, while her toes crunched another pile on a bath towel. She looked microscopically at the lines of her flanks, wondering how soon the fine, slim edifice would begin to sink squat and earthward. In about six years, but now I'll do—in fact I'll do as well as anyone I know.

She was not exaggerating. The only physical disparity between Nicole at present and the Nicole of five years before was simply that she was no longer a young girl. But she was enough ridden by the current youth worship, the moving pictures with their myriad faces of girl-children, blandly represented as carrying on the work and wisdom of the world, to feel a jealousy of youth.

She put on the first ankle-length day dress that she had owned for many years and crossed herself reverently with Chanel Sixteen. When Tommy drove up at one o'clock she had made her person into the trimmest of gardens.

How good to have things like this, to be worshipped again, to pretend to have a mystery! She had lost two of the great arrogant years in the life of a pretty girl—now she felt like making up for them; she greeted Tommy as if he were one of many men at her feet, walking ahead of him instead of beside him as they crossed the garden toward the market umbrella. Attractive women of nineteen and of twenty-nine are alike in their breezy confidence; on the contrary, the exigent womb of the twenties does not pull the outside world centripetally around itself. The former are ages of insolence, comparable the one to a young cadet, the other to a fighter strutting after combat.

But whereas a girl of nineteen draws her confidence from a surfeit of attention, a woman of twenty-nine is nourished on subtler stuff. Desirous, she chooses her apéritifs wisely or, content, she enjoys the caviare of potential power. Happily she does not seem, in either case, to anticipate the subsequent years when her insight will often be blurred by panic, by the fear of stopping or the fear of going on. But on the landings of nineteen or twenty-nine she is pretty sure that there are no bears in the hall.

Nicole did not want any vague spiritual romance—she wanted an "affair"; she wanted a change. She realized, thinking with Dick's thoughts, that from a superficial view it was a vulgar business to enter, without emotion, into an indulgence that menaced all of them. On the other hand, she blamed Dick for the immediate situation, and honestly thought that such an experiment might have a therapeutic value. All summer she had been stimulated by watching people do exactly what they were tempted to do and pay no penalty for it—moreover, in spite of her intention of no longer lying to herself, she preferred to consider that she was merely feeling her way and that at any moment she could withdraw. . . .

In the light shade Tommy caught her up in his white-duck arms and pulled her around to him, looking at her eyes.

"Don't move," he said. "I'm going to look at you a great deal from now on."

There was some scent on his hair, a faint aura of soap from his white clothes. Her lips were tight, not smiling, and they both simply looked for a moment.

"Do you like what you see?" she murmured.

"Parle français."

"Very well," and she asked again in French. "Do you like what you see?"

He pulled her closer.

"I like whatever I see about you." He hesitated. "I thought I knew your face but it seems there are some things I didn't know about it. When did you begin to have white crook's eyes?"

She broke away, shocked and indignant, and cried in English:

"Is that why you wanted to talk French?" Her voice quieted as the butler came with sherry. "So you could be offensive more accurately?"

She parked her small seat violently on the cloth-of-silver chair cushion.

"I have no mirror here," she said, again in French, but decisively, "but if my eyes have changed it's because I'm well again. And being well perhaps I've gone back to my true self—I suppose my grandfather was a crook and I'm a crook by heritage, so there we are. Does that satisfy your logical mind?"

He scarcely seemed to know what she was talking about.

"Where's Dick—is he lunching with us?"

Seeing that his remark had meant comparatively little to him she suddenly laughed away its effect.

"Dick's on a tour," she said. "Rosemary Hoyt turned up, and either they're together or she upset him so much that he wants to go away and dream about her."

"You know, you're a little complicated after all."

"Oh, no," she assured him hastily. "No, I'm not really—I'm just a—I'm just a whole lot of different simple people."

Marius brought out melon and an ice pail, and Nicole, thinking irresistibly about her crook's eyes, did not answer; he gave one an entire nut to crack, this man, instead of giving it in fragments to pick at for meat.

"Why didn't they leave you in your natural state?" Tommy demanded presently. "You are the most dramatic person I have known."

She had no answer.

"All this taming of women!" he scoffed.

"In any society there are certain—" She felt Dick's ghost prompting at her elbow but she subsided at Tommy's overtone:

"I've brutalized many men into shape but I wouldn't take a chance on half the number of women. Especially this 'kind' bullying—what good does it do anybody?—you or him or anybody?"

Her heart leaped and then sank faintly with a sense of what she owed Dick.

"I suppose I've got——"

"You've got too much money," he said impatiently. "That's the crux of the matter. Dick can't beat that."

She considered while the melons were removed.

"What do you think I ought to do?"

For the first time in ten years she was under the sway of a personality other than her husband's. Everything Tommy said to her became part of her forever.

They drank the bottle of wine while a faint wind rocked the pine needles and the sensuous heat of early afternoon made blinding freckles on the checkered luncheon cloth. Tommy came over behind her and laid his arms along hers, clasping her hands. Their cheeks touched and then their lips and she gasped half with passion for him, half with the sudden surprise of its force.

"Can't you send the governess and the children away for the afternoon?"

"They have a piano lesson. Anyhow I don't want to stay here."

"Kiss me again."

A little later, riding toward Nice, she thought: So I have white crook's eyes, have I? Very well then, better a sane crook than a mad puritan.

His assertion seemed to absolve her from all blame or responsibility and she had a thrill of delight in thinking of herself in a new way. New vistas appeared ahead, peopled with the faces of many men, none of whom she need obey or even love. She drew in her breath, hunched her shoulders with a wriggle, and turned to Tommy.

"Have we *got* to go all the way to your hotel at Monte Carlo?"

He brought the car to a stop with a squeak of tires.

"No!" he answered. "And, my God, I have never been so happy as I am this minute."

They had passed through Nice following the blue coast and began to mount to the middling-high Corniche. Now Tommy turned sharply down to the shore, ran out a blunt peninsula, and stopped in the rear of a small shore hotel.

Its tangibility frightened Nicole for a moment. At the desk an American was arguing interminably with the clerk about the rate of exchange. She hovered, outwardly tranquil but inwardly miserable, as Tommy filled out the police blanks—his real, hers false. Their room was a Mediterranean room, almost ascetic, almost clean, darkened to the glare of the sea. Simplest of pleasures—simplest of places. Tommy ordered two cognacs and, when the door closed behind the waiter, he sat in the only chair, dark, scarred, and handsome, his eyebrows arched and upcurling, a fighting Puck, an earnest Satan.

Before they had finished the brandy they suddenly moved together and met standing up; then they were sitting on the bed and he kissed her hardy knees. Struggling a little still, like a decapitated animal, she forgot about Dick and her new white eyes, forgot Tommy himself, and sank deeper and deeper into the minutes and the moment.

. . . When he got up to open a shutter and find out what caused the increasing clamor below their windows, his figure was darker and stronger than Dick's, with high lights along the rope-twists of muscle. Momentarily he had forgotten her too—almost in the second of his flesh breaking from hers she had a foretaste that things were going to be different from what she had expected. She felt the nameless fear which precedes all emotions, joyous or sorrowful, inevitably as a hum of thunder precedes a storm.

Tommy peered cautiously from the balcony and reported:

"All I can see is two women on the balcony below this. They're talking about weather and tipping back and forth in American rocking-chairs."

"Making all that noise?"

"The noise is coming from somewhere below them. Listen."

> *"Oh, way down South in the land of cotton*
> *Hotels bum and business rotten*
> *Look away——"*

"It's Americans."

Nicole flung her arms wide on the bed and stared at the ceiling; the powder had dampened on her to make a milky surface. She liked the bareness of the room, the sound of the single fly navigating overhead. Tommy brought the chair over to the bed and swept the clothes off it to sit down; she liked the economy of the weightless dress and espadrilles that mingled with his ducks upon the floor.

He inspected the oblong white torso joined abruptly to the brown limbs and head, and said, laughing gravely:

"You are all new like a baby."

"With white eyes."

"I'll take care of that."

"It's very hard taking care of white eyes—especially the ones made in Chicago."

"I know all the old Languedoc peasant remedies."

"Kiss me, on the lips, Tommy."

"That's so American," he said, kissing her nevertheless. "When I was in America last there were girls who would tear you apart with their lips, tear themselves too, until their faces were scarlet with the blood around the lips all brought out in a patch—but nothing further."

Nicole leaned up on one elbow.

"I like this room," she said.

He looked around.

"I find it somewhat meagre. Darling, I'm glad you wouldn't wait until we got to Monte Carlo."

"Why only meagre? Why, this is a wonderful room, Tommy—like the bare tables in so many Cézannes and Picassos."

"I don't know." He did not try to understand her. "There's that noise again. My God, has there been a murder?"

He went to the window and reported once more:

"It seems to be two American sailors fighting and a lot more cheering them on. They are from your battleship off shore." He wrapped a towel around himself and went farther out on the balcony. "They have poules with them. I have heard about this now —the women follow them from place to place wherever the ship goes. But what women! One would think with their pay they could find better women! Why, the women who followed Kornilov! Why, we never looked at anything less than a ballerina!"

Nicole was glad he had known so many women, so that the word itself meant nothing to him; she would be able to hold him so long as the person in her transcended the universals of her body.

"Hit him where it hurts!"

"Yah-h-h-h!"

"Hey, what I tell you get inside that right!"

"Come on, Dulschmit, you son!"

"*Yaa-Yaa!*"

"*YA-YEH-YAH!*"

Tommy turned away.

"This place seems to have outlived its usefulness, you agree?"

She agreed, but they clung together for a moment before dressing, and then for a while longer it seemed as good enough a palace as any. . . .

Dressing at last Tommy exclaimed:

"*My God,* those two women in the rocking-chairs on the balcony below us haven't moved. They're trying to talk this matter out of existence. They're here on an economical holiday, and all the American navy and all the whores in Europe couldn't spoil it."

He came over gently and surrounded her, pulling the shoulder strap of her slip into place with his teeth; then a sound split the air outside: Cr-ACK—BOOM-M-m-*m!* It was the battleship sounding a recall.

Now, down below their window, it was pandemonium indeed—for the boat was moving to shores as yet unannounced. Waiters called accounts and demanded settlements in impassioned voices; there were oaths and denials, the tossing of bills too large and change too small; passouts were assisted to the boats, and the voices of the naval police chopped with quick commands through all voices. There were cries, tears, shrieks, promises as the first launch shoved off and the women crowded forward on the wharf, screaming and waving.

Tommy saw a girl rush out upon the balcony below waving a napkin, and before he could see whether or not the rocking Englishwomen gave in at last and acknowledged her presence, there was a knock at their own door. Outside, excited female voices made them agree to unlock it, disclosing two girls, young, thin, and barbaric, unfound rather than lost, in the hall. One of them wept chokingly.

"Kwee wave off your porch?" implored the other in passionate American. "Kwee please? Wave at the boy friends? Kwee, please. The other rooms is all locked."

"With pleasure," Tommy said.

The girls rushed out on the balcony and presently their voices struck a loud treble over the din.

" 'By, Charlie! Charlie, look *up!*"

"Send a wire gen'al alivery Nice!"

"Charlie! He don't see me."

One of the girls hoisted her skirt suddenly, pulled and ripped at her pink step-ins, and tore them to a sizable flag; then, screaming "Ben! Ben!" she waved it wildly. As Tommy and Nicole left the room it still fluttered against the blue sky. Oh, say can you see the tender color of remembered flesh?—while at the stern of the battle-ship rose in rivalry the Star Spangled Banner.

They dined at the new Beach Casino at Monte Carlo . . . much later they swam in Beaulieu in a roofless cavern of white moonlight formed by a circlet of pale boulders about a cup of phosphorescent water, facing Monaco and the blur of Mentone. She liked his bringing her there to the eastward vision and the novel tricks of wind and water; it was all as new as they were to each other. Symbolically she lay across his saddle-bow as surely as if he had wolfed her away from Damascus and they had come out upon the Mongolian plain. Moment by moment all that Dick had taught her fell away and she was ever nearer to what she had been in the beginning, prototype of that obscure yielding up of swords that was going on in the world about her. Tangled with love in the moonlight she welcomed the anarchy of her lover.

They awoke together to find the moon gone down and the air cool. She struggled up demanding the time and Tommy called it roughly at three.

"I've got to go home then."

"I thought we'd sleep in Monte Carlo."

"No. There's a governess and the children. I've got to roll in before daylight."

"As you like."

They dipped for a second, and when he saw her shivering he rubbed her briskly with a towel. As they got into the car with their heads still damp, their skins fresh and glowing, they were loath to start back. It was very bright where they were and as Tommy kissed her she felt him losing himself in the whiteness of her cheeks and her white teeth and her cool brow and the hand that touched his face. Still attuned to Dick, she waited for interpretation or qualification; but none was forthcoming. Reassured sleepily and happily that none would be, she sank low in the seat and drowsed until the sound of the motor changed and she felt them climbing toward Villa Diana. At the gate she kissed him an almost automatic good-bye. The sound of her feet on the walk was changed, the night noises of the garden were suddenly in the past, but she was glad, none the less, to be back. The day had progressed at a staccato rate, and in spite of its satisfactions she was not habituated to such strain.

CHAPTER IX

At four o'clock next afternoon a station taxi stopped at the gate and Dick got out. Suddenly off balance, Nicole ran from the terrace to meet him, breathless with her effort at self-control.

"Where's the car?" she asked.

"I left it in Arles. I didn't feel like driving any more."

"I thought from your note that you'd be several days."

"I ran into a mistral and some rain."

"Did you have fun?"

"Just as much fun as anybody has running away from things. I drove Rosemary as far as Avignon and put her on her train there." They walked toward the terrace together, where he deposited his bag. "I didn't tell you in the note because I thought you'd imagine a lot of things."

"That was very considerate of you." Nicole felt surer of herself now.

"I wanted to find out if she had anything to offer—the only way was to see her alone."

"Did she have—anything to offer?"

"Rosemary didn't grow up," he answered. "It's probably better that way. What have you been doing?"

She felt her face quiver like a rabbit's.

"I went dancing last night—with Tommy Barban. We went——"

He winced, interrupting her.

"Don't tell me about it. It doesn't matter what you do, only I don't want to know anything definitely."

"There isn't anything to know."

"All right, all right." Then as if he had been away a week: "How are the children?"

The phone rang in the house.

"If it's for me I'm not home," said Dick, turning away quickly. "I've got some things to do over in the work-room."

Nicole waited till he was out of sight behind the well; then she went into the house and took up the phone.

"Nicole, comment vas-tu?"

"Dick's home."

He groaned.

"Meet me here in Cannes," he suggested. "I've got to talk to you."

"I can't."

"Tell me you love me." Without speaking she nodded at the receiver; he repeated, "Tell me you love me."

"Oh, I do," she assured him. "But there's nothing to be done right now."

"Of course there is," he said impatiently. "Dick sees it's over between you two—it's obvious he has quit. What does he expect you to do?"

"I don't know. I'll have to—" She stopped herself from saying "—to wait until I can ask Dick," and instead finished with: "I'll write and I'll phone you tomorrow."

She wandered about the house rather contentedly, resting on her achievement. She was a mischief, and that was a satisfaction; no longer was she a huntress of corralled game. Yesterday came back to her now in innumerable detail—detail that began to overlay her memory of similar moments when her love for Dick was fresh and intact. She began to slight that love, so that it seemed to have been tinged with sentimental habit from the first. With the opportunistic memory of women she scarcely recalled how she had felt when she and Dick had possessed each other in secret places around the corners of the world, during the month before they were married. Just so had she lied to Tommy last night, swearing to him that never before had she so entirely, so completely, so utterly. . . .

. . . then remorse for this moment of betrayal, which so cavalierly belittled a decade of her life, turned her walk toward Dick's sanctuary.

Approaching noiselessly she saw him behind his cottage, sitting in a steamer chair by the cliff wall, and for a moment she regarded him silently. He was thinking, he was living a world completely his own, and in the small motions of his face, the brow raised or lowered, the eyes narrowed or widened, the lips set and reset, the play of his hands, she saw him progress from phase to phase of his

own story spinning out inside him, his own, not hers. Once he
clenched his fists and leaned forward, once it brought into his face
an expression of torment and despair—when this passed its stamp
lingered in his eyes. For almost the first time in her life she was
sorry for him—it is hard for those who have once been mentally
afflicted to be sorry for those who are well, and though Nicole often
paid lip service to the fact that he had led her back to the world
she had forfeited, she had thought of him really as an inexhaustible
energy, incapable of fatigue—she forgot the troubles she caused him
at the moment when she forgot the troubles of her own that had
prompted her. That he no longer controlled her—did he know
that? Had he willed it all?—she felt as sorry for him as she had
sometimes felt for Abe North and his ignoble destiny, sorry as for
the helplessness of infants and the old.

She went up to him and, putting her arm around his shoulder
and touching their heads together, said:

"Don't be sad."

He looked at her coldly.

"Don't touch me!" he said.

Confused she moved a few feet away.

"Excuse me," he continued abstractedly. "I was just thinking what
I thought of you——"

"Why not add the new classification to your book?"

"I have thought of it—'Furthermore and beyond the psychoses
and the neuroses——'"

"I didn't come over here to be disagreeable."

"Then why *did* you come, Nicole? I can't do anything for you
any more. I'm trying to save myself."

"From my contamination?"

"My profession throws me in contact with questionable company
sometimes."

She wept with anger at the abuse.

"You're a coward! You've made a failure of your life, and you
want to blame it on me."

While he did not answer she began to feel the old hypnotism
of his intelligence, sometimes exercised without power but always
with substrata of truth under truth which she could not break or
even crack. Again she struggled with it, fighting him with her

small, fine eyes, with the plush arrogance of a top dog, with her nascent transference to another man, with the accumulated resentment of years; she fought him with her money and her faith that her sister disliked him and was behind her now; with the thought of the new enemies he was making with his bitterness, with her quick guile against his wining and dining slowness, her health and beauty against his physical deterioration, her unscrupulousness against his moralities—for this inner battle she used even her weaknesses, fighting bravely and courageously with the old cans and crockery and bottles, the empty receptacles of her expiated sins, outrages, mistakes. And suddenly, in the space of two minutes, she achieved her victory and justified herself to herself without lie or subterfuge, cut the cord forever. Then she walked, weak in the legs and sobbing coolly, toward the household that was hers at last.

Dick waited until she was out of sight. Then he leaned his head forward on the parapet. The case was finished. Doctor Diver was at liberty.

CHAPTER X

AT TWO O'CLOCK THAT night the phone woke Nicole and she heard Dick answer it from what they called the restless bed, in the next room.

"Oui, oui . . . mais à qui est-ce-que je parle? . . . Oui . . ." His voice woke up with surprise. "But can I speak to one of the ladies, Sir the Officer? They are both ladies of the very highest prominence, ladies of connections that might cause political complications of the most serious. . . . It is a fact, I swear to you. . . . Very well, you will see."

He got up and, as he absorbed the situation, his self-knowledge assured him that he would undertake to deal with it—the old fatal pleasingness, the old forceful charm, swept back with its cry of "Use me!" He would have to go fix this thing that he didn't care a damn about, because it had early become a habit to be loved, perhaps from the moment when he had realized that he was the last hope of a decaying clan. On an almost parallel occasion, back in Dohmler's clinic on the Zürichsee, realizing this power, he had made his choice, chosen Ophelia, chosen the sweet poison and drunk it. Wanting above all to be brave and kind, he had wanted, even more than that, to be loved. So it had been. So it would ever be, he saw, simultaneously with the slow archaic tinkle from the phone box as he rang off.

There was a long pause. Nicole called, "What is it? Who is it?" Dick had begun to dress even as he hung up the phone.

"It's the poste de police in Antibes—they're holding Mary North and that Sibley-Biers. It's something serious—the agent wouldn't tell me; he kept saying 'pas de morts—pas d'automobiles,' but he implied it was just about everything else."

"Why on earth did they call on *you*? It sounds very peculiar to me."

321

"They've got to get out on bail to save their faces; and only some property owner in the Alpes Maritimes can give bail."

"They had their nerve."

"I don't mind. However, I'll pick up Gausse at the hotel——"

Nicole stayed awake after he had departed, wondering what offense they could have committed; then she slept. A little after three when Dick came in she sat up stark awake, saying "What?" as if to a character in her dream.

"It was an extraordinary story—" Dick said. He sat on the foot of her bed, telling her how he had roused old Gausse from an Alsatian coma, told him to clean out his cash drawer, and driven with him to the police station.

"I don't like to do something for that Anglaise," Gausse grumbled.

Mary North and Lady Caroline, dressed in the costume of French sailors, lounged on a bench outside the two dingy cells. The latter had the outraged air of a Briton who momentarily expected the Mediterranean fleet to steam up to her assistance. Mary Minghetti was in a condition of panic and collapse—she literally flung herself at Dick's stomach as though that were the point of greatest association, imploring him to do something. Meanwhile the chief of police explained the matter to Gausse, who listened to each word with reluctance, divided between being properly appreciative of the officer's narrative gift and showing that, as the perfect servant, the story had no shocking effect on him.

"It was merely a lark," said Lady Caroline with scorn. "We were pretending to be sailors on leave, and we picked up two silly girls. They got the wind up and made a rotten scene in a lodging house."

Dick nodded gravely, looking at the stone floor, like a priest in the confessional—he was torn between a tendency to ironic laughter and another tendency to order fifty stripes of the cat and a fortnight of bread and water. The lack, in Lady Caroline's face, of any sense of evil, except the evil wrought by cowardly Provençal girls and stupid police, confounded him; yet he had long concluded that certain classes of English people lived upon a concentrated essence of the anti-social that, in comparison, reduced the gorgings of New York to something like a child contracting indigestion from ice cream.

"I've got to get out before Hosain hears about this," Mary pleaded.

"Dick, you can always arrange things—you always could. Tell 'em we'll go right home, tell 'em we'll pay anything."

"I shall not," said Lady Caroline disdainfully. "Not a shilling. But I shall jolly well find out what the Consulate in Cannes has to say about this."

"No, no!" insisted Mary. "We've got to get out tonight."

"I'll see what I can do," said Dick, and added, "but money will certainly have to change hands." Looking at them as though they were the innocents that he knew they were not, he shook his head: "Of all the crazy stunts!"

Lady Caroline smiled complacently.

"You're an insanity doctor, aren't you? You ought to be able to help us—and Gausse has *got* to!"

At this point Dick went aside with Gausse and talked over the old man's findings. The affair was more serious than had been indicated—one of the girls whom they had picked up was of a respectable family. The family were furious, or pretended to be; a settlement would have to be made with them. The other one, a girl of the port, could be more easily dealt with. There were French statutes that would make conviction punishable by imprisonment or, at the very least, public expulsion from the country. In addition to the difficulties, there was a growing difference in tolerance between such townspeople as benefited by the foreign colony and the ones who were annoyed by the consequent rise of prices. Gausse, having summarized the situation, turned it over to Dick. Dick called the chief of police into conference.

"Now you know that the French government wants to encourage American touring—so much so that in Paris this summer there's an order that Americans can't be arrested except for the most serious offenses."

"This is serious enough, my God."

"But look now—you have their cartes d'identité?"

"They had none. They had nothing—two hundred francs and some rings. Not even shoe-laces that they could have hung themselves with!"

Relieved that there had been no cartes d'identité Dick continued.

"The Italian countess is still an American citizen. She is the grand-daughter—" he told a string of lies slowly and portentously, "—of John D. Rockefeller Mellon. You have heard of him?"

"Yes, oh heavens, yes. You mistake me for a nobody?"

"In addition she is the niece of Lord Henry Ford and so connected with the Renault and Citroën companies—" He thought he had better stop here. However, the sincerity of his voice had begun to affect the officer, so he continued: "To arrest her is just as if you arrested a great royalty of England. It might mean—War!"

"But how about the Englishwoman?"

"I'm coming to that. She is affianced to the brother of the Prince of Wales—the Duke of Buckingham."

"She will be an exquisite bride for him."

"Now we are prepared to give—" Dick calculated quickly, "one thousand francs to each of the girls—and an additional thousand to the father of the 'serious' one. Also two thousand in addition, for you to distribute as you think best—" he shrugged his shoulders, "—among the men who made the arrest, the lodging-house keeper, and so forth. I shall hand you the five thousand and expect you to do the negotiating immediately. Then they can be released on bail on some charge like disturbing the peace, and whatever fine there is will be paid before the magistrate tomorrow —by messenger."

Before the officer spoke Dick saw by his expression that it would be all right. The man said hesitantly, "I have made no entry because they have no cartes d'identité. I must see—give me the money."

An hour later Dick and M. Gausse dropped the women by the Majestic Hotel, where Lady Caroline's chauffeur slept in her landaulet.

"Remember," said Dick, "you owe M. Gausse a hundred dollars apiece."

"All right," Mary agreed, "I'll give him a check tomorrow— and something more."

"Not I!" Startled, they all turned to Lady Caroline, who, now entirely recovered, was swollen with righteousness. "The whole thing was an outrage. By no means did I authorize you to give a hundred dollars to those people."

Little Gausse stood beside the car, his eyes blazing suddenly.

"You won't pay me?"

"Of course she will," said Dick.

Suddenly the abuse that Gausse had once endured as a bus boy in London flamed up and he walked through the moonlight up to Lady Caroline.

He whipped a string of condemnatory words about her and, as she turned away with a frozen laugh, he took a step after her and swiftly planted his little foot in the most celebrated of targets. Lady Caroline, taken by surprise, flung up her hands like a person shot as her sailor-clad form sprawled forward on the sidewalk.

Dick's voice cut across her raging: "Mary, you quiet her down! or you'll both be in leg-irons in ten minutes!"

On the way back to the hotel old Gausse said not a word, until they passed the Juan-les-Pins Casino, still sobbing and coughing with jazz; then he sighed forth:

"I have never seen women like this sort of women. I have known many of the great courtesans of the world, and for them I have much respect often, but women like these women I have never seen before."

CHAPTER XI

DICK AND NICOLE WERE accustomed to go together to the barber, and have haircuts and shampoos in adjoining rooms. From Dick's side Nicole could hear the snip of shears, the count of changes, the Voilàs and Pardons. The day after his return they went down to be shorn and washed in the perfumed breeze of the fans.

In front of the Carleton Hotel, its windows as stubbornly blank to the summer as so many cellar doors, a car passed them and Tommy Barban was in it. Nicole's momentary glimpse of his expression, taciturn and thoughtful and, in the second of seeing her, wide-eyed and alert, disturbed her. She wanted to be going where he was going. The hour with the hair-dresser seemed one of the wasteful intervals that composed her life, another little prison. The coiffeuse in her white uniform, faintly sweating lip-rouge and cologne, reminded her of many nurses.

In the next room Dick dozed under an apron and a lather of soap. The mirror in front of Nicole reflected the passage between the men's side and the women's, and Nicole started up at the sight of Tommy entering and wheeling sharply into the men's shop. She knew with a flush of joy that there was going to be some sort of showdown.

She heard fragments of its beginning.

"Hello, I want to see you."

". . . serious."

". . . serious."

". . . perfectly agreeable."

In a minute Dick came into Nicole's booth, his expression emerging annoyed from behind the towel of his hastily rinsed face.

"Your friend has worked himself up into a state. He wants to see us together, so I agreed to have it over with. Come along!"

"But my hair—it's half cut."

"Never mind—come along!"

Resentfully she had the staring coiffeuse remove the towels.

Feeling messy and unadorned she followed Dick from the hotel. Outside Tommy bent over her hand.

"We'll go to the Café des Alliées," said Dick.

"Wherever we can be alone," Tommy agreed.

Under the arching trees, central in summer, Dick asked: "Will you take anything Nicole?"

"A citron pressé."

"For me a demi," said Tommy.

"The Blackenwite with siphon," said Dick.

"Il n'y a plus de Blackenwite. Nous n'avons que le Johnny Walkair."

> *"She's—not—wired for sound*
> *but on the quiet*
> *you ought to try it——"*

"Your wife does not love you," said Tommy suddenly. "She loves me."

The two men regarded each other with a curious impotence of expression. There can be little communication between men in that position, for their relation is indirect, and consists of how much each of them has possessed or will possess of the woman in question, so that their emotions pass through her divided self as through a bad telephone connection.

"Wait a minute," Dick said. "Donnez moi du gin et du siphon."

"Bien, Monsieur."

"All right, go on, Tommy."

"It's very plain to me that your marriage to Nicole has run its course. She is through. I've waited five years for that to be so."

"What does Nicole say?"

They both looked at her.

"I've gotten very fond of Tommy, Dick."

He nodded.

"You don't care for me any more," she continued. "It's all just habit. Things were never the same after Rosemary."

Unattracted to this angle, Tommy broke in sharply with:

"You don't understand Nicole. You treat her always like a patient because she was once sick."

They were suddenly interrupted by an insistent American, of sinister aspect, vending copies of the *Herald* and of the *Times* fresh from New York.

"Got everything here, Buddies," he announced. "Been here long?"

"Cessez cela! Allez ouste!" Tommy cried; and then to Dick, "Now no woman would stand such——"

"Buddies," interrupted the American again. "You think I'm wasting my time—but lots of others don't." He brought a gray clipping from his purse—it cartooned millions of Americans pouring from liners with bags of gold. "You think I'm not going to get part of that? Well, I am. I'm just over from Nice for the Tour de France."

As Tommy got him off with a fierce "allez-vous en," Dick called after him, "When does the Tour de France get here?"

"Any minute now, Buddy."

He departed at last with a cheery wave and Tommy returned to Dick.

"Elle doit avoir plus avec moi qu'avec vous."

"Speak English! What do you mean 'doit avoir'?"

"'Doit avoir?' Would have more happiness with me."

"You'd be new to each other. But Nicole and I have had much happiness together, Tommy."

"L'amour de famille," Tommy said, scoffing.

"If you and Nicole married wouldn't that be 'l'amour de famille'?" The increasing commotion made him break off; presently it came to a serpentine head on the promenade and a group, presently a crowd, of people sprung from hidden siestas lined the curbstone.

Boys sprinted past on bicycles, automobiles jammed with elaborate betasselled sportsmen slid up the street, high horns tooted to announce the approach of the race, and unsuspected cooks in undershirts appeared at restaurant doors as around a bend a procession came into sight. First was a lone cyclist in a red jersey, toiling intent and confident out of the westering sun, passing to the melody of a high chattering cheer. Then three together in a harlequinade of faded color, legs caked yellow with dust and sweat, faces expressionless, eyes heavy and endlessly tired.

Tommy faced Dick, saying: "I think Nicole wants a divorce—I suppose you'll make no obstacles?"

A troupe of fifty more swarmed after the first bicycle racers, strung out over two hundred yards; a few were smiling and self-conscious, a few obviously exhausted, most of them indifferent and weary. A retinue of small boys passed, a few defiant stragglers, a light truck carried the victims of accident and defeat. They were back at the table. Nicole wanted Dick to take the initiative, but he seemed content to sit with his face half-shaved matching her hair half-washed.

"Isn't it true you're not happy with me any more?" Nicole continued. "Without me you could get to your work again—you could work better if you didn't worry about me."

Tommy moved impatiently.

"That is so useless. Nicole and I love each other, that's all there is to it."

"Well, then," said the Doctor, "since it's all settled, suppose we go back to the barber shop."

Tommy wanted a row: "There are several points——"

"Nicole and I will talk things over," said Dick equitably. "Don't worry—I agree in principle, and Nicole and I understand each other. There's less chance of unpleasantness if we avoid a three-cornered discussion."

Unwillingly acknowledging Dick's logic, Tommy was moved by an irresistible racial tendency to chisel for an advantage.

"Let it be understood that from this moment," he said, "I stand in the position of Nicole's protector until details can be arranged. And I shall hold you strictly accountable for any abuse of the fact that you continue to inhabit the same house."

Dick nodded and walked off toward the hotel, with Nicole's whitest eyes following him.

"He was fair enough," Tommy conceded. "Darling, will we be together tonight?"

"I suppose so."

So it had happened—and with a minimum of drama; Nicole felt outguessed, realizing that from the episode of the camphor-rub, Dick had anticipated everything. But also she felt happy and excited, and the odd little wish that she could tell Dick all about it faded quickly. But her eyes followed his figure until it became a dot and mingled with the other dots in the summer crowd.

CHAPTER XII

THE DAY BEFORE DOCTOR DIVER left the Riviera he spent all his time with his children. He was not young any more with a lot of nice thoughts and dreams to have about himself, so he wanted to remember them well. The children had been told that this winter they would be with their aunt in London and that soon they were going to come and see him in America. Fraülein was not to be discharged without his consent.

He was glad he had given so much to the little girl. About the boy he was more uncertain—always he had been uneasy about what he had to give to the ever-climbing, ever-clinging, breast-searching young. But, when he said good-bye to them, he wanted to lift their beautiful heads off their necks and hold them close for hours.

He embraced the old gardener who had made the first garden at Villa Diana six years ago; he kissed the Provençal girl who helped with the children. She had been with them for almost a decade and she fell on her knees and cried until Dick jerked her to her feet and gave her three hundred francs. Nicole was sleeping late, as had been agreed upon—he left a note for her and one for Baby Warren, who was just back from Sardinia and staying at the house. Dick took a big drink from a bottle of brandy three feet high, holding ten quarts, that some one had presented them with.

Then he decided to leave his bags by the station in Cannes and take a last look at Gausse's beach.

The beach was peopled with only an advance guard of children when Nicole and her sister arrived that morning. A white sun, chivied of outline by a white sky, boomed over a windless day. Waiters were putting extra ice into the bar; an American photographer from the AP worked with his equipment in a precarious shade and looked up quickly at every footfall descending the stone steps. At the hotel his prospective subjects slept late in darkened rooms upon their recent opiate of dawn.

When Nicole started out on the beach she saw Dick, not dressed for swimming, sitting on a rock above. She shrank back in the shadow of her dressing-tent. In a minute Baby joined her, saying:

"Dick's still there."

"I saw him."

"I think he might have the delicacy to go."

"This is his place—in a way, he discovered it. Old Gausse always says he owes everything to Dick."

Baby looked calmly at her sister.

"We should have let him confine himself to his bicycle excursions," she remarked. "When people are taken out of their depths they lose their heads, no matter how charming a bluff they put up."

"Dick was a good husband to me for six years," Nicole said. "All that time I never suffered a minute's pain because of him, and he always did his best never to let anything hurt me."

Baby's lower jaw projected slightly as she said:

"That's what he was educated for."

The sisters sat in silence, Nicole wondering in a tired way about things, Baby considering whether or not to marry the latest candidate for her hand and money, an authenticated Hapsburg. She was not quite *think*ing about it. Her affairs had long shared such a sameness that, as she dried out, they were more important for their conversational value than for themselves. Her emotions had their truest existence in the telling of them.

"Is he gone?" Nicole asked after a while. "I think his train leaves at noon."

Baby looked.

"No. He's moved up higher on the terrace and he's talking to some women. Anyhow there are so many people now that he doesn't *have* to see us."

He had seen them though, as they left their pavilion, and he followed them with his eyes until they disappeared again. He sat with Mary Minghetti, drinking anisette.

"You were like you used to be the night you helped us," she was saying, "except at the end, when you were horrid about Caroline. Why aren't you nice like that always? You can be."

It seemed fantastic to Dick to be in a position where Mary North could tell him about things.

"Your friends still like you, Dick. But you say awful things to people when you've been drinking. I've spent most of my time defending you this summer."

"That remark is one of Doctor Eliot's classics."

"It's true. Nobody cares whether you drink or not—" She hesitated, "Even when Abe drank hardest, he never offended people like you do."

"You're all so dull," he said.

"But we're all there is!" cried Mary. "If you don't like nice people, try the ones who aren't nice, and see how you like that! All people want is to have a good time and if you make them unhappy you cut yourself off from nourishment."

"Have I been nourished?" he asked.

Mary was having a good time, though she did not know it, as she had sat down with him only out of fear. Again she refused a drink and said: "Self-indulgence is back of it. Of course, after Abe you can imagine how I feel about it—since I watched the progress of a good man toward alcoholism——"

Down the steps tripped Lady Caroline Sibley-Biers with blithe theatricality.

Dick felt fine—he was already well in advance of the day, arrived at where a man should be at the end of a good dinner, yet he showed only a fine, considered, restrained interest in Mary. His eyes, for the moment clear as a child's, asked her sympathy and stealing over him he felt the old necessity of convincing her that he was the last man in the world and she was the last woman.

. . . Then he would not have to look at those two other figures, a man and a woman, black and white and metallic against the sky. . . .

"You once liked me, didn't you?" he asked.

"*Liked* you—I *loved* you. Everybody loved you. You could've had anybody you wanted for the asking——"

"There has always been something between you and me."

She bit eagerly. "Has there, Dick?"

"Always—I knew your troubles and how brave you were about them." But the old interior laughter had begun inside him and he knew he couldn't keep it up much longer.

"I always thought you knew a lot," Mary said enthusiastically. "More about me than anyone has ever known. Perhaps that's why I was so afraid of you when we didn't get along so well."

His glance fell soft and kind upon hers, suggesting an emotion underneath; their glances married suddenly, bedded, strained together. Then, as the laughter inside of him became so loud that it seemed as if Mary must hear it, Dick switched off the light and they were back in the Riviera sun.

"I must go," he said. As he stood up he swayed a little; he did not feel well any more—his blood raced slow. He raised his right hand and with a papal cross he blessed the beach from the high terrace. Faces turned upward from several umbrellas.

"I'm going to him," Nicole got to her knees.

"No, you're not," said Tommy, pulling her down firmly. "Let well enough alone."

CHAPTER XIII

NICOLE KEPT IN TOUCH with Dick after her new marriage; there were letters on business matters, and about the children. When she said, as she often did, "I loved Dick and I'll never forget him," Tommy answered, "Of course not—why should you?"

Dick opened an office in Buffalo, but evidently without success. Nicole did not find what the trouble was, but she heard a few months later that he was in a little town named Batavia, New York, practising general medicine, and later that he was in Lockport, doing the same thing. By accident she heard more about his life there than anywhere: that he bicycled a lot, was much admired by the ladies, and always had a big stack of papers on his desk that were known to be an important treatise on some medical subject, almost in process of completion. He was considered to have fine manners and once made a good speech at a public health meeting on the subject of drugs; but he became entangled with a girl who worked in a grocery store, and he was also involved in a lawsuit about some medical question; so he left Lockport.

After that he didn't ask for the children to be sent to America and didn't answer when Nicole wrote asking him if he needed money. In the last letter she had from him he told her that he was practising in Geneva, New York, and she got the impression that he had settled down with someone to keep house for him. She looked up Geneva in an atlas and found it was in the heart of the Finger Lakes section and considered a pleasant place. Perhaps, so she liked to think, his career was biding its time, again like Grant's in Galena; his latest note was post-marked from Hornell, New York, which is some distance from Geneva and a very small town; in any case he is almost certainly in that section of the country, in one town or another.

APPENDIX
AND
NOTES

APPENDIX

The Manuscripts of "Tender"

FITZGERALD HAD SAVED MOST of his papers, and his daughter, Mrs. Samuel J. Lanahan, has given them to the Princeton University Library. There the various drafts of *Tender Is the Night* are kept in six big blue cartons, with some additional folders of notes, in the air-conditioned basement of the Manuscript Room. The drafts and notes and false beginnings would repay a closer study than the present editor has been able to give them. They reveal how an author who was not a born novelist, but rather a romantic poet with a gift for social observation, a highly developed critical sense, and a capacity for taking infinite pains, went about the long task of putting his world into a book.

Opening the cartons one after another we can trace the novel in its different versions and trace each scene or chapter through its successive stages: larva, pupa, imago. First there will be notes and observations on the chapter to be written and perhaps a schedule of working hours; then a manuscript pencilled by Fitzgerald in his high, narrow, hasty and unformed, but quite legible scrawl; then a typescript made by his secretary and corrected by the author, with pages crossed out and others written in; then there will be a second typescript—and often this will be rejected as a whole, with the author starting over from the beginning, in pencil, and making new corrections before giving his work to the copyist.

It is possible to distinguish three separate versions of the novel. The first is the Melarky version, which was started on the Riviera in the late summer of 1925. In April of the following year Fitzgerald wrote to his agent, Harold Ober, "The novel is about one-fourth done and will be delivered for possible serialization about January 1st. It will be about 75,000 words long, divided into 12 chapters,

335

concerning tho this is absolutely confidential such a case as that girl who shot her mother on the Pacific coast last year." The background of the novel would be the Riviera, Paris, and Rome. The hero would be Francis Melarky, a young technician from Hollywood with a domineering mother. Francis would fall in love with a woman like Nicole Diver, would go on too many wild parties, would lose control of himself, and would kill his mother in a fit of rage. He would be pursued and punished for the crime, although it seems that the author never decided exactly how he was going to die. Fitzgerald wrote several drafts of four long chapters of the Melarky version and they are in the blue cartons at Princeton. Apparently there was once a draft, now lost or destroyed, of four additional chapters.

The second or Rosemary version of the novel is undated, but it has connections with two of Fitzgerald's published stories—"The Rough Crossing" (1929) and "One Trip Abroad" (1930)—and it must have been written at about the same time. The events of the first two chapters, which are the only ones preserved in the blue cartons, take place on a luxury liner bound for Europe. Lewellen Kelly, as Fitzgerald spelled the new hero's name, is a famous young moving-picture director who has become dissatisfied with his work in Hollywood; he is taking his wife, Nicole, for a two years' vacation in Europe, although he also plans to make some pictures there. Rosemary and her mother appear in this manuscript for the first time. They are travelling in the cheapest class, tourist third, but the mother has Rosemary dress in her best gown and steal into first class through the engine room, so that Kelly will see her and give her a screen test. There is the promise that all the characters will meet again on the summer Riviera. . . . Kelly and his wife reappear in the story "One Trip Abroad" and there they undergo a process of deterioration that is very much like Dick Diver's.

The third or Dick Diver version of the novel was started from a new plan early in 1932 and was carried through to the end. It fills most of the space in the six blue cartons, not only because it is longer but also because it exists in more stages than the other versions: besides the notes for it, the early drafts in pencil, the first and second typescripts, and the corrected carbons, there are also galley and page proofs from *Scribner's Magazine* and proofs of the pub-

lished book with Fitzgerald's revisions, which had no end. Paul
Valéry once said that a work of art is never finished, but merely
abandoned. Fitzgerald was unwilling to abandon *Tender Is the
Night* and even after the novel had appeared in *Scribner's,* complete
in four installments, he worked over it until the last moment, missing his little mistakes but trying to strengthen the big effects; he
omitted half a dozen scenes, shortened many others, and inserted
page after page of typescript into the galley proofs.

Although the three versions differ widely from one another, we
feel no doubt in reading them that they are stages in writing a single
novel. The essential theme is the same in all three: an ambitious
young American goes to Europe and is ruined by his contact with
the leisure class. All three have the same backgrounds—although we
make our first visit to Switzerland in "One Trip Abroad"—and all
have the contrast between hard-working Hollywood people and the
idle rich. Most of the persons mentioned in the first version reappear
in the last, even if some of them have changed their names not once
but twice: thus, Abe North was originally Abe Grant and then became Abe Herkimer, while keeping the same traits. On the other
hand, Nicole Diver loses some of the traits that she had possessed
when she was Dinah Piper and borrows some new traits from her
namesake of the Rosemary version, Nicole Kelly. At first these little
transformations are confusing to follow; but as one continues to
read through the early manuscripts the characters become as familiar
as a close group of friends and behave as we have known our friends
to do—some of them changing in front of our eyes, some dropping
out of sight, and some—like Albert McKisco, for example—remaining always and reassuringly the same. They have adventures that
Fitzgerald describes in one version and omits in another. The file
of manuscripts gives us the picture of a complete little world; the
finished novel gives us only segments of that world, but they are
chosen in such a fashion as to imply the rest of it.

Fitzgerald was both a miser and a spendthrift in his use of material. His first drafts of the various scenes, though interesting in
conception, were sometimes as bald in the telling as boys' stories by
Horatio Alger or G. A. Henty. Almost always, however, they would
contain a few telling phrases or a gesture that revealed character and
Fitzgerald tried never to throw those good things away. They

would reappear in the rewriting of the scene, together with other good phrases that had occurred to him; and if the scene was abandoned they would be copied into his notebook for future use. He saved bits and pieces, like an old man saving ends of string. There is a remark of Abe North's—"Tired of friends. The thing is to have sycophants"—that appears in different scenes scattered through half a dozen manuscripts. On the other hand, Fitzgerald could also be madly improvident. Having reworked a scene many times and having thickened it with the fragments of other scenes, he was capable of throwing it away because his narrative had to move faster or because he judged that the finished episode, no matter how effective in itself, was not essential to the broader effect at which he was aiming.

As examples of many other omissions, there is room in this Appendix for two episodes dropped from the manuscript at various stages. The first is a night piece—Fitzgerald was always good at them—from Chapter IV of the Melarky version. It was first printed by Arthur Mizener in the Autumn 1948 issue of *Kenyon Review,* where it appeared with the preceding scene from the same chapter, under the title of "The World's Fair." Note that Seth and Dinah Piper in the episode are earlier incarnations of Dick and Nicole Diver.

1. WANDA BREASTED

WHEN FRANCIS REACHED THE bar where he had arranged to meet Wanda Breasted, he found her in the company of three other girls. They were tall slender girls with rather small, well-carried heads, groomed to the preciseness of manikins' heads, and charming floating faces. They had evidently been in the bar a long time, but none of them was tight, and when Wanda presented Francis their heads above their black tailored suits waved gracefully at him like cobras' hoods or long-stemmed flowers in the wind. Francis had an immediate feeling that he had met all three of them somewhere before. Wanda whispered to him that they were all having dinner together—she couldn't avoid it, but he was not to pay for anything, for it was Miss Hart's party and there was another young man, now out telephoning, who would join them presently.

Wanda said to the others that he was a friend of Seth Piper's and at once the three women extended themselves toward him, expressing surprise and interest that the Pipers were in Paris. The girl whose mouth twisted kindly under a hooked nose said:

"Not that I should be concerned—after their being so obviously fed up with me."

Then the tallest and handsomest girl said bitterly, "I must say I prefer people whose lives have more corrugated surfaces. Seth might be all right if she'd give him a chance."

Miss Hart, a boyish, jaunty girl who might have been anything between twenty-five and thirty-five, spoke in a hearty voice:

"After all, darling, what's so extraordinary about them? I've met them here and there and after expecting at least Saint Louis and Joan of Arc I haven't been able to get really excited about them."

"Seth's the extraordinary one," said the girl the Pipers were fed up with. "Dinah's just a very loyal, frank person."

"A loyal, frank person," repeated the other bitterly. "Yes—she's got to be that if she has to bitch everybody in the world to do it."

Francis was furious but he was somewhat intimidated by their height and sleekness and by the attentive and finely critical look they bent upon him whenever he opened his mouth to speak. Feeling himself slipping here and there among changing indignations he gave up and told himself how hard and superficial everyone was after Seth and Dinah. They were in any case not talking to him, but to each other. Again they reminded him of something and again it slipped away.

"I don't really think she likes all this changing around of friends," insisted Miss Taube. "Of course my private opinion is that Seth made her up."

"But why the entirely liquid Mr. Grant?" asked Miss Hart.

"That's Mrs. Grant—Seth will stand a lot from anyone capable of telling him in new ways how charming he is."

"My God!" muttered Francis. They all threw him a flinching glance and Miss Taube said conciliatingly:

"After all, I'm only sorry Seth doesn't like me any more—and some day it might be his whim to honor me once again with a moment or so of his attentions, and hand me my self-respect, my justification on a platter, as he has a way of doing."

The handsomest head swayed forward eagerly like a cobra's hood:

"Once I tried to paint him. I know how his face goes, but I always had one eye left over. The answer was that his eyes are too close together."

"My God," said Francis again.

"So are mine, dearest. Seth's great quality is that politeness of his that seems to extend right out of the ordinary world of courtesy. One advantage of politeness like that in a man is to be able to deal with women on our own grounds—please or torture them as it may prove necessary. And not fire random shots from his own camp many miles away—like Big Bertha, you know, accidentally slaying whole congregations."

"What struck me is their self-satisfaction, their positive admiration for their own things——"

"—Which you must admit are usually the best things."

"Oh, they give a good show—I'd be the last one ever to deny that. I remember that famous houseboat party. And I'm willing to admit that Seth is quite amusing—but so Irish; his face begins to move before he says anything in that Irish way. And those phrases he uses over and over: 'Oldest inhabitant gnawed by rodents'—how many times have you heard him say that? And that one way of imitating everything, whether it's an Englishman or a billy goat—he widens his nostrils, waves his head from side to side, and talks through his nose."

"Everybody has only one way of imitating that they use for everything."

Sometime during this conversation they were joined by the young man who had been telephoning. To Francis' disgust he was One of the Boys, and Francis searched vainly for any way he might extricate himself from the situation. He looked reproachfully at Wanda, who smiled back encouragingly, and again his desire for her was renewed. She was a special red-and-white type that always aroused him and certainly the pressure of her hand the other day had been in a sense a promise, of how much he couldn't say.

Through dinner he felt his mind wandering off the company; things were so dead after the Pipers and he wondered what they were doing tonight. They had saved tonight for something, perhaps, he thought with a sudden sense of being shut out—perhaps to be alone.

He drank a lot of champagne at dinner but was taciturn and had the feeling that the three girls didn't like him any more than he liked them. First he felt this only casually but later it deepened, and dancing afterward at the Bœuf sur le Toit he saw they were inclined to be cold with him.

"I'm getting tight and cross," he thought, "I'd better go home. What a rotten evening. What bum people." He asked Wanda if they couldn't go.

"Yes, but wait," she answered. "They'll be furious if I take you off."

"Well, who are they? Why should you care?"

"I don't, but wait."

They were dancing close together and suddenly he told her he wanted her. Surely her smile as she bent back and looked up at him was consent, yet she said:

"Isn't this enough?"

"Of course not."

"Don't you think this is enough?"

He got nothing more than that from her, but his next glass of champagne made him genial at last; he even consented to move on to another place, but Miss Carmichael was in the taxi with Wanda and himself and he could do no more than press her hand.

He knew they were girls of some distinction; he did not make the mistake of lumping them as bluestockings or Lesbians. They were three tall rich American girls and that was the principal thing about them. To be a tall rich American girl is a form of hereditary achievement, whether or not progress does eventually culminate in her insouciant promenade along the steel girder of our prosperity. Nevertheless it was increasingly clear to him that Miss Taube had more immediate concerns—there was a flick of the lip somewhere, a bending of the smile toward some indirection, a momentary lifting and dropping of the curtain over a hidden passage. An hour later he came out of somewhere to a taxi whither they had preceded him and found Wanda limp and drunk in Miss Taube's arms.

"What's the idea?" he demanded furiously.

Miss Taube smiled at him. Wanda opened her eyes sleepily and said, "Hello."

"What's all this business?" he repeated.

"I love Wanda," said Miss Taube.

"Vivian is a nice girl," said Wanda. "Come sit back here with us."

"Why can't you get out of the taxicab and go home with your friends," said Francis harshly to Miss Taube. "You know you have no business to do this. She's tight."

"I love Wanda," repeated Miss Taube good-naturedly.

"I don't care. Please get out."

In answer Wanda drew the girl close to her again, whereupon in a spasm of fury Francis opened the door, took her by the arm, and, before the girl understood his purpose, deposited her in a sitting position on the curb.

"This is perfectly outrageous!" she cried.

"I should say it is," he agreed, his voice trembling. A chasseur and several bystanders hurried up; Francis spoke to the driver and got into the cab quickly. The incident had wakened Wanda.

"Why did you do that?" she demanded. "I'll have to go back."

"Do you realize what she was doing?"

"Vivian's a nice girl."

"Vivian's a——"

"I don't feel good."

"What's your address?"

She told him and he sat back, robbed and glowering. The sight of this almost legendary aberration in action had spoiled some great series of human facts for him, as it had when he had first become aware of its other face some years before. Better Hollywood's bizarre variations on the normal, with George Collins on the phone ordering twelve beautiful girls for dinner, none over nineteen. He wanted to go back and kill that girl.

The cab stopped in front of a cluster of murky brown doors so alike that to be identified it seemed that hers must be counted off from the abutting blackness of an alley.

"Can you get in alone?"

"Maybe." But getting from the cab she wobbled helplessly and he helped her to the door and up an ancient circular stairway to her apartment, where he fumbled in her bag for the key.

It was one room in listless disorder, opening off a bathroom with a tin tub. The daybed was covered with a length of blue felt on which reversed letters of ravelled thread spelled out "Bryn Mawr—1924." Wanda went into the bathroom without speaking and Francis opened a window which looked on a narrow and tubular court, gray as rats, but echoing at the moment to a plaintive and peculiar music. It was two men chanting in an unfamiliar language full of k's and l's—he leaned out but he could not see them; there was obviously a religious significance in the sounds, and tired and emotionless he let them pray for him too, but what for, save that he should never lose himself in the darkness of his own mind, he did not know. He felt no passion, only a lowering of his faculties—but they tightened with a nervous wrench of his heart at the sound of a pistol shot from the bathroom.

"Ah, my!" he gasped.

In a second he opened the door of the bathroom. Wanda faced him weakly with a small pistol wobbling in her hand. It was an old pistol, for as he took it away from her a slice of pearl came off the handle and fell on the floor.

"What do you want to do?" he asked imperatively.

"I don't know, I was just shooting it."

She sat down on the water closet with a coquettish smile. Her eyes, glazed a few minutes since, were full of an impish malice.

"What's the trouble? Are you in any trouble?"

"Nobody's in trouble. Nothing's trouble. Everybody is responsible for what they do."

"You're not, you're tight."

Any minute he expected a knocking at the door, but perhaps from fear or indifference nothing stirred in the house—even the singing in the areaway continued, sad as a flute, and moment by moment they were more alone in the flat.

"You'd better go to bed," he said.

She laughed scornfully. "Go to bed and lie there? What for?"

"Well—" he said after considering unsuccessfully, "I don't want to go away and leave you like this. Are you all right now?"

"Oh, get out!" she said unpleasantly. "Leave me my pistol."

He took out the little shells and handed the gun back to her, but at the look of childish craftiness in her eyes he became disturbed.

"You've got more shells. Look here, you're behaving like an idiot. What's the matter—are you broke?"

She shook her head. "Just lousy with money."

"Is it something about that girl?"

Her eyes narrowed defiantly. "She's a very nice girl. She's been very good to me."

"She wasn't behaving very well tonight."

"She's very nice." Suddenly she seemed to remember. "You were the one. You pulled her out of the cab into the public gutter. She'll never forgive that," she shook her head solemnly, "never—never. Got a cigarette?"

She leaned back comfortably against the waterpipe, as one enjoying the moment at leisure. Francis lit her a cigarette impatiently and waited. He was very tired but he was afraid to leave her alone, as much for himself as for her. At the moment he didn't give a damn whether she killed herself or not because he was so tired, but her friends knew that he had taken her home and there was a concierge below.

"I'm pretty tired," he said—unfortunately, because this gave her an advantage; she wasn't tired; although her mind moved in a tedious half time like a slow moving picture, her nerves were crowded with feverish traffic. She tried to think of some mischief.

"You were after me," she said accusingly.

"What of it?"

She laughed sneeringly.

"I'll go home—if you'll tell me where the rest of the shells are and then hop into bed and get some sleep."

"Oh, s . . .!" she cried. "You'll tuck the baby in, will you—you God damn old fool—you meig me sick to my stomach."

Half an hour passed. When he was silent she took her ease, refusing to leave the bathroom. When he made a motion to go she woke like a watchdog and held him there. He looked in the bureau for shells till she cried, "Let my things alone." He thought of calling the concierge, but that would be to arouse the house surely; dawn was filtering into the bedroom now, the singing had long ago ceased.

He hated her for entangling him in this sordidness—it was unbelievable that he had ever desired her, a hysterical Lesbian, keeping him there as if she had any possible right. He would have liked to hit her—but at the thought of her bruised in all this trouble of hers a complete revulsion of feeling went over him; he went and knelt beside her and put his arm about her shoulder.

"Poor little girl, what is it? Tell me—are you busted or something, or have you gotten mixed up with those Lesbians?"

She broke down suddenly.

"Oh, no," she cried, "I wanted to see if I could—sleep with you—I——"

Then as suddenly she was herself again.

"You can go now," she said after a moment coldly.

"What are you going to do?"

"Going to sleep, what do you think I'm going to do—set myself on fire? Take the pistol if you want."

She began taking off her dress. Without looking at him she turned on the hot water in the wash basin and looked at herself in the mirror.

"Good-bye."

"Bye."

Outside it was morning; he stopped at a workman's bistro for a cup of coffee. "Good God, this is getting to be a hell of a world," he thought. Now ne remembered stories he had heard in California. It was all very depressing and it frightened him, as if someone he knew were being operated on. He wanted to see Seth and Dinah and he made up his mind on a savage impulse to tell the story to his mother. "God damn these women!" he thought.

*

* *

Although Fitzgerald was unable to use the Wanda Breasted passage in *Tender Is the Night,* he managed to salvage part of it. The three tall American girls with heads like cobras appear in Chapter V of Book III and make some of their comments on the Divers. The chant in the unfamiliar language full of k's and l's is heard when Dick and Nicole are visiting the Minghettis, in Chapter IV of Book V. Some of the other incidents and phrases were copied into Fitzgerald's notebooks and were reprinted after his death in *The Crack-Up.*

The second passage from the manuscript is being printed in full for the first time. It comes from a late draft of *Tender* and was omitted by Fitzgerald before the last installment of the novel came out in *Scribner's Magazine.* Describing as it does the last hours of Nicole's first night with Tommy Barban, it belongs at the end of Chapter VIII of Book V.

2. MONSIEUR IRV

At the beach casino in Monte Carlo Nicole was still happy. Several acquaintances looked at them as if to say "Hurray for you—so you're with us at last!" She rather liked their sly smiles, and smiled back confessionally. She and Tommy left early, heading west along the shore. In the deep black of ten o'clock he stopped in front of a tall iron grille at the end of the promontory at Beaulieu.

"We are here," he said to Nicole. "Did you ever read the books of Phillips Oppenheim?"

"I think I've read one."

"He's one of my favorite American writers," Tommy said simply. "He writes about the Riviera, you know. I don't know whether the things he writes about are true but this place is like that."

Standing before the gate they were suddenly bathed in a small floodlight, quick as a flashlight, that left them blinded for a moment. Then a voice from behind the gate:

"Who's this, please?"

"Tell Monsieur Irv that it's Monsieur Tommy. Tell him we can't come in the house but can he come out in the garden a minute."

A section of the gate rumbled open like a safe and they were in a park, following a young Italian-American dandy toward a lighted house. They waited just out of range of the porch light, and presently the door opened and a dark thin man of forty came out and gazed blindly.

"Where you, Tommy?"

"Down here. Don't come. I have a lady with me who wants to remain anonymous."

"How?"

"I've got a lady with me who doesn't want to be seen—like you."

"Oh, I unestand, I unestand."

"We want to swim. Anybody on your beach?"

"Nobody, nobody. Go ahead, Tommy. You want suits, towels?"

"All right, some towels. Nobody's going to come down, are they?"

"No, no, nobody. Say, did you see Du Pont de Nemours went up——"

"No stock market in the presence of ladies."

"All right, excuse me, lady. You wait now—Salve will take you down —don't want you to get in trouble."

As Irv re-entered the house Tommy said, "Probably he's phoning the machine gunner to pass us. He was a fellow townsman of yours in Chicago—now he has the best beach on the Riviera."

Curiously Nicole followed down an intricate path, then through a sliding steel door that operated like a guillotine, out into a roofless cavern of white moonlight, formed by pale boulders about a cup of phosphorescent waters. It faced Monaco and the blur of Mentone be-

yond. She liked his taste in bringing her here—from the high-handed
storming of Mr. Irv's fortress to the eastward vision and the novel tricks
of wind and water, it was all as new as they were to each other. Symbolically she lay across his saddle-bow as surely as if he had wolfed her
from Damascus and they had come out upon the Mongolian plain. Moment by moment all that Dick had taught her fell away and she was
ever near what she had been in the beginning, prototype of that obscure
yielding up of swords that was going on in the world all about her.
Tangled with love in the moonlight she welcomed the anarchy of her
lover.

They awoke together, finding the moon gone down and the air cool.
She struggled up demanding the time and Tommy called it roughly
at three.

"I've got to go home then."

"I thought we'd sleep in Monte Carlo."

"No. There's the governess and the children. I've got to roll in before daylight."

"As you like."

They dipped for a second, and when he saw her shivering he rubbed
her briskly with a towel. Then, as they started back the lane by which
they had come, Tommy tripped over a wire and a faint buzzer sounded
far away.

"My God!" he exclaimed. "That a man should have to live with
this!"

"Is he afraid of burglars?"

"He's afraid of your lovely city and came here with a bodyguard of·
a dozen monkeys—is that the right slang? Maybe Al Capone is after
him. Anyhow he has one period between being drunk and being sober
when he is very nice."

He broke off as again they were momentarily bathed in the ubiquitous
spotlight. Then amber lamps glowed on the porch of the castellated villa
and Monsieur Irv, this time supported by the very neat young man,
came out unsteadily.

"I kept them off the beach, Tommy," he announced.

"Thank you, very much."

"Won't you both change your minds and come in? In *great*est confidence, I have some other ladies here." He raised his voice as if to
address Nicole. "As you are a lady of background you will like 'em."

"It's four o'clock," said Tommy. "We have to get to our background. Good night."

Irv's voice followed them: "You never make a mistake having to do with a lady."

*

*   *

At almost the last moment before the fourth installment of *Tender* was printed in *Scribner's,* Fitzgerald inserted a new chapter, the arrest of Lady Caroline and Mary Minghetti (Book V, Chapter X). That episode in one way takes the place of the visit to the retired bootlegger, by furnishing the same sort of social comment. It is more amusing, too, yet one is sorry about the disappearance of Monsieur Irv and his bodyguard of a dozen gorillas.

Some of the other changes in the novel, before and after its magazine publication, are mentioned in the Notes that follow.—M. C.

Notes

The Title.—The novel in its various stages had a whole series of titles. In the first or Melarky version it was called at different times *The Boy Who Killed His Mother, The Melarky Case, Our Type,* and *The World's Fair.* The second or Rosemary version apparently had no title, although a short story that grew out of it was "One Trip Abroad." The final version was called *The Doctor's Holiday,* then *Doctor Diver's Holiday,* and this last title was retained—Arthur Mizener tells us—until just before the novel began to run in *Scribner's Magazine.* The phrase "tender is the night" comes from the fourth stanza of Keats's "Ode to a Nightingale." Except for the "Ode on a Grecian Urn," that was Fitzgerald's favorite poem and one "which I can never read through without tears in my eyes," he said in a letter to his daughter.

Dedication.—The book is dedicated to Gerald and Sara Murphy, wealthy friends of the Fitzgeralds who entertained them at the Cap d'Antibes in 1925. Fitzgerald's plan for the background of the novel was to make it "one in which the leisure class is at their truly most brilliant and glamorous such as Murphys."

7. The first edition had Doctor Diver "delicately poking at the cervical of a brain," which is impossible. Fitzgerald must have intended "cortical of a brain" and "cortex" is better in this connection.

7. In the first edition the name of Dick's colleague was usually spelled "Gregorovious," a form that is highly improbable in German. At one point, however, it was correctly spelled "Gregorovius" and that gave some warrant for changing it throughout the novel.

11. After Nicole's first letter Fitzgerald put an asterisk in the margin of the Princeton copy of *Tender* and pencilled a note beside

it: "This is my mark to say that I have made final corrections up to this point."

15. "Nicole's mother died when she was eleven" was found on this page of the first edition; but on page 72 of the same edition (114 in this edition) Nicole said to Rosemary, "Just before the war we were in Berlin—I was thirteen, it was just before Mother died." The editor struck a balance and made her age twelve in both passages. Several of these little errors in chronology were scattered through the text.

22. "I've got only one [plan], Franz, and that's to be a good psychologist—maybe the greatest one that ever lived."—This is one of the points where the hero comes closest to the author. "I want to be one of the greatest writers that ever lived, don't you?" Fitzgerald had said to Edmund Wilson when they were just out of Princeton. But note that Dick Diver in his dress and social personality was completely unlike Fitzgerald. Some of the characters in the novel were suggested by living persons; not one of them was merely copied.

23. "He wanted to be loved, too, if he could fit it in."—There are indications that Fitzgerald regarded the need to be loved, or at least to be admired, as the tragic flaw in Dick's character and the cause of his ruin. Later in the novel he would say of Dick, ". . . the old fatal pleasingness, the old forceful charm, swept back with its cry of 'Use me!' "

53. The author hesitated whether to make this chapter the last of Book I or the first of Book II. The arrangement followed here is that of the Princeton copy.

55. On this page are phrases from the Rosemary version of the novel (see Appendix) and from a short story, "One Trip Abroad." Fitzgerald is summarizing a whole discarded portion of the manuscript.

58. The arrival of Rosemary and her mother at Gausse's hotel,

with most of the episodes that follow, is rewritten from the first or Melarky version of the novel. Francis Melarky and his mother reached the Cap d'Antibes and met the Divers (or Pipers) in much the same fashion.

75. Fitzgerald called the man with the monocle "Signor Campion," but his first name, Luis, was Spanish, not Italian.

76. "The name that sounds like a substitute for gasoline or butter" was borne by a substitute man of letters. There are puns or suggestions in the names of other characters besides Albert McKisco, and we learn from Fitzgerald's notes that some of the puns were deliberate. Diver was the man who dived from a high place into obscurity, Campion was given to "camping"—which was 1920 slang for making a parade of effeminacy—and Tommy Barban suggested the barbarian.

84. After "the proud uniqueness of their destinies," eight words of the first edition have been omitted here: "buried under the compromises of how many years." Fitzgerald had used almost the same phrase on page 111.

85. Just before "Under the spell of the climb to Tarmes," there is another omission, this time of eleven words from the first edition: "To resume Rosemary's point of view it should be said that . . ."

90. Fitzgerald wrote, by a slip of the pencil, that McKisco "essayed equally *irrelative* themes."

142. Abe's departure from the Gare Saint-Lazare, in Chapter VII of Book III, is one of the most worked-over scenes in the novel. Fitzgerald had tried many versions of it, saving only the best phrases from each. In the earlier versions it was hinted that Abe's easy life with the Divers had destroyed his ambition and that his hopeless love for Nicole was his excuse for drinking himself to death. . . . At one time Fitzgerald planned to start Book III, "Casualties," with this chapter. It is the point where the story ceases to be told from Rosemary's angle.

153. The French in *Tender* was checked over by a Frenchman, with the result that it came out much better than the Italian or the German, but a good many mistakes crept into it. On this page, for example, the store with shirts in the window belonged to a chain of haberdasheries called *Aux Cent Mille Chemises,* not, as he wrote it, *1000 Chemises.*

154. At the beginning of Chapter IX was the dialogue with an American newspaper vendor (pages 120–121 of the first edition) which Fitzgerald decided to omit.

160. Abe was getting his geography mixed, as well as his telephone conversations. On page 168 we learn that Mr. Peterson came from Stockholm and that the race riot was not in Montmartre but on the other side of the Seine, in Montparnasse.

163. Abe's day in the Ritz bar was described at much greater length in the version of the novel that appeared in *Scribner's Magazine*. It was one of the brilliant passages that Fitzgerald sacrificed without regret, on the principle that his central effect should be obtained with the greatest possible economy of means.

167. The phrase in the first edition, "her face getting big as it came up to him," has been omitted after "Presently she kissed him several times in the mouth." Fitzgerald copied the phrase from his notebook and forgot that it was also being used on page 48.

196. The year is 1928 and the editor has added three words, "One July morning," at the beginning of the chapter to indicate the passage of time. The chronology of the novel requires thirty months, not eighteen, between the Christmas holidays at Gstaad and Dick's waking at the clinic. One can assume that the Divers spent another year on the Riviera while the clinic was being remodelled, and then eighteen months on the Zugersee. We learn from one manuscript that they rented Villa Diana to a movie queen, who tried to seduce Dick at the dinner they gave for her.

211. ". . . he had found something antipathetic in the English

lately."—Dick's racial antipathies, which he displayed on many occasions, were regarded by the author as a symptom of his deterioration. Writing about his own breakdown, in 1936, Fitzgerald would say, ". . . in these latter days I couldn't stand the sight of Celts, English, Politicians, Strangers, Virginians, Negroes (light or dark), Hunting People, or retail clerks, and middlemen in general, all writers (I avoided writers very carefully because they can perpetuate trouble as no one else can)—and all the classes as classes and most of them as members of their class." (*The Crack-Up*, page 73.)

215. "Mac thinks a Marxian is somebody who went to St. Mark's school."—Abe North had gone to St. Mark's, before winning a Prix de Rome while he was still an undergraduate at Harvard. Back in New York, after parting from the Divers, he had stayed sober long enough to write the music for a successful light opera. One learns a lot about Abe from reading the early manuscripts of *Tender*. Fitzgerald could have written a separate novel about him, as he could have written a novel about Rosemary in Hollywood and Europe.

215. The first edition read, "He unscrewed two blooded wire-hairs from a nearby table and departed"—but McKibben was still there and interrupting the conversation on the following page.

220. The woman in the hotel garden at Innsbruck was the McKibbens' governess. There was an account of Dick's meeting with her in the magazine version of the novel.

222. The two paragraphs about boarding a steamer are rewritten from the beginning of a story, "The Rough Crossing"—see *The Stories of F. Scott Fitzgerald*, page 254. Fitzgerald tried to save as much as possible from the stories he didn't intend to republish in a book. In his own phrase, he "junked and dismantled" them—that is, he marked the best passages and had them copied in his notebook, so that they would be available for use in a novel.

225. The second meeting with Rosemary was in January, 1929. Dick, born in 1891, would be thirty-eight in September; Rosemary would be twenty-two in July.

242. The fight with the taxi drivers had a long biographical and fictional history. It began as a misadventure of Fitzgerald's, one that occurred in the winter of 1924–25; ten years later he would describe it in a letter as "just about the rottenest thing that ever happened in my life" (see *The Far Side of Paradise,* page 166). He first retold the experience in a never-published magazine article, "The High Cost of Macaroni"; then he rewrote it as the first chapter of the Melarky version of the novel; then it became the seventh chapter; then finally the whole episode was recast for Dick Diver, with Baby Warren playing the part once written for Francis Melarky's mother.

249. In the paragraph beginning, "The piazza on which it faced," Fitzgerald used seven Italian words and misspelled all seven, a record even for him.

253. The first edition read, ". . . that least palpable"—for "palatable"—"of European types, the Latin moralist."

263. All through this passage the first edition had "Chili" and "Chilians."

275. Fitzgerald says in his 1932 sketch of the novel—the one that was carried through to the end—that Lanier was born in August, 1920 and Topsy in June, 1922.

276. Beginning with, "Another element that distinguished this summer," Fitzgerald planned to omit the rest of this chapter, including the whole visit to the Minghettis. The passage has been retained, however, for reasons explained in the Introduction.

284. From here to the end most of the story is told from Nicole's point of view. Fitzgerald said in his notes for the novel, "Part III" —now Book V—"is as much as possible seen through Nicole's eyes. All Dick's stories such as are *absolutely necessary* . . . must be told without putting in his reactions or feelings. From now on he is mystery man, at least to Nicole with her guessing at mystery."

292. "All right, she would go with him—" Fitzgerald says in his

notes for this section of the book, "Dick is still in control of the situation and thinks of the matter practically. They must separate for both their sakes. In wild bitterness he thinks of one tragic idea" —a double suicide—"but controls himself and manages a saner one instead."

296. This is the transference, the saner idea that Dick has managed. Fitzgerald, always a master of the trivial and the incongruous, has Nicole fling herself at Tommy with a jar of, presumably, Vick's Vaporub.

297. We will be told several times that five years have passed since Rosemary's first visit to the Cap d'Antibes in the summer of 1925. Her second visit, then, was in June, 1930. The date reveals a change in Fitzgerald's plans, since his earlier intention had been to end the story in July, 1929, a few months before the Wall Street crash. There is always a sense of historical events in the background of the novel, like a hushed musical accompaniment, and many episodes in it have the color of a special year. At this point, however, the author needed more elapsed time to accomplish Dick's ruin—five years instead of four—and actually 1930 was better for the historical background than 1929. It was the year when, in spite of the crash, there were more rich Americans in Europe than ever before and when the summer season on the Riviera was the biggest and maddest.

298. ". . . with money as fins and wings." The remark comes from a story, "The Swimmers," one of those that Fitzgerald "junked and dismantled" after they had appeared in the *Saturday Evening Post.* "Americans," the hero of the story liked to say, "should be born with fins, and perhaps they were—perhaps money was a form of fin. In England, property begot a strong place sense, but Americans, restless and with shallow roots, needed fins and wings."

304. Fitzgerald pencilled a note on the margin of this page, in the Princeton copy: "Tiresome stuff! True but why?" Apparently he planned to rewrite the encounter with Mary Minghetti.

311. " 'You've got too much money,' he said impatiently."—Compare this with Gatsby's remark about Daisy Buchanan, in *The Great*

Gatsby: "Her voice is full of money." In a sense both novels have the same theme: a poor young man ruined by his love for a rich woman.

316. The beach at Beaulieu where Nicole and Tommy swam was on the property of Monsieur Irv, the retired bootlegger from Chicago (see Appendix, 2).

321. Chapter X, the arrest of Mary Minghetti and Lady Caroline, was a final episode added to the novel at the last moment before magazine publication. It was a story from life and Fitzgerald sent a telegram to a friend, the one who got the two women out of jail, asking whether he would be embarrassed by its appearance in the novel.

328. The newspaper vendor had appeared before, at the beginning of Chapter IX of Book III, but Fitzgerald omitted the passage from his last revision of the novel. The omission made it necessary to drop two phrases here: "—and Dick recognized it as he saw it," said of the gray clipping that the newspaper vendor produced from his purse, and "Dick identified him as the man who had once hailed him in the Rue des Saints-Anges five years before."

329. One sentence has been omitted from this page: " 'I never did go in for making love to dry loins,' said Dick." Fitzgerald had written to Bennett Cerf, when there was question of reprinting the novel in the Modern Library, "There is not more than one complete sentence that I want to eliminate, one that has offended many people and that I admit is out of Dick's character: 'I never did go in for making love to dry loins.' It is a strong line but definitely offensive."

333. Fitzgerald tried several versions of this farewell to Gausse's beach. In one of them Dick had to be helped away by an attendant; in another he fell on his face after making the papal cross over the bathers. It was a long time before he found what he was always looking for, and found again in the last brief chapter: the exactly right degree of understatement.

M. C.

THE
LAST TYCOON

FOREWORD

Scott Fitzgerald died suddenly of a heart attack (December 21, 1940) the day after he had written the first episode of Chapter 6 of his novel. The text which is given here is a draft made by the author after considerable rewriting; but it is by no means a finished version. In the margins of almost every one of the episodes, Fitzgerald had written comments—a few of them are included in the notes—which expressed his dissatisfaction with them or indicated his ideas about revising them. His intention was to produce a novel as concentrated and as carefully constructed as *The Great Gatsby* had been, and he would unquestionably have sharpened the effect of most of these scenes as we have them by cutting and by heightening of color. He had originally planned that the novel should be about 60,000 words long, but he had written at the time of his death about 70,000 words without, as will be seen from his outline, having told much more than half his story. He had calculated, when he began, on leaving himself a margin of 10,000 words for cutting; but it seems certain that the novel would have run longer than the proposed 60,000 words. The subject was here more complex than it had been in *The Great Gatsby*—the picture of the Hollywood studios required more space for its presentation than the background of the drinking life of Long Island; and the characters needed more room for their development.

This draft of *The Last Tycoon*, then, represents that point in the artist's work where he has assembled and organized his material and acquired a firm grasp of his theme, but has not yet brought it finally into focus. It is remarkable that, under these circumstances, the story should have already so much power and the character of Stahr emerge with so much intensity and reality. This Hollywood producer, in his misery and grandeur, is certainly the one of Fitzgerald's central figures which he had thought out most completely

iii

and which he had most deeply come to understand. His notes on the character show how he had lived with it over a period of three years or more, filling in Stahr's idiosyncrasies and tracing the web of his relationships with the various departments of his business. Amory Blaine and Antony Patch were romantic projections of the author; Gatsby and Dick Diver were conceived more or less objectively, but not very profoundly explored. Monroe Stahr is really created from within at the same time that he is criticized by an intelligence that has now become sure of itself and knows how to assign him to his proper place in a larger scheme of things.

The Last Tycoon is thus, even in its imperfect state, Fitzgerald's most mature piece of work. It is marked off also from his other novels by the fact that it is the first to deal seriously with any profession or business. The earlier books of Fitzgerald had been preoccupied with debutantes and college boys, with the fast lives of the wild spenders of the twenties. The main activities of the people in these stories, the occasions for which they live, are big parties at which they go off like fireworks and which are likely to leave them in pieces. But the parties in *The Last Tycoon* are incidental and unimportant; Monroe Stahr, unlike any other of Scott Fitzgerald's heroes, is inextricably involved with an industry of which he has been one of the creators, and its fate will be implied by his tragedy. The moving-picture business in America has here been observed at a close range, studied with a careful attention and dramatized with a sharp wit such as are not to be found in combination in any of the other novels on the subject. *The Last Tycoon* is far and away the best novel we have had about Hollywood, and it is the only one which takes us inside.

It has been possible to supplement this unfinished draft with an outline of the rest of the story as Fitzgerald intended to develop it, and with passages from the author's notes which deal, often vividly, with the characters and scenes.

It is worth while to read *The Great Gatsby* in connection with *The Last Tycoon* because it shows the kind of thing that Fitzgerald was aiming to do in the latter. If his conception of his subject in *Tender Is the Night* had shifted in the course of his writing it so that the parts of that fascinating novel do not always quite hang together, he had recovered here the singleness of purpose, the sureness of craftsmanship, which appear in the earlier story. In going through the immense pile of drafts and notes that the author had made for this novel, one is confirmed and reinforced in one's impression that Fitzgerald will be found to stand out as one of the first-rate figures in the American writing of his period. The last pages of *The Great Gatsby* are certainly, both from the dramatic point of view and from the point of view of prose, among the very best things in the fiction of our generation. T. S. Eliot said of the book that Fitzgerald had taken the first important step that had been made in the American novel since Henry James. And certainly *The Last Tycoon,* even in its unfulfilled intention, takes its place among the books that set a standard.

EDMUND WILSON

THE
LAST TYCOON

THE LAST TYCOON

CHAPTER I

THOUGH I HAVEN'T ever been on the screen I was brought up in pictures. Rudolph Valentino came to my fifth birthday party—or so I was told. I put this down only to indicate that even before the age of reason I was in a position to watch the wheels go round.

I was going to write my memoirs once, *The Producer's Daughter*, but at eighteen you never quite get around to anything like that. It's just as well—it would have been as flat as an old column of Lolly Parsons'. My father was in the picture business as another man might be in cotton or steel, and I took it tranquilly. At the worst I accepted Hollywood with the resignation of a ghost assigned to a haunted house. I knew what you were supposed to think about it but I was obstinately unhorrified.

This is easy to say, but harder to make people understand. When I was at Bennington some of the English teachers who pretended an indifference to Hollywood or its products, really *hated* it. Hated it way down deep as a threat to their existence. Even before that, when I was in a convent, a sweet little nun asked me to get her a script of a screen play so she could "teach her class about movie writing" as she had taught them about the essay and the short story. I got the script for her, and I suppose she puzzled over it and puzzled over it, but it was never mentioned in class, and she gave it back to me with an air of offended surprise and not a single comment. That's what I half expect to happen to this story.

You can take Hollywood for granted like I did, or you can dismiss it with the contempt we reserve for what we don't understand. It can be understood too, but only dimly and in flashes. Not half a dozen men have ever been able to keep the whole equation of pictures in their heads. And perhaps the closest a woman can come to the set-up is to try and understand one of those men.

The world from an airplane I knew. Father always had us travel back and forth that way from school and college. After my sister died when I was a junior, I travelled to and fro alone, and the journey always made me think of her, made me somewhat solemn and subdued. Sometimes there were picture people I knew on board the plane, and occasionally there was an attractive college boy—but not often during the depression. I seldom really fell asleep during the trip, what with thoughts of Eleanor and the sense of that sharp rip between coast and coast—at least not till we had left those lonely little airports in Tennessee.

This trip was so rough that the passengers divided early into those who turned in right away and those who didn't want to turn in at all. There were two of these latter right across from me, and I was pretty sure from their fragmentary conversation that they were from Hollywood—one of them because he looked like it: a middle-aged Jew, who alternately talked with nervous excitement or else crouched as if ready to spring, in a harrowing silence; the other a pale, plain, stocky man of thirty, whom I was sure I had seen before. He had been to the house or something. But it might have been when I was a little girl, and so I wasn't offended that he didn't recognize me.

The stewardess—she was tall, handsome and flashing dark, a type that they seemed to run to—asked me if she could make up my berth.

"—and, dear, do you want an aspirin?" She perched on the side of the seat and rocked precariously to and fro with the June hurricane, "—or nembutal?"

"No."

"I've been so busy with everyone else that I've had no time to ask you." She sat down beside me and buckled us both in. "Do you want some gum?"

This reminded me to get rid of the piece that had been boring me for hours. I wrapped it in a piece of magazine and put it into the automatic ash-holder.

"I can always tell people are nice," the stewardess said approvingly, "if they wrap their gum in paper before they put it in there."

We sat for awhile in the half-light of the swaying car. It was vaguely like a swanky restaurant at that twilight time between meals. We were all lingering—and not quite on purpose. Even the stewardess, I think, had to keep reminding herself why she was there.

She and I talked about a young actress I knew, whom she had flown West with two years before. It was in the very lowest time of the depression, and the young actress kept staring out the window in such an intent way that the stewardess was afraid she was contemplating a leap. It appeared though that she was not afraid of poverty, but only of revolution.

"I know what mother and *I* are going to do," she confided to the stewardess. "We're coming out to the Yellowstone and we're just going to live simply till it all blows over. Then we'll come back. They don't kill artists—you know?"

The proposition pleased me. It conjured up a pretty picture of the actress and her mother being fed by kind Tory bears who brought them honey, and by gentle fawns who fetched extra milk from the does and then lingered near to make pillows for their heads at night. In turn I told the stewardess about the lawyer and the director who told their plans to Father one night in those brave days. If the bonus army conquered Washington, the lawyer had a boat hidden in the Sacramento River, and he was going to row up stream for a few months and then come back "because they always needed lawyers after a revolution to straighten out the legal side."

The director had tended more toward defeatism. He had an old suit, shirt and shoes in waiting—he never did say whether they were his own or whether he got them from the prop department—and he was going to Disappear into the Crowd. I remember Father saying: "But they'll look at your hands! They'll know you haven't done manual work for years. And they'll ask for your union card." And I remember how the director's face fell, and how gloomy he was while he ate his dessert, and how funny and puny they sounded to me.

"Is your father an actor, Miss Brady?" asked the stewardess. "I've certainly heard the name."

At the name Brady, both the men across the aisle looked up. Sidewise—that Hollywood look, that always seems thrown over one shoulder. Then the young, pale, stocky man unbuttoned his safety strap and stood in the aisle beside us.

"Are you Cecilia *Brady*?" he demanded accusingly, as if I'd been holding out on him. "I *thought* I recognized you. I'm Wylie White."

He could have omitted this—for at the same moment a new voice said, "Watch your step, Wylie!", and another man brushed by him in the aisle and went forward in the direction of the cockpit. Wylie White started, and a little too late called after him defiantly:

"I only take orders from the pilot."

I recognized the kind of pleasantry that goes on between the powers in Hollywood and their satellites.

The stewardess reproved him:

"Not so loud, please—some of the passengers are asleep."

I saw now that the other man across the aisle, the middle-aged Jew, was on his feet also, staring, with shameless economic lechery, after the man who had just gone by. Or rather at the back of the man, who gestured sideways with his hand in a sort of farewell, as he went out of my sight.

I asked the stewardess: "Is he the assistant pilot?"

She was unbuckling our belt, about to abandon me to Wylie White.

"No. That's Mr. Smith. He has the private compartment, the 'bridal suite'—only he has it alone. The assistant pilot is always in uniform." She stood up: "I want to find out if we're going to be grounded in Nashville."

Wylie White was aghast.

"Why?"

"It's a storm coming up the Mississippi Valley."

"Does that mean we'll have to stay here all *night*?"

"If this keeps up!"

A sudden dip indicated that it would. It tipped Wylie White into the seat opposite me, shunted the stewardess precipitately down in the direction of the cockpit, and plunked the Jewish man into a sitting position. After the studied, unruffled exclamations of distaste that befitted the air-minded, we settled down. There was an introduction.

"Miss Brady—Mr. Schwartz," said Wylie White. "He's a great friend of your father's, too."

Mr. Schwartz nodded so vehemently that I could almost hear him saying: "It's true. As God is my judge, it's true!"

He might have said this right out loud at one time in his life—but he was obviously a man to whom something had happened. Meeting him was like encountering a friend who has been in a fist fight or collision, and got flattened. You stare at your friend and say: "What happened to you?" And he answers something unintelligible through broken teeth and swollen lips. He can't even tell you about it.

Mr. Schwartz was physically unmarked; the exaggerated Persian nose and oblique eye-shadow were as congenital as the tip-tilted Irish redness around my father's nostrils.

"Nashville!" cried Wylie White. "That means we go to a hotel. We don't get to the coast till tomorrow night—if then. My God! I was born in Nashville."

"I should think you'd like to see it again."

"Never—I've kept away for fifteen years. I hope I'll *never* see it again."

But he would—for the plane was unmistakably going down, down, down, like Alice in the rabbit hole. Cupping my hand against the window I saw the blur of the city far away on the left. The green sign "Fasten your belts—No smoking" had been on since we first rode into the storm.

"Did you hear what he said?" said Schwartz from one of his fiery silences across the aisle.

"Hear what?" asked Wylie.

"Hear what he's calling himself," said Schwartz. "Mr. *Smith*!"

"Why not?" asked Wylie.

"Oh nothing," said Schwartz quickly. "I just thought it was funny, Smith." I never heard a laugh with less mirth in it: "Smith!"

I suppose there has been nothing like the airports since the days of the stage-stops—nothing quite as lonely, as somber-silent. The old red-brick depots were built right into the towns they marked—people didn't get off at those isolated stations unless they lived there. But airports lead you way back in history like oases, like the stops on the great trade routes. The sight of air travellers strolling in ones and twos into midnight airports will draw a small crowd any night up to two. The young people look at the planes, the older ones look at the passengers with a watchful incredulity. In the big transcontinental planes we were the coastal rich, who casually alighted from our cloud in mid-America. High adventure might be among us, disguised as a movie star. But mostly it wasn't. And I always wished fervently that we looked more interesting than we did— just as I often have at premières, when the fans look at you with scornful reproach because you're not a star.

On the ground Wylie and I were suddenly friends, because he held out his arm to steady me when I got out of the plane. From then on, he made a dead set for me—and I didn't mind. From the moment we walked into the airport it had become plain that if we were stranded here we were stranded here together. (It wasn't like the time I lost my boy—the time my boy played the piano with that girl Reina in a little New England farmhouse near Bennington, and I realized at last I wasn't wanted. Guy Lombardo was on the air playing *Top Hat* and *Cheek to Cheek,* and she taught him the melodies. The keys falling like leaves and her hands splayed over his as she showed him a black chord. I was a freshman then.)

When we went into the airport Mr. Schwartz was along with us, too, but he seemed in a sort of dream. All the time we were trying to get accurate information at the desk, he kept staring at the door that led out to the landing field, as if he were afraid the plane would leave without him. Then I excused myself for a few minutes and something happened that I didn't see, but when I came back he and White were standing close together, White talking and Schwartz looking twice as much as if a great truck had just backed up over him. He didn't stare at the door to the landing field any more. I heard the end of Wylie White's remark . . .

"—I told you to shut up. It serves you right."

"I only said——"

He broke off as I came up and asked if there was any news. It was then half-past two in the morning.

"A little," said Wylie White. "They don't think we'll be able to start for three hours anyhow, so some of the softies are going to a hotel. But I'd like to take you out to the Hermitage, Home of Andrew Jackson."

"How could we see it in the dark?" demanded Schwartz.

"Hell, it'll be sunrise in two hours."

"You two go," said Schwartz.

"All right—you take the bus to the hotel. It's still waiting—*he's* in there." Wylie's voice had a taunt in it. "Maybe it'd be a good thing."

"No, I'll go along with you," said Schwartz hastily.

We took a taxi in the sudden country dark outside, and he seemed to cheer up. He patted my knee-cap encouragingly.

"I should go along," he said, "I should be chaperone. Once upon a time when I was in the big money, I had a daughter—a beautiful daughter."

He spoke as if she had been sold to creditors as a tangible asset.

"You'll have another," Wylie assured him. "You'll get it all back. Another turn of the wheel and you'll be where Cecilia's papa is, won't he, Cecilia?"

"Where is this Hermitage?" asked Schwartz presently. "Far away at the end of nowhere? Will we miss the plane?"

"Skip it," said Wylie. "We ought to've brought the stewardess along for you. Didn't you admire the stewardess? *I* thought she was pretty cute."

We drove for a long time over a bright level countryside, just a road and a tree and a shack and a tree, and then suddenly along a winding twist of woodland. I could feel even in the darkness that the trees of the woodland were green—that it was all different from the dusty olive-tint of California. Somewhere we passed a negro driving three cows ahead of him, and they mooed as he scatted them to the side of the road. They were real cows, with warm, fresh, silky flanks, and the negro grew gradually real out of the darkness with his big brown eyes staring at us close to the car, as Wylie gave him a quarter. He said "*Thank* you—thank you," and stood there, and the cows mooed again into the night as we drove off.

I thought of the first sheep I ever remember seeing—hundreds of them, and how our car drove suddenly into them on the back lot of the old Laemmle studio. They were unhappy about being in pictures, but the men in the car with us kept saying:

"Swell?"

"Is that what you wanted, Dick?"

"Isn't that swell?" And the man named Dick kept standing up in the car as if he were Cortez or Balboa, looking over that gray fleecy undulation. If I ever knew what picture they were in, I have long forgotten.

We had driven an hour. We crossed a brook over an old rattly iron bridge laid with planks. Now there were roosters crowing and blue-green shadows stirring every time we passed a farmhouse.

"I told you it'd be morning soon," said Wylie. "I was born near here—the son of impoverished southern paupers. The family mansion is now used as an outhouse. We had four servants—my father, my mother and my two sisters. I refused to join the guild, and so I went to Memphis to start my career, which has now reached a dead end." He put his arm around me: "Cecilia, will you marry me, so I can share the Brady fortune?"

He was disarming enough, so I let my head lie on his shoulder.

"What do you do, Celia. Go to school?"

"I go to Bennington. I'm a junior."

"Oh, I beg your pardon. I should have known, but I never had the advantage of college training. But a *junior*—why I read in *Esquire* that juniors have nothing to learn, Cecilia."

"Why do people think that college girls——"

"Don't apologize—knowledge is power."

"You'd know from the way you talk that we were on our way to Hollywood," I said. "It's always years and years behind the times."

He pretended to be shocked.

"You mean girls in the East have no private lives?"

"That's the point. They *have* got private lives. You're bothering me, let go."

"I can't. It might wake Schwartz, and I think this is the first sleep he's had for weeks. Listen, Cecilia: I once had an affair with the wife of a producer. A very short affair. When it was over she said to me in no uncertain terms, she said: 'Don't you ever tell about this or I'll have you thrown out of Hollywood. My husband's a much more important man than you!'"

I liked him again now, and presently the taxi turned down a long lane fragrant with honeysuckle and narcissus, and stopped beside the great grey hulk of the Andrew Jackson house. The driver turned around to tell us something about it, but Wylie shushed him, pointing at Schwartz, and we tiptoed out of the car.

"You can't get into the Mansion now," the taxi man told us politely.

Wylie and I went and sat against the wide pillars of the steps.

"What about Mr. Schwartz," I asked. "Who is he?"

"To hell with Schwartz. He was the head of some combine once —First National? Paramount? United Artists? Now he's down and out. But he'll be back. You can't flunk out of pictures unless you're a dope or a drunk."

"You don't like Hollywood," I suggested.

"Yes I do. Sure I do. Say! This isn't anything to talk about on the steps of Andrew Jackson's house—at dawn."

"I *like* Hollywood," I persisted.

"It's all right. It's a mining town in lotus land. Who said that? I did. It's a good place for toughies, but I went there from Savannah, Georgia. I went to a garden party the first day. My host shook hands and left me. It was all there—that swimming pool, green moss at two dollars an inch, beautiful felines having drinks and fun——

"—And nobody spoke to me. Not a soul. I spoke to half a dozen people but they didn't answer. That continued for an hour, two hours—then I got up from where I was sitting and ran out at a dog trot like a crazy man. I didn't feel I had any rightful identity until I got back to the hotel and the clerk handed me a letter addressed to me in my name."

Naturally I hadn't ever had such an experience, but looking back on parties I'd been to, I realized that such things could happen. We don't go for strangers in Hollywood unless they wear a sign saying that their axe has been thoroughly ground elsewhere, and that in any case it's not going to fall on our necks—in other words, unless they're a celebrity. And they'd better look out even then.

"You should have risen above it," I said smugly. "It's not a slam at *you* when people are rude—it's a slam at the people they've met before."

"Such a pretty girl—to say such wise things."

There was an eager to-do in the eastern sky, and Wylie could see me plain—thin with good features and lots of style, and the kicking fetus of a mind. I wonder what I looked like in that dawn, five years ago. A little rumpled and pale, I suppose, but at that age, when one has the young illusion that most adventures are good, I needed only a bath and a change to go on for hours.

Wylie stared at me with really flattering appreciation—and then suddenly we were not alone. Mr. Schwartz wandered apologetically into the pretty scene.

"I fell upon a large metal handle," he said, touching the corner of his eye.

Wylie jumped up.

"Just in time, Mr. Schwartz," he said. "The tour is just starting. Home of Old Hickory—America's tenth president. The victor of New Orleans, opponent of the National Bank, and inventor of the Spoils System."

Schwartz looked toward me as toward a jury.

"There's a writer for you," he said. "Knows everything and at the same time he knows nothing."

"What's that?" said Wylie, indignant.

It was my first inkling that he was a writer. And while I like writers—because if you ask a writer anything, you usually get an answer—still it belittled him in my eyes. Writers aren't people exactly. Or, if they're any good, they're a whole *lot* of people trying so hard to be one person. It's like actors, who try so pathetically not to look in mirrors. Who lean *back*ward trying—only to see their faces in the reflecting chandeliers.

"Ain't writers like that, Celia?" demanded Schwartz. "I have no words for them. I only know it's true."

Wylie looked at him with slowly gathering indignation. "I've heard that before," he said. "Look, Manny, I'm a more practical man than you any day! I've sat in an office and listened to some mystic stalk up and down for hours spouting tripe that'd land him on a nut-farm anywhere outside of California—and then at the end tell me how *prac*tical he was, and *I* was a dreamer—and would I kindly go away and make sense out of what he'd said."

Mr. Schwartz's face fell into its more disintegrated alignments. One eye looked upward through the tall elms. He raised his hand and bit without interest at the cuticle on his second finger. There was a bird flying about the chimney of the house, and his glance followed it. It perched on the chimney pot like a raven, and Mr. Schwartz's eyes remained fixed upon it as he said: "We can't get in, and it's time for you two to go back to the plane."

It was still not quite dawn. The Hermitage looked like a nice big white box, but a little lonely and vacated still after a hundred years. We walked back to the car. Only after we had gotten in, and Mr. Schwartz had surprisingly shut the taxi door on us, did we realize he didn't intend to come along.

"I'm not going to the Coast—I decided that when I woke up. So I'll stay here, and afterwards the driver could come back for me."

"Going back East?" said Wylie with surprise. "Just because——"

"I have decided," said Schwartz, faintly smiling. "Once I used to be a regular man of decision—you'd be surprised." He felt in his pocket, as the taxi driver warmed up the engine. "Will you give this note to Mr. Smith?"

"Shall I come in two hours?" the driver asked Schwartz.

"Yes . . . sure. I shall be glad to entertain myself looking around."

I kept thinking of him all the way back to the airport—trying to fit him into that early hour and into that landscape. He had come a long way from some Ghetto to present himself at that raw shrine. Manny Schwartz and Andrew Jackson—it was hard to say them in the same sentence. It was doubtful if he knew who Andrew Jackson was as he wandered around, but perhaps he figured that if people had preserved his house Andrew Jackson must have been someone who was large and merciful, able to understand. At both ends of life man needed nourishment: a breast—a shrine. Something to lay himself beside when no one wanted him further, and shoot a bullet into his head.

Of course we did not know this for twenty hours. When we got to the airport we told the purser that Mr. Schwartz was not continuing, and then forgot about him. The storm had wandered away into Eastern Tennessee and broken against the mountains, and we were taking off in less than an hour. Sleepy-eyed travellers appeared from the hotel, and I dozed a few minutes on one of those Iron Maidens they use for couches. Slowly the idea of a perilous journey was recreated out of the debris of our failure: a new stewardess, tall, handsome, flashing dark, exactly like the other except she wore seersucker instead of French red-and-blue, went briskly past us with a suitcase. Wylie sat beside me as we waited.

"Did you give the note to Mr. Smith?" I asked, half asleep.

"Yeah."

"Who is Mr. Smith? I suspect he spoiled Mr. Schwartz's trip."

"It was Schwartz's fault."

"I'm prejudiced against steam-rollers," I said. "My father tries to be a steam-roller around the house, and I tell him to save it for the studio."

I wondered if I was being fair; words are the palest counters at that time in the morning. "Still, he steam-rollered me into Bennington and I've always been grateful for that."

"There would be quite a crash," Wylie said, "if steam-roller Brady met steam-roller Smith."

"Is Mr. Smith a competitor of Father's?"

"Not exactly. I should say no. But if he was a competitor, I know where my money would be."

"On Father?"

"I'm afraid not."

It was too early in the morning for family patriotism. The pilot was at the desk with the purser and he shook his head as they regarded a prospective passenger who had put two nickels in the electric phonograph and lay alcoholically on a bench fighting off sleep. The first song he had chosen, *Lost,* thundered through the room, followed, after a slight interval, by his other choice, *Gone,* which was equally dogmatic and final. The pilot shook his head emphatically and walked over to the passenger.

"Afraid we're not going to be able to carry you this time, old man."

"Wha?"

The drunk sat up, awful-looking, yet discernibly attractive, and I was sorry for him in spite of his passionately ill-chosen music.

"Go back to the hotel and get some sleep. There'll be another plane tonight."

"Only going up in ee *air.*"

"Not this time, old man."

In his disappointment the drunk fell off the bench—and above the phonograph, a loudspeaker summoned us respectable people outside. In the corridor of the plane I ran into Monroe Stahr and fell all over him, or wanted to. There was a man any girl would go for, with or without encouragement. I was emphatically with*out* it, but he liked me and sat down opposite till the plane took off.

"Let's all ask for our money back," he suggested. His dark eyes took me in, and I wondered what they would look like if he fell in love. They were kind, aloof and, though they often reasoned with you gently, somewhat superior. It was no fault of theirs if they saw so much. He darted in and out of the role of "one of the boys" with dexterity—but on the whole I should say he wasn't one of them. But he knew how to shut up, how to draw into the background, how to listen. From where he stood (and though he was not a tall man, it always seemed high up) he watched the multitudinous practicalities of his world like a proud young shepherd to whom night and day had never mattered. He was born sleepless, without a talent for rest or the desire for it.

We sat in unembarrassed silence—I had known him since he became Father's partner a dozen years ago, when I was seven and Stahr was twenty-two. Wylie was across the aisle and I didn't know whether or not to introduce them, but Stahr kept turning his ring so abstractedly that he made me feel young and invisible, and I didn't dare. I never dared look quite away from him or quite *at* him, unless I had something important to say—and I knew he affected many other people in the same manner.

"I'll *give* you this ring, Cecilia."

"I beg your pardon. I didn't realize that I was——"

"I've got half a dozen like it."

He handed it to me, a gold nugget with the letter S in bold relief. I had been thinking how oddly its bulk contrasted with his fingers, which were delicate and slender like the rest of his body, and like his slender face with the arched eyebrows and the dark curly hair. He looked spiritual at times, but he was a fighter—somebody out of his past knew him when he was one of a gang of kids in the Bronx, and gave me a description of how he walked always at the head of his gang, this rather frail boy, occasionally throwing a command backward out of the corner of his mouth.

Stahr folded my hand over the ring, stood up and addressed Wylie.

"Come up to the bridal suite," he said. "See you later, Cecilia."

Before they went out of hearing, I heard Wylie's question: "Did you open Schwartz's note?" And Stahr:

"Not yet."

I must be slow, for only then did I realize that Stahr was Mr. Smith.

Afterwards Wylie told me what was in the note. Written by the headlights of the taxi, it was almost illegible.

"Dear Monroe, You are the best of them all I have always admired your mentality so when you turn against me I know it's no use! I must be no good and am not going to continue the journey let me warn you once again look out! I know.

"Your friend

MANNY."

Stahr read it twice, and raised his hand to the morning stubble on his chin.

"He's a nervous wreck," he said. "There's nothing to be done—absolutely nothing. I'm sorry I was short with him—but I don't like a man to approach me telling me it's for *my* sake."

"Maybe it was," said Wylie.

"It's poor technique."

"I'd fall for it," said Wylie. "I'm vain as a woman. If anybody pretends to be interested in me, I'll ask for more. I like advice."

Stahr shook his head distastefully. Wylie kept on ribbing him—he was one of those to whom this privilege was permitted.

"You fall for some kinds of flattery," he said. "This 'little Napoleon stuff.' "

"It makes me sick," said Stahr, "but it's not as bad as some man trying to help you."

"If you don't like advice, why do you pay *me*?"

"That's a question of merchandise," said Stahr. "I'm a merchant. I want to buy what's in your mind."

"You're no merchant," said Wylie. "I knew a lot of them when I was a publicity man, and I agree with Charles Francis Adams."

"What did he say?"

"He knew them all—Gould, Vanderbilt, Carnegie, Astor—and he said there wasn't one he'd care to meet again in the hereafter. Well —they haven't improved since then, and that's why I say you're no merchant."

"Adams was probably a sourbelly," said Stahr. "He wanted to be head man himself, but he didn't have the judgment or else the character."

"He had brains," said Wylie rather tartly.

"It takes more than brains. You writers and artists poop out and get all mixed up, and somebody has to come in and straighten you out." He shrugged his shoulders. "You seem to take things so personally, hating people and worshipping them—always thinking people are so important—especially yourselves. You just ask to be kicked around. I like people and I like them to like me, but I wear my heart where God put it—on the inside."

He broke off.

"What did I say to Schwartz in the airport? Do you remember —exactly?"

"You said, 'Whatever you're after, the answer is No!'"

Stahr was silent.

"He was sunk," said Wylie, "but I laughed him out of it. We took Billy Brady's daughter for a ride."

Stahr rang for the stewardess.

"That pilot," he said, "would he mind if I sat up in front with him awhile?"

"That's against the rules, Mr. Smith."

"Ask him to step in here a minute when he's free."

Stahr sat up front all afternoon. While we slid off the endless desert and over the table-lands, dyed with many colors like the white sands we dyed with colors when I was a child. Then in the late afternoon, the peaks themselves—the Mountains of the Frozen Saw —slid under our propellers and we were close to home.

When I wasn't dozing I was thinking that I wanted to marry Stahr, that I wanted to make him love me. Oh, the conceit! What on earth did I have to offer? But I didn't think like that then. I had the pride of young women, which draws its strength from such sublime thoughts as "I'm as good as *she* is." For my purposes I was just as beautiful as the great beauties who must have inevitably thrown themselves at his head. My little spurt of intellectual interest was of course making me fit to be a brilliant ornament of any salon.

I know now it was absurd. Though Stahr's education was founded on nothing more than a night-school course in stenography, he had a long time ago run ahead through trackless wastes of perception into fields where very few men were able to follow him. But in my reckless conceit I matched my grey eyes against his brown ones for guile, my young golf-and-tennis heart-beats against his, which must be slowing a little after years of over-work. And I planned and I contrived and I plotted—any woman can tell you—but it never came to anything, as you will see. I still like to think that if he'd been a poor boy and nearer my age I could have managed it, but of course the real truth was that I had nothing to offer that he didn't have; some of my more romantic ideas actually stemmed from pictures— *42nd Street,* for example, had a great influence on me. It's more than possible that some of the pictures which Stahr himself conceived had shaped me into what I was.

So it was rather hopeless. Emotionally, at least, people can't live by taking in each other's washing.

But at that time it was different: Father might help, the stewardess might help. She might go up in the cockpit and say to Stahr: "If I ever saw love, it's in that girl's eyes."

The pilot might help: "Man, are you blind? Why don't you go back there?"

Wylie White might help—instead of standing in the aisle looking at me doubtfully, wondering whether I was awake or asleep.

"Sit down," I said. "What's new?—where are we?"

"Up in the air."

"Oh, so that's it. Sit down." I tried to show a cheerful interest: "What are you writing?"

"Heaven help me, I am writing about a Boy Scout—*The* Boy Scout."

"Is it Stahr's idea?"

"I don't know—he told me to look into it. He may have ten writers working ahead of me or behind me, a system which he so thoughtfully invented. So you're in love with him?"

"I should say not," I said indignantly. "I've known him all my life."

"Desperate, eh? Well, I'll arrange it if you'll use all your influence to advance me. I want a unit of my own."

I closed my eyes again and drifted off. When I woke up, the stewardess was putting a blanket over me.

"Almost there," she said.

Out the window I could see by the sunset that we were in a greener land.

"I just heard something funny," she volunteered, "up in the cockpit—that Mr. Smith—or Mr. Stahr—I never remember seeing his name—"

"It's never on any pictures," I said.

"Oh. Well, he's been asking the pilots a lot about flying—I mean he's interested? You *know*?"

"I know."

"I mean one of them told me he bet he could teach Mr. Stahr solo flying in ten minutes. He has such a fine mentality, that's what he said."

I was getting impatient.

"Well, what was so funny?"

"Well, finally one of the pilots asked Mr. Smith if he liked his business, and Mr. Smith said, 'Sure. Sure I like it. It's nice being the only sound nut in a hatful of cracked ones.'"

The stewardess doubled up with laughter—and I could have spit at her.

"I mean calling all those people a hatful of nuts. I mean *cracked* nuts." Her laughter stopped with unexpected suddenness, and her face was grave as she stood up. "Well, I've got to finish my chart."

"Goodbye."

Obviously Stahr had put the pilots right up on the throne with him and let them rule with him for awhile. Years later I travelled with one of those same pilots and he told me one thing Stahr had said.

He was looking down at the mountains.

"Suppose you were a railroad man," he said. "You have to send a train through there somewhere. Well, you get your surveyors' reports, and you find there's three or four or half a dozen gaps, and not one is better than the other. You've got to decide—on what basis? You can't test the best way—except by doing it. So you just do it."

The pilot thought he had missed something.

"How do you mean?"

"You choose some one way for no reason at all—because that mountain's pink or the blueprint is a better blue. You see?"

The pilot considered that this was very valuable advice. But he doubted if he'd ever be in a position to apply it.

"What I wanted to know," he told me ruefully, "is how he ever got to be Mr. Stahr."

I'm afraid Stahr could never have answered that one; for the embryo is not equipped with a memory. But I could answer a little. He had flown up very high to see, on strong wings, when he was young. And while he was up there he had looked on all the kingdoms, with the kind of eyes that can stare straight into the sun. Beating his wings tenaciously—finally frantically—and keeping on beating them, he had stayed up there longer than most of us, and then, remembering all he had seen from his great height of how things were, he had settled gradually to earth.

The motors were off, and all our five senses began to readjust themselves for landing. I could see a line of lights for the Long Beach Naval Station ahead and to the left, and on the right a twinkling blur for Santa Monica. The California moon was out, huge and orange over the Pacific. However I happened to feel about these things—and they were home, after all—I know that Stahr must have felt much more. These were the things I had first opened my eyes on, like the sheep on the back lot of the old Laemmle studio; but this was where Stahr had come to earth after that extraordinary illuminating flight where he saw which way we were going, and how we looked doing it, and how much of it mattered. You could say that this was where an accidental wind blew him, but I don't think so. I would rather think that in a "long shot" he saw a new way of measuring our jerky hopes and graceful rogueries and awkward sorrows, and that he came here from choice to be with us to the end. Like the plane coming down into the Glendale airport, into the warm darkness.

CHAPTER II

It was nine o'clock of a July night and there were still some extras in the drug-store across from the studio—I could see them bent over the pin-games inside—as I parked my car. "Old" Johnny Swanson stood on the corner in his semi-cowboy clothes, staring gloomily past the moon. Once he had been as big in pictures as Tom Mix or Bill Hart—now it was too sad to speak to him, and I hurried across the street and through the front gate.

There is never a time when a studio is absolutely quiet. There is always a night shift of technicians in the laboratories and dubbing rooms and people on the maintenance staff dropping in at the commissary. But the sounds are all different—the padded hush of tires, the quiet tick of a motor running idle, the naked cry of a soprano singing into a nightbound microphone. Around a corner I came upon a man in rubber boots washing down a car in a wonderful white light—a fountain among the dead industrial shadows. I slowed up as I saw Mr. Marcus being hoisted into his car in front of the administration building, because he took so long to say anything, even good night—and while I waited I realized that the soprano was singing, *Come, come, I love you only* over and over; I remember this because she kept singing the same line during the earthquake. That didn't come for five minutes yet.

Father's offices were in the old building with the long balconies and iron rails with their suggestion of a perpetual tightrope. Father was on the second floor, with Stahr on one side and Mr. Marcus on the other—this evening there were lights all along the row. My stomach dipped a little at the proximity to Stahr, but that was in pretty good control now—I'd seen him only once in the month I'd been home.

There were a lot of strange things about Father's office, but I'll make it brief. In the outer part were three poker-faced secretaries who

21

had sat there like witches ever since I could remember—Birdy Peters, Maude something, and Rosemary Schmiel; I don't know whether this was her name, but she was the dean of the trio, so to speak, and under her desk was the kick-lock that admitted you to Father's throne room. All three of the secretaries were passionate capitalists, and Birdy had invented the rule that if typists were seen eating together more than once in a single week, they were hauled up on the carpet. At that time the studios feared mob rule.

I went on in. Nowadays all chief executives have huge drawing rooms, but my father's was the first. It was also the first to have one-way glass in the big French windows, and I've heard a story about a trap in the floor that would drop unpleasant visitors to an oubliette below, but believe it to be an invention. There was a big painting of Will Rogers, hung conspicuously and intended, I think, to suggest Father's essential kinship with Hollywood's St. Francis; there was a signed photograph of Minna Davis, Stahr's dead wife, and photos of other studio celebrities and big chalk drawings of mother and me. Tonight the one-way French windows were open and a big moon, rosy-gold with a haze around, was wedged helpless in one of them. Father and Jacques La Borwitz and Rosemary Schmiel were down at the end around a big circular desk.

What did Father look like? I couldn't describe him except for once in New York when I met him where I didn't expect to; I was aware of a bulky, middle-aged man who looked a little ashamed of himself, and I wished he'd move on—and then I saw he was Father. Afterward I was shocked at my impression. Father can be very magnetic—he has a tough jaw and an Irish smile.

But as for Jacques La Borwitz, I shall spare you. Let me just say he was an assistant producer, which is something like a commissar, and let it go at that. Where Stahr picked up such mental cadavers or had them forced upon him—or especially how he got any use out of them—has always amazed me, as it amazed everyone fresh from the East who slapped up against them. Jacques La Borwitz had his points, no doubt, but so have the sub-microscopic protozoa, so has a dog prowling for a bitch and a bone. Jacques La—oh my!

From their expressions I was sure they had been talking about Stahr. Stahr had ordered something or forbidden something, or defied Father or junked one of La Borwitz' pictures or something catastrophic, and they were sitting there in protest at night in a community of rebellion and helplessness. Rosemary Schmiel sat pad in hand, as if ready to write down their dejection.

"I'm to drive you home dead or alive," I told Father. "All those birthday presents rotting away in their packages!"

"A birthday!" cried Jacques in a flurry of apology. "How old? I didn't know."

"Forty-three," said Father distinctly.

He was older than that—four years—and Jacques knew it; I saw him note it down in his account book to use some time. Out here these account books are carried open in the hand. One can see the entries being made without recourse to lip-reading, and Rosemary Schmiel was compelled in emulation to make a mark on her pad. As she rubbed it out, the earth quaked under us.

We didn't get the full shock like at Long Beach, where the upper stories of shops were spewed into the streets and small hotels drifted out to sea—but for a full minute our bowels were one with the bowels of the earth—like some nightmare attempt to attach our navel cords again and jerk us back to the womb of creation.

Mother's picture fell off the wall, revealing a small safe—Rosemary and I grabbed frantically for each other and did a strange screaming waltz across the room. Jacques fainted or at least disappeared, and Father clung to his desk and shouted, "Are you all right?" Outside the window the singer came to the climax of *I love you only,* held it a moment and then, I swear, started it all over. Or maybe they were playing it back to her from the recording machine.

The room stood still, shimmying a little. We made our way to the door, suddenly including Jacques, who had reappeared, and tottered out dizzily through the anteroom on to the iron balcony. Almost all the lights were out, and from here and there we could hear cries and calls. Momentarily we stood waiting for a second shock—then, as with a common impulse, we went into Stahr's entry and through to his office.

The office was big, but not as big as Father's. Stahr sat on the side of his couch rubbing his eyes. When the quake came he had been asleep, and he wasn't sure yet whether he had dreamed it. When we convinced him he thought it was all rather funny—until the telephones began to ring. I watched him as unobtrusively as possible.

He was grey with fatigue while he listened to the phone and dictograph; but as the reports came in, his eyes began to pick up shine.

"A couple of water mains have burst," he said to Father, "—they're heading into the back lot."

"Gray's shooting in the French Village," said Father.

"It's flooded around the Station, too, and in the Jungle and the City Corner. What the hell—nobody seems to be hurt." In passing, he shook my hands gravely: "Where've you been, Cecilia?"

"You going out there, Monroe?" Father asked.

"When all the news is in. One of the power lines is off, too—I've sent for Robinson."

He made me sit down with him on the couch and tell about the quake again.

"You look tired," I said, cute and motherly.

"Yes," he agreed, "I've got no place to go in the evenings, so I just work."

"I'll arrange some evenings for you."

"I used to play poker with a gang," he said thoughtfully, "before I was married. But they all drank themselves to death."

Miss Doolan, his secretary, came in with fresh bad news.

"Robby'll take care of everything when he comes," Stahr assured Father. He turned to me. "Now there's a man—that Robinson. He was a trouble-shooter—fixed the telephone wires in Minnesota blizzards—nothing stumps him. He'll be here in a minute—you'll like Robby."

He said it as if it had been his life-long intention to bring us together, and he had arranged the whole earthquake with just that in mind.

"Yes, you'll like Robby," he repeated. "When do you go back to college?"

"I've just come home."

"You get the whole summer?"

"I'm sorry," I said. "I'll go back as soon as I can."

I was in a mist. It hadn't failed to cross my mind that he might have some intention about me, but if it was so, it was in an exasperatingly early stage—I was merely "a good property." And the idea didn't seem so attractive at that moment—like marrying a doctor. He seldom left the studio before eleven.

"How long," he asked my father, "before she graduates from college. That's what I was trying to say."

And I think I was about to sing out eagerly that I needn't go back at all, that I was quite educated already—when the totally admirable Robinson came in. He was a bowlegged young redhead, all ready to go.

"This is Robby, Cecilia," said Stahr. "Come on, Robby."

So I met Robby. I can't say it seemed like fate—but it was. For it was Robby who later told me how Stahr found his love that night.

Under the moon the back lot was thirty acres of fairyland—not because the locations really looked like African jungles and French châteaux and schooners at anchor and Broadway by night, but because they looked like the torn picture books of childhood, like fragments of stories dancing in an open fire. I never lived in a house with an attic, but a back lot must be something like that, and at night of course in an enchanted distorted way, it all comes true.

When Stahr and Robby arrived, clusters of lights had already picked out the danger spots in the flood.

"We'll pump it out into the swamp on Thirty-Sixth Street," said Robby after a moment. "It's city property—but isn't this an act of God? Say—look there!"

On top of a huge head of the Goddess Siva, two women were floating down the current of an impromptu river. The idol had come unloosed from a set of Burma, and it meandered earnestly on its way, stopping sometimes to waddle and bump in the shallows with the other debris of the tide. The two refugees had found sanctuary along a scroll of curls on its bald forehead and seemed at first glance to be sightseers on an interesting bus-ride through the scene of the flood.

"Will you look at that, Monroe!" said Robby. "Look at those dames!"

Dragging their legs through sudden bogs, they made their way to the bank of the stream. Now they could see the women, looking a little scared but brightening at the prospect of rescue.

"We ought to let 'em drift out to the waste pipe," said Robby gallantly, "but DeMille needs that head next week."

He wouldn't have hurt a fly, though, and presently he was hip deep in the water, fishing for them with a pole and succeeding only in spinning it in a dizzy circle. Help arrived, and the impression quickly got around that one of them was very pretty, and then that they were people of importance. But they were just strays, and Robby waited disgustedly to give them hell while the thing was brought finally into control and beached.

"Put that head back!" he called up to them. "You think it's a souvenir?"

One of the women came sliding smoothly down the cheek of the idol, and Robby caught and set her on solid ground; the other one hesitated and then followed. Robby turned to Stahr for judgment.

"What'll we do with them, chief?"

Stahr did not answer. Smiling faintly at him from not four feet away was the face of his dead wife, identical even to the expression. Across the four feet of moonlight, the eyes he knew looked back at him, a curl blew a little on a familiar forehead; the smile lingered, changed a little according to pattern; the lips parted—the same. An awful fear went over him, and he wanted to cry aloud. Back from the still sour room, the muffled glide of the limousine hearse, the falling concealing flowers, from out there in the dark—here now warm and glowing. The river passed him in a rush, the great spotlights swooped and blinked—and then he heard another voice speak that was not Minna's voice.

"We're sorry," said the voice. "We followed a truck in through a gate."

A little crowd had gathered—electricians, grips, truckers, and Robby began to nip at them like a sheep dog.

". . . get the big pumps on the tanks on Stage 4 . . . put a cable around this head . . . raft it up on a couple of two by fours . . . get the water out of the jungle first, for Christ's sake . . . that big 'A' pipe, lay it down . . . all that stuff is plastic. . . ."

Stahr stood watching the two women as they threaded their way after a policeman toward an exit gate. Then he took a tentative step to see if the weakness had gone out of his knees. A loud tractor came bumping through the slush, and men began streaming by him—every second one glancing at him, smiling, speaking: "Hello, Monroe. . . . Hello, Mr. Stahr . . . wet night, Mr. Stahr . . . Monroe . . . Monroe . . . Stahr . . . Stahr . . . Stahr."

He spoke and waved back as the people streamed by in the darkness, looking, I suppose, a little like the Emperor and the Old Guard. There is no world so but it has its heroes, and Stahr was the hero. Most of these men had been here a long time—through the beginnings and the great upset, when sound came, and the three years of depression, he had seen that no harm came to them. The old loyalties were trembling now, there were clay feet everywhere; but still he was their man, the last of the princes. And their greeting was a sort of low cheer as they went by.

CHAPTER III

BETWEEN THE NIGHT I got back and the quake, I'd made many observations.

About Father, for example. I loved Father—in a sort of irregular graph with many low swoops—but I began to see that his strong will didn't fill him out as a passable man. Most of what he accomplished boiled down to shrewd. He had acquired with luck and shrewdness a quarter interest in a booming circus—together with young Stahr. That was his life's effort—all the rest was an instinct to hang on. Of course, he talked that double talk to Wall Street about how mysterious it was to make a picture, but Father didn't know the ABC's of dubbing or even cutting. Nor had he learned much about the feel of America as a bar boy in Ballyhegan, nor did he have any more than a drummer's sense of a story. On the other hand, he didn't have concealed paresis like ———; he came to the studio before noon, and, with a suspiciousness developed like a muscle, it was hard to put anything over on him.

Stahr had been his luck—and Stahr was something else again. He was a marker in industry like Edison and Lumière and Griffith and Chaplin. He led pictures way up past the range and power of the theatre, reaching a sort of golden age, before the censorship.

Proof of his leadership was the spying that went on around him —not just for inside information or patented process secrets—but spying on his scent for a trend in taste, his guess as to how things were going to be. Too much of his vitality was taken by the mere parrying of these attempts. It made his work secret in part, often devious, slow—and hard to describe as the plans of a general, where the psychological factors become too tenuous and we end by merely adding up the successes and failures. But I have determined to give you a glimpse of him functioning, which is my excuse for what follows. It is drawn partly from a paper I wrote in college on *A*

Producer's Day and partly from my imagination. More often I have blocked in the ordinary events myself, while the stranger ones are true.

In the early morning after the flood, a man walked up to the outside balcony of the Administration Building. He lingered there some time, according to an eyewitness, then mounted to the iron railing and dove head first to the pavement below. Breakage—one arm.

Miss Doolan, Stahr's secretary, told him about it when he buzzed for her at nine. He had slept in his office without hearing the small commotion.

"Pete Zavras!" Stahr exclaimed, "—the camera man?"

"They took him to a doctor's office. It won't be in the paper."

"Hell of a thing," he said. "I knew he'd gone to pot—but I don't know why. He was all right when we used him two years ago—why should he come here? How did he get in?"

"He bluffed it with his old studio pass," said Catherine Doolan. She was a dry hawk, the wife of an assistant director. "Perhaps the quake had something to do with it."

"He was the best camera man in town," Stahr said. When he had heard of the hundreds dead at Long Beach, he was still haunted by the abortive suicide at dawn. He told Catherine Doolan to trace the matter down.

The first dictograph messages blew in through the warm morning. While he shaved and had coffee, he talked and listened. Robby had left a message: "If Mr. Stahr wants me tell him to hell with it I'm in bed." An actor was sick or thought so; the Governor of California was bringing a party out; a supervisor had beaten up his wife for the prints and must be "reduced to a writer"—these three affairs were Father's job—unless the actor was under personal contract to Stahr. There was early snow on a location in Canada with the company already there—Stahr raced over the possibilities of salvage, reviewing the story of the picture. Nothing. Stahr called Catherine Doolan.

"I want to speak to the cop who put two women off the back lot last night. I think his name's Malone."

"Yes, Mr. Stahr. I've got Joe Wyman—about the trousers."

"Hello, Joe," said Stahr. "Listen—two people at the sneak pre-view complained that Morgan's fly was open for half the picture . . . of course they're exaggerating, but even if it's only ten feet . . . no, we can't find the people, but I want that picture run over and over until you find that footage. Get a lot of people in the projection room—somebody'll spot it."

"Tout passe.—L'art robuste
Seul a l'éternité."

"And there's the Prince from Denmark," said Catherine Doolan. "He's very handsome." She was impelled to add pointlessly, "—for a tall man."

"Thanks," Stahr said. "Thank you, Catherine, I appreciate it that I am now the handsomest small man on the lot. Send the Prince out on the sets and tell him we'll lunch at one."

"And Mr. George Boxley—looking very angry in a British way."

"I'll see him for ten minutes."

As she went out, he asked: "Did Robby phone in?"

"No."

"Call sound, and if he's been heard from, call him and ask him this. Ask him this—did he hear that woman's name last night? Either of those women. Or anything so they could be traced."

"Anything else?"

"No, but tell him it's important while he still remembers. What were they? I mean what kind of people—ask him that, too. I mean were they——"

She waited, scratching his words on her pad without looking.

"—oh, were they—questionable? Were they theatrical? Never mind—skip that. Just ask if he knows how they can be traced."

The policeman, Malone, had known nothing. Two dames, and he had hustled 'em, you betcha. One of them was sore. Which one? One of them. They had a car, a Chevy—he thought of taking the license. Was it—the good looker who was sore? It was one of them.

Not which one—he had noticed nothing. Even on the lot here Minna was forgotten. In three years. So much for that, then.

Stahr smiled at Mr. George Boxley. It was a kindly fatherly smile Stahr had developed inversely when he was a young man pushed into high places. Originally it had been a smile of respect toward his elders, then as his own decisions grew rapidly to displace theirs, a smile so that they should not feel it—finally emerging as what it was: a smile of kindness—sometimes a little hurried and tired, but always there—toward anyone who had not angered him within the hour. Or anyone he did not intend to insult, aggressive and outright.

Mr. Boxley did not smile back. He came in with the air of being violently dragged, though no one apparently had a hand on him. He stood in front of a chair, and again it was as if two invisible attendants seized his arms and set him down forcibly into it. He sat there morosely. Even when he lit a cigarette on Stahr's invitation, one felt that the match was held to it by exterior forces he disdained to control.

Stahr looked at him courteously.

"Something not going well, Mr. Boxley?"

The novelist looked back at him in thunderous silence.

"I read your letter," said Stahr. The tone of the pleasant young headmaster was gone. He spoke as to an equal, but with a faint two-edged deference.

"I can't get what I write on paper," broke out Boxley. "You've all been very decent, but it's a sort of conspiracy. Those two hacks you've teamed me with listen to what I say, but they spoil it—they seem to have a vocabulary of about a hundred words."

"Why don't you write it yourself?" asked Stahr.

"I have. I sent you some."

"But it was just talk, back and forth," said Stahr mildly. "Interesting talk but nothing more."

Now it was all the two ghostly attendants could do to hold Boxley in the deep chair. He struggled to get up; he uttered a single quiet bark which had some relation to laughter but none to amusement, and said:

"I don't think you people read things. The men are duelling when the conversation takes place. At the end one of them falls into a well and has to be hauled up in a bucket."

He barked again and subsided.

"Would you write that in a book of your own, Mr. Boxley?"

"What? Naturally not."

"You'd consider it too cheap."

Movie standards are different," said Boxley, hedging.

"Do you ever go to them?"

"No—almost never."

"Isn't it because people are always duelling and falling down wells?"

"Yes—and wearing strained facial expressions and talking incredible and unnatural dialogue."

"Skip the dialogue for a minute," said Stahr. "Granted your dialogue is more graceful than what these hacks can write—that's why we brought you out here. But let's imagine something that isn't either bad dialogue or jumping down a well. Has your office got a stove in it that lights with a match?"

"I think it has," said Boxley stiffly, "—but I never use it."

"Suppose you're in your office. You've been fighting duels or writing all day and you're too tired to fight or write any more. You're sitting there staring—dull, like we all get sometimes. A pretty stenographer that you've seen before comes into the room and you watch her—idly. She doesn't see you, though you're very close to her. She takes off her gloves, opens her purse and dumps it out on a table——"

Stahr stood up, tossing his key-ring on his desk.

"She has two dimes and a nickel—and a cardboard match box. She leaves the nickel on the desk, puts the two dimes back into her purse and takes her black gloves to the stove, opens it and puts them inside. There is one match in the match box and she starts to light it kneeling by the stove. You notice that there's a stiff wind blowing in the window—but just then your telephone rings. The girl picks it up, says hello—listens—and says deliberately into the phone, 'I've never owned a pair of black gloves in my life.' She hangs up, kneels by the stove again, and just as she lights the match, you glance around very suddenly and see that there's another man in the office, watching every move the girl makes——"

Stahr paused. He picked up his keys and put them in his pocket.

"Go on," said Boxley smiling. "What happens?"

"I don't know," said Stahr. "I was just making pictures."

Boxley felt he was being put in the wrong.

"It's just melodrama," he said.

"Not necessarily," said Stahr. "In any case, nobody has moved violently or talked cheap dialogue or had any facial expression at all. There was only one bad line, and a writer like you could improve it. But you were interested."

"What was the nickel for?" asked Boxley evasively.

"I don't know," said Stahr. Suddenly he laughed. "Oh, yes—the nickel was for the movies."

The two invisible attendants seemed to release Boxley. He relaxed, leaned back in his chair and laughed.

"What in hell do you pay me for?" he demanded. "I don't understand the damn stuff."

"You will," said Stahr grinning, "or you wouldn't have asked about the nickel."

A dark saucer-eyed man was waiting in the outer office as they came out.

"Mr. Boxley, this is Mr. Mike Van Dyke," Stahr said. "What is it, Mike?"

"Nothing," Mike said. "I just came up to see if you were real."

"Why don't you go to work?" Stahr said. "I haven't had a laugh in the rushes for days."

"I'm afraid of a nervous breakdown."

"You ought to keep in form," Stahr said. "Let's see you peddle your stuff." He turned to Boxley: "Mike's a gag man—he was out here when I was in the cradle. Mike, show Mr. Boxley a double wing, clutch, kick and scram."

"Here?" asked Mike.

"Here."

"There isn't much room. I wanted to ask you about——"

"There's lot of room."

"Well," he looked around tentatively. "You shoot the gun."

Miss Doolan's assistant, Katy, took a paper bag, blew it open.

"It was a routine," Mike said to Boxley, "—back in the Keystone days." He turned to Stahr: "Does he know what a routine is?"

"It means an act," Stahr explained. "Georgie Jessel talks about 'Lincoln's Gettysburg routine.'"

Katy poised the neck of the blown-up bag in her mouth. Mike stood with his back to her.

"Ready?" Katy asked. She brought her hands down on the side. Immediately Mike grabbed his bottom with both hands, jumped in the air, slid his feet out on the floor one after the other, remaining in place and flapping his arms twice like a bird——

"Double wing," said Stahr.

—and then ran out the screen door which the office boy held open for him and disappeared past the window of the balcony.

"Mr. Stahr," said Miss Doolan, "Mr. Hanson is on the phone from New York."

Ten minutes later he clicked his dictograph, and Miss Doolan came in. There was a male star waiting to see him in the outer office, Miss Doolan said.

"Tell him I went out by the balcony," Stahr advised her.

"All right. He's been in four times this week. He seems very anxious."

"Did he give you any hint of what he wanted? Isn't it something he can see Mr. Brady about?"

"He didn't say. You have a conference coming up. Miss Meloney and Mr. White are outside. Mr. Broaca is next door in Mr. Reinmund's office."

"Send Mr. Roderiguez in," said Stahr. "Tell him I can see him only for a minute."

When the handsome actor came in, Stahr remained standing.

"What is it that can't wait?" he asked pleasantly.

The actor waited carefully till Miss Doolan had gone out.

"Monroe, I'm through," he said. "I had to see you."

"Through!" said Stahr. "Have you seen *Variety*? Your picture's held over at Roxy's and did thirty-seven thousand in Chicago last week."

"That's the worst of it. That's the tragedy. I get everything I want, and now it means nothing."

"Well, go on, explain."

"There's nothing between Esther and me any more. There never can be again."

"A row."

"Oh, no—worse—I can't bear to mention it. My head's in a daze. I wander around like a madman. I go through my part as if I was asleep."

"I haven't noticed it," said Stahr. "You were great in your rushes yesterday."

"Was I? That just shows you nobody ever guesses."

"Are you trying to tell me that you and Esther are separating?"

"I suppose it'll come to that. Yes—inevitably—it will."

"What was it?" demanded Stahr impatiently. "Did she come in without knocking?"

"Oh, there's nobody else. It's just—me. I'm through."

Stahr got it suddenly.

"How do you know?"

"It's been true for six weeks."

"It's your imagination," said Stahr. "Have you been to a doctor?"

The actor nodded.

"I've tried everything. I even—one day in desperation I went down to—to Claris. But it was hopeless. I'm washed up."

Stahr had an impish temptation to tell him to go to Brady about it. Brady handled all matters of public relations. Or was this private relations. He turned away a moment, got his face in control, turned back.

"I've been to Pat Brady," said the star, as if guessing the thought. "He gave me a lot of phoney advice and I tried it all, but nothing doing. Esther and I sit opposite each other at dinner, and I'm ashamed to look at her. She's been a good sport about it, but I'm ashamed. I'm ashamed all day long. I think *Rainy Day* grossed twenty-five thousand in Des Moines and broke all records in St. Louis and did twenty-seven thousand in Kansas City. My fan mail's way up, and there I am afraid to go home at night, afraid to go to bed."

Stahr began to be faintly oppressed. When the actor first came in, Stahr had intended to invite him to a cocktail party, but now it scarcely seemed appropriate. What would he want with a cocktail party with this hanging over him? In his mind's eye he saw him wandering haunted from guest to guest with a cocktail in his hand and his grosses up twenty-seven thousand.

"So I came to you, Monroe. I never saw a situation where you didn't know a way out. I said to myself: even if he advises me to kill myself, I'll ask Monroe."

The buzzer sounded on Stahr's desk—he switched on the dictograph and heard Miss Doolan's voice.

"Five minutes, Mr. Stahr."

"I'm sorry," said Stahr. "I'll need a few minutes more."

"Five hundred girls marched to my house from the high school," the actor said gloomily, "and I stood behind the curtains and watched them. I couldn't go out."

"You sit down," said Stahr. "We'll take plenty of time and talk this over."

In the outer office, two members of the conference group had already waited ten minutes—Wylie White and Jane Meloney. The latter was a dried-up little blonde of fifty about whom one could hear the fifty assorted opinions of Hollywood—"a sentimental dope," "the best writer on construction in Hollywood," "a veteran," "that old hack," "the smartest woman on the lot," "the cleverest plagiarist in the biz"; and, of course, in addition she was variously described as a nymphomaniac, a virgin, a pushover, a Lesbian and a faithful wife. Without being an old maid, she was, like most self-made women, rather old maidish. She had ulcers of the stomach, and her salary was over a hundred thousand a year. A complicated treatise could be written on whether she was "worth it" or more than that or nothing at all. Her value lay in such ordinary assets as the bare fact that she was a woman and adaptable, quick and trustworthy, "knew the game" and was without egotism. She had been a great friend of Minna's, and over a period of years Stahr had managed to stifle what amounted to a sharp physical revulsion.

She and Wylie waited in silence—occasionally addressing a remark to Miss Doolan. Every few minutes Reinmund, the supervisor, called up from his office, where he and Broaca, the director, were waiting. After ten minutes Stahr's button went on, and Miss Doolan called Reinmund and Broaca; simultaneously Stahr and the actor came out of Stahr's office with Stahr holding the man's arm. He was so wound up now that when Wylie White asked him how he was he opened his mouth and began to tell him then and there.

"Oh, I've had an awful time," he said, but Stahr interrupted sharply.

"No, you haven't. Now you go along and do the role the way I said."

"Thank you, Monro—"

Jane Meloney looked after him without speaking.

"Somebody been catching flies on him?" she asked—a phrase for stealing scenes.

"I'm sorry I kept you waiting," Stahr said. "Come on in."

It was noon already and the conferees were entitled to exactly an hour of Stahr's time. No less, for such a conference could only be interrupted by a director who was held up in his shooting; seldom much more, because every eight days the company must release a production as complex and costly as Reinhardt's *Miracle*.

Occasionally, less often than five years ago, Stahr would work all through the night on a single picture. But after such a spree he felt badly for days. If he could go from problem to problem, there was a certain rebirth of vitality with each change. And like those sleepers who can wake whenever they wish, he had set his psychological clock to run one hour.

The cast assembled included, besides the writers, Reinmund, one of the most favored of the supervisors, and John Broaca, the picture's director.

Broaca, on the surface, was all engineer—large and without nerves, quietly resolute, popular. He was an ignoramus, and Stahr often caught him making the same scenes over and over—one scene about a rich young girl occurred in all his pictures with the same action, the same business. A bunch of large dogs entered the room and jumped around the girl. Later the girl went to a stable and slapped a horse on the rump. The explanation was probably not Freudian; more likely that at a drab moment in youth he had looked through a fence and seen a beautiful girl with dogs and horses. As a trademark for glamor it was stamped on his brain forever.

Reinmund was a handsome young opportunist, with a fairly good education. Originally a man of some character, he was being daily forced by his anomalous position into devious ways of acting and thinking. He was a bad man now, as men go. At thirty he had none of the virtues which either gentile Americans or Jews are taught to think admirable. But he got his pictures out in time, and by manifesting an almost homosexual fixation on Stahr, seemed to have dulled Stahr's usual acuteness. Stahr liked him—considered him a good all-around man.

Wylie White, of course, in any country would have been recognizable as an intellectual of the second order. He was civilized and voluble, both simple and acute, half dazed and half saturnine. His jealousy of Stahr showed only in unguarded flashes, and was mingled with admiration and even affection.

"The production date for this picture is two weeks from Saturday," said Stahr. "I think basically it's all right—much improved."

Reinmund and the two writers exchanged a glance of congratulation.

"Except for one thing," said Stahr, thoughtfully. "I don't see why it should be produced at all, and I've decided to put it away."

There was a moment of shocked silence—and then murmurs of protest, stricken queries.

"It's not your fault," Stahr said. "I thought there was something there that wasn't there—that was all." He hesitated, looking regretfully at Reinmund: "It's too bad—it was a good play. We paid fifty thousand for it."

"What's the matter with it, Monroe?" asked Broaca bluntly.

"Well, it hardly seems worth while to go into it," said Stahr.

Reinmund and Wylie White were both thinking of the professional effect on them. Reinmund had two pictures to his account this year—but Wylie White needed a credit to start his comeback to the scene. Jane Meloney was watching Stahr closely from little skull-like eyes.

"Couldn't you give us some clue," Reinmund asked. "This is a good deal of a blow, Monroe."

"I just wouldn't put Margaret Sullavan in it," said Stahr. "Or Colman either. I wouldn't advise them to play it——"

"Specifically, Monroe," begged Wylie White. "What didn't you like? The scenes? the dialogue? the humor? construction?"

Stahr picked up the script from his desk, let it fall as if it were, physically, too heavy to handle.

"I don't like the people," he said. "I wouldn't like to meet them —if I knew they were going to be somewhere, I'd go somewhere else."

Reinmund smiled, but there was worry in his eyes.

"Well, that's a damning criticism," he said. "I thought the people were rather interesting."

"So did I," said Broaca. "I thought Em was very sympathetic."

"Did you?" asked Stahr sharply. "I could just barely believe she was alive. And when I came to the end, I said to myself, 'So what?'"

"There must be something to do," Reinmund said. "Naturally we feel bad about this. This is the structure we agreed on——"

"But it's not the story," said Stahr. "I've told you many times that the first thing I decide is the *kind* of story I want. We change in every other regard, but once that is set we've got to work toward it with every line and movement. This is not the kind of a story I want. The story we bought had shine and glow—it was a happy story. This is all full of doubt and hesitation. The hero and heroine stop loving each other over trifles—then they start up again over trifles. After the first sequence, you don't care if she never sees him again or he her."

"That's my fault," said Wylie suddenly. "You see, Monroe, I don't think stenographers have the same dumb admiration for their bosses they had in 1929. They've been laid off—they've seen their bosses jittery. The world has moved on, that's all."

Stahr looked at him impatiently, gave a short nod.

"That's not under discussion," he said. "The premise of this story is that the girl did have dumb admiration for her boss, if you want to call it that. And there wasn't any evidence that he'd ever been jittery. When you make her doubt him in any way, you have a different kind of story. Or rather you haven't anything at all. These people are extraverts—get that straight—and I want them to extravert all over the lot. When I want to do a Eugene O'Neill play, I'll buy one."

Jane Meloney, who had never taken her eyes off Stahr, knew it was going to be all right now. If he had really been going to abandon the picture, he wouldn't have gone at it like this. She had been in this game longer than any of them except Broaca, with whom she had had a three-day affair twenty years ago.

Stahr turned to Reinmund.

"You ought to have understood from the casting, Reiny, what kind of a picture I wanted. I started marking the lines that Corliss and McKelway couldn't say and got tired of it. Remember this in the future—if I order a limousine, I want that kind of car. And the fastest midget racer you ever saw wouldn't do. Now—" He looked around. "—shall we go any farther? Now that I've told you I don't even like the kind of picture this is? Shall we go on? We've got two weeks. At the end of that time I'm going to put Corliss and McKelway into this or something else—is it worth while?"

"Well, naturally," said Reinmund, "I think it is. I feel bad about this. I should have warned Wylie. I thought he had some good ideas."

"Monroe's right," said Broaca bluntly. "I felt this was wrong all the time, but I couldn't put my finger on it."

Wylie and Rose looked at him contemptuously and exchanged a glance.

"Do you writers think you can get hot on it again?" asked Stahr, not unkindly. "Or shall I try somebody fresh?"

"I'd like another shot," said Wylie.

"How about you, Jane?"

She nodded briefly.

"What do you think of the girl?" asked Stahr.

"Well—naturally I'm prejudiced in her favor."

"You better forget it," said Stahr warningly. "Ten million Americans would put thumbs down on that girl if she walked on the screen. We've got an hour and twenty-five minutes on the screen —you show a woman being unfaithful to a man for one-third of that time and you've given the impression that she's one-third whore."

"Is that a big proportion?" asked Jane slyly, and they laughed.

"It is for me," said Stahr thoughtfully, "even if it wasn't for the Hays office. If you want to paint a scarlet letter on her back, it's all right, but that's another story. Not this story. This is a future wife and mother. However—*however*——"

He pointed his pencil at Wylie White.

"—this has as much passion as that Oscar on my desk."

"What the hell!" said Wylie. "She's full of it. Why she goes to——"

"She's loose enough," said Stahr, "—but that's all. There's one scene in the play better than all this you cooked up, and you've left it out. When she's trying to make the time pass by changing her watch."

"It didn't seem to fit," Wylie apologized.

"Now," said Stahr, "I've got about fifty ideas. I'm going to call

Miss Doolan." He pressed a button. "—And if there's anything you don't understand, speak up——"

Miss Doolan slid in almost imperceptibly. Pacing the floor swiftly, Stahr began. In the first place he wanted to tell them what kind of a girl she was—what kind of a girl he approved of here. She was a perfect girl with a few small faults as in the play, but a perfect girl not because the public wanted her that way but because it was the kind of girl that he, Stahr, liked to see in this sort of picture. Was that clear? It was no character role. She stood for health, vitality, ambition and love. What gave the play its importance was entirely a situation in which she found herself. She became possessed of a secret that affected a great many lives. There was a right thing and a wrong thing to do—at first it was not plain which was which, but when it was, she went right away and did it. That was the kind of story this was—thin, clean and shining. No doubts.

"She has never heard the word labor troubles," he said with a sigh. "She might be living in 1929. Is it plain what kind of girl I want?"

"It's very plain, Monroe."

"Now about the things she does," said Stahr. "At all times, at all moments when she is on the screen in our sight, she wants to sleep with Ken Willard. Is that plain, Wylie?"

"Passionately plain."

"Whatever she does, it is in place of sleeping with Ken Willard. If she walks down the street she is walking to sleep with Ken Willard, if she eats her food it is to give her strength to sleep with Ken Willard. *But* at no time do you give the impression that she would ever consider sleeping with Ken Willard unless they were properly sanctified. I'm ashamed of having to tell you these kindergarten facts, but they have somehow leaked out of the story."

He opened the script and began to go through it page by page. Miss Doolan's notes would be typed in quintuplicate and given to them, but Jane Meloney made notes of her own. Broaca put his hand up to his half-closed eyes—he could remember "when a director was something out here," when writers were gag-men or eager and ashamed young reporters full of whiskey—a director was all there was then. No supervisor—no Stahr.

He started wide-awake as he heard his name.

"It would be nice, John, if you could put the boy on a pointed roof and let him walk around and keep the camera on him. You might get a nice feeling—not danger, not suspense, not pointing for anything—a kid on the roof in the morning."

Broaca brought himself back in the room.

"All right," he said, "—just an element of danger."

"Not exactly," said Stahr. "He doesn't start to fall off the roof. Break into the next scene with it."

"Through the window," suggested Jane Meloney. "He could climb in his sister's window."

"That's a good transition," said Stahr. "Right into the diary scene."

Broaca was wide-awake now.

"I'll shoot up at him," he said. "Let him go away from the camera. Just a fixed shot from quite a distance—let him go away from the camera. Don't follow him. Pick him up in a close shot and let him go away again. No attention on him except against the whole roof and the sky." He liked the shot—it was a director's shot that didn't come up on every page any more. He might use a crane—it would be cheaper in the end than building the roof on the ground with a process sky. That was one thing about Stahr—the literal sky was the limit. He had worked with Jews too long to believe legends that they were small with money.

"In the third sequence have him hit the priest," Stahr said.

"What!" Wylie cried, "—and have the Catholics on our neck."

"I've talked to Joe Breen. Priests have been hit. It doesn't reflect on them."

His quiet voice ran on—stopped abruptly as Miss Doolan glanced at the clock.

"Is that too much to do before Monday?" he asked Wylie.

Wylie looked at Jane and she looked back, not even bothering to nod. He saw their week-end melting away, but he was a different man from when he entered the room. When you were paid fifteen hundred a week, emergency work was one thing you did not skimp, nor when your picture was threatened. As a "free lance" writer Wylie had failed from lack of caring, but here was Stahr to care, for all of them. The effect would not wear off when he left the office—not anywhere within the walls of the lot. He felt a great purposefulness. The mixture of common sense, wise sensibility, theatrical ingenuity, and a certain half-naïve conception of the common weal which Stahr had just stated aloud, inspired him to do his part, to get his block of stone in place, even if the effort were foredoomed, the result as dull as a pyramid.

Out of the window Jane Meloney watched the trickle streaming toward the commissary. She would have her lunch in her office and knit a few rows while it came. The man was coming at one-fifteen with the French perfume smuggled over the Mexican border. That was no sin—it was like prohibition.

Broaca watched as Reinmund fawned upon Stahr. He sensed that Reinmund was on his way up. He received seven hundred and fifty a week for his partial authority over directors, writers and stars who got much more. He wore a pair of cheap English shoes he had bought near the Beverly Wilshire, and Broaca hoped they hurt his feet, but soon now he would order his shoes from Peel's and put away his little green Alpine hat with a feather. Broaca was years ahead of him. He had a fine record in the war, but he had never felt quite the same with himself since he had let Ike Franklin strike him in the face with his open hand.

There was smoke in the room, and behind it, behind his great desk, Stahr was withdrawing further and further, in all courtesy, still giving Reinmund an ear and Miss Doolan an ear. The conference was over.

[*Stahr was to have received the Danish Prince Agge, who "wanted to learn about pictures from the beginning" and who in the author's cast of characters is described as an "early Fascist."*]

"Mr. Marcus calling from New York," said Miss Doolan.

"What do you mean?" demanded Stahr. "Why, I saw him here last night."

"Well, he's on the phone—it's a New York call and Miss Jacobs' voice. It's his office."

Stahr laughed.

"I'm seeing him at lunch," he said. "There's no aeroplane fast enough to take him there."

Miss Doolan returned to the phone. Stahr lingered to hear the outcome.

"It's all right," said Miss Doolan presently. "It was a mistake. Mr. Marcus called East this morning to tell them about the quake and the flood on the back lot, and it seems he asked them to ask you about it. It was a new secretary who didn't understand Mr. Marcus. I think she got mixed up."

"I think she did," said Stahr grimly.

Prince Agge did not understand either of them, but, looking for the fabulous, he felt it was something triumphantly American. Mr. Marcus, whose quarters could be seen across the way, had called his New York office to ask Stahr about the flood. The Prince imagined some intricate relationship without realizing that the transaction had taken place entirely within the once brilliant steel-trap mind of Mr. Marcus, which was intermittently slipping.

"I think she was a very new secretary," repeated Stahr. "Any other messages?"

"Mr. Robinson called in," Miss Doolan said, as he started for the commissary. "One of the women told him her name, but he's forgotten it—he thinks it was Smith or Brown or Jones."

"That's a great help."

"And he remembers she says she just moved to Los Angeles."

"I remember she had a silver belt," Stahr said, "with stars cut out of it."

"I'm still trying to find out more about Pete Zavras. I talked to his wife."

"What did she say?"

"Oh, they've had an awful time—given up their house—she's been sick——"

"Is the eye-trouble hopeless?"

"She didn't seem to know anything about the state of his eyes. She didn't even know he was going blind."

"That's funny."

He thought about it on the way to luncheon, but it was as confusing as the actor's trouble this morning. Troubles about people's health didn't seem within his range—he gave no thought to his own. In the lane beside the commissary he stepped back as an open electric truck crammed with girls in the bright costumes of the

Regency came rolling in from the back lot. The dresses were fluttering in the wind, the young painted faces looked at him curiously, and he smiled as it went by.

Eleven men and their guest, Prince Agge, sat at lunch in the private dining room of the studio commissary. They were the money men—they were the rulers; and unless there was a guest, they ate in broken silence, sometimes asking questions about each other's wives and children, sometimes discharging a single absorption from the forefront of their consciousness. Eight out of the ten were Jews— five of the ten were foreign-born, including a Greek and an Englishman; and they had all known each other for a long time: there was a rating in the group, from old Marcus down to old Leanbaum, who had bought the most fortunate block of stock in the business and never was allowed to spend over a million a year producing.

Old Marcus still managed to function with disquieting resilience. Some never-atrophying instinct warned him of danger, of gangings up against him—he was never so dangerous himself as when others considered him surrounded. His grey face had attained such immobility that even those who were accustomed to watch the reflex of the inner corner of his eye could no longer see it. Nature had grown a little white whisker there to conceal it; his armor was complete.

As he was the oldest, Stahr was the youngest of the group—not by many years at this date, though he had first sat with most of these men when he was a boy wonder of twenty-two. Then, more than now, he had been a money man among money men. Then he had been able to figure costs in his head with a speed and accuracy that dazzled them—for they were not wizards or even experts in that regard, despite the popular conception of Jews in finance. Most of them owed their success to different and incompatible qualities. But in a group a tradition carries along the less adept, and they were content to look at Stahr for the sublimated auditing, and experience a sort of glow as if they had done it themselves, like rooters at a football game.

Stahr, as will presently be seen, had grown away from that particular gift, though it was always there.

Prince Agge sat between Stahr and Mort Fleishacker, the company lawyer, and across from Joe Popolos the theatre owner. He was hostile to Jews in a vague general way that he tried to cure himself of. As a turbulent man, serving his time in the Foreign Legion, he thought that Jews were too fond of their own skins. But he was willing to concede that they might be different in America under different circumstances, and certainly he found Stahr was much of a man in every way. For the rest—he thought most business men were dull dogs—for final reference he reverted always to the blood of Bernadotte in his veins.

My father—I will call him Mr. Brady, as Prince Agge did when he told me of this luncheon—was worried about a picture, and when Leanbaum went out early, he came up and took his chair opposite.

"How about the South America picture idea, Monroe?" he asked.

Prince Agge noticed a blink of attention toward them as distinct as if a dozen pairs of eyelashes had made the sound of batting wings. Then silence again.

"We're going ahead with it," said Stahr.

"With that same budget?" Brady asked.

Stahr nodded.

"It's out of proportion," said Brady. "There won't be any miracle in these bad times—no *Hell's Angels* or *Ben Hur,* when you throw it away and get it back."

Probably the attack was planned, for Popolos, the Greek, took up the matter in a sort of double talk.

"It's not adoptable, Monroe, in as we wish adopt to this times in as it changes. It what could be done as we run the gamut of prosperity is scarcely conceptuable now."

"What do you think, Mr. Marcus?" asked Stahr.

All eyes followed his down the table, but, as if forewarned, Mr. Marcus had already signalled his private waiter behind him that he wished to rise, and was even now in a basket-like position in the waiter's arms. He looked at them with such helplessness that it was hard to realize that in the evenings he sometimes went dancing with his young Canadian girl.

"Monroe is our production genuis," he said. "I count upon Monroe and lean heavily upon him. I have not seen the flood myself."

There was a moment of silence as he moved from the room.

"There's not a two million dollar gross in the country now," said Brady.

"Is not," agreed Popolos. "Even as if so you could grab them by the head and push them by and in, is not."

"Probably not," agreed Stahr. He paused as if to make sure that all were listening. "I think we can count on a million and a quarter from the road-show. Perhaps a million and a half altogether. And a quarter of a million abroad."

Again there was silence—this time puzzled, a little confused. Over his shoulder Stahr asked the waiter to be connected with his office on the phone.

"But your budget?" said Fleishacker. "Your budget is seventeen hundred and fifty thousand, I understand. And your expectations only add up to that without profit."

"Those aren't my expectations," said Stahr. "We're not sure of more than a million and a half."

The room had grown so motionless that Prince Agge could hear a grey chunk of ash fall from a cigar in midair. Fleishacker started to speak, his face fixed with amazement, but a phone had been handed over Stahr's shoulder.

"Your office, Mr. Stahr."

"Oh, yes—oh, hello, Miss Doolan. I've figured it out about Zavras. It's one of these lousy rumors—I'll bet my shirt on it. . . . Oh, you did. Good. . . . good. Now here's what to do: send him to my oculist this afternoon—Dr. John Kennedy—and have him get a report and have it photostated—you understand?"

He hung up—turned with a touch of passion to the table at large.

"Did any of you ever hear a story that Pete Zavras was going blind?"

There were a couple of nods. But most of those present were poised breathlessly on whether Stahr had slipped on his figures a minute before.

"It's pure bunk. He says he's never even been to an oculist— never knew why the studios turned against him," said Stahr. "Somebody didn't like him or somebody talked too much, and he's been out of work for a year."

There was a conventional murmur of sympathy. Stahr signed the check and made as though to get up.

"Excuse me, Monroe," said Fleishacker persistently, while Brady and Popolos watched. "I'm fairly new here, and perhaps I fail to comprehend implicitly and explicitly." He was talking fast, but the veins on his forehead bulged with pride at the big words from N. Y. U. "Do I understand you to say you expect to gross a quarter million short of your budget?"

"It's a quality picture," said Stahr with assumed innocence.

It had dawned on them all now, but they still felt there was a trick in it. Stahr really thought it would make money. No one in his senses——

"For two years we've played safe," said Stahr. "It's time we made a picture that'll lose some money. Write it off as good will—this'll bring in new customers."

Some of them still thought he meant it was a flyer and a favorable one, but he left them in no doubt.

"It'll lose money," he said as he stood up, his jaw just slightly out and his eyes smiling and shining. "It would be a bigger miracle than *Hell's Angels* if it broke even. But we have a certain duty to the public, as Pat Brady has said at Academy dinners. It's a good thing for the production schedule to slip in a picture that'll lose money."

He nodded at Prince Agge. As the latter made his bows quickly, he tried to take in with a last glance the general effect of what Stahr said, but he could tell nothing. The eyes, not so much downcast as fixed upon an indefinite distance just above the table, were all blinking quickly now, but there was not a whisper in the room.

Coming out of the private dining room, they passed through a corner of the commissary proper. Prince Agge drank it in—eagerly. It was gay with gypsies and with citizens and soldiers, with the sideburns and braided coats of the First Empire. From a little distance they were men who lived and walked a hundred years ago, and Agge wondered how he and the men of his time would look as extras in some future costume picture.

Then he saw Abraham Lincoln, and his whole feeling suddenly changed. He had been brought up in the dawn of Scandinavian socialism when Nicolay's biography was much read. He had been told Lincoln was a great man whom he should admire, and he hated him instead, because he was forced upon him. But now seeing him sitting here, his legs crossed, his kindly face fixed on a forty-cent dinner, including dessert, his shawl wrapped around him as if to protect himself from the erratic air-cooling—now Prince Agge, who was in America at last, stared as a tourist at the mummy of Lenin in the Kremlin. This, then, was Lincoln. Stahr had walked on far ahead of him, turned waiting for him—but still Agge stared.

This, then, he thought, was what they all meant to be.

Lincoln suddenly raised a triangle of pie and jammed it in his mouth, and, a little frightened, Prince Agge hurried to join Stahr.

"I hope you're getting what you want," said Stahr, feeling he had neglected him. "We'll have some rushes in half an hour and then you can go on to as many sets as you want."

"I should rather stay with you," said Prince Agge.

"I'll see what there is for me," said Stahr. "Then we'll go on together."

There was the Japanese consul on the release of a spy story which might offend the national sensibilities of Japan. There were phone calls and telegrams. There was some further information from Robby.

"Now he remembers the name of the woman. He's sure it was Smith," said Miss Doolan. "He asked her if she wanted to come on the lot and get some dry shoes, and she said no—so she can't sue."

"That's pretty bad for a total recall—'Smith.' That's a great help." He thought a moment: "Ask the phone company for a list of Smiths that have taken new phones here in the last month. Call them all."

"All right."

CHAPTER IV

"How ARE YOU, Monroe," said Red Ridingwood. "I'm glad you came down."

Stahr walked past him, heading across the great stage toward the set of a brilliant room that would be used tomorrow. Director Ridingwood followed, realizing after a moment that, however fast he walked, Stahr managed to be a step or two ahead. He recognized the indication of displeasure—he had used it himself. He had had his own studio once and he had used everything. There was no stop Stahr could pull that would surprise him. His task was the delivery of situations, and Stahr by effective business could not outplay him on his own grounds. Goldwyn had once interfered with him, and Ridingwood had led Goldwyn into trying to act out a part in front of fifty people—with the result that he had anticipated: his own authority had been restored.

Stahr reached the brilliant set and stopped.

"It's no good," said Ridingwood. "No imagination. I don't care how you light it——"

"Why did you call me about it?" Stahr asked, standing close to him. "Why didn't you take it up with Art?"

"I didn't ask you to come down, Monroe."

"You wanted to be your own supervisor."

"I'm sorry, Monroe," said Ridingwood patiently, "but I didn't ask you to come down."

Stahr turned suddenly and walked back toward the camera set-up. The eyes and open mouths of a group of visitors moved momentarily off the heroine of the picture, took in Stahr, and then moved vacantly back to the heroine again. They were Knights of Columbus. They had seen the host carried in procession, but this was the dream made flesh.

Stahr stopped beside her chair. She wore a low gown which dis-

50

played the bright eczema of her chest and back. Before each take, the blemished surface was plastered over with an emollient, which was removed immediately after the take. Her hair was of the color and viscosity of drying blood, but there was starlight that actually photographed in her eyes.

Before Stahr could speak, he heard a helpful voice behind him: "She's radiant. Absolutely radiant."

It was an assistant director, and the intention was delicate compliment. The actress was being complimented so that she did not have to strain her poor skin to bend and hear. Stahr was being complimented for having her under contract. Ridingwood was being remotely complimented.

"Everything all right?" Stahr asked her pleasantly.

"Oh, it's fine," she agreed, "—except for the ——ing publicity men."

He winked at her gently.

"We'll keep them away," he said.

Her name had become currently synonymous with the expression "bitch." Presumably she had modelled herself after one of those queens in the Tarzan comics who rule mysteriously over a nation of blacks. She regarded the rest of the world as black. She was a necessary evil, borrowed for a single picture.

Ridingwood walked with Stahr toward the door of the stage.

"Everything's all right," the director said. "She's as good as she can be."

They were out of hearing range, and Stahr stopped suddenly and looked at Red with blazing eyes.

"You've been photographing crap," he said. "Do you know what she reminds me of in the rushes—'Miss Foodstuffs.'"

"I'm trying to get the best performance——"

"Come along with me," said Stahr abruptly.

"With you? Shall I tell them to rest?"

"Leave it as it is," said Stahr, pushing the padded outer door.

His car and chauffeur waited outside. Minutes were precious most days.

"Get in," said Stahr.

Red knew now it was serious. He even knew all at once what was the matter. The girl had got the whip hand on him the first day with her cold lashing tongue. He was a peace-loving man and he had let her walk through her part cold rather than cause trouble.

Stahr spoke into his thoughts.

"You can't handle her," he said. "I told you what I wanted. I wanted her *mean*—and she comes out bored. I'm afraid we'll have to call it off, Red."

"The picture?"

"No. I'm putting Harley on it."

"All right, Monroe."

"I'm sorry, Red. We'll try something else another time."

The car drew up in front of Stahr's office.

"Shall I finish this take?" said Red.

"It's being done now," said Stahr grimly. "Harley's in there."

"What the hell——"

"He went in when we came out. I had him read the script last night."

"Now listen, Monroe——"

"It's my busy day, Red," said Stahr, tersely. "You lost interest about three days ago."

It was a sorry mess, Ridingwood thought. It meant he would have slight, very slight loss of position—it probably meant that he could not have a third wife just now as he had planned. There wasn't even the satisfaction of raising a row about it—if you disagreed with Stahr, you did not advertise it. Stahr was his world's great customer, who was always—almost always—right.

"How about my coat?" he asked suddenly. "I left it over a chair on the set."

"I know you did," said Stahr. "Here it is."

He was trying so hard to be charitable about Ridingwood's lapse that he had forgotten that he had it in his hand.

"Mr. Stahr's Projection Room" was a miniature picture theatre with four rows of overstuffed chairs. In front of the front row ran long tables with dim lamps, buzzers and telephones. Against the wall was an upright piano, left there since the early days of sound. The room had been redecorated and reupholstered only a year before, but already it was ragged again with work and hours.

Here Stahr sat at two-thirty and again at six-thirty watching the lengths of film taken during the day. There was often a savage tensity about the occasion—he was dealing with *faits accomplis*—the net result of months of buying, planning, writing and rewriting, casting, constructing, lighting, rehearsing and shooting—the fruit of brilliant hunches or of counsels of despair, of lethargy, conspiracy and sweat. At this point the tortuous manœuvre was staged and in suspension—these were reports from the battle-line.

Besides Stahr, there were present the representatives of all technical departments, together with the supervisors and unit managers of the pictures concerned. The directors did not appear at these showings—officially because their work was considered done, actually because few punches were pulled here as money ran out in silver spools. There had evolved a delicate staying away.

The staff was already assembled. Stahr came in and took his place quickly, and the murmur of conversation died away. As he sat back and drew his thin knee up beside him in the chair, the lights in the room went out. There was the flare of a match in the back row—then silence.

On the screen a troop of French Canadians pushed their canoes up a rapids. The scene had been photographed in a studio tank, and at the end of each take, after the director's voice could be heard saying "Cut," the actors on the screen relaxed and wiped their brows and sometimes laughed hilariously—and the water in the tank stopped flowing and the illusion ceased. Except to name his choice from each set of takes and to remark that it was "a good process," Stahr made no comment.

The next scene, still in the rapids, called for dialogue between the Canadian girl (Claudette Colbert) and the *courrier du bois* (Ronald Colman), with her looking down at him from a canoe. After a few strips had run through, Stahr spoke up suddenly.

"Has the tank been dismantled?"

"Yes, sir."

"Monroe—they needed it for——"

Stahr cut in peremptorily.

"Have it set up again right away. Let's have that second take again."

The lights went on momentarily. One of the unit managers left his chair and came and stood in front of Stahr.

"A beautifully acted scene thrown away," raged Stahr quietly. "It wasn't centered. The camera was set up so it caught the beautiful top of Claudette's head all the time she was talking. That's just what we want, isn't it? That's just what people go to see—the top of a beautiful girl's head. Tell Tim he could have saved wear and tear by using her stand-in."

The lights went out again. The unit manager squatted by Stahr's chair to be out of the way. The take was run again.

"Do you see now?" asked Stahr. "And there's a hair in the picture—there on the right, see it? Find out if it's in the projector or the film."

At the very end of the take, Claudette Colbert slowly lifted her head, revealing her great liquid eyes.

"That's what we should have had all the way," said Stahr. "She gave a fine performance too. See if you can fit it in tomorrow or late this afternoon."

Pete Zavras would not have made a slip like that. There were not six camera men in the industry you could entirely trust.

The lights went on; the supervisor and unit manager for that picture went out.

"Monroe, this stuff was shot yesterday—it came through late last night."

The room darkened. On the screen appeared the head of Siva, immense and imperturbable, oblivious to the fact that in a few hours it was to be washed away in a flood. Around it milled a crowd of the faithful.

"When you take that scene again," said Stahr suddenly, "put a couple of little kids up on top. You better check about whether it's reverent or not, but I think it's all right. Kids'll do anything."

"Yes, Monroe."

A silver belt with stars cut out of it. . . . Smith, Jones or Brown. . . . Personal—will the woman with the silver belt who——?

With another picture the scene shifted to New York, a gangster story, and suddenly Stahr became restive.

"That scene's trash," he called suddenly in the darkness. "It's badly written, it's miscast, it accomplishes nothing. Those types aren't tough. They look like a lot of dressed up lollipops—what the hell is the matter, Lee?"

"The scene was written on the set this morning," said Lee Kapper. "Burton wanted to get all the stuff on Stage 6."

"Well—it's trash. And so is this one. There's no use printing stuff like that. She doesn't believe what she's saying—neither does Cary. 'I love you' in a close up—they'll cluck you out of the house! And the girl's overdressed."

In the darkness a signal was given, the projector stopped, the lights went on. The room waited in utter silence. Stahr's face was expressionless.

"Who wrote the scene?" he asked after a minute.

"Wylie White."

"Is he sober?"

"Sure he is."

Stahr considered.

"Put about four writers on that scene tonight," he said. "See who we've got. Is Sidney Howard here yet?"

"He got in this morning."

"Talk to him about it. Explain to him what I want there. The girl is in deadly terror—she's stalling. It's as simple as that. People don't have three emotions at once. And Kapper——"

The art director leaned forward out of the second row.

"Yeah."

"There's something the matter with that set."

There were little glances exchanged all over the room.

"What is it, Monroe?"

"You tell *me*," said Stahr. "It's crowded. It doesn't carry your eye out. It looks cheap."

"It wasn't."

"I know it wasn't. There's not much the matter, but there's something. Go over and take a look tonight. It may be too much furniture—or the wrong kind. Perhaps a window would help. Couldn't you force the perspective in that hall a little more?"

"I'll see what I can do." Kapper edged his way out of the row, looking at his watch.

"I'll have to get at it right away," he said. "I'll work tonight and we'll put it up in the morning."

"All right. Lee, you can shoot around those scenes, can't you?"

"I think so, Monroe."

"I take the blame for this. Have you got the fight stuff?"

"Coming up now."

Stahr nodded. Kapper hurried out, and the room went dark again. On the screen four men staged a terrific socking match in a cellar. Stahr laughed.

"Look at Tracy," he said. "Look at him go down after that guy. I bet he's been in a few."

The men fought over and over. Always the same fight. Always at the end they faced each other smiling, sometimes touching the opponent in a friendly gesture on the shoulder. The only one in danger was the stunt man, a pug who could have murdered the other three. He was in danger only if they swung wild and didn't follow the blows he had taught them. Even so, the youngest actor was afraid for his face and the director had covered his flinches with ingenious angles and interpositions.

And then two men met endlessly in a door, recognized each other and went on. They met, they started, they went on.

Then a little girl read underneath a tree with a boy reading on a limb of the tree above. The little girl was bored and wanted to talk to the boy. He would pay no attention. The core of the apple he was eating fell on the little girl's head.

A voice spoke up out of the darkness:

"It's pretty long, isn't it, Monroe?"

"Not a bit," said Stahr. "It's nice. It has nice feeling."

"I just thought it was long."

"Sometimes ten feet can be too long—sometimes a scene two hundred feet long can be too short. I want to speak to the cutter before he touches this scene—this is something that'll be remembered in the picture."

The oracle had spoken. There was nothing to question or argue. Stahr must be right always, not most of the time, but always—or the structure would melt down like gradual butter.

Another hour passed. Dreams hung in fragments at the far end of the room, suffered analysis, passed—to be dreamed in crowds, or else discarded. The end was signalled by two tests, a character man and a girl. After the rushes, which had a tense rhythm of their own, the tests were smooth and finished; the observers settled in their chairs; Stahr's foot slipped to the floor. Opinions were welcome. One of the technical men let it be known that he would willingly cohabit with the girl; the rest were indifferent.

"Somebody sent up a test of that girl two years ago. She must be getting around—but she isn't getting any better. But the man's good. Can't we use him as the old Russian Prince in *Steppes*?"

"He *is* an old Russian Prince," said the casting director, "but he's ashamed of it. He's a Red. And that's one part he says he wouldn't play."

"It's the only part he could play," said Stahr.

The lights went on. Stahr rolled his gum into its wrapper and put it in an ash-tray. He turned questioningly to his secretary.

"The processes on Stage 2," she said.

He looked in briefly at the processes, moving pictures taken against a background of other moving pictures by an ingenious device. There was a meeting in Marcus' office on the subject of *Manon* with a happy ending, and Stahr had his say on that as he had had before—it had been making money without a happy ending for a century and a half. He was obdurate—at this time in the afternoon he was at his most fluent and the opposition faded into another subject: they would lend a dozen stars to the benefit for those the quake had made homeless at Long Beach. In a sudden burst of giving, five of them all at once made up a purse of twenty-five thousand dollars. They gave well, but not as poor men give. It was not charity.

At his office there was word from the oculist to whom he had sent Pete Zavras that the camera man's eyes were 19-20: approximately perfect. He had written a letter that Zavras was having photostated. Stahr walked around his office cockily while Miss Doolan admired him. Prince Agge had dropped in to thank him for his afternoon on the sets, and while they talked, a cryptic word came from a supervisor that some writers named Tarleton had "found out" and were about to quit.

"These are good writers," Stahr explained to Prince Agge, "and we don't have good writers out here."

"Why, you can hire anyone!" exclaimed his visitor in surprise.

"Oh, we hire them, but when they get out here, they're not good writers—so we have to work with the material we have."

"Such as what?"

"Anybody that'll accept the system and stay decently sober—we have all sorts of people—disappointed poets, one-hit playwrights—college girls—we put them on an idea in pairs, and if it slows down, we put two more writers working behind them. I've had as many as three pairs working independently on the same idea."

"Do they like that?"

"Not if they know about it. They're not geniuses—none of them could make as much any other way. But these Tarletons are a husband and wife team from the East—pretty good playwrights. They've just found out they're not alone on the story and it shocks them—shocks their sense of unity—that's the word they'll use."

"But what does make the—the unity?"

Stahr hesitated—his face was grim except that his eyes twinkled.

"I'm the unity," he said. "Come and see us again."

He saw the Tarletons. He told them he liked their work, looking at Mrs. Tarleton as if he could read her handwriting through the typescript. He told them kindly that he was taking them from the picture and putting them on another, where there was less pressure, more time. As he had half expected, they begged to stay on the first picture, seeing a quicker credit, even though it was shared with others. The system was a shame, he admitted—gross, commercial, to be deplored. He had originated it—a fact that he did not mention.

When they had gone, Miss Doolan came in triumphant.

"Mr. Stahr, the lady with the belt is on the phone."

Stahr walked into his office alone and sat down behind his desk and picked up the phone with a great sinking of his stomach. He did not know what he wanted. He had not thought about the matter as he had thought about the matter of Pete Zavras. At first he had only wanted to know if they were "professional" people, if the woman was an actress who had got herself up to look like Minna, as he had once had a young actress made up like Claudette Colbert and photographed her from the same angles.

"Hello," he said.

"Hello."

As he searched the short, rather surprised word for a vibration of last night, the feeling of terror began to steal over him, and he choked it off with an effort of will.

"Well—you were hard to find," he said. *"Smith*—and you moved here recently. That was all we had. And a silver belt."

"Oh, yes," the voice said, still uneasy, unpoised, "I had on a silver belt last night."

Now, where from here?

"Who *are* you?" the voice said, with a touch of flurried bourgeois dignity.

"My name is Monroe Stahr," he said.

A pause. It was a name that never appeared on the screen, and she seemed to have trouble placing it.

"Oh, yes—yes. You were the husband of Minna Davis."

"Yes."

Was it a trick? As the whole vision of last night came back to him—the very skin with that peculiar radiance as if phosphorus had touched it—he thought whether it might not be a trick to reach him from somewhere. Not Minna and yet Minna. The curtains blew suddenly into the room, the papers whispered on his desk, and his heart cringed faintly at the intense reality of the day outside his window. If he could go out now this way, what would happen if he saw her again—the starry veiled expression, the mouth strongly formed for poor brave human laughter.

"I'd like to see you. Would you like to come to the studio?"

Again the hesitancy—then a blank refusal.

"Oh, I don't think I ought to. I'm awfully sorry."

This last was purely formal, a brush-off, a final axe. Ordinary skin-deep vanity came to Stahr's aid, adding persuasion to his urgency.

"I'd like to see you," he said. "There's a reason."

"Well—I'm afraid that——"

"Could I come and see you?"

A pause again, not from hesitation, he felt, but to assemble her answer.

"There's something you don't know," she said finally.

"Oh, you're probably married," he was impatient. "It has nothing to do with that. I asked you to come here openly, bring your husband if you have one."

"It's—it's quite impossible."

"Why?"

"I feel silly even talking to you, but your secretary insisted—I thought I'd dropped something in the flood last night and you'd found it."

"I want very much to see you for five minutes."

"To put me in the movies?"

"That wasn't my idea."

There was such a long pause that he thought he had offended her.

"Where could I meet you?" she asked unexpectedly.

"Here? At your house?"

"No—somewhere outside."

Suddenly Stahr could think of no place. His own house—a restaurant? Where did people meet?—a house of assignation, a cocktail bar?

"I'll meet you somewhere at nine o'clock," she said.

"That's impossible, I'm afraid."

"Then never mind."

"All right, then, nine o'clock, but can we make it near here? There's a drug-store on Wilshire——"

It was a quarter to six. There were two men outside who had come every day at this time only to be postponed. This was an hour of fatigue—the men's business was not so important that it must be seen to, nor so insignificant that it could be ignored. So he postponed it again and sat motionless at his desk for a moment, thinking about Russia. Not so much about Russia as about the picture about Russia which would consume a hopeless half hour presently. He knew there were many stories about Russia, not to mention The Story, and he had employed a squad of writers and research men for over a year, but all the stories involved had the wrong feel. He felt it could be told in terms of the American thirteen states, but it kept coming out different, in new terms that opened unpleasant possibilities and problems. He considered he was very fair to Russia— he had no desire to make anything but a sympathetic picture, but it kept turning into a headache.

"Mr. Stahr—Mr. Drummon's outside, and Mr. Kirstoff and Mrs. Cornhill, about the Russian picture."

"All right—send them in."

Afterwards from six-thirty to seven-thirty he watched the afternoon rushes. Except for his engagement with the girl, he would ordinarily have spent the early evening in the projection room or the dubbing room, but it had been a late night with the earthquake, and he decided to go to dinner. Coming in through his front office, he found Pete Zavras waiting, his arm in a sling.

"You are the Aeschylus and the Euripides of the moving picture," said Zavras simply. "Also the Aristophanes and the Menander."

He bowed.

"Who are they?" asked Stahr smiling.

"They are my countrymen."

"I didn't know you made pictures in Greece."

"You're joking with me, Monroe," said Zavras. "I want to say you are as dandy a fellow as they come. You have saved me one hundred percent."

"You feel all right now?"

"My arm is nothing. It feels like someone kisses me there. It was worth doing what I did, if this is the outcome."

"How did you happen to do it here?" Stahr asked curiously.

"Before the Delphic oracle," said Zavras. "The Oedipus who solved the riddle. I wish I had my hands on the son-of-a-bitch who started the story."

"You make me sorry I didn't get an education," said Stahr.

"It isn't worth a damn," said Pete. "I took my baccalaureate in Salonika and look how I ended up."

"Not quite," said Stahr.

"If you want anybody's throat cut anytime day or night," said Zavras, "my number is in the book."

Stahr closed his eyes and opened them again. Zavras' silhouette had blurred a little against the sun. He hung on to the table behind him and said in an ordinary voice.

"Good luck, Pete."

The room was almost black, but he made his feet move, following a pattern, into his office and waited till the door clicked shut before he felt for the pills. The water decanter clattered against the table; the glass clacked. He sat down in a big chair, waiting for the benzedrine to take effect before he went to dinner.

As Stahr walked back from the commissary, a hand waved at him from an open roadster. From the heads showing over the back he recognized a young actor and his girl, and watched them disappear through the gate, already part of the summer twilight. Little by little he was losing the feel of such things, until it seemed that Minna had taken their poignancy with her; his apprehension of splendor was fading so that presently the luxury of eternal mourning would depart. A childish association of Minna with the material heavens made him, when he reached his office, order out his roadster for the first time this year. The big limousine seemed heavy with remembered conferences or exhausted sleep.

Leaving the studio, he was still tense, but the open car pulled the summer evening up close, and he looked at it. There was a moon down at the end of the boulevard, and it was a good illusion that it was a different moon every evening, every year. Other lights shone in Hollywood since Minna's death: in the open markets lemons and grapefruit and green apples slanted a misty glare into the street. Ahead of him the stop-signal of a car winked violet and at another crossing he watched it wink again. Everywhere floodlights raked the sky. On an empty corner two mysterious men moved a gleaming drum in pointless arcs over the heavens.

In the drug-store a woman stood by the candy counter. She was tall, almost as tall as Stahr, and embarrassed. Obviously it was a situation for her, and if Stahr had not looked as he did—most considerate and polite—she would not have gone through with it. They said hello, and walked out without another word, scarcely a glance —yet before they reached the curb Stahr knew: this was just exactly a pretty American woman and nothing more—no beauty like Minna.

"Where are we going?" she asked. "I thought there'd be a chauffeur. Never mind—I'm a good boxer."

"Boxer?"

"That didn't sound very polite." She forced a smile. "But you people are supposed to be such *horrors*."

The conception of himself as sinister amused Stahr—then suddenly it failed to amuse him.

"Why did you want to see me?" she asked as she got in.

He stood motionless, wanting to tell her to get out immediately. But she had relaxed in the car, and he knew the unfortunate situation was of his own making—he shut his teeth and walked around to get in. The street lamp fell full upon her face, and it was difficult to believe that this was the girl of last night. He saw no resemblance to Minna at all.

"I'll run you home," he said. "Where do you live?"

"Run me home?" She was startled. "There's no hurry—I'm sorry if I offended you."

"No. It was nice of you to come. I've been stupid. Last night I had an idea that you were an exact double for someone I knew. It was dark and the light was in my eyes."

She was offended—he had reproached her for not looking like someone else.

"It was just that!" she said. "That's funny."

They rode in silence for a minute.

"You were married to Minna Davis, weren't you?" she said with a flash of intuition. "Excuse me for referring to it."

He was driving as fast as he could without making it conspicuous.

"I'm quite a different type from Mirna Davis," she said, "—if that's who you meant. You might have referred to the girl who was with me. She looks more like Minna Davis than I do."

That was of no interest now. The thing was to get this over quick and forget it.

"Could it have been her?" she asked. "She lives next door."

"Not possibly," he said. "I remember the silver belt you wore."

"That was me all right."

They were northwest of Sunset, climbing one of the canyons through the hills. Lighted bungalows rose along the winding road, and the electric current that animated them sweated into the evening air as radio sound.

"You see that last highest light—Kathleen lives there. I live just over the top of the hill."

A moment later she said, "Stop here."

"I thought you said over the top."

"I want to stop at Kathleen's."

"I'm afraid I'm——"

"I want to get out here myself," she said impatiently.

Stahr slid out after her. She started toward a new little house almost roofed over by a single willow tree, and automatically he followed her to the steps. She rang a bell and turned to say good night.

"I'm sorry you were disappointed," she said.

He was sorry for her now—sorry for them both.

"It was my fault. Good night."

A wedge of light came out the opening door, and as a girl's voice inquired, "Who is it?" Stahr looked up.

There she was—face and form and smile against the light from inside. It was Minna's face—the skin with its peculiar radiance as if phosphorus had touched it, the mouth with its warm line that never counted costs—and over all the haunting jollity that had fascinated a generation.

With a leap his heart went out of him as it had the night before, only this time it stayed out there with a vast beneficence.

"Oh, Edna, you can't come in," the girl said. "I've been cleaning and the house is full of ammonia smell."

Edna began to laugh, bold and loud. "I believe it was you he wanted to see, Kathleen," she said.

Stahr's eyes and Kathleen's met and tangled. For an instant they made love as no one ever dares to do after. Their glance was slower than an embrace, more urgent than a call.

"He telephoned me," said Edna. "It seems he thought——"

Stahr interrupted, stepping forward into the light.

"I was afraid we were rude at the studio, yesterday evening."

But there were no words for what he really said. She listened closely without shame. Life flared high in them both—Edna seemed at a distance and in darkness.

"You weren't rude," said Kathleen. A cool wind blew the brown curls around her forehead. "We had no business there."

"I hope you'll both," Stahr said, "come and make a tour of the studio."

"Who are you? Somebody important?"

"He was Minna Davis's husband, he's a producer," said Edna,

as if it were a rare joke, "—and this isn't at all what he just told me. I think he has a crush on you."

"Shut up, Edna," said Kathleen sharply.

As if suddenly realizing her offensiveness, Edna said, "Phone me, will you?" and stalked away toward the road. But she carried their secret with her—she had seen a spark pass between them in the darkness.

"I remember you," Kathleen said to Stahr. "You got us out of the flood."

Now what? The other woman was more missed in her absence. They were alone and on too slim a basis for what had passed already. They existed nowhere. His world seemed far away—she had no world at all except the idol's head, the half open door.

"You're Irish," he said, trying to build one for her.

She nodded.

"I've lived in London a long time—I didn't think you could tell."

The wild green eyes of a bus sped up the road in the darkness. They were silent until it went by.

"Your friend Edna didn't like me," he said. "I think it was the word Producer."

"She's just come out here, too. She's a silly creature who means no harm. *I* shouldn't be afraid of you."

She searched his face. She thought, like everyone, that he seemed tired—then she forgot it at the impression he gave of a brazier out of doors on a cool night.

"I suppose the girls are all after you to put them on the screen."

"They've given up," he said.

This was an understatement—they were all there, he knew, just over his threshold, but they had been there so long that their clamoring voices were no more than the sound of the traffic in the street. But his position remained more than royal: a king could make only one queen; Stahr, at least so they supposed, could make many.

"I'm thinking that it would turn you into a cynic," she said. "You didn't want to put me in the pictures?"

"No."

"That's good. I'm no actress. Once in London a man came up to me in the Carlton and asked me to make a test, but I thought awhile and finally I didn't go."

They had been standing nearly motionless, as if in a moment he would leave and she would go in. Stahr laughed suddenly.

"I feel as if I had my foot in the door—like a collector."

She laughed, too.

"I'm sorry I can't ask you in. Shall I get my reefer and sit outside?"

"No." He scarcely knew why he felt it was time to go. He might see her again—he might not. It was just as well this way.

"You'll come to the studio?" he said. "I can't promise to go around with you, but if you come, you must be sure to send word to my office."

A frown, the shadow of a hair in breadth, appeared between her eyes.

"I'm not sure," she said. "But I'm very much obliged."

He knew that, for some reason, she would not come—in an instant she had slipped away from him. They both sensed that the moment was played out. He must go, even though he went nowhere, and it left him with nothing. Practically, vulgarly, he did not have her telephone number—or even her name; but it seemed impossible to ask for them now.

She walked with him to the car, her glowing beauty and her unexplored novelty pressing up against him; but there was a foot of moonlight between them when they came out of the shadow.

"Is this all?" he said spontaneously.

He saw regret in her face—but there was a flick of the lip, also, a bending of the smile toward some indirection, a momentary dropping and lifting of a curtain over a forbidden passage.

"I do hope we'll meet again," she said almost formally.

"I'd be sorry if we didn't."

They were distant for a moment. But as he turned his car in the next drive and came back with her still waiting, and waved and drove on, he felt exalted and happy. He was glad that there was beauty in the world that would not be weighed in the scales of the casting department.

But at home he felt a curious loneliness as his butler made him tea in the samovar. It was the old hurt come back, heavy and delightful. When he took up the first of two scripts that were his evening stint, that presently he would visualize line by line on the screen, he waited a moment, thinking of Minna. He explained to her that it was really nothing, that no one could ever be like she was, that he was sorry.

That was substantially a day of Stahr's. I don't know about the illness, when it started, etc., because he was secretive, but i know he fainted a couple of times that month because Father told me. Prince Agge is my authority for the luncheon in the commissary where he told them he was going to make a picture that would lose money —which was something, considering the men he had to deal with and that he held a big block of stock and had a profit-sharing contract.

And Wylie White told me a lot, which i believed because he felt Stahr intensely with a mixture of jealousy and admiration. As for me, I was head over heels in love with him then, and you can take what i say for what it's worth.

CHAPTER V

Fresh as the morning, I went up to see him a week later. Or so I thought; when Wylie called for me, I had gotten into riding clothes to give the impression I'd been out in the dew since early morning.

"I'm going to throw myself under the wheel of Stahr's car, this morning," I said.

"How about this car?" he suggested. "It's one of the best cars Mort Fleishacker ever sold second-hand."

"Not on your flowing veil," I answered like a book. "You have a wife in the East."

"She's the past," he said. "You've got one great card, Celia—your valuation of yourself. Do you think anybody would look at you if you weren't Pat Brady's daughter?"

We don't take abuse like our mothers would have. Nothing—no remark from a contemporary means much. They tell you to be smart, they're marrying you for your money, or you tell them. Everything's simpler. Or is it? as we used to say.

But as I turned on the radio and the car raced up Laurel Canyon to *The Thundering Beat of My Heart,* I didn't believe he was right. I had good features except my face was too round, and a skin they seemed to love to touch, and good legs, and I didn't have to wear a brassiere. I haven't a sweet nature, but who was Wylie to reproach me for that?

"Don't you think I'm smart to go in the morning?" I asked.

"Yeah. To the busiest man in California. He'll appreciate it. Why didn't you wake him up at four?"

"That's just it. At night he's tired. He's been looking at people all day, and some of them not bad. I come in in the morning and start a train of thought."

"I don't like it. It's brazen."

"What have you got to offer? And don't be rough."

"I love you," he said, without much conviction, "I love you more than I love your money, and that's plenty. Maybe your father would make me a supervisor."

"I could marry the last man tapped for Bones this year and live in Southampton."

I turned the dial and got either *Gone* or *Lost*—there were good songs that year. The music was getting better again. When I was young during the depression, it wasn't so hot, and the best numbers were from the twenties, like Benny Goodman playing *Blue Heaven* or Paul Whiteman with *When Day Is Done*. There were only the bands to listen to. But now I liked almost everything except Father singing *Little Girl, You've Had a Busy Day* to try to create a sentimental father-and-daughter feeling.

Lost and *Gone* were the wrong mood, so I turned again and got *Lovely to Look At,* which was my kind of poetry. I looked back as we crossed the crest of the foothills—with the air so clear you could see the leaves on Sunset Mountain two miles away. It's startling to you sometimes—just air, unobstructed, uncomplicated air.

"Lovely to look at—de-lightful to know-w," I sang.

"Are you going to sing for Stahr?" Wylie said. "If you do, get in a line about my being a good supervisor."

"Oh, this'll be only Stahr and me," I said. "He's going to look at me and think, 'I've never really seen her before.' "

"We don't use that line this year," he said.

"—Then he'll say 'Little Cecilia,' like he did the night of the earthquake. He'll say he never noticed I have become a woman."

"You won't have to do a thing."

"I'll stand there and bloom. After he kisses me as you would a child——"

"That's all in my script," complained Wylie, "and I've got to show it to him tomorrow."

"—he'll sit down and put his face in his hands and say he never thought of me like that."

"You mean you get in a little fast work during the kiss?"

"I bloom, I told you. How often do I have to tell you I bloom."

"It's beginning to sound pretty randy to me," said Wylie. "How about laying off—I've got to work this morning."

"Then he says it seems as if he was always meant to be this way."

"Right in the industry. Producer's blood." He pretended to shiver. "I'd hate to have a transfusion of that."

"Then he says——"

"I know all his lines," said Wylie. "What I want to know is what you say."

"Somebody comes in," I went on.

"And you jump up quickly off the casting couch, smoothing your skirts."

"Do you want me to walk out and get home?"

We were in Beverly Hills, getting very beautiful now with the tall Hawaiian pines. Hollywood is a perfectly zoned city, so you know exactly what kind of people economically live in each section, from executives and directors, through technicians in their bungalows, right down to extras. This was the executive section and a very fancy lot of pastry. It wasn't as romantic as the dingiest village of Virginia or New Hampshire, but it looked nice this morning.

"*They asked me how I knew,*" sang the radio, "*—my true love was true.*"

My heart was fire, and smoke was in my eyes and everything, but I figured my chance at about fifty-fifty. I would walk right up to him as if I was either going to walk through him or kiss him on the mouth—and stop a bare foot away and say "Hello" with dis-arming understatement.

And I did—though of course it wasn't like I expected: Stahr's beautiful dark eyes looking back into mine, knowing, I am dead sure, everything I was thinking—and not a bit embarrassed. I stood there an hour, I think, without moving, and all he did was twitch the side of his mouth and put his hands in his pocket.

"Will you go with me to the ball tonight?" I asked.

"What ball?"

"The screen-writers' ball down at the Ambassador."

"Oh, yes." He considered. "I can't go with you. I might just come in late. We've got a sneak preview in Glendale."

How different it all was from what you'd planned. When he sat down, I went over and put my head among his telephones, like a sort of desk appendage, and looked at him; and his dark eyes looked back so kind and nothing. Men don't often know those times when a girl could be had for nothing. All I succeeded in putting into his head was:

"Why don't you get married, Celia?"

Maybe he'd bring up Robby again, try to make a match there.

"What could I do to interest an interesting man?" I asked him.

"Tell him you're in love with him."

"Should I chase him?"

"Yes," he said smiling.

"I don't know. If it isn't there, it isn't there."

"I'd marry you," he said unexpectedly. "I'm lonesome as hell. But I'm too old and tired to undertake anything."

I went around the desk and stood beside him.

"Undertake me."

He looked up in surprise, understanding for the first time that I was in deadly earnest.

"Oh, no," he said. He looked almost miserable for a minute. "Pictures are my girl. I haven't got much time——" He corrected himself quickly, "I mean any time."

"You couldn't love me."

"It's not that," he said and—right out of my dream but with a difference: "I never thought of you that way, Celia. I've known you so long. Somebody told me you were going to marry Wylie White."

"And you had—no reaction."

"Yes, I did. I was going to speak to you about it. Wait till he's been sober for two years."

"I'm not even considering it, Monroe."

We were way off the track, and just as in my day-dream, somebody came in—only I was quite sure Stahr had pressed a concealed button.

I'll always think of that moment, when I felt Miss Doolan behind me with her pad, as the end of childhood, the end of the time when you cut out pictures. What I was looking at wasn't Stahr but a picture of him I cut out over and over: the eyes that flashed a sophisticated understanding at you and then darted up too soon into his wide brow with its ten thousand plots and plans; the face that was aging from within, so that there were no casual furrows of worry and vexation but a drawn asceticism as if from a silent self-set struggle—or a long illness. It was handsomer to me than all the rosy tan from Coronado to Del Monte. He was my picture, as sure as if he had been pasted on the inside of my old locker in school. That's what I told Wylie White, and when a girl tells the man she likes second best about the other one—then she's in love.

I noticed the girl long before Stahr arrived at the dance. Not a pretty girl, for there are none of those in Los Angeles—one girl can be pretty, but a dozen are only a chorus. Nor yet a professional beauty—they do all the breathing for everyone, and finally even the men have to go outside for air. Just a girl, with the skin of one of Raphael's corner angels and a style that made you look back twice to see if it were something she had on.

I noticed her and forgot her. She was sitting back behind the pillars at a table whose ornament was a faded semi-star, who, in hopes of being noticed and getting a bit, rose and danced regularly with some scarecrow males. It reminded me shamefully of my first party, where mother made me dance over and over with the same boy to keep in the spotlight. The semi-star spoke to several people at our table, but we were busy being Café Society and she got nowhere at all.

From our angle it appeared that they all wanted something.

"You're expected to fling it around," said Wylie, "—like in the old days. When they find out you're hanging on to it, they get discouraged. That's what all this brave gloom is about—the only way to keep their self-respect is to be Hemingway characters. But underneath they hate you in a mournful way, and you know it."

He was right—I knew that since 1933 the rich could only be happy alone together.

I saw Stahr come into the half-light at the top of the wide steps and stand there with his hands in his pockets, looking around. It was late and the lights seemed to have burned a little lower, though they were the same. The floor show was finished, except for a man who still wore a placard which said that at midnight in the Hollywood Bowl Sonja Henie was going to skate on hot soup. You could see the sign as he danced becoming less funny on his back. A few years before there would have been drunks around. The faded actress seemed to be looking for them hopefully over her partner's shoulder. I followed her with my eyes when she went back to her table——

—and there, to my surprise, was Stahr talking to the other girl. They were smiling at each other as if this was the beginning of the world.

Stahr had expected nothing like this when he stood at the head of the steps a few minutes earlier. The "sneak preview" had disappointed him, and afterwards he had had a scene with Jacques La Borwitz right in front of the theatre, for which he was now sorry. He had started toward the Brady party when he saw Kathleen sitting in the middle of a long white table alone.

Immediately things changed. As he walked toward her, the people shrank back against the walls till they were only murals; the white table lengthened and became an altar where the priestess sat alone. Vitality welled up in him, and he could have stood a long time across the table from her, looking and smiling.

The incumbents of the table were crawling back—Stahr and Kathleen danced.

When she came close, his several visions of her blurred; she was momentarily unreal. Usually a girl's skull made her real, but not this time—Stahr continued to be dazzled as they danced out along the floor—to the last edge, where they stepped through a mirror into another dance with new dancers whose faces were familiar but nothing more. In this new region he talked, fast and urgently.

"What's your name?"

"Kathleen Moore."

"Kathleen Moore," he repeated.

"I have no telephone, if that's what you're thinking."

"When will you come to the studio?"

"It's not possible. Truly."

"Why isn't it? Are you married?"

"No."

"You're not married?"

"No, nor never have been. But then I may be."

"Someone there at the table."

"No." She laughed. "What curiosity!"

But she was deep in it with him, no matter what the words were.

Her eyes invited him to a romantic communion of unbelievable intensity. As if she realized this, she said, frightened:

"I must go back now. I promised this dance."

"I don't want to lose you. Couldn't we have lunch or dinner?"

"It's impossible." But her expression helplessly amended the words to, "It's just possible. The door is still open by a chink, if you could squeeze past. But quickly—so little time."

"I must go back," she repeated aloud. Then she dropped her arms, stopped dancing, and looked at him, a laughing wanton.

"When I'm with you, I don't breathe quite right," she said.

She turned, picked up her long dress, and stepped back through the mirror. Stahr followed until she stopped near her table.

"Thank you for the dance," she said, "and now really, good night."

Then she nearly ran.

Stahr went to the table where he was expected and sat down with the Café Society group—from Wall Street, Grand Street, Loudon County, Virginia, and Odessa, Russia. They were all talking with enthusiasm about a horse that had run very fast, and Mr. Marcus was the most enthusiastic of all. Stahr guessed that the Jews had taken over the worship of horses as a symbol—for years it had been the Cossacks mounted and the Jews on foot. Now the Jews had horses, and it gave them a sense of extraordinary well-being and power. Stahr sat pretending to listen and even nodding when something was referred to him, but all the time watching the table behind the pillars. If everything had not happened as it had, even to his connecting the silver belt with the wrong girl, he might have thought it was some elaborate frame-up. But the elusiveness was beyond suspicion. For there in a moment he saw that she was escaping again—the pantomime at the table indicated goodbye. She was leaving, she was gone.

"There," said Wylie White with malice, "goes Cinderella. Simply bring the slipper to the Regal Shoe Company, 812 South Broadway."

Stahr overtook her in the long upper lobby, where middle-aged women sat behind a roped-off space, watching the ballroom entrance.

"Am I responsible for this?" he asked.

"I was going anyhow." But she added almost resentfully, "They talked as if I'd been dancing with the Prince of Wales. They all stared at me. One of the men wanted to draw my picture, and another one wanted to see me tomorrow."

"That's just what I want," said Stahr gently, "but I want to see you much more than he does."

"You insist so," she said wearily. "One reason I left England was that men always wanted their own way. I thought it was different here. Isn't it enough that I don't want to see you?"

"Ordinarily," agreed Stahr. "Please believe me, I'm way out of my depth already. I feel like a fool. But I must see you again and talk to you."

She hesitated.

"There's no reason for feeling like a fool," she said. "You're too good a man to feel like a fool. But you should see this for what it is."

"What is it?"

"You've fallen for me—completely. You've got me in your dreams."

"I'd forgotten you," he declared, "—till the moment I walked in that door."

"Forgotten me with your head perhaps. But I knew the first time I saw you that you were the kind that likes me——"

She stopped herself. Near them a man and woman from the party were saying goodbye: "Tell her hello—tell her I love her dearly," said the woman, "—you both—all of you—the children." Stahr could not talk like that, the way everyone talked now. He could think of nothing further to say as they walked toward the elevator except:

"I suppose you're perfectly right."

"Oh, you admit it?"

"No, I don't," he retracted. "It's just the whole way you're made. What you say—how you walk—the way you look right this minute—" He saw she had melted a little, and his hopes rose. "Tomorrow is Sunday, and usually I work on Sunday, but if there's anything you're curious about in Hollywood, any person you want to meet or see, please let me arrange it."

They were standing by the elevator. It opened, but she let it go.

"You're very modest," she said. "You always talk about showing me the studio and taking me around. Don't you ever stay alone?"

"Tomorrow I'll feel very much alone."

"Oh, the poor man—I could weep for him. He could have all the stars jumping around him and he chooses me."

He smiled—he had laid himself open to that one.

The elevator came again. She signalled for it to wait.

"I'm a weak woman," she said. "If I meet you tomorrow, will you leave me in peace? No, you won't. You'll make it worse. It wouldn't do any good but harm, so I'll say no and thank you."

She got into the elevator. Stahr got in too, and they smiled as they dropped two floors to the hall, cross-sectioned with small shops. Down at the end, held back by police, was the crowd, their heads and shoulders leaning forward to look down the alley. Kathleen shivered.

"They looked so strange when I came in," she said, "—as if they were furious at me for not being someone famous."

"I know another way out," said Stahr.

They went through a drug-store, down an alley, and came out into the clear cool California night beside the car park. He felt detached from the dance now, and she did, too.

"A lot of picture people used to live down here," he said. "John Barrymore and Pola Negri in those bungalows. And Connie Talmadge lived in that tall thin apartment house over the way."

"Doesn't anybody live here now?"

"The studios moved out into the country," he said, "—what used to be the country. I had some good times around here, though."

He did not mention that ten years ago Minna and her mother had lived in another apartment over the way.

"How old are you?" she asked suddenly.

"I've lost track—almost thirty-five, I think."

"They said at the table you were the boy wonder."

"I'll be that when I'm sixty," he said grimly. "You will meet me tomorrow, won't you?"

"I'll meet you," she said. "Where?"

Suddenly there was no place to meet. She would not go to a party at anyone's house, nor to the country, nor swimming, though she hesitated, nor to a well-known restaurant. She seemed hard to please, but he knew there was some reason. He would find out in time. It occurred to him that she might be the sister or daughter of someone well-known, who was pledged to keep in the background. He suggested that he come for her and they could decide.

"That wouldn't do," she said. "What about right here?—the same spot."

He nodded—pointing up at the arch under which they stood.

He put her into her car, which would have brought eighty dollars from any kindly dealer, and watched it rasp away. Down by the entrance a cheer went up as a favorite emerged, and Stahr wondered whether to show himself and say good night.

This is Cecilia taking up the narrative in person. Stahr came back finally—it was about half past three—and asked me to dance.

"How are you?" he asked me, just as if he hadn't seen me that morning. "I got involved in a long conversation with a man."

It was secret, too—he cared that much about it.

"I took him for a drive," he went on innocently. "I didn't realize how much this part of Hollywood had changed."

"Has it changed?"

"Oh, yes," he said, "—changed completely. Unrecognizable. I couldn't tell you exactly, but it's all changed—everything. It's like a new city." After a moment he amplified: "I had no idea how much it had changed."

"Who was the man?" I ventured.

"An old friend," he said vaguely, "—someone I knew a long time ago."

I had made Wylie try to find out quietly who she was. He had gone over and the ex-star had asked him excitedly to sit down. No: she didn't know who the girl was—a friend of a friend of someone —even the man who had brought her didn't know.

So Stahr and I danced to the beautiful music of Glenn Miller playing *I'm on a See-Saw*. It was good dancing now, with plenty of room. But it was lonely—lonelier than before the girl had gone. For me, as well as for Stahr, she took the evening with her, took along the stabbing pain I had felt—left the great ballroom empty and without emotion. Now it was nothing, and I was dancing with an absent-minded man who told me how much Los Angeles had changed.

They met, next afternoon, as strangers in an unfamiliar country. Last night was gone, the girl he had danced with was gone. A misty rose-and-blue hat with a trifling veil came along the terrace to him, and paused, searching his face. Stahr was strange, too, in a brown suit and a black tie that blocked him out more tangibly than a formal dinner coat, or when he was simply a face and voice in the darkness the night they had first met.

He was the first to be sure it was the same person as before: the upper half of the face that was Minna's, luminous, with creamy temples and opalescent brown—the cool-colored curly hair. He could have put his arm around her and pulled her close with an almost family familiarity—already he knew the down on her neck, the very set of her backbone, the corners of her eyes, and how she breathed— the very texture of the clothes that she would wear.

"Did you wait here all night," she said, in a voice that was like a whisper.

"I didn't move—didn't stir."

Still a problem remained, the same one—there was no special place to go.

"I'd like tea," she suggested, "—if it's some place you're not known."

"That sounds as if one of us had a bad reputation."

"Doesn't it?" she laughed.

"We'll go to the shore," Stahr suggested. "There's a place there where I got out once and was chased by a trained seal."

"Do you think the seal could make tea?"

"Well—he's trained. And I don't think he'll talk—I don't think his training got that far. What in *hell* are you trying to hide?"

After a moment she said lightly: "Perhaps the future," in a way that might mean anything or nothing at all.

As they drove away, she pointed at her jalopy in the parking lot.

"Do you think it's safe?"

"I doubt it. I noticed some black-bearded foreigners snooping around."

Kathleen looked at him alarmed.

"Really?" She saw he was smiling. "I believe everything you say," she said. "You've got such a gentle way about you that I don't see why they're all so afraid of you." She examined him with approval—fretting a little about his pallor, which was accentuated by the bright afternoon. "Do you work very hard? Do you really always work on Sundays?"

He responded to her interest—impersonal yet not perfunctory.

"Not always. Once we had—we had a house with a pool and all—and people came on Sunday. I played tennis and swam. I don't swim any more."

"Why not? It's good for you. I thought all Americans swam."

"My legs got very thin—a few years ago, and it embarrassed me. There were other things I used to do—lots of things: I used to play handball when I was a kid, and sometimes out here—I had a court that was washed away in a storm."

"You have a good build," she said in formal compliment, meaning only that he was made with thin grace.

He rejected this with a shake of his head.

"I enjoy working most," he said. "My work is very congenial."

"Did you always want to be in movies?"

"No. When I was young I wanted to be a chief clerk—the one who knew where everything was."

She smiled.

"That's odd. And now you're much more than that."

"No, I'm still a chief clerk," Stahr said. "That's my gift, if I have one. Only when I got to be it, I found out that no one knew where anything was. And I found out that you had to know why it was where it was, and whether it should be left there. They began throwing it all at me, and it was a very complex office. Pretty soon I had all the keys. And they wouldn't have remembered what locks they fitted if I'd given them back."

They stopped for a red light, and a newsboy bleated at him: "Mickey Mouse Murdered! Randolph Hearst declares war on China!"

"We'll have to buy his paper," she said.

As they drove on, she straightened her hat and preened herself. Seeing him looking at her, she smiled.

She was alert and calm—qualities that were currently at a

premium. There was lassitude in plenty—California was filling up with weary desperadoes. And there were tense young men and women who lived back East in spirit while they carried on a losing battle against the climate. But it was everyone's secret that sustained effort was difficult here—a secret that Stahr scarcely admitted to himself. But he knew that people from other places spurted a pure rill of new energy for awhile.

They were very friendly now. She had not made a move or a gesture that was out of keeping with her beauty, that pressed it out of its contour one way or another. It was all proper to itself. He judged her as he would a shot in a picture. She was not trash, she was not confused but clear—in his special meaning of the word, which implied balance, delicacy and proportion, she was "nice."

They reached Santa Monica, where there were the stately houses of a dozen picture stars, penned in the middle of a crawling Coney Island. They turned down hill into the wide blue sky and sea and went on along the sea till the beach slid out again from under the bathers in a widening and narrowing yellow strand.

"I'm building a house out here," Stahr said, "—much further on. I don't know why I'm building it."

"Perhaps it's for me," she said.

"Maybe it is."

"I think it's splendid for you to build a big house for me without even knowing what I looked like."

"It isn't too big. And it hasn't any roof. I didn't know what kind of roof you wanted."

"We don't want a roof. They told me it never rained here. It—"

She stopped so suddenly that he knew she was reminded of something.

"Just something that's past," she said.

"What was it?" he demanded, "—another house without a roof?"

"Yes. Another house without a roof."

"Were you happy there?"

"I lived with a man," she said, "a long, long time—too long. It was one of those awful mistakes people make. I lived with him a long time after I wanted to get out, but he couldn't let me go. He'd try, but he couldn't. So finally I ran away."

He was listening, weighing but not judging. Nothing changed

under the rose and blue hat. She was twenty-five or so. It would have been a waste if she had not loved and been loved.

"We were too close," she said. "We should probably have had children—to stand between us. But you can't have children when there's no roof to the house."

All right, he knew something of her. It would not be like last night when something kept saying, as in a story conference: "We know nothing about the girl. We don't have to know much—but we have to know something." A vague background spread behind her, something more tangible than the head of Siva in the moonlight.

They came to the restaurant, forbidding with many Sunday automobiles. When they got out, the trained seal growled reminiscently at Stahr. The man who owned it said that the seal would never ride in the back seat of his car but always climbed over the back and up in front. It was plain that the man was in bondage to the seal, though he had not yet acknowledged it to himself.

"I'd like to see the house you're building," said Kathleen. "I don't want tea—tea is the past."

Kathleen drank a coke instead and they drove on ten miles into a sun so bright that he took out two pairs of cheaters from a compartment. Five miles further on they turned down a small promontory and came to the fuselage of Stahr's house.

A headwind blowing out of the sun threw spray up the rocks and over the car. Concrete mixer, raw yellow wood and builders' rubble waited, an open wound in the seascape, for Sunday to be over. They walked around front, where great boulders rose to what would be the terrace.

She looked at the feeble hills behind and winced faintly at the barren glitter, and Stahr saw—

"No use looking for what's not here," he said cheerfully. "Think of it as if you were standing on one of those globes with a map on it—I always wanted one when I was a boy."

"I understand," she said after a minute. "When you do that, you can feel the earth turn, can't you?"

He nodded.

"Yes. Otherwise it's all just *mañana*—waiting for the morning or the moon."

They went in under the scaffolding. One room, which was to be the chief salon, was completed even to the built-in book shelves and the curtain rods and the trap in the floor for the motion picture projection machine. And to her surprise, this opened out to a porch with cushioned chairs in place and a ping-pong table. There was another ping-pong table on the newly laid sod beyond.

"Last week I gave a premature luncheon," he admitted. "I had some props brought out—some grass and things. I wanted to see how the place felt."

She laughed suddenly.

"Isn't that real grass?"

"Oh, yes—it's grass."

Beyond the strip of anticipatory lawn was the excavation for a swimming pool, patronized now by a crowd of seagulls, which saw them and took flight.

"Are you going to live here all alone?" she asked him, "—not even dancing girls?"

"Probably. I used to make plans, but not any more. I thought this would be a nice place to read scripts. The studio is really home."

"That's what I've heard about American business men."

He caught a tilt of criticism in her voice.

"You do what you're born to do," he said gently. "About once a month somebody tries to reform me, tells me what a barren old age I'll have when I can't work any more. But it's not so simple."

The wind was rising. It was time to go, and he had his car keys out of his pocket, absent-mindedly jingling them in his hand. There was the silvery "hey!" of a telephone, coming from somewhere across the sunshine.

It was not from the house, and they hurried here and there around the garden, like children playing warmer and colder—closing in finally on a tool shack by the tennis court. The phone, irked with delay, barked at them suspiciously from the wall. Stahr hesitated.

"Shall I let the damn thing ring?"

"I couldn't. Unless I was sure who it was."

"Either it's for somebody else or they've made a wild guess."

He picked up the receiver.

"Hello . . . Long distance from where? Yes, this is Mr. Stahr."

His manner changed perceptibly. She saw what few people had

seen for a decade: Stahr impressed. It was not discordant, because he often pretended to be impressed, but it made him momentarily a little younger.

"It's the President," he said to her, almost stiffly.

"Of your company?"

"No, of the United States."

He was trying to be casual for her benefit, but his voice was eager.

"All right, I'll wait," he said into the phone, and then to Kathleen: "I've talked to him before."

She watched. He smiled at her and winked, as an evidence that while he must give this his best attention, he had not forgotten her.

"Hello," he said presently. He listened. Then he said, "Hello" again. He frowned.

"Can you talk a little louder," he said politely, and then: "Who? . . . What's that?"

She saw a disgusted look come into his face.

"I don't want to talk to him," he said. "No!"

He turned to Kathleen:

"Believe it or not, it's an orang-outang."

He waited while something was explained to him at length; then he repeated:

"I don't want to talk to it, Lew. I haven't got anything to say that would interest an orang-outang."

He beckoned to Kathleen, and when she came close to the phone, he held the receiver so that she heard odd breathing and a gruff growl. Then a voice:

"This is no phoney, Monroe. It can talk and it's a dead ringer for McKinley. Mr. Horace Wickersham is with me here with a picture of McKinley in his hand——"

Stahr listened patiently.

"We've got a chimp," he said, after a minute. "He bit a chunk out of John Gilbert last year. . . . All right, put him on again."

He spoke formally as if to a child.

"Hello, orang-outang."

His face changed, and he turned to Kathleen.

"He said 'Hello.'"

"Ask him his name," suggested Kathleen.

"Hello, orang-outang—God, what a thing to be!—Do you know

your name? . . . He doesn't seem to know his name. . . . Listen, Lew. We're not making anything like *King Kong,* and there is no monkey in *The Hairy Ape.* . . . Of course I'm sure. I'm sorry, Lew, goodbye."

He was annoyed with Lew because he had thought it was the President and had changed his manner, acting as if it were. He felt a little ridiculous, but Kathleen felt sorry and liked him better because it had been an orang-outang.

They started back along the shore with the sun behind them. The house seemed kindlier when they left it, as if warmed by their visit—the hard glitter of the place was more endurable if they were not bound there like people on the shiny surface of a moon. Looking back from a curve of the shore, they saw the sky growing pink behind the indecisive structure, and the point of land seemed a friendly island, not without promise of fine hours on a further day.

Past Malibu with its gaudy shacks and fishing barges they came into the range of human kind again, the cars stacked and piled along the road, the beaches like ant hills without a pattern, save for the dark drowned heads that sprinkled the sea.

Goods from the city were increasing in sight—blankets, matting, umbrellas, cookstoves, reticules full of clothing—the prisoners had laid out their shackles beside them on this sand. It was Stahr's sea if he wanted it, or knew what to do with it—only by sufferance did these others wet their feet and fingers in the wild cool reservoirs of man's world.

Stahr turned off the road by the sea and up a canyon and along a hill road, and the people dropped away. The hill became the outskirts of the city. Stopping for gasoline, he stood beside the car.

"We could have dinner," he said almost anxiously.

"You have work you could do."

"No—I haven't planned anything. Couldn't we have dinner?"

He knew that she had nothing to do either—no planned evening or special place to go.

She compromised.

"Do you want to get something in that drug-store across the street?"

He looked at it tentatively.

"Is that really what you want?"

"I like to eat in American drug-stores. It seems so queer and strange."

They sat on high stools and had tomato broth and hot sandwiches. It was more intimate than anything they had done, and they both felt a dangerous sort of loneliness, and felt it in each other. They shared in varied scents of the drug-store, bitter and sweet and sour, and the mystery of the waitress, with only the outer part of her hair dyed and black beneath, and, when it was over, the still life of their empty plates—a sliver of potato, a sliced pickle and an olive stone.

It was dusk in the street, it seemed nothing to smile at him now when they got into the car.

"Thank you so much. It's been a nice afternoon."

It was not far from her house. They felt the beginning of the hill, and the louder sound of the car in second was the beginning of the end. Lights were on in the climbing bungalows—he turned on the headlights of the car. Stahr felt heavy in the pit of his stomach.

"We'll go out again."

"No," she said quickly, as if she had been expecting this. "I'll write you a letter. I'm sorry I've been so mysterious—it was really a compliment because I like you so much. You should try not to work so hard. You ought to marry again."

"Oh, that isn't what you should say," he broke out protestingly. "This has been you and me today. It may have meant nothing to you—it meant a lot to me. I'd like time to tell you about it."

But if he were to take time it must be in her house, for they were there and she was shaking her head as the car drew up to the door.

"I must go now. I do have an engagement. I didn't tell you."

"That's not true. But it's all right."

He walked to the door with her and stood in his own footsteps of that other night, while she felt in her bag for the key.

"Have you got it?"

"I've got it," she said.

That was the moment to go in, but she wanted to see him once more and she leaned her head to the left, then to the right, trying to catch his face against the last twilight. She leaned too far and too long, and it was natural when his hand touched the back of her upper arm and shoulder and pressed her forward into the darkness of his throat. She shut her eyes, feeling the bevel of the key in her tight-clutched hand. She said "Oh" in an expiring sigh, and then "Oh" again, as he pulled her in close and his chin pushed her cheek around gently. They were both smiling just faintly, and she was frowning, too, as the inch between them melted into darkness.

When they were apart, she shook her head still, but more in wonder than in denial. It came like this then, it was your own fault, now far back, when was the moment? It came like this, and every instant the burden of tearing herself away from them together, from it, was heavier and more unimaginable. He was exultant; she resented and could not blame him, but she would not be part of his exultation, for it was a defeat. So far it was a defeat. And then she thought that if she stopped it being a defeat, broke off and went inside, it was still not a victory. Then it was just nothing.

"This was not my idea," she said, "not at all my idea."

"Can I come in?"

"Oh, no—no."

"Then let's jump in the car and drive somewhere."

With relief, she caught at the exact phrasing—to get away from here immediately, that was accomplishment or sounded like it—as if she were fleeing from the spot of a crime. Then they were in the car, going down hill with the breeze cool in their faces, and she came slowly to herself. Now it was all clear in black and white.

"We'll go back to your house on the beach," she said.

"Back there?"

"Yes—we'll go back to your house. Don't let's talk. I just want to ride."

When they got to the coast again the sky was grey, and at Santa Monica a sudden gust of rain bounced over them. Stahr halted beside the road, put on a raincoat, and lifted the canvas top. "We've got a roof," he said.

The windshield wiper ticked domestically as a grandfather's clock. Sullen cars were leaving the wet beaches and starting back into the city. Further on they ran into fog—the road lost its boundaries on either side, and the lights of cars coming toward them were stationary until just before they flared past.

They had left a part of themselves behind, and they felt light and free in the car. Fog fizzed in at a chink, and Kathleen took off the rose-and-blue hat in a calm, slow way that made him watch tensely, and put it under a strip of canvas in the back seat. She shook out her hair and, when she saw that Stahr was looking at her, she smiled.

The trained seal's restaurant was only a sheen of light off toward the ocean. Stahr cranked down a window and looked for landmarks, but after a few more miles the fog fell away, and just ahead of them the road turned off that led to his house. Out here a moon showed behind the clouds. There was still a shifting light over the sea.

The house had dissolved a little back into its elements. They found the dripping beams of a doorway and groped over mysterious waist-high obstacles to the single finished room, odorous of sawdust and wet wood. When he took her in his arms, they could just see each other's eyes in the half darkness. Presently his rain coat dropped to the floor.

"Wait," she said.

She needed a minute. She did not see how any good could come from this, and though this did not prevent her from being happy and desirous, she needed a minute to think how it was, to go back an hour and know how it had happened. She waited in his arms, moving her head a little from side to side as she had before, only more slowly, and never taking her eyes from his. Then she discovered that he was trembling.

He discovered it at the same time, and his arms relaxed. Immediately she spoke to him coarsely and provocatively, and pulled his face down to hers. Then, with her knees she struggled out of something, still standing up and holding him with one arm, and kicked it off beside the coat. He was not trembling now and he held her again, as they knelt down together and slid to the raincoat on the floor.

Afterwards they lay without speaking, and then he was full of such tender love for her that he held her tight till a stitch tore in her dress. The small sound brought them to reality.

"I'll help you up," he said, taking her hands.

"Not just yet. I was thinking of something."

She lay in the darkness, thinking irrationally that it would be such a bright indefatigable baby, but presently she let him help her up. . . . When she came back into the room, it was lit from a single electric fixture.

"A one-bulb lighting system," he said. "Shall I turn it off?"

"No. It's very nice. I want to see you."

They sat in the wooden frame of the window seat, with the soles of their shoes touching.

"You seem far away," she said.

"So do you."

"Are you surprised?"

"At what?"

"That we're two people again. Don't you always think—hope that you'll be one person, and then find you're still two?"

"I feel very close to you."

"So do I to you," she said.

"Thank you."

"Thank *you*."

They laughed.

"Is this what you wanted?" she asked. "I mean last night."

"Not consciously."

"I wonder when it was settled," she brooded. "There's a moment when you needn't, and then there's another moment when you know nothing in the world could keep it from happening."

This had an experienced ring, and to his surprise he liked her even more. In his mood, which was passionately to repeat yet not recapitulate the past, it was right that it should be that way.

"I *am* rather a trollop," she said, following his thoughts. "I suppose that's why I didn't get on to Edna."

"Who is Edna?"

"The girl you thought was me. The one you phoned to—who lived across the road. She's moved to Santa Barbara."

"You mean she was a tart?"

"So it seems. She went to what you call call-houses."

"That's funny."

"If she had been English, I'd have known right away. But she seemed like everyone else. She only told me just before she went away."

He saw her shiver and got up, putting the raincoat around her shoulders. He opened a closet, and a pile of pillows and beach mattresses fell out on the floor. There was a box of candles, and he lit them around the room, attaching the electric heater where the bulb had been.

"Why was Edna afraid of me?" he asked suddenly.

"Because you were a producer. She had some awful experience or a friend of hers did. Also, I think she was extremely stupid."

"How did you happen to know her?"

"She came over. Maybe she thought I was a fallen sister. She seemed quite pleasant. She said 'Call me Edna' all the time—'Please call me Edna,' so finally I called her Edna and we were friends."

She got off the window seat so he could lay pillows along it and behind her.

"What can I do?" she said. "I'm a parasite."

"No, you're not." He put his arms around her. "Be still. Get warm."

They sat for awhile quiet.

"I know why you liked me at first," she said. "Edna told me."

"What did she tell you?"

"That I looked like—Minna Davis. Several people have told me that."

He leaned away from her and nodded.

"It's here," she said, putting her hands on her cheekbones and distorting her cheeks slightly. "Here and here."

"Yes," said Stahr. "It was very strange. You look more like she actually *looked* than how she was on the screen."

She got up, changing the subject with her gesture as if she were afraid of it.

"I'm warm now," she said. She went to the closet and peered in, came back wearing a little apron with a crystalline pattern like a snowfall. She stared around critically.

"Of course we've just moved in," she said, "—and there's a sort of echo."

She opened the door of the veranda and pulled in two wicker chairs, drying them off. He watched her move, intently, yet half afraid that her body would fail somewhere and break the spell. He had watched women in screen tests and seen their beauty vanish second by second, as if a lovely statue had begun to walk with the meagre joints of a paper doll. But Kathleen was ruggedly set on the balls of her feet—the fragility was, as it should be, an illusion.

"It's stopped raining," she said. "It rained the day I came. Such an awful rain—so loud—like horses weeing."

He laughed.

"You'll like it. Especially if you've got to stay here. Are you going to stay here? Can't you tell me now? What's the mystery?"

She shook her head.

"Not now—it's not worth telling."

"Come here then."

She came over and stood near him, and he pressed his cheek against the cool fabric of the apron.

"You're a tired man," she said, putting her hand in his hair.

"Not that way."

"I didn't mean that way," she said hastily. "I meant you'll work yourself sick."

"Don't be a mother," he said.

"All right. What shall I be?"

Be a trollop, he thought. He wanted the pattern of his life broken. If he was going to die soon, like the two doctors said, he wanted to stop being Stahr for awhile and hunt for love like men who had no gifts to give, like young nameless men who looked along the streets in the dark.

"You've taken off my apron," she said gently.

"Yes."

"Would anyone be passing along the beach? Shall we put out the candles?"

"No, don't put out the candles."

Afterwards she lay half on a white cushion and smiled up at him.

"I feel like Venus on the half shell," she said.

"What made you think of that?"

"Look at me—isn't it Botticelli?"

"I don't know," he said smiling. "It is if you say so."

She yawned.

"I've had such a good time. And I'm very fond of you."

"You know a lot, don't you?"

"What do you mean?"

"Oh, from little things you've said. Or perhaps the way you say them."

She deliberated.

"Not much," she said. "I never went to a university, if that's what you mean. But the man I told you about knew everything and he had a passion for educating me. He made out schedules and made me take courses at the Sorbonne and go to museums. I picked up a little."

"What was he?"

"He was a painter of sorts and a hell-cat. And a lot besides. He wanted me to read Spengler—everything was for that. All the history and philosophy and harmony was all so I could read Spengler, and then I left him before we got to Spengler. At the end I think that was the chief reason he didn't want me to go."

"Who was Spengler?"

"I tell you we didn't get to him," she laughed, "and now I'm forgetting everything very patiently, because it isn't likely I'll ever meet anyone like him again."

"Oh, but you shouldn't forget," said Stahr, shocked. He had an intense respect for learning, a racial memory of the old *schules*. "You shouldn't forget."

"It was just in place of babies."

"You could teach your babies," he said.

"Could I?"

"Sure you could. You could give it to them while they were young. When I want to know anything, I've got to ask some drunken writer. Don't throw it away."

"All right," she said, getting up. "I'll tell it to my children. But it's so endless—the more you know, the more there is just beyond, and it keeps on coming. This man could have been anything if he hadn't been a coward and a fool."

"But you were in love with him."

"Oh, yes—with all my heart." She looked through the window, shading her eyes. "It's light out there. Let's go down to the beach."

He jumped up, exclaiming:

"Why, I think it's the grunion!"

"What?"

"It's tonight. It's in all the papers." He hurried out the door, and she heard him open the door of the car. Presently he returned with a newspaper.

"It's at ten-sixteen. That's five minutes."

"An eclipse or something?"

"Very punctual fish," he said. "Leave your shoes and stockings and come with me."

It was a fine blue night. The tide was at the turn, and the little silver fish rocked off shore waiting for 10.16. A few seconds after the time they came swarming in with the tide, and Stahr and Kathleen stepped over them barefoot as they flicked slip-slop on the sand. A negro man came along the shore toward them, collecting the grunion quickly, like twigs, into two pails. They came in twos and threes and platoons and companies, relentless and exalted and scornful, around the great bare feet of the intruders, as they had come before Sir Francis Drake had nailed his plaque to the boulder on the shore.

"I wish for another pail," the negro man said, resting a moment.

"You've come a long way out," said Stahr.

"I used to go to Malibu, but they don't like it, those moving picture people."

A wave came in and forced them back, receded swiftly, leaving the sand alive again.

"Is it worth the trip?" Stahr asked.

"I don't figure it that way. I really come out to read some Emerson. Have you ever read him?"

"I have," said Kathleen. "Some."

"I've got him inside my shirt. I got some Rosicrucian literature with me, too, but I'm fed up with them."

The wind had changed a little—the waves were stronger further down, and they walked along the foaming edge of the water.

"What's your work," the negro asked Stahr.

"I work for the pictures."

"Oh." After a moment he added, "I never go to movies."

"Why not?" asked Stahr sharply.

"There's no profit. I never let my children go."

Stahr watched him, and Kathleen watched Stahr protectively.

"Some of them are good," she said, against a wave of spray; but he did not hear her. She felt she could contradict him and said it again, and this time he looked at her indifferently.

"Are the Rosicrucian brotherhood against pictures?" asked Stahr.

"Seems as if they don't know what they *are* for. One week they for one thing and next week for another."

Only the little fish were certain. Half an hour had gone, and still they came. The negro's two pails were full, and finally he went off over the beach toward the road, unaware that he had rocked an industry.

Stahr and Kathleen walked back to the house, and she thought how to drive his momentary blues away.

"Poor old Sambo," she said.

"What?"

"Don't you call them poor old Sambo?"

"We don't call them anything especially." After a moment, he said, "They have pictures of their own."

In the house she drew on her shoes and stockings before the heater.

"I like California better," she said deliberately. "I think I was a bit sex-starved."

"That wasn't quite all, was it?"

"You know it wasn't."

"It's nice to be near you."

She gave a little sigh as she stood up, so small that he did not notice it.

"I don't want to lose you now," he said. "I don't know what you think of me or whether you think of me at all. As you've probably guessed, my heart's in the grave—" He hesitated, wondering if this was quite true. "—but you're the most attractive woman I've met since I don't know when. I can't stop looking at you. I don't know now exactly the color of your eyes, but they make me sorry for everyone in the world——"

"Stop it, stop it!" she cried laughing. "You'll have me looking in the mirror for weeks. My eyes aren't any color—they're just eyes to see with, and I'm just as ordinary as I can be. I have nice teeth for an English girl——"

"You have beautiful teeth."

"—but I couldn't hold a candle to these girls I see here——"

"*You* stop it," he said. "What I said is true, and I'm a cautious man."

She stood motionless a moment—thinking. She looked at him, then she looked back into herself, then at him again--then she gave up her thought.

"We must go," she said.

Now they were different people as they started back. Four times they had driven along the shore road today, each time a different pair. Curiosity, sadness and desire were behind them now; this was a true returning—to themselves and all their past and future and the encroaching presence of tomorrow. He asked her to sit close in the car, and she did, but they did not seem close, because for that you have to seem to be growing closer. Nothing stands still. It was on his tongue to ask her to come to the house he rented and sleep there tonight—but he felt that it would make him sound lonely. As the car climbed the hill to her house, Kathleen looked for something behind the seat cushion.

"What have you lost?"

"It might have fallen out," she said, feeling through her purse in the darkness.

"What was it?"

"An envelope."

"Was it important?"

"No."

But when they got to her house and Stahr turned on the dashboard light, she helped take the cushions out and look again.

"It doesn't matter," she said, as they walked to the door. "What's your address where you really live?"

"Just Bel-air. There's no number."

"Where is Bel-air?"

"It's a sort of development, near Santa Monica. But you'd better call me at the studio."

"All right . . . good night, Mr. Stahr."

"*Mister* Stahr," he repeated, astonished.

She corrected herself gently.

"Well, then, good night, Stahr. Is that better?"

He felt as though he had been pushed away a little.

"As you like," he said. He refused to let the aloofness communicate itself. He kept looking at her and moved his head from side to side in her own gesture, saying without words: "You know what's happened to me." She sighed. Then she came into his arms and for a moment was his again completely. Before anything could change, Stahr whispered good night and turned away and went to his car.

Winding down the hill, he listened inside himself as if something by an unknown composer, powerful and strange and strong, was about to be played for the first time. The theme would be stated presently, but because the composer was always new, he would not recognize it as the theme right away. It would come in some such guise as the auto horns from the technicolor boulevards below, or be barely audible, a tattoo on the muffled drum of the moon. He strained to hear it, knowing only that music was beginning, new music that he liked and did not understand. It was hard to react to what one could entirely compass—this was new and confusing, nothing one could shut off in the middle and supply the rest from an old score.

Also, and persistently, and bound up with the other, there was the negro on the sand. He was waiting at home for Stahr, with his pails of silver fish, and he would be waiting at the studio in the morning. He had said that he did not allow his children to listen to Stahr's story. He was prejudiced and wrong, and he must be shown somehow, some way. A picture, many pictures, a decade of pictures, must be made to show him he was wrong. Since he had spoken, Stahr had thrown four pictures out of his plans—one that was going into production this week. They were borderline pictures in point of interest, but at least he submitted the borderline pictures to the negro and found them trash. And he put back on his list a difficult picture that he had tossed to the wolves, to Brady and Marcus and the rest, to get his way on something else. He rescued it for the negro man.

When he drove up to his door, the porch lights went on, and his Philippino came down the steps to put away the car. In the library, Stahr found a list of phone calls:

"La Borwitz
Marcus
Harlow
Reinmund
Fairbanks
Brady
Colman
Skouras
Fleishacker," *etc*.

The Philippino came into the room with a letter.

"This fell out of the car," he said.

"Thanks," said Stahr. "I was looking for it."

"Will you be running a picture tonight, Mr. Stahr?"

"No, thanks—you can go to bed."

The letter, to his surprise, was addressed to Monroe Stahr, Esq. He started to open it—then it occurred to him that she had wanted to recapture it, and possibly to withdraw it. If she had had a phone, he would have called her for permission before opening it. He held it for a moment. It had been written before they met—it was odd to think that whatever it said was now invalidated; it possessed the interest of a souvenir by representing a mood that was gone.

Still he did not like to read it without asking her. He put it down beside a pile of scripts and sat down with the top script in his lap. He was proud of resisting his first impulse to open the letter. It seemed to prove that he was not "losing his head." He had never lost his head about Minna, even in the beginning—it had been the most appropriate and regal match imaginable. She had loved him always and just before she died, all unwilling and surprised, his tenderness had burst and surged forward and he had been in love with her. In love with Minna and death together—with the world in which she looked so alone that he wanted to go with her there.

But "falling for dames" had never been an obsession—his brother had gone to pieces over a dame, or rather over dame after dame after dame. But Stahr, in his younger days, had them once and never more than once—like one drink. He had quite another sort of adventure reserved for his mind—something better than a series of emotional sprees. Like many brilliant men, he had grown up dead cold. Beginning at about twelve, probably, with the total rejection common to those of extraordinary mental powers, the "See here: this is all wrong—a mess—all a lie—and a sham—," he swept it all away, everything, as men of his type do; and then instead of being a son-of-a-bitch as most of them are, he looked around at the barrenness that was left and said to himself, "*This* will never do." And so he had learned tolerance, kindness, forbearance, and even affection like lessons.

The Philippino boy brought in a carafe of water and bowls of nuts and fruit, and said good night. Stahr opened the first script and began to read.

He read for three hours—stopping from time to time, editing without a pencil. Sometimes he looked up, warm from some vague happy thought that was not in the script, and it took him a minute each time to remember what it was. Then he knew it was Kathleen, and he looked at the letter—it was nice to have a letter.

It was three o'clock when a vein began to bump in the back of his hand, signalling that it was time to quit. Kathleen was really far away now with the waning night—the different aspects of her telescoped into the memory of a single thrilling stranger, bound to him only by a few slender hours. It seemed perfectly all right to open the letter.

"Dear Mr. Stahr.
"In half an hour I will be keeping my date with you. When we say goodbye I will hand you this letter. It is to tell you that I am to be married soon and that I won't be able to see you after today.

"I should have told you last night but it didn't seem to concern you. And it would seem silly to spend this beautiful afternoon telling you about it and watching your interest fade. Let it fade all at once —now. I will have told you enough to convince you that I am Nobody's Prize Potato. (I have just learned that expression—from my hostess of last night, who called and stayed an hour. She seems to believe that everyone is Nobody's Prize Potato—except you. I think I am supposed to tell you she thinks this, so give her a job if you can.)

"I am very flattered that anyone who sees so many lovely women—

I can't finish this sentence but you know what I mean. And I will
be late if I don't go to meet you right now.
"With All Good Wishes
"KATHLEEN MOORE."

Stahr's first feeling was like fear; his second thought was that the
letter was invalidated—she had even tried to retrieve it. But then
he remembered "Mister Stahr" just at the end, and that she had
asked him his address—she had probably already written another
letter which would also say goodbye. Illogically he was shocked by
the letter's indifference to what had happened later. He read it
again, realizing that it foresaw nothing. Yet in front of the house
she had decided to let it stand, belittling everything that had happened, curving her mind away from the fact that there had been
no other man in her consciousness that afternoon. But he could not
even believe this now, and the whole adventure began to peel away
even as he recapitulated it searchingly to himself. The car, the
hill, the hat, the music, the letter itself, blew off like the scraps of
tar paper from the rubble of his house. And Kathleen departed,
packing up her remembered gestures, her softly moving head, her
sturdy eager body, her bare feet in the wet swirling sand. The skies
paled and faded—the wind and rain turned dreary, washing the
silver fish back to sea. It was only one more day, and nothing was
left except the pile of scripts upon the table.

He went upstairs. Minna died again on the first landing, and he
forgot her lingeringly and miserably again, step by step to the top.
The empty floor stretched around him—the doors with no one sleeping behind. In his room, Stahr took off his tie, untied his shoes and
sat on the side of his bed. It was all closed out, except for something
that he could not remember; then he remembered: her car was still
down in the parking lot of the hotel. He set his clock to give him
six hours' sleep.

This is Cecilia taking up the story. I think it would be most
interesting to follow my own movements at this point, as this is
a time in my life that I am ashamed of. What people are ashamed
of usually makes a good story.

When I sent Wylie over to Martha Dodd's table, he had no success in finding out who the girl was, but it had suddenly become my chief interest in life. Also, I guessed—correctly—that it would be Martha Dodd's. To have had at your table a girl who is admired by royalty, who may be tagged for a coronet in our little feudal system—and not even know her name!

I had only a speaking acquaintance with Martha, and it would be too obvious to approach her directly, but I went out to the studio Monday and dropped in on Jane Meloney.

Jane Meloney was quite a friend of mine. I thought of her rather as a child thinks of a family dependent. I knew she was a writer, but I grew up thinking that writer and secretary were the same, except that a writer usually smelled of cocktails and came more often to meals. They were spoken of the same way when they were not around—except for a species called playwrights, who came from the East. These were treated with respect if they did not stay long— if they did, they sank with the others into the white collar class.

Jane's office was in the "old writers' building." There was one on every lot, a row of iron maidens left over from silent days and still resounding with the dull moans of cloistered hacks and bums. There was the story of the new producer who had gone down the line one day and then reported excitedly to the head office.

"Who are those men?"

"They're supposed to be writers."

"I thought so. Well, I watched them for ten minutes and there were two of them that didn't write a line."

Jane was at her typewriter, about to break off for lunch. I told her frankly that I had a rival.

"It's a dark horse," I said. "I can't even find out her name."

"Oh," said Jane. "Well, maybe I know something about that. I heard something from somebody."

The somebody, of course, was her nephew, Ned Sollinger, Stahr's office boy. He had been her pride and hope. She had sent him through New York University, where he played on the football team. Then in his first year at medical school, after a girl turned him down, he dissected out the least publicized section of a lady corpse and sent it to the girl. Don't ask me why. In disgrace with fortune and men's eyes, he had begun life at the bottom again, and was still there.

"What do you know?" I asked.

"It was the night of the earthquake. She fell into the lake on the back lot, and he dove in and saved her life. Someone else told me it was his balcony she jumped off of and broke her arm."

"Who was she?"

"Well, that's funny, too—"

Her phone rang, and I waited restlessly during a long conversation she had with Joe Reinmund. He seemed to be trying to find out over the phone how good she was or whether she had ever written any pictures at all. And she was reputed to have been on the set the day Griffith invented the close-up! While he talked she groaned silently, writhed, made faces into the receiver, held it all in her lap so that the voice reached her faintly—and kept up a side chatter to me.

"What is *he* doing—killing time between appointments? . . . He's asked me every one of these questions ten times . . . that's all on a memorandum I sent him.". . .

And into the phone:

"If this goes up to Monroe, it won't be my doing. I want to go right through to the end."

She shut her eyes in agony again.

"Now he's casting it . . . he's casting the minor characters . . . he's going to have Buddy Ebson. . . . My God, he just hasn't anything to do . . . now he's on Walter Davenport—he means Donald Crisp . . . he's got a big casting directory open in his lap and I can hear him turn the pages . . . he's a big important man this morning, a second Stahr, and for Christ sake I've got two scenes to do before lunch."

Reinmund quit finally or was interrupted at his end. A waiter came in from the commissary with Jane's luncheon and a Coca-Cola for me—I wasn't lunching that summer. Jane wrote down one sentence on her typewriter before she ate. It interested me the way she wrote. One day I was there when she and a young man had just lifted a story out of *The Saturday Evening Post*—changing the characters and all. Then they began to write it, making each line answer the line before it, and of course it sounded just like people do in life when they're straining to be anything—funny or gentle or brave.

I always wanted to see that one on the screen, but I missed it somehow.

I found her as lovable as a cheap old toy. She made three thousand a week, and her husbands all drank and beat her nearly to death. But today I had an axe to grind.

"You don't know her name?" I persisted.

"Oh—" said Jane, "that. Well, he kept calling her up afterwards, and he told Katy Doolan it was the wrong name, after all."

"I think he found her," I said. "Do you know Martha Dodd?"

"Hasn't that little girl had a tough break, though!" she exclaimed with ready theatrical sympathy.

"Could you possibly invite her to lunch tomorrow?"

"Oh, I think she gets enough to eat all right. There's a Mexican—"

I explained that my motives were not charitable. Jane agreed to coöperate. She called Martha Dodd.

We had lunch next day at the Bev Brown Derby, a languid restaurant, patronized for its food by clients who always look as if they'd like to lie down. There is some animation at lunch, where the women put on a show for the first five minutes after they eat, but we were a tepid threesome. I should have come right out with my curiosity. Martha Dodd was an agricultural girl, who had never quite understood what had happened to her and had nothing to show for it except a washed-out look about the eyes. She still believed that the life she had tasted was reality and this was only a long waiting.

"I had a beautiful place in 1928," she told us, "—thirty acres, with a miniature golf course and a pool and a gorgeous view. All spring I was up to my ass in daisies."

I ended by asking her to come over and meet Father. This was pure penance for having had "a mixed motive" and being ashamed of it. One doesn't mix motives in Hollywood—it is confusing. Everybody understands, and the climate wears you down. A mixed motive is conspicuous waste.

Jane left us at the studio gate, disgusted by my cowardice. Martha had worked up inside to a pitch about her career—not a very high pitch, because of seven years of neglect, but a sort of nervous acquiescence, and I was going to speak strongly to Father. They never did anything for people like Martha, who had made them so much money at one time. They let them slip away into misery eked out with extra work—it would have been kinder to ship them out of town. And Father was being so proud of me this summer. I had to keep him from telling everybody just how I had been brought up so as to produce such a perfect jewel. And Bennington—oh, what an exclusive—dear God, my heart. I assured him there was the usual proportion of natural-born skivvies and biddies tastefully concealed by throw-overs from sex Fifth Avenue; but Father had worked himself up to practically an alumnus. "You've had everything," he used to say happily. Everything included roughly the two years in Florence, where I managed against heavy odds to be the only virgin in school, and the courtesy début in Boston, Massachusetts. I was a veritable flower of the fine old cost-and-gross aristocracy.

So I knew he would do something for Martha Dodd, and as we went into his office, I had great dreams of doing something for Johnny Swanson, the cowboy, too, and Evelyn Brent, and all sorts of discarded flowers. Father was a charming and sympathetic man— except for that time I had seen him unexpectedly in New York— and there was something touching about his being my father. After all, he was *my* father—he would do anything in the world for me.

Only Rosemary Schmiel was in the outer office, and she was on Birdy Peters' phone. She waved for me to sit down, but I was full of my plans and, telling Martha to take it easy, I pressed the clicker under Rosemary's desk and went toward the opened door.

"Your father's in conference," Rosemary called. "Not in conference, but I ought to——"

By this time I was through the door and a little vestibule and another door, and caught Father in his shirtsleeves, very sweaty and trying to open a window. It was a hot day, but I hadn't realized it was that hot, and thought he was ill.

"No, I'm all right," he said. "What is it?"

I told him. I told him the whole theory of people like Martha Dodd, walking up and down his office. How could he use them and guarantee them regular employment? He seemed to take me up excitedly and kept nodding and agreeing, and I felt closer to him than I had for a long time. I came close and kissed him on his cheek. He was trembling and his shirt was soaked through.

"You're not well," I said, "or you're in some sort of stew."

"No, I'm not at all."

"What is it?"

"Oh, it's Monroe," he said. "That goddam little Vine Street Jesus! He's in my hair night and day!"

"What's happened?" I asked, very much cooler.

"Oh, he sits like a little goddam priest or rabbi and says what he'll do and he won't do. I can't tell you now—I'm half crazy. Why don't you go along?"

"I won't have you like this."

"Go along, I tell you!" I sniffed, but he never drank.

"Go and brush your hair," I said. "I want you to see Martha Dodd."

"In here! I'd never get rid of her."

"Out there then. Go wash up first. Put on another shirt."

With an exaggerated gesture of despair, he went into the little bathroom adjoining. It was hot in the office as if it had been closed for hours, and maybe that was making him sick, so I opened two more windows.

"You go along," Father called from behind the closed door of the bathroom. "I'll be there presently."

"Be awfully nice to her," I said. "No charity."

As if it were Martha speaking for herself, a long low moan came from somewhere in the room. I was startled—then transfixed, as it came again, not from the bathroom where Father was, not from outside, but from a closet in the wall across from me. How I was brave enough I don't know, but I ran across to it and opened it, and Father's secretary, Birdy Peters, tumbled out stark naked—just like a corpse in the movies. With her came a gust of stifling, stuffy air. She flopped sideways on the floor, with the one hand still clutching some clothes, and lay on the floor bathed in sweat—just as Father came in from the bathroom. I could feel him standing behind me, and without turning I knew exactly how he looked, for I had surprised him before.

"Cover her up," I said, covering her up myself with a rug from the couch. "Cover her *up*!"

I left the office. Rosemary Schmiel saw my face as I came out and responded with a terrified expression. I never saw her again or Birdy Peters either. As Martha and I went out, Martha asked: "What's the matter, dear?"—and when I didn't say anything: "You did your best. Probably it was the wrong time. I'll tell you what I'll do. I'll take you to see a very nice English girl. Did you see the girl that Stahr danced with at our table the other night?"

So at the price of a little immersion in the family drains I had what I wanted.

I don't remember much about our call. She wasn't at home was one reason. The screen door of her house was unlocked, and Martha went in calling "Kathleen" with bright familiarity. The room we saw was bare and formal as a hotel; there were flowers about, but they did not look like sent flowers. Also, Martha found a note on the table, which said: "Leave the dress. Have gone looking for a job. Will drop by tomorrow."

Martha read it twice but it didn't seem to be for Stahr, and we waited five minutes. People's houses are very still when they are gone. Not that I expect them to be jumping around, but I leave the observation for what it's worth. Very still. Prim almost, with just a fly holding down the place and paying no attention to you, and the corner of a curtain blowing.

"I wonder what kind of a job," said Martha. "Last Sunday she went somewhere with Stahr."

But I was no longer interested. It seemed awful to be here—producer's blood, I thought in horror. And in quick panic I pulled her out into the placid sunshine. It was no use—I felt just black and awful. I had always been proud of my body—I had a way of thinking of it as geometric which made everything it did seem all right. And there was probably not any kind of place, including churches and offices and shrines where people had not embraced—but no one had ever stuffed me naked into a hole in the wall in the middle of a business day.

"If you were in a drug-store," said Stahr, "—having a prescription filled——"

"You mean a chemist's?" Boxley asked.

"If you were in a chemist's," conceded Stahr, "and you were getting a prescription for some member of your family who was very sick——"

"—Very ill?" queried Boxley.

"Very ill. *Then* whatever caught your attention through the window, whatever distracted you and held you would probably be material for pictures."

"A murder outside the window, you mean."

"There you go," said Stahr, smiling. "It might be a spider working on the pane."

"Of course—I see.'"

"I'm afraid you don't, Mr. Boxley. You see it for *your* medium, but not for ours. You keep the spiders for yourself and you try to pin the murders on us."

"I might as well leave," said Boxley. "I'm no good to you. I've been here three weeks and I've accomplished nothing. I make suggestions, but no one writes them down."

"I want you to stay. Something in you doesn't like pictures, doesn't like telling a story this way——"

"It's such a damned bother," exploded Boxley. "You can't let yourself go——"

He checked himself. He knew that Stahr, the helmsman, was finding time for him in the middle of a constant stiff blow—that they were talking in the always creaking rigging of a ship sailing in great awkward tacks along an open sea. Or else—it seemed at times—they were in a huge quarry—where even the newly-cut marble bore the tracery of old pediments, half-obliterated inscriptions of the past.

"I keep wishing you could start over," Boxley said. "It's this mass production."

"That's the condition," said Stahr. "There's always some lousy condition. We're making a life of Rubens—suppose I asked you to do portraits of rich dopes like Bill Brady and me and Gary Cooper and Marcus when you wanted to paint Jesus Christ! Wouldn't you feel you had a condition? Our condition is that we have to take people's own favorite folklore and dress it up and give it back to them. Anything beyond that is sugar. So won't you give us some sugar, Mr. Boxley?"

Boxley knew he could sit with Wylie White tonight at the Troc raging at Stahr, but he had been reading Lord Charnwood and he recognized that Stahr like Lincoln was a leader carrying on a long war on many fronts; almost single-handed he had moved pictures sharply forward through a decade, to a point where the content of the "A productions" was wider and richer than that of the stage. Stahr was an artist only, as Mr. Lincoln was a general, perforce and as a layman.

"Come down to La Borwitz' office with me," said Stahr. "They sure need some sugar there."

In La Borwitz' office, two writers, a shorthand secretary and a hushed supervisor, sat in a tense smoky stalemate, where Stahr had left them three hours before. He looked at the faces one after another and found nothing. La Borwitz spoke with awed reverence for his defeat.

"We've just got too many characters, Monroe."

Stahr snorted affably.

"That's the principal idea of the picture."

He took some change out of his pocket, looked up at the suspended light and tossed up half a dollar, which clanked into the bowl. He looked at the coins in his hands and selected a quarter.

La Borwitz watched miserably; he knew this was a favorite idea of Stahr's and he saw the sands running out. At the moment everyone's back was toward him. Suddenly he brought up his hands from their placid position under the desk and threw them high in the air, so high that they seemed to leave his wrist—and then he caught them neatly as they were descending. After that he felt better. He was in control.

One of the writers had taken out some coins, also, and presently rules were defined. "You have to toss your coin through the chains without hitting them. Whatever falls into the light is the kitty."

They played for half an hour—all except Boxley, who sat aside and dug into the script, and the secretary, who kept tally. She calculated the cost of the four men's time, arriving at a figure of sixteen hundred dollars. At the end, La Borwitz was winner by $5.50, and a janitor brought in a step-ladder to take the money out of the light.

Boxley spoke up suddenly.

"You have the stuffings of a turkey here," he said.

"What!"

"It's not pictures."

They looked at him in astonishment. Stahr concealed a smile.

"So we've got a real picture man here!" exclaimed La Borwitz.

"A lot of beautiful speeches," said Boxley boldly, "but no situations. After all, you know, it's not going to be a novel. And it's too long. I can't exactly describe how I feel, but it's not quite right. And it leaves me cold."

He was giving them back what had been handed him for three weeks. Stahr turned away, watching the others out of the corner of his eye.

"We don't need *less* characters," said Boxley. "We need *more*. As I see it, that's the idea."

"That's the idea," said the writers.

"Yes—that's the idea," said La Borwitz.

Boxley was inspired by the attention he had created.

"Let each character see himself in the other's place," he said. "The policeman is about to arrest the thief when he sees that the thief actually has *his* face. I mean, show it that way. You could almost call the thing *Put Yourself in My Place*."

Suddenly they were at work again—taking up this new theme in turn like hepcats in a swing band and going to town with it. They might throw it out again tomorrow, but life had come back for a moment. Pitching the coins had done it as much as Boxley. Stahr had recreated the proper atmosphere—never consenting to be a driver of the driven, but feeling like and acting like and even sometimes looking like a small boy getting up a show.

He left them, touching Boxley on the shoulder in passing—a deliberate accolade—he didn't want them to gang up on him and break his spirit in an hour.

Doctor Baer was waiting in his inner office. With him was a colored man with a portable cardiograph like a huge suitcase. Stahr called it the lie detector. Stahr stripped to the waist, and the weekly examination began.

"How've you been feeling?"

"Oh—the usual," said Stahr.

"Been hard at it? Getting any sleep?"

"No—about five hours. If I go to bed early, I just lie there."

"Take the sleeping pills."

"The yellow one gives me a hangover."

"Take two red ones, then."

"That's a nightmare."

"Take one of each—the yellow first."

"All right—I'll try. How've *you* been?"

"Say—I take care of myself, Monroe, I save myself."

"The hell you do—you're up all night sometimes."

"Then I sleep all next day."

After ten minutes, Baer said:

"Seems O.K. The blood pressure's up five points."

"Good," said Stahr. "That's good, isn't it?"

"That's good. I'll develop the cardiographs tonight. When are you coming away with me?"

"Oh, some time," said Stahr lightly. "In about six weeks things'll ease up."

Baer looked at him with a genuine liking that had grown over three years.

"You got better in thirty-three when you laid up," he said. "Even for three weeks."

"I will again."

No he wouldn't, Baer thought. With Minna's help he had enforced a few short rests years ago and lately he had hinted around, trying to find who Stahr considered his closest friends. Who could take him away and keep him away? It would almost surely be useless. He was due to die very soon now. Within six months one could say definitely. What was the use of developing the cardiograms? You couldn't persuade a man like Stahr to stop and lie down and look at the sky for six months. He would much rather die. He said differently, but what it added up to was the definite urge toward total exhaustion that he had run into before. Fatigue was a drug as well as a poison, and Stahr apparently derived some rare almost physical pleasure from working lightheaded with weariness. It was a perversion of the life force he had seen before, but he had almost stopped trying to interfere with it. He had cured a man or so—a hollow triumph of killing and preserving the shell.

"You hold your own," he said.

They exchanged a glance. Did Stahr know? Probably. But he did not know when—he did not know how soon now.

"If I hold my own, I can't ask more," said Stahr.

The colored man had finished packing the apparatus.

"Next week same time?"

"O.K., Bill," said Stahr. "Goodbye."

As the door closed, Stahr switched open the dictograph. Miss Doolan's voice came through immediately.

"Do you know a Miss Kathleen Moore?"

"What do you mean?" he asked startled.

"A Miss Kathleen Moore is on the line. She said you asked her to call."

"Well, my God!" he exclaimed. He was swept with indignant rapture. It had been five days—this would never do at all.

"She's on now?"

"Yes."

"Well, all right then."

In a moment he heard the voice up close to him.

"Are you married?" he asked, low and surly.

"No, not yet."

His memory blocked out her face and form—as he sat down, she seemed to lean down to his desk, keeping level with his eyes.

"What's on your mind?" he asked in the same surly voice. It was hard to talk that way.

"You did find the letter?" she asked.

"Yes. It turned up that night."

"That's what I want to speak to you about."

He found an attitude at length—he was outraged.

"What is there to talk about?" he demanded.

"I tried to write you another letter, but it wouldn't write."

"I know that, too."

There was a pause.

"Oh, cheer up!" she said surprisingly. "This doesn't sound like you. It *is* Stahr, isn't it? That very nice Mr. Stahr?"

"I feel a little outraged," he said almost pompously. "I don't see the use of this. I had at least a pleasant memory of you."

"I don't believe it's you," she said. "Next thing you'll wish me luck." Suddenly she laughed: "Is this what you planned to say? I know how *aw*ful it gets when you plan to say anything——"

"I never expected to hear from you again," he said with dignity; but it was no use, she laughed again—a woman's laugh that is like a child's, just one syllable, a crow and a cry of delight.

"Do you know how you make me feel?" she demanded. "Like a day in London during a caterpillar plague when a hot furry thing dropped in my mouth."

"I'm sorry."

"Oh, please wake up," she begged. "I want to see you. I can't explain things on the phone. It was no fun for me either, you understand."

"I'm very busy. There's a sneak preview in Glendale tonight."

"Is that an invitation?"

"George Boxley, the English writer, is going with me." He surprised himself. "Do you want to come along?"

"How could we talk?"

She considered. "Why don't you call for me afterwards," she suggested. "We could ride around."

Miss Doolan on the huge dictograph was trying to cut in on the line with a shooting director—the only interruption ever permitted. He flipped the button and called "Wait" impatiently into the machine.

"About eleven?" Kathleen was saying confidentially.

The idea of "riding around" seemed so unwise that if he could have thought of the words to refuse her he would have spoken them, but he did not want to be the caterpillar. Suddenly he had no attitude left except the sense that the day, at least, was complete. He had an evening—a beginning, a middle and an end.

He rapped on the screen door, heard her call from inside, and stood waiting where the level fell away. From below came the whir of a lawn mower—a man was cutting his grass at midnight. The moon was so bright that Stahr could see him plainly, a hundred feet off and down, as he stopped and rested on the handle before pushing it back across his garden. There was a midsummer restlessness abroad—early August with imprudent loves and impulsive crimes.

With little more to expect from summer, one tried anxiously to live in the present—or, if there was no present, to invent one.

She came at last. She was all different and delighted. She wore a suit with a skirt that she kept hitching up as they walked down to the car with a brave, gay, stimulating, reckless air of "Tighten up your belt, baby. Let's get going." Stahr had brought his limousine with the chauffeur, and the intimacy of the four walls whisking them along a new curve in the dark took away any strangeness at once. In its way, the little trip they made was one of the best times he had ever had in his life. It was certainly one of the times when, if he knew he was going to die, it was not tonight.

She told him her story. She sat beside him cool and gleaming for a while, spinning on excitedly, carrying him to far places with her, meeting and knowing the people she had known. The story was vague at first. "This Man" was the one she had loved and lived with. "This American" was the one who had rescued her when she was sinking into a quicksand.

"Who is he—the American?"

Oh, names—what did they matter? No one important like Stahr, not rich. He had lived in London and now they would live out here. She was going to be a good wife, a real person. He was getting a divorce—not just on account of her—but that was the delay.

"But the first man?" asked Stahr. "How did you get into that?"

Oh, that was a blessing at first. From sixteen to twenty-one the thing was to eat. The day her stepmother presented her at Court they had one shilling to eat with so as not to feel faint. Sixpence apiece, but the stepmother watched while she ate. After a few months the stepmother died, and she would have sold out for that shilling but she was too weak to go into the streets. London can be harsh—oh, quite.

Was there nobody?

There were friends in Ireland who sent butter. There was a soup kitchen. There was a visit to an uncle, who made advances to her when she had a full stomach, and she held out and got fifty pounds out of him for not telling his wife.

"Couldn't you work?" Stahr asked.

"I worked. I sold cars. Once I sold a car."

"But couldn't you get a regular job?"

"It's hard—it's different. There was a feeling that people like me forced other people out of jobs. A woman struck me when I tried to get a job as chambermaid in a hotel."

"But you were presented at Court?"

"That was my stepmother who did that—on an off chance. I was nobody. My father was shot by the Black-and-Tans in twenty-two when I was a child. He wrote a book called *Last Blessing*. Did you ever read it?"

"I don't read."

"I wish you'd buy it for the movies. It's a good little book. I still get a royalty from it—ten shillings a year."

Then she met "The Man" and they travelled the world around. She had been to all the places that Stahr made movies of, and lived in cities whose name he had never heard. Then The Man went to seed, drinking and sleeping with the housemaids and trying to force her off on his friends. They all tried to make her stick with him. They said she had saved him and should cleave to him longer now, indefinitely, to the end. It was her duty. They brought enormous pressure to bear. But she had met The American, and so finally she ran away.

"You should have run away before."

"Well, you see, it was difficult." She hesitated, and plunged. "You see, I ran away from a king."

His moralities somehow collapsed—she had managed to top him. A confusion of thoughts raced through his head—one of them a faint old credo that all royalty was diseased.

"It wasn't the King of England," she said. "My king was out of a job as he used to say. There are lots of kings in London." She laughed —then added almost defiantly, "He was very attractive until he began drinking and raising hell."

"What was he king of?"

She told him—and Stahr visualized the face out of old news reels.

"He was a very learned man," she said. "He could have taught all sorts of subjects. But he wasn't much like a king. Not nearly as much as you. None of them were."

This time Stahr laughed.

"You know what I mean. They all felt old-fashioned. Most of them tried so hard to keep up with things. They were always advised to keep up with things. One was a syndicalist, for instance. And one used to carry around a couple of clippings about a tennis tournament when he was in the semi-finals. I saw those clippings a dozen times."

They rode through Griffith Park and out past the dark studios of Burbank, past the airports, and along the way to Pasadena past the neon signs of roadside cabarets. Up in his head he wanted her, but it was late and just the ride was an overwhelming joy. They held hands and once she came close into his arms saying, "Oh, you're *so* nice. I *do* like to be with you." But her mind was divided—this was not his night as the Sunday afternoon had been his. She was absorbed in herself, stung into excitement by telling of her own adventures; he could not help wondering if he was getting the story she had saved up for The American.

"How long have you known The American?" he asked.

"Oh, I knew him for several months. We used to meet. We understand each other. He used to say, 'It looks like a cinch from now on.' "

"Then why did you call me up?"

She hesitated.

"I wanted to see you once more. Then, *too*—he was supposed to arrive today, but last night he wired that he'd be another week. I wanted to talk to a friend—after all, you *are* my friend."

He wanted her very much now, but one part of his mind was cold and kept saying: She wants to see if I'm in love with her, if I want to marry her. Then she'd consider whether or not to throw this man over. She won't consider it till I've committed myself.

"Are you in love with The American?" he asked.

"Oh, yes. It's absolutely arranged. He saved my life and my reason. He's moving half-way around the world for me. I insisted on that."

"But are you in love with him?"

"Oh, yes. I'm in love with him."

The "Oh, yes" told him she was not—told him to speak for himself—that she would see. He took her in his arms and kissed her deliberately on the mouth and held her for a long time. It was so warm.

"Not tonight," she whispered.

"All right."

They passed over suicide bridge with the high new wire.

"I know what it is," she said, "but how stupid. English people don't kill themselves when they don't get what they want."

They turned around in the driveway of a hotel and started back. It was a dark night with no moon. The wave of desire had passed and neither spoke for awhile. Her talk of kings had carried him oddly back in flashes to the pearly White Way of Main Street in Erie, Pennsylvania, when he was fifteen. There was a restaurant with lobsters in the window and green weeds and bright lights on a shell cavern, and beyond behind a red curtain the terribly strange brooding mystery of people and violin music. That was just before he left for New York. This girl reminded him of the fresh iced fish and lobsters in the window. She was Beautiful Doll. Minna had never been Beautiful Doll.

They looked at each other and her eyes asked, "Shall I marry The American?" He did not answer. After awhile he said:

"Let's go somewhere for the week-end."

She considered.

"Are you talking about tomorrow?"

"I'm afraid I am."

"Well, I'll tell you tomorrow," she said.

"Tell me tonight. I'd be afraid——"

"——find a note in the car?" she laughed. "No there's no note in the car. You know almost everything now."

"Almost everything."

"Yes—almost. A few little things."

He would have to know what they were. She would tell him tomorrow. He doubted—he wanted to doubt—if there had been a maze of philandering: a fixation had held her to The Man, the king, firmly and long. Three years of a highly anomalous position—one foot in the palace and one in the background. "You had to laugh a lot," she said. "I learned to laugh a lot."

"He could have married you—like Mrs. Simpson," Stahr said in protest.

"Oh, he was married. And he wasn't a romantic." She stopped herself.

"Am I?"

"Yes," she said unwillingly, as if she were laying down a trump. "Part of you is. You're three or four different men but each of them out in the open. Like all Americans."

"Don't start trusting Americans too implicitly," he said smiling. "They may be out in the open, but they change very fast."

She looked concerned.

"Do they?"

"Very fast and all at once," he said, "and nothing ever changes them back."

"You frighten me. I always had a great sense of security with Americans."

She seemed suddenly so alone that he took her hand.

"Where will we go tomorrow?" he said. "Maybe up in the mountains. I've got everything to do tomorrow, but I won't do any of it. We can start at four and get there by afternoon."

"I'm not sure. I seem to be a little mixed up. This doesn't seem to be quite the girl who came out to California for a new life."

He could have said it then, said, "It *is* a new life," for he knew it was, he knew he could not let her go now; but something else said to sleep on it as an adult, no romantic. And not to tell her till tomorrow. Still she was looking at him, her eyes wandering from his forehead to his chin and back again, and then up and down once more, with that odd slowly-waving motion of her head.

. . . It is your chance, Stahr. Better take it now. This is your girl. She can save you, she can worry you back to life. She will take looking after and you will grow strong to do it. But take her now— tell her and take her away. Neither of you knows it, but far away over the night The American has changed his plans. At this moment his train is speeding through Albuquerque; the schedule is accurate. The engineer is on time. In the morning he will be here.

. . . The chauffeur turned up the hill to Kathleen's house. It seemed warm even in darkness—wherever he had been near here was by way of being an enchanted place for Stahr: this limousine, the rising house at the beach, the very distances they had already covered together over the sprawled city. The hill they climbed now gave forth a sort of glow, a sustained sound that struck his soul alert with delight.

As he said goodbye he felt again that it was impossible to leave her, even for a few hours. There were only ten years between them, but he felt that madness about it akin to the love of an aging man for a young girl. It was a deep and desperate time-need, a clock ticking with his heart, and it urged him, against the whole logic of his life, to walk past her into the house now and say, "This is forever."

Kathleen waited, irresolute herself—pink and silver frost waiting to melt with spring. She was a European, humble in the face of power, but there was a fierce self-respect that would only let her go so far. She had no illusions about the considerations that swayed princes.

"We'll go to the mountains tomorrow," said Stahr. Many thousands of people depended on his balanced judgment—you can suddenly blunt a quality you have lived by for twenty years.

He was very busy the next morning, Saturday. At two o'clock, when he came from luncheon, there was a stack of telegrams—a company ship was lost in the Arctic; a star was in disgrace; a writer was suing for one million dollars. Jews were dead miserably beyond the sea. The last telegram stared up at him:

I was married at noon today. Goodbye; and on a sticker attached *Send your answer by Western Union Telegram.*

CHAPTER VI

I KNEW NOTHING about any of this. I went up to Lake Louise, and when I came back didn't go near the studio. I think I would have started East in mid-August—if Stahr hadn't called me up one day at home.

"I want you to arrange something, Cecilia—I want to meet a Communist Party member."

"Which one?" I asked, somewhat startled.

"Any one."

"Haven't you got plenty out there?"

"I mean one of their organizers—from New York."

The summer before I had been all politics—I could probably have arranged a meeting with Harry Bridges. But my boy had been killed in an auto accident after I went back to college, and I was out of touch with such things. I had heard there was a man from *The New Masses* around somewhere.

"Will you promise him immunity?" I asked, joking.

"Oh, yes," Stahr answered seriously. "I won't hurt him. Get one that can talk—tell him to bring one of his books along."

He spoke as if he wanted to meet a member of the "I am" cult.

"Do you want a blonde or a brunette?"

"Oh, get a man," he said hastily.

Hearing Stahr's voice cheered me up—since I had barged in on Father it had all seemed a paddling about in thin spittle. Stahr changed everything about it—changed the angle from which I saw it, changed the very air.

"I don't think your father ought to know," he said. "Can we pretend the man is a Bulgarian musician or something?"

"Oh, they don't dress up any more," I said.

It was harder to arrange than I thought—Stahr's negotiations with the Writers' Guild, which had continued over a year, were approaching a dead end. Perhaps they were afraid of being corrupted, and I was asked what Stahr's "proposition" was. Afterwards Stahr told me that he prepared for the meeting by running off the Russian Revolutionary films that he had in his film library at home. He also ran off *Doctor Caligari* and Salvator Dali's *Le Chien Andalou,* possibly suspecting that they had a bearing on the matter. He had been startled by the Russian films back in the twenties, and on Wylie White's suggestion he had had the script department get him up a two-page "treatment" of the *Communist Manifesto.*

But his mind was closed on the subject. He was a rationalist who did his own reasoning without benefit of books—and he had just managed to climb out of a thousand years of Jewry into the late eighteenth century. He could not bear to see it melt away—he cherished the parvenu's passionate loyalty to an imaginary past.

The meeting took place in what I called the "processed leather room"—it was one of six done for us by a decorator from Sloane's years ago, and the term stuck in my head. It was *the* most decorator's room: an angora wool carpet the color of dawn, the most delicate grey imaginable—you hardly dared walk on it; and the silver panelling and leather tables and creamy pictures and slim fragilities looked so easy to stain that we could not breathe hard in there, though it was wonderful to look into from the door when the windows were open and the curtains whimpered querulously against the breeze. It was a lineal descendant of the old American parlor that used to be closed except on Sunday. But it was exactly the room for the occasion, and I hoped that whatever happened would give it character and make it henceforth part of our house.

Stahr arrived first. He was white and nervous and troubled—except for his voice, which was always quiet and full of consideration. There was a brave personal quality in the way he would meet you—he would walk right up to you and put aside something that was in the way, and grow to know you all over as if he couldn't help himself. I kissed him for some reason, and took him into the processed leather room.

"When do you go back to college?" he asked.

We had been over this fascinating ground before.

"Would you like me if I were a little shorter?" I asked, "I could wear low heels and plaster down my hair."

"Let's have dinner tonight," he suggested. "People will think I'm your father but I don't mind."

"I *love* old men," I assured him. "Unless the man has a crutch, I feel it's just a boy and girl affair."

"Have you had many of those?"

"Enough."

"People fall in and out of love all the time, don't they?"

"Every three years or so, Fanny Brice says. I just read it in the paper."

"I wonder how they manage it," he said. "I know it's true because I see them. But they look so con*vinced* every time. And then suddenly they don't look convinced. But they get convinced all over."

"You've been making too many movies."

"I wonder if they're as convinced the second time or the third time or the fourth time," he persisted.

"More each time," I said. "Most of all the last time."

He thought this over and seemed to agree.

"I suppose so. Most of all the last time."

I didn't like the way he said this, and I suddenly saw that under the surface he was miserable.

"It's a great nuisance," he said. "It'll be better when it's over."

"Wait a *min*ute! Perhaps pictures are in the wrong hands."

Brimmer, the Party Member, was announced, and going to meet him I slid over to the door on one of those gossamer throw-rugs and practically into his arms.

He was a nice-looking man, this Brimmer—a little on the order of Spencer Tracy, but with a stronger face and a wider range of reactions written up in it. I couldn't help thinking as he and Stahr smiled and shook hands and squared off, that they were two of the most alert men I had ever seen. They were very conscious of each other immediately—both as polite to me as you please, but with a softening of the ends of their sentences when they turned in my direction.

"What are you people trying to do?" demanded Stahr. "You've got my young men all upset."

"That keeps them awake, doesn't it?" said Brimmer.

"First we let half a dozen Russians study the plant," said Stahr. "As a model plant, you understand. And then you try to break up the unity that makes it a model plant."

"The unity?" Brimmer repeated. "Do you mean what's known as The Company Spirit?"

"Oh, not that," said Stahr, impatiently. "It seems to be *me* you're after. Last week a writer came into my office—a drunk—a man who's been floating around for years just two steps out of the bughouse—and began telling me my business."

Brimmer smiled.

"You don't look to me like a man who could be told his business, Mr. Stahr."

They would both have tea. When I came back, Stahr was telling a story about the Warner Brothers and Brimmer was laughing with him.

"I'll tell you another one," Stahr said. "Balanchine the Russian Dancer had them mixed up with the Ritz Brothers. He didn't know which ones he was training and which ones he was working for. He used to go around saying, 'I cannot train these Warner Brothers to dance.'"

It looked like a quiet afternoon. Brimmer asked him why the producers didn't back the anti-Nazi League.

"Because of you people," said Stahr. "It's your way of getting at the writers. In the long view you're wasting your time. Writers are children—even in normal times they can't keep their minds on their work."

"They're the farmers in this business," said Brimmer pleasantly. "They grow the grain but they're not in at the feast. Their feeling toward the producer is like the farmers' resentment of the city fellow."

I was wondering about Stahr's girl—whether it was all over between them. Later, when I heard the whole thing from Kathleen, standing in the rain in a wretched road called Goldwyn Avenue, I figured out that this must have been a week after she sent him the telegram. She couldn't help the telegram. The man got off the train unexpectedly and walked her to the registry office without a flicker of doubt that this was what she wanted. It was eight in the morning, and Kathleen was in such a daze that she was chiefly concerned about how to get the telegram to Stahr. In theory you could stop and say, "Listen, I forgot to tell you but I met a man." But this track had been laid down so thoroughly, with such confidence, such struggle, such relief, that when it came along, suddenly cutting across the other, she found herself on it like a car on a closed switch. He watched her write the telegram, looking directly at it across the table, and she hoped he couldn't read upside down. . . .

When my mind came back into the room, they had destroyed the poor writers—Brimmer had gone so far as to admit they were "unstable."

"They are not equipped for authority," said Stahr. "There is no substitute for will. Sometimes you have to fake will when you don't feel it at all."

"I've had that experience."

"You have to say, 'It's got to be like this—no other way'—even if you're not sure. A dozen times a week that happens to me. Situations where there is no real reason for anything. You pretend there is."

"All leaders have felt that," said Brimmer. "Labor leaders, and certainly military leaders."

"So I've had to take an attitude in this Guild matter. It looks to me like a try for power, and all I am going to give the writers is money."

"You give some of them very little money. Thirty dollars a week."

"Who gets that?" asked Stahr, surprised.

"The ones that are commodities and easy to replace."

"Not on my lot," said Stahr.

"Oh, yes," said Brimmer. "Two men in your shorts department get thirty dollars a week."

"Who?"

"Man named Ransome—man named O'Brien."

Stahr and I smiled together.

"Those are not writers," said Stahr. "Those are cousins of Cecilia's father."

"There are some in other studios," said Brimmer.

Stahr took his teaspoon and poured himself some medicine from a little bottle.

"What's a fink?" he asked suddenly.

"A fink? That's a strikebreaker or a company tec."

"I thought so," said Stahr. "I've got a fifteen hundred dollar writer that every time he walks through the commissary keeps saying 'Fink!' behind other writers' chairs. If he didn't scare hell out of them, it'd be funny."

Brimmer laughed.

"I'd like to see that," he said.

"You wouldn't like to spend a day with me over there?" suggested Stahr.

Brimmer laughed with genuine amusement.

"No, Mr. Stahr. But I don't doubt but that I'd be impressed. I've heard you're one of the hardest working and most efficient men in the entire West. It'd be a privilege to watch you, but I'm afraid I'll have to deny myself."

Stahr looked at me.

"I like your friend," he said. "He's crazy, but I like him." He looked closely at Brimmer: "Born on this side?"

"Oh, yes. Several generations."

"Many of them like you?"

"My father was a Baptist minister."

"I mean are many of them Reds. I'd like to meet this big Jew that tried to blow over the Ford factory. What's his name—"

"Frankensteen?"

"That's the man. I guess some of you believe in it."

"Quite a few," said Brimmer dryly.

"Not you," said Stahr.

A shade of annoyance floated across Brimmer's face.

"Oh, yes," he said.

"Oh, no," said Stahr. "Maybe you did once."

Brimmer shrugged his shoulders.

"Perhaps the boot's on the other foot," he said. "At the bottom of your heart, Mr. Stahr, you know I'm right."

"No," said Stahr, "I think it's a bunch of tripe."

"—you think to yourself, 'He's right,' but you think the system will last out your time."

"You don't really think you're going to overthrow the government."

"No, Mr. Stahr. But we think perhaps you are."

They were nicking at each other—little pricking strokes like men do sometimes. Women do it, too; but it is a joined battle then with no quarter. But it is not pleasant to watch men do it, because you never know what's next. Certainly it wasn't improving the tonal associations of the room for me, and I moved them out the French window into our golden-yellow California garden.

It was midsummer, but fresh water from the gasping sprinklers made the lawn glitter like spring. I could see Brimmer look at it with a sigh in his glance—a way they have. He opened up big outside—inches taller than I thought and broad-shouldered. He reminded me a little of Superman when he takes off his spectacles. I thought he was as attractive as men can be who don't really care about women as such. We played a round robin game of ping-pong, and he handled his bat well. I heard Father come into the house singing that damn *Little Girl, You've Had a Busy Day,* and then breaking off, as if he remembered we weren't speaking any more. It was half past six—my car was standing in the drive, and I suggested we go down to the Trocadero for dinner.

Brimmer had that look that Father O'Ney had that time in New York when he turned his collar around and went with father and me to the Russian Ballet. He hadn't quite ought to be here. When Bernie, the photographer, who was waiting there for some big game or other, came up to our table, he looked trapped—Stahr made Bernie go away, and I would like to have had the picture.

Then, to my astonishment, Stahr had three cocktails, one after the other.

"Now I know you've been disappointed in love," I said.

"What makes you think that, Cecilia?"

"Cocktails."

"Oh, I never drink, Cecilia. I get dyspepsia—I've never been tight."

I counted them: "—two—*three.*"

"I didn't realize. I couldn't taste them. I thought there was something the matter."

A silly glassy look darted into his eye—then passed away.

"This is my first drink in a week," said Brimmer. "I did my drinking in the Navy."

The look was back in Stahr's eye—he winked fatuously at me and said:

"This soap-box son-of-a-bitch has been working on the Navy."

Brimmer didn't know quite how to take this. Evidently he decided to include it with the evening, for he smiled faintly, and I saw Stahr was smiling, too. I was relieved when I saw it was safely in the great American tradition, and I tried to take hold of the conversation, but Stahr seemed suddenly all right.

"Here's my typical experience," he said very succinctly and clearly to Brimmer. "The best director in Hollywood—a man I never interfere with—has some streak in him that wants to slip a pansy into every picture, or something on that order. Something offensive. He stamps it in deep like a watermark so I can't get it out. Every time he does it the Legion of Decency moves a step forward, and something has to be sacrificed out of some honest film."

"Typical organization trouble," agreed Brimmer.

"Typical," said Stahr. "It's an endless battle. So now this director tells me it's all right because he's got a Director's Guild and I can't oppress the poor. That's how you add to my troubles."

"It's a little remote from us," said Brimmer smiling. "I don't think we'd make much headway with the directors."

"The directors used to be my pals," said Stahr proudly.

It was like Edward the Seventh's boast that he had moved in the best society in Europe.

"But some of them have never forgiven me," he continued, "for bringing out stage directors when sound came in. It put them on their toes and made them learn their jobs all over, but they never did really forgive me. That time we imported a whole new hogshead full of writers, and I thought they were great fellows till they all went red."

Gary Cooper came in and sat down in a corner with a bunch of men who breathed whenever he did and looked as if they lived off him and weren't budging. A woman across the room looked around and turned out to be Carole Lombard—I was glad that Brimmer was at least getting an eyeful.

Stahr ordered a whiskey and soda and, almost immediately, another. He ate nothing but a few spoonfuls of soup and he said all the awful things about everybody being lazy so-and-so's and none of it mattered to *him* because he had lots of money—it was the kind of talk you heard whenever Father and his friends were together.

I think Stahr realized that it sounded pretty ugly outside of the proper company—maybe he had never heard how it sounded before. Anyhow he shut up and drank off a cup of black coffee. I loved him, and what he said didn't change that, but I hated Brimmer to carry off this impression. I wanted him to see Stahr as a sort of technological virtuoso, and here Stahr had been playing the wicked overseer to a point he would have called trash if he had watched it on the screen.

"I'm a production man," he said, as if to modify his previous attitude. "I like writers—I think I understand them. I don't want to kick anybody out if they do their work."

"We don't want you to," said Brimmer pleasantly. "We'd like to take you over as a going concern."

Stahr nodded grimly.

"I'd like to put you in a roomful of my partners. They've all got a dozen reasons for having Fitts run you fellows out of town."

"We appreciate your protection," said Brimmer with a certain irony. "Frankly we *do* find you difficult, Mr. Stahr—precisely because you are a paternalistic employer and your influence is very great."

Stahr was only half listening.

"I never thought," he said, "that I had more brains than a writer has. But I always thought that his brains be*longed* to me—because I knew how to use them. Like the Romans—I've heard that they never invented things but they knew what to do with them. Do you see? I don't say it's right. But it's the way I've always felt—since I was a boy."

This interested Brimmer—the first thing that had interested him for an hour.

"You know yourself very well, Mr. Stahr," he said.

I think he wanted to get away. He had been curious to see what kind of man Stahr was, and now he thought he knew. Still hoping things would be different, I rashly urged him to ride home with us, but when Stahr stopped by the bar for another drink I knew I'd made a mistake.

It was a gentle, harmless, motionless evening with a lot of Saturday cars. Stahr's hand lay along the back of the seat touching my hair. Suddenly I wished it had been about ten years ago—I would have been nine, Brimmer about eighteen and working his way through some mid-western college, and Stahr twenty-five, just having inherited the world and full of confidence and joy. We would both have looked up to Stahr so, without question. And here we were in an adult conflict, to which there was no peaceable solution, complicated now with exhaustion and drink.

We turned in at our drive, and I drove around to the garden again.

"I must go along now," said Brimmer. "I've got to meet some people."

"No, stay," said Stahr. "I never have said what I wanted. We'll play ping-pong and have another drink, and then we'll tear into each other."

Brimmer hesitated. Stahr turned on the floodlight and picked up his ping-pong bat, and I went into the house for some whiskey—I wouldn't have dared disobey him.

When I came back, they were not playing, but Stahr was batting a whole box of new balls across to Brimmer, who turned them aside. When I arrived, he quit and took the bottle and retired to a chair just out of the floodlight, watching in dark dangerous majesty. He was pale—he was so transparent that you could almost watch the alcohol mingle with the poison of his exhaustion.

"Time to relax on Saturday night," he said.

"You're not relaxing," I said.

He was carrying on a losing battle with his instinct toward schizophrenia.

"I'm going to beat up Brimmer," he announced after a moment. "I'm going to handle this thing personally."

"Can't you pay somebody to do it?" asked Brimmer.

I signalled him to keep quiet.

"I do my own dirty work," said Stahr. "I'm going to beat hell out of you and put you on a train."

He got up and came forward, and I put my arms around him, gripping him.

"Please *stop* this!" I said. "Oh, you're being so bad."

"This fellow has an influence over you," he said darkly. "Over all you young people. You don't know what you're doing."

"Please go home," I said to Brimmer.

Stahr's suit was made of slippery cloth and suddenly he slipped away from me and went for Brimmer. Brimmer retreated backward around the table. There was an odd expression in his face, and afterwards I thought it looked as if he were saying, "Is *this* all? This frail half-sick person holding up the whole thing."

Then Stahr came close, his hands going up. It seemed to me that Brimmer held him off with his left arm a minute, and then I looked away—I couldn't bear to watch.

When I looked back, Stahr was out of sight below the level of the table, and Brimmer was looking down at him.

"Please go home," I said to Brimmer.

"All right." He stood looking down at Stahr as I came around the table. "I always wanted to hit ten million dollars, but I didn't know it would be like this."

Stahr lay motionless.

"Please go," I said.

"I'm sorry. Can I help——"

"No. Please go. I understand."

He looked again, a little awed at the depths of Stahr's repose, which he had created in a split second. Then he went quickly away over the grass, and I knelt down and shook Stahr. After a moment he came awake with a terrific convulsion and bounced up on his feet.

"Where is he?" he shouted.

"Who?" I asked innocently.

"That American. Why in hell did you have to marry him, you damn fool?"

"Monroe—he's gone. I didn't marry anybody."

I pushed him down in a chair.

"He's been gone half an hour," I lied.

The ping-pong balls lay around in the grass like a constellation of stars. I turned on a sprinkler and came back with a wet handkerchief, but there was no mark on Stahr—he must have been hit in the side of the head. He went off behind some trees and was sick, and I heard him kicking up some earth over it. After that he seemed all right, but he wouldn't go into the house till I got him some mouthwash, so I took back the whiskey bottle and got a mouthwash bottle. His wretched essay at getting drunk was over. I've been out with college freshmen, but for sheer ineptitude and absence of the

Bacchic spirit it unquestionably took the cake. Every bad thing happened to him, but that was all.

We went in the house; the cook said Father and Mr. Marcus and Fleishacker were on the veranda, so we stayed in the "processed leather room." We both sat down in a couple of places and seemed to slide off, and finally I sat on a fur rug and Stahr on a footstool beside me.

"Did I hit him?" he asked.

"Oh, yes," I said. "Quite badly."

"I don't believe it." After a minute he added: "I didn't want to hurt him. I just wanted to chase him out. I guess he got scared and hit me."

If this was his interpretation of what had happened, it was all right with me.

"Do you hold it against him?"

"Oh, no," he said. "I was drunk." He looked around. "I've never been in here before—who did this room?—somebody from the studio?"

"Somebody from New York."

"Well, I'll have to get you out of here," he said in his old pleasant way. "How would you like to go out to Doug Fairbanks' ranch and spend the night?" he asked me. "I know he'd love to have you."

That's how the two weeks started that he and I went around together. It only took one of them for Louella to have us married.

The manuscript stops at this point. The following synopsis of the rest of the story has been put together from Fitzgerald's notes and outlines and from the reports of persons with whom he discussed his work:

Soon after his interview with Brimmer, Stahr makes a trip East. A wage-cut has been threatened in the studio, and Stahr has gone to talk to the stockholders—presumably with the idea of inducing them to retrench in some other way. He and Brady have long been working at cross-purposes, and the struggle between them for the control of the company is rapidly coming to a climax. We do not know about the results of this trip from the business point of view, but, whether or not on a business errand, Stahr for the first time visits Washington with the intention of seeing the city; and it is to be presumed that the author had meant to return here to the motif introduced in the first chapter with the visit of the Hollywood people to the home of Andrew Jackson and their failure to gain admittance or even to see the place clearly: the relation of the moving-picture industry to the American ideals and tradition. It is mid-summer; Washington is stifling; Stahr comes down with summer grippe and goes around the city in a daze of fever and heat. He never succeeds in becoming acquainted with it as he had hoped to.

When he recovers and gets back to Hollywood, he finds that Brady has taken advantage of his absence to put through a fifty percent pay-cut. Brady had called a meeting of writers and told them in a tearful speech that he and the other executives would take a cut themselves if the writers would consent to take one. If they would agree, it would not be necessary to reduce the salaries of the stenographers and the other low-paid employees. The writers had accepted this arrangement, but had then been double-crossed by Brady, who had proceeded to slash the stenographers just the same. Stahr is revolted by this; and he and Brady have a violent falling-out. Stahr, though opposed to the unions, believing that any enterprising office-boy can make his way to the top as he has done, is an old-fashioned paternalistic employer, who likes to feel that the people who work for him are contented, and that he and they are on friendly terms. On the other hand, he quarrels also with Wylie White, who he finds has become truculently hostile to him, in spite of the fact that Stahr was not personally responsible for the pay-cut. Stahr has been patient in the past with White's drinking and his practical jokes, and he is hurt that the writer should not feel toward him the same kind of personal loyalty—which is the only solidarity that Stahr understands in the field of business relations.

"The Reds see him now as a conservative—Wall Street as a Red."
But he finds himself driven by the logic of the situation to fall in
with the idea which has been proposed and is heartily approved
by Brady, of setting up a company union.

As for his own position in the studio, he had in Washington
already thought of quitting; but, intimately involved in the struggle,
ill, unhappy and embittered though he is, it is difficult for him to
surrender to Brady. In the meantime, he has been going around with
Cecilia. The girl in a conversation with her father about the attentions Stahr has apparently been paying her, has carelessly let Brady
know that Stahr is in love with someone else. Brady finds out about
Kathleen, whom Stahr has been seeing again, and attempts to black-
mail Stahr. Stahr in disgust with the Bradys abruptly drops Cecilia.
He on his side has known for years—having learned it by way
of his wife's trained nurse—that Brady had had a hand in the death
of the husband of a woman with whom he (Brady) had been in
love. The two men threaten one another with no really conclusive
evidence on either side.

But Brady has an instrument ready to his hand. The man whom
Kathleen has married—whose name is W. Bronson Smith—is a
technician working in the studios, who has been taking an active
part in his union. It is impossible to tell precisely how Scott Fitzgerald imagined the labor situation in Hollywood for the purposes
of his story. At the time of which he is writing, the various kinds of
technicians had already been organized in the International Alliance
of Theatrical Stage Employees; and it is obvious that he intended
to exploit the element of racketeering and gangsterism revealed in
this organization by the case of William Bioff. Brady was to go to
Kathleen's husband and play upon his jealousy of his wife. We do
not know what Fitzgerald intended that these two should try to do
to Stahr. Robinson, the cutter (see the notes on this character), was
originally to have undertaken to murder him; but it seems more
probable from the author's outline that Stahr was to be caught in
some trap which would supply Kathleen's husband with grounds
for bringing a suit against Stahr for alienation of his wife's affection.
In Fitzgerald's outline below, the theme of Chapter VIII is indicated
by the words, "The suit and the price." This is evidently partly
explained by the following note of material which Fitzgerald in-

tended to make use of, though it is impossible to tell how it was to be modified to meet the demands of the story: "One of the ———— brothers is accused by an employee of seducing his wife. Sued for alienation. They try to settle it out of court, but the man bringing suit is a labor leader and won't be bought. Neither will he divorce his wife. He considers rougher measures. His price is that ———— shall go away for a year. ————'s instinct is to stay and fight it, but the other brothers get to a doctor and pronounce death sentence on him and retire him. He tries to get the girl to go with him, but is afraid of the Mann Act. She is to follow him and they'll go abroad."

In any case, Stahr is to be saved by the intervention of the camera man, Pete Zavras, whom he has befriended at the beginning of the story, when Zavras had lost his standing with the studios.

In the meantime, Stahr is now seriously ill. He and Kathleen have been "taking breathless chances." They have succeeded in having "one last fling," which has taken place during an overpower-ing heat wave in the early part of September. But their meetings have proved unsatisfactory. The author has indicated in an early sketch that Kathleen was to "come of very humble parents"—her father was to have been the captain of a Newfoundland fishing smack; and in another place he says that Stahr has found it difficult to accept her as a permanent part of his life because she is "poor, unfortunate, and tagged with a middle-class exterior which doesn't fit in with the grandeur Stahr demands of life." It is possible that the labor conflict in which her husband has become involved was intended to alienate her and Stahr. Stahr is now being pushed into the past by Brady and by the unions alike. The split between the controllers of the movie industry, on the one hand, and the various groups of employees, on the other, is widening and leaving no place for real individualists of business like Stahr, whose successes are personal achievements and whose career has always been invested with a certain personal glamor. He has held himself directly responsible to everyone with whom he has worked; he has even wanted to beat up his enemies himself. In Hollywood he is "the last tycoon."

Stahr has not been afraid, as we have seen in the conference in Chapter III, to risk money on unpopular films which would afford him some artistic satisfaction. He has had a craftsman's interest in the pictures, and it has been natural for him to want to make them better. But he has been "lying low" since the wage-cut and has ceased to make pictures altogether. There was to have been a second series of scenes showing him at a story conference, at the rushes and on the sets, which was to have contrasted with the similar series in Chapters III and IV, and to have shown the change that has taken place in his attitude and status.

He must, however, stand up to Brady, who he knows will stop at nothing. He evidently fears Brady will murder him, for he now decides to resort to Brady's own methods and get his partner murdered. For this he apparently goes straight to the gangsters. It is not clear how the murder is to be accomplished; but in order to be away at the time, Stahr arranges a trip to New York. He sees Kathleen for the last time at the airport, and also meets Cecilia, who is going back to college on a different plane. On the plane he has a reaction of disgust against the course he has taken; he realizes that he has let himself be degraded to the same plane of brutality as Brady. He decides to call off the murder and intends to wire orders as soon as the plane descends at the next airport. But the plane has an accident and crashes before they reach the next stop. Stahr is killed, and the murder goes through. The ominous suicide of Schwartz in the opening chapter of the story is thus balanced by the death of Stahr. In the note that Schwartz had sent him, he had been trying to warn him against Brady, who had long wanted to get Stahr out of the company.

Stahr's funeral, which was to have been described in detail, is an orgy of Hollywood servility and hypocrisy. Everybody is weeping copiously or conspicuously stifling emotion with an eye on the right people. Cecilia imagines Stahr present and can hear him saying "Trash!" The old cowboy actor, Johnny Swanson, who has been mentioned at the beginning of Chapter II and for whom in his forlorn situation Cecilia has later had the idea of trying to do something at the time of her visit to her father's office, has been invited to the funeral by mistake—through the confusion of his name with someone else's,—and asked to officiate as pall-bearer along with the most intimate and important of the dead producer's friends. Johnny goes through with the ceremony, rather dazed; and then finds out, to his astonishment, that his fortunes have been gloriously restored. From this time on, he is deluged with offers of jobs.

In the meantime, a final glimpse of Fleishacker, the ambitious company lawyer, a man totally without conscience or creative brains, was to have shown him as prefiguring the immediate future of the moving-picture business. There was also to have been a passage toward the end between Fleishacker and Cecilia, in which the former, who has been to New York University and who was perhaps to have tried to marry Cecilia, was to have attempted a conversation with her on an "intellectual" plane.

Cecilia, on the rebound from Stahr, has had an affair with a man she does not love—probably Wylie White, who has been after her from the first and who represents the opposition to Stahr. As a result of the death of Stahr and the murder of her father, she now breaks down completely. She develops tuberculosis, and we were to learn for the first time at the end that she has been putting together her story in a tuberculosis sanitarium. (See the first of the fragments under *Cecilia*.)

We were to have had a final picture of Kathleen standing outside the studio. She has presumably separated from her husband as a result of the plot against Stahr. It had been one of her chief attractions for Stahr that she did not belong to the Hollywood world; and now she knows that she is never to be part of it. She is always to remain on the outside of things—a situation which also has its tragedy.

NOTES

Chapter I

The author has written at the top of his last draft of the first chapter, as given here:

Rewrite from mood. Has become stilted with rewriting. Don't look [at previous draft]. Rewrite from mood.

Page 20. Fitzgerald's first sketch for the end of the chapter perhaps conveys his idea more completely than he had succeeded in doing in this draft:

This will be based on a conversation that I had with ——— the first time I was alone with him in 1927, the day that he said a thing about railroads. As near as I can remember what he said was this:

We sat in the old commissary at ——— and he said, "Scottie, supposing there's got to be a road through a mountain—a railroad, and two or three surveyors and people come to you and you believe some of them and some of them you don't believe, but all in all, there seem to be half a dozen possible roads through those mountains, each one of which, so far as you can determine, is as good as the other. Now suppose you happen to be the top man, there's a point where you don't exercise the faculty of judgment in the ordinary way, but simply the faculty of arbitrary decision. You say, 'Well, I think we will put the road there,' and you trace it with your finger and you know in your secret heart, and no one else knows, that you have no reason for putting the road there rather than in several other different courses, but you're the only person that knows that you don't know why you're doing it and you've got to stick to that and you've got to pretend that you know and that you did it for specific reasons, even though you're utterly assailed by doubts at times as to the wisdom of your decision, because all these other possible decisions keep echoing in your ear. But when you're planning a new enterprise on a grand scale, the people under you mustn't ever know or guess that you're in any doubt, because they've all got to have something to look up to and they mustn't ever dream that you're in doubt about any decision. Those things keep occurring."

At that point, some other people came into the commissary and sat down, and the first thing I knew there was a group of four and the intimacy of the conversation was broken, but I was very much impressed by the shrewdness of what he said—something more than shrewdness—by the largeness of what he thought and how he reached it at the age of twenty-six, which he was then.

So I think that this last episode will be when Stahr goes up and sits with the pilot up in front and rides beside the pilot, and the pilot recognizes in Stahr someone who in his own field must be just as sure, just as determined, just as courageous as he himself is. Very few words are exchanged between Stahr and the pilot—in fact, it is an episode that we may see entirely through the eyes of Cecilia peeping in, of the stewardess reporting to Cecilia what she saw peeping through the cockpit, or Schwartz still trying to get to Stahr before they get to Los Angeles. It is quite possible that we may not be alone with Stahr through this entire episode down to the very end, but at the very end I want to go into that strong feeling that I had in that undeveloped note about the motor shutting off and the plane settling down to earth and the lights of Los Angeles, and for a minute there, I want to give an all-fireworks illumination of the intense passion in Stahr's soul, his love of life, his love for the great thing that he's built out here, his, perhaps not exactly, satisfaction, but his feeling certainly of coming home to an empire of his own—an empire he has made.

I want to contrast this sharply with the feeling of those who have merely gypped another person's empire away from them like the four great railroad kings of the coast . . . or the feeling that ——— would have. He's not interested in it because he owns it. He's interested in it as an artist because he has made it, and mixed up with his great feeling of triumph and happiness there must inevitably be a feeling of sadness with all acts of courage—a feeling that it is to some extent a finished thing, and doubt as to the next step as to how far he can go.

After the plane comes down, it may be best to finish the chapter with that fireworks—repeat my own fear when I landed in Los Angeles with the feeling of new worlds to conquer in 1937 transferred to Stahr, or it may be best to end with a cacophony of a rival.

Chapter II

Page 24. Fitzgerald had written Only fair *opposite the paragraph which begins,* "Robby'll take care of everything when he comes," Stahr assured Father. *This was to have been the first appearance of a character who was to play an important role, and the author wanted presumably, at this casual introduction, to give a sharper impression of him. His notes on Robinson will be found below among the preliminary sketches for the characters.*

Chapter III

This chapter had not been cut and organized to the author's complete satisfaction. It is given here as it stands in the manuscript, with only a few changes to make it self-consistent.

In the manuscript, the passage on page 46 reads as follows:

Probably the attack was planned, for Popolos, the Greek, took up the matter in a sort of double talk that reminded Prince Agge of Mike Van Dyke, except that it tried to be and succeeded in being clear instead of confusing.

The author had written a scene with which he was dissatisfied, in which the Prince had encountered Mike Van Dyke, the old gag-man; but the double talk of Mike Van Dyke was intended to figure in some other place. The passages that deal with it follow:

"Hello, Mike," said Monroe. He introduced him to the visitor: "Prince Agge, this is Mr. Van Dyke. You've laughed at his stuff many times. He's the best gag-man in pictures."

"In the world," said the saucer-eyed man gravely, "—the funniest man in the world. How are you, Prince? . . ."

Immediately the Prince found himself engaged in conversation with Mike Van Dyke. He answered politely without quite getting the gist of his words. Something about the commissary, where Mr. Van Dyke thought he had seen the Prince trying to order what sounded like "twisted fish and a cat's handlebar," though the Prince was certain he misunderstood.

He tried to explain that he had not been to the commissary, but by this time they were so far into the subject that he thought the quickest way was to admit that he had, and merely parry Mr. Van Dyke's mistaken statements as to what he had done there. Mr. Van Dyke was not so much insistent as convinced, and he seemed to talk very fast. . . .

The Prince was introduced to Mr. Spurgeon and to Mr. and Mrs. Tarleton, but he was now so involved in the conversation with Mr. Van Dyke that he heard himself stammering, "I'm glad to meet me," because he was explaining to Van Dyke that he had *not* seen Technigarbo in Gretacolor. Again he had misunderstood. Was his name Albert Edward Butch Arthur Agge David, Prince of Denmark? "That's my cousin," he almost said, his head reeling.

Stahr's voice, clear and reassuring, brought him back to reality. "That's enough, Mike.—That was 'double-talk'," he explained to Prince Agge. "It's considered funny here in the lower brackets. Do it slow, Mike."

Mike demonstrated politely.

"In an income at the gate this morning—" He pointed at Stahr. "—or did he?"

Baffled, the Dane bit again.

"What? Did he what?" Then he smiled: "I see. It is like your Gertrude Stein."

Chapter IV

Fitzgerald has the following note on the episode with the director at the beginning of this chapter:

What is missing in Ridingwood scene is passion and imagination, etc. What an extraordinary thing that it should all have been there for Ridingwood and then not there.

Chapter V

Page 97. After the words, And so he had learned tolerance, kindness, forbearance, and even affection like lessons, *the author has written for his own guidance*: (Now the idea about young and generous).

Note following the section that ends on page 98:

This may not be terse and clear enough here. Or perhaps I mean strong enough. It may be the place for the doctor's verdict. I would like to leave him on a stronger note.

Two Outlines

The following letter and outline throw some light on the course of the story and show how it developed and changed from the author's first conception of it.

A letter written by Fitzgerald, September 29, 1939, explaining his original plans for the novel to his publisher and to the editor of a magazine in which he hoped to serialize it:

The story occurs during four or five months in the year 1935. It is told by Cecilia, the daughter of a producer named Bradogue in Hollywood. Cecilia is a pretty, modern girl, neither good nor bad, tremendously human. Her father is also an important character. A shrewd man, a gentile, and a scoundrel of the lowest variety. A self-made man, he has brought up Cecilia to be a princess, sent her East to college, made of her rather a snob, though, in the course of the story, her character evolves *away from this*. That is, she was twenty when the events that she tells occurred, but she is twenty-five when she tells about the events, and of course many of them appear to her in a different light.

Cecilia is the narrator because I think I know exactly how such a person would react to my story. She is *of* the movies but not *in* them. She probably was born the day *The Birth of a Nation* was previewed and Rudolf Valentino came to her fifth birthday party. So she is, all at once, intelligent, cynical, but understanding and kindly toward the people, great or small, who are of Hollywood.

She focuses our attention upon two principal characters—Milton Stahr and Thalia, the girl he loves.

In the beginning of the book I want to pour out my whole impression of this man Stahr as he is seen during an airplane trip from New York to the coast—of course, through Cecilia's eyes. She has been hopelessly in love with him for a long time. She is never going to win anything more from him than an affectionate regard, even that tainted by his dislike of her father.

Stahr is overworked and deathly tired, ruling with a radiance that is almost moribund in its phosphorescence. He has been warned that his health is undermined, but, being afraid of nothing, the warning is unheeded. He has had everything in life except the privilege of giving himself unselfishly to another human being. This he finds on the night of a semi-serious earthquake (like in 1935) a few days after the opening of the story.

It has been a very full day even for Stahr—the burst water mains, which cover the whole ground space of the lot to the depth of several feet, seem to release something in him. Called over to the outer lot to supervise the salvation of the electrical plant (for he has a finger in every pie of the vast bakery), he finds two women stranded on the roof of a property farmhouse and goes to their rescue.

Thalia Taylor is a twenty-six-year-old widow, and my present conception of her should make her the most glamorous and sympathetic of my heroines. Glamorous in a new way, because I am in secret agreement with the public in detesting the type of feminine arrogance that has been pushed into prominence in the case of ——, etc. People simply do not sympathize deeply with those who have had *all* the breaks, and I am going to dower this girl, like Rosalba in Thackeray's *Rose and the Ring,* with "a little misfortune." She and the woman with her (to whom she is serving as companion) have come secretly on the lot through the other woman's curiosity. They have been caught there when the catastrophe occurred.

Now we have a love affair between Stahr and Thalia, an immediate, dynamic, unusual, physical love affair—and I will write it so that you can publish it. At the same time I will send you a copy of how it will appear in book form somewhat stronger in tone.

This love affair is the meat of the book—though I am going to treat it, remember, as it comes through to Cecilia. That is to say by making Cecilia, at the moment of her telling the story, an intelligent and observant woman, I shall grant myself the privilege, as Conrad did, of letting her imagine the actions of the characters. Thus, I hope to get the verisimilitude of a first person narrative, combined with a Godlike knowledge of all events that happen to my characters.

Two events beside the love affair bulk large in the intermediary chapters. There is a definite plot on the part of Bradogue, Cecilia's father, to get Stahr out of the company. He has even actually and factually considered having him murdered. Bradogue is the monopolist at his worst—Stahr, in spite of the inevitable conservatism of the self-made man, is a paternalistic employer. Success came to him young, at twenty-three, and left certain idealisms of his youth unscarred. Moreover, he is a worker. Figuratively he takes off his coat and pitches in, while Bradogue is not interested in the making of pictures save as it will benefit his bank account.

The second incident is how young Cecilia herself, in her desperate love for Stahr, throws herself at his head. In her reaction at his indifference, she gives herself to a man whom she does not love. This episode is *not* absolutely necessary to the serial. It could be tempered, but it might be best to eliminate it altogether.

Back to the main theme: Stahr cannot bring himself to marry Thalia. It simply doesn't seem part of his life. He doesn't realize that she has become necessary to him. Previously his name has been associated with this or that well-known actress or society personality, and Thalia is poor, unfortunate, and tagged with a middle-class exterior which doesn't fit in with the grandeur Stahr demands of life. When she realizes this she leaves him temporarily, leaves him not because he has no legal intentions toward her but because of the hurt of it, the remainder of a vanity from which she had considered herself free.

Stahr is now plunged directly into the fight to keep control of the company. His health breaks down very suddenly while he is on a trip to New York to see the stockholders. He almost dies in New York and comes back to find that Bradogue has seized upon his absence to take steps which Stahr considers unthinkable. He plunges back into work again to straighten things out.

Now, realizing how much he needs Thalia, things are patched up between them. For a day or two they are ideally happy. They are going to marry, but he must make one more trip East to clinch the victory which he has conciliated in the affairs of the company.

Now occurs the final episode which should give the novel its quality—and its unusualness. Do you remember about 1933 when a transport plane was wrecked on a mountain-side in the Southwest, and a Senator was killed? The thing that struck me about it was that the country people rifled the bodies of the dead. That is just what happens to this plane which is bearing Stahr from Hollywood. The angle is that of three children who, on a Sunday picnic, are the first to discover the wreckage. Among those killed in the accident besides Stahr are two other characters we have met. (I have not been able to go into the minor characters in this short summary.) Of the three children, two boys and a girl, who find the bodies, one boy rifles Stahr's possessions; another, the body of a ruined ex-producer; and the girl, those of a moving picture actress. The possessions which the children find, symbolically determine their attitude toward their act of theft. The possessions of the moving picture actress tend the young girl to a selfish possessiveness; those of the unsuccessful producer sway one of the boys toward an irresolute attitude; while the boy who finds Stahr's briefcase is the one who, after a week, saves and redeems all three by going to a local judge and making full confession.

The story swings once more back to Hollywood for its finale. During the story *Thalia has never once been inside a studio.* After Stahr's death as she stands in front of the great plant which he created, she realizes now that she never will. She knows only that he loved her and that he was a great man and that he died for what he believed in. . . .

There's nothing that worries me in the novel, nothing that seems uncertain. Unlike *Tender is the Night,* it is not the story of deterioration—it is not depressing and not morbid in spite of the tragic ending. If one book could ever be "like" another, I should say it is more "like" *The Great Gatsby* than any other of my books. But I hope it will be entirely different—I hope it will be something new, arouse new emotions, perhaps even a new way of looking at certain phenomena. I have set it safely in a period of five years ago to obtain detachment, but now that Europe is tumbling about our ears this also seems to be for the best. It is an escape into a lavish, romantic past that perhaps will not come again into our time.

THIS DIAGRAM IS THE LAST OUTLINE MADE BY THE AUTHOR

EPISODES			Chapter	Act
A	June 28th		Chapter (A) Introduce Cecilia, Stahr, White, Schwartz.	Act I June (The Plane) 6,000
	1. The plane. 2. Nashville. 3. Up forward. Different.	6000		STAHR
B	July 28th		Chapter (B) Introduces Brady, Kathleen, Robinson and secretaries. Atmosphere of night—sustain.	Act II July—early August (The Circus) 21,000
	4. Johnny Swanson—Marcus leaving—Brady. 5. The earthquake. 6. The back lot.	3000		
C	July 29th		Chapters (C & D) are equal to guest list and Gatsby's party. Throw everything into this, with selection. They must have a plot, though, leading to 13.	
	7. The camera man. Stahr's work and health. From something she wrote. 8. First conference. 9. Second conference and afterwards. 10. Commissary and idealism about non-profit pictures. Rushes. Phone call, etc.	5000		STAHR and KATHLEEN
D				
	11. Visit to rushes. 12. Second meeting that night. Wrong girl—glimpse.	2500		
E	August 6th		Chapter (E) Three episodes. Atmosphere in 15 most important. Hint of Waste Land of the house too late.	
	13. Cecilia and Stahr and ball. 14. Malibu seduction. Try to get on lot. Dead middle. 15. Cecilia and father. 16. Phone call and wedding.	6000		

142

F	17. The dam breaks with Brimmer. 18. The cummerbund—market—(The theatre with Benchley). 19. The four meet. Renewal. Palomar. 20. Wylie White in office.	August 10th August 20th 5000	Chapter (F) This belongs to the women. It introduces Smith (for the first time?)	Act III August—early Sept. (The Underworld) 11,500
G	21. Sick in Washington. To quit? 22. Brady and Stahr—double blackmail. Quarrel with Wylie. 23. Throws over Cecilia, who tells her father. Stops making pictures. A story conference—rushes and sets. Lies low after cut. 24. Last fling with Kathleen. Old stars in heat wave at Encino.	August 28th—Sept. 14th 6500	Chapter (G) The blow falls on Stahr. Sense of heat all through, culminating in 25.	THE STRUGGLE
H	25. Brady gets to Smith. Fleishacker and Cecilia. 26. Stahr hears plan. Camera man O.K. Stops it—very sick. 27. Resolve problem. Kathleen at airport; Cecilia to college.	Sept. 15th–30th 7000	Chapter (H) The suit and the price.	Act IV (The Murderers) DEFEAT 7,000
I	28. The plane falls. Foretaste of the future in Fleishacker. 29. Outside the studio. 30. Johnny Swanson at funeral.	Sept. 30th–Oct. 4500	Chapter (I) Stahr's death.	Act V (The End) October EPILOGUE 4,500
				51,000

CECILIA

*The first of the following fragments was originally written to
stand as an introduction to the story; but Fitzgerald decided to discard it because he was afraid it would make the opening too depressing. The picture of Cecilia in the tuberculosis sanitarium was,
however, to appear at the end of the book.*

We two men were fascinated by that young face. A few months
ago, we had made a short trip to the canyons of the Colorado as if
for a last gape at life; now back at the hospital this girl's face in the
sunset, and with the fever, seemed to share some of the primordial
rose tints of that "natural wonder."

"Go on tell us," we said. "We don't know about such things"
She started to cough, changed her mind—as one can.

"I don't mind telling *you*. But why should our friends, the
asthmas, have to hear?"

"They're going," we assured her.

We three waited, our heads leant back on our chairs, while a
nurse marshalled a flustered little group that must have heard the
remark—and edged them toward the sanitarium. The nurse cast a
reproachful glance back at Cecilia as if she wanted to return and slap
her—but the glance changed its mind and the nurse hurried in after
her flock.

"They're gone. Now tell us."

Cecilia stared up at the brilliant Arizona sky. She regarded it—
the blue air, which to us had once stood for hope in the morning
—not with regret but rather with the cocksure confusion of those the
depression caught in mid-adolescence. Now she was twenty-five.

"Anything you want to know," she promised. "I don't owe *them*
any loyalty. Oh, they fly over and see me sometimes, but what do I
care—I'm ruined."

"We're all ruined," I said mildly.

She sat up, the Aztec figures of her dress emerging from the
Navajo pattern of her blanket. The dress was thin—gone native for
the sun country—and I remembered the round shining knobs of
another girl's shoulders at another time and place, but here we must
all stay in the shadow.

"You shouldn't talk like that," she assured me. "I'm ruined, but you're just two good guys who happened to get a bug."

"You don't grant us any history," we objected with senescent irony. "Nobody over forty is allowed a history."

"I didn't mean that. I mean you'll get *well*."

"In case we don't, tell us the story. You still hear this stuff about him. What was he: Christ in Industry? I know boys who worked on the Coast and hated his guts. Were you crazy about him? Loosen up, Cecilia. Something for a jaded palate! Think of the hospital dinner we'll face in half an hour."

Cecilia's glance suspected, then rejected our existence—not our right to live, but our right to any important feeling of loss or passion or hope or high excitement. She started to talk, waited for a tickle to subside in her throat.

"He never looked at me," she said indignantly, "and I won't talk about him when you're in this mood."

She threw off the blanket and stood up, her center-parted hair falling from her wan temples, ripples from a brown dam. She was high-breasted and emaciated, still perfectly the young woman of her time. Superiority was implicit in her heel taps as she walked through the open door into the corridor of the building—our only road to wonderland. Apparently Cecilia believed in nothing at present, but it seemed she had once known another road, passed by it a long time ago.

We were sure, nevertheless, that some time she would tell us about it—and so she did. What follows is our imperfect version of her story.

———

This is Cecilia taking up the story. I should probably explain why I spent so much of the summer hanging around the studio. Well, for one thing, I was too big to keep out now and I knew how to do it without bothering people. Secondly, I had had a difference with Wylie White about who had the say about my body, so there was a man named X whom I didn't intend to marry who was playing the man who *al*most got the girl in three pictures at once and had to be on the lot. And thirdly, most important, I had nothing else to do. (Fourth, with description of Hollywood boys.)

———

[*Cecilia and Kathleen*]

She wore a little summer number from Saks, about $18.98, and a pink and blue hat that had been stepped on on one side. Her nails were pale pink, almost natural, and her hair you couldn't be absolutely sure of. She was polite and rather overwhelmed. X spent some time trying to convey who I was, but kept bumping against the flat fact that Kathleen Moore had never heard of my father.

"I've been looking for a job," she said.

"What kind of a job?"

"I've been going through the advertisements. What is a swami?"

X explained—it was very interesting.

"He was the most encouraging," Kathleen said. "But I'm afraid it wouldn't do—that filthy towel about his head."

Father used to have great scraps with the Jews over Jewish and Irish tricks. The Jews claimed he always oversold his points. Father thought he was just right. For instance, [his] weeping trick.

STAHR

Stahr's day would begin often enough right in the studio. Since his wife's death, he frequently slept there; his suite contained a bath and dressing-room, and his divan made a bed. With the immense distances of Los Angeles County—three hours a day in an automobile is not exceptional—this was a great saving of time.

Never wanted his name on pictures—"I don't want my name on the screen because credit is something that should be given to others. If you are in a position to give credit to yourself, then you do not need it."

I want to tell also of his great failing of surrounding himself with men who were very far below him. However, this may have been because of a sureness about his health, because he felt in his 20's that he himself was able to keep a direct eye on everything, and, therefore, would have been hindered rather than helped by men who were positive-minded supervisors. His relation with directors, his importance in that he brought interference with their work to a minimum, and while he made enemies—and this is important—up to his arrival the director had been King Pin in pictures since Griffith made *The Birth of a Nation*. Now, therefore, some of the directors resented the fact that he reduced their position from one of complete king to being simply one element in a combine. His interest in the lot itself is important, his utter democracy, his popularity with the rank and file of the studio.

However, this is not really thinking out Stahr from the beginning. I must go back into his childhood and remember that remark of his mother: "We always knew that Monroe would be all right." . . . Remember also that he was a fighter even though he was a small man—certainly not more than 5′6½″, weighing very little (which is one reason he always liked to see people sitting down), and remember when the man tried to get fresh with his wife at Venice how he lost his temper and got into a fight. . . . He must have been a scrapper from early boyhood, probably a neighborhood scrapper. Remember also how popular he was with men from the beginning in a free and easy way, that is to say, as a man that liked to sit around with his feet up and smoke and "be one of the boys." He was essentially more of a man's man than a ladies' man.

There was never anything priggish or superior in his casual conversation that makes men uneasy in the company of other men. He used to run sometimes with a rather fast crowd of directors— many of them heavy drinkers, though he wasn't one himself. And they accepted him as one of themselves in a "hale fellow, well met" spirit—that is: in spite of the growing austerity which overwork forced on him in later years, Stahr never had any touch of the prig or the siss about him, and I think this was real and not an overlay. To that extent he was Napoleonic and actually liked combat—which leads me back to the supposition that probably he was a scrapper as a boy and had always been that way. If, after he came into full power, he sometimes resorted to subterfuge to have his way, that was the result of his position rather than anything in his nature. I think, by nature, he was very direct, frank, challenging. Try to analyze what his probable boyhood was from the above.

This chapter must not develop into merely a piece of character analysis. Each statement that I make about him must contain at the end of every few hundred words some pointed anecdote or story to keep it alive. I do not want it to have the ring of an analysis. I **want it to have** as much drama throughout as the story of old **Laemmle himself** on the telephone.

———

Stahr knew he had a working knowledge of technics, but because he had been head man for so long and so many apprentices had grown up during his sway, more knowledge was attributed to him than he possessed. He accepted this as the easiest way and was an adept though cautious bluffer. In the dubbing-room, which was for sound what the cutting-room was for sight, he worked by ear alone and was often lost amid the chorus of ever newer terms and slang. So on the stops. He watched the new processes of faking animated backgrounds, moving pictures taken against the background of other moving pictures, with a secret child's approval. He could have understood easily enough—often he preferred not to, to preserve a sensual acceptance when he saw the scene unfold in the rushes. There were smart young men about—Reinmund was one—who phrased their remarks to convey the impression that they understood everything about pictures. Not Stahr. When he interfered, it was always from his own point of view, not from theirs. Thus his function was different from that of Griffith in the early days, who had been all things to every finished frame of film.

———

It is doubtful if any of these head men read through a single work of the imagination in a year. And Stahr, who had no time whatever to read and must depend on synopses, began to doubt that any of his supervisors read more than what was ordered; he doubted that his casting people (note for a character here) covered the range he would have wanted them to. A show played a year and a half in San Francisco—the specialty in it was discovered only after it reached Los Angeles, where young teats drew a tired sabled audience, and the specialty was in a boom market within a week. And had to be paid for against important budgets where alertness would have bought it for nothing.

———

In order to forgive Stahr for what he did that afternoon, it should
be remembered that he came out of the old Hollywood that was
rough and tough and where the wildest bluffs hold. He had manu-
factured gloss and polish and control of the new Hollywood, but
occasionally he liked to tear it apart just to see if it was there.

But now as he stood there and the orchestra began to play and
the dancers stood up, a sentence spoke in his mind that surprised
him: "I am bored beyond measure," it said.

Even the words did not sound like him. "Beyond measure" was
theatrical, he wondered if he had read it recently. He did not go out
often enough to be bored or to think of it like that. He knew how
to elude bores, and he had grown to accept deference and admiration as something to wear with humility and grace; and he almost
always had a good time.

Some men came up to him, and he talked to them with his hands
in his pockets. One was an agent who hated him and always referred
to him, so Stahr was told, as "The Vine Street Jesus," "The Walking
Oscar," or "The Back-to-Use Napoleon."

At some point after censorship, Monroe revolts against childish-
ness.

Show Stahr hiding in retreat or avoiding people without hurting
them.

Like many men, he did not like flowers except a few weedy ones
—they were too highly evolved and self-conscious. But he liked leaves
and peeled twigs, horse chestnuts and even acorns, unripe, ripe and
wormy fruit.

Stahr is miserable and embittered toward the end.

Before death, thoughts from *Crack-Up*.
Do I look like death? (in mirror at 6 P.M.)

Men who have been endowed with unusual powers for work or analysis or ingredients that go to make big personal successes, seem to forget as soon as they are rich that such abilities are not evenly distributed among the men of their kind. So when the suggestion of a Union springs out of this act of Bradogue's [Brady's], Stahr seems to reverse his form, join the other side and almost to ally himself with Bradogue. Note also in the epilogue that I want to show that Stahr left certain harm behind him just as he left good behind him. That some of his reactionary creations such as the Screen Playwrights existed long after his death just as so much of his valuable creative work survived him. However, remember this is to play a small part in this chapter and must be written epigrammatically, cleverly and perhaps placed in the mouth of one whom we may see leaving Hollywood in this chapter [the final departure of Stahr in the plane]. In any case, it must not be allowed to interfere with the mood of this short chapter, which would, whether treated in a close-up or remotely, belong to Thalia [Kathleen] and leave Thalia to linger in the reader's mind.

KATHLEEN

The realization came to her that the tracks of life would never lead anywhere and were like tracks of the airplane; that no one knew of their place, since there was no Daniel Boone to hack trees; that the world had to go on and that it wasn't going to be inside her and there still had to be those tracks. It was an awful lonesome journey.

———

She thought of electric fans in little restaurants with lobsters on ice in the windows, and of pearly signs glittering and revolving against the obscure, urban sky, the hot, dark sky. And pervading everything, a terribly strange, brooding mystery of roof tops and empty apartments, of white dresses in the paths of parks, and fingers for stars and faces instead of moons, and people with strange people scarcely knowing one another's names.

———

Bright unused beauty still plagued her in the mirror.

———

[Kathleen and her husband?]

He found her in the cabin, just standing, thinking. He was afraid of her when she thought, knowing that in the part of her most removed from him, there was taking place a tireless ratiocination, the synthesis of which has always a calm sense of the injustice and unsatisfactions of life. He knew the [?] with which her mind worked, but he was always surprised that it brought forth in the end protests that were purely abstract, and in which he figured only as an element as driven and succorless as herself. This made him more afraid than if she said, "It was your fault," as she frequently did—for by it she seemed to lift the situation and its interpretation out of his grasp. In that region his mind was more feminine than hers—he felt light, and off his balance—and a little like the Dickens character who accused his wife of praying against him.

STAHR AND KATHLEEN

Object: I wanted a seduction—very Californian, yet new—very Hollywood, say. If he has no illusion, he has at least great pity and excitement, friendliness, stimulus, fascination.

Where will the warmth come from in this? Why does he think she's warm? Warmer than the voice in *Farewell to Arms*. My girls were all so warm and full of promise. What can I do to make it honest and different?

The sea at night. Como. St.-Pol (used in *Tender*). Why are French romances cold and sad *au fond?*—why was Wells warm?

———

General Mood. Shaken by the flare-up, they go back, she still thinking she can withdraw. She could not bear to think. It was tonight. It is a murky, rainy dusk, a dreary day (change former time to sunset). They left the hotel a little more than three hours ago, but it seemed a long time. Get them there quickly. Odd effect of the place like a set. The mood should be two people—free. He has an overwhelming urge toward the girl, who promises to give life back to him—though he has no idea yet of marriage—she is the heart of hope and freshness. *He seduces her because she is slipping away—* she lets herself be seduced because of overwhelming admiration (the phone call). Once settled, it is sensual, breathless, immediate, then gentle and tender for awhile.

———

She was very ready and it was right. It would have been good any time, but for the first time it was much more than he had hoped or expected. Not like very young people, but wise and fond and chokingly sweet, as it had been with Minna when sometimes they had gone for many days. He was away for a hundred miles for a visit to himself, but he did not let her see.

———

This girl had a life—it was very seldom he met anyone whose life did not depend in some way on him or hope to depend on him.

ROBINSON

These passages about Robinson all relate to an earlier plan for the story. The author had discarded his original idea of having Kathleen have a love affair with Robinson, but the latter was perhaps still to figure as the agent selected by Brady to put Stahr out of the way. Kathleen is here called Thalia.

I would like this episode to give a picture of the work of a cutter, camera man or second unit director in the making of such a thing as *Winter Carnival,* accenting the speed with which Robinson works, his reactions, why he is what he is instead of being the very high-salaried man which his technical abilities entitle him to be. I might as well use some of the Dartmouth atmosphere, snow, etc., being careful not to impinge at all on any material that Walter Wanger may be using in *Winter Carnival* or that I may have ever suggested as material to him.

I could begin the chapter through Cecilia's eyes, who is a guest at the carnival, skip quickly to Robinson and have them perhaps meet at a telegraph desk where she sees him sending a wire to Thalia. But by this time and through the material I choose—photographing backgrounds for the snow picture—I should not only develop the character of Robinson as he is, but leave a loophole showing the possibility of his being later corrupted. In a very short transition or montage, I bring the whole party West on the Chief. Cecilia, perhaps with friends of her own, coaxes the producer who has been in charge (ineffectual producer) and Robinson.

The man chosen tentatively to put Stahr out of the way is Robinson the cutter. Must develop Robinson character so that this is possible—that is, Robinson now has three aspects. His top possibility as a sort of Sergeant————character as planned. His relation with the world, which is conventional and rather stereotyped and trite; and this new element, in which it would be possible for him to be so corrupted by circumstances as to be drawn into such a matter and used by Bradogue. To do this it is practically necessary that there must be from the beginning some flaw in Robinson in spite of his courage, his resourcefulness, his technical expertness and the Sergeant ————virtues I intend to give him. Some secret flaw—perhaps something sexual. It might be possible, but if I do that, then he could have had no relation with Thalia, who certainly would not have accepted a bad lover. Perhaps he would have some flaw, not sexual—not unmanly—in any case have no special idea at present, and this must be invented. In any case, his having loved Thalia would make him a very natural tool for Bradogue to use in playing on his natural jealousy of Stahr.

————————

[Thalia] has been having an affair intermittently, of which she is half ashamed, with the character whom I have called Robinson, the cutter, who is in his (and this is very important) professional life an extraordinarily interesting and subtle character on the idea of Sergeant————in the army or that cutter at United Artists whom I so admired or any other person of the type of trouble shooter or film technician—and I want to contrast this sharply with his utter conventionality and acceptance of banalities in the face of what might be called the cultural urban world. Women can twist him around their little finger. He might be able to unravel the most twisted skein of wires in a blinding snowstorm on top of a sixty-foot telephone pole in the dark with no more tools than an imperfect pair of pliers made out of the nails of his boots, but faced with the situation which the most ignorant and useless person would handle with urbanity he would seem helpless and gawky—so much so as to give the impression of being a Babbitt or of being a stupid, gawky, inept fellow.

This contrast at some point in the story is recognized by Stahr, who must at all points, when possible, be pointed up as a man who sees below the surface into reality.

Her attitude towards this man has been that even in the niceties of love-making she has had to be his master, and his deep gratitude to her is allied to his love for her, though throughout the story he always feels that she is inevitably the superior person. Stahr at some point points it out to her that this is nonsense and I want to show here something different in men's and women's points of view: particularly that women are prone to cling to an advantage or rather have less human generosity in points of character than men have, or do I mean a less wide point of view?

————

Stahr nodded and walked along at the head of his gang. Robinson, who was almost beside him, but a little behind, was a hard-jawed technician—supposed to be the best cutter in Hollywood. I didn't come in contact with that class, but I know Robinson was such a good cutter that often he had been asked to direct a picture. He had tried once, back in the silent days, and it was a failure. Never, never would a man like Jack Robinson want to steer a venture, if I know what I'm talking about. From the time he was called from his job on top of telephone posts in Michigan thunderstorms to the intricate task of trying, as a sergeant, to establish tangible liaison with the artillery in his infantry division. At that point when he found that an uneducated trouble-shooter was worth a dozen hit-or-miss shave-tails, called "signal officers," he had lost faith in his superiors and never afterward wanted to be anything except a liaison between what was commanded from above and what could be done below.

There was something warm about him that Stahr liked. Often he would edge up to Stahr, sensing the truth or falsity in some story—but in practice his advice faded to, "Oh, what the hell—what do these ————s know? All right. Go on. Where do we run these wires? *Sure,* it's a great idea."

CRASH OF THE PLANE

Fitzgerald had sketched in some detail the episode of the children finding the fallen plane, which is mentioned in the letter to his publisher. He had at one point decided to discard this, as he thought that the account of Stahr's funeral would make a better epilogue; but a note evidently written at a later time shows that he was still considering it.

It is important that I begin this chapter with a delicate transition, because I am not going to describe the fall of the plane, but simply give a last picture of Stahr as the plane takes off, and describe very briefly in the airport the people who are on board. The plane, therefore, has left for New York, and when the reader turns to Chapter X, I must be sure that he isn't confused by the sudden change of scene and situation. Here I can make the best transition by an opening paragraph in which I tell the reader that Cecilia's story ends here and that what is now told was a situation discovered by the writer himself and pieced together from what he learned in a small town in Oklahoma, from a municipal judge. That the incidents occurred one month after the plane fell and plunged Stahr and all its occupants into a white darkness. Tell how the snow hid the wreck and that in spite of searching parties the plane was considered lost, and then will resume the narrative—that a curtain first went up during an early thaw the following March. (I have to go over all the chapters and get the time element to shape up so that Stahr's second trip to New York, the one on which he is killed, takes place when the first snow has fallen on the Rockies. I want this plane to be like that plane that was lost for fully two months before they found the plane and the survivors.) Consider carefully whether if possible by some technical trick it might not be advisable to conceal from the reader that the plane fell until the moment when the children find it. The problem is that the reader must not turn to Chapter X and be confused, but, on the other hand, the dramatic effect, even if the reader felt lost for a few minutes, might be more effective if he did not find at the beginning of the chapter that the plane fell. In fact, almost certainly that is the way to handle it, and I must find a method of handling it in that fashion. There must be an intervening paragraph to begin Chapter X which will reassure the reader that he is following the same story, but it can be evasive and confine itself to leading the reader astray thinking that the paragraph is merely to explain that Cecilia is not telling this next part of the story without telling the reader that the plane ran into a mountain top and disappeared from human knowledge for several months.

When I have given the reader some sense of the transition and prepared him for a change in scene and situation, break the narrative with a space or so and begin the following story. That a group of children are starting off on a hike. That there is an early spring thaw in this mountain state. Pick out of the group of children, three whom we will call Jim, Frances, and Dan. That atmosphere is that particular atmosphere of Oklahoma when the long winter breaks. The atmosphere must be an all-cold climate where the winter breaks very suddenly with almost a violence—the snow seems to part as if very unwillingly in great convulsive movements like the break-up of an ice floe. There's a bright sun. The three children get separated from the teacher or scoutmaster or whoever is in charge of the expedition, and the girl, Frances, comes upon a part of the engine and fly-wheel of a broken airplane. She has no idea what it is. She is rather puzzled by it and at the moment is engaged rather in a flirtation with both Jim and Dan. However, she is an intelligent child of thirteen or fourteen and while she doesn't identify it as part of an airplane, she knows it is an odd piece of machinery to be found in the mountains. First she thinks it is the remains of some particular mining machinery. She calls Dan and then Jim, and they forget whatever small juvenile intrigue they were embarking on in their discovery of other debris from the fall of the plane. Their first general instinct is to call the other members of the party, because Jim, who is the smartest of the children (both the boys' ages about fifteen), recognizes that it is a fallen plane—though he doesn't connect it with the plane that disappeared the previous November—when Frances comes upon a purse and an open travelling case which belonged to the actress. It contains the things that to her represent undreamt of luxuries. In it there's a jewel box. It has been unharmed—it has fallen through the branches of a tree. There are flasks of perfume that would never appear in the town where she lives, perhaps a negligee or anything

I can think of that an actress might be carrying which was absolutely the last word in film elegance. She is utterly fascinated.

Simultaneously Jim has found Stahr's briefcase—a briefcase is what he has always wanted, and Stahr's briefcase is an excellent piece of leather—and some other travelling appurtenances of Stahr's. Things that are notably possessions of wealthy men. I have no special ideas at present, but think what a very wealthy, well-equipped man might be liable to have with him on such an expedition and then Dan makes the suggestion of "Why do we have to tell about this? We can all come up here later, and there is probably a lot more of this stuff here, and there's probably money and everything—these people are dead, they will never need it again—then we can say about the plane or let other people find it. Nobody will know we have been up here."

Dan bears, in some form of speech, a faint resemblance to Bradogue. This must be subtly done and not look too much like a parable or moral lesson, still the impression must be conveyed, but be careful to convey it once and not rub it in. If the reader misses it, let it go—don't repeat. Show Frances as malleable and amoral in the situation, but show a definite doubt on Jim's part, even from the first, as to whether this is fair dealing even towards the dead. Close this episode with the children rejoining the party.

Several weeks later the children have now made several trips to the mountain and have rifled the place of everything that is of any value. Dan is especially proud of his find, which includes some rather disreputable possessions of Ronciman. Frances is worried and definitely afraid and tending to side with Jim, who is now in an absolutely wretched mood about the whole affair. He knows that searching parties have been on a neighboring mountain—that the plane has been traced and that with the full flowering of spring the secret will come out and that each trip up he feels that the danger is more and more. However, let that be Frances' feeling, because Jim has, by this time, read the contents of Stahr's briefcase and late at night, taking it from the woodshed where he has concealed it, has gotten an admiration for the man. Naturally, by the time of this episode all three children are aware of what plane it was and who was in it and whose possessions they have.

One day also they have found the bodies, though I do not want to go into this scene in any gruesome manner, of the six or seven victims still half concealed by the snow. In any case, something in one of Stahr's letters that Jim reads late at night decides him to go to Judge ——— and tell the whole story, which he does against the threats of Dan, who is bigger than he is and could lick him physically. We leave the children there with the idea that they are in good hands, that they are not going to be punished, that they have made full restoration, and the fact that, after all, they could plead in court that they did not know anything more about the situation than "finders keepers." There will be no punishment of any kind for any of the three children. Give the impression that Jim is all right—that Frances is faintly corrupted and may possibly go off in a year or so in search of adventure and may turn into anything from a gold digger to a prostitute, and that Dan has been completely corrupted and will spend the rest of his life looking for a chance to get something for nothing.

I cannot be too careful not to rub this in or give it the substance or feeling of a moral tale. I should [show] very pointedly that Jim is all right and end perhaps with Frances and let the readers hope that Frances is going to be all right and then take that hope away by showing the last glimpse of Frances with that lingering conviction that luxury is over the next valley, therefore giving a bitter and acrid finish to the incident to take away any possible sentimental and moral stuff that may have crept into it. Certainly end the incident with Frances.

———

Effect on children idea persists. Plane might fall in suburb of Los Angeles. He thinks it was hills, but it's right there—a desolation he helped to create.

HOLLYWOOD, ETC.

It is impossible to tell you anything of Stahr's day except at the risk of being dull. People in the East pretend to be interested in how pictures are made, but if you actually tell them anything, you find they are only interested in Colbert's clothes or Gable's private life. They never see the ventriloquist for the doll. Even the intellectuals, who ought to know better, like to hear about the pretensions, extravagances and vulgarities—tell them pictures have a private grammar, like politics or automobile production or society, and watch the blank look come into their faces.

I could try, for instance, to make you understand what Stahr meant by his peculiar use of the word "nice," something like what Saint-Simon meant by *la politesse,* and you would classify what I had said as a lecture on taste.

The Warner Brothers narrative writing and the Metro dramatic, packed—cut back and forth writing from Stahr.

[*Stahr and Prince Agge*]

"Come on: we'll go get some lunch." Casually he added: "Broaca is the best man in Hollywood except Lubitsch and Vidor. But he's getting old and it makes him cross. He doesn't see that a director isn't everything in pictures now. That comes from the days when they shot off the cuff."

"The cuff?"

They started out the door. Stahr laughed.

"The director was supposed to have the plot on his cuff. There wasn't any script. Writers were all called gag-men—usually reporters and all souses. They stood behind the director and made suggestions, and if he liked it and it fitted with what was on his cuff, he staged it and took his footage."

The situation on the big lot was that every producer, director and scenarist there could adduce proof that he was a money-maker. With the initial distrust of the industry by business, with the weeding out of better men from the needs of speed, with the emphasis as in a mining camp on the lower virtues; then with the growing complication of technique and the elusiveness it created—it could fairly be said of all and by all of those who remained that they had made money—despite the fact that not a third of the producers or one-twentieth of the writers could have earned their living in the East. There was not one of these men, no matter how low-grade or ıncompetent a fellow, who could not claim to have participated largely in success. This made difficulty in dealing with them.

Remember my summing-up in *Crazy Sunday*—don't give the impression that these are bad people.

Actress—introduced so slowly, so close, so real that you believe in her. Somehow she's first sitting next to you, not an actress but with all the qualifications, loud and dissonant in your ear. Then she *is* one, but don't let it drift away in detailed description of her career. Keep her close. Never ıust use her name. Always begin with a mannerism.

The Beard. Monty Woolley's beard. 50 peddle the muff. Family supported by beard. It hasn't worked for seven weeks. It was wonderful in *Hurricane*. It got a poor deal Wednesday. For a gag going to cut it off—work I lose. How much prestige, *amour propre*. Damage to ego. $30,000. Fake beard cut off.

Tillie Losch worried about what "exotic" meant.

He was so new as a scenarist that when the agent came ın, he thought he wanted him to write something for the paper. [This refers to the habit of the Hollywood trade papers of shaking down new-comers for ads under threat of giving them bad publicity or none.]

Man [from Hollywood trade paper] advising me not to read the book.

Character of X, *poor* producer.
—— saying afterwards that he died with silent pictures.
We need a new formula.

The cleverly expressed opposite of any generally accepted idea is worth a fortune to somebody.

Joke about "Shoot it both ways."

"We could tap out something," she said—as a colored maid says, "I'll rinse out your stockings," to minimize the work.

Great masses of wires on floor—can hear everyone through dictophone.

Her ash-blond hair seemed weather-proof save for a tiny curtain of a bang that was evidently permitted, even expected, to stir a little in a mild wind. She had an unmistakable aura about her person of being carefully planned. Under minute scallops that were scarcely brows, her eyes, etc. Her teeth were so white against the tan, her lips so red, that in combination with the blue of her eyes, the effect was momentarily startling—as startling as if the lips had been green and the pupils white.

She feared the black cone hanging from the metal arm, shrilling and shrilling across the sunny room. It stopped for a minute, replaced by her heartbeats; then began again.

Hollywood child. The little hard face of a successful street-walker on a jumping-jack's body, the clear cultured whine of the voice.

Most of us could be photographed from the day of our birth to the day of our death and the film shown, without producing any emotion except boredom and disgust. It would all just look like monkeys scratching. How do you feel about your friends' home movies about their baby or their trip? Isn't it a godawful bore?

A football team on a blazing hot July day. Two hot teams mousing around at $500 a day. Actors, extras and a camera crew. High in the empty stadium, Stahr and his girl.

There was, for example, a man who in all seriousness asked him this favor: Stahr was to say, "Hello, Tim," and slap him on the back in front of the commissary one morning. Stahr had the man's record traced, and then slapped him on the back. The man ascended into Heaven.

Almost literally, for he was taken into one of the best agencies— which is what George Gershwin referred to when he said, "It's nice work if you can get it." He sits there today, with a picture of his wife and children on the wall, and has his nails manicured at the Beverly Hills Hotel. His life is one long happy dream.

———

Stahr remembered how they had used the three freaks back in 1927. X was being bothered by a really appalling woman. The day before the case came to trial, he sent a dwarf and [two other freaks] to her with messages. His counsel opened by stating that the woman was crazy. On the stand she told about her visitors—the jury shook their heads, winked at each other and acquitted.

———

Cecilia's uncle is an idiot like ————'s brother.

"—the rugged individualism of Tommy Manville, Barbara Hutton and Woolie Donahue." Never forgiven Wylie for slipping it into his speech when he was supporting Landon.

———

There is a place for a hint somewhere of a big agent, to complete the picture.

———

A tall round-shouldered young man with a beaked nose and soft brown eyes in a sensitive face.

———

The awful reverberating thunder of his absence.

———

[*Airplane Trip*]

My blue dream of being in a basket like a kite held by a rope against the wind.

———

It's fun to stretch and see the blue heavens spreading once more, spreading azure thighs for adventure.

———

Girl like a record with a blank on the other side.

———

There are no second acts in American lives.

———

Tragedy of these men was that nothing in their lives had really bitten deep at all.
Bald Hemingway characters.

———.

wily plagiarist
exigent overlordship
not one survived the castration

———

Don't wake the Tarkington ghosts.

———

ACTION IS CHARACTER.